Javaid Laghari, PhD, has served as a senator and Chairman of Higher Education Commission in Pakistan. A close associate of Benazir Bhutto, two-time prime minister of Pakistan who was killed by terrorists, he also served as president of a private university and as a professor of Electrical and Computer Engineering at SUNY, Buffalo.

This is his fourth book and his first novel, the first three books being on leadership. He loves to read and travel, and lives with his wife and two sons in Houston.

To all those brave men and women who lost their lives fighting terrorism.

Javaid Laghari

IFRIT

AUSTIN MACAULEY PUBLISHERS
LONDON • CAMBRIDGE • NEW YORK • SHARJAH

Copyright © Javaid Laghari (2019)

The right of Javaid Laghari to be identified as author of this work has been asserted by him in accordance with section 77 and 78 of the Copyright, Designs and Patents Act 1988.

All rights reserved. No part of this publication may be reproduced, stored in a retrieval system, or transmitted in any form or by any means, electronic, mechanical, photocopying, recording, or otherwise, without the prior permission of the publishers.

Any person who commits any unauthorized act in relation to this publication may be liable to criminal prosecution and civil claims for damages.

A CIP catalogue record for this title is available from the British Library.

ISBN 9781528906623 (Paperback)
ISBN 9781528906630 (Hardback)
ISBN 9781528906647 (E-Book)

www.austinmacauley.com

First Published (2019)
Austin Macauley Publishers Ltd
25 Canada Square
Canary Wharf
London
E14 5LQ

I have always been a great fan of mystery and adventure books since childhood. Growing up with reading books written by Enid Blyton, Erle Stanley Gardner, Ian Fleming, and Alistair MacLean among others, and watching thriller movies religiously, I always aspired to be a writer myself. But it was really the Dan Brown series that motivated me to write my first thriller novel at a time when I was at the peak of my professional career as an academic and scientist.

The idea of introducing the power of mystical Islam into a thriller was not something I had forethought. Over the years, I was introduced to the beliefs and myths that many followed and practiced in life, from family to business, and from politics to terrorism. When I was living in Islamabad, the whole region was rocked by terrorism, and in particular, colleges and schools were being attacked by fanatics who wanted to suppress progressive thought and impose their own version of Islam. Treading the thin and sensitive line between fact and fiction on the power of mysticism is not easy in a society that is closed to open discussion on religion, and to use that theme in a plot on terrorism was like sitting on a keg of dynamite. Despite the threat, the developing events led me to write this book.

Ifrit is not my creation alone but is the mind of many who made it possible. There are many who chose not to be identified for reasons of secrecy and are, therefore, not named below but are acknowledged for their contribution. At the same time, I am grateful to the following individuals and organizations who became a source of inspiration and encouragement, and for the information that forms the core of the book.

I am grateful to my wife, Pari; and to my children, Asad and Zaid, who sacrificed their personal time by providing me with opportunities to meet certain people and experience firsthand their mystical practices, as well as helping me edit this book. Asad was the source of so many lively discussions that I had to create a character based on him. And to my mother, whose love and training molded me into what I am today; and to my father, who taught me to always speak out for truth and justice, even at the cost of one's life.

To my former roommate Daniel Inman, with whom I learnt the American way of life; to my friend Larry Wallace, who himself survived a terrorist attack in Karachi when I first met him, for many of the Washington insights; and to my Afghani friend Taj Ayubi, who was the source of ongoing socio-political developments between Afghanistan and Pakistan.

To Seymour Hersh, Pulitzer Prize winning journalist and author, who provided me with the encouraging feedback on my manuscript; and to Lejla Kucukalic at Khalifa University, for her useful insight on science fiction. To

Will Norton Jr. at the University of Mississippi, for his enthusiastic interest in the topic of the book and the search for a book agent; and to Nancy Scannell at the University of Illinois Springfield, for helping me find a suitable publisher.

I am also grateful to many other friends, including Martha Dillman, for the discussions on countering evil forces through the power of spirituality; Syed Zeeshan Arshad, who interpreted many of the confusing aspects between religion and science; and Abdul Munaf, for his insight on jinn and end of times.

There are others who have silently contributed to the topic, including spiritual scholars, healers, and astrologers who specifically asked not to be named and have been a great source of knowledge, to "Moti Nivas", "Motley Gang", "Café Unity", "SZABIST", "ODTU", and "SUNY", and to my friends in the Pakistan parliament, vice chancellors, faculty and scholars, school principals, teachers, students, civil society, and the social media for being a source of interactive discussions. All references to the Quran are from The Noble Quran, http://www.pdf-koran.com/ File Version 2.0, Jan 17, 2006.

I would also like to acknowledge my friends in the Pakistan armed forces and the intelligence agencies who were a useful source of information and are leading the fight against terrorism, and to many unnamed friends in the diplomatic community in Islamabad and Karachi, particularly those from the US Embassy and USAID.

At this point, I would like to remember my mentor, friend, and leader Benazir Bhutto, who stood up against terrorism even at the cost of her own life. The torch that she lit continues to be carried by those who believe in tolerance, social justice, and the democratic rights of the people to decide their own fate without fear.

Finally, to the editorial staff at Austin Macauley for their very professional and untiring support in making this book a reality.

In the end, let me reiterate that there is a fine line between myth and reality. Many believe and have experienced firsthand the power of mysticism, while others write it off as superstition or a figment of imagination. While it is coincidental that many of the facts and experiences in the book may be true, the reader must realize that it is only a piece of fiction, so he or she must simply sit back and enjoy reading it without delving deep into what is true or false. Only time will tell!

Table of Contents

Chapter 1   13
Jihad

Chapter 2   79
Dreams and Prayers

Chapter 3   175
Black Magic

Chapter 4   237
Jinn

Chapter 5   305
Apocalypse

'Solomon said to his own men: "Ye chiefs! Which of you can bring me her throne before they come to me in submission?"
Said an Ifrit of the Jinns: "I will bring it to thee before thou rise from thy council: indeed, I have full strength for the purpose, and may be trusted."'

Al-Quran, Verses 27:38 and 27:39

Key Characters

Samir Baloch, Advisor to the Prime Minister on Education 13
Sanam Shah, Prime Minister of Pakistan 13
Marvi Brohi, Assassinated Prime Minister of Pakistan 15
Mike Johnson, Former US Special Envoy 21
Hameed Khan, Vice Chancellor of Mingora University 23
Harry Walker, Foreign Security Agency Contractor 31
Hakeem Luqman, Expert on Medicine of the Prophet 34
Khalifa, ISIS Head in Afghanistan 35
Shaday, Samir's wife 36
Hasan, Samir's son, Graduate of Psychology 36
Jadoo Baba, Magician and Spiritual Healer 39
Murtaza Brohi, Former Prime Minister of Pakistan 41
Latif Orakzai, Vice Chancellor of Global Muslim University 41
Zaid Brohi, Son of Murtaza Brohi, Former Prime Minister of Pakistan 41
William Bush, US Special Envoy 60
Timur, Senior Commander and Recruiter for TTP 67
Qari, Trainer and Suicide Bomber for TTP 74
Wazir, Deputy Emir of Al-Qaeda and Head of Operations in Afghanistan and Pakistan 76
Qabza Khan, Jinn Master and Magician 77
Ifrit, Powerful Jinn 78
Lal Bux Jillani, Sajjada Nasheen and Caretaker of Bari Imam Shrine 91
Iblis, King Jinn 99
Allama Malik, Scholar on Spiritual Islam 104
Ali Harmeen, Suicide Bomber 124
Baba Sain, Spiritual Healer and Protector 125
Pir Wasim, Religious Guide 182
Najumi Jamali, Astrologer 188
Colonel Khalid, Chief of Security where nuclear fuel is stored 194
Numbers 1, 2, 3, 4, and 5 TTP recruits 197
Colonel Asad, Anti-Terrorist Special Force 204
Major Farooq, Nuclear Emergency Task Force 204
Shams Hashmi, Spiritual Scholar on Jinn 237
Nafis Alibhoy, University Scientist 266
Colonel Zamin, Base Commander where nuclear arsenal is stored 278
Captain Tariq, Security Incharge at Miranshah 281
Brigadier Aftab, Special Forces Army Headquarters 288
Robert Forster, US Secretary of State 314
Captain John USAF 329

Second Lieutenant Tom USAF 329
Rasool Bux, Sajjada Nasheen and Caretaker of Lal Shahbaz Qalandar Shrine 342

This is a work of fiction. Names, characters, businesses, organizations, places, events, beliefs, and incidents are either the products of the author's imagination or used in a fictitious manner. Any resemblance to actual persons, living or dead, or actual events is purely coincidental.

Chapter 1
Jihad

'On that account: We ordained for the children of Israel that if any one slew a person—unless it be for murder or for spreading mischief in the land—it would be as if he slew the whole people: and if any one saved a life, it would be as if he saved the life of the whole people. Then, although there came to them Our messengers with clear signs, yet, even after that, many of them continued to commit excesses in the land.'

Al-Quran, Verse 5:32

To Charsadda

Samir Baloch had just stepped into his office when his personal secretary Rashid barged in and shouted in an almost hysterical voice, "Ali Khan University at Charsadda has been attacked by armed gunmen...it is breaking news on television!"

"What?" Samir exclaimed, "Another terrorist attack?"

He was not used to such shocking news first thing in the morning, but this was serious and required urgent attention. Terrorism had plagued Pakistan, and the most recent targets were schools and colleges. He immediately switched on the wall-mounted TV in his office to catch up on the breaking news.

Samir was the Advisor to the Prime Minister on Education. He was about 55 years old, tall and slim with dark curly hair. A professor of electrical and computer engineering at the State University of New York (SUNY) at Buffalo, and one of their youngest faculty to be tenured, he was asked by Prime Minister Sanam Shah to be her advisor when she was elected two years ago. He reluctantly agreed, took leave from the university, and joined a few months later.

He and Sanam had been good friends since long. She was completing her masters in international relations at Harvard when he was finishing up his doctorate at MIT. They had spent many evenings together at coffee shops strategizing the struggle for democracy and in the holding of free and fair elections in Pakistan.

Samir was known to have a liberal mindset, and was an outspoken critic of fundamental Islam. For him, religion was between man and God, and Islam had similar values of love as were found in all other faiths. He believed the pseudo religious scholars of Islam had indoctrinated the illiterate masses with incorrect teachings of hatred towards those who would not follow their religion. He supported freedom of speech and expression, advocated tolerance and compassion, and believed in a pluralistic society, which was another reason Sanam had asked him to be her advisor. He and Sanam shared the same viewpoints on Islam.

Most of his friends were either from the academic community, or were intellectuals who had a liberal mindset. He would not accept anything or any belief at face value unless there was a scientific or logical explanation for it. Because of that, he was despised by many religious fundamentalists who would even call him a 'kafir' or a non-believer in their private gatherings. It made very little difference to how Samir approached life.

His office was on the outskirts of Islamabad, from where one could see the Margalla Hills through the windows, with the beautiful Faisal Mosque in the foreground at its footsteps. Islamabad was considered one of the most beautiful capitals of the world, till it was struck by terrorism, converting it into a war zone. The last one year had been exceptionally violent and explosive in Pakistan.

There had been numerous terrorist attacks on schools and colleges in Pakistan since the military operation against the terrorists had begun over a year ago. It felt war-like with news of suicide bombings and terrorist attacks in public places, airports, schools, and colleges almost on a weekly basis. This was the price Pakistan was paying for its 'Operation Zarb-e-Azb' against the terrorists. Zarb-e-Azb, named after Prophet Muhammad's sword, also meaning sharp and cutting strike, was the offensive conducted by the Pakistan Army against militant groups, including Al-Qaeda and the Tehrik-i-Taliban Pakistan, commonly referred to as the TTP, who had many hideouts mainly in the northern tribal areas particularly in the region bordering Afghanistan.

The TTP, also referred to as the Pakistani Taliban, were different from the Taliban operating in Afghanistan. Among the TTP's stated objectives were jihad against the Pakistani state and enforcement of their interpretation of sharia. TTP was actually an organization of over a dozen, maybe more, orthodox Sunni Islamist militant groups mainly based in the northwestern Federally Administered Tribal Areas, or FATA, and northern Balochistan along the Afghan border, and in southern Punjab in Pakistan. The TTP had almost exclusively targeted the Pakistani security agencies, its schools and colleges, religious minorities, and some high-profile figures. However, it had also claimed responsibility for the Camp Chapman attack in Afghanistan in which seven CIA officials were killed, and the New York Times Square attempted car bombing.

The Afghan Taliban, on the other hand, operating out of Afghanistan, had declared their jihad against the international coalition and Afghan security forces and were opposed to targeting the Pakistani state. The West had always considered them the assets of the Pakistan intelligence agency, the ISI, which was polled as the best in the world by an American TV channel. The Afghan Taliban had morphed from the courageous Mujahidin of the Afghan-Russian war of the 70s. When the Russians pulled back in 1988, the American support vanished overnight, leaving the Mujahidin to their fate in lawless and war-torn Afghanistan. They had overrun Kabul, formed an Islamic government based on the sharia, or Islamic laws, and were granted full recognition by Saudi Arabia and Pakistan. They were also fully dependent on the Pakistan forces and Saudi aid till 9/11 struck.

Fast forwarding to the present, Maulana Fazlullah had become the new leader of the TTP following the killing of Baitullah Mehsud in FATA in an American drone attack. It was estimated that there could be over 15,000 TTP and other militants operating in and out of the northern tribal areas, including some from other pockets in southern Punjab and Balochistan. They had declared an independent Islamic state along the porous border with Afghanistan. ISIS, or Daesh as so called by the Middle Eastern Arabs, was also stretching its muscles to extend its domain to eastern Afghanistan and then on to western Pakistan where they had their eye on the strategic nuclear assets. They had been eying TTP as a potential partner to form the Islamic State Khorasan Province or ISKP, the chapter of Islamic State in Afghanistan, Pakistan, and Central Asia,

Zarb-e-Azb was, therefore, launched by the Pakistan Army in North Waziristan along the Pakistan-Afghanistan border as a decisive battle against the TTP in the wake of an attack on the International Airport in Karachi, 900 miles to the south of Islamabad and the commercial hub of Pakistan, for which the TTP had claimed responsibility. Ten militants armed with automatic weapons, rocket launchers, suicide vests, and grenades attacked the Airport in which 36 people were killed, including all 10 attackers. The attackers were of Uzbek origin who belonged to the Islamic Movement of Uzbekistan, an Al-Qaeda linked militant organization that worked closely with TTP.

A few months later, seven gunmen disguised as military men and affiliated with the TTP conducted a terrorist attack on the Army Public School in the northwestern Pakistani city of Peshawar. The militants, all foreign nationals, included one Chechen, three Arabs, and three Afghans, entered the school and opened fire on school staff, and children, killing over 150 people, including 132 school-children, ranging between eight and 18 years of age. Pakistan Army's Special Services Group killed all seven terrorists and rescued about a thousand people. Four more militants picked up later through a search operation were hanged within days.

And only recently, the Global Muslim University in the suburbs of the nation's capital, Islamabad, was attacked in twin suicide attacks in which six people, including three women, were killed, and as many as 40 people injured, 25 of them women. The attacks had prompted the authorities to close all schools and colleges throughout the country, which had only opened after the educational institutes were directed by the government to provide extra security to the students and staff.

The breaking news continued to flash on all TV channels, "Heavily armed gunmen have stormed the Ali Khan University campus in Charsadda, killing many students…the campus is still under attack…army personnel from a nearby base are moving into the area…"

Samir's cell phone started to ring continuously. He knew the calls would be from the media, each one scurrying to get him live on their TV channels first. With these attacks on campuses, he was one of the most sought-after officials in the capital in view of his position as Advisor on Education to the Prime Minister, Sanam Shah.

After graduation from US, Sanam had moved to Pakistan to join the struggle with Marvi Brohi, a former prime minister of Pakistan, against the authoritarian regime of General Mehmood Ali. Samir had moved on to the West Coast to NASA's Jet Propulsion Lab on a sabbatical and returned back to SUNY a year later. He was the point man and a trustworthy aide for her continued contacts with the US administration and the congress.

Marvi, who was living in self-exile in Dubai, had returned much earlier to Pakistan and survived a major suicide attack on her life on arrival at Islamabad in which 180 people were killed and over 500 were injured. It was assumed that the

TTP was behind the attack, but the authoritarian government in Pakistan was less than willing to catch the planners of the attack. The attack was meant to warn her to return back to the US. The military general in power was not willing to accommodate her into power. However, elections were held five months later under international pressure, but were conveniently rigged to bring the general's man and a protégé of former General Zain, Rahim Aziz as Prime Minister.

Rahim had his own vision of implementing the sharia laws. Under his weak administration, the TTP were able to expand their bases throughout Pakistan. They collaborated with other militant groups and got involved in cross-border terrorist activities, including in India. After all, Rahim owed his rise to power indirectly to Al-Qaeda, as it was alleged by Marvi that Rahim was financed at one time by Osama bin Laden, the mastermind of 9/11, to consolidate his political position in Pakistan.

The attack on Taj Mahal Hotel in Mumbai, India, took place soon after. India laid its finger on the Pakistan Intelligence support of the militant operation operating out of Pakistan, which was dismissed by the government. It appeared that the supporters of rightist parties who believed in militancy and jihad as a way of life and governance had penetrated the ranks and files of the government, and were supporting militancy in various forms.

Immediately afterwards, an airbase in India was attacked in which six soldiers were killed. The attackers were alleged by India to have crossed over from across the border which was vehemently denied by Pakistan.

When Osama was killed in his hideout in a surprise US raid at Abbottabad, the government had demonstrated its helplessness and inability of not being able to locate him on Pakistan soil for all these years.

Marvi's struggle against the Rahim government and for democracy thus gained momentum with the support of western powers. Her struggle bore fruit, and two years later, the government was forced to conduct yet another election under the supervision of international observers. The militants tried to sabotage and postpone the elections through yet another deadly attack against her in a public rally in Lahore in which she, along with 24 of her supporters, were killed.

The struggle for democracy was then led by Sanam, who was her close associate and second in command, and their party eventually won the election by a landslide.

Immediately after being sworn in as Prime Minister, Sanam declared that Pakistan will not allow its soil to be used by terrorists and other militant groups, and all their hideouts would be weeded out. Within a few months, she replaced the Army Chief, General Khalil, who had served under former Prime Minister Rahim, and appointed General Zaheer Khan, a blue-blooded professional soldier as the new army chief. She then gave him a free-hand to bring on his own team at the commander's level and take on the militants. Operation Zarb-e-Azb on the terrorists was declared six months later. It was the decisive moment for Pakistan.

"Call up the VCs of all KP universities, and ask them to meet me at Charsadda in two hours," Samir blurted out to his secretary. VC was the common abbreviation for the Vice Chancellor, or the president of the university. Samir wanted to send a clear signal to the terrorists, "…come what may…we will not be bullied or frightened by the attacks, and we will not shut down!"

Charsadda was 90 miles to the west of Islamabad and a mere 20 miles away from Peshawar, the capital of KP province. KP stood for Khyber Pukhtunkhwa, which was the new name given by the parliament to the North-Western Frontier Province, or NWFP, named by the British before independence and partitioning of South Asia into Pakistan, India, and Bangladesh in 1947. KP borders Afghanistan in the west. The land of the fiercely independent and warlike Pathan, or Pashtun as they are ethnically called, KP is also the site of the ancient kingdom Gandhara, including the ruins of its capital, Pushkalavati, now Charsadda, and of the oldest Buddhist learning center at Takht-i-Bahi in the beautiful valley of Swat. It was first a Zoroastrian complex which, after the later arrival of Buddhism, was converted into a Buddhist monastery, and is over 2,000 years old.

How times had now changed! In 2009, the valley of Swat was completely taken over by the TTP. Girl schools were shut down, and the burqa, a complete covering of the head and body, was enforced. Those who refused to wear it were publicly flogged. Some blamed it on the weak administration of the Rahim government, while others blamed it on his rightist leanings and the intentional overlook by the civilian government when the militants were reinforcing themselves. This was when the Pakistan Army unilaterally moved into Swat and commenced Operation Rah-e-Rast, meaning the correct path, and killed most militants who had set up base there while the remaining escaped to FATA and Afghanistan. However, the TTP kept hitting back, and a few years back, a young girl, Shazia, who was an outspoken proponent of girl's education, while boarding her school bus, was shot three times by the TTP. Being in critical condition, she was moved out to a foreign hospital, recovered, and eventually won a major global prize, the youngest person ever to do so.

Over the centuries, KP had been invaded by the Persians, Greeks, Mauryans, Kushans, Shahis, Ghaznavids, Mughals, Sikhs, and the British Empire giving them their warlike character.

The Pashtun population extends into Balochistan in Pakistan and into Afghanistan where the majority population is Pashtun as well. Bacha Khan, the Frontier Gandhi, wanted to unite the Pashtun, but died before he could fulfill his dream. He is buried at Jalalabad in Afghanistan. Another university in Charsadda is named after him to honor his struggle for the Pashtun race.

The Pashtun fiercely resisted the Russian invasion of 1979. The Mujahidin, who were mostly Pashtun, then became the darlings and heroes of the west. Their resistance to the Soviet occupation ultimately led to the withdrawal of the Soviet troops in 1989, and to the disintegration of the USSR in 1991. However, the tides turned after 9/11 in which over 3,000 civilians were killed and over 6,000 injured as a result of the worst terrorist attack on US soil. The Pashtun have since then been eyed suspiciously as terrorists by the western powers even though none of the 9/11 hijackers were Pashtun. It was only when the Taliban leader, Mulla Omar, a Pashtun, refused to hand over Osama bin Laden to the Americans that they bore the wrath of the west. The mulla had honored the Pashtunwali, which is a non-written ethical code and traditional lifestyle which the Pashtun people follow. Pashtunwali dates back to ancient pre-Islamic times. During the Pashtun-dominated Taliban regime, Pashtunwali was practiced throughout the Islamic Emirate of Afghanistan. Osama was a guest of the Taliban and, according to the code, could not be handed over to his enemies without his consent. A Pashtun would rather die than break the code.

The Pashtun constitute the second largest ethnic group in the Pakistan Army, second only to Punjabis, who are from the largest province of Punjab. But now, the Pashtun were under attack not just in the West but by the terrorists, as well.

It would take about 90 minutes on M1 Motorway to reach Peshawar driving though the same land which Alexander of Macedonia took around 326 BCE. Then it would take another 15 minutes to reach Charsadda via the Peshawar ring road.

As the car reached the suburbs of Islamabad, while passing the campus of the Global Muslim University, Samir's mind drifted to the earlier attack last month at this campus. The boundary wall that had been damaged from the blowing up of the suicide bomber had been repaired. A group of girls, some covered in veil, others in hijab, carrying books, were entering the gate where a scanner had been placed. A female security guard was taking the girls into a small room meant for body searches. One could only imagine the horror the female students must have undergone when the terrorists had blown themselves up in the middle of the cafeteria with chants of 'Allah-o-Akbar', or God is great.

A few minutes out of Islamabad, another road forked off to Taxila where Buddha did his teachings. When Alexander came to Taxila, he found a university there the like of which had not been seen in Greece, a university which taught the three Vedas of the Hindu mythology.

The motorway then passed through the outskirts of Wah Military cantonment where Pakistan's largest ordinance factory is located. Just a few months ago, there had been a double suicide attack at the factory in which 70 military personnel were killed and over 100 wounded. This was the deadliest attack by the terrorists on a military site. The bombers had detonated themselves at the factory's gates while workers were changing shifts.

The Cadet College at Hasan Abdal passed to the right where many a fine generals and bureaucrats had received their school education. Located here also is the Gurdwara Panja Sahib, which is one of the holiest places of worship of Sikhism. At the Gurdwara temple is a rock believed to have the hand print of Guru Nanak imprinted on it when he had visited the place in 1521. Sikhs visit this Gurdwara from all over the world.

The six-lane M1 motorway stretched out for miles on a level field without a turn. It had been specially designed to handle F-16 and Mirage jet fighter's takeoff and landings during times of war. Pakistan and India have fought three wars since their independence from the British in 1947, and had many skirmishes and cross-border firing incidents across the Line-of-Control on a regular basis. The M1 passed through the region of the martial races of Pakistan in northern Punjab and KP.

A little further down the motorway, they reached an intersection where the road on the right led to Abbottabad, a military garrison town about 80 miles away. This was Osama bin Laden's hideout till he was killed in the US SEAL raid. It had become a matter of national debate whether the Pakistan military knew of his whereabouts and were protecting him, or whether they were equally surprised when Osama was found a stone's throw away from the Army garrison. There was yet a larger viewpoint of the people living in Abbottabad that Osama was not present in the house, and it was a make-believe raid by the SEALS who claimed they had killed him and had disposed of his body in the sea, while in fact he had died of kidney failure many years ago in the Tora Bora mountain ranges in Afghanistan bordering Pakistan. Whatever it was, the US suspected that certain pockets in the Pakistan intelligence agencies had a hand in harboring and protecting various militant groups which were the nurseries for the TTP, the Al-Qaeda and now ISIS.

The road to the left led to the Pakistan Air Force Aeronautical Complex at Kamra. The Complex comprises an Airbase, Avionics Production Factory, Aircraft Rebuild Factory, Aircraft Manufacturing Factory, and the French Fighter plane Dassault Mirage Rebuild Factory. It is the center of aircraft manufacturing and overhauling for Pakistan and is now commonly known as the Aviation City.

There had been three terrorist attacks just at Kamra alone within a span of last twelve months. A year back, a school bus carrying children during the morning rush hour was attacked by a suicide bomber, injuring seven. A month later, terrorists fired four rockets at the base, including two at the Mirage Rebuild Factory but no casualties were reported. Then seven months later, nine TTP militants assaulted the air force base. After a pitched battle, in which four security personnel died, all nine attackers were killed while two Pakistani security officials also died. The base commander was reported wounded in the attack, as well. The militants also destroyed one Saab 2000 Erieye plane and damaged a few others.

Next, the car passed the exit to Swabi leading to the GIK Institute of Science and Technology named after a former president of Pakistan. The institute is located right next to the Tarbela Dam, which is the largest earth filled dam in the world. Samir's mind wandered to the day in 1992 when he was offered the position of the provost by the president himself, a position that he had politely declined due to the nature of his research work funded by the US department of defense. The institute was Dr. Wali Khan's baby, considered the godfather of the Pakistan's nuclear bomb, and it was perhaps the nature of Samir's work in high energy density pulsed power systems that had attracted him to Khan.

A nuclear science program was initiated at the GIK Institute in the earlier years, but was quietly relocated to more secure institutions run by the Pakistan Atomic Energy Commission (PAEC), such as at the Khan Research Laboratories (KRL) at Kahuta, and at two other institutes, PIEAS and PINSTECH at Nilore, in the outskirts of Islamabad. However, most of the nuclear fuel reprocessing and four plutonium enrichment facilities run by the military had been moved to other locations, including Khushab, about 100 miles south of Islamabad and near the PAF Sargodha base where the nuclear fuel is stored underground at undisclosed locations. It was estimated by western intelligence agencies that Pakistan has over 150 nuclear bombs, stored at various top secret and secure locations across the country, and its arsenal is continuing to grow at a much faster pace than neighboring India.

The National Command Authority (NCA), established in 2000 with the Strategic Plans Division (SPD) as its secretariat, has broad power over 'all issues relating to nuclear and space technologies' in Pakistan, bringing all national strategic organizations under its authority. They remain the focal point for Pakistan's missile development programs. They have also developed Pakistan's first land attack cruise missiles, and their inaugural test-flight stunned many observers both for its technological complexity and its undetected development.

According to intelligence reports, as many as 66% of Pakistan's nuclear warheads are mounted on land-based and mobile missile systems. Among the developed missiles include the Hatf, with a minimum range of 60 miles, Ghauri 800 miles, Shaheen 1,500 miles, Ghaznavi 200 miles, Babur 200 miles, Nasr 40 miles, and very recently, the Ababeel with a range of 1,500 miles. Most missiles could also be delivered with the US made F-16s and French Mirage 111/V.

Ababeel is the latest ballistic missile developed by Pakistan which can carry nuclear warheads, and uses multiple independently targetable reentry vehicles (MIRV), a technology yet to be developed by India. The missile's name of 'Ababeel' or 'Swallow' is a reference to a pre-Islamic event during the 'Year of the Elephant' when an army comprising of war elephants attacked the Kaaba. A flock of 'ababil' appeared and dropped stones upon the attacking army destroying them. The Ababeel missile makes reference to this historical event on two grounds: a MIRV attack would resemble falling stones; and an army of elephants would suggest the attacking force is Indians.

The Nasr has also been developed as a top of the line missile. A short-range, state-of-art, solid fueled tactical 'Multi-tube Ballistic Missile'. It can carry and deliver multiple nuclear warheads of appropriate yield, with high accuracy. It was developed as a counter to the 'Cold Start Doctrine' developed by the Indian Army for use in a war with Pakistan. The Cold Start Doctrine is intended to allow India's conventional forces to perform holding and shallow attacks in order to prevent a nuclear retaliation from Pakistan. The Nasr missile is seen as the solution providing flexible deterrence options for an appropriate response to Cold Start rather than massive nuclear retaliation against India. Nasr missiles are stored, fully armed and in battle ready conditions, at a number of strategic and secret locations around the country. Nasr proponents argue that by maintaining a credible linkage between limited conventional war and nuclear escalation, the Nasr missile will deter India from carrying out its plan of attacking Pakistan.

The car reached near the end of the motorway where a sign clearly marked the exit to Charsadda about 10 miles to the right. One could see a security check point with multiple army vehicles moving in and out. The road had been blocked off for general traffic, and two army helicopters were hovering in the air. Straight ahead on the motorway were the city limits to Peshawar.

Peshawar dates back to 539 BCE, making it one of the oldest cities in Pakistan. Peshawar was called Purusapura in Sanskrit, meaning 'city of men'. The city is also mentioned in the Zend Avesta as Vaekereta, the seventh most beautiful place on earth created by Ahura Mazda, the Zoroastrian God. It was the crown Jewel of Bactria and held sway over Takshashila, now Taxila. The Museum at Peshawar holds relics of civilization from the Zoroastrian, Buddhist, Hindu, Greek, and Islamic periods, and is considered one of the richest museums in the world. However, it had been shut down for the last one year due to threats by the TTP to blow it up. The TTP believes that display of relics is un-Islamic, and is akin to deity worship. The Taliban had also blown up the Bamyan statues of Buddha who were carved into a valley north of Kabul. It is much like what the ISIS believe who blew up Palmyra and many other historical sites in Syria and Iraq.

The colleges in and around Peshawar were continuously under attack. The VC of a college was kidnapped by TTP few years back. He was taken to North Waziristan where he was also made to meet Hakimullah Mehsud who was his captor. Only last year, after four years in captivity, and being moved around at least 20 times, he returned home. His family speaks of the time without him in terms of days, not years—1,451 days as opposed to four years—to underscore the anguish of their long wait of their lives on hold. Whether the government paid the ransom or swapped TTP prisoners for him was not clear. The TTP chief had claimed the professor was swapped for three Taliban commanders.

Yet another VC of a KP university 50 miles from Peshawar was kidnapped a year earlier, but released only after six months in captivity. Again, there were rumors that the previous government had released a top TTP commander for his release. This had led to the precedence and a surge in kidnapping soft targets. Only few years back, the sons of a former president and of a former chief minister were kidnapped in bright daylight by unknown militants, and were only recently released.

Peshawar itself had also been subject to a severe attack by the terrorists only a few months back. Fourteen terrorists had entered from Afghanistan and stormed a Pakistan Air Force base killing 29 airmen despite the high level of security at the base. The security personnel were confused as to how the attackers could have penetrated the base. Pakistan army retaliated immediately and killed all terrorists. Strange tattoos were found on the bodies of all attackers, and the local media had speculated that black arts were practiced and used by the terrorists in these attacks. Samir recalled he had shrugged them off as hocus pocus. However, it had left a deep mark on the capability of the Pakistan's military to protect its installations and to secure itself against terrorist attacks. The western media was quick to point out that Pakistan's nuclear weapons had become extremely susceptible as a result of these militant attacks.

There was growing concern that Pakistan was now under the continued growing menace of the TTP and the Al-Qaeda, and there were reports that they were working as surrogates of ISIS in Pakistan, which was expanding its base from Syria and Iraq to the East. It had dreams of establishing an Islamic Caliphate from Morocco to Bangladesh. The TTP was a willing local partner, and the threat of extremist groups were lurking all around the country. If ISIS or Al-Qaeda could get their hands on nuclear weapons then one could only imagine the destruction that could be cast by these fanatics.

ISIS already had its presence in the Jalalabad district of Afghanistan and in the Tora Bora mountains, which borders Peshawar district of Pakistan. This was less than three hours away by road from Pakistan's top secret and heavily guarded nuclear installations. Calling it the Islamic State Khorasan Province, it comprised fighters mainly from existing militant groups in Afghanistan and Pakistan, the majority coming from the TTP. A US presidential candidate had also expressed concern about jihadi coups and suicide nuclear bombers during the last election campaign.

Samir's phone rang. It was his friend, Mike Johnson, from the US who had served as attorney general of the State of Arkansas, and was previously special envoy for a US president for South Asia. He was still well connected with the intelligence community in the US.

"I heard about the university attack from my friends," he was referring to the CIA. "They have shown concern for your life as you are on the hit list of the militants, as well. Please be careful. We pray for your safety."

Mike had friends in the US administration and was a big help in getting support for the education programs in Pakistan through the USAID and the department of state. Over $300 million of aid were already provided by the US just in support of higher education in Pakistan within two years during Samir's tenure, and was considered one of the largest aid programs in education for any country.

"Don't worry, Mike, we will all be very careful. Your president correctly defined these terrorists when he said terrorists do not worship God, they worship death!"

The car arrived at a security checkpoint. It slowed down and was stopped by two SSG commandos both wielding submachine guns. They asked for identities, and checked the trunk and underneath the car for any suspicious objects. After confirming the identity of the passenger, one of them apologized for stopping a top government functionary due to security reasons, and waved to the driver to pass through.

Ali Khan University was a mere 15 minutes away, and the road was swarming with over a dozen army trucks. Some army men had taken up positions on both sides of the road and around the small bridges that passed over the tributaries of river Kabul. The army was carrying out a search operation of the nearby villages to seek any terrorists or facilitators. Samir wondered where the security was when the terrorists had crossed multiple checkpoints on way to Charsadda. It was a frightening thought that the supporters of the various terrorist's groups could penetrate the ranks and files of the security agencies. There were rumors floating in the media after the Peshawar attack that some terrorists had acquired powers through the use of black magic, and were in control of supernatural entities called jinn that many Muslims believe in. Samir shrugged them off as a figment of imagination and rubbish.

The car was stopped near the main entrance to the university. A young army captain was in charge. He had received advance word from the earlier security checkpost of the visitors. He recognized Samir and saluted him.

"Sir, we believe all terrorists—four, I believe—that attacked have been killed, but we are still ensuring everything is safe. It is likely that there may be accomplices in the nearby areas. It is also possible that timed bombs may have been placed inside the buildings and around the campus, so it is not yet safe to go in."

Samir understood. "What are our casualties like?"

One could feel the pain in his reply, "15 shaheed, over 50 injured, and still counting, sir." Shaheed was the local word for martyred.

A voice suddenly crackled on the wireless, "Building four now cleared. Six more bodies found."

Samir felt the situation was getting out of control.

"We are concerned over similar attacks on our universities, and I have called an urgent meeting of all KP VCs…"

The captain interrupted, "Yes, sir! Some of them have already arrived. As the university is still not clear, we have arranged your meeting in the building across the road."

Samir walked over to the agriculture extension service building, which was about 100 yards on the other side of the road. It had not been attacked, because from outside, it appeared like a normal residence found in this part of the province.

Most of them were like mansions, large in size, with huge doors and multiple windows, having a large courtyard. It was, in fact, the residence of a former chief minister who had leased it out to the university at very favorable terms. Two heavily armed commandos were at the gate, and after receiving a nod from the captain, let Samir into the building.

Ali Khan University

Samir walked through the entrance and into the main lounge of the building. Seven VCs of KP universities had already arrived. They all appeared visibly disturbed. It was a group of men mostly in their upper fifties to early sixties. All were Pashtun hailing from various regions in KP: Peshawar, Mardan, Haripur, D.I. Khan, Bannu, Kohat, and Charsadda itself.

There was a sound of another car pulling up in front of the building. The door behind Samir opened, and a six-foot-tall hulky man, wearing a traditional white shalwar-qameez, the local dress, and pathani shoes, walked in. Hameed Khan, the VC from Mingora University in KP, was considered a die-hard religious fundamentalist and a very patriotic Pakistani. He had a strong built body with a six-inch black beard that was well-trimmed. Most knew he had strong views against terrorism but sometimes would make statements blaming the government for its failure for not opening up a dialogue with them. It was no secret that he had friends on both sides of the divide.

"Salam alaikum. My apologies for being late." Salam alaikum is the Muslim greeting meaning peace be upon you.

As they entered, someone who appeared to be a senior official of Ali Khan University and was badly shaken, started speaking up. "I was in my office when the gunfire erupted…luckily, it was early in the morning, and most of the students had not shown up yet. I had a feeling it was coming…"

Samir interrupted, "Had you taken the security measures as were directed?"

"We had six armed guards at the main entrance…they couldn't have entered from there…maybe they scaled the walls…there are possibly hundreds shaheed and many more injured…"

"Did you not have security cameras?"

The official was still trembling, "Yes. There were cameras after every 200 feet. I am surprised how they could have gotten in undetected."

Further questions on security could wait. The dead and the injured were more important now.

Samir snapped, "We need to go inside and check for casualties, and talk to the faculty and students, as well."

The captain walked in, "Sir! We have just received clearance to go in. But I will strongly recommend you stay together and walk within the perimeter of the army personnel. We will have six SSG commandos escorting you inside."

The view inside was like a slaughterhouse. There was blood all over the lawn, and on the walkways. The main building was up front. A part of the reception area had been blown away, and there were human parts all over the seating area. This is where the first suicide bomber had blown himself up. There was blood on the walls, the floor, and the furniture. The bodies of the students had been removed, and the stench of body parts had not yet set in.

The room beyond the reception was the auditorium. The survivors had been rounded up in the auditorium and were now under the protection of the army. There were around 40 or so badly shaken staff members and students standing. Many were still trying to make use of their cell phones to contact their families, but the signals had been jammed by the army by now. As they saw the group of VCs walk in, there was panic in the room, and everyone tried to speak at the same time.

"The government is responsible for all these deaths…"

"We can't let these maniacs go free…"

"Can someone let us know where we stand…"

"Who are the shaheed…"

The army captain signaled the crowd to order.

"We are fully in control now. There is no need to panic anymore. You will all be free to go in a few minutes once we get the clearance that there are no more bombers in the vicinity."

Samir knew it was necessary to talk to the staff and students to pacify them. He could see they were badly shaken. It was important to build up the morale and confidence of the victims, and to inform them of the reasons of the attack, as they would be sought out by the media for their personal experience during the attack. The message had to come out clear to the terrorists, and the world at large, that Pakistan will not be pushed back.

He moved to the center of the crowd, and spoke in a confident tone to soothe the horror, "We are fighting this war against terrorism. The terrorists are not humans by any definition. They are not Muslims though they claim they are. Killing is strongly forbidden in Islam. God in the Holy Quran, in Chapter 5, Verse 32, has clearly ordained that if any one slew a person, it would be as if he slew the whole people: and if any one saved a life, it would be as if he saved the life of the whole people."

Samir continued, "There has been a lot of collateral damage, more so in colleges and universities than anywhere else. We understand we have been the main targets of the terrorist attacks. There have been many casualties, and we are still picking up the pieces. But we cannot afford to stop this war!"

"But why us? Why don't the terrorists attack the west instead of killing us Muslims…"

Samir looked at him for a moment, and continued to speak, "You need to understand that foremost of all, there is no one single terrorist group or ideology. Some are lost souls who are misled by those who themselves are lost souls. Some want jihad and impose sharia laws. Others are paid mercenaries to create chaos and further chaos. Yet, some are working on foreign agendas. There are some who want to avenge deaths of close ones, whether in a drone attack or in some international troop operation in a foreign land…"

"But this has been going on since 9/11. Why us? Will we ever see the end of it?"

"The terrorists need media attention. More so in the west than in the east. But since it is difficult for them to hit at the west, the east is a soft target for them. Be it Pakistan, Afghanistan, Syria, Iraq, or Turkey, it makes no difference to them. Their ideology and training comes from the madrassah and the militant training camps. And they have been fairly successful in accomplishing their goals. The media has been captured by terrorists. Polls show that a large number identify terrorism as the most important national problem. Some politicians are starting to call the battle against terrorism as World War III."

Samir continued, "Terrorists are more interested in capturing attention and putting their issue at the forefront of the agenda than in the number of deaths they cause. ISIS particularly broadcasts the barbaric beheadings through social media to create terror in the minds of those watching. Al-Qaeda did the same thing. They just want to inspire fear. This university attack is meant to create terror in all our colleges so that students stop coming to college to seek education."

"But terrorism kills…"

"Terrorism is not the biggest killer. Terrorism kills far fewer people than car accidents. One is more likely to be struck by lightning than to be killed by a terrorist."

"You can't be serious?" asked another person in bewilderment.

"In a recent study in the US, of those killed in a year, 31 were killed by lightning in one year, over 11,000 were shot by another American, 21 were shot by armed toddlers, but only nine were killed by jihadists…"

Another one interrupted, "But we have fundamentalist groups within Pakistan who sympathize with these terrorists."

"I agree! There are many who sympathize with them. Such groups are searching for a pure Islamic Caliphate. They have delusions of grandeur of the Caliphate that existed at the time of Caliph Omar. It was perfect then. However, the same ground reality and economic conditions do not exist now. Muslims are much diversified and now extend to over 50 Muslim majority countries with different languages and cultures. They also extend to and are an integral part of the communities from the US to Europe to Australia. We have some of the best educated Muslims, artists, and scholars, as well. Technology has become the norm now. Even our women are working in Muslim countries and outside, as well. Many work in films and television. They are on billboards and advertisements which the fundamentalist mind does not accept. They want an enslaved woman, be it their mother, sister, wife, or daughter. The extremist jihadi thought, however, will eventually be defeated by us. But greater are the external factors which are fueling it, perhaps for a wider global agenda."

Samir did not want to tread into this domain with this crowd, as he had been into a highly classified foreign policy and security briefing at the intelligence agency headquarter only last month. The agencies had reason to believe that multiple intelligence agencies from around the region, including the Indian intelligence agency RAW, Afghanistan's Khad, Iran's VAJA, the Gulf countries, Israeli Mossad, American CIA, and the British MI5 all had their finger in the pie. There were multiple conspiracy theories, as well.

The oldest one was that it was primarily India which had never accepted the partitioning of the sub-continent into India and Pakistan in 1947. The first war between the two newly formed countries was fought over Kashmir in 1947, which got divided into two Kashmirs. The second was again due to the Kashmir insurgency and the Rann of Kutch dispute in 1965. Both sides claimed victory. The third was in 1971 where India had a decisive victory and Bangladesh was created out of East Pakistan. Then there was the Kargil war of 1999, which also took place in Kashmir. Both nations were now nuclear armed to the teeth, with full delivery capability. The possibility of a conventional war across the full-fledged border had now diminished because of 'mutually assured destruction' as they would literally destroy each other with nuclear weapons.

Both nations had now resorted to the 'fourth generation' warfare tactics, which included acts of cross-border terrorism, cultural, media, and economic warfare. Pakistan believed all these acts of terrorism were Indian financed and sponsored. Every now and then, someone caught in Pakistan would be blindfolded and paraded on national TV as a RAW agent. This had gone to that extreme that even some of the mainstream political parties in Pakistan, leading private television channels, newspapers, TV anchorpersons, and writers were accused of being Indian agents without an iota of evidence. Their only 'crime' being they were advocating peace and trade with India. What was happening in India was no different.

However, the most popular conspiracy theory doing the rounds was that the terrorists wanted to get their hands on the nuclear device ever since Pakistan had exploded the nuclear bomb. They felt it would be like snatching candy from a baby. This was their territory, their domain, their people. Pakistan was after all a Muslim country, and everyone would sympathize with them since the 'kafir', or unbelievers, were killing thousands of Muslims every year in the Middle East, Africa, everywhere. Someone had to get even and teach them a lesson. They believed they could easily infiltrate the security protecting these devices. They had been able to do it at the Air Force base, the Naval base, and at the GHQ at Islamabad itself. They were planning to attack Kahuta or wherever the bombs were hidden.

However, they had underestimated the security measures the armed forces had undertaken to protect their nuclear arsenal. According to the intelligence briefings, Pakistan's nuclear arsenal security was fool-proof, not just from the terrorists, but even from any western plan to capture and destroy these weapons. The weapons were hidden away from crowded population, in safe locations, and safeguarded with triple layers of security by specially trained SSG commandos. And the weapons were always on the move. Samir had pointed out at the briefings that this actually made them less secure, as any of the security personnel could become sympathetic to the jihadi cause, or when the weapons are on the move, the containers could be easily hijacked. And if not the whole device, then by getting their hands on the nuclear fuel at a minimum, they could easily make a 'dirty bomb' by combining the radioactive fuel with conventional explosives, and blow them in a crowded area, like a city center, airport, or metro station. A dirty bomb, however, is not a weapon of mass destruction and is not capable of causing death by tens of thousands, but the radioactive damage it could inflict would create panic and terror, causing secondary deaths in hundreds or perhaps a thousand years into the future, as well. However, military intelligence believed the nuclear weapons and their fuel were fully secure and protected, as well, and there was nothing to fear. The west did not think so.

The latest conspiracy theory for chaos and terrorism doing the rounds was the China Pakistan Economic Corridor, called CPEC. China was investing over $62 billion and the corridor is considered to be an extension of China's ambitious proposed 21st century Silk Road initiative called 'One Belt, One Road'. The CPEC would provide the shortest route from China through Pakistan into the warm waters of the Arabian Sea. The sleepy deep-water port at Gwadar was being upgraded to handle the increased Chinese cargo that would pass through it and by land from

Pakistan to China. China had diplomatically acquired access to the warm waters of the Arabian Sea peacefully, what the Soviets could not through the invasion of Afghanistan, and through their designs on Balochistan.

The Strait of Malacca currently provides China with its shortest maritime access to Europe, Africa, and the Middle East for over $2 trillion of exports. Also, over 80% of Chinese energy and other raw material imports pass through the Strait. As the world's biggest oil importer, energy security is a key concern for China while current sea routes used to import Gulf oil are frequently patrolled by the United States' Navy.

In case of any hostile action from terrorism or any act of war, energy imports through the Strait could be halted, which in turn would paralyze the Chinese economy in a scenario that is frequently referred to as the 'Malacca Dilemma'. The CPEC project will allow Chinese energy imports to circumvent these contentious areas, as well as allow a shorter and faster route of exports to the world. It is estimated that shipping time for Chinese trade to the Middle East and the west would reduce by 35 days.

For Pakistan, in addition to the advantages of Chinese transit trade, the region around the trade route would trigger a heap of economic and industrial activity. Multiple projects under development and construction include power plants, metro transit in cities and supply and service among others. At the far end, Gwadar itself was being visualized to be another Dubai, or mini Dubai. Gwadar would be a competitor to Dubai.

India had also announced it would finance a port at Chabahar, in Iran, just a couple of hours across the border from Pakistan and from Gwadar. This would allow easy access to the open seas via Iran to war-stricken Afghanistan and the land locked central Asian states, including Russia. India would, thus, be able to circumvent Pakistan to reach out to the emerging economies in central Asia for their natural resources and for trade purposes.

It is estimated that there are deposits of over $3 trillion worth of Lithium and rare earth in Afghanistan and in the tribal belt of Pakistan, to which all regional and global powers want their hands on. There are also has huge deposits of gold, silver, and copper in addition to oil and gas in North Waziristan, making the whole region among the richest in this part of the world. It sounded like the plot to the science fiction movie 'Avatar' was being implemented in Afghanistan.

So, according to the various conspiracy theories doing the rounds, the state and non-state actors who would like to jeopardize the CPEC through a fourth generation warfare, and including terrorism, bombings, abductions of workers, killings, and creating chaos include India, who for obvious reasons would not want Pakistan or China to flourish; US, which would not want Chinese influence to spread in Southwest Asia, or lay its hands on the rare minerals in the region; UAE, whose ports and economy would suffer if Gwadar takes off; Afghanistan and Iran, who want to play a similar role for the land-locked Central Asian Republic states including Russia through the port of Chabahar in Iran; Israel, who would want an unstable and weak nuclear Pakistan; and UK who is always suspected as the surrogate of the US in Commonwealth countries. The destabilization had already reached out to Karachi, considered the commercial capital of Pakistan, and into Balochistan, bordering Iran and Afghanistan, on the Arabian Sea, where Gwadar is located.

Hameed Khan, the VC from KP, spoke up loudly from the back, "We have lost our ways, and deviated from the real Islam and the sharia. Our media is full of obscene shows. Our leaders are corrupt and have no fear of Allah or the life after. The Taliban are the real followers of the sharia. They are teaching us a lesson to come back to the correct path. We should be indebted to them."

There was deafening silence. Hameed Khan had always projected his religious fundamentalist views. Only last week, he had posted a notice on his campus that boys and girls are not allowed to sit or walk together within the campus or outside, and if anyone was found violating this policy would be fined, and an emergency meeting would be called with the parents. He had made many such policies. It was rumored that his first cousin was a member of the Taliban Shura, or the supreme council. He had survived his position as VC because he was also an important conduit to the extremists and Taliban through his cousin for the intelligence agencies and the government. He had always advocated a dialogue with the Taliban because he believed it was in the best interest of Pakistan. Samir knew Hameed was always a good source to get deep information on what the other side was thinking or planning, or perhaps even to reach out to them if the need arose.

Hameed also had an extremist view and believed that all non-Muslims in an occupied territory should either convert to Islam, or pay the necessary tax, called jizya. He continued, "Dr. Sahib: do you know a recent fatwa claims that it is permissible for Muslim men to take non-Muslim women into slavery, or even rape them, in order to humiliate them. Personally, I disagree with this extreme viewpoint but this fatwa has come from no other than a female Islamic professor from a leading Arab university during an interview with a TV channel…"

Samir shook his head in disbelief, "Hameed, while I respect your views, but I do not know where you get some of the stories from. You are an intelligent and responsible person, and you should filter out what is trash. These stories are fake and are planted on the net by the enemies of Islam. You very well know that Muslims are among the most hospitable nations. They are supposed to be hospitable to everyone, including non-Muslims. Even though some Muslims consider the Jews the biggest enemies of Islam, but Jews, Christians, and Muslims have lived together in Jerusalem side by side as family for hundreds of years.

"You also know that the Albanian Muslims during World War II saved over 2,000 Jews by risking their lives. They followed a code of honor called Besa. During the Nazi occupation, they hid Jewish families in their homes. The Albanian prime minister had given secret orders that Muslims should make sure that the Jew children sleep with their children, eat same food, and live as one family. This is what Islam and other religions are all about."

Sohail, a young VC from KP spoke up, "Allow me to intervene, but the suicide bombers are just an offshoot of religious extremism and radical Islam. Most people are poor today due to bad political governance, thanks to our corrupt politicians. Poverty leads to resentment. The poorest of the poor, many with large families, and unmarried young daughters, and almost everyone unemployed, the choice is between being a beggar or a martyr. Having no education on top of that leads to easy manipulations by the so-called religious leaders who are clever. They can easily manipulate and play on prejudices and superstitions prevailing culturally among Muslims. It becomes so easy to indoctrinate them and make them militants, or even terrorists, ready to give their life for Islam, become martyrs, and live a permanent luxurious life in the hereafter."

Sohail was one of the outspoken, liberal VCs who would take every opportunity to bash at the extremists without fear. Samir knew he was one of the few who spoke sense.

He continued to communicate his viewpoint, "What is surprising though is that it is no more poverty or illiteracy that is driving the jihadi mindset. If you look at the 9/11 hijackers, they were all educated and from middle class families. The Times Square bomber was educated, with an MBA from an American university, and lived a comfortable life in US. Even in our country, we have seen educated people becoming extremists, militants, and even terrorists. A faculty member from a top private university in Karachi was giving hate lectures in the classroom. There has also been a case of a student from a leading private business school from Lahore involved in terrorism. What we are seeing today is radical Islam and a hate mindset in educated people who are ready to die for Islam. So, it is not poverty and illiteracy that creates religious extremism; instead it is extremism that creates poverty and illiteracy."

Samir nodded in agreement. "I fully agree with your viewpoint."

Sohail looked around to everyone, "It is not about self-glory. Many of the educated and well to do are 'reawakened Muslims' if I could call them that. They have a desire for changing the life of their fellowmen, or the country. They are sick of corruption and have become radicals. Islam promises a clear solution to every problem. The Taliban had first become popular in Afghanistan because they provided quick justice, even as harsh as amputation of the limbs. Crime disappeared almost overnight. Today, in Pakistan, or in the Muslim world, we see rampant corruption, bad governance, and class difference between the rich and poor, or between the powerful and the powerless. People desire change. They want a better life. Islam promises them this life."

"That is exactly what I was conveying," added Hameed.

Sohail was expecting this but did not want to contradict Hameed, "Islam certainly promises a better life if practiced properly and correctly. Jihadists are misusing Islam. According to a news report published a few months back, a few women in Karachi were found collecting funds for ISIS. Some of them were educated and from well-off families. They wrongly collect these funds in the name of Zakat, or the mandatory charity given in the name of Islam. Nobody knows where these funds are going. Three women were also accused of abetting the Safoora bus carnage…" Safoora carnage referred to an incident last year when eight gunmen attacked a bus in Safoora, a suburb of Karachi, and killed over 46 people, who were all from a minority Muslim sect.

Sohail continued, "What is even more concerning is that a female medical college student, who herself was the daughter of a well-known professor at another university, was arrested by the police for abetting terrorism. She later confessed that ISIS had planned to use her as a suicide bomber…"

Samir shook his head in disbelief, "This was indeed very shocking when I heard her confessional statement on local television. This shows how radical Islam is creeping into the colleges and schools. But that is not all! The problem is far more severe. A private university VC in Karachi was also arrested for facilitating terrorists. He had been allegedly funding Al-Qaeda and was also a business partner of the terrorists involved in Safoora killing. He also disclosed that they have established a network in the educational institutions…almost like a secret society. This network is giving Islamic lectures which are not based on facts and polluting the mind of the youth and the females by the thousands, and recruiting extremists by the hundred…"

Samir's sentence was interrupted by the sound of a loud explosion right outside the auditorium, and the remaining glass windows that were still intact shattered inwards. Splinters from the wall and the roof fell on the people inside. Some screamed, others ducked. This was followed by the sound of machine-gun fire, which continued for a few minutes. Then there was silence. No one moved. The silence outside remained for another few minutes, then one could hear the sound of people running and shouting. Time froze. The only audible voice was that of a few people inside the auditorium reciting verses from the Quran.

The door suddenly opened, and those inside panicked, and the faces of some of those inside whitened, expecting a terrorist to walk in and blow himself up in their midst and kill everyone. There was a sigh of relief when it was the Captain, toting his gun, who walked in and asking everyone to stay calm.

"What happened?" asked a terrified VC.

"It is not very clear, sir. The whole area had been cleared and searched one more time. There was no sign of any terrorist inside the compound. The whole area was secured. All those martyred were removed. But somehow one more terrorist appeared as if out of thin air. With bombs tied to his chest. He was fast moving towards this auditorium. We got him in time."

"How is it possible that no one saw him?"

Hameed frowned, "Dr. Sahib. I am surprised that you do not know that. I have tried to explain it to you many times before but you fail to listen or understand, because you have a scientific mindset. An army of a thousand cannot stop even one individual if he has the protection of Allah. There are miracles in Islam. The Quran is full of miracles and our history is filled with such stories of victory. Reciting certain 'Ayat' or verses from the Quran can give one supernatural powers! Only a few can kill a hundred if they could read these sacred verses, or wear certain Islamic symbol. He can become invisible or even fly through the air. Then there are powers of the jinn…"

"Stop it, Hameed," Samir snapped. He had heard enough of these stories from people who frequented small time madrasahs and magicians. It was nothing but the blind preaching to the blind. The lure of magic by the so-called scholars had attracted the poor, the needy and particularly the women to their centers. They had then fallen into traps of blind faith, and the weak men were easily inducted into the so-called jihad. The cities were full of flyers and billboards by 'aamil', or the learned religious men who could perform white or black magic to resolve any issue or solve any problem. They could make a difficult lover comply with one's desires or have them succeed in their business. Some claimed they could even make a man invisible or make him fly. Others claimed to possess 'jinn', the supernatural beings in the Quran who are created out of a smokeless fire, and who could perform any supernatural act in a flash of a second. They could change into any form, including animals, and pass by unnoticed. They had tremendous strength. Many aamil also claim to possess 'mukil', a jinn-like being which some classify as angels who can do any task, even capture a jinn.

Hameed appeared annoyed but continued anyway, "Such stories are in the Hadith. By closing your eyes, you are denying the facts." Hadith are the books about the life and teachings of Prophet Muhammed written a few hundred years after the death of the Prophet. The majority of Muslims believe in their authenticity and follow his practices and way of life very religiously as described in these books. However, Samir knew there were many versions of the Hadith, which Muslims quote frequently, but only those are reliable that do not contradict the Quran.

Samir spoke up, "There is no evidence of such an invisibility cloak, or flying through the air by anyone. We should leave these fictional stories to other times. Anyway, if the area is now clear, we should all head back. And thank you again, particularly the VCs who drove from far away at my call just to show solidarity with our educational system. We will not back down, we will not surrender, and Inshallah, God willing, we will destroy these monsters!"

Samir bade goodbye to all, applauded the soldiers in their fight against the terrorists and walked to his car. As he drove back to Islamabad, his mind drifted to these horror stories of aamil who many people believed could perform miracles and do magic! Were they really miracles, or an illusion created by them? And if they could really do miracles, like become invisible, or fly through the air, then why would they attack a civilian target like a university. Why not a military base? Were they just testing their powers? Was it a prelude to something much larger, something more disastrous? If one were to believe what one heard or saw, it appeared that the real prize for the terrorists lay elsewhere. And they would resort to any means to obtain it, whether by magic or through the control of the supernatural entities called jinn.

But the key question was: was it possible to acquire these powers and use them or were these just superstitious beliefs and folklore stories?

Contractor

It was a few months earlier that Harry Walker was contacted by a leading security agency for an overseas assignment. The Pentagon usually outsourced security services to defense contractors and various other agencies like Blackwater in many regions around the world, including in Afghanistan, Pakistan, Iraq, and Libya, among others, where it did not want to be caught red handed with its fingers in the pie or go through various congressional oversights.

Harry had served in the Special Forces and the Marines before taking early retirement. He was a computer programmer and was considered top notch in nuclear espionage. He could decode any nuclear triggering device. But above that, he was also considered a fighting machine, one of the best! He wanted to spend his retirement years living out of his mountain lodge in Washington State, hunting big game and mountain climbing. His physical appearance was like a typical commando: tall, strong muscles, and army cut hair. He had blue eyes and blonde hair.

It was during one of his hunting wild bear trips when he was contacted by a leading private security service which had major overseas contracts in the Middle East and South Asia. He had heard of the company's reputation as one of the best, and knew they were pay masters. They offered him a handsome contract for his short-term services overseas which would only be for 3 months. It was too good to be true. He could easily buy the Hummer H1 that he long aspired. He immediately agreed.

He was to be stationed for one month in a location outside the US and then taken to another country for a specific operation. He would be briefed upon arrival.

He packed his knapsack, making sure he tucked in his favorite Glock 18 fully automatic machine pistol. His Glock had many a times saved his life. A chopper picked him up within a few hours.

Boarding a military aircraft at Seattle, he arrived after a short refueling stop at Frankfurt at Bagram Air Base in Afghanistan, which he immediately recognized, as he had served there for a full year prior to taking early retirement from the Special Forces. He could speak fluent Pashto which he had learnt quickly. He always believed the key to survival is knowing the local language. A Willy's Jeep was waiting for him to take him to Kabul, which was about 30 minutes away.

He hated Islam even though he had served most of his time in Muslim countries. He believed that the biggest problem with Muslims was their jihadi viewpoint and their beliefs in the so-called sharia laws'. He believed Muslims were retarded people as a result of inbreeding by marrying first cousins. To him, it was incest, which was legally allowed in Islam. This practice had been prohibited among Jews since Moses, and later by the Christians. Scientifically also, if one had a child with one's cousin, there is a strong likelihood that there will be a genetic problem. Muhammad himself had married cousins. In Pakistan, half the marriages are among cousins. Those born as a result of inbreeding have mental and schizophrenic sickness, and physical retardation.

The Sultans of Turkey, who considered themselves Caliphs, never married and only had concubines. Their offsprings were all born out of wedlock. Polygamy is allowed in Islam. This practice has been going on for more than 1,400 years. Having multiple wives living together was common among the Muslims, especially among the Pashtun. According to Harry, the race was full of bastards.

Stoning to death, or beheadings were common in this part of the world, while others watched and cheered. Women were treated like slaves. They were imprisoned in homes, and wore burqas from head to toe when out on streets. The Muslim countries had the highest rates of illiteracy and poverty anywhere. Their leaders were corrupt to the core. He recalled a major US paper presenting Islam more negatively than cancer or cocaine. In US media, the most frequent terms associated with Muslims include 'rebel' and 'militant'. In a survey, none of the 25 most frequently occurring terms about Muslims were positive.

He recalled the ugly incident in Afghanistan two years back when their helicopter was shot down by the Taliban, and the three of them were surrounded by Al-Qaeda terrorists. In a gruesome battle that lasted a few hours in which the other two, including the young Ryan who was only 21 years old and a cheerful young chap who loved music, were badly injured. They were captured, and instead of making them prisoners or taking them to camp, the two injured were slaughtered right before his eyes. They were beheaded, their bodies cut in pieces, and their heads stuck on a pole as a sign of victory. He could never forget the look in Ryan's eyes before he was beheaded. He had vowed that if he ever lived, he would avenge him. He did not know why he was not killed like the others, but was sure he would be beheaded later while a video would be shot of him to show to the world. He was made to walk barefoot on hot burning rocks two miles to their nearby camp.

A day later, the camp was attacked by another rebel group in the night. He made his escape, walking for hours, before being picked up by US forces who were patrolling the area. He directed the forces back to the camp, and attacked the surviving terrorists and massacred every single one. They then gave a decent burial to Ryan and the other corporal.

He had since then considered Muslims the biggest terrorists anywhere in the world. It did not matter to him whether they were Al-Qaeda, the Taliban, or Pakistanis.

He now had his opportunity to set his own agenda to rid the world of this menace. If he could help the world get rid of the Muslims, it would be a much better place to live.

Healer

At a madrassah, somewhere in the mountains of Swat, about 20 tall green turbaned men wearing traditional white clothes with long beards and no mustaches, sat on the floor in a circle facing each other, and were reciting some holy verses from the Quran in unison. They belonged to a secret society called the Harmeen. It was a militant offshoot of the Wahhabis, which believed in a return to puritanical Islam. The Harmeen believed that the world should revert back by 1,400 years and Muslims should continue with the practices of the Prophet. For them, all the evils of the present world were due to Muslims adopting modern beliefs and practices, including a belief in sciences, and in the use of technology. Harmeen were like the 'Muslim Amish', but believed in the use of force to cleanse and to ensure that Muslims revert back to the old-fashioned traditional ways. For them, the modern Muslim reformer was misleading and misguiding the society. Those who believed in modern science, like the theory of evolution, or the big bang theory of universe, were kafir, and deserved to be eliminated. For them, the schools, colleges, and universities, and the scientific conferences taking place were only propaganda machines established by 'the Jews and the Romans'. Their mission was to 'save Islam and take it back to the traditional ways of 1,400 years ago'.

At their center was a large pile of a few thousand beads. Verses were being chanted together in rhythm, and when a verse was completed, a bead was picked up by the man wearing a green scarf sitting at the head of the group, and placed on the side into another pile. This exercise, or praying together in unison, had continued uninterrupted for the last few hours.

In the adjoining room, three other men, who looked more militant as they carried guns, were sitting together. Lying on a cot in the middle of the room was a shirtless man who appeared badly injured from what appeared to be multiple gunshots. A white scarf was tied around his chest, which showed signs that there was considerable bleeding that had taken place earlier and had dried up into clots now. He was half conscious and was sometimes moving his head or slightly lifting his hands as if coming back to life.

A turbaned man, who appeared to be a hakeem, or a local doctor, wearing a green shirt and scarf, was sitting next to him. He seemed to be in authority and was nursing him with lightly rubbing his chest and blowing into the wounds. He had a small silver crucible lying on the side of the head, which had the verses of the Quran inscribed on the inner side. It was filled with some liquid, a potion, which was prepared as per teachings of the Prophet to heal people. Such a treatment was in accordance with 'Tibb-e-Nabvi' or the medicine of the Prophet, which had gained popularity among the poor and the middle class in recent years. Many who had lost all hope in life reverted to the spiritual treatment. The hakeem, a tibb-e-nabvi expert, and known by the name of Luqman, was the healer. He was using a dab of cotton and was feeding a few drops at a time into the injured person's mouth alternating with rubbing his chest too.

Downstairs at the small entrance to the madrassah stood two more men with semi-automatics slung around their shoulders. Nobody seemed to notice them or their guns as people passed by. Many of the people themselves carried guns which was the norm in this part of the world. The madrassah had a sign outside in Urdu, the local language, with a few verses from the Quran written on it along with a green crescent.

The locals knew that the Hakeem had great spiritual powers and could literally bring back the dead back to life without any medicine. Many a people from all over the country, including from neighboring Afghanistan and Iran, had brought their friends, family members, including those with terminal illness to the Hakeem at the madrasahs and the clinics he frequented, with great success. The reputation had gone far and wide. More recently, with the Operation Zarb-e-Azb, many an injured had been brought here, and had miraculously healed. Hakeem Luqman was known as the wise one with the wisdom and the magical power of healing.

In Islamic traditions, Luqman, who lived around 1100 BCE, was a wise man from Ethiopia. Some people believe him to be a prophet, though the Quran makes no such reference. The belief is that when God wanted to gift him power or wisdom, he chose wisdom. Luqman had a cure for all diseases of the world, and therefore the most knowledgeable physicians in the Muslim world are referred to as Hakeem Luqman. The turbaned man was identified as such. The chanting of the verses continued late into the night.

Mulla Maqsood

Samir had just entered his office when a message by Mulla Maqsood was posted on the net. The mulla was the factional head of TTP in KP and was claiming responsibility for the deadly attack at Charsadda. He had been very close to Hakimullah Mehsud, the TTP Emir in Pakistan, before Mehsud was killed in a CIA drone missile attack.

Mulla Maqsood was also claimed by TTP to be the mastermind of the massacre at a school in Peshawar in which 132 children were killed. He has posted a similar video on the net after the school killing in which the TTP had said that the school attack was in retaliation for a military offensive carried out by the Pakistani army. Mulla was also close to Maulana Fazlullah who had ordered assassins to kill the schoolgirl Shazia in Swat.

According to some captured Taliban, Maqsood had received high school education in Islamabad and later studied in a madrassah. He also spent time working in Karachi as a laborer before joining the TTP in 2007.

"He was very strict from the start when he joined," an arrested TTP commander had said. "He left many commanders behind if they had a soft corner in their heart for the government."

The video message posted after the Charsadda attack was very similar to the school attack message. It showed Khalifa, meaning an Islamic leader, Maqsood, with three of the suicide bombers on his right and two on his left, all heavily armed. Three were masked and three, including Maqsood, did not disclose their identities on the video. They all carried long and thick and beards and wore caps. Some of the words were inaudible and not clear.

The message ran as follows in broken Pashto language:

"I want to say two or three things to the…Muslims. Firstly, the fake rulers of Pakistan have challenged the supremacy of Allah for over 50 years. And for not imposing the rule of Allah, they are punished in various ways…earthquakes, floods, storms…and instead of repenting, their…keeps on increasing. They should remember how Allah destroyed them in the past…if Pakistan does not refrain from their sins and democracy does not repent, then Sindh and Punjab like KP will suffer…God has decided if any country commits a sin, then there will be a severe punishment for them…and we started with Ali Khan University because the system of democracy, the leadership, the political rule…is corrupt. Here they are nurtured. Judges, magistrates, lawyers are trained here. Law colleges are here. Their mind is poisoned. They make laws against the laws of Allah.

"The Pakistan army is a terrible organization. The captains, majors, colonels, brigadiers, corps commanders, lieutenant generals, major generals, generals are fighting us! We, who are the real saviors and have raised their voice for Allah…Pakistan and its senate are useless. The cabinet, and ministers of defense, foreign, interior, governors, chief ministers, are useless. They go to national assembly and make laws against the law of Allah…so after a lot of discussion and consultation, we have reached the conclusion that from today, colleges, schools, and universities will be attacked, and not the army in camps, or lawyers in courts, or the politicians in the senate or the national assembly and parliament. But here in schools, colleges and universities where they are trained. Inshallah, we will kill them here and destroy these foundations, and till they are not finished, we will continue attacking schools, colleges and universities.

"We want to tell the Islamic scholars that Torah was based on 4,000-year-old laws, and when the children of Israel made changes to the Torah, and then Allah declared everyone to be kafir. So, in Pakistan, the whole system is kafir. After our attack on the school, the government announced a National Action Plan, based on 21 points, so why doesn't Pakistan become kafir then? Bani Israel was declared kafir after a small amendment. So, now all Pakistan system is kafir. So, why is it not kafir? We demand Pakistani scholars that in front of all the Islamic world, they should speak up the facts, otherwise on doomsday, our hands and that of other 'fedayeen' will be on your collar…you should clarify that the Quran is a law that God has sent us, including the basic law. We have started cleansing this process practically, through schools, colleges, and universities. The system that has come from UK and USA and made by men, and imposed on us, we want to destroy it, and finish its basis. We want to impose Allah's system, and Allah's rule. Salam."

The phone rang. Samir's wife, Shaday, called from Miami, where she had been visiting Samir's sister. She had been trying for the last two hours to check on his welfare but the signals were jammed at Charsadda.

She informed him that there had been a big shoot out at a gay bar in Orlando. The news was flashing all over the TV that yet another jihadi, a Muslim, had attacked a gay bar in Orlando and massacred over 50 people. Some called it the worst terror attack since 9/11. She was worried about him and their younger son Hasan who was visiting Pakistan during his summer break.

Hasan was 22 years old, handsome with curly hair like his father. He had just graduated in psychology and was still 'discovering' himself. He had read a lot on mystical Islam, had a passion for spiritualism and sufism, and had researched well into the Islamic beliefs in mystics, dreams, black magic, and jinn. In the US, he had spent many evenings discussing these aspects with his father, who would usually write them off as nonsense.

"Dad, prayers and dreams have miraculous powers. It is true for all religions and beliefs. It connects the soul to the supernatural. Likewise, magic has existed for thousands of years, from Babylon to the pharaohs to the times of our Prophet and the present times. It is believed and practiced in every religion and region. Also, the jinn are a real entity, mentioned in the Quran, with superhuman powers, although it is forbidden in our religion to make contact with them or use them to our advantage."

Hasan had a very pragmatic view of such beliefs.

"Hasan is fine and safe, and is currently in Karachi with his friends."

Samir knew Hasan had planned to visit some of the famous sufi shrines, including the Lal Shahbaz Qalandar in Sehwan, which is frequented by Muslims, Hindus, and Christians alike, the Shah Abdul Latif Shrine in Hala, revered by all Sindhis, and the Abdullah Ghazi Shrine in Karachi, overlooking the Arabian Sea. It is believed that many cyclones and tsunamis, which were destined to hit Karachi, were diverted by the spiritual power of Abdullah Ghazi. He is considered the savior saint of Karachi.

"I am just worried and hope he is not influenced by any negativity."

Samir was least worried about his children. Hussain, the elder one, had just graduated with a degree in medicine and was the nerdy type like his father and very scientific oriented. Hasan, on the other hand, was artistic, creative, and social, always wanting to reach out and make new friends.

"Don't worry! He has a lot of friends in Karachi and knows his ways around. He will be here with me in Islamabad within the next few days."

As Samir hung up, his phone rang again. It was Hameed.

"Did you hear about the Orlando attack? This is exactly what I have been telling you. These are part of false flag operations. This attack is a set-up because the Muslim world, including the whole of US, have just mourned the death of the greatest sportsman who ever lived—Muhammad Ali—and Ali's religion was Islam. TV channels were projecting stories about his humane side, and how he helped everyone—Christians, Jews, Muslims, black or white, old or young. He was a Muslim fighter, a truth jihadi, a man willing to sacrifice everything for truth and justice. The humanitarian side of Islam was making world headlines. It was the best week Islam had in the US since 9/11. This was clearly not acceptable to those who hated Muslims."

"And why would they do it?" asked Samir.

"The haters and our enemies had yet another fear that the US president was going to support a resolution in the UNSC that recognized and officially established the State of Palestine within its pre-1967 borders."

Hameed continued, "The haters have responded with a massive attack in Orlando to make the world forget Muhammad Ali and to force the US president to not support the resolution. They need to keep the clash of civilizations going, and Israel expanding."

"And who would lose from this? The Muslims?" asked Samir. Hameed made sense to a certain extent. It certainly appeared like a hate crime, and not a jihadi-inspired shoot-out.

"The Muslims, of course! How is it possible that there was only one shooter and there were 50 dead? He must be the best shot in the world! And he was not even a commando or from the special services, but just a petty security guard. There is certainly something fishy here!"

Samir could feel Hameed raising the tone of his voice, who hated all such allegations made against the Muslims. "Just see the pattern of how all Muslim terrorists can hijack and remotely fly three planes at the same time, how they can take down two tall towers in the heart of New York City, how they can blow up any building with a few fire-crackers, and the funny thing is that in each of these incidents, they also leave behind at the scene of terrorism their passports or ID cards, which somehow never burn or are even parched despite the heat and explosion. We must be extra-competent Superman and Batman in one, or the team of Avengers put together. Yet, on the other end, we are projected as a bunch of least competent fools who can't even light a match to ignite the fuse, or to remember that they have forgotten their underwear at home so they have no place to hide the explosives."

He continued without stopping, "The majority of the terrorist attacks in the US are not committed by the Muslims, but rather by Jews, Christians, and those with a screwed-up mind.

"All the plots and attacks attributed to Muslims are concocted by the CIA, the Zionist lobby, the ultra-far right, the KKK, and the hidden state within the state."

Hameed paused for a few seconds as if to catch his breath, and then added, "Look at this: the Jewish controlled US media, immediately after projecting Allah-o-Akbar on the screen for hours, claimed that 'the shooter had pledged allegiance to ISIS'. How convenient, when ISIS itself is the baby of the west. This only proves that the shooting was an inside job."

"But what about the shooter being from Afghanistan?" asked Samir.

"His parents were born in Afghanistan. The secret hands were setting him up for the massacre, as they knew he was gay himself, and used to frequent the bar! This was nothing but a hate crime, a gay, which Islam also curses, targeting out other gays due to jealousy or something! Maybe he was just a jilted lover."

Hameed seemed convinced that the massacre was a conspiracy planned by someone else.

He went on, "It is possible that he may just have fired a few shots. But then he was set up, and then professional multiple killers completed the job.

"It is also reported somewhere in the media that his father was a hardcore CIA asset and was told that he would be the future Afghan president. He is a staunch anti-Pakistan, pro-TTP, pro-India, CIA agent and wants to divide Pakistan. The whole Orlando shooting is a CIA operation."

Samir's mind floated back to yet another fateful shooting in San Bernardino, California last year where 14 innocent people were killed and 22 were injured in a mass shooting and attempted bombing. The shooters were Farook and Tashfeen, a married Muslim couple of Pakistani descent who had attacked a holiday party. Farook was a US born citizen while Tashfeen was a permanent resident.

The FBI had subsequently investigated and found that the couple had been inspired by foreign terrorist groups and were not part of any cell or network. They had become radicalized, consuming 'poison on the internet', and had expressed a leaning to jihadism and martyrdom in messages to each other. They had also been to Saudi Arabia for pilgrimage purposes. There was no evidence at this stage if they had made any physical contact with terrorist networks. A large supply of weapons, ammunition, and bomb-making equipment had been subsequently discovered at their home. What was most shocking was that they had left their six-month-old daughter with Farook's mother the morning of the attack, saying they had a clinical appointment and would return soon.

The couple, during the attack, had worn ski masks and black tactical gear, fired around 70 bullets, and escaped the massacre. Sources reported that Tashfeen had pledged allegiance to ISIS on a Facebook account associated with her as the attack was underway. However, it was later found that the posting was made on their behalf. The police eventually caught up with the SUV that was used in the attack. After an exchange of fire with the police, both were killed.

Farook was born in Chicago and had attended California State University, San Bernardino, and received a bachelor's degree in environmental health. He also attended the California State University, Fullerton, as a graduate student in environmental engineering for one semester in 2014 and had dropped out. According to friends, Farook was a practicing Muslim, and had performed the Haj, or the pilgrimage to Mecca, in 2013. He regularly attended prayers at the Islamic Center of Riverside. However, he had stopped going to the mosque since 2014 following his marriage to Tashfeen.

Tashfeen was born in Pakistan but lived most of her life in Saudi Arabia. She studied pharmacology at a university in Multan, a city which is considered the center of sufism. However, a large number of sectarian and extremist organizations also flourished in Multan, including Lashkar-e-Jhangvi, a Sunni supremacist and jihadist militant organization and the Sipah-e-Sahaba, yet another Sunni organization. Tashfeen became very conservative and wore both the niqab, a veil covering the face, and the burqa, a full veil covering the body. She reportedly had ties to the radical Red Mosque in Islamabad though it was not confirmed at any stage.

While in Multan, Tashfeen attended the local center of a religious academy for women with branches across Pakistan, US, and Canada. The school was aligned with the conservative form of Sunni Islam, and draws much of its support from educated, middle and upper middle-class women. Most women attending these lectures had personal problems, including matrimonial, financial or issues with in-laws or children. They could find solace in her lectures, and sometimes a solution as well.

Samir wondered, finding solace from problems is one thing, but if educated middle class Pakistanis like Farook and Tashfeen could be brainwashed on the net into becoming militants, ending up by sacrificing their career, families and a daughter, embracing 'shahadat', or martyrdom, then there was certainly a problem in the teachings at the universities, and in academies across the country. He wanted to get to the core of the issue of how the students were being radicalized so it could be stopped. This was part of his job after all.

To get some of these answers, he decided to make his next stop at the Global Muslim University in Islamabad, which was considered a scholarly Islamic university with heavy funding from the Saudis. Recently, the university itself had been attacked by terrorists. One could therefore only wonder whose side the terrorists were on!

Aamil

Jadoo Baba was one of the most famous aamil in Hasan Abdal, a spiritual healer, conjurer and man of magic who could make anything happen. He could make divorces happen for a jealous lover, or destroy another's career. He could arrange a big financial loss for someone, he could touch someone on the forehead and render him unconscious, or even cast a spell so that the person would die a slow painful death. He also claimed he could even make people fly and transport them from one place to another in an instant, or even have them become invisible, a claim that could not be confirmed by reliable sources. Nevertheless, his magical powers were well-known and people flocked to him by the hundreds from far and wide.

He was slim and very tall, over six feet, with sharp piercing eyes and looked like a wicked magician even in his appearance, and lived and worked from a small house off a narrow street in the most crowded part of the city. The road outside was full of uncollected garbage with the gutter overflowing onto the sidewalk. There were many small shops in the area, some selling milk and bread, one cell phone repair shop, and one selling fresh juices and soft drinks. There were a few men who appeared to be doing nothing except indulging in small talk. A woman wearing a burqa, or a full-length veil, with a small child passed them and entered the house. The hallway was crowded with men, about 20 of them, and there was hardly enough room for her to pass through to the women's secluded area.

There were three men sitting outside a closed door. They were all tall and were whispering to each other in Pashto. One carried a small briefcase and was holding it tightly. Another got up to offer the woman a seat. She declined without answering as she preferred the room where 'purdah', or seclusion, could be observed.

The door opened, and everyone looked up. A man walked out carrying a small colored plastic box in his hand covered in a black scarf. He was handling it very carefully as if it was something volatile and could explode. He had a satisfied look on his face as if he got what he wanted. He hurriedly walked towards the exit and left without looking back.

The man sitting inside the room on the floor, who was the famous aamil Jadoo Baba, was tall and thin. He was wearing a black dress with an orange necklace round his neck which had strange charms, and had a long black beard with mustaches. He had what one would call a wicked face. The three men sitting outside immediately walked in before anyone else could move and shut the door behind them. No one actually moved as the body language of these men showed them to have some degree of authority.

The walls inside the room had many charts with various strange symbols, numbers, and words on them. One had some Arabic verses, another carried the picture of what appeared to be a holy man with a light shining around his head, and a third had a picture of what looked like a cat with large claws flying through the air. There were a number of candles lighted around the room, and a collection of small bottles and plastic containers in one corner of the room on a table. A small fridge was in the other corner. The door of the fridge appeared to be smeared in dried blood. People knew it carried animal, and sometimes even human organs, stolen by digging out fresh corpses from graves and cutting them apart to take out a liver or heart. The room had a strong stench of stale raw meat.

The short man waived to the others to sit down and not speak. He then closed his eyes, recited a mantra, concentrated for a minute, took a pinch of a powder from a small napkin lying in front of him, and tossed it up in the air. He knew what these men were here for. The task in hand had been discussed earlier.

"What you ask for is difficult but not impossible. I have already accomplished one task for you with success. This one, what you ask now, needs far more resources."

He was making it very clear that this task will cost more. He was a greedy man.

The first man replied, "Money is not an issue. We would like to have our hands on a treasure which is well guarded, and we know you can make this happen. He then placed the briefcase on the floor and opened it. It was full of hundred-rupee bills.

The aamil's eyes almost opened wide as he looked at the money. He had never been offered so much before by anyone, not even by them. He smiled and then closed his eyes to focus on the difficult nature of the task for a minute or two. He recited some mantra or verses, then slowly opened his eyes, looked hard at the first man, and finally spoke, "I need the hair locks of the men who would go in to get the treasure in order to make them invisible, to make them fly, and to protect them. I also need a close personal item of the commander in charge of the guards. It has to be an item, or a piece of cloth, that has touched his body. I also need to know the name of his mother. We will make him blind, deaf, and dumb at the very moment when you want to steal the treasure."

"It will be done!" the first man replied. "We will be back in a few days with what you want."

The aamil then continued with his mantra for a few more minutes, and sprinkled another pinch of powder in the air. He then took the briefcase full of money and placed it to his side.

"It will be done. Your men will not fail!"

The men walked out with grinning faces.

Global Muslim University

Global Muslim University, known locally as GMU, lies at the foothills of the Margalla ranges in Islamabad, right next to the Faisal Mosque. Faisal Mosque, the largest mosque in Pakistan, was completed in 1986, and was named after King Faisal of Saudi Arabia who was killed in 1975. The mosque was designed by a Turkish architect. It is shaped like an Arab bedouin's tent, and is the iconic symbol of Islamabad in Pakistan. The mosque has covered area of 54,000 sq. ft. and can accommodate 10,000 worshipers in its main prayer hall, 24,000 in its porticoes, 40,000 in its courtyard, and another 200,000 in the adjoining grounds. General Zain, the martial law dictator who overthrew the democratic government of Murtaza Brohi, the father of Marvi, and hanged him, lies buried in the courtyard. He was killed in a plane explosion along with a senior US official of that time.

It is still not known who was responsible for his death, but the local grapevine accused the Russians, since he supported the jihad against the Soviet occupation of Afghanistan. Another theory blamed the CIA, as they wanted him out of the way after the Geneva Accord was signed for the withdrawal of troops from Kabul, and cessation of all hostilities in Afghanistan, to which he was not willing. He had a dream of conquering Afghanistan after the Soviet withdrawal making it a part of greater Pashtunistan in Pakistan. It was not meant to be. Yet, a third theory attributed his killing to the Al-Murtaza militant group, led by Zaid, a diehard rebel son of the hanged Prime Minister Murtaza Brohi, who wanted to avenge his father's death, and had chosen the revolutionary way to overthrow General Zain with the financial support of Colonel Kaddafi of Libya. Marvi had instead chosen the democratic way to overthrow Zain.

Both GMU and Faisal Mosque were heavily funded and influenced by the Saudis. No VC of the university could be appointed without Saudi consent, neither could the imam of the mosque. The current VC Latif Orakzai was a Pashtun and considered a top-notch religious scholar. He was well-respected for his knowledge of geopolitical affairs and was also known as a religious fundamentalist with strong ties to all religious parties. He was tall and handsome with blue eyes and a trimmed beard.

"Salam alaikum," Latif excitedly blurted out as Samir walked unexpectedly into his office overlooking the minarets of the Faisal Mosque. "Dr. Sahib, what brings you here? You could have asked for me, and I would have honored you with my presence in your office."

Samir jumped straight to the point. There was no need to brief this man who perhaps knew much more geopolitics than many others in the country. He could perhaps give a better insight why these terrorist attacks were being carried out in Pakistan on a regular basis.

"Latif! As you know, the Ali Khan University was attacked this morning by terrorists and we have lost 22 students including one professor. The video message of the TTP honcho was very clear…they will be attacking universities and schools from now on. How can we prevent this catastrophe from hitting our institutions, and the country? What are they trying to achieve? Why the colleges and what is their real agenda?"

"Dr. Sahib: This is a war that the West has imposed on us. It is to get the Pashtun people and wipe them clean off the face of this Earth."

He paused to let the message sink in, "Pashtun are a martial race but at the same time, the most hospitable race of the world. We stretched all the way west to Persia and Persepolis, and east to Lahore and Delhi. The West has hit the innocent Pashtun throughout history. Alexander, who was a westerner and an alien to our culture, invaded our territory over 2,000 years ago and destroyed our peaceful civilization. They then left us at the mercy of the Indians. The British Empire used us to fight their dirty war first against the Turkish Empire, and then against the Nazis and the Japs. They too left us at the disposal of the Punjabis. Punjabis then used us to fight the Hindus in Kashmir and then abandoned us. Americans then used us to fight the Soviets after the invasion of Afghanistan. After we won the war for them, they too abandoned us."

Samir couldn't agree more. He added, "Pashtun are a martial race that have survived centuries…"

Latif didn't hear him, "The final nail in our coffin came after 9/11. The Pashtun were not even involved in the destruction of the World Trade Towers. The terrorists were all Arabs. But this was a Zionist agenda to wipe out the Pashtun. The key question is that how is it possible that 19 hijackers were led by a man in a cave in Afghanistan, who was on dialysis, with the main hijacker being a smoker of cocaine and an alcoholic? How is it possible that the planes were flown by amateur pilots? No fighter jets intercepted them. Then one of the planes supposedly crashes into the Pentagon, right on target into the very room where papers on the $ 2.3 trillion budget totals were missing. Someone in the defense department must be smiling. It was a clean missile type of hit, and there was no evidence of plane parts. And the hijacker's passport copy was found near the World Trade Center. It is an insult to our intelligence."

Latif's face turned red with anger, "The whole operation was planned and financed by the Jewish lobby. It has been reported in the media, and then hushed up, that two key Jewish businessmen had bought the buildings, which were nothing but a liability—full of asbestos—and the cost of extracting asbestos was to be in billions. It is a confirmed fact that half the buildings were unoccupied. So, it was a huge financial drain on these Jews. They bought the lease on it, and within six weeks, things come down! And in these six weeks, they doubled the insurance policy."

Latif paused for a moment so as to let the gravity of his argument sink in, and then continued.

"If it was Muhammad, instead of the Jewish businessmen, the media would have immediately highlighted it. Jewish billionaires don't buy buildings which are financial liability. It appeared they were friends of the Israeli prime minister. The workers had been working in the building for weeks—no one knows what they were bringing in and out. Explosives obviously. Some Mossad agents were reportedly caught by the police as well, but were let go without any investigation. Clearly, the collapse was masterminded by the Mossad. Bombs were obviously planted in buildings the day before. It has also been reported that neither the CEO of the building nor his daughters showed up to work that day. They had put a hefty insurance policy on the two buildings. It was a conspiracy similar to the Pearl Harbor attack, so that America would be sucked into the war. The whole scheme was to destroy the Pashtun because the hardcore Jews believe the Pashtun will one day destroy them. The Americans want to occupy our region for its trillion-dollar resources, as well."

He continued with his argument, "If you also recall, there was the David Malone incident, who was a contractor with the CIA and was caught in Lahore. Allegedly, David was in touch with a CIA-financed doctor who had provided information on Osama bin Laden's whereabouts to him. David killed two armed men in Lahore and was jailed with charges of double murder and the illegal possession of a firearm. Yet, another car which came to help him killed a third man. David was being provided sensitive information by Mossad and RAW. David was released after the US government paid $2.4 million in blood money. What hypocrisy of the Americans! On one hand, they are against the sharia laws, and on the other hand, they apply the sharia law to have their mercenary released!

"Now, David has come up with his bull-shit version of the incident in his recent book. It is nothing but a propaganda against our intelligence agencies!"

He paused for a moment, expecting Samir to add something, and then continued, "We all know David was taking pictures of sensitive spots in Pakistan, including where the US intelligence assumed the nuclear arsenal is kept. But David was not the only one involved in spying. There was an earlier incident as well when four contractors, dressed as Taliban and fluent in Pashto, were arrested in a vehicle about two miles from the sensitive Kahuta Nuclear Plant. Explosives and sensitive equipment were found in their vehicle. Under influence from the US government, they were released. In both cases, the plan was that once the information was confirmed, the TTP, aided by US intelligence agencies, would attack these bases to get hold of at least one bomb. The world community would then have a strong case to ask Pakistan to reverse and dismantle its nuclear program. In retaliation, the plan was to heavily bomb the Pashtun areas in Pakistan like they did in Afghanistan after 9/11 to finish this race before it annihilates Israel! They want to hold the Pashtun and the ISI responsible for everything so they have a reason to attack us!"

Samir interrupted, "But statements of the westerner David Headley, who was born Daood Sayed Gilani, is that he, not the ISI, conspired with the Lashkar-e-Taiba, abbreviated LeT, and literally meaning the 'Army of the Pure', in some of the terrorist activities, like plotting the 2008 Mumbai attacks. Headley did at least five spying trips to Mumbai to plan these attacks, and was arrested in Chicago airport on his way to Pakistan in October 2009. For the Indian authorities, Headley is the equivalent of Osama bin Laden. The US court has already sentenced Headley to 35 years in prison for his role in the Mumbai attacks!"

Latif's eyes shone as if he knew of the conspiracy, "Headley is being prosecuted by a Mumbai special court, who want him deported to India. They want the blame shifted to Pakistan so it can be attacked by India. Supposedly, in a video link from his prison cell, he has claimed that the ISI had supported the militants."

Samir had also heard of that conspiracy. "It makes no sense to me, as I am sure Pakistan had no role in the Mumbai attacks."

Latif moved towards the window, and paused to take a sip of water. "It is much deeper than that if you know what I mean. The American fundamentalists, the extreme die-hard neo-conservative, believe that Christ will come after a major war in the Middle East and after Israel has destroyed its enemies. Some of the proponents of this belief want to start a huge war in the Middle East so that Jesus can come soon. What we are seeing today in Iraq and Syria is an outcome of such beliefs. The US presidency wanted the Iraq war to bring on the apocalypse in the Middle East."

He continued, "The Christian fundamentalists also believe that Gog and Magog are the people who are prophesied to come from the east and destroy Israel. We believe they were trapped behind a wall built by Zul-Qarnain who they believe to be a prophet. Some believe they will come from the Levent region, hence the wars in Iraq and Syria to destroy them. Others think they are the Chinese behind the Great Wall. However, there are quite a few fundamentalist Christians who believe the Gog and Magog to be central Asians from the Khorasan, notably the Pashtun. Hence, we see multiple wars in Afghanistan, from the Russian invasion in the 70s to the 9/11 catastrophe, both meant to destroy the Pashtun."

Samir blurted in, "But in 1979, it was the Russians who invaded Afghanistan. The Americans only came in to liberate them."

Latif chuckled, "That is what we are made to believe. It was all planned. The Soviets were given a green signal and were led by the Americans to invade Afghanistan, just like Saddam was led into attacking Kuwait. The Americans then stepped in, as they had planned the war in Afghanistan, like they did in Iraq, to ensure that the destruction continues."

He continued, "However, the Pashtun are a resilient nation. Haven't you noticed that despite the first war with a super power like the Russians, which lasted over 10 years, the Pashtun won and came out smiling. And now even in the second war with the Americans, and with the joint International Security Assistance Forces, or ISAF in short, established by the United Nations Security Council in which many other countries, including NATO countries, have contributed its forces, and with the use of highly sophisticated and technologically advanced weapons deployed by the Americans, the Pashtun, with their primitive weapons, are still winning this war. If the prophecy is correct, it is ordained that the Pashtun will be the ones to destroy Israel. There is no way the Pashtun will get destroyed by the Christians and Jews even if they team up."

Samir could see Latif was proud of his race and ethnic background.

Latif continued, "The plan of this Christian fundamentalist mafia is to lead the whole region into World War III, followed by Armageddon, the Second Coming of the Christ and the Rapture. But leave the Christian fundamentalists aside. Many Americans believe that the Bible predicts the future and that we are living in the last days. This lot of believers make up about one-third of America's 40 or 50 million evangelical Christians. They believe that Israel will play a central role during judgement day when the world will be destroyed. They also believe that the Bible's prophecies are being fulfilled very accurately and in quick succession. Peace is nowhere prophesied until Jesus comes and brings it himself, and anyone who talks peace is ignoring or defying God's plan for the end of the world. All this is reported in a research conducted by an American organization…"

Samir interrupted to ask Latif a fundamental question, "Where are the terrorists operating from, where are their bases, and who is supporting them?"

"From Afghanistan, of course, aided by RAW and Mossad. The conspirators in America are supporting the TTP and the Afghan government as well against Pakistan. We have a number of checkposts at the Afghan border to stop the intrusion of terrorists from Afghanistan into Pakistan. However, this has made the

Americans very unhappy. If you recall, sometime back, NATO helicopters, gunships and fighter jets had attacked the Salala checkpost. They had violated the Pakistan airspace by entering over two miles into the Pakistani border area one early morning from Afghanistan and opened fire at two checkposts killing 28 Pakistani soldiers. This attack had led to a deterioration of relations between Pakistan and the US. We reacted by closing the Shamsi Airfield in Balochistan, which was one of the bases from where the US drones were taking off, and closed the NATO supply line, as well, which badly hurt the Americans. Subsequently, it was proven that Pakistan was right and the US secretary of state officially apologized for these attacks. Pakistan then reopened the NATO supply line."

"It was accidental!"

Hameed shook his head, "The neo-conservatives in America do not trust the Pakistan army and have always used different means in the past to stop military aid and weaken the army. If you recall, the biggest one of them was the Memo-gate controversy. It was about the memorandum allegedly written by a senior Pakistani official, whom many believe was on the American payroll as well, after Osama bin Laden was killed in the US raid in Abbottabad. The so-called memo was addressed to the chairman of the joint chiefs of staff, and sent through an intermediary friend, seeking help of the US government to prevent a military takeover of Pakistan. It requested the US government to help the civilian government in controlling the Pakistan Army. Under pressure from our military, it led to the resignation of the official and a supreme court investigation, which could not be completed as the records were found missing, obviously facilitated by our civilian government. The official has since then sought refuge in the US and continues to write anti-military articles."

Samir concluded that Latif's mind, like that of Hameed, was so much infiltrated with conspiracy theories that it seemed impossible to get any reasonable information from him.

Latif, however, continued with his hypothesis, "We all know that TTP are not true Taliban but have been created by RAW and CIA to defame Afghan Taliban. They are 'khawarij' as mentioned in various Hadith, and are declared to be so by a number of Islamic academies. They attack and kill innocent Muslims. On the other hand, the Afghan Taliban never kill innocent people but they have only been fighting against the invading forces in Afghanistan who are out to exterminate them."

Samir had heard of the khawarij but wanted to hear Latif's opinion on them, "Who are the khawarij?"

"The Outsiders! The khawarij are people that rebelled after the death of Muhammad when choosing a leader to lead the newly found religion. They revolted against Caliph Ali after he agreed to arbitration with his rival, Muawiyah, to decide on the succession to the caliphate. A khawarij later assassinated Ali, and for hundreds of years, the khawarij were a source of insurrection against the caliphate."

There was grief in his argument, "Islam has unfortunately divided into many sects. Sunni and Shia are the predominant ones, which are led by the Saudi and the Irani schools of thoughts, respectively. Within Sunni are various sects, including the hard-core fundamentalist Salafis. The Wahhabi movement, led by Abdulwahhab in the 18th century, is the other side of the same coin. Both have the same ideas and beliefs, which is about returning to pure Islam and fighting modern science and innovation. The militant followers of 'puritanical Islam' include the Taliban, the Al-Qaeda, and ISIS among many other groups operating around the world, including Boko Haram in Nigeria and the Al-Nusra group in Syria. The Harmeen are yet another secret society in Pakistan that believe in implementing sharia through violence. Then there are the Deobandi, who have followers mostly in India and Pakistan. They are led by religious scholars and in full control of many madrassahs preaching Islam. This Deoband school of thought had erupted in the city of Deoband in pre-partition British India as a counter to British education. Many madrassahs were set up by them so the Muslim student could get Islamic education. The Deoband school of thought is influenced by Wahhabism, and does not believe in saints or shrines."

Samir recalled that Wahhabism and Salafism are based on the teachings of Sheikh Taqi ibn Taymiyyah, a 13th century Islamic scholar and reformer. They preach that it is not enough for Muslims to carry out the daily prayers, fast during Ramadan, give alms, attempt to make the pilgrimage to Mecca, and affirm that 'there is no god but God', but Islamic practices and religion itself need to be purified. Muslims must also renounce all beliefs and practices that negate, implicitly or explicitly, the oneness of God. Some militant groups within these sects like the Harmeen believe those who do not repent or practice their puritanical version of Islam are to be executed. Wahhab condemned building or visiting shrines or even marking graves, honoring death, displaying images of animals, humans, or angels. He condemned the enactment of any law that is contrary to sharia, or the Islamic law. Saudis insist they do not follow Wahhabism, but Salafism which is based on the early followings of the Prophet. Some Salafists consider the term Wahhabi to be derogatory.

Latif continued describing the various sects of Islam popular in South Asia. "The Barelvi, on the other hand, are far more liberal in their views of Islam. It is a Sunni Hanafi school of jurisprudence which originated in Bareilly, India and has a very large following, estimated at over 100 million. The followers are also referred to as ahle-sunnat-wal-jama'at. The movement is a synthesis of sharia with sufi practices and includes the veneration of saints. It also emphasizes personal devotion to the Prophet Muhammad. Its devotees sing qawwali, which are certain types of religious songs sung in chorus, to honor the saints and God.

"Similar other smaller sufi sects include, among others, the Qadri, Naqshabandi, Qallandri, and the Chistia, named after the saint they revere. These are followers of mystical Islam. The sufis find God in everything, especially in their inner self, and preach love, and have adopted various methods of worship, including meditation, dancing, and music. They have found a large following among all segments of the society, including the educated and in the west as well. The Wahhabi find the sufis unacceptable to their belief, as they consider their way of worship as 'shirk' or sin."

He then moved on to describe the Shia, "The Shia are the second largest sect of Islam, mostly concentrated in Iran and Iraq, where most of their holy places are located. They are divided into many sects. The largest of them are called the Twelver Shia or the Ithnashariyyah, also called Imami or Jafari. They follow the doctrine of believing in twelve 'Imams' or leaders. The Wahhabis consider the Shia 'wajib-ul-qatil'. Wajib-ul-qatil means they should be killed for their beliefs.

"But yet another sect of the Shia, the Ismaili, a very liberal sect, are led by the Aga Khan. They are very business-oriented, much like another Shia sect, the Bohri, whose women wear colorful burqas and the men wear round caps."

Samir had many friends in these communities. "I have great respect for the Ismaili and the Bohri. They are both moderate and liberals. The founder of Pakistan, Muhammad Ali Jinnah, was an Ismaili. He married a Parsi girl out of love. That is the model of tolerance he gave us. The Ismaili readily adopt the local western culture wherever they are settled."

Latif disagreed. "Have you seen the Aga Khani women and how liberal they are? They do not cover up their hair and will burn in hell. We must follow the Arab way of life, as it is in Saudi Arabia that Islam first came. We must make it mandatory to speak and understand Arabic and dress like them, as well."

Samir disagreed, "We must respect all cultures and beliefs. We must learn to tolerate and live together. South Asia has hundreds of faiths. Muslims, Hindus, Christians, Parsi, Sikh, Bahai, and so on. Our former Prime Minister Murtaza Brohi's mother was a Hindu. The great Nobel Laureate in Physics, Dr. Abdus Salam was an Ahmadiyya. The Pakistan parliament had no business deciding who is Muslim and who is not." The parliament in 1974 declared the Ahmadiyya as non-Muslims.

Latif was a traditional conservative Muslim, and had two wives living with him in the same house who both wore burqas. He believed in equality for all wives according to the Islamic beliefs, and practiced it well. He also believed in seclusion and purdah for women, and even had his house windows completely covered so that his wives could not look out, nor anyone look in.

Samir disagreed. "Muslims in general are not required to cover up. It has evolved over time in different cultures and countries to promote modesty. It is a fact that only a few hundred out of five million Muslim women wore burqa in France before they were banned. They recently introduced the burkini at the beaches which the western women find distasteful. The two main countries that require the covering of the women's body, Saudi Arabia and Iran, don't even make up 6 % of the world Muslims.

"Secondly, being a Muslim is not the same as being an Arab. Only one fifth of the Muslims are Arabs. Two thirds of the Muslims don't even live in the Middle East. This is akin to one fifth of the global Christian population being African. Yet, Africans are not considered the mainstream representation of Christianity."

Samir believed Muslims were open minded and progressive, "Islam is not stuck in the dark ages. We are very open-minded in our beliefs. Think of this: half of the American Muslims believe in evolution, compared to a quarter of Evangelical Christians. The Islamic golden age was very scientific and revolutionized almost every field of human thought. Mathematics and science owe its advancement to Muslim scholars, even though it was picked up from where the Greeks left it."

He continued. "Islam is also a very compassionate religion. Mercy, plea, and compassion are mentioned in the Quran 355 times, while the word jihad is mentioned only 41 times. We believe saving one life is equivalent to saving all of humanity."

"However, people have misinterpreted and misrepresented Islam. Only in the last decade it has become hostage to the indoctrination of Sheikh Taqi ibn

Taymiyyah. All Al-Qaeda, ISIS and terrorist ideologies originate from his school of thought. The so called jihadi hardly quote the Quran but refer to the Mardin fatwa of Ibn Tamiyyah."

Latif interrupted, "He was one of the leading Islamic scholars, a liberator and a hero!"

Samir has reservations on that, "He couldn't be! I have read that Ibn Taymiyyah justified carnage and killings in his fatwas, and these beliefs have permeated into today's terrorism. He lived and died hundreds of years ago. He was born in the year 1263 in Mardin, Turkey and died in 1328. How could one apply his doctrine to this era?"

Samir had strong views against such beliefs, "The fatwas and dogma of this radical Islamist scholar are behind all the fundamentalist Islamic organizations and Salafist jihadists such as Al-Qaeda, ISIS and its branches. When these terrorists kill and slit throats, the terrorists produce jurisprudence to support their killings, which dates back to Ibn Taymiyyah."

"The fatwas have no expiry dates!"

"They cannot be applicable in today's pluralistic society!" Samir snapped. "The occupation of Mardin by the Mongols occurred when Ibn Taymiyah was seven years old. Ibn Taymiyah regarded the Mongol occupiers who ruled them as unbelievers, murderers, and thieves. The Mongols carried out numerous atrocities against the Muslims, hence he justified jihad and their killing, as well. The same belief against non-believers who occupy one's land continues to the present day, be they ISAF countries in Afghanistan or the Americans in Iraq or Libya. ISIS justifies its holy war based on the Mardin fatwa, the Salafist jihadi ideology perceive this fatwa as a permission to wage war to impose Islamic laws, or sharia. Ibn Taymiyyah in another fatwa on collateral damage stipulated that the Mujahedin who intended to target infidels were allowed to kill other Muslims who might stand in the way of reaching the Mujahedin's goal. Al-Qaeda used this fatwa to justify the killing of large numbers of Iraqis through suicide bombers, and car bombs after the US invasion in 2003. As for cutting off hands and heads, jizya tax imposition on non-Muslims, female genital mutilation, destruction of tombs and shrines, and other practices carried out by ISIS, they are all enshrined in the doctrines set forth mainly by Ibn Taymiyyah. I understand his doctrines are gathered in a book titled 'Majmu' al-Fatawa' written by him."

"This is the ideology of Ibn Taymiyyah!" commented Latif.

Samir shook his head. "There are many ideologies floating around in the Muslim world, most of which are based on incorrect interpretation of Islam. The Muslim Brotherhood ideology, for example, considers all countries of the world as infidel states. By mixing these two concepts, radical Islamists see the need to wage war and establish an Islamic caliphate. Islamic eschatology prophesizes Muslims will rule the world before the end of times. The fact is that these doctrines are taught regularly in schools and universities in Pakistan and many Arab countries. Abu Bakr al-Baghdadi, the current leader of ISIS who proclaimed himself as the Caliph, or ruler, of the Muslim world studied his doctrines in the Faculty of Islamic Sciences in Baghdad. We need to change that thinking in Pakistan by cleaning out the education system."

Latif spoke, "Dr. Sahib, I partially agree but disagree with you as well. The Zionists want to redraw the Muslim world map and break it into small volatile pieces and control its resources. Hence, they got rid of Saddam Hussain and Kaddafi. It has led to more turmoil in these countries. If you had been watching the American media during the presidential race in US, one of the presidential candidates admitted that the Middle East was better off with Saddam Hussain and Kaddafi in power. By toppling these leaders, these countries are now in control of all types of leaders, from bad guys to radical Islamic guys. Since the start of the Iraq War, deaths from terrorism has increased over 4,500% just between 2002 and 2014. Suicide attacks were unheard of in Pakistan before 9/11, and in Iraq before 2003. Not one! Since the 2003 invasion of Iraq, there have been over 1,900 attacks just in Iraq alone, over 500 in Pakistan, 88 in Somalia, 85 in Yemen, 30 in Libya, 91 in Nigeria, and over 165 in Syria!"

Latif was certainly well rehearsed with numbers.

He continued on with his argument. "Just in 14 years, the US has spent over $6 trillion in Iraq and Afghanistan alone. It amounts to $75,000 per US household; most of it is borrowed money. Even if a part of this used for the welfare of the Muslim world, these problems would not have happened. US would have been considered a savior then. What has happened now? Over 7,000 US personnel have died! I have also read that about 22 veterans commit suicide every day. That means thousands more are dying. Was it worth it? The war on terror has brought us more wars, and more terror. They have brought the war to our region. We were very peaceful people."

Samir did not entirely agree with the above contention. "You have forgotten or not read history. The Muslim states of North Africa were the first countries to declare war on the newly formed United States. From 1783, until the Presidency of George Washington in 1789, the newborn Republic had no strong central authority, and that is when the pirates from North Africa struck.

"The First Barbary War, as it was called, lasted four years, from 1801 to 1805, and was the first of two wars between the United States and the four North African Muslim states known collectively as the 'Barbary States'. Three of these, Tripoli, Algiers, and Tunis, were nominal provinces of the Turkish Ottoman Empire, while the fourth was the independent Sultanate of Morocco. The cause of the war was similar to what is happening today off the coast of Somalia: pirates from the Barbary States seizing American merchant ships and holding the crew for ransom, demanding the US pay tribute to the Barbary rulers. President Thomas Jefferson refused to pay this tribute. Tripoli then declared war on the United States which led to the first Barbary War."

This was all documented history. Americans were the first victims of Muslim pirates.

Samir reminded Latif of history, "The American President Thomas Jefferson, knew he was up against jihad. His words and actions are well documented even today:

*'The ambassador answered us that it was founded on the laws of their Prophet, that it was written in their Koran, that all nations who should not have acknowledged their authority were sinners, that it was their right and duty to make war upon them wherever they could be found, and to make slaves of all they could take as prisoners, and that every Muslim who should be slain in battle was sure to go to Paradise.'"

Samir let this sink into Latif for a moment, and then continued, "It was in 1805 that the US Marines from Egypt came into Tripolitania and forced the surrender of Tripoli and freed the kidnapped Americans who were made slaves. We are seeing a repeat of what happened 200 years ago! We nurture dangerous people through incorrect ideologies."

Latif disagreed. He bent over to pick up a printed paper from his desk and read from it, "US is more dangerous to world peace than Afghanistan, Iran, North Korea, and Pakistan combined. This is as per a poll conducted in 2014 which interviewed 66,000 people in 65 countries. US was officially named the country that posed the greatest threat to world peace. Since the disintegration of the Soviet Union in 1991, the US is now the world's sole superpower. Today, it possesses over 5,000 weapons of mass destruction, including nuclear warheads, chemical and biological weapons.

"In 2011, the US spent over $700 billion on military resources, which is the total of the next 14 largest military expenditures. With US being the world's largest economic and military power, and unchallenged, we should ask ourselves how dangerous it really is. Despite the fact that congress last declared war in 1941, since World War II, US has been engaged in more wars than any other country. Since the country was founded in 1776, it has been at war for more than 93% of its existence. War is the fundamental strategy of the US domination of the world."

Latif paused to let that sink in and added, "In 2003, US invaded Iraq under the pretext of seeking WMDs, but in 2007, the former head of US military operations in Iraq admitted that the real motive was to access Iraq's massive oil reserve so US could remain a self-sufficient nation. Since the 9/11 attack, days later, congress authorized the use of military force against global terrorism. Because of this authorization, US was involved in secret wars in 134 countries. It includes combat missions and training foreign forces."

"Most of these countries were not democracies…"

He disagreed with this notion. "US has supported military dictators, and monarchs around the world. In addition, it is the only country that has deployed and used nuclear weapons during warfare. In 1945, nuclear bombs were dropped in Nagasaki and Hiroshima killing an estimated 250,000 people, forcing Japan into surrender. Pearl Harbor was another false flag operation. It made US immediately gain political and diplomatic advantage over USSR in post-war settlement in both Asia and Europe.

"Also, in the Vietnam war in the 60s and 70s, the US used weapons against the civilian population. Newly developed chemical weapons like Napalm and Agent Orange were used. More than four million people were exposed causing serious illness which is still evident generations later. At least 150,000 new-borns suffer from deformities caused by use of chemical weapons. 50% of the deaths were civilian because of firepower directed at heavily populated areas."

Latif paused for a moment as if to take a breath and then continued, "US has also supported in overthrowing popular leaders. In 1961, CIA was involved in the assassination of the democratically elected prime minister of Congo. In Cuba, CIA made 638 attempts against Castro as per Cuban intelligence. Have you also forgotten the Iran-Contra affair?

"Have you also forgotten that it was a former secretary of state who threatened your beloved leader Murtaza Brohi that he will make an example out of him.

Murtaza was overthrown in a military coup, all because he refused to tow the American line, and was later hanged."

Samir had read of that in the memoirs of Murtaza which he had written from his death cell. He couldn't disagree more.

Latif knew he had scored a point. "You also probably know but do not want to admit that Marvi Brohi, his daughter, was also assassinated because she wanted to pursue an independent foreign policy after her return from self-exile, even though the Americans had facilitated her return. We think she was shot by American mercenaries with a high-powered laser gun."

"I don't think so! The US was facilitating her return. She was a friend of the Americans…"

"Sure! Like we are friends of the Israelis. These are just temporary strategic alliances between the powerful and the powerless to serve the needs of the powerful. They get long term strategic benefits while we get peanuts. Don't you know that during the Russian occupation of Afghanistan, Israel and Pakistan had a strategic partnership for exchange of military information. While Pakistan does not recognize Israel, we have worked closely with them in Afghanistan during the occupation in the 80s. This happened because General Zain, who hanged Murtaza Brohi, was a favorite of the Israelis and had worked closely with them in the past, as well."

Samir interrupted, "Zain was a diehard fundamentalist who destroyed Pakistan's moderate fabric!"

"Yes, he was. He also led a successful operation against the Palestinians in Jordan in 1970 and was awarded Jordan's highest honor for the services rendered in exterminating the Palestinians. In this war, around 7,000 Palestinians were killed, although Yasser Arafat claimed more than 25,000 were killed. The operation made the Israeli general very happy who commented to King Hussein that: 'Hussein killed more Palestinians in 11 days than Israel could kill in 20 years'. The Israelis looked up to Zain since then and he became the only figure in Pakistan army whom they could trust and could use to make good political and military relations.

"During the Afghan war, Israel supplied Russian weapons which they had captured from the PLO in Lebanon, as well as training to the Afghan Mujahidin against the Russians. Poor Zain did not realize that he was being used by both the Americans and the Russians to exterminate the Afghanis. He played into their hands when he called upon the PLO to recognize the Jewish state."

Latif certainly knew history well, "Pakistan's ISI had good relations with Israel's Mossad under Zain and regularly passed intelligence information to Mossad, such as Israeli civilians who could be targeted in a terrorist attack in India in 2008. Wiki Leaks had reported that Pakistan's ISI chief was in direct contact with Mossad. Only recently, Britain's Department for Business, Innovation and Skills revealed that in 2011, Israel had provided military equipment, including electronic warfare systems and aircraft parts, to Pakistan through Britain."

Samir interrupted. "Israel is a reality and will not go away. It is one of the most educated and developed countries in West Asia. The Jews, Muslims, and Christians have lived side by side in that region for thousands of years. There have been many intermarriages over thousands of years. Many Muslim countries have relations with Israel. The Brits, like they did in the sub-continent, divided the land erroneously.

The Jewish nation could very well have had land to live side by side with the Palestinians. Even General Mehmood knew that Israel is a reality and insisted on good relations with them. Pakistan should readjust its diplomatic stand toward Israel based on the mere fact that it exists and will not go away. We can all live peacefully together without treading on each other's toes as long as Palestinians have a separate and independent homeland."

Latif disagreed, "If only Zain had lived for another few years, we would have seen an Islamic Empire, a revival of the caliphate, centered in Pakistan and including Kashmir, Afghanistan, Central Asian States, Kurdistan, Iran, and Turkey. We would have dominated and guaranteed the security of all Arab states as well, who would now have looked towards us for their protection instead of to the US or elsewhere. We would have been a real superpower, and an Islamic one. We would have spread real Islam to all these countries. We know we are the chosen ones, the ones mentioned in the Hadith who will come from the east, from Khorasan, to liberate the world from the unbelievers before the end of times."

"So, you think it will be the Pashtun that will lead the Islamic army to victory?"

"Yes! We have a very old history. There are some who also believe that Pashto, the language of the Pashtun, is the language of the jinn. Legend has it that one of the sons of Prophet Solomon was called Afghan. He wanted to learn the language of the jinn who were serving in Solomon's army, so Solomon told the jinn to teach them the language. The children of Afghan then moved eastward to a land in the Khorasan now called Afghanistan, or the land of the Afghans.

"Today, some Jews are claiming that the Pashtun are descendants from the 10 lost tribes of Israel. They want to protect themselves by connecting their roots with our brave race."

He continued with a gleam in his eyes, "When Prophet Muhammed proclaimed Islam in Mecca, the Afghan leader Qais Baba went to the Prophet to accept Islam and then returned back to Khorasan. When Mecca was attacked by the kafirs, the Prophet sent one of his top commanders Khalid bin Walid to ask Qais for help. Mecca was liberated from the kafirs by the Pashtun."

Samir was dumbfounded at what Latif believed in! Do the Pashtun really believe they are the saviors of Islam and of the world? But the problem was that it was not only the Pashtun who believed this, but the fundamental Christians and Jews believed it too, and wanted to exterminate this race before they themselves could be wiped out by the Pashtun.

Samir looked out the window and could see the mosque where General Zain was buried in the courtyard. His plane had exploded in midair, and all that was recovered of the remains from the burning wreckage was his jaw. His mind wandered to what Pakistan had inherited under Zain: intolerance, hatred, fundamentalism, radicalism, extremism, and terrorism. So many extremist and terrorist groups were now operating from within the country that it was becoming difficult to keep track. A new splinter group kept cropping up every now and then. They were becoming a hydra with multiple heads, cut one off and another one appears. His mind rewound to some of these terrorist groups:

Lashkar-e-Taiba, abbreviated LeT and considered by the West and India as one of the largest and most active terrorist organizations in South Asia, allegedly operates mainly from Pakistan. Founded in 1987 by Hafiz Saeed and others, allegedly with funding from Osama bin Laden, it reportedly has its headquarters near Lahore in Punjab and operates several training camps in Pakistan-administered Kashmir. Its stated objective is to introduce an Islamic state in South Asia and to 'liberate' Muslims residing in Indian Kashmir.

LeT had been accused by India of the 2001 Indian parliament attack and the 2008 Mumbai attacks. The organization is banned as a terrorist organization by US, UK, India, and many other countries including Pakistan. However, the political arm of LeT, called Jamat-ud-Dawah, continues to work openly as LeT's charitable wing. LeT continues to carry out its activities with the support of many individuals.

Jaish-e-Mohammed, abbreviated JeM, and literally the Army of Muhammad, is considered by the West and India as an Islamist terrorist group in Kashmir. It aims to separate Kashmir from India and has carried out several attacks in Indian-held Kashmir. It has been banned in Pakistan since 2002 but somehow is still active in Kashmir. It recently carried out its most deadly attack on an army base in Indian-held Kashmir in which 17 Indian soldiers were killed, and over 22 injured. This incident almost led to a war between both India and Pakistan, with both armies being placed on full alert.

Hizb-ul-Mujahidin, literally the 'Party of Holy Warriors', is a Kashmiri separatist group, designated a terrorist organization by the West and India. It is pro-Pakistan and is considered to be the largest militant organization in Kashmir with more than 10,000 fighters. It has made life difficult for the Indian security forces.

But the one that had threatened Islamabad, the capital of Pakistan, were the militants who were recruited at the Red Mosque, a few miles south of the university.

The Lal Masjid, or the Red Mosque, is named for its red walls and interiors. It was one of the largest recruiting centers for Mujahedin's during the Soviet war in Afghanistan. Being in the heart of Islamabad, and within a short distance of the ISI headquarters, it had occasionally received support and patronage from some influential government functionaries. The seminaries nearby accommodate a few thousand male and female students.

After the imam of the mosque was assassinated, his sons Abdul Rab and Abdul Wali took over the mosque, making it a center for fundamentalist teachings. Abdul Rab was the sermon giver till he was removed for issuing a controversial sermon against the army, in which he proclaimed that no Pakistani army officer deserved an Islamic burial if he died fighting the Taliban. A few years later, a stand-off between the madrassah students barricaded inside the mosque and the government resulted in bloody gun battles in which estimates ranged from 20 to 70 people killed and over one hundred others injured. Abdul Rab was arrested while he was trying to escape. Abdul Wali was killed in crossfire. The government had claimed the mosque was taken over by foreign militants, however, the religious political parties claimed that there were no foreigners inside the mosque.

Following the attack, those attending the funeral of Abdul Wali called for jihad. Ayman al-Zawahiri, Al-Qaeda's then second in command, released a message saying: "Your salvation is only through jihad."

Abdul Rab, in a later interview to a major TV channel, clearly identified Osama bin Laden as a hero and a martyr. He said they created awareness about jihad in the children of their 27 madrassahs, which numbered to over 5,000.

The Muslim world has suffered globally since 9/11 because the attack was carried out by the terrorist organization called the Al-Qaeda. Al-Qaeda, literally meaning the base, or the fundamental, is a militant Sunni Islamist multi-national organization founded in 1988 by Osama bin Laden and others who fought the Soviet invasion of Afghanistan.

Osama was Saudi Arabian, a member of the wealthy bin Laden family. He first gained visibility in 1979 when he joined Mujahidin forces in Pakistan fighting against the Soviets in Afghanistan. He was the darling of the west as he helped fund the Mujahidin by funneling arms, money and fighters from the Arab world into Afghanistan, and also gained popularity among many Arab countries. As his power increased, he formed Al-Qaeda in 1988 at the time of the Soviet withdrawal from Afghanistan, and expanded his activities to the Arab countries as well, including to Africa. In 1992, he was banished from Saudi Arabia, and shifted to Sudan. However, he left Sudan in 1996 after he realized the US had located his base. He then established a new base in Afghanistan and declared war against the US, being responsible for a number of bombings. Osama was on the FBI's lists of Ten Most Wanted Fugitives and Most Wanted Terrorists for his involvement in the 1998 US embassy bombings.

Al-Qaeda was involved in the 1998 US embassy bombings, the 9/11 attacks, the 2002 Bali bombings and many other acts of violence, as well. Al-Qaeda leaders regard liberal Muslims, Shia, sufis, and other sects as heretics and have attacked their mosques and gatherings. Like the ISIS, Al-Qaeda envisioned the creation of a caliphate ruling over the entire Muslim world.

Right after 9/11 from 2001 to 2011, bin Laden was a major target of the war on terror, as the FBI placed a $25 million bounty on him. He was among the most wanted and searched fugitive from justice, till he was killed in a covert operation by US SEALS on May 2, 2011 inside a residential compound in Abbottabad. His body was never displayed or photographed, and the Americans claimed his body was taken and thrown in the Arabian Sea right after the operation. This claim is disputed by many locals of Abbottabad, who claim to this day that Osama never lived there, and died of kidney failure many years ago in the Tora Bora mountain range in Afghanistan. Only for gaining political and military mileage was the whole drama enacted by the US and Pakistani forces.

One of the biggest casualties because of Osama's killing became the polio vaccination program in Pakistan, one of the few countries left in the world with the polio virus. In 2007, Maulana Fazlullah, the head of the TTP at that time, had already announced a ban on polio vaccinations in Swat because he announced that this was a part of the US and Jewish conspiracy to sterilize all Muslims, so that their population is substantially reduced. The tribal population became even more resentful against the vaccination programs after the CIA, through a fake Hepatitis B vaccination program organized by a local doctor, tried to obtain information about Osama Bin Laden in order to identify him and kill him.

However, after the death of Osama bin Laden, the support for Al-Qaeda dropped considerably according to Pew polls. Even in Saudi Arabia, only 10 percent have a favorable view of Al-Qaeda. ISIS has taken over most of Al-Qaeda role but with a much harsher tone. Al-Qaeda is now led by Ayman al-Zawahiri and the two terrorist organizations, Al-Qaeda and ISIS, do not see eye to eye as they both lay claims to lead the Islamic world. However, most believe they are one and the same, the same hydra with two heads, funded and financed by the same groups, and the TTP in Pakistan is yet another surrogate child. These organizations work together when they have a common interest or for money.

Samir bade Latif goodbye. His next stop was to go to the prime minister, as she had left a message for him to see her. He had to brief her about all these attacks by the terrorists on university campuses. He did not have an answer as to how they could be stopped, but was beginning to get a feel of their power. Where and when the next attack would take place, he did not and could not know. But he was determined to find out how and where they planned it, and wanted to put a stop to it!

Prime Minister

As Samir entered the gates of the prime minister's residence, there was another devastating news. Terrorists had attacked a government hospital in Quetta at the opportune moment when a large crowd of lawyers has assembled after the president of the lawyers association had just been gunned down by unknown assailants. The suicide bombing in their midst killed over 70 and injured more than 130 others, mostly lawyers. The attack was immediately claimed by various Islamist groups including ISIS. This would be the worst nightmare for Pakistan if ISIS ideology gained ground here. They were already strengthening their base next door in Afghanistan in Tora Bora mountain ranges.

ISIS was created after the situation in Iraq and Syria worsened due to the civil war in Syria, and the Sunni-Shia divide. ISIS, or the Islamic State of Iraq and Syria, also known as ISIL, Islamic State of Iraq and Levant, a region defined as the eastern Mediterranean, and by its Arabic language acronym Daesh. It is a jihadist militant group that follows an extremist Wahhabi doctrine of Sunni Islam. Many believe ISIS and Al-Qaeda are one and the same as they believe in the same Sunni agenda. Many believed the Zionist groups in Israel and their supporters in the US were behind the formation of ISIS.

ISIS began identifying itself as an Islamic State in June 2014, when it proclaimed itself a worldwide caliphate, and Abu Bakr al-Baghdadi was proclaimed as the caliph. With this pronouncement, it assumed it had religious, political, and military authority over the whole Islamic world, with its capital at Mosul. However, its influence by force continues to be limited to Syria and Iraq, with some operations in Libya, Nigeria, and Afghanistan. It had recently got a foothold in Pakistan, considered a prize catch because of its nuclear arsenal, through its affiliates like the TTP. ISIS is considered a terrorist organization like many others and is declared so by the UN, EU, US, and by many Muslim countries.

ISIS claims it has over 40,000 fighters, and access to large oil revenues from Iraq. It also got its hands-on cash worth tens of millions of dollars from the banks they had managed to loot in Iraq. The UN reported few years ago that 34 militant groups from around the world had reportedly pledged allegiance to ISIS and this number was expected to rise. The UN report also said that ISIS is 'the world's wealthiest terrorist organization' generating about half a billion dollars a year from oil wealth despite an embargo. According to the UN mission in Iraq, money looted from banks located in regions under ISIS control totaled over a billion dollars. The report also estimated that a tax collected from trucks entering IS controlled-territory generated an additional billion dollars a year. Using its influence of wealth, ISIS continues to maintain its presence in both Syria and Iraq and is expanding its influence on the poorer Muslim countries.

ISIS had gathered the attention of the whole world through its videos of beheadings, the imprisonments of minority women as sex slaves, and then its destruction of cultural and historical heritage sites. Muslim leaders around the world condemned its actions, as they do not reflect Islam's real teachings or virtues. However, there is very little they have done to contain its spread except to save their own autocratic rules and monarchies.

The merger of ISIS with Al-Nusra Front to form ISIL, was announced by al-Baghdadi himself in April 2013, but was rejected by Al-Nusra leader Al-Julani, and denounced by Al-Qaeda leader al-Zawahiri.

The news flashed on the radio as Samir pulled up into the prime minister's house. The ISIS leader in Afghanistan and Pakistan, Hafiz Saeed, was killed in a drone attack in the border area. "They got him," the US official said, speaking on condition of anonymity ahead of any official announcement. This was good news. It was a major setback for ISIS as it was trying to establish a foothold in Pakistan and Afghanistan, beyond its caliphate in Iraq and Syria. A number of Taliban splinter groups had joined them. This was the second major setback for the militants after the former TTP head, Mulla Akhtar Mansour, was killed in a US drone strike inside Pakistan a few months earlier.

As Samir walked into the prime minister's office, she appeared tense due to the Ali Khan University incident.

"Samir, we have got a put an end to the attacks on the campuses. Are the VCs not putting up enough security at the campuses? Why can't we get early intel on these attacks?"

Samir explained, "We do get these intelligence reports sometimes, but most of them are fake and planted in advance incorrectly to distract the security. In most cases, multiple sites are identified, and one of them may be the target. So, it is not clear where the attack could take place, and when! The terrorists are like the hydra. You chop them out at one place, they show up at another. They are working with the support of a number of organizations and groups sympathetic to them, and there is a large flow of foreign funds to these groups. You know ISIS has more money than we can possibly spend to counter them."

The prime minister was disturbed, "Pakistan is getting very bad publicity in the western media. Recently, the New York Times reported that region's triumvirate of violent jihad is living openly in Pakistan."

She paused for a moment, reaching out for a glass of water, took a sip, and continued.

"They reported Al-Qaeda's leader, Ayman al-Zawahri, enjoys sanctuary in Pakistan—placing him in Balochistan. They say he uses this base to set up training camps in Afghanistan. US forces say that they are fighting a new group supported by Al-Qaeda from Pakistan. This group has claimed responsibility for the killing of a number of people in Karachi.

"Then there is Sirajuddin Haqqani, the leader of the Haqqani network, and second in command of the Taliban. He is among the most wanted in the US as he has made life miserable for both the US forces as well as the Afghan Government.

The paper reports that he moves freely around Pakistan, and has even visited the Pakistani intelligence headquarters of the Afghan campaign in Rawalpindi. They have forgotten that he was one of the best Mujahidin commanders in Afghanistan working for the US. How come this has happened and I am kept in the dark?"

Samir was at loss for words.

She was unhappy, "And this last leader of the Taliban, Mulla Akhtar Mansour, who was just eliminated by the CIA in a drone attack inside Pakistan, I have read that he used to openly meet his military commanders in Quetta. If true, how come the intelligence agencies have not been able to keep tab of such movements and disallowed it. Under him, the Taliban have mounted some of the most offensive attacks in Afghanistan, in Kunduz, and in Helmand where they seized control."

She was clearly concerned about the reported free movement of the militants within Pakistan. She looked Samir in the eye, and her tone became harsher.

"The Afghanis, who are like our brothers, are concerned. They think that unless Pakistan clamps down on these groups, their country may not survive for long. We always had good ties with that country till General Zain messed it up. But the truth is that Afghanistan has many internal failings: political divisions, weak institutions, warlords, and corruption.

"We are now clearing their sanctuaries in the tribal area of North Waziristan—Taliban bases, torture chambers and ammunition dumps have been busted. But someone informed the militants early, and hundreds escaped over the border to Afghanistan."

Samir nodded in agreement. "The top brass is trying to control those leaks, but we certainly have informers in our midst who tip them off…"

She cut him off. "India is trying to use its influence in Afghanistan to cut us off, which we cannot allow. Pakistan regards Afghanistan as its backyard and gives us strategic depth. Our military considers the Taliban as our best ally after the US has left. We cannot allow Indian influence there.

"But what is more disturbing is the report that Pakistan has a role in the rise of the ISIS. Taliban, yes, I can understand, but clearly neither the Al-Qaeda nor ISIS."

She took another sip of water and continued, "They base this report on the fact that prior to our operation in North Waziristan, hundreds of foreign fighters, who were all Sunni Wahhabi, left to fight against President Bashar al-Assad in Syria, because he is a Shia. Reports from the area say they went first to a gulf country, and from there went to Syria via Turkey. Many travelled by road, as well. They all arrived in time to make inroads for ISIS into Iraq, and for the creation of the Islamic State itself."

She paused for a second to let it sink in. "We have been accused in the past also of training the Chinese Uyghur in Afghanistan, though we had nothing to do with it. And Bosnians and Chechnyans though we had no role in it. And with Kashmiris which may be true as we lay our claim to it. Now, more recently, we have been accused of harboring Osama in a military town, where no one would ever dream of looking for him."

She looked at Samir, as if expecting a response, and continued, "What is worse is that ISIS has made a unilateral declaration that they will avenge the Babri Masjid demolition, and massacre of Muslims in Kashmir and Gujrat. The West and India think we are behind this declaration, even though the person in the ISIS video was an Indian national with a sword in hand, one whom many have identified.

"The video has even gone to the limit of thinking India is Iraq. It has asked Indians to accept any of the three conditions if they wish no retaliation: to accept Islam, to pay Jizya, or to prepare to be slaughtered. How can that be?"

Samir interrupted to remind her about the Indian threat to Pakistan.

"The Indians have threatened to get involved in Balochistan like they did in East Pakistan, and dismembered the country in two parts in 1971. We have even nabbed one of their top spies in Balochistan who was inciting terrorism…"

She disagreed. "This time, it's different. The Chinese are interested in developing Balochistan along with Pakistan under CPEC. One of the influential think-tanks in China has already warned India that China will get involved if India formants trouble in Balochistan."

There was a slight knock on the door before the ADC walked in to remind her of her next appointment.

She waved him off.

"Do you have anything else to discuss?"

Samir wanted to bring up another subject using this opportunity with her to seek her support for academic freedom in Pakistan, as a counter to suppression of free thought and radicalization.

"Prime Minister, Both the state and non-state actors are infringing upon academic freedom of those few who are opposing the right-wing ideology and radicalism that was encouraged by the Zain school of thought for long. This was the subject of a recent seminar at a university and is forging a sense of insecurity and fear in the academia. As an academic, I am concerned that some elements in the security agencies are interfering and pointing out that some research being done in the universities is anti-Pakistan."

"This should not happen. Please talk to the ISI chief."

"Even a recent notification from a ministry official has highlighted the same concern, directing that any discussion or presentation contrary to the ideology and principles of Pakistan must be avoided. They have asked the VCs to remain vigilant and stop any such activity that is contrary to the ideology and principles of Pakistan. I disagree as universities must be free to pursue free thought and expression."

"I totally agree with you. Please ask for an explanation from the official who wrote this nasty memo."

Samir wanted to take this advantage to discuss yet another matter of concern to him which was encouraging extreme viewpoint and radicalism on campuses.

"I am sorry for infringing on your time, but there is yet another item: that of imparting quality science education across the board to all disciplines, which is necessary to suppress radical thought among students."

"What is that?"

"One of the Pakistani professors wrote recently that depriving or imparting poor quality science and math education is more lethal than RAW, and I tend to agree with him."

"How can that be?"

"According to this article, the success of the human species over other forms of life depends on science and math education. Without science and math, the pyramids could not have been built, navigation would have been impossible and

America would not have been discovered, electricity would not have been discovered, nor computers invented."

Samir was wearing his academic hat again, "This professor has explained it well in his article. Math and science demand mental capacity and concentration. They need logic, each link connected to the preceding one. By not laying a strong foundation for science, technology, engineering, and math at our schools and universities, and not teaching them science at all, not questioning the teachers, or for that matter our own existence or evolution, we are creating human robots who take their orders from the religious fundamentalists and the moulvi who are misguiding the youth. The professor has correctly pointed out that as long as teachers and students remain shackled to the madrassah mindset, they will remain mentally stunted. The real challenge lies in figuring out how to set their minds free. Critical thinking must be encouraged and introduced in the curricula."

The door opened again. It was the ADC reminding her again of the appointment.

This time, she dismissed Samir with a stern reminder. "Remind me prior to the cabinet meeting to discuss this issue. In the meantime, I would like you to see the American envoy for South Asia who is here for a day and clarify that Pakistan, particularly our government, had no role in the formation of ISIS, or the harboring of Osama. We would like to fully cooperate with the west in eliminating the menace of terrorism and their bases in the region. But we need their support to resolve the Kashmir issue with India, for without the resolution of the Kashmir issue, there can be no peace between India and Pakistan."

Kidnappings

The diplomatic enclave in Islamabad is a high security red zone where one has to go through two checkposts and identify oneself before entering. Normally, the host would inform the posts in advance of the visiting guest. As Samir drove into the diplomatic enclave to visit the American embassy, his mind wandered to two high profile kidnappings that had taken place earlier, including one from the high security enclave. It was rumored that the hostages in both cases were subsequently released after an undisclosed agreement.

Tanveer, son of a former president, was kidnapped from the diplomatic enclave in broad daylight by Al-Qaeda militants when he was campaigning for a parliamentary seat. After three years, he was recovered in a joint operation by Afghan and US forces in Afghanistan. According to him, he was also taken to North Waziristan and chained for two years. He was kept in a small room and not allowed to see the sky for more than a year. He had forgotten how the sun felt on his skin. He said he always feared an air raid or a drone strike in which he could be killed along with other Al-Qaeda terrorists. He felt like he was in a warzone. Sometimes, there were even up to five drones at a time. Samir wondered how the kidnappers were able to not only penetrate the enclave but take the kidnapped out as well away from the eyes of all the security checks. He recalled Hameed's words at Charsadda where he had said the militants, through magic, could have acquired the powers to become invisible and fly through the air. He shrugged off the thought and reminded himself to thank the American envoy personally for the American forces rescuing Tanveer.

In the other high-profile kidnapping, Saleem, son of an outspoken former chief minister, was kidnapped by militants over four and a half year ago. He was recently recovered from Balochistan. The chief minister himself was killed by his armed guard accusing him of blasphemy. The kidnappers who had picked him up from a posh locality of Lahore were part of a local Punjabi gang which a few days earlier had kidnapped an American. The gang then sold him to the Uzbeks fighters of the Islamic Movement of Uzbekistan, who were dreaded even in jihadi groups because they were considered inhumane and ruthless. They were feared and untouchable as their sympathies lay with ISIS. The TTP were usually paid a share in the extortions and kidnappings which were happening all over Pakistan.

Saleem had suffered torture from his captors, who had plucked out his nails and sent them in a packet to his family. North Waziristan was considered the unofficial state of the Islamic Emirates in the north and out of bounds for army, as they did not recognize the authority of the Pakistani state. Prior to Zarb-e-Azb, even the army had not moved into these areas. It was only due to the flushing operation of the military due to Zarb-e-Azb that the Uzbek captors had to be on the run from their North Waziristan hideout. Here Haqqani had trained his forces and here the notorious Hakimullah Mehsud was killed in a drone strike as well. So, the Uzbeks took Saleem into Afghanistan.

Within Afghanistan, the Taliban considered both the Uzbeks and ISIS as vying for their influence and territory, hence the Uzbeks came under attack from the Taliban. Saleem found an opportunity in the cross fire to run for his life, but was now captured by the Taliban, who thought he was an Uzbek too. He remained a prisoner of the Taliban for a few months, trying to convince them of his identity and offering money for his release. Finally, a deal was struck. Grapevine has it that Saleem was released in exchange for over a dozen prisoners and a few tens of millions of ransom money. The Taliban gave him some money to survive and helped him cross the border on motorcycle back into Balochistan in Pakistan. In a small town, he made a phone call to his family to have him picked up. The security forces arrived and secured him subsequently.

Samir's thoughts were interrupted as he entered the gate of the US Embassy.

Envoy

The US Special Envoy to South Asia, William Bush, welcomed Samir into his embassy office. William had worked for Samir's friend, Mike, as an associate during the Clinton years, and had heard of Samir. After all, Mike had spoken highly of Samir as a friend of US and democracy.

After thanking the envoy on Tanveer's rescue, Samir came straight to the point.

"The prime minister is concerned that there is developing a misunderstanding between our two governments. The US president recently referred to Pakistan as an 'abysmally dysfunctional country'. The chairman of the joint sub-committee of the committee on foreign affairs is also on record saying that US should completely cut off all funding to Pakistan, and then, a State Sponsor of Terrorism declaration.

"Our enemies want the world to conclude that Pakistan is the epicenter of terror, and that our military and ISI are behind every act of terror committed in Afghanistan or India. We all know of the role your and our governments played together with the Taliban to get the USSR out of Afghanistan. But we are also following that a US presidential candidate accused a former secretary of state in his role in the rise of the Islamic State, the spread of Al-Qaeda and the complete mess in Iraq and Syria, and in Libya."

The above sentence got the envoy's attention.

Samir's tone was harsh, "The US keeps asking Pakistan to 'do more' while we have done more than enough. Over 80,000 Pakistanis have been killed in the war on terror. We are not just saying so, but it has been authenticated also by independent reports, such as a study conducted by a group of international physicians' organization." Samir was referring to a report released by a Nobel Prize winning organization.

"Terrorism is a world phenomenon, not just confined to Pakistan. There are terrorists in the US, as well. Only recently, a former security advisor has clearly highlighted this fact in his book. He writes that since 9/11, hundreds of born Americans have been indicted or convicted of terrorism charges. Many others have been involved in terrorism abroad: an American was involved in the Mumbai attacks. Many more have been charged due to their involvement with ISIS. We all remember the incidents that took place at Fort Hood, the Boston Marathon, and in San Bernardino. What motivated them, where, and how are they trained? Clearly, Pakistan was not a part of it. Shall we call US a terrorist nation as well just because a few hundred nationals were involved in terrorism?"

The envoy was struck back, "Most Americans are inspired by jihadi literature distributed through off shore websites."

"We can say the same for Pakistan, as well. The most notorious of the terrorists killed were not of Pakistani origin. The book expresses it well. They were foreigners, either from Afghanistan, or from Central Asian Republics. Likewise, in the US, Anwar al-Awlaki was the New Mexico-born radical cleric who was the first US citizen killed by a CIA drone, and who mentored the Charlie Hebdo shooters. Likewise, another US national Samir Khan's online broadcasts have inspired terrorists around the world, including the Tsarnaev brothers. Omar Hammami was an Alabama native who regularly appeared in al Shabaab's videos.

"Even the recent NY and NJ attempted bombing by an Afghani-American is being tied to Pakistan, just because he visited Pakistan a few times, including for his marriage to an Afghani. You know he was already in the FBI list for the last two years, when his own father had called him a terrorist. This is a weakness of your own intel, and now they trying to lay it on Pakistan."

Samir knew he had caught the envoy's attention. "Muslims living in the US, of which I am one, are living in fear because you have a biased view that most of them are potential terrorists. They are being harassed and hounded by all intelligence and security agencies, from the department of homeland security to the FBI to the NYPD. Even the mosques and Islamic centers are under surveillance; and one of your presidential candidates has even gone to the extent of proposing new laws to register them and monitor all activities."

The envoy shook his head. "It was American politics at its worst."

Samir knew William had a soft corner for the Muslims, having worked with Mike before. However, he continued to drive across his point, "Since 9/11, 94 people have been killed in the United States in ten attacks carried out by a total of 12 radical Islamist terrorists. Each of the attackers was either an American citizen or a legal resident. More than half of the 94 murders occurred last year, when Omar Mateen, who was born on Long Island, killed almost 50 people at a night club in Orlando."

William did not comment and let Samir continue to speak.

"According to the comprehensive terrorism database maintained by an American organization, since 9/11, there have been 396 people involved in American terrorism cases, which New America defines as 'individuals who are charged with or died engaging in jihadist terrorism or related activities inside the United States, and Americans accused of such activity abroad'. 83% of these individuals were American citizens or permanent residents. 17% were non-residents or had an unknown status."

Samir was sure of his statistics, "Hate crimes against Muslims in the US have been up by 78% since 9/11. All of this is leading to a backlash there, since a large number of US citizens are of Pakistan origin. And most of them are professionals: doctors, software engineers, professors, and the business community. More Pakistani professionals go to work in Silicon Valley than to any other region of the US. It is now becoming more difficult for Pakistanis to obtain US student or visitor visas, work or business visas, or the green card. Actually, more and more Pakistanis are now opting for other destinations such as Canada and Australia. All of this is affecting bilateral relations between our countries. It may affect the technological strength of the US in the long run, as the H-1B program is called the secret weapon of the US."

William smiled and nodded his head in agreement, "I understand and know that. However, the US is equally concerned about the wave of bombings and killings that have taken place in Europe. There has been London, Brussels, Paris, Nice, and Istanbul. It is the Atlantic that has saved us."

"But none of them were Pakistani," interrupted Samir, "you have enough of your own homegrown terrorists. I recall distinctly the Virginia Tech killings by a senior in which he killed 32 students before committing suicide. We have crazy lunatics in every country."

William agreed, "Yes, except when the lunatic kills for religion. What happened at Lahore this year on Easter, when Christian families were in a festive mood? Over 75 were killed and 340 injured. And this is not the first time that Christians or other minorities have been attacked. Two years back, at an attack on a church in Peshawar, 85 people were killed. These happen under the pretext of blasphemy under most cases. A couple was burnt alive only recently in a brick kiln. Aasiya, who is a minor, is serving a death sentence. Salman Taseer, the governor, died because he uttered a few sympathetic words for her. Few years ago, a Christian minister, Shahbaz Bhatti, was killed because he was an outspoken critic of the blasphemy laws."

Samir disagreed, "These people are misusing Islam and not following in the traditions of our Prophet. At the St. Catherine Monastery, in Mount Sinai in Egypt, built between 548 and 565 CE on the site where Prophet Moses spoke to God, and where the fire burnt in the bushes, is preserved a sacred document with Prophet Muhammed's seal, which clearly ordains the Muslims not to destroy or damage churches, and to respect the praying places of the Christians. This was the Prophet's promise to the Christians till the end of time. These people today are butchers and murderers, and not Muslims, and should be punished accordingly."

"The minorities are being victimized..."

"Not by the State. TTP claimed responsibility for Shahbaz's killing and called him a blasphemer. Also, for the Easter killings, a group associated with the TTP claimed responsibility. The TTP is a terrorist organization that does not accept Pakistan either.

"But it is not just the Christians that are being targeted by non-state actors. Other minorities are under attack too by the fanatics. Last year, there were two major incidents on the Shia minorities. Gunmen stormed a bus carrying Shias in Karachi and killed 45 people. Two weeks earlier, a bus was hijacked near Pishin in Balochistan killing 22 people. A few months prior to that, a suicide bomber killed 23 Shiite pilgrims returning from Iran. Another 81 were killed in Quetta the same year. There have been many more such attacks in the past..."

"I recall 10 foreign climbers were also killed by militants on Nanga Parbat Mountain around the same time," William reminded.

Samir shook his head. "There are psychopaths and perverts in every religion and communities. The Christians have the Klu Klux Klan. So, are they Christians? Likewise, ISIS claims to be representative of Muslims but they are not, and neither are they Muslims!"

William nodded his head in agreement. "Security is always breached everywhere whenever such incidents happen. We have our conspiracy theories too, but we always like to give the benefit of the doubt to the Pakistan security agencies. However, we would be very concerned if such groups were to infiltrate the security set-up at the nuclear installations. Our president, at this year's nuclear security summit, delivered a clear warning that madmen could kill and injure hundreds of thousands of innocent people using only plutonium the size of an apple."

Samir agreed. He feared just that as a likely scenario. But such events could be stopped with both the US and Pakistan cooperating with each other instead of stabbing each other in the back.

Samir brought up another issue of mistrust between the two governments, "Our government is also very concerned over the flight of a US drone into Balochistan which killed the Afghan Taliban leader Mulla Akhtar Mansour. He was the successor to Mulla Omar and the undisputed leader of the Taliban. His death is likely to have major ramifications for Pakistan and on US-Pakistani relations."

The envoy was skeptical, "The US knows how the Quetta Shura functions. Omar was under your protection and had been dead for two years before the news was leaked out. ISI was aware of this. They then needed a new leader who would play puppet to their orders."

Samir couldn't disagree more. "This would have had severe consequences for the Americans. As you know, a successor was quickly chosen; otherwise the whole game would have fallen into the hands of the surrogates of the ISIS who are trying to get a footprint in Pakistan. They have only recently got one in the killing of the lawyers in Quetta. For us, relatively the Taliban are angels. Our worst enemies are the TTP, Al-Qaeda and now ISIS. But they are seeking support of the Afghans and Indians to secure a hold into Balochistan."

The differences appeared quite evident between the US and Pakistan as William spoke, "Our administration is growing less patient with your government's failure to move against the Afghan Taliban. While your military has cooperated in the strikes against Al-Qaeda and the TTP in the tribal areas, Balochistan has been kept off limits."

Samir disagreed, "We do not consider the Afghan Taliban as counter-productive to Pakistan's interest. They also represent the Afghan population. We have been working with them to join the talks with the US. Even the US considers them as representatives of the larger Afghan Pashtun population in the south; hence, it wants them to join the peace talks. But the TTP, Al-Qaeda and ISIS are nothing but terrorist groups. We are concerned that the TTP enjoys sanctuary in Afghanistan under American control. If America does not 'do more' to weed them out, I am afraid we won't be able to stop our military to go after them. This may lead to collateral damage and worsening of our relations, worse than what happened after the Salala incident."

The envoy shook his head, "Maulvi Haibatullah Akhundzada, a Sunni Deobandi Pashtun, is now the new leader of the Taliban. We know he is based in Quetta as well and heads the Quetta Shura."

Samir could not see eye to eye with the envoy, "But he was a religious scholar and has never been a fighter. He was the head of the Taliban's Islamic courts and had issued many fatwas. He remained in Afghanistan during the war.

"Pakistan has suffered a lot since 9/11, but we would like to tell the global community and particularly the US that we have done more than our share in our fight against terrorism, and now it's time for us and the global community to pick up the pieces, to put this region of the world back in order."

Samir waited for a few seconds to let his comments sink in, "I am also asked to convey that the China Pakistan Economic Corridor, or the CPEC in short, has become the target of conflicting interests. There is a convergence of interests to derail it, which we clearly will not allow to happen. We hope that the US understands that CPEC is not against American economic interests. India thinks it is a nightmare for them, and is trying to find every single excuse to stop it. Today, we have a new geo-political positioning taking place in South and Central Asia, and Pakistan is at the center of it."

Samir threw in his parting comment which was a bitter pill.

"Our government is also very upset over your decision to manufacture F-16s in India, while we, who had even paid for them, were denied delivery for many years. I believe if US goes ahead with these plans, our military may be forced to look towards the Russians to manufacture their MIGs here. We have invited them for a joint military exercise for the first time ever. However, clearly, we would prefer a balance of power if the US is willing to play ball."

With these parting sentences, Samir left the envoy's office. He wondered if the Americans were really friends or foes. Pakistan and US had walked together a very long way, but now conflicting interests in this region were tearing these relations apart and was threatening peace in South Asia. But he knew this threat would not just be confined to this region, but would engulf most of Asia, perhaps striking into Europe and US, as well.

It was important that all regional powers work together for enduring peace in the area.

Madrassah

It was a large madrassah about two miles away from a university at Swat, which was located at Saidu Sharif, the capital of Swat. It boasted a long alumni list, including a number of religious scholars that were serving both the Taliban and the Al-Qaeda. It was said that a lot of the Taliban school of thought was nurtured here. A few of those who spoke Arabic had even made their way to Iraq and Syria and had become ISIS scholars and part of the inner circle to their leader al-Baghdadi. People from far and wide flocked to this madrassah. Many came from Afghanistan while some even came from as far as Uzbekistan.

It was a huge three-story building with a large courtyard and had a large mosque in one corner of the yard which could easily accommodate over three hundred inside and another 600 in the open courtyard. There was one entry gate to the premises which was vigilantly guarded by two men carrying guns. They seemed to know everyone who walked in or out as their eyes scrutinized everyone. Occasionally, some were stopped for body searches. There was a long stream of people entering the madrassah after each muezzin call for prayers.

About 200 children, from the age of 8 to 17 lived within the premises of the madrassah. There were multiple rooms that served as classrooms. Free meals were served to all who lived there, and the locals, including some anonymous Muslim donors from outside the country contributed a lot to its expenditures. It was said that Haqqani himself had lectured here quite a few times, so had a number of other Taliban leaders. The imam of the Red Mosque was a very frequent speaker. Most of those who attended came from lower class backgrounds. Most were illiterate. These were people who were unemployed or worked on a measly daily salary. The madrassah offered hope for them, both in this word and the hereafter.

It was a very popular recruiting ground for the Taliban, and a number of other militant groups. Those who would provide them and their family the best delusions of grandeur would succeed in recruiting the militants. Only those who had been attendees to the sermons for a few months at least would be acceptable. A few of these who would qualify would join the jihadi forces. They would then be sent to the training camps in North Waziristan and a few other scattered camps in the country, including in Afghanistan. Their families would be provided financial support in their absence. In case of martyrdom, the family would be given a handsome reward.

General Mehmood wanted to win over the religious parties so he could remain president. During his time, graduation was made a requirement to contest the parliamentary elections. Therefore, to give favor to the religious parties, Mehmood had accorded recognition to the madrassah's graduates as equivalent to university graduates. The education advisor prior to Samir was Mehmood's friend and gave carte blanche approval to this recognition. A number of leading academics had pointed out that a graduation from the madrassah was substandard and does not meet the newly defined qualification framework of the education ministry as equivalent to graduation. Samir knew reversing the decision would mean a large number of parliamentarians would be disqualified. He had held a number of meetings with the Chairman of the Islamic Council and the madrassah authority at the ministry but they were not helpful. It appeared that the religious right enjoyed strong political support, including from the military headquarters. The ministry officials were afraid to reverse the decision for fear of their life. Even Samir in not so clear terms was warned not to touch the issue. But he was adamant to review the decision of the past government, and the prime minister had agreed to open the case. Subsequently, he had received a few anonymous death threats.

Samir had requested Hameed that he would like to visit the madrassah in Swat so he could learn of the preaching and the teachings in this seminary first hand. Samir knew Hameed was influential and could arrange that. However, Hameed was hesitant at first, and instead offered to arrange a visit to one of the Islamabad madrassahs. Samir insisted on visiting this particular one in Swat or another one in the tribal belt of which he had heard were active in recruiting the college students. He was concerned because the ministry had decided to open a university in the tribal belt, and this could then become a fertile valley for recruitment. Samir had personally wanted to visit a couple of tribal agencies to check on the logistics but was warned by the intelligence agencies to stay within the state jurisdiction. So, Swat was a safe bet to visit the madrassah. He already had a visit lined up to visit the universities in Swat and check out their new development work which was financed by the government.

He informed Hameed that he would be in Swat next week and that he would like to meet with the VCs of the KP region at a local university for a short meeting. Samir reiterated that during this visit, he would like to visit the madrassah along with Hameed, and asked if he could arrange that. Hameed was still hesitant, so had to be bribed first with a hefty grant for his university for building a new hostel.

Samir's phone rang a day before the visit. It was Hameed.

"I have arranged that we will be visiting the madrassah you had requested after the meeting of the VCs in Swat."

That was good news. This madrassah was off limits to government functionaries. Hameed was influential and must have provided his personal assurances to the sponsors of the madrassah. Samir knew Hameed may be a die-hard religious fundamentalist, but he was a patriotic Pakistani at heart. Maybe through him, Samir could get to the core of the recruiting, and be able to get some insight on threats and possible terrorist targets in Pakistan. He was also interested in trying to find out how the terrorists were able to evade detection despite the high security. Were magic or supernatural forces really at play here like Hameed had earlier indicated? He hoped he would be able to get these answers soon with Hameed's help.

The meeting at the university ended late afternoon just prior to sunset. Hameed signaled Samir to leave so they could offer the maghrib or sunset prayers at the madrassah. Samir was already informed in advance to wear the local shalwar-qameez dress instead of the western suit. Hameed had also brought a Swati shawl and a local cap and asked Samir to wear it so as not to draw any attention in the madrassah.

They left the university and walked across the road to the madrassah which was just about a mile away through the main bazaar. The weather was pleasant and walking across turned out to be a pleasant experience for Samir from the elitist type of events they were usually accustomed to.

There were two armed Pashtun at the entrance who eyed everyone as they walked in through the small doorway inside the green grilled gate. Hameed walked upfront, and the guard recognized him. Hameed signaled that he had someone with him. The guard stopped Samir to frisk him and check for any hidden objects. When the guard was satisfied there were none, he let both of them walk through.

The main praying area was on the left with the open courtyard in front. The mosque was already starting to fill up. There were about 200 devotees who had come to pray, including about 150 or so children between the ages of 8 and 17, who were residents at the madrassah. The imam was on a speaker which could only be heard inside the premises. Hameed led Samir to a place upfront and they sat down on the floor along with others.

At the call of the muezzin, everyone stood up to offer their prayers in congregation. The prayer congregation was followed by everyone completing their remaining prayers. They then continued to sit down waiting for any further announcement by the imam. Hameed and Samir waited.

When almost all had offered their prayers, the imam came back to the microphone and announced that they are fortunate that someone important, an aalim, or scholar, from North Waziristan is with them today to give a lecture on the afterlife, and asked everyone to move to the main courtyard. Samir and Hameed followed the crowd and sat among the last rows.

A tall man entered the courtyard with the imam from the side entrance. He was wearing a black shalwar-qameez and was almost $6^{1/2}$ feet tall, slim with a short beard and was escorted by two men with guns. He did not look Pashtun but had strong central Asian features, like a Mongol. He could have been an Uzbek.

"He is Timur, a senior recruiter and commander for the TTP," whispered Hameed.

Timur started with a few versus on jihad and the day of judgment from the Quran.

He then continued on to describe the signs of the end of times, which he said would be upon us any moment. These signs have all been clearly described in the Hadith, as described by the Prophet. There will be ten minor signs, followed by 10 major signs.

He said of the minor signs, nine have already appeared, which include all the sins in this world, such as people not offering prayers, accepting falsehood, committing adultery, fornication and homosexuality, widespread ignorance, listening to music, Satan worshiping, bribery, worldly gains, and not respecting elders. He said he believed that the tenth may already have happened, which is the birth of the 'Mahdi'. Mahdi is just a title, but his real name will be Muhammad and his father's name will be Abdullah, who will be from the tribe of Quraish, which was the tribe of the holy Prophet. Mahdi will be born in Medina, but he may have been born already. At the age of 30 or 40, he will come to Mecca to perform Haj. During this time, there will be a war between three kings or tribes to take over Mecca to acquire the treasure that is buried under the Kaaba. He emphasized that these wars are already happening all around us, in Yemen, in Syria, and Iraq, and between the Shia and Sunni. So, Mahdi's appearance at Mecca can't be far. When the Mahdi will appear, and will stand between the black stone and the 'Maqam Ibrahim', or place where Prophet Ibrahim, or Abraham, stood, which are both at the Kaaba, he will then be chosen as the leader unanimously by the people to lead them to victory. Muslim forces from the East, from Khorasan, bearing black flags, will then announce that they are joining him for jihad. He will lead the force of Islam and move into Syria to defeat the forces of the unbelievers at Dabiq.

Samir recalled Dabiq is a town in Syria near the Turkish border and features in Islamic eschatology as the site of an end-of-times showdown between Muslims and their 'Roman' enemies. According to most Hadith, Muslims will defeat the Romans at Dabiq and then proceed west to conquer Constantinople from the Romans, which is now modern-day Istanbul. Samir wondered if the speaker realized that Constantinople was already conquered by the Mehmet, the seventh Sultan of the Ottoman Empire in 1453!

The speaker continued that Muslims will then conquer Jerusalem, and Islam will rule the world for seven years, bringing peace and justice. 'Dajjal', the one-eyed false messiah, will then appear. He would live for 40 days where 'one day would be like one year, next one would be like one month, next one would be like one week'. The Prophet Isa, or Jesus, will then appear from heaven to join Mahdi. Mahdi will lead the prayers at the white minaret, east of Damascus, and Isa will then kill Dajjal. Isa will live for 40 years and die a natural death, and will be buried in Medina next to Prophet Muhammad.

He continued that Gog and Magog people will then appear and take over the world. There will be three major earthquakes: one in the east, one in the west, and one in Arabia. Smoke would rise from Yemen. There will be no more Islam and not one Muslim will be left. The sun will then rise from the west and the world, including Mecca, Medina, and the Al-Aqsa Mosque in Jerusalem, will be destroyed. This is the day of resurrection where we will all be judged for our sins.

This sounded like Armageddon, thought Samir.

The speaker went on to his punch line to emphasize that we all will be judged for whether we delivered on the five obligatory duties, foremost of which includes whether we joined the jihad or not.

"The time to take up arms against the kafir and declare jihad is now!" he declared.

The crowd appeared to be in a trance, because whatever he spoke was written in the Hadith and the Quran. It is Muslims that had deviated from it, and they would all burn in the fire of hell forever, unless they corrected their ways and joined jihad against the kafir and the yahudi, who are the Jews and the Americans.

Samir thought the speaker was propagating the eschatology version of the Sunni. The Shias think slightly differently. The Shias believe that the Mahdi is their twelfth imam and was already born hundreds of years ago, but had vanished then and will reappear towards the end of times in Khorasan. However, he is around us all the time and in frequent contact with the religious leaders like the Ayatullah. Some Shias also believe that real pious believers can contact him if they pray in a certain mosque in Iran. They believe that Mahdi will lead his army with black flags, destroy the Gog and Magog people, and then move west to defeat Dajjal and live till the end of time, where Islam will be the supreme religion under him. Both Sunni and Shia associate Dajjal with the Jewish leadership, believing at one time it was Moshe Dayan.

Samir went down memory lane. He recalled that historically, over 30 people have claimed to be Mahdi so far. The last incident was at the time of the takeover of the Grand Mosque in Mecca by a group of fanatics who claimed themselves to be the Mahdi and his followers. On November 20, 1979, which was the first day of the Islamic New Year, the year being 1400 of the Islamic calendar, at the early morning fajr prayers, a couple of hundred militants led by a man named Juhayman

Al-Otaybi, fully armed with weapons, took over the mosque and held a few thousand worshippers hostage. He claimed the Mahdi was here with him, who happened to be his brother-in-law, and whose name was Muhammad, was also the son of Abdullah and from the Quraish tribe.

The day and year of the take-over also coincided with the year when Prophet Muhammad had said the end of times will begin. The man asked Muhammad to stand between the Black Stone and Maqam Ibrahim near the Kaaba, and asked the people to owe allegiance to him as per Hadith. The people were confused, and some did, while others tried to run away, only to be fired upon by the militants. The gates were sealed, and it was announced through the speakers on the minarets that unless the House of Saud gives up its westernization and its allegiance to Satan America, the siege would continue. It took the Saudi forces, with assistance from the SSG Commandos from the Pakistan army, two weeks to clear them out. Muhammad was killed in the army action and Juhayman, along with some of his commanders, was captured alive, later beheaded in public by the Saudis. It is believed that over 250 worshippers and military personnel died in the incident.

Samir also remembered the burning of the American Embassy in Islamabad, when the Iranian Supreme Leader Ayatullah Khomeini had declared the take-over of the Grand Mosque in Mecca to be the works of Satan America. There were violent demonstrations against the Americans all over the Muslim world, the worst being in Islamabad.

Samir recalled that Christians and Jews also believe in the reappearing of the Christ, and they believe Dajjal is the Anti-Christ, and that Gog and Magog will be the evil forces that will come from Khorasan, and the Messiah Jesus will defeat these forces and there will be Christianity or Judaism that will rule Jerusalem till the end of times. In the recent past, they had associated these forces with Osama bin Laden and Al-Qaeda, with Saddam and the Iraqi forces, with the Taliban and the Pashtun, and more recently with ISIS who some believed will be aided by the Pashtun. Hence, the urge to destroy them in order for the fundamentalist Christians or Jews to rule the world. Samir thought believers of all these beliefs were ignorant and still living in medieval times.

Samir wanted to meet the speaker to learn more about him, and he signaled to Hameed. Hameed got up and signaled to the man standing next to the speaker. He came to the back and Hameed communicated something to him. He returned back and whispered something to the speaker, who nodded his head. Hameed signaled to Samir to get up and they walked towards the exit to wait.

As they reached the exit door, one of the armed guards who had accompanied the speaker came and directed his message to Hameed:

"Timur will meet you tonight in Mingora, and wants you to bring your visitor."

"I will be there, and tell Timur we may have some good news to share with him."

Hameed turned to Samir and said, "That was a bait. Timur is his nickname, named after the great Uzbek leader who was from the Mongols. He is a senior commander for the TTP who is well connected to the hierarchy and we will be lucky to meet him. But he is also dangerous. He knows a lot more than what he pretends to know."

Recruiting Center

Mingora is the largest commercial city in Swat, and is located about two miles away from Saidu Sharif. It was considered one of the recruiting grounds for the jihadi in Swat. A pick-up truck came to the guest house of the university to pick up Hameed and Samir around 10 P.M. Hameed had asked Samir to dress up very conservatively like a local Swati. It took them about 30 minutes to reach Mingora. Then they drove over to the other side of town, over the Swat River, past a large mosque, and then entered a side dirt road. A few miles later was a barrier which was guarded by two local Swati. They recognized the vehicle, but regardless shone a torch through the window to ensure who was inside. They recognized the escort, and then lifted the barrier to let them pass through. A couple of hundred yards past the barrier was an old farmhouse. There were five men sitting outside, each armed with a gun. Two of them looked central Asian, and could be Uzbek or Tajik. The driver parked the vehicle, and a heavy man with a thick beard came to greet them.

"Salam alaikum."

"Walaikum salam," which was the return salutation.

"Timur has been waiting for you. He will meet you after he is done with his talk. I hope you are not carrying a mobile phone or a camera." Hameed confirmed in the negative.

The man guided them inside the farmhouse which had a large hall in the middle with a high roof and a raised platform at one end. There were a number of smaller rooms on the side which had locks on them. One man who appeared to be guarding them stood next to the doors.

There were about 30 men seated on the floor in front of the raised platform. A man who looked like Timur was standing on the platform and giving a speech. Hameed and Samir took up a position along the side wall on the floor away and from the others. Timur saw them and continued to give what appeared to be an emotional talk. Samir could only catch bits and pieces of it as Timur spoke with a strong Uzbek accent.

"...the infidels, polytheists, and the kafir have influenced the Muslim leaders....for polytheism, kufr, apostasy, and blasphemy, the punishment is death, and death only...one must follow the right path, and only then one has the right to implement the Islamic ways of life...the Taliban will be rewarded on this earth and in heaven for implementing the sharia law in the regions they control...God willing, soon they will drive the infidels out of Afghanistan and bring in a perfect Islamic system, the way of the Prophet...all Muslim governments are illegal, as they are not following the sharia...once we have the power, we will overthrow them...there can only be one government of Muslims: that of khilafat, or the caliphate, which will implement the sharia law...the seeds of khilafat have already been planted in Syria and Iraq, and these will extend to Afghanistan, Pakistan, and Kashmir...we will inshallah soon have a large and powerful Muslim empire like it was in the days of Caliph Omar...all national governments in the Muslim world are kufr, and have no place in Islam...God has determined that Muslims are the most superior of all races, and non-Muslims are born only to be ruled by Muslims...inshallah the day is not far when the whole world will be ruled by Islam...

"...join in the struggle of the supremacy of Islam...those who die in the cause of Islam are shaheed...those who live are ghazi...God has promised they will be given eternal lives of comfort on earth and in heaven with the most beautiful women...this is only a temporary world...God is testing whether you follow the earthy goods, or follow in His way and earn the heavenly rewards..."

The crowd was listening very attentively to him. Hameed said to Samir, "Oh! I have heard this before. You will enjoy this and would want to sign up too. Listen to this."

"...forget your wives, the whores and prostitutes in this world...imagine what God has prepared for you in heaven...prepare yourself for the 72 houris that God will reward you with in heaven."

Samir whispered, "Ah! The same old line. Always sells in these conservative societies."

"...their eyes will be like almonds and beautiful...each houri will have 70 exquisite dresses to wear just for you...they will be waiting for you on satin embroidered cushions...they will be more beautiful than you can ever imagine...silken transparent skin that you will be able to see their marrow through the bones too.

"...these beautiful women will not be there just for your hugging or kissing, but you can sleep with them and have sex, as much as you want...and the enjoyment will be much superior than what you have ever experienced in this world...here you probably discharge within a few minutes, but there in heaven, you will have the sexual stamina and strength of a hundred men—and you can use these women in any way you like and as much as you like, with the stamina of a 100..."

Hameed was enjoying this.

"...and when you are finally tired of one, the next one will be standing over your shoulder, tapping you on the shoulder, and when you turn your head, you will see that she is more beautiful than the women under you...she will then say in the sweetest sexiest voice, 'Please leave her and come to me...I also have some right over you...' then she will take you and you will enjoy even more than the previous one...

"...God created women to serve you. That is why he had created Eve...to serve Adam...women are meant to serve you not just eternally in heaven but in this world as well...all women who do not believe in Islam are there to be our slaves once we conquer them...it is your right to rape them and make them your slaves...not one, not two, but as many as you can afford...and you can enter them any way you like...these slaves are yours to keep and enjoy and make them work and take care of your needs...and you can sell later after you are tired of them."

Timur turned to the man guarding the room to the side who seemed to have the key.

"...we have many kafir women we have captured from the infidels. You can join us and have your own treasure once you capture them...if you die in the way of God, you will have many more in heaven...some of our fighters have brought a few slaves for you to see for yourself the treasures of jihad..."

He signaled to the man to open the door and bring forth to the stage what was behind

Two women, wearing a full black burqa, were led by the guard to the stage. Only their palms, which were white as snow, and large black beautiful eyes, were visible.

"...this treasure belongs to our brother, Waleed, and they travel with him...they serve him food, massage him, do his laundry, and give him a good time...they were captured in Iraq and are Yazidi girls. There are many more like them to be captured..."

He waved his hand, and the girls were taken back to the inner room.

Timur continued for a few more minutes, then got off the platform and went into a side room. A man walked over to Hameed and signaled to follow him.

Samir and Hameed entered the side room, which appeared like living quarters. There was a cot in the middle, an old computer was placed on a table, and there was a TV set with a player connected. The room had one closet which was locked. It looked like the Osama bin Laden room in Abbottabad where he was killed that was shown on TV.

"Welcome brother, Hameed. My apologies I could not talk to you earlier at the madrassah. We only arrived this afternoon and must be on our way early morning tomorrow. You promised me some good news."

"Brother. This is my friend and brother, Samir. He is a teacher and comes from Sindh province."

"What can he do for us fighting for Islam?"

"Samir has influence in the government. He can get some of your people out of prison."

"Mashallah, that is good news. We got many of our brothers out in exchange for that boy who was the son of a minister, only if it had not been for the yahudi, we may have gotten more out. What does your brother seek in return?"

"Brother. Samir would like to meet the khalifa who is your emir."

"That is difficult and dangerous. The emir is on the move every day. The vultures are after him. The drones are after him. The kafir forces are after him."

"You know there was an attack in Charsadda today by the army of Mulla Maqsood. We want such attacks to stop at our schools."

"These kafir schools who teach non-Islamic laws? There can only be one law which is sharia. Once the government announces that, all attacks will cease. We will then join the forces of Pakistan to create a new khilafat.

"You know what, Hameed, you are a brother. Maybe you can talk it over with the deputy emir. He is from Al-Qaeda and heads the operation in the region and will be in Kohat tomorrow on an important assignment. He does not meet anyone and stays mostly in Afghanistan. Why don't both of you come to Kohat, and stay at the Afghan Sarai. We will contact you there. But under no circumstance should you communicate this to anyone at all."

"You have our word," nodded Hameed in agreement.

Timur knew a Pashtun would never go back on his word.

Training Camp

Samir and Hameed had just checked into the Sarai at Kohat, when two men came, asking them to join them in a pick-up truck. They were asked to leave their mobile phones and weapons behind, and were frisked first before they drove off towards the mountain range in the direction of the tribal agencies.

They crossed two security posts, manned by the Pakistan army, and upon informing them that they were going over to attend a wedding ritual, and after showing their identities, were let through. The captain on duty, however, had a word of warning for Samir and Hameed, as he recognized them both as high-ranking officials. He asked them to be extra careful and to be on the lookout for kidnappers. He also offered, if they wanted, for any military personnel to accompany them. Samir thanked and declined. The captain warned them that cellular phones did not work in this area, so they will be on their own. Hameed informed them that they were not carrying phones anyway. The captain, however, told them that if they were not back in six hours, he would send a search team looking for them.

It had turned dark, and nothing was visible except the front of the road where the headlights shone. They drove for another 20 miles into the tribal zone zigzagging through various passes between the hills, the last 5 miles literally being a dirt trail, and reached the end of the trail. Two armed men were waiting there for them, and accompanied them along the side of the mountain. They walked for another 30 minutes through the mountain terrain, and Samir felt as if they were being watched from the hilltops. Finally, they reached a barrier, which had another two men with guns guarding it, and crossed over.

The other side had a small hut, and a large courtyard, which seemed like some training ground. It had barriers, obstacles, pits, ropes hanging from a couple of poles, and one long one connected between two poles. A small generator was purring in the background, and a cable ran to a small projector that was set up in front of a small screen. There was a cave at the foot of the mountain, with a large boulder in front of it. It made the cave not visible from the air. It probably served as temporary accommodation for the fighters.

There were about 20 men who were seated in front of the screen. A movie with a bad resolution was being shown on the screen. It was like it was made on a cell phone, and was blown up to view on a 6 by 6 screen. It showed a smiling truck driver, showing a V sign with his fingers, and reading the 'kalima' which proclaim that there is only one God Allah and Muhammad is his Prophet. It also showed him having an electronic detonator in his hand, and the camera then focused on the boxes of explosives under his seat, before he drove off to what looked like a government building in the background about half a mile away. The background score was recitation of what appeared to be Allah-o-Akbar songs and relevant jihadi verses from the Quran. There was also a banner of the Emirates of Islamic Afghanistan in the background. The men watched as the truck reached the building, and exploded in a ball of fire, what looked like a huge explosion. It was a suicide attack on what could be an Afghan government office which was recorded live. The men watching all jeered shouting, "Allah-o-Akbar."

Timur appeared from inside the cave and walked over to the visitors.

"Salam alaikum. Welcome to camp Ghazi." Ghazi meant a soldier fighting for Islam. "The deputy emir has sent his apologies that he could not come. Actually, we have received information that the army is combing the area as they suspect he is in the area. Some filthy dog must have provided this information and will be beheaded once caught."

Samir spoke up, "We are as much wanting peace in the area, and Afghanistan to be ruled by the people, but you must call off all such suicide attacks. If you surrender, we can talk to the government to grant you a state pardon."

"Dr. Sahib: we don't need a state pardon. Surrender is an insult to us. We are either ghazi or shaheed. We will rather die fighting the dogs. We want the Americans out of Afghanistan and out of all the Muslim countries. If they don't do it soon enough, we will carry this war into their mainland. We have many Farooks and Tashfeens in the US already in our sleeper cells willing to carry out this task."

"But you can't kill innocent civilians…"

"How many innocent Muslims have these kafir and yahudi killed in Afghanistan, in Iraq, in Syria, in Palestine, in Libya? Unless we kill that many, we will not rest."

"You are killing Muslims too in Pakistan."

"Stop calling them Muslims. Your military are the stooges of the yahudi. They get training, arms, and ammunition from them. Zain killed thousands of Palestinians in Jordan. Now, you are carrying out a similar operation in North Waziristan at the behest of the Americans, and killing our tribal brothers. If you hit us, we will hit you."

He turned around to look at the men who were watching the video, "Let me introduce you to some of our warriors who are willing to give their lives for Islam."

He called out a name, and a small 20-year-old boy got up from amongst the crowd. He did not look like a Pashtun and had a short beard with no mustache. He came walking over like a robot.

"Meet Qari. This is his nick name. He is from Lahore. He is not a madrassah graduate like you think our fighters are, but has passed matric in a city school. He was converted to our cause at the Lal Masjid. He tried to enroll himself at the mosque, but was rejected, as we suspected he could be from the agencies. So, we asked him to go to Miranshah. There he was kept in a camp for three months to check his background and to teach him real Islam. When we were sure that he had converted to our mission of jihad, we agreed to train him for nine months. He has turned out to be one of our best and now, he himself is a trainer at this camp, and at a few other camps. He has trained many a good men who are ready to embrace shahadat. He himself is ready to die and has been asking us to send him on his last mission. He is looking forward to his shahadat as he wants to meet his creator and be rewarded with houris in heaven."

Timur sounded like a professor whose student had received an offer to join a Fortune 500 company. The boy beamed as if he had graduated and was ready to receive his reward in heaven.

Timur was boastful of his student, "We have trained him in making his own explosives and have provided him with ammunition. He can make suicide jackets, bombs, and mines. He is well rehearsed in jihad and prays five times a day. Most of our recruits you see here at this camp are from Punjab and are trained by him.

"Some trainers are also from Punjab. The Pashto trainers are in the tribal zones and in Afghanistan. Those who can speak Arabic have moved to Iraq. Some are also college graduates. They are doing it for a cause, not money. There is a lot of financial support from people who want sharia laws imposed in Pakistan. Plus, there are many who want revenge for what is happening around the world. We have a long list of trained suicide bombers waiting for orders…close to 300, and another 500 are in training. We lose 10 to 15 suicide bombers for one single successful attack, but it is worth it!"

Timur then looked at Qari expecting him to say something. Qari started speaking like a programmed robot giving a sermon in a mosque.

"Inshallah, soon we will see Taliban Government in Pakistan and Afghanistan, and one country and one Emirate. This will be our success. Millions of people will rise from Islamabad and Rawalpindi and join our struggle at our call. Then more people will join from Waziristan. Before that it used to be a struggle just in Afghanistan. It was the US that wanted to destabilize Pakistan. Not anymore.

"Today, we want shariat in Pakistan. Our jihad is against the kafir and munafiq, who are the unbelievers and the opportunists. First, we will fight the Pakistani rulers. The government says wrong is done by Taliban, not by other sides, which is incorrect. Baitullah Masood people used to go to Afghanistan to fight there. Even now more than 400 of his supporters have gone there. Now, they have been called back to fight in Pakistan where the real battle will take place."

He was cynical, "The media only shows one side, as if we are doing wrong, and never the other side for their wrong doings. Hence, we target the media too. Now, we are targeting Punjab. KP is already in our hands. Waziristan is already with us. Inshallah, Balochistan will also break away with the help of our friends. We will also start bloodshed in Karachi soon…"

Timur interrupted, "Enough, Qari. You are our prime fighter. Allah will reward you in heaven."

A group of men had by now lit a charcoal fire, and were spreading the burning coal over a larger area, about 15 feet by 2 feet.

"Let me show you what our fighters are capable of."

Timur led them to the fire, which the men by now had circled. At the far end, a man who appeared to be some type of a religious leader stood. He had a rosary in his hand and was reciting some verses.

"He is an aamil who can perform the magic that has passed down from his forefathers. It is a secret art not known to many. Watch what we can do now! I am glad you are witnessing it first-hand," Timur beamed.

A man walked over to the edge of the burning coal. He took off his sandals, kneeled down in prayers touching his head to the ground. The aamil recited something and sprinkled some powder over the man's head and blew on him. Then with a prayer on his lips, the man shouted, "Allah-o-Akbar," and stepped over the burning cinders, and walked over to the other side, on the burning coal, without an expression of pain on his face. The men applauded with shouts of Allah-o-Akbar. He fell down again in prostration, bowing to Allah. The aamil gleamed with pleasure.

"Wait and see more of our powers, and the miracles we can achieve with our magic."

Another man walked over to the end of the burning coal. The aamil again recited some mantra and sprinkled some powder over the man's head. This man did not remove his sandals but approached the burning coal and jumped slightly. As if by magic, it appeared that he had elevated one foot into the air. He then seemed to glide across over to the other side without his feet even touching the burning coal. He stepped down on the other side, and went into prostration to

Allah. The crowd jeered with more shouts of Allah-o-Akbar. Was it magic or an illusion, Samir thought. The aamil beamed with a larger smile.

Timur said, "The unbelievers can't win against us. Allah is on our side. We can walk on fire and survive explosions without burning. We can fly though the air as you witnessed yourself. We can also become invisible. Our injured can heal themselves miraculously. Gunshots don't bother them. We are invincible since we have now have the magical powers. Look what happened at the university in Charsadda, and at the American University of Kabul. You couldn't stop us since we flew into both without being seen. We can fly into any base, and we can kill anyone without being seen. You would not have believed it but now you have seen it for yourself.

"But that is not all! We are acquiring even more powers through jinn. These are not American movie stories but real. Only when you will taste it you will realize our strength."

He spoke confidently, "We will soon be ready for an all-out war with the whole Pakistan Army, the whole US Army, the whole NATO and ISAF Army, who will be destroyed by just a few hundred of our fighters. They will not even know what hit them. It is mentioned in the sayings of the Prophet that this land will be their graveyard. We are preparing for it and their time is coming. You will see it very soon."

"You are mistaken! You are no match for the Pakistan Army…"

"Aha! Didn't you see that we now have the knowledge of the magic that has existed from the times of the pharaohs and from Prophet Solomon's times in Babylon? Haven't you read the story of Harut and Marut in the Quran? It is all in our hands now. Not only that, but very soon, we will be able to control the jinn, as well. Don't you know of the power of the jinn? These are not fiction but facts if you have read the Quran!"

"These were thousands of years ago and don't exist anymore," interrupted Hameed.

Timur smiled, "That is where you are badly mistaken. This knowledge exists even today and we have acquired it after a lot of effort. Have you not heard of the famous Jadoo Baba from Hasan Abdal…"

His sentence was interrupted with the sound of a machine gun fire and some scurrying near the entrance to the camp. It was not clear who was firing. Hameed immediately asked Samir to lay low.

"Someone has attacked this camp. It could either be a rebel group or the Pakistan Army has moved in."

Timur and Qari disappeared in a flash. The other men just raised their hands not wanting a fight. There was some more firing, and a bomb exploded a hundred feet to the right of Samir.

A group of soldiers, heavily armed, moved in. Someone wearing the stripes of a captain was holding a flashlight.

"Please don't move. Anyone who moves even an inch will be shot!"

It appeared the captain knew Samir and Hameed would be here. He shone the flashlight at their faces, and immediately recognized Samir.

"Sir! We had been asked to be careful. We are after the deputy emir, a man named Wazir, who is the Al-Qaeda leader in this region and a prized catch. We had received intelligence information he would be here. But it looks like he was tipped off."

"The deputy emir was not here but another of the senior commander from TTP…" before Samir could complete his sentence, Hameed had nudged him hard in the ribs.

The captain did not notice. He asked his lieutenant if all have been taken into custody. The lieutenant reported a few had managed to escape and the rest were rounded up.

Samir could not see Timur or Qari or the aamil among those detained. Where did they disappear? Could they have flown away? Or had they turned invisible? Samir shrugged off the thought. It was not possible even though he had seen first-hand a man flying in the air. Clearly, they must have had an escape route to disappear, like through a tunnel in the cave, something that would be discovered soon.

But what Samir had seen today was frightening. He had witnessed something strange first-hand. Was it an illusion, magic or real, he was not sure, but he was certainly confused. If the terrorists could indeed acquire these powers, or had acquired them, or what Timur was hinting at like controlling the jinn, it would be very difficult to stop these attacks. The thought was frightening!

Samir decided he had to learn more about these mystical powers such as magic or the power of jinn. He had to find out whether they were true or not, and if they were really possible to acquire, how they could be blocked. He had heard about mystical powers in Islam and had always written it off. But if the terrorists had acquired these powers, they must be stopped before they could carry out any major disastrous attack with them!

Samir was now determined to learn more about these mystical powers.

Jinn Master

It was a dark night. The graveyard that was high up in an isolated part of the mountain in the tribal belt was quiet except for the sound of the man who was encircling a small fire that he had lit next to a grave. Qabza Khan had a face that could scare anyone in the dark and was reciting what appeared to be holy verses or a magic mantra. He was short-heighted and was wearing a red dress. His face was covered with a scarf except for his eyes which protruded outwards making him look wicked like his appearance. He was an aamil, or a magician who practiced the dark arts, and was locally known as a jinn master.

He was moving barefoot on one foot in a rhythmic motion on a circle that he had marked. A Star of David, with strange symbols inside, was etched inside the circle which had six candles burning at its points. Every now and then, he was looking up towards the sky as if expecting a spirit or a supernatural entity to come talk to him. He had been practicing this ritual every night, all night, for the last many nights and would do so till he completed forty nights.

He was confident and determined to succeed to whomsoever or whatever he was calling out to. He had seen many others practice this ritual of 'chilla', or encircling the star, for 40 nights to reach out to the supernatural entities called the jinn. This was the minimum number of days required to make contact with the jinn. During the chilla, the jinn would do everything within its powers to distract the chilla goer. It could come in the form of one's mother, child, or a beloved, acting in very strange ways, to distract the ritual. It was considered very dangerous, and those who would get distracted, leave it halfway or doing it incorrectly would be killed a painful death by the jinn.

His cousin had only completed five days of the chilla last year when he was thrown off a cliff by an invisible hand as he faltered. Yet another tale he had heard was that some other chilla goer only last month was butchered into two halves, the mountain cats had devoured his body halves, while the remaining body parts were eaten up by vultures. There were countless such stories that had gone from mouth to mouth over the years. There were many more who had attempted similar rites, and their bodies or their parts were nowhere to be found. No one had yet completed the chilla successfully, though many falsely claimed they did, including himself, he smiled!

This graveyard, which was a few hundred years old, had eerily marked graves. The graveyard was considered a popular settlement for the jinn as strange noises would be heard in the night. No one would dare come close to it during the day or night. There had been no burial here for the last many years since one of the holy men in a nearby shrine had asked the locals to keep away from it.

Not deterred by these horror stories, the man was determined to succeed. He knew this time the prize was something big. The man who had paid him to do this task had come fully covered in a black cloak, as if he was the Satan himself. There was something about the man that he just couldn't say no.

He also knew he was not the only jinn master who had been contacted by the man in black. He had heard from his fraternity that many others like him in the region had been contacted to do what he had been asked to do: capture a jinn! He had also heard that some had already failed and had been killed either by the jinn or the men in black. The men in black were onto something big, and failure was clearly not an option for them. They had spent a lot of money and had contacted many jinn masters in the region. He knew if he succeeded, not only would he be handsomely rewarded, but he could become the most famous aamil. He was a greedy man and therefore determined not to fail!

He recalled his grandfather had single-handedly fought a mukil in this very graveyard and overcome it, taken it home, and had made it a slave. He had then become a pir, and many would come to him from far and wide with their desires to be fulfilled, which were fulfilled by the mukil. One day, the mukil got free, killed his grandfather and escaped.

This time, he was trying to reach out to a different jinn, a very powerful jinn, one who had never been contacted before. This powerful one was mentioned in the Quran as Ifrit. He was a warrior jinn who was a commander in Prophet Solomon's army. If the smaller and less powerful jinn could be possessed, why not capture the most powerful one himself!

It was an extremely dangerous task, for which he could easily lose his life. But he knew that if he succeeded, he would become the most famous jinn master and could perhaps control the world as well!

He continued his ritual late into the night.

Chapter 2
Dreams and Prayers

Remember in thy dream Allah showed them to thee as few: if He had shown them to thee as many, ye would surely have been discouraged, and ye would surely have disputed in your decision; but Allah saved you: for He knoweth well the secrets of all hearts.

And remember when ye met, He showed them to you as few in your eyes, and He made you appear as contemptible in their eyes: that Allah might accomplish a matter already enacted. For to Allah do all questions go back for decision?

Al-Quran, Verses 8:43 and 8:44

Dreams

"Dad, you need to understand that all these beliefs and superstitions which grandma told us are real. There is the power of visions, the power of dreams, the power of prayers, the power of magic, and the power of jinn who are mentioned as supernatural beings in the Quran. But all these powers are only meant to be channeled positively. Those who misinterpret, exploit or misuse them become victims themselves and will burn in hell forever." Hasan was very much sure of his convictions.

Samir shrugged his shoulders. He was not superstitious at all and did not believe in such fairy tales. But in the back of his mind, he knew that spiritual powers did very much exist in Islam as he had read much about them. He had sometimes also experienced them first-hand, but it could just have been like a placebo effect, rather than these events being influenced by supernatural forces.

Millions flock to Mecca and Medina to pray. They go to mosques to pray. They go to shrines to pray. They pray at home. They pray on roadsides and wherever they could prostrate. But where the power of humans ended, the power of the supernatural begun. And God was much above all of that.

"What about dreams? Can one prophesize an event or the future through dreams, or are dreams just stories and images that are subconsciously created while we sleep?

"Most people do not remember dreaming, and 95% actually forget what they dreamt by the time they get out of bed. It is generally assumed that everyone dreams a number of times every night, each dream lasting from a few minutes to longer."

Hasan put on his psychology hat, "Dreams are a universal human experience and are nothing but a state of consciousness characterized by sensory, cognitive, and emotional occurrences during sleep. Psychoanalysts try to understand the meaning of dreams and relate them to past and present happenings in a dreamer's life."

"What about the 'I have a dream' or the eureka moment?" Samir wanted to hear from his son.

"Dreams are conjured visions, or something one aspires to achieve. Martin Luther King's 'I have a dream' speech was delivered by him on the steps of the Lincoln Memorial in Washington, DC in 1963, in which he called for an end to racism, and for civil and economic rights for the African-Americans. The speech became the basis of the American Civil Rights Movement."

He continued, "Dreams are also eureka moments. Niels Bohr saw the structure of the atom in his dream. Inventor Elias Howe invented the sewing machine after seeing a needle penetrating a fabric in his dream. Some even say Albert Einstein developed his theory of relativity when he dreamt himself sledding down a mountainside faster than the speed of light…"

"What about in Islam? What do our scriptures tell us about dreams?"

"Dreams are mentioned in the Quran. There are stories and lessons to be learnt. However, many Muslims have strong beliefs in dreams. They let their dreams control their lives and live their lives according to their dreams, which is so wrong! There was a recent case in which a man killed his business partner because he dreamt he was cheating on him. Another recently divorced his wife because he dreamt that she had an illicit relation with someone else. There are so many stories of such beliefs that people live by. While a dream may have some interpretation, which we do not understand, people misunderstand or misinterpret them.

"Some also believe that when we sleep, our spirit leaves our body and returns back when we wake up. They classify sleep as a minor death and as a warning from God that the major death is coming soon."

Hasan continued, "Hadith has its own interpretation, though not all people believe all Hadith is authentic. According to some Hadith, dreams are of three types: a dream from God, a dream from Satan, and a dream which is about what he or she normally thinks about or does on a daily basis. Some moulvi say if anyone sees a negative dream, he should spit to his left three times, and seek refuge from God, and turn over from the side on which he was sleeping. Some also say we should not be sharing our bad dreams with anyone at least for three days because that causes it to become true…"

Samir smiled, "Surely, you don't believe that, do you?"

"No, Dad. But you will be amazed how much faith people have in dreams. They live their lives according to it. It is a sin to do that. Historically, battles have been lost as a result of dreams. There have been many an accident endured by dreamers who misinterpreted their dreams. Many incorrectly interpret dreams at face value which is not correct."

He continued, "There are incidences of dreams in the Quran though. The dream of Prophet Yusuf or Joseph, in which he saw 11 stars and the sun and the moon bowing to him. His father had warned him not to reveal his dream to his brothers, but he did so, and had to go through a lot of pain just because he shared his dream with his brothers.

"When Yusuf was in prison, the king of Egypt had a dream in which he saw seven lean cows eating seven fat cows; and seven green ears of corn and seven dry. He was called upon to interpret the king's dream, which he did. He interpreted that for seven years the kingdom shall have a good crop, but must save, as after that will come seven bad years, so they will eat from what they have saved earlier. Only the following year will they have abundant water to grow again, with a good crop of olives and vine."

"Yusuf was a prophet empowered by God to interpret dreams!" Samir commented.

"He could, yes! There is also the dream of Prophet Abraham, in which God commanded him to sacrifice his son. He obeyed without any hesitation, even though Satan tried to persuade him not to do so, and at the last moment, the son was replaced by a ram. Based on these stories in the Quran, many still believe that through dreams and visions, God speaks to the believer…"

Samir shook his head, "Nowhere in the Quran has God ordained for the common man that dreams have a message. This power was only given by God to some of his prophets!"

"Yes, you are right! Even Prophet Muhammad had dreamt that there were lesser numbers of the enemies than what they were when he was going into battle against them. This is mentioned in Chapter 8, verses 43 and 44 of the Quran. However, God made it clear in the Quran that this was done intentionally so they would not lose courage against a much larger invading army. So, in this case, it is clear that a dream should not be interpreted at face value. Those who do so are wrong. Dreams are just dreams and not a prophecy. Those who believe in it are non-followers of Islam."

"But what about the famous dream of the Roman Emperor Constantine…"

Hasan had studied his history well. "That is the most famous dream which saved Christianity. Christians, right after Jesus, were persecuted for centuries by Romans and were living a very obscure life hidden from all in secluded monasteries and dwellings. In 312 CE, the Roman Emperor Constantine was engaged in one of the greatest battles of his life. He was faced with an army twice the size of his own, and realized that they would certainly lose and all would die in battle. He was very depressed, but that night, in a dream, an angel appeared bearing the image of a cross, and said, 'By this symbol, you shall conquer'. When he got up, he immediately ordered all shields to be adorned with the symbol of the cross. When he went into battle against a much larger army, he won! The Roman Empire was saved. It dawned on him that this religion was indeed the truthful one, and God wanted him to save it. He then proclaimed Christianity to be the official religion of one of the greatest empires of the world. Some die-hard Christians believe in dreams as much as the Muslim's do."

Samir felt the belief in dreams was in every religion, faith, belief or region. But there was also a life out there beyond dreams. There was the power of belief, of prayers, of the divine knowledge, and of superstition and supernaturals that had become a religion in itself.

Was it possible that, like the Prophet Muhammad's dream, the terrorists were relying on the power of the dream, and the power of the prayer to plan and achieve their goals? These terrorists are clearly no prophet or men of religion! Or was it something even beyond dreams which they were following to achieve their goals?

Samir had heard of sufism in which the followers of many sufis believed in what they dreamt, and followed them religiously. But this belief of dreams was not across all sects of sufism.

Were the terrorists relying on the spiritual powers of the sufis to achieve their goals, Samir wondered. He decided to do some exploring and pay a visit to the local sufi shrine with Latif, the VC of GMU who was knowledgeable about the sufis, and to learn more about the power of dreams and prayers. He knew Latif could give him a more religious insight into sufism and how they perceive dreams.

Sufism

Thursday evenings are generally considered the best times to visit a shrine, or dargah or mazaar, as locally called, of a religious person who is considered close to God by his followers.

Friday is a day of sabbath for Muslims, when prayers are obligatory at the mosque. Since the Islamic day begins at sunset the day before, many flock to the shrines on Thursday evenings at the onset of the Muslim day.

Latif picked up Samir from his residence after work, both clad in traditional shalwar-qameez dress, with a dab of attar, or non-alcoholic perfume which many religious Muslims prefer over the alcoholic cologne or perfume. There were a number of shrines within driving distance of Islamabad, however, the most famous of them was the shrine of Bari Imam, or the patron saint of Islamabad. He was quite well-respected and visited by the 'Who's-Who' of Islamabad, including all prime ministers and presidents who served in the capital, to have their desires fulfilled.

Bari Imam, born in 1617, had visited a number of religious places in his youth, which each had many famous shrines. These included Kashmir in the sub-continent, where Jesus himself is believed to have visited, and Bukhara in Uzbekistan, famous for where Imam Muhammad Al-Bukhari came from, who wrote one of the most famous Hadith called 'Sahih Bukhari', and of the famous sufi mystic Baha al-Din al-Naqshbandi who is buried in Bukhara. Bari Imam had also travelled to Mashhad in Iran, Baghdad in Iraq, and Damascus in Syria which are all famous holy cities and themselves have many shrines. He not only received spiritual knowledge in these places but also held discussions with scholars belonging to different schools of thought on various beliefs. It is also believed that the great Mughal Emperor Aurangzeb himself came to this location to pay respects to Bari Imam.

There is a strong belief among the devotees that when one visits shrines and prays, their wishes or desires are fulfilled. Whether it is a want of a child, a spouse, or a job, people flock to the shrines by millions all over the world and pray.

Samir himself did not believe in the power of such saints, except that they should be respected for being spiritual guides for many of their followers.

"Do people pray to the saint or God?" asked Samir.

Latif turned a corner, looked at Samir in the eye, and replied, "Some believe it is to the power of the saint, as he is considered very close to God. Since the saint can be directly reached by us mortals at the shrine, to the extent of hearing us directly and audibly, people pray to him and ask him to recommend their wishes to God. They find it a short-cut to communicate with God. Others pray to God directly at the shrine, asking God to fulfill their wishes for the saint's sake whom He loves. Either way, wishes made at shrines are mostly fulfilled."

"Maybe like a placebo effect, I guess. How do you view sufism?" asked Samir, wanting to learn directly from Latif who was quite knowledgeable on the subject.

Latif thought that one over for a moment first before replying. "Sufism is a simplistic religious order which cuts across many beliefs. There are many sects within sufism, and they mostly preach love for humanity. Many live in their inner self, and try to find God within themselves."

Samir agreed. "I love Bulley Shah who has rendered one of the best sufi verses. His message is for all humanity. I particularly like his narration that God resides in one's heart. It goes like this:

'Tear down the mosque and temple too, break all that divides,
But do not break the human heart as it is there that God resides.'"

Latif was surprised to hear Samir narrate from Bulley. He had thought of Samir more like a nerd rather than being associated with literature and poetry. He nodded his head in appreciation and continued to explain, "Sufism is considered by many of its Muslim followers as the inner mystical dimension of Islam. Those who follow sufism usually congregate around a saint whose ancestry can be traced back to the Prophet Muhammad. They follow an order or 'silsila' which meets regularly at the shrine or any other meeting place for spiritual sessions and their own reawakening. Usually, there is praise of the God and Prophet through remembrance and mention. Most follow the Sunni school of thought, though there are Shia and non-Muslim followings of sufism, as well.

"Sufis are spread all over the Muslim world, particularly in South Asia. However, the practice is also popular in African countries such as Tunisia, Algeria, Morocco, and Senegal as well, where it is seen as a mystical expression of Islam. It has gained popularity in Africa particularly because it can easily accommodate local beliefs and customs, which tend toward the mystical. In the western world, it has also gained popularity among non-Muslims as well such as in Spain which at one time was under Muslim domination."

"Sufi following is picking up in the US, as well. What is their main mode of practice?" Samir asked.

"Dhikr, or zikr, is one of them, which is mentioning and praising Allah as is commanded in the Quran. This is done through various acts, such as repetition of divine names, and Allah has 99, recitation of verses, chanting, music, and singing. The well-known singing form is the 'qawwali', the devotional singing in Pakistan and India. There are many devotional songs sung by both sufi and non-sufi singers, such as the well-known Nusrat Fateh Ali Khan, well-known for his qawwali, who passed away a number of years back. Abida Parveen today stands out as a well-known devotional singer who sings the verses of the sufis.

"Sometimes, there is dancing as well, like the Tanoura dance in Egypt, the whirling dervishes of Konya and the 'dhamaal' at the shrine of Lal Shahbaz Qalandar. 'Wajd' or 'haal' is yet another spiritual ecstasy which is induced by remembrance of God while hearing recitation of the Quran. Most practices depend on the silsila being followed."

Samir could relate to the whirling dervishes at the shrine of the great sufi and spiritual leader, Jalaluddin Rumi, at Konya and to the dhamaal at shrine of Lal Shahbaz Qalandar.

He had visited Rumi's shrine when he was a graduate student in Turkey. Rumi is well-known as the Islamic Shakespeare. His teachings resonate in the world with today's happenings so more and more people are now relating to him. Rumi's poetry is well-read in the western world as well.

Rumi passed away on Dec 17, 1273. This date is known as 'Sheb-i Arus' meaning 'The Wedding Night'. Every year, the 17th of December is celebrated at Konya as the night of Rumi's reunion with his Beloved. Rumi, in his lifetime, described it in his poetry as follows:

"When I die, when my coffin is being taken out
You must never think I am missing this world.
Don't shed any tears, don't lament or feel sorry. I'm not falling into a monster's abyss.
When you see my corpse is being carried,
Don't cry for my leaving.
I'm not leaving, I'm arriving at eternal love.
When you leave me in the grave, don't say goodbye.
Remember a grave is only a curtain for the paradise behind.
You'll only see me descending into a grave, now watch me rise.
How can there be an end? When the sun sets
Or the moon goes down, it looks like the end,
It seems like a sunset, but in reality, it is a dawn.
When the grave locks you up, that is when your soul is freed.
Have you ever seen a seed fallen to earth not rise with a new life?
Why should you doubt the rise of a seed named human?
When for the last time you close your mouth,
Your words and soul will belong to the world of no place, no time."

Samir also recalled the ecstatic dhamaal dancing at the shrine of Lal Shahbaz Qalandar in Sindh, "The popular dhamaal at Qalandar is the dancing connection to God, and leads one to a state of mental intoxication," he added.

Latif agreed, "'Qalandars' are saints who achieve a very high level of spirituality, and have a very strong affinity for God's creation. They feel they are not bound with time and space, and hold a very high order among all saints. Their followers, who are from all religions, believe that every part of the universe is at their disposal but these holy people are far above temptation, greed or lust, and that they have been appointed by God for this very purpose."

Samir knew more about Lal Shabaz Qalandar from Sindh, "He was called 'Lal', or red colored after his usual red attire, 'Shahbaz' to denote a noble and divine spirit and 'Qalandar' as he was a wandering holy man who had achieved a very high level of spirituality. He is reputed for performing many miracles and is seen as a very holy figure in Sindh across many beliefs. He has a very large Hindu following as well, who believe he is the reincarnation of their revered god Jhulelal, which means red bridegroom. Jhulelal was the deity of River Indus, and is himself considered an incarnation of the Hindu God Varuna. Lal Shahbaz Qalandar is therefore also referred to as 'Jhulelal Qalandar'. The Sindhi folk song, 'Dama Dam Mast Qalandar' is one of the most popular sufi songs in South Asia, and most events and celebrations end with the whole crowd dancing to this song."

Samir continued, "In Multan, he met Bahauddin Zakria of the Suhrwardiyya, Baba Fariduddin Ganjshakar of the Chishtiyya, and Syed Jalaluddin Bukhari also of the Suhrawardiyya order. The friendship of these four became legendary, and was known as the four lanterns, or 'Chahar Yar', meaning four friends. They are also referred to in his mast qalandar song. Shahbaz was a profound scholar of many religions and was fluent in many languages, including Pashto, Persian, Turkish, Arabic, Sindhi, and Sanskrit.

"Lal Shahbaz Qalandar holds among the highest order in Pakistan and India!" Samir agreed.

Latif continued, "Pakistan probably has the largest number of famous sufi shrines, and has many fake ones too. Shah Abdul Latif, Abdullah Ghazi and Sachal Sarmast are also notable in Sindh, while in Punjab, Data Ganj Ali Hajveri of Lahore holds a very high order. Multan has many saints, and is known as the city of sufis in Pakistan, where caravans of scholar used to come from Central Asia, the Middle East and Persia and from South Asia and East Asia to learn about Islam. Bahauddin Zakria and Rukn-e-Alam, and some believe Shams Tabrizi, who was the spiritual mentor of Jalaluddin Rumi, also lie in Multan.

"Outside Pakistan, Pir Abdul Qadir Jillani in Baghdad, who is among the direct descendant of the Prophet, enjoys a very high status among the sufis, and has a very strong following in Pakistan and India, where many Jillanis claim heredity to the Pir. Another famous sufi Naqshbandi lies buried in Bukhara in Uzbekistan."

Samir was going down memory lane, "Yes. I have visited most of them and am certainly inspired by their teachings."

Latif was surprised to hear this, "In India, Saleem Chisti is credited with the birth of Mughal Emperor Jehangir, to whom his father, the great Emperor Akbar walked barefoot from Delhi asking him to pray for a son. When his son was born, he named him after the saint as Saleem, known to all as Emperor Jehangir. Another sufi Nizamuddin Auliya lies at Delhi. But the most famous of all, Moinuddin Chishti at Ajmer Sharif, has a following of millions of Hindus and Muslims in the subcontinent."

Samir added, "Both our Prime Ministers, Murtaza and Marvi, were devoted followers of Ajmer Sharif and of Lal Shahbaz Qalandar…"

"So are so many Bollywood stars and celebrities. Most Indian movies in India are only released after the producer, director, and the actors pray for its success at the shrine. Free food, prepared in large quantities and called 'langar', is offered to thousands of devotees every day…"

"Hasn't there been a women saint too?"

"All lineage from the Prophet are saintly, including Hazrat Aisha and Hazrat Fatima, the Prophet's wife and daughter, who hold the highest honors among all women. But if you mean sufi saint, Rabia al-Adawiyya, also known as Rabia Basri, lies in the port city of Basra in Iraq. She is well-known for her famous prayer:

'O God! If I worship You for fear of hell, burn me in hell, and if I worship You in hope of paradise, exclude me from paradise. But if I worship You for Your Own sake, grudge me not Your everlasting beauty.'"

"Who are the 'murshids'?" asked Samir, seeking a clarification on a word commonly used by the followers of sufism.

"A murshid is a spiritual guide or teacher. The path of sufism starts when a student, called the 'murid', or follower or student, takes an oath, called the 'baith', with the spiritual guide. Those who pledge to the murshid pledge it through him to God. The students take advice from their murshid who is their tutor and guide."

"What about the 'pir' and the 'sajjada nasheen'?"

"The pir and the sajjada nasheen are titles for the descendant of a saint, and in some instances descendant of a disciple of a sufi, and are thought of by the illiterate masses as conduits to God. They can offer prayers for their followers which they claim can solve many problems, give success or protect them. People give 'nazrana', or token money of appreciation or respect, to the pir or sajjada nasheen, who mints them by the millions. Because of their following, they hold immense power. The more the number of followers, the more their status. As a result, they also enjoy political patronage of the governments. Many a member of parliaments and ministers, particularly from your province of Sindh and south Punjab are pir, or syed, who claim direct ancestry to the Prophet. The former prime minister of Pakistan, and a number of chief ministers of Sindh, were all syed. Then there are fake pir and syed, as well."

"How many sufi silsila are there?"

"There are as many as there are sufis. There is the Mevlevi, Chistiya, Naqshbandi, Shadhiliya, Suhrawardiyya, Qadiriyya, and Qalandariyya among others depending on the sufi they follow."

Samir remembered his discussions with Hasan on the subject. Qalandariyya are on one end of the spectrum, who are like Faqirs, wearing colorful clothes and beaded necklaces and bracelets, are mostly travelers found lying by the roadsides, without any desire of worldly or materialistic things, and are not followers of the sharia, or Islamic laws, as they seek God within themselves. Naqshbandi, on the other hand, follow the sharia. The Chistiya are somewhere in between, who sing the qawwali, yet respect most sharia laws. There is a belief among some sufi followers that all orders will merge before the end of times, and consolidate under Imam Mahdi to assist him in establishing one Islamic order in the world.

"Aren't sufi followers persecuted in Pakistan?"

"Historically, including to the present times, they have been persecuted by extreme viewpoints and by militant organizations. Persecution has included destruction of sufi shrines and mosques, suppression of orders, and discrimination against followers. Kamal Ataturk after the Turkish revolution banned all sufi orders and abolished their institutions after the sufis opposed the new secular order. The Iranian Islamic Republic has harassed Shia sufis. In other Muslim countries, like Pakistan, attacks on sufi shrines have come from the Islamist militant organizations who believe that celebration of birthdays of sufi saints, called 'urs' and the praying, singing, and dancing at the shrines or graves, is 'shirk', or praying to a deity."

"There is also faith healing at the shrines?"

"Faith healing has become a business at the shrines! The pir offer prayers which they claim can heal the sick. The shrines are also swarming with fake faith healers and fakirs, who live there endlessly in colorful rags leading a very simple life, and who claim they get the power of the praying or healing from the saint, and in some cases, from God himself."

"Isn't magic also practiced at the shrines?" Timur had talked of magic, and Samir was alluding to the possibility that terrorists perhaps had acquired the services of magicians at shrines, even though they were not followers of sufism.

"Magic has been practiced at Sufi shrines, notably in India and Pakistan. This practice, which is not part of sufism, flourishes when the sufi order is incorrectly exploited as a means to gain wealth and power. Magical practices and superstition are common now at most shrines practiced by those who continue to exploit spirituality for their gains. It has become a million-rupee business to mint money from the illiterate poor followers of the sufi. Many others flock to them as well."

"Could terrorists have exploited them?"

"Not a possibility. These men who practice magic at the shrine are mostly there 'to make a wish come true'," Latif smiled.

"What about the practice of dreams in sufism?"

"Some sufis believe that the Prophet Muhammad listens to them when they call upon him. Sufis seeing the Prophet in a dream is a common claim. Many more strive to do so, and if they so visualize, they tend to interpret or misinterpret these dreams as well. At the same time, many believe that the saint's spirit hovers around the shrine and gives blessings to the devotee in person and comes in their dreams as well."

Samir interrupted, "This has clearly led to the wrong practice of devotees praying to the shrine instead of to God Himself. It is a sin to pray to anyone else other than God. This is shirk or a sin in all monotheistic religions."

Latif smiled, "They don't know whom they are praying to."

"The followers of sufism are from all religions and faiths. It is at the shrine which becomes the melting pot for all faiths!" commented Samir, "but then unfortunately, they are targeted for the same reasons."

Recently a number of sufi shrines had been attacked in Pakistan. A suicide bombing took place inside the Shrine of Lal Shahbaz Qalandar in which at least 90 people were killed and over 300 injured. The shrine is frequented with Muslims, Hindus, and Christians alike. ISIS had claimed responsibility for the attack. The Shah Noorani shrine in Balochistan was also attacked earlier that killed over 60 devotees and wounded over 100. ISIS claimed their suicide bomber had carried out the bombing and targeted polytheists. The shrine was popular with both Shiite and Sunni sects. Sunni extremists regard both Shiites and sufis as heretics. In an earlier attack on the Data Ganj shrine in Lahore in 2010, over 50 devotees, mostly belonging to the Sunni sect, were killed by two suicide bombers.

Some also object to women going to shrines, as they believe according to certain Hadith that women should not go to graves, even though the shrines are mostly thronged with women. More recently, in India, a women society won a petition in the court to keep shrines open to visit by women. The male keepers of the Haji Ali shrine had banned women from entering it.

Samir knew of parallel world of beliefs and superstitions built around the shrines, as many of his own friends were themselves syed and pir, and even though well-educated, believed in these powers.

"What about fortune telling, or predicting the future, by these pir?"

"Many a politicians and businessmen flock to the pir and murshid to know of the future, or that of their business or of their political future. All prime ministers that I know, and many a leading businessman, believe in these powers of the pir and the shrine, and flock to them regularly for advice before making a major decision."

Samir figured this practice was not just confined to the politicians and the businessmen, but religious scholars could also be a source of advice and guidance for the militants and extremists who would seek advice prior to their actions.

"Haven't you read the prophesies of Shah Naimatullah Wali?" asked Latif.

Samir had heard of him, and of his prophesies, claimed to have been made over 600 years ago, but not in much detail. But he was not the only one who prophesized the future. There were many in almost all beliefs, including the famous prophecies being of St. John Bosco and Nostradamus.

He recalled St. John Bosco's most famous prophecy, made in 1,868, which had a vision of hell. They say St. John regularly used to have visions in his dreams since he was nine years old, and that even impressed Pope Pius IX so much that he ordered St. John to write down his dreams for the encouragement of his congregation.

Nostradamus, on the other hand, was a reputed seer who made many prophecies. His first book, *Les Propheties*, was published in 1,555, which is still widely read. He is credited with predicting many major world events. Most of his prophesies are so generic that anything at any time could fit into them. Samir recalled the rise of Colonel Kaddafi, of Saddam Hussain and the Gulf War were all 'prophesized' by Nostradamus.

Likewise, the prophesies of Shah Naimatullah Wali were based on earlier sayings and the Hadith, but were tampered with over the years to fit every event happening around the world. Samir thought it was a blind belief of his followers that Naimatullah prophesized everything till the end of times. He wanted to hear of it from Latif.

Shah Naimatullah

"Shah Naimatullah Wali was born in Syria and was said to be more than 100 years old when he died near Kirman in Iran in 1431. It is amazing that all his prophesies, which were about the future and the end of times, have come true. He made it clear that he was not saying it out of knowledge of astrology, but with the grace of God. Many of his prophesies about the forthcoming future are yet to be fulfilled."

"Haven't most of his writings been lost?"

"We believe he wrote more than 2,000 verses out of which less than 250 are available even today. We continue to search for this lost treasure!"

"I read somewhere that when the oldest manuscript was obtained by a visiting scholar Edward Browne in 1888, there were only around 50 or so verses that were found?"

Latif looked at Samir in the eye, "The Viceroy of India Lord Curzon, during the British occupation of India, had banned his manuscripts because Shah had prophesized that the English will rule India for only 100 years. This eventually turned out to be true if you don't count the rule under East India Company. The

British wanted to rule forever, but Shah had predicted that a 6-year war against the Germans, despite the English winning, will weaken their system of rule, and they will leave India. Eventually, when the British left, the people started searching for his lost manuscripts. More of his manuscripts were found later.

"Shah had even predicted the World War II will start 21 years after the first war, and it would be more violent, lethal, destructive and ruinous then the first one. All his prophesies have come true! Now, through his prophesies we have a road map to the future events and how the world will shape."

Samir recalled that most of his prophesies were actually based on the Hadith and what was prophesized during the early Islamic period. He was skeptical, "But did not the later found prophesies, which were not in the Hadith, only covered events which had already happened?"

Latif was unsure, "Hazrat Naimatullah had predicted not only about the British but events prior to that by both name and duration. He predicted Timur, and after him the King of Kabul Babar will rule India, followed by his son Himayun, who will be challenged by Sher Shah, and will flee to Iran. He will return to rule, followed by his sons Akbar, Jahangir, and Shah Jahan. He predicted the Mughals would rule for 300 years. He also predicted the appearance of Nanak, who is the patron saint of the Sikhs. He predicted the partitioning of India into India and Pakistan, and of the breakup of Pakistan into Pakistan and Bangladesh. He predicted the 17-day 1965 war between India and Pakistan."

Latif continued, "He predicted in the World War I, 13.1 million people would be killed…"

Samir interrupted, "That's impossible! Only God can be that accurate."

"This is exactly the point. He had a vision. It was God who told him of all these future happenings. It couldn't be manmade."

"So, what did he predict about the future?"

"Listen to what he predicted about the present first. Whatever is happening today was predicted by him 600 years ago. These are also the minor signs of the end of times, as described in the Hadith and expressed by our Prophet. Corrupt rulers will rule us, officials will take bribes. The educated and knowledgeable like us will mourn. The media will make them blind, dumb, and deaf. Everyone will be busy dancing and listening to songs."

"Well, it is not a new prediction!"

Latif continued without listening, "Incest will be common. Sister with brother, boy with his mother, and father with his daughter. Even mothers will cheat their daughters. Murders, adultery, and homosexuality will spread throughout. Muslims will commit such criminal and disgusting acts. The clerics will issue baseless decrees…"

Samir smiled, "That is certainly what they are doing, and are good at! That is the only part of the prophecy I would agree with."

Latif went on speaking, as if his heart was paining, "Muslims will forget what is 'halal', or allowed, and what is 'haram', or forbidden. Because of kidnappings and rapes, women will lose their dignity and respect. Hatred will be common; women will be without veil, will look innocent but in reality, will be like prostitutes and whores. Some people will even sell their daughters and act as pimps."

It read like the encyclopedia of the sin and the bad, Samir thought.

Latif went on like on autopilot, "Shah prophesized that governments will be formed through deceit and through lies. Hypocrisy will spread in the east and in the west, and in all four directions. Common people will accept the widespread evil and sins. You'll not see anyone defending the truth. They will honor the thieves and robbers. Scholars will give satanic suggestions, while they sit in their homes with their lovers. Fasting, prayers, and obedience will disappear suddenly. Zikr and religious chants will be hypocritical…"

"Well! Our nation has become corrupt because our leaders are corrupt. We reap what we sow, but we hope to change that. But what did Shah prophesize about the future? Now that the minor signs of the end of times are already here, can Imam Mahdi be far away?" Samir asked cynically.

"Shah saw complete victory for the Muslims. Particularly the Muslims of Pakistan. He prophesized that an army of warriors of the Turks, Arabs, Persians, and from the Middle East will come to help Pakistan. Even the Chinese will come to the aid of Pakistan.

"Our nations of Pashtun will lead the forces. The big battle in the subcontinent will be fought in Chitral, Nanga Parbat, Gilgit, and Tibet. There will be bloodshed. River Attock will become red with the blood of the kafir. Eventually, after a six-month long war, India will be cleansed from the Hindu rituals and conquered again by the Muslims from the northwest. All those beautiful women you see in Bollywood movies will be among the spoils of war…"

Samir shook his head in disagreement, "War is not an option anymore. Both countries are nuclear powers. There can never be a conventional war between them in which one side will be the victor, and nuclear is out of the question."

Latif turned and looked at Samir, "That is not all! Like India, the west too will have bad luck. Shah prophesized that the third world war will begin soon!"

Samir agreed, "With what is happening around the world today, Afghanistan, Syria, Iraq, Yemen, Libya, and now in North Korea, it is already the equivalent of a great war!"

Latif looked up, "Shah prophesized 600 years ago that the superpowers of today will be destroyed by the Muslims in this great war."

He took a deep breath and continued, "Out of England and America, one will be completely destroyed by Russia. Weapons of mass destruction will be used in the war. Russia will then be devastated by China. Only through some last minutes diplomacy will it be able to save itself."

Samir wondered if the Russians had read these prophesies. He couldn't believe the nonsense in the prophesies. It appeared they were all made up in recent years.

"What is in fate for the Muslims according to the prophecy?"

"The Mahdi will then appear! It will be the last of the minor signs to the end of times and the day of judgment. News of his appearance will spread around the world. Dajjal will then appear from the city of Isfahan. Prophet Isa, or Jesus, will then return back to earth to help Mahdi kill Dajjal!"

"Really! I think most of it is plagiarized from the Hadith, and some has been made up and added in recent years to make it look appealing and authentic. If the terrorists are hearing of these sermons from their religious leaders, and believing in them, then God give them wisdom to distinguish the truth from the lies!"

Latif pretended not to hear and turned into the lane of the shrine and found a convenient place to park near the entrance. They both got down from the car, and as they walked to the shrine, Samir wondered if the most educated and the elite among Muslims believed in such prophesies, what to talk of the average person, and specially the uneducated. No wonder the jihadi had found so much blind support from the countless illiterates who believed Muslims will defeat India, the Christians, the Jews, and the superpowers, and will eventually rule the world. And on top of that they would also be rewarded with those beautiful Bollywood girls as well!

Sajjada Nasheen

Lal Bux Jillani had inherited the position of sajjada nasheen of the Bari Imam shrine from his father eight years ago. He was around 70 years old but looked over 80 and fragile. He had lived and spent all his life listening to the sermons of his father, and had travelled wide and far to most Muslim countries where he had a large following. The who's who of Islamabad would frequent him regularly, sit at his footstep for advice and guidance. The former prime minister would not make any decisions unless it had his blessings. He was the Imam, or the lead priest at the shrine, as was addressed as such.

He was wearing a white shalwar-qameez with a green turban when he received them at the main entrance of the shrine. He had applied 'surma' to his eyes which is a fine black powdered ore used like the mascara, and red henna to his hair, both in the traditions of the Prophet. Modern science has discovered that surma contains lead and is not beneficial for the eyes, however, the traditional belief of applying surma is held among the conservative Muslims.

He was very clear in his message, "Allah is all powerful. He reigns all, and it is to Him that we should call to. Bari Imam facilitates our call to Allah, as Allah listens to him. Whatever we ask of Bari Imam, he never ever turns it down, and asks Allah of the same, and it is instantly fulfilled."

"But don't many go back empty handed as well?" Samir was inquisitive.

He looked Samir in the eye disapprovingly, shook his head, and said, "Man does not know what Bari Imam does. He overseas everything. If Bari Imam feels the fulfilling of a certain prayer would be detrimental to the person asking, it is turned down for his own good. We never question what is not fulfilled as it is all the will of Allah."

Samir came straight to the point, "Imam sahib: Our country is being attacked by various terrorist groups who claim they are the champions of Islam. I believe they frequently visit shrines too for guidance. I am sure many of them come here to pray and seek guidance as well. Can we seek Bari Imam's help and stop them from carrying out their acts?" He had to use the language that the devotees of the shrine understood.

The Imam appeared pleased. "Many a disaster in Islamabad were averted because of his presence. Last year, the parliament building was going to be blown up. Bari Imam warned me in my dream, and I alerted the agencies. The extra precautions they took saved the lives of a few hundred parliamentarians..."

"Can he not alert us before every attack?"

"Yes, he can, but you must reform and improve your ways first. Look at the Islamabad night life. I am ashamed to say that what is happening in the villas and farmhouses by our elected representatives and those who hold public offices does not reflect our values." He coughed and continued, "People have adopted the ways of the non-believers. Drinking, dancing, and corruption are all widespread. These are the signs of the end of times. We should follow in the steps of our Prophet and the sharia. No harm will come to us then. Even the superpowers like America, or Russia, or even India can do us no harm if we seek help from Allah."

"But we do that all the time. Millions pray in the mosques every day for our welfare and of the country…"

"But not with 'niyat'." Niyat meant with sincerity and real intention. "Prayers to Allah from the heart can protect anyone from the impossible. Prophet Abraham was thrown into the fire by the king of Babylon, Nimrod, with his own father watching, but the fire became a garden because of Abraham's prayer to Allah. Just one prayer, as given in the Quran in chapter 3, verse 173, saved him when he called out:

'Allah is sufficient for me and He is the best Disposer of affairs.'

"Today, millions pray but prayers are not heard because they do not pray with niyat. If only the world of Islam follows in the footsteps of the prophets, we Muslims can dominate and rule the world."

Latif added, "It is like the story of Prophet Yunus and his prayer at the time of distress when he was swallowed by a fish."

The Imam picked up the story, "There are lessons to be learnt from the Quran. Prophet Yunus, also referred to as Jonah in the Bible, was sent by Allah to the people of Nineveh, a town in the area of Mosul in northern Iraq. He called his people to the message of Allah and truth, but initially, they rejected his message and persisted in their disbelief and wrongdoings. Disappointed and frustrated, Prophet Yunus left them in anger, threatening them with punishment after three days. However, soon Allah guided the hearts of his people and they realized their mistakes and went out to the desert asking for Allah's forgiveness. On this, Allah spared them from the punishment."

He continued, "Prophet Yunus, after leaving his people, went on to board a ship that got caught up in a storm and its people thought that they would drown. In such a desperate situation when the ship was being pounded by waves on all sides, and they were at risk of drowning, they drew lots to decide to throw someone out of the ship in an effort to lighten the load. Prophet Yunus lost the draw three times. However, the people of the ship did not want to throw him out of the ship. So, he took off his garment to throw himself into the sea. After he jumped into the sea, Allah sent from the sea a large fish which swallowed Prophet Yunus. Allah inspired that large fish not to devour his flesh or break his bones. When in the belly of the fish, Prophet Yunus realized his mistake and called out to Allah from the depths of darkness, a prayer commonly referred to as 'Ayat Kareema' which is given in chapter 21 verse 87:

'There is no God but You, Glorified be You! Truly, I have been of the wrongdoers.'"

He pointed to a side room, where about 20 worshippers were seated in a circle on the floor, with a pile of small shells in the center. They were reading something in a soft tone, again and again, picking up a shell, and placing it on the side.

"This recitation, in which Ayat Kareema is repeated again and again, happens thousands of times by various groups who come here all day and night long to pray and have their desires fulfilled."

He was convinced of the power of collective prayers, "Muslims collectively recite the Ayat Kareema over and over again repeating it at least 125,000 times at times of distress, asking for forgiveness and help from God. Allah always listens to this particular prayer and saves one from the distress. It is guaranteed help from God!"

"How do you know that?" asked Samir.

"Allah made it known that had it not been for Prophet Yunus's sincere repentance and his invocations to Him, he would have stayed in the fish's stomach till the day of judgment. So, it is clearly ordained in the Quran that when we are in a difficulty or a distressful situation and turn to Allah and call upon Him with sincere repentance, especially with these words of Ayat Kareema, Allah will respond to our call. This is an important lesson we have not forgotten. Without being sincere, if we repent and call out to Allah, we cannot come out of distress!"

"Can reciting the Ayat Kareema over and over again save us from these attacks?" Samir was inquisitive.

"Allah has tremendous powers. The cases of Prophets Yunus and Abraham are in the Quran. Allah saved one from the fire, and the other from the belly of the fish. These terrorist attacks are very minor. But only if mankind regrets and prays to Allah with sincerity like Prophets Yunus and Abraham did."

"Collective prayers are far more effective," added Latif. "Worshippers flock to mosques and shrines during worship times to pray collectively so the divine energy is synergized and praying becomes far more effective. Prophet Muhammed always asked his followers to pray at the mosque when possible, but definitely during Friday prayers."

"Could the terrorists not make use of the same collective power of prayers to fulfill their desires and cause more terror?" Samir was curious.

The imam gave a look of disapproval, "This prayer is only to fulfill desires and one that that causes no harm to anyone. Would you not like to pray at Bari Imam?"

Without waiting for an answer, the imam led the way into the shrine. There were devotees by the hundreds. Some were worshiping, some reading from the Quran or other smaller booklets, while some were just sitting on the floor with a rosary in hand, reciting something inaudible.

There was another line-up of devotees outside a window in the courtyard. Thousands were being fed free food which was distributed every day. The whole street outside the shrine had commercial kitchens where one could order or buy a whole 'degh' or large metal cooking pot, so it can be distributed free to the worshippers, the homeless, or the travelers. No one would go back hungry from this place. On Thursdays and Fridays, there were 'langars', which was food cooked in very large quantities and distributed free to the visitors. Samir recalled that the langars at the shrine of Moinuddin Chisti at Ajmer, India, were among the largest in the world, and would feed people by the hundreds of thousands at the annual congregation.

Thousands came to Bari Imam and to all the other shrines every day, and particularly on Thursday nights to pray and ask for fulfillment of their desires. The sajjada nasheen led them close to the grave of Bari Imam and asked the three of them to raise their hands to Allah and ask for His help and His blessings.

Samir prayed to God, and wondered whether people prayed to God or to Bari Imam. If they desired their wishes from Bari Imam, then did Bari Imam really have the power to fulfill their desires? Many shrines had been attacked in recent years, and if the saints could not even protect their own resting places and shrines, how could they protect their devotees?

The group quietly prayed and focused on their personal desires for the next few minutes, stretching out their open palms upwards towards the sky as if receiving God's blessings, ending the prayers by lightly rubbing their palms on their faces, which was traditional. It was like the grace of God had collected in their open palms and transferred from the palms into their faces and body.

Samir could only imagine why the Muslims had become lethargic. They wanted God or Bari Imam or any other sufi or saint to do everything for them, instead of doing it themselves. Praying with devotion certainly helped, but it is essential that both praying and efforts to complete a task are done side by side, and not just by praying alone. If God just listened to prayers, and to those who gave alms, and who distributed free food, then one didn't need to do any effort to achieve what they wanted. The devotees only wanted Allah or the saint to do everything for them without doing anything themselves! *What a crooked thinking,* thought Samir.

As Samir and Latif walked back to their car, the sajjada nasheen put his hand on Samir's shoulder and whispered, "I just heard from Bari Imam! He asked you to be careful as you are treading on dangerous grounds. He said your life is in danger, but he said he will protect you since you came to pay respects to him and pray at the shrine. He will be with you always to protect you."

Samir was confused. He did not know whether to believe him or not. But he did feel something like an aura of protection around him as he walked away from the shrine. Was it a real feeling or only an imagination, only time would tell.

Drive

Latif was a good guide and source of information on Islam, "We will next stop at the Islamic Center, which a world apart from what is taught at the madrassahs run by the religious imams, or dictated at the shrines. It is staffed by university scholars, has a library with online connectivity to the Al-Azhar University Library and other leading Islamic universities and databases around the world. The center is an excellent forum for intellectual thought and invites excellent speaker from around the world. Some of the lectures are also brought in through live streaming as well. Today's lecture, as you know, is on spiritualism of Islam."

Samir nodded his head. He knew who the speaker was as he himself had arranged for him to come to Pakistan and speak at a conference, which was to take place at a science conference at the ministry within a few days. He and Samir shared similar views on Islam.

Samir expressed his views on Islam, "The simple submission is to Allah. This is what Islam is all about. Religion is between humans and God, and God lies in our hearts. Hence, we must love the fellow human being. That is what the sufis believe in too."

Samir continued, "I do not believe in extremist and primitive views about Islam. One must be tolerant and respect everyone's beliefs. I believe that even if one human reforms, and learns to love others, the entire society will reform collectively. Unfortunately, the society has deviated from true faith, and a certain extreme and fundamentalist version is being projected into the society by the so called moulvis, maulanas, pirs, syeds, and by external forces who want to bring a bad name to our religion. This view has been imposed onto the Muslims over hundreds of years by these pseudo-religious scholars. Even an alternate viewpoint or room for discussion is not allowed. If one proposes an alternate viewpoint, then it is considered blasphemous, and is punishable by death, not just by the state, but by self-proclaimed guardians of Islam. Hence, everyone is afraid to speak up.

"Governor Taseer was killed for the same reason. Aasiya, a Christian girl, is under the death penalty for insulting the Prophet, an accusation which she denies. Many other minorities are scapegoated and persecuted by accusing them of blasphemy. Hundreds other die for similar reasons. Only yesterday's papers mentioned someone jailed for 25 years for accidently disposing off the pages of the Quran in a trash can instead of placing it in flowing water. The governments are silent bystanders as they cannot afford to take on the wrath of the moulvis. The politicians are equally to blame for not speaking out against blasphemous laws which are misinterpreted and misapplied."

Latif remained silent, as this was such a sensitive subject, which could cost anyone their life. However, Samir continued, "We Muslims portray God and his angels as always prying and watching every single move we make, or how we think. Every second, the two angels dedicated to each individual are busy compiling and updating our good-deed bad-deed record. We do not even have one second of privacy. Hence, everyone is afraid to speak up."

"Nothing is hidden from God!"

"That we know. But the so-called good Muslims are always pleasing God so they can enter heaven: from wearing a dress which fully covers their body to reading prayers five times a day, or even more, to reciting from the Quran, and countless, hundreds, maybe thousands of teachings in the Hadith. Muslims are afraid of God. There is more fear of God than love of God in most of us. We focus more on avoiding sin which will punish us in hell and less on doing the good deeds as ordained in Islam. The female sufi, Rabia, propagated exactly this viewpoint."

Samir continued, "The conservatives, and the fundamentalists, believe that God can become annoyed over the smallest of things, from even glancing or smiling at a woman, or eating with the left hand, or standing up and peeing. From birth to death, all Muslims believe worshiping Allah will give them eternal life in heaven, with bountiful fruits, gardens and shades, and houris for men.

"All sermons of clerics during prayers emphasize on the punishment and reward system. Punishments are graphically described, projecting God as a judge and jury, and having everyone being afraid of him, while He is actually most loving, kind, and forgiving. While judges follow the law, God is actually kind and can forgive one for his or her one single good deed."

Latif shook his head, "The sinners will be certainly punished. The soul leaves the body at the time of death. It is then taken by the angel of death to the windows of heaven and hell, informing him of his fate, and then brought back to the body. He is asked three critical questions about his faith and the Prophet. If he answers them correctly, he is given comfort in his grave and left to fate till the final day of judgment. If not, he would rot with insects and snakes till that day."

Latif had his beliefs about life after death, "On the day of the judgement, everyone would become alive and appear before the court of Allah at Mount Ararat, the same ground where Haj is performed. Billions of people, born and dead from Adam to the present or future time, would come alive at the same time and head towards the throne of God. No one would recognize anyone, not even a mother her child. There would be complete chaos. Their deeds will be read out. They would then have to cross a bridge having a width thinner than the hair. Below the bridge would be the fires of hell and those who will not be able to cross will fall down."

Samir shook his head, "You create fear and terror in people's heart instead of love for humanity. And talking of the bridge that one needs to cross, don't you guys believe that the same lamb whom you sacrificed during Eid would help you cross the bridge, while all others would fall below to burn in hell, including those who have not slaughtered lambs. Isn't that why you feed the best grass, nuts and milk to the sacrificial animals, and decorate them before running a knife around their throat?" Samir asked cynically.

Latif pretended not to hear, "Those who cross over will go to paradise."

Samir disagreed, "Millions of goats and lamb are slaughtered during haj and Eid in one day. God had asked Abraham to sacrifice whatever is dearest to him, and not really a ram. That is the real spirit of Eid…learning to sacrifice. I believe it would be better if we helped the poor with this money instead.

"Also, look at how the heaven is projected to the poor Muslim. Isn't it described as a fantasy world which the Arabs of Saudi Arabia living 1,400 years ago could relate to? The honey, the rare fruits that were imported from the Mediterranean coast, the sweet fragrant water, the rivers of milk, and the shades have all been deficient in the Arabic desert. Polygamy was common. So, the bonus is many beautiful virgins with large eyes, and big boobs, to fulfill one's endless desire. And on top of that the moulvis say a man will not tire of having sex with each one, and with many endlessly. This endless sex could go on for a billion years. No wonder Muslims only look forward to the next permanent world instead of making this world a better place to live in!"

"Heaven and hell are in every religion!" commented Latif.

"But among Muslims, those who propagate the belief that the jihadi and only those who pray and worship will go to heaven ruins it all. It makes Muslims lethargic and not wanting to do anything constructive for humanity in this world. There are those who just want to pray to God five times a day, and fast 30 days in Ramadhan. The rich and the playful party all night and sleep all day even in Ramadhan. They go for haj and umrah, the off-season pilgrimage, multiple times because they can afford it, even with corruption money. They can afford to give alms to the poor, even with stolen money. They beat up women. If she resists, they send her off to her family, or even divorce her. Divorce is as simple as a three-letter word. Then they marry again, multiple times. Or they marry even if their wife is around…up to four times at the same time."

Samir could not subscribe to these practices, "Just listen to sermons given by the illiterate who put further fear of God in you. They promise you an eternal and comfortable life in paradise. No need to work. No wonder the Muslim countries are among the most backward in the world. Finally, for the poorest and the most illiterate, and those influenced by extreme religious thought, there is an easy short cut: Pick up a gun, or tie a bomb around your waist. Kill a few kafir. Blow yourself up. And its heaven and houris for you. Exactly what ISIS or Al-Qaeda is doing!"

There was silence for a few moments. Latif was speechless. He understood the complications but was afraid of speaking up on controversial subjects lest he lose his position as a religious scholar or even as a VC.

The car by now had reached the toll to the motorway. Latif slowed down and paid the toll. There was a female beggar on the side of the road, completely clad up in chador, which is a large scarf. There was a younger female beggar with her with blue eyes who had her hair uncovered. Samir noticed the peculiarity. Latif slowed down and gave him some short change, ensuring he used his right hand. Muslims believe all good deeds must be done with the right hand, including eating food. Left is considered negative or unlucky or sinful. Samir wondered what would the left-handed people did. Would they all go to hell?

Samir thought that the average Muslim was a 'hidden fundamentalist' in their private lives, except that he or she would not admit it in public. There was a local saying for it, something like 'a beard hidden in your trousers!'

The Islamic Center was another 20 minutes away. Samir thought this was a good time to explore further from Latif what that the average Muslim believed in and practiced.

Samir asked, "Why are Muslims so superstitious and believe in 1,400 old traditions, or in beliefs that make no sense. Why does the fundamentalist Muslim grow a long beard, but no mustache?"

Latif, who himself had a beard and no mustache, was quick to reply, "Jews do that too. We love our Prophet and wish to follow in his traditions. Hadith is the way of the Prophet, his sayings, his likings, his practices. The details on how a Muslim should live are in the Hadith. We must follow it as everything is not detailed in the Quran as it is not a handbook or a manual."

Samir disagreed, "But aren't there so many volumes of Hadith, each written by a different scholar, and were they not written a few hundred years after the Prophet died? With no written books then, it was all word of mouth passed down from generation to generation. I can't even remember how my grandmother lived or what she said, even in this age of printing press, audio recording, and camera. Maybe my mother can remember a few things, but I can't! No wonder there is so much disagreement between the various Hadith? Most rely on a couple of them which they say is 'sahih' or authentic. Isn't that one of the reasons there are so many sects in Islam?"

Latif turned to look at Samir, "Christians have many sects too. We Sunni follow the traditions of the Prophet and his four caliphs: Abu Bakr, Omar, Osman, and Ali. The Shias do not believe in the first three. We follow the way the Prophet lived as narrated by his companions, also called the 'sahaba' These were carried from mouth to mouth till the learned men compiled them into Hadith. Some of these Hadith are very authentic!"

Samir shook his head in disagreement again.

"But not all! So, the Hadith asks men to grow beards, and not wear shorts, and wear their pants above the ankles, while women are to be fully covered?"

Latif replied, "Only her eyes are to be visible in front of men. Even her sound of walking, or her fragrance, should not reach other man, as it leads to temptation. Our women wear the burqa, while the ones in the gulf countries wear the abaya. There is some disagreement whether a woman should be fully covered, but in all cases, it is the woman's hair that must be fully covered, hence the hijab or the chador is compulsory!"

Samir continued to disagree. "Hijab is not mentioned in the Quran. It was introduced by the Arabs much later. The Quran says women must dress up with decency and modesty. Some even say the so-called purdah was only for the wives of the Prophet. I am sure you will disagree. Isn't it a fact that the women, including the Prophet's daughter, have fought wars and led armies, not just during the early Islamic period but in South Asia as well? We turn blind to such facts and misinterpret many others.

"The hijab is now more of an identity for the Muslim women living in the west. I don't recall any girl during my school and college days wearing a hijab. My mother and sister would just use a dupatta, or a long scarf, to cover their hair, which was also a fashion statement rather than anything else. Today, you still find Muslim girls by the millions not covering their hair."

Latif kept on his driving without offering any comment.

Samir had his strong views on the way a woman must cover herself, "Hijab has now become a Muslim identity in the west only after the events of 9/11. A rebellion by our young generation, or a fashion statement, if you will. The Ataturk school of thought in Turkey objects even to the hijab, which was not allowed in universities and official events. Erdogan is changing all of that. The new fashion statement of the Muslim women on the beach in Europe has become the 'burkini'. I believe dress code is purely cultural, or in tune with fashion, as long as it is not provocative. Many an educated Pakistani woman do that!"

Latif took the next exit into a side road which led to Rawalpindi, the twin city of Islamabad. Latif asked if he could make a small stop at the university guest house next to a small creek, which had a small garden. Samir said it was okay.

Latif led Samir to the plant nursery.

"I would like to show you a flowering plant that we imported from Azerbaijan. It is unique in the sense that its flower opens up with the sound of a muezzin calling for prayers."

"Have you seen it open up yourself?"

"We are trying to make it flower, but so far without success. I saw a video of it on YouTube, and then asked someone going to Central Asia to bring a sapling. The flower is called Azan, meaning call to prayers. The Quran clearly says the seven heavens and the earth, and all beings therein, declare His glory: there is not a thing but celebrates His praise."

Samir took it with a pinch of salt. "It is only a video. You know how many hoax videos are floating around the net. But this will certainly be a miracle if you could demonstrate it live to the world at large whenever you are able to make it flower!"

Latif made no comment.

As they walked towards the gate, there was the sound of a wedding taking place next door with loud music playing, and men dancing.

"Damn these people for the music and dance. It is forbidden in Islam!"

Samir disagreed, "I think music is the global language of love. How can the folk 'ho jamalo' from Sindh, or 'bhangra' from Punjab, which are part of our folklore, or for that matter the 'qawwali', which are religious songs in praise of God, and sung at shrines, be haram?"

"Music distracts people from praying, and leads to sinful thoughts and actions…"

Samir took it with a pinch of salt. He knew Hasan loved music and played the guitar, and recalled what Hasan had told him about music. "Christians believe that Lucifer, before he became Satan, was an angel in the court of God and in charge of music. His music played all over heaven even before mankind was created. He was considered the most beautiful of all angels. Muslims, however, believe that Lucifer was the jinn Iblis who was raised to the level of an angel but was not an angel himself. In either case, he was thrown out of heaven because he rebelled against God. But it only shows that music was played in the heaven of God…"

Latif was adamant, "Satan was in charge of music in heaven, and he now plays the same music to distract the believers. We must not listen to music…"

"You sound like our former president who urged the people not to observe Valentine's Day, saying that it was not a part of Muslim tradition, but of the West. Even one of the courts made a similar observation," Samir interrupted cynically.

Latif moved to another point, "Valentines, love affairs and weddings…you know use of alcoholic perfumes is also forbidden. Only the nonalcoholic attar, which essentially is the essence or oils of flowers, is allowed and can be worn."

"C'mon Latif. We are not drinking perfumes and getting intoxicated with alcohol…"

"Couples also wear silk and gold in a wedding. Gold and silk are also considered haram for man to wear."

"You got to be kidding. I have seen many a youngsters wear gold chain and bracelets…"

"It is in the sayings of the Prophet that gold and silk are forbidden for man. We believe that gold and silk are something that people wear to beautify themselves, but a man is not meant to do this because he is perfect. He doesn't have to wear jewelry or silk clothing to attract a woman, unlike what a woman does to attract man. A woman has to look beautiful to attract her husband, and create a bond with him. Hence, a woman can wear gold."

Samir smiled, "This is like saying women are objects of sex…"

"What is in the sharia, we do not question."

Latif took a left turn into the road, and slowed down as the traffic was jammed. A stray dog crossed the road. Samir was almost sure Latif swore at the dog and muttered, "Dogs are impure animals."

"Dogs are considered man's best friend," Samir said. "What is impure about them?"

"Angels do not enter a house where there is a dog. Also, if a dog licks anything which has food, one should throw the food away and wash the utensil seven times."

"But there is nothing in the Quran that forbids people from keeping dogs as pets or from touching them. Many believe that a dog can be kept for hunting, guarding livestock or guarding crops. There is even a story of the sleepers and their watch dog in the Quran. Some even say a dog has all the attributes of an animal who deserves to go to heaven. They are more faithful and trustworthy than most humans are…"

Latif interrupted, "It is not hygienic to keep a dog in the house. Do you know owning a dog in Iran could result in 74 lashes? Even in Malaysia, moulvis were angered after a dog patting event was held in a public park. Cats are preferred."

"Why is that? Don't cats lick too?" Samir asked cynically.

"Our Prophet appreciated cats and was kind towards them. He even had a favorite cat called Muezza. He loved his cat so much that once, when it was worship time, and Muezza was sleeping on one of his sleeves, he cut off the sleeve instead of waking the cat.

"It is also said that the Prophet stroked the cat three times which granted the cats seven lives and the ability to land on its feet at all times!"

Samir wondered about the multitude of other animals if they were allowed as pets. He certainly knew horses and camels were revered by the Arabs. He also knew that the Hindus believed in the medicinal properties of cow urine, while some Muslims believed in the medicinal properties of camel urine. He wanted to ask why dog saliva was filth but camel urine was okay, but did not want to get into a detailed discussion on this subject.

They passed a bank on the right, which had the name of the bank identified as an 'Islamic Bank'.

"What makes a bank Islamic?"

"Interest is haram, or forbidden in Islam, either giving or receiving, so Islamic banks have their finance system based on profit sharing rather than interest."

"But isn't it the same thing? Interest is basically inflation plus administrative fee plus some profits. Islamic banks combine all three to make it 'halal' and call it profit. Some banks I have seen actually charge more 'profit' on loans than the regular commercial banks charge interest!"

"Riba, which is interest, is clearly forbidden in the Quran!"

"There is a clear distinction between 'riba' and interest. Riba misuses money to fleece the poor. If a poor person takes a loan of Rs. 100,000, he pays Rs. 1,000 riba every month for the rest of his life, while the loan amount does not reduce. On the other hand, with nominal interest, the principal is also paid off every month. I agree riba should not be allowed but if banks stop giving loans, then the world economy will stop! No one has enough savings to buy houses, or cars, with 100% payment upfront. The world economy will crash overnight."

"One should not take or give interest!"

"No one will deposit their money in the bank if there is no catching up with inflation. The economy would melt down. Today, we are dealing with a global economy, and institutions like the World Bank and IMF provide billions to the poor countries for development, to build dams, roads, hospitals, etc. There has to be a minimum interest payable to cover costs and inflation."

Latif had made the final turn onto the road to the center. The road was blocked with a truck unloading sand for construction.

Samir took this final moment to drive across how he grew up and what he believed faith is.

"When we went to kindergarten at a missionary school in Hyderabad, we were taught by fathers and nuns whom we considered were the best teachers. They were mostly Catholics of Portuguese origin. We learnt to respect and love them and others. This is also what my mother taught us when we grew up at home. I still recall distinctly a poem we learnt by heart in kindergarten about Abou bin Adam written by Leigh Hunt."

"I have not heard of it. What did it narrate?"

Samir cleared his throat and recited loudly,

"Abou Ben Adam, may his tribe increase!
Awoke one night from a deep dream of peace,
And saw, within the moonlight in his room,
Making it rich, and like a lily in bloom,
An Angel writing in a book of gold—
Exceeding peace had made Ben Adam bold,
And to the Presence in the room he said,
"What writest thou?"—The vision raised its head,
And with a look made of all sweet accord,
Answered, "The names of those who love the Lord."
"And is mine one?" said Abou. "Nay, not so,"
replied the Angel. Abou spoke more low,
But cheerly still, and said, "I pray thee, then,
Write me as one that loves his fellow men."
The Angel wrote, and vanished. The next night
It came again with a great wakening light,
And showed the names whom love of God had blessed,
And lo! Ben Adam's name led all the rest."

Latif seemed to like it. "This is certainly a masterpiece. We should make it compulsory for everyone to read it."

"Not just read it, but follow it! We did not go to madrassahs, but we had a subject we studied in kindergarten called Character Building. In it, we learned about humanity and about love. When we were seven years old, we had a moulvi who used to come and teach us how to read the Quran in Arabic. We went through the whole excise and completed reading the Quran in six months without understanding a single word of it. It was only much later, when I was in college, that I read the translation and its commentary in English. It raised more questions than gave answers. Anyone I asked for an explanation told me not to question what is in the Quran or the Hadith but to accept it at face value by saying 'Allah knows best'. That is what I did then, but questions remained in my heart. Many have been answered in due course of time, while many still remain unanswered. The Quran specifically tells us to read and understand."

"You could ask your questions at the Islamic Center. Maybe you will get some answers."

"The big question I always have is why we were created. God already had billions and billions of angels whose only job was to worship God day and night nonstop for billions and billions of years ever since they were created. He also had jinn whom He created after He created the angels, and even honored Iblis with the kingdom on earth much before man was created, according to the Hadith. Then He created man, and asked the angels to bow before Him, and all did except Iblis. Then God threw him out of heaven, saying He knows what Iblis did not know.

"The Quran clearly says God created men and jinn to serve Him. If we were created only to worship God day and night like the angels do, then clearly, we were not needed as there are billions of angels already doing that. Instead, God gave us a heart and a brain, which is emotion and love, and knowledge and intelligence, which he did not give to the angels. Angels cannot think or make decisions on their own, or love or hate. Only humans can and are allowed to with the power and the conscious and emotions that God gave us. We must use them for the welfare of humanity!"

Samir continued, "Humans multiplied into a civilization, into countries and communities speaking different languages. Now, we are faced with the challenges of mankind, with good and evil. It is a fight between good and evil. We are to use our heart and brain to distinguish between the two, to help mankind, to make this world of ours a better place than what it was before we were born.

"By fulfilling this role, which I think is what God created us for, either as teachers, doctors, nurses, even a plumber or a carpenter, or even a spiritual guide, we can help others with our skills. We can use our brain and improve on things around us, have passion and love in our heart for mankind, animals, plants, the environment, everything that God created, I think this is our biggest test and our universal religion. It is not about this prophet or that, but what each prophet was preaching. The message is the same as is being preached by each and every prophet, by each wise man, by scholars, by scientists, by many others and by all religions, beliefs and faiths. We are all messengers of God in the classical sense, and not in religious sense. If we all strive to propagate the message of peace and love and understanding, there will be no killing then, no war and no jihad!"

"You have put it well. Maybe you would one day like to lecture at the center as well!"

"I would love to do that in due course of time. Today, people are quoting the Hadith and the sayings of the Prophet and not the Quran in every matter of life. The Quran is the direct word of God and is a guide for all humanity. It has remained unchanged for 1,400 years. The Hadith, on the other hand, is a third-party collection of the sayings of the Prophet written 200 years after his death. There are at least 6 'Sunni' Hadith, 14 'other' Hadith, and 3 'Shia' Hadith. What is authentic and what is not is debatable!"

Samir was skeptical, and continued speaking, "The Quran offers solutions to all evils of this world. Let us take the case of black magic and jinn. The Quran has the four 'Qul' which are very short chapters. These are chapters 109, 112, 113, and 114. Two of these were specially bestowed by God to the Prophet for protection from black magic and jinn.

"For all rounded protection in one's daily life, the Quran has Ayat-ul-Kursi called the 'Verse of the Throne'. These five together are the most powerful verses and prayers in themselves for protection from evil and are self-sufficient."

"We have many more prayers," commented Latif

Samir appeared not to have listened to him, "I have seen people carry books and books of prayers written by moulvis. They quote the Prophet to read this prayer or that prayer for each and every action of one's life, confusing the follower even more. I agree they may be from the Hadith, but when the direct word of God is there for protection, why not follow that directly! There is no need to resort to other prayers from elsewhere when the Quran itself offers the direct solution.

"I personally read the four Qul and the Ayat-ul-Kursi every day in the morning before going out, and before going to bed, and I believe God will protect me from all harm and from the threats of these terrorists."

Latif interrupted, "There are other verses too in the Quran which you can read for protection. The last three verses of the second chapter of the Quran, called Al-Baqarah, or The Cow, protects the home from all evil. It is said that if one recites it in their home every day, no jinn or Satan will ever come to your house."

Samir had heard of those verses too for protection from black magic and jinn. "Islam is not rocket science. I believe two things are certain and common to all mankind since the creation of humans: birth and death! Where we come from, no one knows, and where we go is written in the Quran and other sacred books…"

"We believe Quran is the word of God!"

"But the Quran itself says its interpretation is for men of understanding. It doesn't say men of understanding are the moulvis with their fatwas, but in my view, these are the scholars and the scientists who understand life and death, and the black holes and the universe. We live in a new world of science and technology, and every ten or so years, we need to explain our existence in light of new theories that are developed. That is why I have called for this conference on Islam and Science next week. Let there be a debate, a better understanding. I do not know why such a constructive discussion is not allowed by the moulvis. I have received many threats to call it off!"

The sound of a plane that flew overhead interrupted their conversation, as the airport was only a few miles away.

Latif looked up towards the sky, "We leave everything in God's hand. He is the most powerful. That is why the air crew reads prayers on the sound system for the welfare of the plane and its passengers when every plane is about to take off. And it works!"

He smiled and added, "With the pathetic condition our airline is in, perhaps that is exactly what we need to make our planes fly…"

Samir shook his head in bewilderment, "So, the pilots and the crew have no role in its flying? You sound like the owners of the airline started by a Hindu couple in Malaysia a few years ago. They said that since all other Malaysian airlines break Islamic traditions, God has punished them with accidents, like the recent crashes of MH370 and MH17. So, this airline takes off by worshiping God first followed by prayers. It serves no liquor and only halal food. The attendants wear hijab as well. They think this makes the airline safer as compared to all the safety checks. Only three other airlines in the world follow a similar conservative rule."

By now they had arrived at the center. As Latif found a place to park, Samir's phone rang. It was the VC from one of the Balochistan universities.

"There has been a major attack on the lawyer's community at a hospital where they all had gathered to mourn the death of a colleague. Over 70 lawyers have been killed. An entire generation of lawyers has been wiped out…" he almost choked.

"This is unbelievable. Has anyone claimed responsibility?"

"TTP and ISIS have both claimed responsibility for the attack. They have announced their next attack will be even more deadly."

Samir wondered why the security agencies were not able to stop such attacks. The phone rang again. It was a 'caller identity blocked' number, typically used by intelligence agencies. The calls are usually encrypted.

Samir answered. The voice sounded familiar.

"Dr. Samir. This is Timur. If you recall, we have met."

Timur the terrorist! How could Samir forget him. He wondered how Timur got his number. Maybe Hameed must have passed it on to him.

"Timur. This attack in Quetta…"

Timur interrupted, "That is exactly why I called to confirm to you of our powers. We have already claimed responsibility for this attack. Do you even wonder why no one could see us when we attacked? We have acquired new powers through magic and can now become invisible! We can even fly when we want to. No one can stop us from carrying out more attacks!"

"But killing civilians is inhumane…"

"I have been asked to warn you again that we want sharia laws in Pakistan announced otherwise there will be far more deadly attacks. Mark my words, with the new powers we are now acquiring through the jinn, no one will be able to stop us." He then hung up the phone.

Samir was shocked. If what Timur was saying was correct, and if the terrorists really could acquire the powers he had earlier mentioned through prayers, dreams or magic, or perhaps even using supernatural entities like the jinn to work for them, could they be stopped? But the question was how?

Samir knew he had to get these answers really fast!

Islamic Center

The Islamic Center was a medium sized building that was a hub of intellectual activity on Islamic thought in Islamabad. It was built along contemporary lines, without domes, minarets, or circular shapes which are the characteristics of many Islamic buildings. Only the sign in front was the giveaway. There were two security guards at the main gate, and upon identifying Samir and Latif, lifted the barrier to let them in. There was no need for any further identification.

Many a scholar, including from outside the country, had delivered lectures on various aspects of Islam, and on other beliefs at the center. Topics had ranged from pre-Islamic civilization, inter-faith harmony, spiritualism and mysticism, and even jihad in Islam. Some of the lectures were considered controversial, and a number of times in the past, there had been threats to the center, but no untoward incident had taken place so far.

Today's speaker was Allama Malik from Houston, whom Samir had known from his days at Turkey, and had invited him to give the talk. They were both doing their Master's degree, Samir in engineering and Allama in Mystical Islam. They had remained house-mates for a year, and had many discussions over late nights on mysticism and spirituality in Islam. Allama and Samir had then moved on to the US to complete their PhDs from different universities. Allama was invited to be a keynote speaker at the Islam and Science Conference next week, and was currently on a lecture spree across the country.

The parking lot, though not very big, was full of cars. They entered the center through the front main entrance. There was a security scanner through which everyone had to pass. On the other side was the main lobby with two doors leading to the auditorium, and a number of other doors which were offices of the support staff.

At the center was a group of people, about eight to ten young women, with a couple wearing the hijab, and the rest had their hair uncovered. They appeared to be university types engulfed in a discussion with the man in the center. He was clean shaven and was wearing a jacket and trousers without a tie. Allama Malik was known as an outspoken and liberal speaker, who after earning his PhD from Yale, had spent a year as a post-doc at Harvard, then had travelled across the Middle East lecturing at universities on mysticism and spiritualism of Islam. Some of his views had not gone well with the religious fundamentalist and hardcore Islamists, and many a times he had faced death threats. But he was known to be a fearless man. Samir and Allama had always kept in touch with each other in the US.

As Samir and Latif walked up to the speaker, he saw them and excused himself from the crowd. "Samir, what a pleasure to see you again. Thanks for inviting me to your conference." He looked around and added, "I see we have a very exciting audience today."

Samir smiled and in a low voice said, "You know your and my interpretation of Islam does not go down well with the fundamentalists in this country. We have been warned about holding the conference, but I do not worry about such things. I hope it does not bother you."

Allama smiled, and before he could say anything, a bell rang, indicating it was time for everyone to be seated. Samir, Latif, and Allama walked into the auditorium together.

The auditorium could hold about 150 people which was almost full. Most were women, young and middle aged, roughly a quarter with hijabs, and almost half of them with hair uncovered. There appeared to be some staff from the Muslim embassies as well, and a few westerners, mostly journalists, Samir presumed. The body language of the attendees spoke somewhat about both the liberal and intellectual nature of the audience. All questions could presumably be asked without fear.

The allama moved to the stage, and like is traditional for all events, started with a formal recitation of a verse from the Quran followed by its translation. In all official events in the Islamic Republic of Pakistan, a verse relevant to the occasion or event is always recited at the beginning, much like an invocation at events.

He started by reciting the last verse from the Chapter Al-Baqarah, which is the second and the longest chapter in the Quran with 286 verses. This chapter immediately follows the Al-Fatiha, the opening chapter, which has only seven verses which is always recited with every worship. He read verse 286 in Arabic, followed by its translation in English:

'On no soul doth Allah place a burden greater than it can bear. It gets every good that it earns, and it suffers every ill that it earns. Pray: "Our Lord! Condemn us not if we forget or fall into error; our Lord! Lay not on us a burden like that which Thou didst lay on those before us; Our Lord! Lay not on us a burden greater than we have strength to bear. Blot out our sins, and grant us forgiveness. Have mercy on us. Thou art our Protector; Help us against those who stand against faith."'

He paused for a moment to let the meaning of the verse sink in.

"There is a very important message in this verse that many followers tend to overlook. Please feel free to interrupt to ask questions and interrupt me any number of times so that the discussion is in context always."

He continued, "There is one point I would, however, like to emphasize upfront. My talk is mostly based on the Quran, which is the direct word of God. While there may be a disagreement in the various versions of the Hadith, there is only one Quran. So, we must base our firm beliefs on the Quran!"

He further emphasized, "Surprisingly, what is floating on the net is sometimes misquoted and many a times incorrect as there is no immediate reference. One, therefore, has to be careful and verify first himself or herself directly instead of believing in hearsay."

Samir was glad Allama had brought this point upfront, because those who were resorting to militancy, to terrorism, and to jihad were quoting things incorrectly and out of context.

Allama continued, "The Quran is a complete book for men of understanding. So, my interpretation of Islam is based on the Quran only."

He started his talk with the very basics of Islam. "Islam has five pillars. Accepting and practicing these makes you a full Muslim. Period. Everything else is just icing on the cake.

"The first is the basic acknowledgement of being a Muslim and being witness to the fact that there is only one God, Allah and Muhammad is His Prophet. That is equivalent to declaring yourself a Muslim and is the most important. The four other pillars are worshiping five times a day, fasting for 30 days in the month of Ramadhan, giving Zakat, and performing Haj, which is the pilgrimage at least once in your lifetime. These are the five obligations in Islam!

"However, as I recited in the opening verse, God has made it clear that there is no compulsion in religion."

He paused for a moment to continue, "Despite these five pillars being obligatory, God has ordained that on no person has He placed a burden greater than he or she can bear. Thus, there are many exemptions and relaxations should one not wish to be burdened."

He knew he was treading into delicate territory which could earn him the wrath of the fundamentalists and charged for blasphemy, "The five obligatory worships are read before sunrise, Fajr; after midday being Zuhr; then a couple of hours before sunset Asr; then at sunset Maghrib, and the last one a couple of hours after sunset, Isha.

"Let us see how there can be no obligation in even these obligations!" He smiled and continued, "There is relaxation in the worship, which we all know. One can only read the 'farz', or the obligatory units, and not the optional ones called 'sunnat' during worship if one is pressed for time, which only takes a few minutes. Also, if one is on travel, or sick, the number of worships in a day can be reduced during that period. One can also do it almost anywhere and in any position.

"One can also worship later in case one missed any regular prayers. It is called 'qazaa'. In this case, the farz, or obligatory part of worship are to be read, and not the optional parts. Also, if one cannot worship while standing up, one can do so while lying down. If one cannot wash up for prayers, for example if there is no water, then one can use clean earth, which is also mentioned in Chapter 5 Verse 6 of the Quran. We normally wash before prayers because water extinguishes or cools down the fire, which is what Satan is made up of. Under extreme conditions, if one cannot pray, even the intention to pray will do.

"Likewise, when one is sick, yet another obligation which is fasting, can be deferred to yet another day.

"Zakat and Haj are only for those who can afford it. God has placed other relievers in lieu of fasting, which is by offering food to the needy, if one couldn't fast for certain reasons like being in old age."

Allama summarized his comments, "So, as you see, God has only made it easy for you to worship, or follow the five pillars and be a true Muslim. He does not wish to burden you beyond what you can do."

Allama had put it correctly that there is no compulsion in religion. Samir wondered why the extremists and the fundamentalists had made religion so difficult! Maybe that is how they liked to show their power and control the masses.

A young student sitting in the front asked. "Is any particular worship time more important than the other, or are all equal?"

"Friday afternoon prayers are the most important. They are specifically mentioned in the Quran in Chapter 62 Verses 9 and 10, in which it is mentioned that when there is the call to prayers on Friday, one must leave off all business and attend to prayers. Friday prayers are like the Sunday Mass for Muslims.

"Other than Friday prayers, while all other prayers are important, Chapter 50 Verse 39 says praise of your Lord 'before the rising of the sun and before its setting'. We understand that to be the fajr and the asr prayers as being specially emphasized in the Quran.

"Also, Chapter 103 is titled Al-Asr, which is one of the worship times, and God refers to Asr in its first verse as well, relating to its importance. Some believe it includes the Zuhr prayers as well in the afternoon, which is after midday and before the sun setting."

Another hijab clad girl at the back raised her hand to ask the next question.

"My mother herself worships more than five times every day and also asks me to worship more often. How important are the additional worships?"

"One can pray to God at any time and as many times asking for His help. It is not the time of the day or number of times that is important. However, the five prayers are obligatory."

He continued, "Surprisingly, sometimes a big importance is given to a sixth prayer called tahajjud by many a religious people, which is read in the last one third of the night between sunset and sunrise. Some specially wake up to perform it because the Prophet himself was observed as performing the tahajjud prayer regularly himself. This practice is not obligatory on anyone. Tahajjud, which were very early morning prayers, eventually led the way to the tarawih prayers, which are performed during the month of Ramadhan only. However, both are not obligatory.

"Then there are a few other optional prayers of worship: Hajjat, Chash, Ishraq, and Istiqfaar. You may not even have heard of most of them, but many religious people read them. None of these are essential or obligatory."

"So, remember, the five obligatory worships are important, and with the obligatory times of prostration," Allama emphasized.

Someone in the front asked, "What about 50 times? I have read that 50 worships a day were becoming obligatory, until the Prophet went on his Mairaj, or the spiritual journey to the heavens, and got it reduced to five?"

"Same answer. It is not a matter of worshiping 5 or 50 or 500 times. What is more important is how clean is your heart first, how sincere you are, and how devoted you are to Him, before you even bow down. We must be selfless and think of humanity as well."

Samir realized fundamentalism rather than spiritualism had crept in religion. He signaled to Allama that he would like to add something. Allama nodded.

Samir got up, faced the crowd, and with a deep voice, said, "Allow me to add something relevant from Bulley Shah, who is one of my favorite Sufi poets. He has very beautifully narrated the same thing in his poetry:

"Going to Makkah is not the ultimate
Even if hundreds of prayers are offered
Going to River Ganges is not the ultimate
Even if hundreds of cleansing are done
Going to Gaya is not the ultimate
Even if hundreds of worships are done
Bulley Shah the ultimate is
When the 'I' is removed from the heart!"

Allama beamed. "Exactly what I said. It is not about how many times one prays but it is what comes from the heart. What is clear is that the Prophet himself requested God to reduce the number of prayers to five per day, which God for the love of humanity accepted."

"But that is not the complete message. Bulley Shah says, and I agree, that none of the prayers would be accepted if the ego is not killed first!" added Samir.

"Why do we wash ourselves before every prayer?" asked another participant.

Allama smiled. "Cleanliness is next to Godliness. But then just use your common sense. God created the Satan from fire, and Satan is one of the jinn. Man is created from clay, which is a cool substance. Water is meant to cool the clay from the fire of the jinn. By washing ourselves before every worship, we take out and discard the hot effects of the jinn, and cool ourselves, so we can pray to God with a cool and clean heart and not be distracted or influenced with the evil of jinn."

"What about the power of supplication, the 'dua'?" asked another participant.

"Dua is communicating one's own personal wishes, desires or needs directly with God. It is thanking God and asking for forgiveness. It is asking God for our health and happiness, to guide us and show us the right way, and to grant us heaven. All these are so beautifully portrayed in the 'Opening Chapter' of the

Quran, the Al-Fatiha, which has only seven verses and is considered the 'mother of the book'. It is the biggest dua one can imagine and is nothing but a supplication to Almighty God. Just focus on its every line which is the essence of Islam."

He read it in Arabic followed by its English translation.

"In the name of Allah, Most Gracious, Most Merciful
Praise be to Allah, the Cherisher and Sustainer of the worlds
Most Gracious, Most Merciful
Master of the Day of Judgment
Thee do we worship, and Thine aid we seek
Show us the straight way
The way of those on whom Thou hast bestowed Thy Grace, those whose portion is not wrath, and who go not astray."

"Its importance is such that it is recited at each and every worship and for each unit, or rakat, of prayer. So, those who worship regularly five times a day would recite it at least 17 times every day just with the obligatory parts of the worship. How many more dua do you need? Even at the death of someone, Al-Fatiha is also recited by individuals, or at their grave, to give them Allah's blessings and forgiveness."

Samir recalled that Al-Fatiha is among the most widely decorated verses of the Quran in homes and offices held in frames, beautifully inscribed in calligraphy form. The mosque walls and pillars have these engraved inscriptions, and roadside vendors sell small tablets or plastic pages with this verse written on it. These lines are a constant reminder to us to seek the right path, and not be led astray.

Allama looked at Samir and could feel he wanted to comment on the verse, "With your background in space sciences, I am sure you would like to add something."

Samir nodded, stood up, and turning towards the crowd, added, "Al-Fatiha makes reference to 'the worlds'. Science only recently has begun to identify 'worlds and multiverses' instead of one universe. Stephen Hawking has spoken and written extensively about it. He theorizes how the universe has expanded since the big bang, and if this expansion was constant at the speed of light or even faster than that, he proposes that the most probable history of the universe would be like the surfaces of the bubbles. Bubbles would appear and disappear, while some would not. They would grow to a larger size, and would start expanding at an ever-increasing rate, called inflation. This phenomenon would lead to formation of new galaxies or universes. People are shocked at this discovery, or theory, even today where we have advanced so much. Yet, the Quran, 1,400 years ago, through this verse, mentioned there are multiverses and not just a single universe!"

There was pin drop silence after this comment, as most of what Samir had said sounded rocket science to them. Everyone was still trying to grasp the authenticity of the Quran from a new angle they had never thought of before.

Samir continued, "We will be having more discussion on this subject at the Islam and Science Conference next week. Hope you will be able to come and participate in the discussions as well."

Allama reverted back to his talk, "Today, I will also talk of yet another miracle verse that Ayat-ul-Kursi, called the 'Verse of the Throne', is. Like the Al-Fatiha, the opening chapter, it is one of the most widely read verses and among the highest ranking. It is Verse 255 of the second Chapter Al-Baqarah."

Allama asked the crowd to focus again on its every line, and recited the Ayat-ul-Kursi in Arabic followed by its English translation:

"Allah! There is no god but He—the Living, the Self-subsisting, Eternal. No slumber can seize Him nor sleep. His are all things in the heavens and on earth. Who is there can intercede In His presence except as He permitteth? He knoweth what appeareth to His creatures as before or after or behind them. Nor shall they encompass aught of His knowledge except as He willeth. His throne doth extend over the heavens and on earth, and He feeleth no fatigue in guarding and preserving them, For He is the most high. The Supreme in glory."

Samir recalled again that like the Al-Fatiha, Ayat-ul-Kursi is also among the most widely decorated verses of the Quran displayed for protection in homes and offices. Mosque have these engraved inscriptions, and vendors sell small frames or plastic pages with the verse written on it. Muslims believes this verse protects them well, whether they read it or display it.

Allama continued, "Let me point out the miracle in the composition of this verse, which many of you may have not even noted."

He paused and then continued, "The verse has nine sentences, but has another hidden treasure. Have you noticed the symmetry in these nine sentences, a mirror reflection between the firsts and the lasts?

"The first sentence has two of Allah names, the ninth also has two names of Allah. The second sentence speaks of drowsiness when one is tired and sleepy; the eighth says that guarding the skies and earth does not exhaust Allah. The third says He owns whatever is in the sky and the earth, which is Maalik, meaning ownership. The seventh says His throne extends to the sky and the earth, from Malik, which is mean king or kingdom. The fourth sentence asks who can intercede unless He gives permission, the sixth says they know nothing of His knowledge except whenever He gives knowledge. The central fifth sentence emphasizes Allah knows what is ahead and what is behind!"

There was complete silence while the crowd seemed to grasp the meaning of the similarities in the sentences. Very few had realized it despite the fact that they recite it almost every day or it is on a frame hanging in their homes or offices. Who could have written that masterpiece except God Himself?

Allama continued to comment on other key verses of the Quran.

"Another important series of verses are the 'Four Qul'.

Samir edged forward in his chair, as this is something he wanted to hear. Allama was speaking on the importance of these verses. "These four Qul are among the smallest chapters of the Quran and are placed at its very end. Chaptered 109, 112, 113, and 114, they are titled Al-Kafirun, Al-Ikhlas, Al-Falaq, and Al-Nas, meaning 'Those Who Reject Faith', 'The Purity of Faith', 'The Daybreak', and 'Mankind'.

"All these Chapter start with the word 'Qul' which in English translates to 'say'. These four Qul are known to be the protecting chapters. Al-Kafirun and Al-Ikhlas protect from 'shirk' which is the sin of practicing idolatry or polytheism, while Al-Falaq and An-Naas protect from mischief of created things, envy, magic, and the whisperings of the jinn."

Allama then in a high-pitched voice read the four Qul with their translation one after the other:

"Al-Kafirun or Those Who Reject Faith
Say: O ye that reject faith!
I worship not that which ye worship,
Nor will ye worship that which I worship.
And I will not worship that which ye have been wont to worship,
Nor will ye worship that which I worship.
To you be your way, and to me mine.

"Al-Ikhlas or The Purity of Faith
Say: He is Allah, the One and Only;
Allah, the Eternal, Absolute;
He begetteth not, nor is He begotten;
And there is none like unto Him.

"Al-Falaq or The Daybreak
Say: I seek refuge with the Lord of the dawn
From the mischief of created things;
From the mischief of darkness as it overspreads;
From the mischief of those who practise secret arts;
And from the mischief of the envious one as he practises envy.

"Al-Nas or Mankind
Say: I seek refuge with the Lord and Cherisher of Mankind,
The King or Ruler of Mankind,
The Allah for judge of Mankind,
From the mischief of the whisperer of evil, who withdraws after his whisper,
The same who whispers into the hearts of mankind,
Among Jinns and among men."

The reference to secret arts and the jinn was the one Samir wanted to hear. The Quran did allude to black magic and jinn. Allama had said that these verses were antidote to magic and jinn just like he had heard before. He would definitely want to learn more about it later as now was not the forum.

He also recalled that the four Qul were also among the most widely decorated verses of the Quran. They are displayed and read for protection from jealousy, the evil eye, the evil spirits, and the jinn. Likewise, homes and offices hold these verses in frames, mosque have engraved inscriptions, and vendors sell small frames or plastic pages with the verses written on it. All Muslims believe in the power of its protection.

Someone from the side raised his hand and asked, "You have elaborated on the Al-Fatiha, the Ayat-ul-Kursi, and the four Qul, what about the 99 names of God?"

"I was coming to that." He paused and continued, "Invoking the 99 names of God has tremendous powers. These 99 names, or attributes of God, have been identified from the verses as well as the Hadith according to various Islamic scholars of the past, though there are some variations in these names. The master list has more names depending upon how they are interpreted or identified. 99 are the most common ones and are chosen, as odd numbers are preferred in Islam."

Allama was referring to how God is addressed in the Quran, "It really doesn't matter if you address God as Allah, or Ar-Rahman, as God Himself says in Chapter 17 Verse 110 to call Him Allah, or call Him Ar-Rahman, by whatever name one calls upon Him, for to Him belong the most beautiful names.

"We also believe that each name of God has a unique attribute or hidden power according to Hadith, and that reciting any of these names multiple times has its benefits. An example, he who recites Al-Aziz, meaning the Mighty or the Victorious, 41 times after the morning prayers will gain honor after a defeat or disgrace."

This one caught Samir's attention too! Did reciting a particular name a certain number of times give one tremendous powers? Was it possible that the terrorists were making use of these sacred powers? He shook his head. No! Sacred names cannot be used for a negative purpose or they will backfire.

Allama interrupted Samir's thoughts. "It is also believed that calling out certain names repeatedly has its health benefits and a cure for certain disease or illness."

Samir knew of hospitals, where the names of God are recited which gave spiritual healing to the ill. He had heard of Chapter Ar-Rahman being recited in hospitals to heal the terminally sick. He also wondered if the terrorists were also using the power of these sacred names to protect themselves. Or at least they believed they could do so, thereby giving them more confidence to carry out these attacks boldly. No one could stop the devil from invoking the name of God! In that case, they were certainly trying to misuse Islam.

One of the younger faculty sitting in the front row raised his hand to ask another question.

"What about the mysterious letters in the Quran? They are at the opening of certain chapters, and are very confusing to me, as no one understands their meanings. Is it astrology, numerology, magic, or what?"

Allama shifted his position and replied, "That is a very good question. I was wondering if anyone would actually ask about these letters.

"The 'mysterious letters', or the secret letters, as they are sometimes referred to, are disjoined or disconnected letters, and are combinations of between one and five Arabic letters. They figure at the beginning of 29 out of the 114 Chapters of the Quran and are placed just after the opening Bismillah-ar-Rahman-ar-Rahim, which means 'In the name of Allah, the most Merciful, the most Beneficent'. The mysterious letters are called the 'muqattaat'. Most of you read them without realizing what they mean. The letters used in them, 14 in total, comprise exactly half the letters of the Arabic alphabet. These letters are also known as 'openers' as they form the opening verse of their respective chapters. Three chapters begin with only one solitary letter, ten with two letters, twelve with three letters, two with four letters, and two with five. All these letters are read separately rather than joined, like 'Ta-Ha' or 'Ya-Sin'. Four Chapters are actually named after these individual or disconnected letters: 'Ṭa-Ha', 'Ya-Sin', 'Saad', and 'Qaaf'."

"Many believe these mysterious letters carry tremendous power!"

This got Samir's attention. Some of these letters were found on the bullet riddled bodies of terrorists. But then he realized these letters could not save them from being killed. Certainly, this was a misuse of sacred letters for an evil purpose so they did not and could not work!

Allama looked at Samir as if he could read his mind. He continued, "Do they really have special powers? Let us understand what they mean or how they came about.

"The original significance of the letters is unknown. As you know, reading and understanding of the Quran is obligatory for Muslims so as to make clear the meanings of each verse. The interpretation of these letters is one of the controversial topics in Quran. Some Islamic scholars, however, believe there is a secret message encoded in these letters, revolving around the number 19, based on a verse that they think is connected to it. Some only identify nine of these disjoined letters as the most important ones, and read them regularly to seek spiritual help from God, or decorate them as frames in their homes or place of business.

"There are, however, many interpretations of these 29 disjoined and mysterious letters. There are conservative, numerological, phonetical-etymological, philosophical, mystical, or being an abbreviation view of them. Some say it has no meaning and only ascribe it to the initials or the monogram of the scribe who wrote the chapter for the first time. Others to the tradition of those times when the Arab poet would use such letters at the beginning of their poetry to seek attention.

He frowned, "But the confusion does not end here. A Christian scholar even interpreted these characters at the front of Chapter 19.1 titled 'Mary' through the Abjad numerology. He showed that these disjoined alphabets actually referred to Christ. However, he was unable to give a similar explanation for the rest of the letters."

He continued with his analysis of the letters, "One of the scientific explanations has been given by a scholar from Malaysia who did seven different analysis of the whole Quran, including size-based analysis, character frequency based analysis, lexical analysis, philosophical analysis, character N-gram based analysis, Quran based analysis, and arithmetic analysis. He concluded that these mysterious letters were employed as a signature for the authentication of the Holy Quran.

"Despite all these explanations by the mortals, the Quran itself in Chapter 3 Verse 7 says,

'He it is who has sent down to thee the Book: In it are Verses basic or fundamental of established meaning; they are the foundation of the Book: others are allegorical. But those in whose hearts is perversity follow the part thereof that is allegorical, seeking discord, and searching for its hidden meanings, but no one knows its hidden meanings except Allah. And those who are firmly grounded in knowledge say: "We believe in the Book; the whole of it is from our Lord:" and none will grasp the Message except men of understanding.'

"So clearly, while the Quran itself is referring to the hidden meaning of the letters, and saying only men of understanding will be able to grasp its meaning, we can only interpret it according to the level of our highest intelligence which may not be correct!"

These letters were certainly being misinterpreted and misused by many, including the terrorists, thought Samir. These terrorists were misguiding their fighters that by inscribing these letters on their bodies, no bullet could pierce them. Clearly, it was not true.

He made a note to himself to tell the security forces to display these letters on dead bodies on the media so the militants would know the truth that these mysterious letters will not protect them.

Another participant referred to a popular chapter which started with disjoined words.

"What about the Chapter 'Yasin'? Isn't that considered the heart of the Quran?" asked one of the participant.

"It certainly is! Yasin is the 36th Chapter of the Quran and has 83 verses. As we discussed earlier in the special letters in the Quran, the name of the Chapter comes from the two letters of the first verse of the chapter, the meaning of which is unknown. Some believe that Yasin is also one of the names of Prophet Muhammad, as reported in a saying of Ali, who said God has named the Prophet by seven names in the Quran: Muhammad, Ahmad, Taha, Yasin, Muzammil, Mudaththir, and Abdullah.

"This chapter focuses on establishing the Quran as a divine source. It warns of the fate of those that mock God's revelations, and reminds of the punishments of nonbelievers in the past as a warning to all. What is most beautiful about the chapter is that it reiterates God's sovereignty as exemplified by His creations through various natural signs that are visible to mankind. Yasin presents the message of the Quran in a very powerful and rhythmic manner."

Allama continued, "To those who accused the Prophet of being a poet and scribing the Quran, God clearly asserts that He has not taught the Prophet any poetry, nor could the Prophet ever have been a poet.

"Yasin concludes by reaffirming God's sovereignty and absolute power. The closing passage is absolute and powerful and carries an essential message of the Quran. It reads in its last three Verses 36:81–83:

"'Is not He who created the heavens and the earth able to create the like thereof?"—Yea, indeed! for He is the Creator Supreme, of skill and knowledge infinite!

Verily, when He intends a thing, His command is, "be", and it is!

So, glory to Him in whose hands is the dominion of all things: and to Him will ye be all brought back.'

"Allah bless us all and this whole mankind that he created," Allama added his prayers at the end.

Someone from the back raised his hand and asked, "There is another important chapter in the Quran. What about Al-Kahf. Many emphasize one must read it every Friday to earn the blessings of Allah!"

"Reading any chapter will earn you the blessings of God. However, it is not about reading Al-Kahf, translated as The Cave, blindly but understanding its true meaning! Have you wondered why the Prophet asked us to recite this every Friday?"

He paused and looked around to see if anyone could answer that. The audience looked around to see if there was any raised hand, but there were none.

Allama chuckled, "One must recite only to understanding the true meaning of the chapter and not to recite like a parrot, which many do! There is a major lesson to be learnt from Al-Kahf, which is Chapter 18 in the Quran. It is a lesson of life, of management, of self-restraining and self-development. All those management gurus of today teach the same lesson over and over again what the Quran did 1,400 years ago!

"In this chapter, God gives us four different stories. Each has a lesson. Let us check it out!

"First is the people of the cave, which is the story of young men who lived in a disbelieving town, so they decide to migrate for the sake of Allah and run away. Allah rewards them with mercy in the cave and protection from the elements of nature. The lesson of this story is the 'Trial of Faith'.

"Second is the owner of two gardens. A story of a man whom Allah blessed with two beautiful gardens, but the man forgot to thank the One who blessed him with everything and he even dared to doubt Allah regarding the afterlife. So, his garden was destroyed—he regretted it, but was too late and his regret did not benefit him. The lesson of this story is the 'Trial of Wealth'."

Allama paused for a moment to let the first two lessons sink in. One could clearly see that he had the attention of the crowd. They were eagerly waiting for him to continue.

"The third is about Prophets Moses and Khidr. When Moses was asked, 'Who is the most knowledgeable of the people of Earth?' Moses replied that it was him as he assumed he was the only prophet on Earth at the time. But Allah revealed to him that there's someone who knows more than him about certain things. Moses traveled around looking for him and learned how divine wisdom can sometimes be hidden in matters which we perceive as bad. The lesson of this story is the 'Trial of Knowledge'.

"The fourth story is global and is about 'Zul-Qarnain'. Allah mentions the story of a great king who was given knowledge and power, travelling the world helping people and spreading all that's good. Some associate him with Alexander of Macedonia. He was able to overcome the problem of Gog and Magog by building a massive wall with the help of people whom he could not even understand. The lesson of this story is the 'Trial of Power'.

Samir could feel the management lesson had made a deep impact with the participants. Hidden in every divinity and verse of the Quran was a clear message to follow. No wonder the Quran was for men of understanding, and was not to be read blindly without understanding or questioning what was not clear. They could now see that God gave them four kinds of stories relating to four kinds of trials which they all had to pass in their day to day lives.

Allama was not finished. He could sense the crowd was mesmerized with his interpretation of the Chapter Al-Kahf. He took the interpretation another step forward.

"It is believed that the Prophet said that one who reads and remembers verses of this chapter will be protected from the trials of the one-eyed monster Dajjal during the end of times!"

He paused to let that sink in.

"How is that possible?" asked a participant enthusiastic to learn more.

"Dajjal will appear before the day of judgement with four trials: He will ask people to worship him and not Allah, which is the trial of faith.

"Then he will be given powers to start and stop the rain and tempt people with his wealth, which is the trial of wealth!

"He will tempt people with knowledge and the news that he will give and gives them, which is the trial of knowledge!

"Finally, he will control huge parts of earth, which is the trial of power!

"So, if one remembers the wordings of this chapter and is steadfast before the day of judgment, Dajjal will not be able to tempt him!"

The crowd was flabbergasted with the hidden meaning in this chapter. Who could have though the Quran had the first of motivational lectures?

An elderly faculty member with grey hair and sitting in the front intervened, "I believe that Dajjal, the one-eyed monster, is the monitor of the TV, the computer, the laptop, the tablet, the smart phone. This is the one eye technically which we fail to see. It has penetrated our lives and is destroying our young generation. People are literally worshipping the smart phone today every single minute of the day. They hold it by their heart. There are apps to control everything. Imagine with the 'Internet of Things', '5G'; and the 'Fourth Industrial Revolution' coming around the corner, which will fuse physical, digital, and biological worlds, the hand-held device will become like a deity to many, Dajjal to others."

He turned around to face the participants and spoke like he was lecturing in a classroom, "The smart phone today has access to information which is more than hundreds of libraries put together, even more than the Library of Congress, the largest library in the world with over 162 million items and over 838 miles of shelves. Most systems today are remotely controlled, from power stations to railways to metros to airports to financial systems. Hacking can destroy economies, interfere in election results, and lead to world wars. Cyber security has become so important today. How much more power can one imagine which can be held in your hand now. It is all controlled by the modern Dajjal which is the tablet or the smart phone."

Another got up to agree, "The IT culture is destroying the young generation rather than making it. Rather have one on one interaction and warmth of relationship, WhatsApp, Instagram, Viber, and Facebook has created more distances and destroyed the personal touch between friends and family. How many a times we see a circle of friends sitting together talking to each other, or playing with each other? They are all on their phones talking or texting to someone at a distance and ignoring the real person sitting next to him. The Dajjal is already here. Can the end of world be far away?"

Allama looked to Samir wanting to answer it in detail, but Samir intervened, "Let us continue to learn from the wisdom of the Allama. We can leave the scientific discussion for the conference."

Allama referred to his notes and continued, "Just note the virtues hidden in the Chapter Al-Kahf. There is mention of good companionship in the 28th verse, knowing the truth of this world in the 45th verse, humility in 69th, sincerity in 110th, calling to Allah in 27th verse, and remembering the hereafter in $47\text{-}49^{th}$ verses. Now when you recite the Chapter Al-Kahf on a Friday or any other day, you will understand and appreciate the message it gives. There is no need to read any more motivational books," he smiled.

"Let us take a short break before we continue into yet another important aspect of Islam, that of dreams."

Another interesting subject that he badly wanted to listen to and get Allama's expert opinion, thought Samir.

The crowd moved towards the tea tables set up in the lobby.

During break time, Samir's mind went to the terrorist warnings who wanted sharia imposed in the country. Clearly, Islam was not about violence, but was such a compassionate and simplistic religion, as Allama had clearly put it. The most important verses which every home, office, mosque, and madrassah were decorated with spoke only of love and care. Why couldn't anyone just read and practice them every single day of their lives. The Quran had the best management and motivational lessons, written hundreds of years ago, which never preached violence but only forgiveness. All the names of Allah are loving and compassionate. If God had created man in His own image, one only needed to become a replica of these 99 names themselves.

The bell rung and everybody walked back into the auditorium.

Allama went up to the podium and said, "There had been a lot of earlier requests that I speak on the 'istikhara', which is the power of dreams. They believe it holds the secret powers to have your desire or wish fulfilled, or to seek guidance to what you intend to do! I had intentionally left it to the second half of my talk, and it was important to first clearly understand our religion first before getting into what people visualize its supernatural powers, like that of dreams."

Samir leaned forward in his chair. This is something he wanted to hear and needed to learn from the Allama himself. Hasan had also told him about the power of dreams, and how many followed their dreams blindly, even in war. He felt sure all these Islamist terrorists, who claimed to be Muslims, were planning every single attack after a 'visionary dream'. Was it the istikhara they were performing first and then following up on their dreams? Or was it something else? Could the istikhara help them win battles?

Allama set the direction of his discussion first, "Some believe the istikhara prayer guides you to the correct path, others believe it leads to a dream which can be interpreted, yet many guide their future course of action on what they dreamt after the istikhara.

"These are two different views on the interpretation and follow-up after doing istikhara. In one school of thought, the followers believe that after worshiping two units of prayers very early in the morning before daybreak, one recites the istikhara prayer and then goes back to sleep again. He or she will then see a dream, which is interpreted by the dreamer himself or herself or by a religious man as to clearly guide what one has to do. If there is no dream, istikhara prayer is repeated for a number of mornings till the dream or interpretation is clear. The believer blindly follows his or her dream unfortunately. Such a dream could unfortunately lead to a violent or negative action as well, and there have been many reported cases! Istikhara is being misused or misinterpreted by many."

One participant interrupted by raising her hand, "I like to seek guidance from the istikhara, but it does not work for me! I have been doing it for the last 15 days and still see no dream? I also pray intensely and read many other verses of the Quran to aid me but alas, I see nothing. What does that mean?"

Another elderly woman added, "In my case, I see a dream which has no meaning and is not even connected to what I ask for? Should I ask my pir for the interpretation?"

A third got up to ask, "My dreams are very clear what I should do. But I am not even sure if it is the right guidance as the dream leads to something negative and violent. Common sense tells me I should do otherwise. Please let me know if we really should follow our dreams after the istikhara blindly?"

Allama smiled. "Very good and pertinent questions, as they cover all aspects of the power of dreams. First of all, let me emphasize that the power to interpret dreams was only given by God to Prophet Yusuf, or Joseph as he is known in the Bible. The average man or woman does not have that power. So, those who claim they can interpret your dreams, or you think you have a certain dream and can interpret what it means, certainly cannot be right or can be misinterpreted. Dreams are the culminations of what is in one's mind, not God's way of telling you what to do. So, if you are following your dream, you are being misled."

That is exactly what Hasan had said about dreams, thought Samir.

"Second, istikhara has been wrongly practiced and interpreted."

He let that sink in and continued, "This is the second school of thought which I believe is the correct one. Istikhara is not about dreams! It is only a prayer seeking help from God to guide one to the correct decision. By reading this prayer, one is only asking God for guidance. What natural course follows should be in your favor. It is not a matter of choices or interpretation or doing something according to your dreams."

Samir seemed to nod his head in agreement. He himself had read that praying istikhara is only seeking guidance from God when one is confused in making a decision, or has a choice to make and cannot decide on the merits or demerits of each. Those, including the militants and the religious fundamentalists, were doing it all wrong and therefore misinterpreting it! They were certainly being misguided by their religious gurus who perhaps were making up these dreams. He was glad Allama had cleared the confusion in his mind.

"How does one do the istikhara prayers then?" asked the elderly lady.

"Elementary, my dear Watson," smiled Allama, "the Prophet's advice was very clear: if any one of us is concerned or confused about a decision he or she has to make, then let him or her pray two units of non-obligatory worship right after the obligatory worship and recite the istikhara prayers focusing on what it is one is seeking. The istikhara prayer spells it all out:

"O Allah, I seek Your counsel by Your knowledge and I seek Your assistance by Your power and I ask You from Your immense favor, for verily You are able while I am not, and verily You know while I do not, and You are the knower of the unseen. O Allah, You know the issue at hand, and mention the issue here, to be good for me in relation to my religion, my life and aftermath, my present and future, then decree it and facilitate it for me, and bless me with it, and if You know this issue to be ill for me concerning my religion, my life and end, my present and future, then remove it from me and remove me from it, and decree for me what is good, whatever it may be, and make me satisfied with it."

"As you see, Istikara is not rocket science! It is just a prayer that our Prophet used to do. By praying istikhara, only what is best for you will or may happen automatically if you believe in it. However, the merchants of Islam have made it a business and a way to create their constituency over the helpless and the misguided."

Samir knew the misguided were misguiding the masses of what to do.

Allama was not done, "There are also other simple prayers that many follow if they wish to have their desires fulfilled. Ayat Kareema, given in Chapter 21 Verse 87, is based on the notion of asking for forgiveness. It is the same prayer that Prophet Yunus read when he was in the belly of a whale as is given in the Quran itself. He remained in the belly for days and recited this verse as an invocation to God as a result of which he finally succeeded in getting out of his misery and be among the people once again. The translation is as follows:

'There are none worthy of worship besides You. Glorified are You. Surely, I am from the wrongdoers.'"

Samir recalled this was the same verse that the worshippers at the Bari Imam shrine were reciting and repeating thousands of times to have their desire fulfilled.

Allama continued, "There are some who believe this verse is a cure or prevention from black magic. Others believe it is the best treatment for incurable diseases. Yet others believe it defeats and overpowers enemies and tyrant leaders. Most read, or have it read by a third party, or a group of friends or relatives, sometimes even by strangers in a mosque by paying a certain amount of money as charity. They recite it about 125,000 times within a defined period and then they are certain their desire will be fulfilled. How misleading! Can one really buy prayers? Then there are others who identify it as very 'jalali', or powerful, in the sense that if done wrong, or for an evil purpose, the opposite will most likely happen.

"Didn't you read in the papers the other day that in a raid carried out by the army, ten militants were rounded up who were reading this Ayat. Upon interrogation, they confessed they were seeking help from God in planning their next attack. No wonder their plan failed and they were caught as they were using these sacred verses for the wrong reason."

"Ayat Kareema is a simple prayer of seeking forgiveness from God. And this prayer must come from the individual himself, and not by a paid group of readers. Many claim they had it recited thousands of times in a mosque or a madrassah, or even in their home by others, and had their wishes fulfilled. The news then spreads like wildfire and then everyone starts resorting to having read Ayat Kareema by others to fulfill their desires."

"Remember one's body has the power to heal itself, and at least one third of all healings have to do with placebo effect, that is, healing occurs without anybody doing anything. If there is a strong belief that the verse will work, then most likely it will certainly work.

"The same is in all beliefs and faiths. It is a belief in the all-powerful. If you believe it will work, and have faith in it, then it certainly will work."

Allama checked his watch, "We seem to be running overtime. However, I would like to add something on spiritualism and sufism in Islam. It is because of the prayers of the living pious, the sufis and the saints that mankind is protected from the evil of the world. They are our warriors who fight the evil forces that are out to harm us, such as Iblis and other jinn who are there to misguide us. Sometimes, we do not even know that we are under heavy attack by an army of jinn, but these are the saints and their spirits that fight them to protect us because God told them to be our bodyguards. When people visit shrines of the saints and pray to bless them, it is God that protects us from all evil.

"God is everywhere. He is inside us like the sufis and the saints say, he is in the flower we admire, and he is all around in the universe. Nothing goes unnoticed or unheard by God any second of the day. Mark my words! The Quran and its verses are sacred and have the powers to help mankind, but if used to harm mankind, the reverse effect will happen. Be kind to mankind and God will always be there for you!"

With that comment, Allama walked down from the stage and shook Samir's hand.

"Thank you for inviting me to the lecture. I will see you at the conference next week."

"Khuda Hafiz," said Samir, which is a farewell salutation meaning God protect you. This is what he had always said ever since he was young. However, nowadays the so-called religious people were relating that to blasphemy, saying 'khuda' is a foreign god, and Muslims must only say Allah Hafiz. Samir disagreed with that.

Samir, Latif, and Allama walked out together to the parking lot. Allama bid goodbye and drove away first, and then Samir and Latif got into their car and hit the road.

Allama's lecture had reinforced a lot of things in Samir's mind, and the way one perceives religion. He was glad Allama's views about religion were similar to his. But above all, it cleared the notion what the fundamentalist and the militant believed in regarding the power of the Quran and its verses. They could not be used for a negative purpose.

There was much damage to control, and to be able to change the way people thought about religion or the power of prayers or dreams or jihad. They were being brainwashed by these make-believe sermons floating around on WhatsApp, on other social media, in religious gatherings, in the mosques and in the madrassahs. The truth had to be told boldly even at the cost of one's life, otherwise the whole society would revert into fundamentalism.

Islam was being hijacked by the fanatics and the fundamentalists, who were misinterpreting Islam, the Quran and its message of love and compassion. The fanatics were using the positive energy of the Quran in a negative way, and Samir was determined to stop them at all costs.

Much more still had to be learnt about mysticism and spirituality, and about the power of secret arts, of magic and of jinn in Islam, before one could counter these terrorist attacks.

Reflections

As Samir and Latif drove back, there was already a lot on Samir's mind as a result of the lecture by Allama. What the Allama spoke was the core of Islam. It is a simple, peaceful and compassionate religion. It wants everyone to do good and stay away from evil. Nothing more! He recalled that was exactly how he had grown up. All religions were good, spiritual, and personal. Bad is considered bad and good is considered good in every faith and religion. Even the standard seven deadly sins are the same in every religion: pride, greed, lust, envy, gluttony, wrath, and sloth.

Samir was born in a traditional Muslim household. Praying, reading the Quran, fasting during the month of ramadhan, and giving charity to the poor was a normal way of life. He had performed umrah with his parents as a teenager, when they had visited most holy places, including Mecca, Medina, Damascus, Baghdad, Karbala, Najaf, and Mashad. Being a Shia or a Sunni did not matter at all. Their own family friends and neighbors were people of all faiths and beliefs, and they never cared nor asked. There was only love, care and concern for each other. Everyone lived as one large happy family.

He went to a Christian missionary school where he had spent the best ten years of his life reforming himself. Some of his best friends were Hindus and Christians. His teachers were 'Dutch fathers and Portuguese nuns', to whom he owed a lot of what he was today. They started the day at school with an assembly and morning prayers led by the fathers. Political Islam did not exist anywhere then. He recalled even praying to God as a teenager at the Notre Dame Cathedral in Paris, and also at the St. Patrick's Cathedral in New York City. For him, there was only one and the same God that all humanity prayed to.

During his study years abroad, his friends and teachers were of all faith and beliefs. When he was teaching at SUNY, he had many American students and friends, and from all over the world, and he did not even care what faith or religion they followed. He recalled his own mentors in the US, from whom he had learned a lot, were perhaps of Jewish or Mormon faith, but he never cared to ask. His housemate, George, was an American, a professor of aerospace engineering, who was born and raised in Michigan, and was a very outgoing and a lively person. They had regular Bring-Your-Own-Booze wine-and-cheese parties in the house they shared, which were the talk of the university. More than a hundred faculty and staff members from the university fraternity used to gate crash their parties every month which used to last till early in the morning. Samir himself never drank alcohol. George and Samir became best friends, and had continued to remain in touch over the years.

Among Samir's own PhD students were two Hindus from India, with one from Kerala and the other from Gujrat, two from Lebanon, one a Druze and the other a Muslim, two Roman Catholics from Poland, both brothers, a female Coptic Christian from Egypt, and a female Zoroastrian from Pakistan. They all enjoyed and partied together. Religion and beliefs were never discussed.

He had made many other friends in the US. Mike was his caring friend whom he had met through Marvi, when he had accompanied her on her return from exile along with a huge team of friends. She had assigned Samir to be his host, and since then they had become very good friends. Mike had always been concerned about Samir moving back to Pakistan after Marvi's assassination, and used to call him regularly asking about his welfare, and always giving him advice for his protection.

Samir's wife, Shaday, though had strong religious views and dressed conservatively, never enforced her views on him. She would regularly worship five times a day, and recite the Quran every morning. She would always pray for

Samir's safety, and would keep reminding him that he also needed to worship and pray regularly for his own spiritual cleansing and protection from external forces and evils.

Samir, on the other hand, was not regular in his worshipping, but would worship whenever he would find the time. 'Worshiping to thank God for His blessings is more important than not worshiping at all', was Samir's justification, however incorrect it may sound to others. He had performed multiple umrahs with his family, and believed he was serving humanity through educating others, which was equivalent to worshiping, much like the poem about Adam he had learnt in kindergarten.

He would, however, always worship at the mosque for Friday prayers which is mandatory in Islam. However, he could not relate to the 'khutba' or the Friday sermon given by the Imam in Arabic. No one could understand that. Why not in the local language? He recalled when he was a student in the US, the Friday sermon used to be given in English by anyone, whether a graduate student or a faculty, and the topic was always something related to what the community was facing. In Pakistan, listening to the Imam in Arabic meant nothing, as hardly anything could be understood. Hence, Samir stopped going early to the mosque so that the sermon could be skipped. It was not mandatory anyway.

Shaday always reminded Samir of praying, "There is so much evil that you need to read the Ayat-ul-Kursi and the four Qul at least twice every day, once in the morning before leaving home, and once at night before sleeping. They will ensure you are protected from jealousy, evil eye, magic, jinn, as well as others who may wish to harm you. There is no better protection than this."

Samir had ensured that he religiously followed this advice every day. Even when he travelled on a busy schedule, he would remind himself to read these verses for protection. He always regularly fasted during Ramadhan during which would ensure he worshipped all five times a day during fasting. In other words, Samir was a 'good Muslim' but not a 'devout Muslim' and had grown up that way. He considered himself a good human being above all.

Shaday herself religiously followed many of the prayers for protection and safety, for entering and while leaving home, while travelling, for the children to make them a better person, for resolving problems, for health, for illness, and recovery.

She strongly believed in charity, and in helping the poor. Charity would consist of the obligatory 'zakat', which is one of the five pillars of Islam, amounting to 2.5% of one's total worth, 'khairat' which was helping the poor above and beyond zakat for any meaningful purpose, and 'sadqa' which was given for a particular reason, like warding off evils, for recovery from illness, and for protection from all types of evil. There would be a stream of poor people who would always come asking for help, and she would never let anyone go back empty handed.

The old and traditional culture of animal sacrifices had carried forward from thousands of years. Sacrificial goats were offered as 'sadqa', which were in addition to the animal sacrifice or 'qurbani' carried out at Eid-Al-Adha, the festival to celebrate Haj or pilgrimage. In case of sadqa, people believed that the animal sacrificed, upon whom the name of Allah has been invoked, would protect the person from the danger or threat facing him or her. A black goat was preferred according to historical old traditions and beliefs. Sacrificing animals, and sometimes even humans, for protection or blessing of the deity has been practiced for thousands of years. Shaday would regularly offer sadqa for Samir's protection.

This belief of animal sacrifices for protection was not just confined to individuals and families but to the state as well. After a recent crash of the national airline in the northern mountains, a black goat was sacrificed on the tarmac before every flight. Even a former president of Pakistan during all his five years of office was known to have sacrificed a black goat every day in the presidency for his protection and to prolong his rule. It is said that this had caused a shortage of black goats in Islamabad, and herds of black goats were bought from outside the city for the sacrifices on a regular basis.

Samir personally disliked an animal being slaughtered, and preferred money be given instead to help the poor. Maybe the prayers of the needy for the welfare of the donor would reach higher levels than the woes of the animal. But then others argued one does not know what evil forces are at work which are blood thirsty, so better that the blood of an animal be spilled, and the meat distributed to the poor, rather than face the wrath of the invisible supernatural forces.

But the way the qurbani, or slaughter, is carried out was inhumane, according to Samir, even though the proponents of qurbani argued it is a painless procedure for the animals by slitting their jugular vein.

The poor animal is strongly held down by a few strong men. If the animal is strong, then they tie up his legs as well. Then preferably the person in whose name the qurbani is done is made to slit the throat and jugular vein with a sharp saber-like knife, while others hold the struggling animal down till the last ounce of blood has oozed out from the body and it becomes lifeless. It appears as if the humans are dealing with a bloodthirsty enemy and avenging him for many gruesome murders he has committed. No one cares how much pain the animals must have undergone. It gave Samir the shivers. There had to be a more humane way for sacrifice.

The same brutality is now replicated by ISIS and Al-Qaeda while slaughtering the throats of their prisoners. How can one be painful and the other not! Muslims believed that they are carrying out the traditions of Prophet Abraham sacrificing his son Ismail from Hajrah, identified as Ishmael and Hagar in the Bible, while the Jews believe the sacrifice was for Isaac from Sarah. In either case, it is the poor animal that suffers.

To add fuel to sarcasm, during the sacrificial Eid festival, the animals are decorated with henna and colorful ribbons, paraded through the streets, and sometimes fed with nuts and good food, only because many a Muslims believe that it is the same animal that will help them cross the thin bridge into heaven. Samir thought if he were the animal, he would have thrown them all into the deep canyon while crossing the bridge!

Over two and a half million Muslims perform the pilgrimage, or haj, every year and slaughter animals. Many perform haj more than once, while the non-haj season pilgrimage called 'umrah' is performed by an equal number of pilgrims round the clock. Many perform umrah again and again, because they have the financial resources to do so, while many others do it many times over due to 'their love of God'. Samir had always articulated his position with family and friends that while a single haj is obligatory for those who can afford it, and maybe one umrah as well to visit the sacred sites, those who do haj and umrah multiple times are doing no one a favor but are instead wasting money that could have been wisely spent on helping many a poor, marrying off many an orphan, treating many an ill, or could have been given to support education, or to a homeless person to build a house. But the conservatives were not willing to accommodate his viewpoint and would write them off as nonsense. Those Muslims wished to spend their wealth on themselves, even if it was acquired through ill means, so that they can be assured a place in heaven. What irony! Samir would rather spend his hard-earned money on the poor.

Samir's minds continued to walk the memory lane while they drove silently through the rest of the distance.

Harmeen

It was a cold blistery night and after the night prayers when a group of Harmeen met in an open ground around a fire.

The young one, known as Ali, and who was a young 30 years old tall and slim firebrand, spoke, "The time has come. It is God sent. I have come to know from my cousin who works at the ministry of education that a large congregation of Muslim kafir is taking place this week in Islamabad. The super kafir of them all, Dr. Samir, has called a large meeting of scientists to discuss Islam, and it is being funded by the CIA and the Americans. You know Dr. Samir is their agent to destroy the teachings of Islam in schools. He is evil and is their agent in Pakistan like the other kafir, Dr. Abdus Salam, was."

"What are they trying to prove? That the Quran and the Hadith is all wrong?" asked another.

"Exactly! The teachers and a group of scientists will be issuing a fatwa in the end that a big explosion took place many millions of years ago, much like the atom bomb, which created the universe, and then following the explosion, the giant animals came, then the monkeys, and finally, the humans were evolved."

"How sinful! God punish them! You mean they will say there was no Adam and Eve created directly by God as is clearly described in the Quran? This is blasphemy and they deserve to die!"

"My cousin also overheard a meeting discussing the agenda of the conference that even Mairaj, or the Prophet's journey to the heavens on the winged horse, Buraq, was imaginary, as no such journeys are possible even today. They are saying that at that time, there were no planes or even cars, so how could the journey to heaven be made on a horse!"

"God burn them all in hell!" commented a younger one. "What else did he tell you?"

"That there will be a big discussion on the Quran itself. They think the Quran is based on numbers, a tradition which the Hindus and the pharaohs follow. It is all haram and kuffar, and forbidden in Islam to discuss this."

"They deserve death!" said one outspoken younger one.

"I agree," said another. All the others nodded their head in unison.

The old man sitting at the center, with a long grey beard, whom they looked up to as their spiritual leader, looked up and said, "I agree with you. They all deserve death. But we would need guidance from God himself before we make any decision what to do. We need God to guide us what to do."

"What are we going to do?" asked Ali.

"I will do an istikhara tonight, and tell you what the dream says you should do. Do you agree?"

No one could challenge the authenticity of the istikhara, especially when it was done by their spiritual leader. Everyone nodded their head in agreement.

"I will let you know as soon as I receive guidance from Allah what to do next."

They decided to meet again the next day.

As soon as the rest walked away, the old man got on his cell phone.

"It is all arranged. We will teach the kafir a lesson they will not forget ever, and burn in hell."

He had an evil look in his eyes.

Amulets and Stones

Along the way, Latif asked Samir if he would like to stop by a spiritual man who advises and provides guidance on how to protect oneself. Baba Sain, a spiritual protector, was an inspiration to many. He could perhaps throw more light to the answers Samir was seeking regarding the mystical powers in Islam. Many would visit Baba Sain to find answers, to seek protection, to have their problems solved, to pass an exam, to find a job, to have a cure for illness, or even to 'tame' a wife or husband.

"Baba Sain will not do anything that is harmful to anyone. Everyone speaks high of him. He will listen to the problem with patience. He has no fee. People just leave a donation with him whatever they can afford. Some will give him a token money, others return back after their problem has been resolved to donate even more money. He never advertises himself. It is only through word of mouth that people flock to him by the hundreds every day."

"A spiritual doctor then? How does he solve problems?"

"Not a traditional doctor or healer like Luqman, but more like a spiritual healer and protector. He would listen to you first, and then based on the severity of the problem, he would prescribe an amulet, a stone, or a talisman to wear or carry with you, or read a prayer for you, or give you a prayer to recite regularly to protect you. You need this protection now since you have put your hand in the hornet's nest. Baba Sain is considered one of the best spiritual protectors. Everyone speaks high of him."

Samir never believed wearing amulets could protect someone. However, there was no harm in seeing someone and learning more about this secret art practiced in Islam and many other faiths. Many a terrorist who were killed were found to be wearing amulets on their arms or a ring on their fingers. If these did not protect them, how could it protect anyone, wondered Samir.

They took a side road and detoured past the main bazaar into another street, where Latif parked the car. They got out, and went into an inner small side street to a house. There was no sign outside. Latif opened the door and walked in. There were about a dozen men and women, some in burqas, segregated in two separate areas. A person sat on a stool outside a door. There was no numbering system. He would remember who came first, and would ask that person to go in next, when the previous person had left.

It appeared the attendant sitting on the stool knew Latif well, as he got up to greet him. Latif spoke something in Pashto to him, and he nodded. "I have told him we have an important issue to discuss and would like to seek Baba's advice. The attendant's brother works for my office, so sometimes pulling strings work. Otherwise, we would have to wait for at least an hour or two."

The inner door opened, and a couple walked out. The attendant beckoned to Latif to go in next. No one objected as these visitors appeared important. They walked into the inner room.

Baba Sain was around 70 years old, but looked much older and frail for his age. He had grey hair and beard, and was sitting on a mat in one corner of the room. There were a few cabinets, which were open, which seemed to have a collection of stones of various colors, some rosaries, and few books. A table on another corner had some papers, a felt pen, a bottle of what appeared to be yellow golden ink, and a few more books. The walls had many frames with Quranic verses on it, and a few charts having symbols and tables on it.

Baba Sain expected the visitors to speak first. Latif started, "Baba Sain. My friend here is from USA. He is working for the government, and his job is very important but dangerous. He has been threatened with his life. We need something to protect him with."

Baba Sain looked at Samir, then scanned his whole body as if he had X-ray eyes. He spoke very softly, "I can see the danger lurking over you. It is very severe and following you around. You could already have been harmed, but I also see an aura of protection around you. It is only because of that protection that no harm has yet come to you."

Was he just making it up just because Latif told him upfront that his life is threatened, wondered Samir. Anyway, he decided to carry it though and observe how these spiritual healers worked.

Samir spoke, "Baba Sain. I read the Ayat-ul-Kursi and the four Qul every day and night for my protection. My wife and my mother, they also pray for my safety every day…"

"My son! You already know how to protect yourself from evil. Ayat-ul-Kursi is the most powerful verse for protection. And the Qul give protection from other evils like jinn, black magic, and jealousy. These should be sufficient for you. You don't need anything more."

He then paused for a minute as if focusing on the issue at hand, and said, "Those who endanger your life are into black magic and many other evil practices. These secret arts are very powerful and sometimes it is difficult to protect oneself as every time an aura of protection builds around you, they break it down with their evil practices. Black magic is very powerful as it even affected our Prophet. But Allah has provided us with additional knowledge on how to counter and seek protection from such evils. But they work only if followed properly."

Samir wondered what type of black magic was it that the terrorists practiced that even the sacred verses would not be sufficient and he would need additional protection.

Latif barged in trying to explain, "Muslims, Christians and Jews, and almost all beliefs, including the Hindus, believe in the protective and healing power of the 'taweez', which is an amulet. They are usually worn on the body as a necklace or a band. They can also be placed in close proximity of the person as well, but that will dilute its powers. These are mostly Quranic verses or other sacred words. The amulet sometimes includes the whole micro-copy of the Holy Quran, or some of its verses which have powers to protect, or the 99 names of God. Others use the disconnected mysterious words from the Quran. Most Muslims feel safe in wearing Quranic verses.

"Sometimes religious narratives also carry powers for the amulet. The story of the miracle of the seven sleepers in Chapter 18: The Cave carries miraculous powers for some. Likewise, an image of Caliph Ali's sword gives physical powers to the wearer."

Baba Sain interrupted, "We are dealing with evil people here. They practice black magic and use numbers, alphabets or symbols conjured through astrology or some secret knowledge passed down through generations such as from the magical times in Babylon during the times of Prophet Solomon. The use of symbols in a taweez is demonic and used in black magic!"

He continued, "Prophet Solomon was very powerful and had the ability to talk to animals and jinn, and was renowned for his wisdom, which also converted the Queen of Sheba to his beliefs. The Seal of Solomon, also known as the Star of David, a six-pointed star or hexagram, is a powerful symbol and is used in black magic. The stargazing priests during the times of pharaohs had first used it as a secret symbol, which was later adopted by David. It is used even today in both in kabbala and in Islamic beliefs, with other letters inscribed within the star."

Baba Sain walked to the table, picked up the felt pen, dipped it in the yellow ink, and made a hexagram. The ink had a fragrance and smelled like saffron, which many use to write verses of the Quran in amulets.

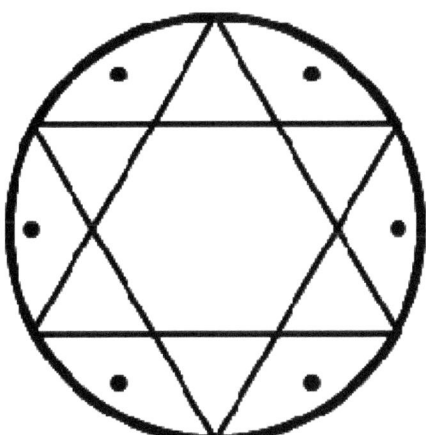

"I am going to give you a taweez that you must always wear on your right hand."

He then wrote some names of Allah within the stars in a particular order, then folded the paper, put it in a small cloth capsule, and sealed it.

"Wear it at all times on your right forearm. Inshallah, no harm will come to you."

Samir was never a believer of the taweez. But he knew many, including the former Prime Minister Marvi when she was returning to Pakistan, did. She had consulted a spiritual reader, who had warned her of the impeding danger. He had given her a taweez as well, and had said no harm will come to within 50 feet of her if she wore it. She was wearing it on the day of the Islamabad attack, and miraculously while 150 people died and over 500 were injured in that attack, she was totally unharmed, despite being the main target of the attack.

He then got up and moved to his cabinet, and took out a yellow colored stone.

"This is an aqeeq stone, which our Prophet also used to wear for protection. Wear it on a silver ring on your little finger of the right hand, facing inwards towards your palm, so that it touches your skin. God willing, you will not only be protected but the stone will impart positive energy in you as well."

Samir recalled stones have a place in all religions since times immemorial. The Bible refers to the twelve stones symbolizing the twelve tribes of Israel. The Book of Revelations mentions twelve stones as the foundation stones of the wall of Jerusalem. Temples and places of worship of all religions are adorned with stones: the moonstones in India, malachite and azurite in Egypt, agates in Rome, jade in China, crystal in Japan, turquoise in Persia, amethyst in Europe, and the black stone of Kaaba at Mecca.

He knew there is belief in gemstones in many faiths. Stones have significance in Hinduism, Jainism, Buddhism, and Sikhism as well, and are considered sacred. Navaratna in Sanskrit means nine gems: ruby for the Sun, pearl for the Moon, red coral for Mars, emerald for Mercury, yellow sapphire for Jupiter, diamond for Venus, blue sapphire for Saturn, hessonite for the ascending Lunar node, and cat's eye for the descending Lunar node. The traditional setting and arrangement of these nine gems always has the ruby representing the Sun at the center, surrounded clockwise from the top by the diamond, pearl, red coral, hessonite, blue sapphire, cat's eye, yellow sapphire, and emerald. Wearing the nine gems is said to provide an astrological balance and benefit to the wearer.

He knew stones have also been used as a form of healing in different ways. Sometimes, just the presence of stones was sufficient to heal. Some theorize that stones have vibrations which are aligned with the forces of nature. The vibrational qualities of the gemstones can further help achieve balance and awareness on physical, emotional, mental, and spiritual levels. The energy of each such element creates an energy exchange when touching the body.

Latif interrupted, "The aqeeq, also known as agate or carnelian, is the most important stone in Islam and the most favorite stone of the Prophet, and therefore his followers. Some believe that it was the first stone to affirm the existence of God and the Prophet. According to some Hadith, there are mountains of aqeeq in heaven. Aqeeq is known to protect people from evil as well.

Samir had studied in Turkey also. He knew like the aqeeq, another popular amulet, even with tourists to the Middle East, particularly in Turkey, is a turquoise eye-shaped amulet, called 'nazar'. This is believed to protect against the evil eye. The belief is that if a person is complimented a lot, they will be jinxed and often sick the next day unless the amulet is worn, or a verse of the Quran is recited. However, in South Asia, the effect of nazar, which in this case is the evil or jealous eye, is neutralized through the physical encircling of the head of the affected person of dried red chillies, which are then burnt.

On the other hand, the 'khamsa', meaning five, depicting the open right hand with five fingers, is yet another popular protective amulet which is popular in North African cultures. These are adopted by Muslims, particularly the Shias,

Christians, and Jews alike. However, many Sunni Muslims consider it a Shia amulet.

Baba Sain added, "There is yet another practice of the fulfillment of desires. At shrines of religious figures, particularly those who follow sufis practices, people tie a piece of ribbon or colorful cloth, mostly green, to a tree or a gate or window as a sign of respect, of devotion and love, and of remembrance. Others leave a ribbon after asking for something, for help, for answers, or for protection, so they leave a bit of themselves. However, many Muslims call it 'shirk' akin to worshipping another deity. I believe it is perfectly fine to tie a ribbon at a shrine for protection."

Baba Sain then went back to the cabinet, and took out a rosary with 99 beads which had the names of Allah written on it. "This is not shirk, or sin. It is from Medina and has been blessed with the Prophet's grave by being placed on it overnight. Keep it with you at all times. Hang it on the mirror of your car to remind you to recite it as well as it will protect you in the car. Recite the 99 names of Allah whenever you have time while travelling by road or air. Allah's names have many powers. Inshallah, no harm will come to you."

He continued, "Just remember, only Allah's name will protect, whether by invoking His names, or thorough His words, like the Ayat-ul-Kursi and the four Qul, which He has blessed us with for protection! His names and words cannot be used to cause harm to anyone, or for any negative things or motives. Those who are trying to harm you are trying to do exactly that. It will backfire for those who do that, and they will always burn in hell!"

As Samir thanked the person and walked out, he felt very grateful at the simple pious person, who gave away the agate, the rosary, and the amulet without even asking for any money or for his services. He had not resorted to any magic or voodoo, but had just asked him to wear an agate ring and an amulet which had the names of Allah for protection. He had also reminded him to continue reading his prayers of protection, and had just asked him to recite the names of Allah whenever he could. No hocus pocus here.

As he left the building, Samir dug into his pocket, took out his wallet, and inserted whatever money he had in the metal box sitting in one corner for donations. Latif did exactly the same.

But Samir wondered if the rosary, the agate, and the amulet would really protect him? Was he beginning to start believing in the supernatural, and the power of the spirituality to protect him from black magic? He never used to believe in these things, but now he was confused!

Healing Center

Hameed picked up Samir in the afternoon for a rendezvous with the well-known spiritual and herbal healer, Hakeem Luqman, at a hospital in Swat. He had heard only a few spiritual and herbal healers in the country used 'Tibb-e-Nabvi' or 'Medicine of the Prophet' which had become very popular in recent years, and Hakeem Luqman was one of them. Tibb-e-nabvi healing was based on the sayings of the Prophet, as documented in many a Hadith, and isolated into a single volume compiled by Ibn Al Qayyam Al Jauziah in the 14th century.

"Tibb-e-nabavi is a complete code of medicine, both for the health of heart soul and physical fitness," Hameed knew about its origin, "We ignored it many hundreds of years, and because of that, it is not even listed as a form of alternative medicine. Today, you find many practitioners of Ayurveda, Unani, Homeopathy, Herbalism, Naturopathy, etc. all over the world but one hardly finds any credible practitioner of tibb-e-nabavi for healing even in the Muslim world!"

"But wasn't so called Islamic medicine based on ancient Greek which the Arabs adopted, and is called Unani or Eastern Medicine today?" Samir was inquisitive.

"Between the 10th to 14th century, leading Muslim physicians and scientists like Ibne Sina, Al Biruni, Tamimi, etc., combined both the ancient Greek and early Islamic, based on tibb-e-nabvi, to revolutionize medicine, and this came to be known as Unani medicine!"

"So, why it is still not widely adopted today?"

"People will only benefit from tibb-e-nabvi if they acknowledge it and have faith in it!"

Luqman's name was well-known in the northern areas and people used to say he had a spiritual and healing touch. The hospital was supposedly frequented by militants and religious fanatics as well. The reason Samir wanted to visit the hospital was because sources had informed him that many a Taliban fighter from across the border used to frequent the hospital in case of combat injury or even illness. He had also wanted to meet the Hakeem as well to learn of his knowledge as he was one of the few practitioners of tibb-e-nabvi in the country.

The huge building was in the center of the city with a green crescent on the roof, and a number of billboards all projecting various verses from the Quran. It looked like both a madrassah and a hospital.

There was a large crowd of people, all turbaned, hanging out on the street near the main gate. There were also many street vendors selling food or the Quranic verses on frames, and religious books, across the street. Many beggars were sprawled on the sidewalk. It looked like a fair rather than an area outside a hospital. A number of people were trickling in and out. The Hakeem would mostly be on travel across the country, and it was rumored that he also travelled to Afghanistan to heal many an injured wounded in combat. He would show up at his base hospital every other week or so. People would wait for days for him to come so they could seek his treatment.

Samir and Hameed went past the front door into the reception area. Hameed spoke to the attendant in Pashto, saying they had an appointment with the Hakeem. The attendant replied that Hakeem has been expecting them, but will join them later as he is with some critical patients. However, he had asked his assistant to guide them through the premises in the meantime. The assistant led them through the door into an inner hall.

This was like a general ward of a hospital. There were around 20 beds, each one occupied with patients, many of whom appeared to be in pain. Every bed had one or two persons attending, who appeared to be a close relative, to look after their well-being. A couple of male nurses in green apron were seen walking about.

Some of the sick were injured, as they had heavy bandages, with some traces of blood. They could have been Taliban fighters or the injury could have been due to tribal feuds. No questions were asked from the patients when they arrived.

Hameed led Samir to a side room, which was like a changing room. It had a number of traditional dresses hanging from various hooks. They had big spots of dried blood on them. The injured were most likely wearing them when they arrived at the hospital. Hameed pulled one from the hook and showed it to Samir. It has some verses of the Quran engraved on it.

"When tribals go to fight enemies, some of the very religious ones wear these for protection. This is like an armor to them. They believe no bullet will penetrate the dress, not will a knife pierce through them. This protective armory has been used in this part of the world since the times of the Arab commander Muhammad bin Qasim, who invaded India around 712 with a much smaller army as compared to that of the Hindu ruler Raja Dahir. The Raja had superior weapons and his army rode elephants. Yet, the Arab commander defeated him."

He continued, "Likewise, the army of the Berber Commander Tariq bin Ziyad who conquered Spain at the Rock of Gibraltar wore such inscribed uniforms. An army of only 7,000 men were able to defeat an army of over 100,000 in the enemy territory across the sea. Such inscribed dresses were also used by the Mongols of central Asia during their invasion of India. The commanders in the Mughal army used to wear them as they conquered the rest of India

"Now, the same is being practiced and worn by the TTP, the Taliban, Al-Qaeda, and ISIS believing no harm will come to them. By wearing this protective armor, they believe they are invulnerable, and even a small group of militants will defeat the Pakistan army or the foreign forces…"

Samir interrupted, "God only provides protection if the war is to protect humanity and is against persecution and evil forces. Such a dress will not protect the evil forces, even if they have the whole Quran inscribed on them. It will not protect the suicide bomber out to take the lives of innocent civilians."

Hameed turned to look at Samir as if disagreeing, "We all know who the occupiers of our lands are, while we Pashtun are the ones being persecuted!"

They then all walked into another room, which had 10 patients lying on beds. They all appeared to be in very critical condition, some were in great pain, some unconscious, while others were motionless and only their eyes open. It looked like an Intensive Care Unit of a hospital.

Each bed had a table on the side with a glass of water on the side with some medicine and a chart. There was only one male attendant present. A CD player on a table at the far end, with small speakers, was playing some Quranic verses. These were echoing across the hall.

Hameed identified the verses, "Chapter 55 Ar-Rahman, the Most Gracious. There is a strong belief among many Muslims that these verses have the power to cure and to heal. It can even bring back the terminally ill from near death. Even a number of major hospitals around the country have started to play these verses to their patients multiple times a day. There are CDs available in every video store with these verses that claim that hearing it regularly will cure one from all disease. The energy of these verses is transferred to the human system, as well as transferred to the water placed next to the bedside. The patients regularly take sips of the 'recited' water throughout the day. The treatment is supplemented with the patients taking herbal medicine based on tibb-e-nabvi. We believe cure is 100% guaranteed within a few days!"

"Really!" Samir exclaimed with a bit of sarcasm, "This must have a better track record than the Cleveland Clinic. Could it just be another placebo effect?"

"Clearly not, as millions have been healed using the ways of the Prophet. Modern medicine is still amazed how healing happens, call it a miracle if you like, but if one has faith in the treatment, it definitely works!"

"Maybe it should go in a modern health sciences curriculum!" Samir again commented sarcastically.

"I guarantee you your opinion will change once you have walked through these premises," replied Hameed, "slowly some of these methods are being adopted in certain hospitals as well. A government hospital in Lahore, where top bureaucrats go, has recently reported that this is the best treatment they follow for their patients. Surprisingly, the spiritual healer there is a western educated doctor, but he regularly prescribes tibb-e-nabvi alongside listening to these verses.

"With the medicine of the Prophet, many have come back from near death, and many a hepatitis and cancer patients have recovered after adopting this treatment and listening to Ar-Rahman continuously for days. All this is documented in the hospital records and reported on media. How the body cells align themselves, how the immune system is strengthened against disease when the verses or Allah's name are being played is not known. As a biologist, I believe that the vibration from the verses or names increases the level of energy in the body of the patient. It repairs at the cell level where microconidia is getting damaged and where oxygenation is not taking place."

"So, why don't you do clinical trials and conduct such scientific investigations at your university? There is nothing that stops you from doing so."

Hameed did not reply, instead he walked up to a person on the bed who was half awake, and spoke to him in Pashto. The man replied back. After a few exchange of sentences, Hameed turned to Samir and said, "He was carried in here, half dead, with shrapnel wounds and major loss of blood when his vehicle drove over a roadside mine in the tribal area outside the TTP zone. Everyone in the vehicle died except him. There was no hope for his survival, and the local doctor had given him a day to live, till he was brought here. In four days only, and under the spiritual treatment of Hakeem, and hearing these verses every day, has given him strength and energy. He can walk to the washroom now by himself, and expects to be out of here within days. He will go back to avenge his injuries. This is a living proof. What other evidence do you want?"

Hameed continued, "Spiritual healing is in every belief and faith. God revealed the Quran to guide mankind to a straight path and to soothe the spirit when recited. Listening to the verses is a healing of the spirit while the herbs healing the body. Once the healed mind takes over, the body gains strength! A lot of today's neuropsychologists believe in that as well. Our Prophet taught that to us 1,400 years ago!

"It is important that the spiritual healing is supplemented with herbal medicine of the Prophet. This is one of the very few tibb-e-nabvi hospitals in the country, and people travel from far and wide to come here after their treatment has failed everywhere else. The laboratories medicinal mixtures are prepared in one of the laboratories upstairs using local herbs and given to the patient. The herbs are organic and pure. We believe no medicine or treatment can work unless there is God's willingness. The medicine does not have the power, it is God that does. Hence, we ask the patient to pray to God first for healing before taking any dose of medicine."

Samir did not offer any comment, because what he was seeing with his own eyes was too good to be true. Tibb-e-nabvi did work! But he was not yet willing to acknowledge that.

But was this type of spiritual healing giving strength to the militants to fight and keep going back to continue fighting more?

They walked over to another smaller room, with a few soft chairs and a couple of beds. An individual was lying on the bed without a shirt, and an attendant was doing a certain procedure on his neck, which looked like some type of surgery. There were a few blood stains on the bedsheet, while the trash can had many cotton swabs with dried blood on it.

"Cupping! It is an ancient form of alternative medicine which dates back to ancient Egyptian, Chinese, Greek, Middle Eastern, and Islamic cultures. It is mentioned by Hippocrates as well, who is considered the father of modern medicine. One of the oldest medical textbooks in the world, the Ebers Papyrus, describes how the ancient Egyptians used cupping therapy in 1550 BCE. In today's cupping, a therapist puts special cups on your skin and creates some suction, so blood is then drawn to the area. In wet cupping, some blood is also drawn out. Those who practice it believe it cures of many disease, but it has not been backed by research.

"Among Muslims, wet cupping is called 'hijama', which forms part of tibb-e-nabvi. According to the Hadith, the best of remedies is the hijama, while another Hadith identifies the 17th, 19th, and 21st day of the Islamic lunar month as the best days, and during the daytime, between sunrise and sunset, to perform hijama. The best areas in the body are two veins at the side of the neck and the base of the neck according to the traditions. Since the Prophet used to have it done himself, Muslims believe regular cupping gives health and is also the cure for many diseases."

Samir wondered why cupping on certain days only worked better, but since he was not a pathologist or an astrologer, he let it go without any follow-up questions.

They walked into another hall, which was a dining hall for about 40 people. Ten tables with four chairs each. A kitchen at one end had a number of stoves, two refrigerators, and a water cooler. A few men who did not appear to be sick, or had recovered, were at the tables eating their food. Two attendants were serving the tables.

The side door opened, and a tall and thin man walked in. He had a light beard which had turned half grey with age. He recognized Hameed and greeted the visitors with a smile and the Islamic salutation, 'Salam alaikum' and shook hands. He was Hakeem Luqman.

Hakeem was pleased to see them, "I am glad you scientists and the educated have found time to visit my hospital. We don't practice modern medicine, or allopathy. All our treatments are based on tibb-e-nabvi and the Islamic ways. They are 100% effective. This is what you should be teaching in your medical colleges."

Hameed replied, "Hakeem sahib, we would like to do that, but unfortunately can only do so if it is approved by PMDC, the Pakistan Medical Council. Herbal medicine can only be prescribed if it backed by research and clinical trials. They then need approval from the pharmacy council and other foreign regulatory agencies like the FDA…"

"Ha! Those are nothing but corporate mafias out to mint money for the rich! For years they said cholesterol is bad, and after having consumers spend billions of dollars on medication, they say the results are mixed and cholesterol is okay. Many a good and cheap herbal treatments have been suppressed by them. One very good example is that the seed of the apricot fruit can cure cancer. But the FDA gives a warning not to consume it in large numbers or it may cause death. We have treated many a cancer patients right here in this hospital with apricot seeds and without chemotherapy!"

He continued, "The proof is in the pudding. There is no dead body that leaves these premises. Those who come on stretchers or wheel chairs walk out by themselves. Our treatments are free in all our hospitals. People provide charity. Some put cash in the boxes outside, others send us checks. Yesterday, we received one donation of Rs. 500,000 from an anonymous donor. He could have been one of our patients. Others send truckloads of food supplies every day. We don't ask names or addresses. We only treat because that is what God wants us to do."

He sounded like Mother Teresa in her role as a doctor.

"Certainly, I see a lot of patients here. Besides recitations from the Quran and cupping, what else do you offer to the sick?"

"The food, fruits and herbs mentioned in the Quran, and those recommended by the Prophet, are a complete cure that will give one a long and healthy life. The sick heal faster when they eat what we prescribe. The west is only learning it now. What do they call it? Organic? GMO free?

"There are 25 prophets mentioned in the Quran, out of thousands that lived, most of them lived to be 100 years or more. Prophet Adam lived 930 years, Noah 1,450 years, Abraham 195 years, and Moses 123 years as an example. They did hard work, had many wives and offspring, and never fell sick. Why is that? It was just the combination of submission to Allah and following His directives in the way of spiritual treatment, and eating and drinking only what he ordained. Shall we sit down?"

They sat at the table, and an attendant immediately brought in three small glasses of water which had engraved Quranic verses on its rim. Hakeem read something on the water, blew on it, and lifted one glass as if to toast.

"'Zamzam' water. The healthiest of them all, which comes from the underground spring under the Kaaba. This is the same water that Prophet Ismail struck when he was left in the middle of the desert by his father Prophet Abraham. For over few thousand years, the spring has not dried, and it feeds millions every year, who not only drink it there, but carry it in jerry cans and bottles home. Just a few sips of this holy and sacred water every day will ensure you do not fall sick, and if you are sick, it will heal you completely."

"Any scientific claim to the strength of this water?"

Hakeem smiled. "I am sure you must have read the secrets of zamzam water. It is naturally alkaline, which only now the doctors are saying is beneficial for health. A Japanese scientist has also shown and proven that zamzam water is different from all other waters. Its drops cannot be crystallized like all other types of water. The scientist couldn't crystallize it unless he diluted the water by 1,000 at least. When he froze it, he got two crystals, one on top of the other, implying the two words connected together: zam and zam. When one of his Muslim colleagues recited Quranic verses over the water, he got the most perfectly-shaped crystals.

Then he played the 99 names of Allah, and each name produced a uniquely-shaped crystal."

He couldn't stop himself from describing the wonderful properties of the zamzam water, "When he completed these experiments, which lasted 15 years, he published a five-volume book called 'Messages from Water'. In his book, he wrote: 'I have proven that water, that peculiar liquid, is capable of thinking, fathoming, feeling, getting excited, and expressing itself.' He also wrote, 'The quality of zamzam water cannot be found anywhere on this earth.' He found that by mixing one drop of zamzam water mix in 1,000 drops of regular water, regular water will get the same quality like zamzam water. Subhanallah! That is the water that God has blessed us with."

Samir spoke, "I have read the works of that scientist as well. While he has done a lot of work on regular water properties, which does act peculiar, there is very little documented research on zamzam. Maybe Hameed can verify these claims in his laboratory if they are true. An Institute at Stuttgart has also discovered that regular water has memory…"

Hakeem interrupted, "Zamzam has collected memory from thousands of years since the times of Prophet Abraham. Imagine a water that has memory of our Prophets as well. But while the zamzam water is too holy, even ordinary water, when recited with select verses of the Quran, becomes charged at the atomic level and gets the power to heal. Those who don't have access to zamzam have this less expensive solution as a cure to their illness by reciting verses on the water and blowing on it. The power of the Quranic verses is then stored in the water, and drinking it will heal you. We regularly read these verses before we serve it to our patients."

"Yes, we saw that in one of the rooms. But I have also heard somewhere that drinking camel urine also heals?" asked Samir sarcastically with disgust on his face.

"It is in tibb-e-nabvi that the Prophet prescribed camel urine as a cure for certain ailments. We have found a few drops of camel urine mixed with camel milk and taken daily is a cure for cancer."

Hameed intervened, "It is a fact proven through research. A Saudi scientist has discovered that nano-particles in the urine of camels can attack cancer cells with success. She was inspired by the Prophet's medical advice and that camel urine consists of natural substances that work to eradicate malignant cells and maintain the number of healthy cells in a cancer patient. There is definitely something in the urine of certain animals, like cows for instance, that even Hindus have adopted."

Samir just couldn't hide his disgust at the thought of any urine.

"Not just the urine, but also the milk and meat of camel have tremendous benefits. The milk of the camel, which was our Prophet's favorite, has a higher nutritious value than that of cow. It is now becoming very popular in the west as well, and I read that California and Texas now have a number of camel farms. Camel meat has its own advantages too. A staple diet of camel milk and meat a day will keep the doctor away," Hakeem added with a smile.

Hakeem continued, "But that is not all. The Prophet has recommended herbs which will make you live almost forever. 'Kalonji', also called black seed, and which looks like black cumin or onion seed, is the most powerful herb mentioned in tibb-e-nabvi. The Prophet said that there is cure for every disease in kalonji except death. There are more than 100 cures for all types of ailments using kalonji with other ingredients. Today, too, thousands of years later, even the west is acknowledging that kalonji seed oil is the best cure for cancer and many other types of ailments!"

Samir had heard of the tremendous benefits of kalonji from his wife, who used to add this herb in almost every food, and also swallow it raw every morning. He wanted to check its nutritional composition, and punched in kalonji on google search. A whole spectrum of links appeared. He read out one quickly, "These seeds are the small black granules found in the fruits of nigella sativa plant. This is native plant of south west Asia that is abundantly cultivated in India, Bangladesh, Turkey, and other eastern countries."

It was unbelievable what he read next on the net.

"The chemical composition of kalonji is very rich and diverse. Aside from its primary ingredient, crystalline nigellone, this seed contains 15 amino acids, proteins, carbohydrates, essential fatty acids, volatile oils, non-volatile oils, alkaloids, saponin, crude fiber, and other minerals. The kalonji seed contains more than hundred valuable nutrients. It contains proteins, carbohydrates and plant fats and oils. Other ingredients include Linoleic acid, Oleic acid, Calcium, Potassium, Iron, Zinc, Magnesium, Selenium, Vitamin A, Vitamin B, Vitamin B2, Niacin, and Vitamin C. It further said that it is used traditionally to cure asthma, hypertension, diabetes, inflammation, cough, bronchitis, headache, eczema, fever, dizziness, and influenza. Its main component, thymoquinone, possess antioxidant, anti-inflammatory, and hepatoprotective properties."

Samir wondered how could the Prophet have known about all the power that was packed in kalonji seeds. Hakeem and Hameed nodded their heads with a smile.

Hakeem continued, "That is not all. Fenugreek and turmeric are other magic herbs. The Prophet once said, 'If my people knew what there is in Fenugreek seed, they would have bought and paid its weight in gold.'"

Samir knew also of Fenugreek seeds and checked on the net again. They are known for their anti-diabetic property. They are also considered excellent to treat arthritis and to reduce blood cholesterol. Fenugreek contains natural expectorant properties and is considered ideal for treating sinus and lung congestion. It also helps in loosening and removing excess mucus and phlegm. The mucilage content of the seeds helps to cure external boils, burns, and ulcers. Likewise, turmeric contains an active ingredient, curcumin, which is anti-inflammatory and one of the world's best cures for arthritis and even cardiac related diseases. Both wonder herbs. How that could have been known 1,400 years ago, he wondered!

"You see, we serve our patients with the most nutritious and spiritual food that not only heals them in no time, but also strengthens them against any attacks in the future. They become supermen. We also serve the fruits that the Quran says we will have in heaven, one that will make us live a disease-free eternal life and with tremendous sexual powers: pomegranate and figs. Saffron is yet another herb with healing powers. Only now science has identified them as aphrodisiacs. The benefits of olives have been known since then. It was the favorite of the Prophet to regularly eat olives.

"We also serve the super dates 'ajwa' that come only from Medina, which the Prophet himself planted with his own hands. They have the miraculous powers to heal. According to the Hadith, the Prophet said that whoever will eat seven ajwas in the morning, no poison or magic will hurt him that day. All these nutritious foods are the food of heaven and have been promised to us. You would be surprised that even the seed of ajwa dates, taken in powdered form, is very good for the heart and for cholesterol."

He continued, "Above all is sweetest nectar of all: honey. Honey is mentioned in the Quran as a healing for people. There will be rivers of honey in heaven. To our patients, we feed the best sidr honey that comes from the Dho'an Valley in the Hadramaout Desert east of Yemen. It was our Prophet's favorite. We treat our patients to a tablespoon of the best raw, organic, unprocessed honey with a pinch of kalonji. It not only gives someone super human powers but even the worst cases of illness or injury recover within days. Islamic honey has the ability to kill all types of bacteria."

Samir wondered if these superfoods were what the terrorists were relying on to become strong and invincible. But then he wondered what the Hakeem meant by Islamic honey. A marketing gimmick? Some billboards in cities market their honey as Islamic. He recalled reading an article recently by a university professor who questioned all 'Islamic products' like Islamic honey, Islamic nuts, Islamic food, Islamic cosmetics, soaps and pastes, Islamic finance, Islamic tourism, Islamic toothbrush, Islamic clothing, Islamic pharmaceuticals, and halal foods. The merchants were just capitalizing on Islam and fooling the masses, while they just had to advertise its origin or ingredients for their health benefits. But then, if there is a market for selling Islam, and people that can be fooled and money made, why not!

The server brought in the food on a tray: some minced camel meat cooked in traditional herbs like kalonji and fenugreek, brown rice, a small glass of camel milk, with a few ajwa dates dipped in honey as dessert, and some peeled pomegranate, water melon cubes, olives and some pink salt on the side. Hakeem asked his guests to say 'Bismillah'. One must only start eating food by invoking the name of God. Samir remembered Christians do that too by thanking God for His blessings.

He started with a pinch of pink salt and then with the fruits, a tradition that the Prophet followed. "Fruits should be eaten on an empty stomach. If you eat fruit first, it will play a major role to detoxify your system, supplying you with a great deal of energy for weight loss and other life activities. It was recommended by our Prophet. Science is only beginning to discover it now."

He ate the watermelon first, "Watermelon is excellent on an empty stomach. It completely detoxifies your digestive system." He then took the pomegranate slice and started peeling the seeds out from the skin, and popping them in his mouth. Others followed.

"Eat every single kernel of pomegranate. We believe there is one kernel at least in each pomegranate that comes from heaven and is blessed. That is the one with the greatest healing power. It is also a great aphrodisiac," he smiled.

Hakeem and Hameed then dug into the rice and minced meat with their right hands, scooping up the food with their thumb and the first two fingers, and eating. Samir was not used to eating with his hands and instead requested a fork, and some paper tissues.

"Our Prophet used to sit on the floor and then eat with his fingers using his right hand. Eating with the left hand is forbidden. We must follow in the traditions and practices of the Prophet. It gives us strength."

Samir wondered why so much taboo in eating food. He always used his left hand to hold the fork and the right for the knife. He wondered how the left-handed Muslims ate food if there were such beliefs being followed.

Hakeem continued, "We add kalonji and fenugreek as an herb to every dish we cook."

He then took a small sip of camel milk. "All liquids must be consumed in three sips, not with one gulp. Preferably, they must be consumed much before a meal, and only in a short quantity, and just a few sips during the meal if you feel the need for it, but never after a meal. At least not for 30 minutes. This is our Prophet's tradition. Also, one must also never drink while standing up, but be seated. It has its advantages in the digestion."

Samir finished first and grabbed the tissue to wipe the edge of his lips. Some itsy-bitsy bits of rice were still on the plate. A few minutes later, both Hakeem and Hameed scooped up the last kernels of rice from the plate with their fingers, almost wiping it clean, and licked all their five fingers, pushing them deep into their mouths all the way in, then tightening their lips around it, and pulling them out so they were clean with saliva.

"One must never leave food on the plate. It is haram. It makes God unhappy who has provided us with so much food that we must be thankful to Him instead of wasting food. Our Prophet has taught us to preserve things, not waste them. Now, I read that there are restaurants in Germany and Japan that actually put a surcharge on your food if you leave it on the plate to throw away. And one must never fill up the stomach, only two thirds at most. And his way of eating with the fingers and licking them with your own mouth has its own advantages."

"What is that?"

"Licking fingers helps produce more saliva, which aids in digesting food. Secondly, it has only recently been discovered by scientists that the tips of our fingers produce a certain enzyme that when ingested actually helps with the digestion of our food. Therefore, by licking your fingers you are actually ingesting this 'newly found' enzyme."

After finishing the main meal, Hakeem took the honey-dipped ajwa in his fingers and dropped it in his mouth. "Having something sweet after a meal is in the traditions of our Prophet. Nothing can be more nutritious or sweeter than ajwa dates dipped in honey."

He turned to Samir and said, "Western doctors and the pharmaceutical firms mint hundreds of billions of dollars from the people. Allopathy has its side effects. People get drug addicted as well due to opioids. Here, we follow a simple lifestyle, one which is very inexpensive, and is 100% guaranteed not only to heal but to give one energy, strength, and long life. Only a few hundred Muslims, 1,400 years ago, fought wars to protect themselves against thousands and won! Each man had the strength of a dozen! Each man also had many wives," he smiled.

Samir wondered if this was the national diet of all those militants who were out to fight jihad and conquer the world! They must be believing it made them invincible!

Luqman changed the conversation to his patients, "We see many injured come back almost from the dead. Many journalists and scholars come visit my hospital, and they are surprised at our success. We do not distinguish between who is who, their nationalities or faiths. We don't ask how they got sick or injured. They could be militants, freedom fighters or jihadi to some, terrorists to others. It makes no difference to us. We treat everyone. They leave when they are cured. They donate at will in the box outside, or drop money at the reception. Sometimes, they send tons of food for the patients. We sometimes have no place to store them."

The Hakeem got up and reached for a 'miswak', a type of a chewing stick, made from the twigs of the arak tree. "The teeth must be cleaned with miswak after every meal. It is in the traditions of our Prophet. If you do so, you will not lose any teeth or have gum disease even if you are 100!"

Hameed added, "Hadith tells us the ancient man used miswak for centuries. It provides us with spiritual benefit as well as everyday maintenance of mouth, gums, and teeth."

Samir figured they had learnt enough about the Hakeem. He was just a spiritual healer, and was not protecting any one or group in particular. But what surprised him were the simple ways of healing of the Prophet which as claimed were far more healthy and nutritious and worked better than prescription medicine or complicated surgeries. Maybe more research was needed in tibb-e-nabvi and in spiritual foods and healing before it was accepted at par with other scientific methods approved by the health agencies.

Samir wondered how medical care had become a business, while it should have been a free public service. People living in the mountains in the Hunza valley few hundred miles north of here were known to live a very healthy lifestyle. The food was pure and the natural unpolluted water melted from the Himalayan glaciers were laden with minerals. The produce and fruits were fresh, locally grown and organic by any definition. The air was clean. Everyone led an active life, working and walking from early mornings to evenings, whether in the farms or at home. There were no radio signals, whether for cellular phones or television, and there were no electric lines. Illness was unheard of. There were no feuds or conflicts among people. They were all happy. They all lived to be well over hundred without even a doctor within a hundred miles of them.

He also now knew where the militants believed they got their strengths from. In addition to what they believed they were fighting and dying for a cause, right or wrong, they led a healthy life-style which was giving them the same strength, energy, and confidence as the Muslim fighters had 1,400 years ago when they had set out from the Arab peninsula in small numbers to conquer the world!

Samir and Hameed thanked the Hakeem for so much information as they asked to be excused, and walked out of the healing center.

Black Magic

The aamil Jadoo Baba at Hasan Abdal was expecting his clients to return soon. After all, they had prepaid a large amount of money in advance for stealing a certain treasure from the military camp. He knew it was not money or gold, and had a fairly good idea what they wanted. Everyone knew that Pakistan had the 'atom bomb' which a certain engineer had made for the army by stealing its blueprints from a 'farangi' or foreign country. Murtaza Brohi, the former prime minister of Pakistan had rightly said that if there can be a Christian bomb, a Jew Bomb, a Hindu bomb, then why can't there be a Muslim bomb. He had told the nation that even if the country had to eat grass, let it be, but we will make the bomb. He did and became a national hero. A farangi minister had said they will make a horrible example out of him. They did and had him killed by the Pakistan Army itself. He died a hero's death, a Shaheed, and is remembered even today as the founder of the bomb. Many more bombs have been made since then. They are stored in military camps safe from the Hindu and the farangi army, who are next door in Afghanistan. They both have an agenda to destroy these bombs and then to destroy Pakistan.

It knew his clients wanted to steal the bombs and use them on the Hindus. Let it be. He would certainly help them at any cost. He was also getting paid for it, he smiled. Let the Hindus who had massacred thousands of Muslims in Kashmir, and over the last thousand years, die. They are also responsible for the attack on the Babri mosque, and for the killings in Gujrat. The money, of course, would be a bonus that he needed to buy a larger house so he would have more clients. He knew even the presidents and the prime ministers whosoever were elected believed in magic. Magic was real and mentioned in both the Quran and the Hadith. Everyone believed in it, from housewives to businessmen to politicians. If he could deliver the bombs, and word gets around, his reputation would be very much enhanced. Muslims and even kings from all over the world would want to see him to seek his advice. He himself would become a hero and the king of aamil.

It was another few days when his clients returned. It was late in the night. They had a briefcase, but this time, it was not full of money.

They walked into his room, bypassing the last few customers sitting outside, closed the door behind them, lay the briefcase on the table, and opened it. In it was one brown paper bag, and one white bag. The man carrying the case carefully took out the brown bag first.

"In it are the hair locks of the five men who would go in. Their locks are all tied separately by a rubber band. We want the men to become invisible when they go in and return safe with the treasure. Then there is a sixth lock tied separately which is of the man who would deliver the treasure to a certain place. We want him also to arrive there safe and unseen and not be caught. We know you can do it as you have done it for us before."

He then took out the other bag, opened it, and took out a vest which appeared unwashed.

"This belongs to the man in charge of the security. It took us a couple of days to steal it from the washer man who does his laundry. But it certainly is his, as it has his name written on it with black dye."

"Perfect!" said Jadoo Baba. "Please sit down and give me a few minutes."

He got up and pulled a book from his cabinet which appeared all worn out and falling apart, and opened it to find the right pages.

"This book belongs to my grandfather who migrated from Iraq many years ago. He inherited it from his own grandfather, who was one of the famous magicians of his time. It has many symbols in it, with an explanation on their powers. Some of them still cannot be deciphered. My grandfather taught me how to use the symbols and the signs, otherwise the magic is meaningless. It is believed that the symbols have the same magical powers as were used thousands of years ago by the Babylonians. All forms of magic were practiced there. No aamil has the knowledge or can do what I can do now with these spells."

With that, he got up to light six candles which he placed at the points of the Star of David on a red mat. Then he took out a small plastic box from his cabinet, which had some brown powder in it that smelled like some animal excrement. He turned off all lights except for one, and sprinkled a pinch of powder on the flames. The flames changed color to bright orange for a few seconds before reverting back to their original color. Then he reached for the brown bag, took out the hair locks, and placed them on the mat next to each of the candles forming the triangles, with the sixth at the center.

He then took out the vest next, asked for the name of the person along with his mother's name, wrote it on a piece of paper which had some symbols on it, placed it on the vest's sleeve, knotted its three times to enclose the piece of paper, at the same time murmuring something, and placed it at the center of the triangle. He then opened the book to a certain page, and started reading some mantra. He continued with it for about five minutes, every now and then taking a pinch of power and sprinkled it on the candles. The flames changed color every time. After he stopped reading, he held each of the hair lock one by one with his fingers and burnt its edge in the flame of the candle next to it, mumbling some more words. Then he opened the vest, placed all hair locks on it, sprinkled some powder, and placed a dried lemon in it. He stuck some needles in the lemon, and read something again for a minute. Then he blew onto the hair and the vest, and rolled them up as one package. He placed them in the white bag, and got up and turned on the lights.

"We need to go to the Misri Shah graveyard which is about 10 miles from here. The timing is perfect as it is already past the night prayer time."

They walked out together, making a passing comment to the few that were waiting outside, that he will not be back tonight, so they can come tomorrow morning.

They drove together, in the old Willy's Jeep that the three visitors had come in, to the corner of the town, past the stadium and a huge open space, then onto a dirt road that went for a few miles to a secluded area behind some large trees that looked like an old graveyard. It appeared to be overflowing with graves with hardly any room to walk between graves. It was at least a few hundred years old and not maintained at all. The older graves were typically reused for new bodies after a few years, if they had no visitors, unless a price was paid to the caretaker.

Jadoo Baba greeted the caretaker, and passed on a few large notes in his hand. The caretaker smiled and pointed his flashlight to a new grave a few hundred feet inside the graveyard. He went back into his shed, and returned with a couple of spades.

They all walked together past the 50 or so graves to the fresh mound that looked like someone had just been buried today. He handed one spade to the aamil, and they both started to scrap away at the mound of fresh dirt, and into the grave till they reached a wooden slab. They removed it to reveal a white cloth coffin which held the corpse. They both pulled it out, lay it on the side, and Jadoo Baba took out a sharp scimitar-like knife from his pocket, and pierced open the belly of the dead to expose the liver.

He took out the white paper bag, and placed its contents right next to the liver. He covered the belly again with the skin. He then took out an amulet from his vest pocket, which carried some of the secret symbols from the book, forcibly opened the mouth of the corpse, and inserted it into its mouth. They then pushed the corpse back into the grave. He then read out something in a strange language, blew on the corpse, and asked the caretaker to put the wooden slab and the dirt back on the grave. Together, they remade the mound to make it look like as it exactly was before they had dug into it.

The caretaker brought a jug of water, and they both washed up the dried blood on their hands and on the knife.

"Your work is done. Go onto your mission without fear. All those men will be invisible to everyone. But complete your mission before the full moon."

The four men walked back, smiling, to the jeep.

Safe House

Harry had checked into a safe house arranged by his agency in Islamabad. The agents would stay at different places each time. Hotels were not safe as there was too much traffic of individuals. They also had a lot of their own internal security as well who would check everything and everyone entering the hotel.

He avoided staying at a five-star hotel in the secure zone of Islamabad because he recalled it had been the subject of attack by terrorists in 2008 hours after the president of Pakistan had made his first speech to the parliament. 54 people had died and another 266 injured. It was also reported in local papers that about 30 US marines, scheduled to go to Afghanistan, were staying at the hotel, and were believed to have been the target of the bombing. It happened when a dump truck filled with explosives gate crashed and exploded in the driveway as it couldn't get past the barriers. 600 kg, which is over 1,300 pounds, of RDX mixed with TNT were used in the attack. No one was held responsible for these attack, though the government pointed the finger at TTP while the Americans blamed Al-Qaeda. The owner of the hotel, though, blamed the attack on the president due to some personal enmity of the president with him.

The parliament, the presidency, the prime minister's office, and the supreme court were all within a couple of miles of the hotel. It was generally considered the safest in Islamabad, and yet, the deadly attack had taken place. There were road blocks everywhere, and security was tight, yet the infiltrators knew how to get around the security. There were informers, and sometimes local plants in the service sector would facilitate entry and exit as well.

Harry had a map of Islamabad, which he laid out on the bed, and marked a one-mile radius where most of the VIP buildings would come within the circle. Any explosion here would be a perfect hit.

He had travelled on a fake passport from Kabul to Dubai, and then had arrived in Islamabad on a flight from Dubai on yet another fake passport. He was posing as a mountaineer travelling to the northern mountainous areas. He knew tourists drew the least attention. He was, however, very careful in ensuring that he was not followed or was not raising suspicious eyebrows wherever he went. He was to make contact with the TTP here, who would pose as his guides. The money for this operation to the local facilitators had exchanged hands by other agents from his security agency at another location in Lahore.

He walked down to the dining room. The server asked him if he wanted breakfast, He declined and ordered a regular coffee.

"I am expecting my guides to come in any moment. Please bring them here."

About ten minutes later, three men, who looked like those from the northern areas, much like from Gilgit, with strong central Asian features, walked in. Most guides were from the Gilgit-Baltistan province, which had an abundance of mountain climbing and skiing activity this season. So, people from Gilgit making contact with foreigners was considered a norm and did not attract much attention. He had received pictures of the men on WhatsApp on his cell phone, which was well encrypted. He waved at them and they walked over.

"Thank you for coming," he said. "I believe you have received your payment from my brother last week. I hope all arrangements have been made for the trip." The tallest of the three nodded.

"You can call me Samad. We have completed all arrangements. Everything is in place. It should happen within the next few days. Like all our deliveries before, this one will also take place tomorrow on time. Please let us know where you would like the mountain gear delivered." Mountain gear was the code for the nuclear fuel.

"As soon as you have the gear, please bring it to this place. I will be waiting here with further directions for you."

"I understand that the gear is to be transported across the border. We have our men ready to do that also. It will cost you more…and like before, we expect all payments in advance in American dollars."

"We will have the cash delivered to you like before."

"I have also received message from our emir that you need one of our best men to carry out his last mission." Emir was a title and usually referred to the boss. "The emir asked me to tell you that one of our best, known as Qari, will be here when the gear arrives." The men were clearly instructed by their emir not to ask any questions.

"I want everything carried out with precision and on time."

"Have we ever failed you?"

As the three men walked away, Harry's thought reverted back to his last briefing at Kabul by his commander.

"We have made all arrangements with our local surrogates to steal a cylinder of nuclear fuel from an agriculture institute in Rawalpindi which is working under the supervision of the federal government and doing research on radio-isotopes. They normally require a very small amount, but we have received credible information that due to a team of Chinese scientists arriving there next week for some important experiments on preservation of fruits, they have requested a few kilograms of enriched radioactive isotope. It will be delivered before the team arrives."

"Isn't that institute well-guarded?"

"Usually it is moderately-guarded, as many students and faculty move in and out every day and evening to attend classes. It normally does not carry any large amounts of radioisotopes or nuclear fuel. It is not like Noshab, where fuel is processed, or their other underground locations in Chakwal, Sargodha, and other remote locations in Balochistan where the fuel or even the nukes are stored."

The commander continued, "After the fuel is stolen, our local operators will arrive immediately at your safe house. Your job is to verify and secure the contents. Then you will hand over the cylinder to another team of operators who will be waiting at another safe house. It will be their responsibility to transport the cylinder across the Pakistan-Afghanistan border through the northern region. The complete chain is in place."

"What are my instructions after that?"

"You will receive a call from US that your mother is terribly ill, and you will take the next flight out of Islamabad back to Dubai. From Dubai, you will fly to Kabul and onto Jalalabad, and await the delivery of the cylinder."

Harry did not ask any further question. He knew through his friends at the agency in Kabul that once the fuel had arrived in Afghanistan, it will be transported back to one of the tribal agencies in the northern areas of Pakistan. Then a mock operation will be carried out by NATO forces, and the contraband cylinder will be recovered along with 'plans' to transport the fuel to the mainland American by sea, where it was to be detonated as a 'dirty bomb'. This would create enough noise in the United Nations, including in China and Russia that the Security Council will be asked to vote, asking Pakistan to disband its nuclear program immediately under UN supervision or face sanctions.

His agency had proposed a similar operation in Iraq before the Gulf War, but the White House had shot it down. Had such an operation been approved, America would have 'recovered' WMDs from Baghdad, and the whole war would have been justified. Sometimes, politicians are dumb and have no vision. But this time around, after its failure in Iraq, it was supported by the 'secret lobby', who were financing the whole operation.

But Harry had his own agenda. How could he return back the fuel after he had his hands on it? The bastard Pakistanis and the Muslims must have a taste of it. He had no plans to send the cylinders to Kabul, but instead have them detonated right here in Islamabad. He had planned well with his TTP friends that after the cylinders were delivered, one of their best suicide bombers would carry them to the heart of Islamabad and detonate them there. There were enough VIP buildings around the area, and with the Parliament being in session, it would wipe out the top leadership in Pakistan. With so many other government buildings in the neighborhood, including the presidency, the prime minister's office, the supreme court, and the federal ministries, it would avenge all the terrorism they have done and supported all over the world in one go! It would serve as a lesson to the rest of the Muslim world as well. He would actually be doing a good favor to the 200 million Pakistanis to get rid of their corrupt politicians in one go. They can perhaps then choose better people who are more responsible to their own society and to the world.

The detonation would also serve the main mission of the agency as well. They should actually be grateful instead of questioning him. With such an explosion of the dirty bomb in the heart of Islamabad, Pakistan would face sanctions anyway, and all its nuclear facilities would be rolled back under international pressure. It was like killing two birds with one stone.

Chilla

It was a dark and cloudy night. He had completed 40 days of the chilla without interruption. Many a times there had been distractions caused by the jinn by creating false illusions which looked real, such as a beautiful woman appearing and luring him and inviting him for sex. At another time, his two children had shown up, who had appeared as if they were bleeding to death, and were asking him for his help. There had been many such distractions on a daily basis. He knew it was always the jinn distracting him to stop the chilla. He knew if he stopped it or stepped out of the chilla, he would be killed by the jinn. Only the most determined could survive such distractions. He was very determined and continued going round and round the chilla without stopping or even being distracted. He recollected that no one except his grandfather had ever completed the chilla. Qabza Khan sat down next to the lighted candles, kept looking up and calling out to the jinn. He kept repeating the call to jinn.

"Oh, Iblis! I have kept my promise. I have done everything that was required of me. I have not had a shower or washed myself, or cleansed myself after relieving myself for the last 40 days. I have only eaten 'haram' meat of dead animals and of reptiles that are forbidden to eat. I have drunk my own urine. I have read the Quran backwards. I have done every single thing that would please you. I have worshipped you. Now, you keep your promise. You come to me and I will bow down to you in obedience. I will be your slave."

He had repeated the call for over three hours now without giving up, continuously looking up, when there was a sound of thunder and lightning. The lightning sometimes would be very severe, and one could clearly see the strikes between clouds, and the whole valley would light up. He did not stop his call and continued them at an even higher pitch.

Another severe strike occurred, which hit the tree tops in the adjacent mountain. Yet another strike, and it seemed to get closer. He knew and felt something was happening. Either he would be hit soon after the next few strikes, and die like many others before him who had tried to reach out to the jinn, or he would have succeeded in reaching out and contacting Iblis. The next strike hit the tree at the corner of the graveyard. The tree caught fire. He could feel the heat from the strike and the flame.

He felt the heat was moving closer to him. He felt very uneasy and frightened, and did not want to give up. He knew he had succeeded in reaching out, but was it a jinn or their king, Iblis, himself? Would it attack him and kill him like it had done to many others before? He kept on calling out to him.

He could feel something move around him, but he could not see anything. There was a gush of hot air that he could feel encircling him, but nothing was visible. He felt his hair stand up as if by an invisible magnetic force. He felt certain he had made contact with Iblis.

"Oh, my Lord. I worship you as my god. You were right in not bowing down to Adam. He has become a selfish creature, thinking out only for himself, as if he would live forever. He is greedy and he kills people like you knew he would. You were right. I want to be your soldier to get rid of this menace once and for all so we can prove that we were right. I want you to rule this earth again. Together, we can carry out our plan. I need your help to carry out this plan, which will support you to become king of the universe again. You have the energy and the strength, while I have only the capacity to plan."

He felt as if the flame had touched him. It was hot and almost burnt him. It was painful but he did not budge. He could see no one, but he was sure a jinn or Iblis himself was around him. He had succeeded so far. If only he could convince him to listen to him and agree to his plan.

He somehow felt as if the jinn wanted him to continue to speak. Perhaps then he would gain his trust and expose himself.

He continued to speak to the jinn, "Men have acquired the capability and they think they can make this a better world. There have been so many men preaching the goodness of God. Many in this world are doing humane work, healing the sick, helping the poor, feeding the hungry, housing the orphans, and so on. If they succeed, then you fail. They must be stopped!

"But the opposite is also true. Man has acquired destructive capability as well. They are our partners and friends and can destroy mankind many times over. There have been wars and thousands and millions have died in these wars. We need to continue with your agenda to have more wars so that mankind can destroy themselves. We can help them do it."

He felt a burning on his skin, he did not want to cry out with pain. He had to be determined to continue with his call. He felt as if Iblis was speaking to him. Was it real or was he hallucinating? He knew he was high on 'bhang', a local marijuana which grew wild in these mountains, one which always gave him visions. Somehow, this time, he felt it was real.

He felt like he heard something say, "What would you want me to do?"

For a second, he could not believe it. He had to act fast before he lost the moment and the jinn disappeared. He immediately went down in prostration, and said, "Oh great one. Oh, my lord, I know you can do many things. You are very knowledgeable. The end of times is very near when we would present our case against men. We need to do one big task together before the end of time."

"What do you want me to do?" he felt the jinn repeat himself.

"This task is too small for you. You are the king. I just need to talk to one of your warriors who is the strong one. With your blessings, we will both do it together. My plan and his strength."

"How can I trust you? If you are lying, I will cut you up in pieces and feed you to the wolves," again he had the feeling the voice was real and the jinn was speaking to him.

"Trust me! I am your humble slave. No one can do what I have done for you for the last 40 days. I can do anything else you want me to do to prove myself. You need my services as much as I need you. You have the power and I have the mind!"

There was silence for a moment. Then the jinn spoke as if putting him to test, "You will need to do something more for me which will make me happy."

Qabza fell down on his knees, put both his palms together as if begging, and pleaded, "Command what you would like me to do, and it will be done!"

The jinn spoke, "I want you to go and come back with the biggest sacrifice you can make. If you are able to do this, I will then be able to trust you and send you my strong warrior."

Jadoo knew God had asked Prophet Abraham for the biggest sacrifice, and Abraham was read to sacrifice his son for Him. The jinn wanted him to do the same for him.

Before he could reply, the thunder and lightning suddenly stopped, and it became all quiet. He looked up and could see the clouds clearing away, and the moon becoming visible. The whole valley was illuminated with moonlight. The jinn had gone.

He was overjoyed. He knew he was successful, and had done what none of the others were able to do in a long time. He now had to go and give the good news to the man who had asked him to do this.

He rushed down the mountain. It was a long walk. He had to find him and tell him the good news. He would get his reward, but he had already won a reward which was far more precious and worthy. But first, he had to deliver on his promise of accomplishing the task for the jinn. The biggest sacrifice he could make!

He reached the village. It was late night with no lights anywhere. The only illumination was from the moon. He reached the same spot where he had met the man. Where and how would he find him? But he was confident. If he could find and meet the jinn, then he could find him as well.

He kept searching for them. He knew the man was assigned for this task so he had to be around someplace.

He soon saw a group of men. They were all wearing a black cloak much like the one the man who had met him wore. He knew they had been watching him and perhaps been tracking his movements to the graveyard every day. After what had happened tonight, the thunderstorm and the lightening, they had a feeling that he could have contact with the jinn.

The group of men came close to him. They all looked devilish in their appearance.

The man in the middle, who looked like their leader, spoke out, "I can see you are back from your chilla and have survived the task. Have you succeeded in reaching out to the jinn?"

"Yes, my master. Not only that, but I have been able to do more than that. I have reached out to their leader, Iblis himself. He has agreed to send his strong warrior for what you want done."

The men looked at each other and smiled. They knew he could not be lying, as he would be beheaded if he lied. They felt they had finally succeeded in their task after a long time. However, they still wanted evidence if the aamil was telling the truth.

"We will need to see proof of your contact. Then we will let you know what we want the jinn to do after you have the jinn in your possession."

The leader took out a wad of local notes from his cloak pocket, and handed it to him. He had never seen so much money before. "This is just a small amount. After the task is done, we will give you double of this one. When can we see the jinn and talk to him?"

"My master, give me one day. The jinn has asked me for the biggest sacrifice. I will show it to him tomorrow night. You can accompany me to the graveyard then."

"We will meet you tomorrow here at sunset. However, you know your fate if you have lied."

"Yes, my master."

The group of men walked away.

There was a smile and a satisfied look on the leader's face, who thought to himself, *Our brothers have wasted so much time and lost so many lives going after small targets. We don't need an army of fighters or suicide bombers to fight our war if we could control only one jinn. One and only one! Then we can go even after the big targets.*

I am glad the emir finally agreed to our plan and financed it. With so many aamil working on capturing the jinn, I knew we would find one who was bound to succeed, and we have finally succeeded through this aamil. Now, I will not be killed by the emir for failure but honored and promoted to commander in place of Timur. The world will soon know of our power. Everyone will hear of us after we have destroyed Satan America. Then we will rule the world.

Plan

The older Harmeen with the long grey beard had sent an urgent message at noon that they should meet immediately after the mid-day prayers at the mosque. The others immediately knew the istikhara must have yielded some results. After all, their leader was a pious man, who prayed regularly five obligatory times, plus worshipped other times as well including tahajjud.

"I did an istikhara after early morning prayers today asking for His guidance. Then I went to sleep and saw a dream. The vision was very clear. Allah clearly wants us to do something."

"What is it?" the younger one asked enthusiastically.

"I saw in my dream a big stage and lots of farangi eating food. It was around sunset. I also saw a lot of books on the tables. Then I saw three birds swooping down on the party. The birds started dropping stones and the people started dying."

The younger one asked, "What does it mean?"

"Chapter 105 Verses 1 to 5 says Allah sent birds in flocks to pelt the Abyssinians with stones of petrified clay. The Abyssinians had tame elephants and were going to attack the Kaaba. They were very rich and possessed the treasures of the Queen of Sheba.

"Each bird held three stones: one in its beak and one in its each leg. The birds dropped these stones on the Abyssinians killing them. Allah also sent a severe wind that added to the speed and strength of the stones and caused the majority of the army to perish."

The younger one couldn't control his smile, "Then we must kill them all."

The old man nodded and replied with authority and confidence, "You must attack the conference when they are having dinner!"

Everyone agreed to the interpretation of the istikhara by the wise man. After all, an istikhara can never be wrong, as it is the message conveyed by God to man through the dream.

"You will altogether be three who will attack, as that is what the istikhara has shown. By following what God has ordained, you will be blessed and successful!

"We will make sure you are protected with the holy verses of God as well. You must wear the verses of protection inside your clothing. It will protect the bodies from bullets and stray shrapnel, should there be any, and no harm will come to you. You can easily find these printed vests from the kiosks at the local market."

They nodded, as it everyone knew most religious artifacts were commonly available at the local market.

"Please let us know how we can plan the attack."

The elderly man spoke with a level confidence as if he had it all planned already, "You will all come in the afternoon of the first day of the conference to the Farmers Market near the conference site in sector I-8. I will meet you there. Indeed, Allah has His ways and has facilitated us already. The catering to the conference is being done by the owner of one of the large shop at the market, who is a Harmeen."

He smiled and continued, "He is my follower and will do whatever I tell him. I will tell him that some of my visiting relatives need to earn some money for a few days, so will request him for employment for you serving food with his agency. He will not refuse me. You will then become part of his serving team to the conference. He does not know anything and will also not be able to suspect anything."

"What about the explosives? Where can we get those?" They had never bought explosives before.

"Don't worry. I will get them from a local who sells arms and explosives. It is a black-market business but he knows me well. I will get the explosives and bring them with me to the market. There is so much fresh produce that moves in and out of the market every day that hardly anything is checked by security. I will place the explosives in a basket covered with vegetable and wait for you.

"When you arrive, you will take transfer it into a serving pot and carry it with the food to be served at the conference venue which is very close. No one will suspect you. The vehicle will have the catering logo, and you will have identities as employees as well, so entry into the lawns of the venue will not be difficult, where the food will be served."

He paused to check if they had absorbed his instructions before proceeding further.

"You will take the food inside the conference site and plant the pot under the main table while laying out the dishes. You will then make your escape to a safe distance as you will have the remote control. When you press the button on the remote, the bomb will explode! There will be so much chaos that you will easily make your escape out of the conference venue. Nothing can go wrong."

He emphasized it again, "With the istikhara, nothing will and can go wrong. In Chapter 8, Al-Anfal, The Spoils of War, Verse 30, it very clearly says,

'But they plan, and Allah plans. And Allah is the best of planners.'"

All others nodded their heads in agreement. It was a fool proof plan. Allah's plan can never go wrong.

The old man smiled to himself. The bait had been planted. He would call up his superiors and convey the good news.

Islam and Numbers

The Conference on Islam and Science was to take place in the auditorium of the education ministry in Sector I-8 of Islamabad. Sector I-8 was a defined education zone and included many schools, colleges, and universities. It was a considerable distance away from the city center and the high security zones of Islamabad.

There were many commercial entities in the vicinity, including the farmers market, where a large number of shoppers came to do their weekly shopping. As there were no offices needing high security in this area, there was no checking of automobiles or of individuals and families by the police as they entered or left this sector.

Samir read his morning prayers, and his daily 'dose' of Ayat-ul-Kursi and the four Qul prior to his breakfast. He knew Shaday must also be praying for his safety as always.

The phone rang. He wondered who could call this early in the morning. It was his mother. She was over 85 and lived in their ancestral home in Hyderabad. She always used to pray for his welfare and safety like most mothers do. He was surprised to receive her unexpected call this early in the morning. She was somehow worried about him as he had not called to talk to her for a few days, and she was worried. She had called him specially to give him her blessings.

"I am all right, Mom, just a little too busy that is why I could not call you for the last few days," Samir apologized.

Samir's mother would always have the same advice for him, "Please make sure you read your prayers. Thank God always for whatever He has given you, and always ask for forgiveness. I have a strange feeling today that made me call you and give you my blessings. May you be happy and always have the protection of Allah."

Mothers have strange vibes as if they are connected to the supernatural, Samir thought. But prayers by his mother meant a lot to him. He always prayed for her health and long life. He was whatever he was today because of her. He owed her a lot.

He remembered that Baba Sain had asked him to wear the amulet on his right arm, and the aqeeq ring on his right small finger. He did not believe in amulets and never wore amulets or rings in his life, and was therefore a little hesitant in doing so. However, he decided there was no harm in carrying them with him in his pocket.

While driving, he remembered what Baba Sain had told him: to read the 99 names of Allah for protection and blessings. He took the rosary from where it was hanging on the rear-view mirror and started reciting the names of God. Calling out to God would always protect. His mind went back to what the sajjada nasheen at Bari Imam had warned him of: the danger to his life, but had immediately added that Bari Imam will protect you.

He wondered why his mother had called him so early in the morning out of the blue. Were all these connected? He had this strange feeling of imminent danger, but was not sure if he was just scared or what. He, however, felt an aura of protection because of his mother's call and his own readings of the protective verses. Every other protection was only secondary.

His phone rang. It was his friend, Mike. Mike would never call him that early in the morning unless he had something urgent and important to convey. He would never beat around the bush.

"Samir, I have just heard from my friends that there is possibly an attack planned by a certain militant group at the conference which is taking place at your premises today. I would recommend you should immediately pull out and cancel the conference!"

Samir was not surprised. Mike seemed to have his ways of getting information from the agencies. Mike was a patriotic US citizen and of course had American interests but he always stood out for his friends.

"Mike, thanks for calling. I have been warned and informed of this danger by others as well who do not have intel like you do but rely on something which you don't have: their mystical powers. This may be something new to you, but somehow today, I feel more protected than I ever could feel by increasing security around me. I will tell you about it one day when we meet."

"I am concerned for your safety. Please ensure you have full security. Take care, my friend. My phone is right next to me!"

Samir arrived at the auditorium well in time. There were about 200 attendees. Roughly one third were women. Many had arrived from various Muslim countries, including the US, Egypt, Turkey, Malaysia, UAE, Qatar, Iran, and Saudi Arabia. One could see the hostility between the Saudis and the Iranians over their differing view on Islamic practices. One could imagine they both would be presenting their own viewpoint. The majority of attendees were from Pakistan as was expected. Most of them were staying at hotels or guest houses in the vicinity of the conference. The ministry had arranged for local transport.

The conference was to run for two days. The first day evening was to be the grand dinner. There were two keynote speakers on the first day. One was a leading professor of mathematics from an Egyptian university and the other one was a science scholar from a private university in Turkey. He was also the author of a book that had discussed numbers in the Quran. Allama was to be the keynote speaker on the second day.

The conference opened on time. Allama was asked to recite the opening invocation. He started by reciting the first revelation to the Prophet, from Chapter 96, Al-Alaq or The Clot:

'Read in the name of thy Lord and Cherisher, Who created
Created man, out of a mere clot of congealed blood
Proclaim! And thy Lord is Most Bountiful
He Who taught the use of the pen
Taught man that which he knew not.'

Samir thought the verse was so appropriate for an academic conference of this nature. He then gave the welcome address.

In his opening statement, he pointed out that God says in the Quran that one should not accept any information unless they have verified it for themselves. God has given humans the gift of hearing, seeing, and thinking, and they are responsible for using them. The Quran and its interpretation is for men of understanding.

He said the theme of the conference is to examine the beliefs in Islam in the context of science. Be it evolution, or the big bang, or the Prophet's journey to the heavens, there has to be a logical explanation for everything which is not a contradiction. The religious scholars have not been able to explain it since they are not rehearsed in science or math. On the other hand, the scientists, mathematicians, and astronomers may be in a better position to at least touch the tip of the iceberg, however they were less knowledgeable on the teachings of the Quran. There is still very limited knowledge today, as science has only evolved rapidly over the last 50 or so years due to many scientific breakthroughs.

He said the early ancestors, homo erectus, first appeared in Africa possibly about two to three million years ago, the earth itself is estimated to be about 4.5 billion years old, while the universe is estimated to be between 12 to 14 billion years old. There is so much time gap in between which even science has been unable to explain.

"Was Adam an homo erectus?" he asked.

"Let me also add that this is a conference that is based on theories in Islam and science that already exist in the literature. These have been around and are scattered all over the net. This conference is not based on presentation of new research. The idea of this conference is to put most of everything together, or the important ones together, on one platform, and deliberate on it how they can make sense.

"Let this be an open discussion. I believe in open discussion and an open forum. The freedom to express oneself is the cornerstone of academic life."

"The opening session of the conference is confined to numbers, as some of my mathematician friends say, God is a mathematician!

"The following session will be on Islam and Science."

With these opening words, Samir opened the conference.

The first invited keynote was a mathematician from Egypt. His presentation was on the importance of numbers in human history. He said he believes God has made everything according to a mathematical model. Mathematicians and astrologers have tried over the years to understand the mathematical codes of the universe. Using numbers, they have also tried to predict future events. While some numbers have been interpreted, and form the basis of many mystical arts like numerology, tarot and kabbala, and in the use of amulets and in magic, but many more numbers and their sequence still lie un-interpreted. Many have used these numbers, and their combinations, to control events and control the destiny of the world. Man is still trying to understand numbers in their quest to control the world.

He said in Islam, odd numbers hold importance in Islam. Certain numbers are important; however, they are only man's interpretation. Some of these numbers include numbers 1, 5, 7, 19, and 99! On the other hand, 786 being an even number is also important.

The number 99 holds importance because there are 99 names of God in the Quran.

Because of that, he said the Muslim rosary has 99 beads, which enables a prayer to repeat names of God, or recite other prayers 99 times each, or its multiples.

He said another basic number of importance is 5, which is a number of balance. There are five pillars of Islam. These are 'shahadah', meaning sincerely reciting the Muslim profession of faith, 'salat', that is performing ritual prayers in the proper way 'five' times each day, 'zakat', which is the paying of alms or charity tax to benefit the poor and the needy, 'sawm', fasting during the month of Ramadan, and 'haj', which is pilgrimage to Mecca for those who can afford it.

He added other than odd numbers, even numbers also hold significance in Islam. He said another significant number in Islam is 786, found written on top at the opening of most books, documents, agreements, and letters.

The Arabic letters of the opening phrase of the Quran 'Bismillah-ar-Rahman-ar-Rahim', meaning, 'In the name of Allah, the most Merciful, the most Beneficent', sums up to the numerical value 786 using the abjad numerals, thus explaining its significance.

The abjad numerals are a decimal number system where the 28 letters of the Arabic alphabet are assigned numerical values. They have been used in the Arabic-speaking world since before the eighth century when Arabic numerals were adopted. In modern Arabic, the word abjadiyah means 'alphabet' in general. In the abjad system, the first letter of the Arabic alphabet represents 1; the second letter represents 2, etc. Individual letters also represent 10s and 100s.

He then switched gears and said he will now speak about a miracle of number pairs in the Quran. He said it is mathematical genius. No human over 1,500 years ago could have thought about it if they had conceived such a book.

"An Islamic scholar has discovered equality in the number of times some words are mentioned in the Quran. I only quote what he has presented on the net, and have not verified it myself:

"The number of times the word woman and man both appear in the Quran is 24, projecting equality between the two sexes.

"Life is mentioned 115 times and so is the hereafter

"Angels and Satan are both mentioned 88 times

"Life and Death are mentioned 145 times each.

"Other pairings include Benefit and Corrupt, 50 each

"People and Messengers, 50 each

"King of Devil Iblis 11, and so is Seeking Refuge from Iblis

"Calamity is 75 and so is Thanks

"Spending and Satisfaction are 73 each

"People who are Mislead and Dead People are 17 each

"Those who follow Muslim practices, and Jihad are 41 each

"Gold is 8 and so is Easy Life

"Magic and Misleading are 60 each

"Zakat or Muslim Tax and Blessings of Wealth are 32 each

"Mind and Enlightenment are 49 each

"Tongue and Sermon, 25 each

"Speaking Publicly and Publicizing, 18 each

"Hardship and Patience, 114 each

"Prophet Mohammed and his Teachings, 4 each

"Hardship and Patience 114 each."

He continued, "Also note that Worshiping is mentioned 5 times, which is the number of times Muslims pray each day.

"Month are mentioned 12 times, and Day 365 times

"What is even more astonishing is that Sea is mentioned 32 times and Land 13 times, which gives a ratio of 71% to 29%, which is the water-land surface area on earth. This is something which was only proved in the last century!"

He received a big round of applause, as many had not even heard of this pairing. One could see the participants exchanging short murmurs of approval or astonishment.

In the discussion session, one participant pointed out that the usage of 786 is extremely popular in South Asia as a talisman. However, some Muslims consider using 786 as 'bidaah', or an innovation in religion, for which there is no room, also arguing that this numbering system has been taken from Jewish sources and Kabbalah. He said others claim it is from Hinduism as Lord Hari Krishna can also be linked to 786. Yet, other Hindus say 786 written in Sanskrit from right to left, then flipped around like a mirror image, and connected calligraphically, will look like an equivalent of 'Om' of the Dharma, or India based religions. He added that is why many Muslims refrain from writing 786.

Another participant pointed out that the number five holds other Islamic significance as well.

Panj-Tan, or 'The Five', also called the 'People of the Cloak, refers to the Prophet Muhammad; his daughter, Fatimah; his cousin and son-in-law Ali; and his two grandsons Hasan and Hussain. It is one of the foundations of the Shia conception of the Imamah, which states that patrilineal descendants of Muhammad's daughter have a special divine spiritual leadership over the Muslim community. They are also called the 'People of the House', or the family of Prophet Muhammad.

The second speaker spoke on the number 19, which in numerology adds up to 10, and reduces to 1. In Islam, it is considered a very important and a mystery number. He requested additional time for his presentation and said he would also use the whiteboard to make his points clear.

He said 19, which is also an odd number, represents a very significant number for Muslims because this number is specifically mentioned in the Quran. In 74:30, it says, 'over it are 19', the number 19 referring to angels appointed to guard hell. The Quran continues with 'We have fixed their number only as a trial for the unbelievers'. Based on this verse in the Quran, he said Muslims claim that 19 is a miraculous number and mathematicians have made many attempts to prove it.

He continued that the mathematical analysis of the Quranic verses show the number 19 as a common denominator. Because of this, many refer to the number 19 as the mathematical number of the Quran. This has been researched by many Islamic scholars.

"The numerical value of the Arabic word 'Wahid', which means one, is 19, as $19=1+9=10=1+0=1$. Thus, number 19 represents the Oneness of God which is a very important doctrine in Islam."

He then went on to signify the importance of the number 19 in our solar system.

"Astronomically, when the Earth rotates once around the sun, it revolves 365 times around itself, which is one year, and the moon will have revolved around itself and the earth 12 times. After a year, the Earth returns to the same point from which it started rotating around the sun. However, at the end of this time, the moon will not have returned to its starting point. The moon and the Earth meet at the same starting point once every 19 years. So, when the Earth has rotated around the sun 19 times and the moon has rotated around the Earth around 235 times, an ecliptic cycle is completed. This ecliptic cycle which occurs once every 19 years has been scientifically used to match the solar and lunar years. Hence, astronomers give significance to this ecliptic cycle and the number 19.

"Every 19 years then, we have the rotations of the Earth and the moon coincide with each other when they return to the same co-ordinate.

"Hence, the solar system runs according to the number of the Quran!"

He added, "Also the word 'year' occurs in the Quran 7 times and 'years' occurs 12 times. Thus, the total count is 19 times."

"The number of letters that are in the opening phrase of the Quran and of most chapters, '*In the name of Allah, the most Compassionate, most Merciful*' is 19. The first word is repeated 19 times in Quran, the second Allah is repeated 2698 times, which is 19 x 142, the third Rahman is repeated 57 times, which is 19 x 3, and the fourth Rahim is repeated 114 times, which is 19 x 6 in the Quran. So, the root words that make up the opening phrase are repeated 2,888 times in the Quran, which is equal to 19 x 152."

He continued, "As mentioned above, the first verse in the Quran has 19 Arabic letters. This same exact verse is placed atop the first 8 chapters. Chapter 9 does not have the opening statement. The missing 'Bismillah' in Chapter 9 is compensated for in Chapter 27, and 27 is 8 plus 19. Chapter 19 in the Quran is the first of the three Chapter in which the word Allah occurs 8 times."

"Additionally, 29 Chapters in the Quran are initialed by letters that prefix the chapters in which they occur. The letters in these chapters also conform to the mathematical system based on the number 19. For example, the total frequency of the letter 'Q' in Chapter 50 is 57 or 19×3."

He went to the smart board and started writing some numbers and continued, "According to Quranic code in the Wiki, the total number of verses in the Quran is 6,346, or 19×334. Also note that $6 + 3 + 4 + 6 = 19$."

"The Bismillah occurs 114 times, despite its conspicuous absence from Chapter 9. This is because it occurs twice in Chapter 27. Note that 114 is 19 times 6. Also, from the missing Bismillah of Chapter 9 to the extra Bismillah of Chapter 27, there are precisely 19 Chapters. It follows that the total of the Chapter numbers from 9 to 27, that is $9 + 10 + 11 + 12 +...+ 26 + 27$ is 342, or 19×18. This total 342 also equals the number of words between the two Bismillah of Chapter 27, and 342 = 19×18."

He continued, "The famous first revelation to the Prophet, which is placed in Chapter 96, Al-Alaq or The Clot, reads, in the first five verses:

'Read in the name of thy Lord and Cherisher, Who created
Created man, out of a mere clot of congealed blood
Proclaim! And thy Lord is Most Bountiful
He Who taught the use of the pen
Taught man that which he knew not'

"It consists of 19 words. This 19-worded first revelation consists of 76 letters which is 19×4. Chapter 96, first in the chronological sequence, consists of 19 verses. This first chronological chapter is placed atop the last 19 chapters.

"Chapter 96 consists of 304 Arabic letters, and 304 equals 19×16.

"The last revelation, Chapter 110, Al-Nasr, or The Help, consists of 19 words. The first verse of the last revelation consists of 19 letters.

"Fourteen different Arabic letters form 14 different sets of Quranic initials, and prefix 29 Chapters. These numbers add up to 14 + 14 + 29 = 57 = 19×3.

"The total of the 29 Chapter numbers where the Quranic initials occur is 2 + 3 + 7 +...+ 50 + 68 = 822, and 822 + 14, where 14 are the 14 sets of initials, equals 836, or 19×44.

"Between the first initialed chapter, which is Chapter 2, and the last initialed chapter, which is Chapter 68, there are 38 un-initialed chapters, which is 19×2.

"Between the first and last initialed chapter, there are 19 sets of alternating initialed and 'un-initialed' chapters. The Quran mentions 30 different numbers: 1, 2, 3, 4, 5, 6, 7, 8, 9, 10, 11, 12, 19, 20, 30, 40, 50, 60, 70, 80, 99, 100, 200, 300, 1,000, 2,000, 3,000, 5,000, 50,000, and 100,000. The sum of these numbers is 162,146, which equals 19×8534.

"No wonder many think of God as a mathematician!"

He paused for a moment to let that information sink in, and then continued, "In addition to the mathematical aspects of the literary aspects of the Quran, there are also allegedly other dimensions to this system. It is said, for example, that when recited, the first chapter of the Quran, generally known as 'The Key', results in the lips touching a total of 19 times on the letters B and M. 15 for the letter M and 4 for the letter B. Additionally, it has been observed that based on geometrical values used during the time of the Quran and prior, B has a value of 2 and M has a value of 40. The total sum of these 19 occurrences thus comes out to 608 or 19×32."

He paused, and then continued, "19 is significant not just in the Quran, but biologically also, the number 19 is significant. The number of bones in our hand is 19. In mathematics, 1 and 9 are like A and Z in English. They signify the first and the last.

"Zero independently has no value. Next to our hand, there are 8 bones in our wrist. 19 is the 8th prime number: 2, 3, 5, 7, 11, 13, 17, and 19."

He closed his argument with another example, "There are other astronomical miracles too relating to number 19. The light from the Sun reaches earth in 499 seconds. This is a scientific average as the distance between the Sun and Earth changes. 499 seconds is 8 minutes and 19 seconds.

"I thank the organizers for allowing me the extra time, and thank you all for your patience as it was a lot of information crammed within a short time."

The crowd was stunned with all these revelations regarding the number 19. One participant from the back raised his hand, and added that the number 19 is considered a powerful number by the terrorists too, as from the reported news, there were 19 who participated in the 9/11 attack. Likewise, there had been many incidents where the number of attackers were reported to be 19! Does that mean the terrorists believe that the number 19 is so sacred that it cannot be defeated?

The speaker disagreed and said that that any sacred number used for any evil design will reverse the effects. That is why despite the attacks, the terrorists could not carry further their evil designs and were all killed themselves.

Another participant pointed out that in kabbalah, 19 is the number of spiritual activity, and in tarot, it represents the Sun, and all the goodness associated with it, such as happiness, honor, success, and courage.

The third speaker spoke on the significance of the number seven in Islam.

He said that the number seven has a very high significance in Islam.

There are seven verses in the opening chapter of the Quran.

While performing the rituals of the pilgrimage in Mecca, whether for haj or for umrah, the pilgrims walk around the black cube Kaaba seven times.

He said during pilgrimage, the pilgrims also walk or run between the two mounds called Mount Safa and Mount Marwah seven times. This is a reminder of Bibi Hajira, called Hagar in the Bible, and the mother of Prophet Ismail, when according to Islamic beliefs, she desperately ran between the two hills in search for water to save her dying son. An angel appeared who hit the ground from where a spring gushed out saving the lives of mother and child. This spring water is called zamzam, which is considered the holiest of all waters by all Muslims, who carry it back home in bottles and cans to feed the sick for health, and to sprinkle it on their cloth coffins so as to receive solace in life after death.

"Pilgrims are also required to throw seven pebbles at each of the three walls representing the devil. The 'stoning of the devil' is performed at Mina, just outside of Mecca."

He continued, "In Chapter 18 of the Quran, in Al-Kaif, we can read about the seven sleepers. This story is also in the Bible in which a group of youths hid inside a cave outside the city of Ephesus around the year 250 CE, to escape a persecution. God had sent Angel Gabriel to reveal the story of the seven sleepers to Muhammad."

"There are seven heavens according to the Quran. The lowest heaven has lights and is fully protected from any evil, while there are six other heavens that we cannot see."

He continued, "According to the Quran, Prophet Muhammad went on a journey to all seven heavens in a single night where he met seven prophets. This has been described as both a physical and spiritual journey for all Muslims. Muhammad travelled 'from the sacred Mosque to the farthest mosque' according to the Quran. Then according to the narration in the Hadith, Muhammad travelled on the steed Buraq, a winged horse, literally the plural of light, Barq, where he toured the seven heavens.

"Each of these heavens are associated with certain prophets, according to the beliefs. First with Adam, second with Yahya, who is John the Baptist in the Bible, third with Yusuf, who is Joseph, fourth with Akhnukh, who is Enoch, fifth with Harun, who is Aaron, sixth with Musa, who is Moses, and seventh with Ibrahim, who is Abraham. Prophet Muhammad leads all these seven Prophets in a prayer. The Dome of the Rock mosque, from where the Prophet ascended, is separated into seven sections in honor of this experience.

"He is then taken to Sidrat al-Muntaha—a holy tree that even Gabriel was not allowed to pass. According to Islamic tradition, God instructed Muhammad that Muslims must pray 50 times per day; however, Muhammad asked for a reduction, until finally it was reduced to five times per day."

Why did he not request for even lesser number of times every day, Samir wondered.

The speaker went on, "There are also the seven gates of hell according to the Quran, each layered above the other, and increasing in the order of severity of punishment. They are called, from the first to the seventh, Jahannam, Ladha, Saqar,

Al Hutamah, Jaheem, Sa'eer, and Al-Haawiyah, within which 'there is an appropriate punishment for each inhabitant' according to the Quran. According to the beliefs, those who enter Al-Haawiyah will never come out! The Quran says, 'The Haawiyah will embrace him like a mother embraces her child. And what will make you know what Al-Hawiyah is? It is a kindled fire burning hot.' It will be so hot that the breeze of fire it lets out will be so powerful that all of the fires in the other levels of hell will seek refuge in God from it."

Samir recalled even the Jews make mention of seven compartments of hell, just as there are seven divisions of heaven. However, Dante in The Inferno depicts hell as nine concentric circles of suffering located within the Earth instead of seven! Seven or nine, within earth or in space, it did not matter as there was certain hell for the unbelievers! But would all unbelievers really be sent to hell? He was not sure.

The speaker continued on to associate the number seven to cultural practices. "'Aqiqa' is a Muslim custom in honor of a new born child. The tradition varies from culture to culture and region to region. One of the beliefs is that when the new born child is seven days old, the hair is shaved off and the child is given a name. Immediately after the child has received a name, sheep are slaughtered. Two sheep or goats are sacrificed if the baby is a boy and one sheep if the baby is a girl. The numbers vary also according to belief.

"The sufis also hold seven in great reverence, in which they have seven stages towards enlightenment, which are the valleys that one has to travel through to unite with their beloved.

"In other religions too in South Asia, seven is a strong number. The Hindus strongly believe in numerology. In addition to many other numbers, they also strongly believe in seven. They believe in the seven planes each above and below the earth. They have seven chakras. They believe in seven levels of consciousness as well. They have seven vows of marriage which they take with the seven 'pheras' or encircling of the fire," The Tibetan Buddhists believe the soul rests in an intermediate stage after death for 49 days, which is 7 times 7.

He ended with a light note, "There are also seven days in a week, and seven colors of the rainbow, though not physically correct, and the pH 7 being neutral, which is what maintains life!

"And on top, there are seven wonders of the world, and seven volumes of the Harry Potter series!"

Everyone smiled.

An attendee commented the number seven is also associated to black magic. Before Islam in Babylon and Damascus, people used to worship seven 'stars', including the Sun, Moon, Saturn, Jupiter, and Mars among others, and the old gates of Damascus also have these seven stars on them. There were no comments from the audience and the next speaker was called in.

He spoke about 666.

"Some think that the number 666 is associated with evil and danger. This mostly followed from a Hollywood movie, The Omen, in which 666 was identified as the 'Number of the Beast'. In Christian theology, the number of the Beast, 666, in Revelation 13:18 has given rise to much controversy, and may refer only to the numerical value of the letters.

"However, it is a trick of Iblis to prevent the people approaching 666 because Iblis knows it is a sacred number.

"Six is the first perfect number in mathematics. Perfect numbers by definition are numbers that the sum of their factors equal to the same number. 6 is divisible by 3, 2, and 1. Thus, 3, 2, and 1 are factors of 6. Six is the only number that the sum of its factors and also the product of its factors equal to the same number. In the Quran, it says that God created the heavens and the earth and all in between in 6 days. The biological life is based on Carbon which has 6 electrons. The numerical value of the word Allah is also 66, which is $1 + 30 + 30 + 5$."

It was not a compelling argument, and a few seemed to disagree.

One got up and after turning around to face the crowd, said in a loud voice that he was convinced 666 is the sign of the reappearance of Iblis, which will reflect the end of the world. He said 666 will be etched as a natural tattoo on the forehead of a person who will be Dajjal. A number of participants nodded their head agreeing with him.

One got up to support the previous person and added that when the number 666 will appear in the sky, it will be the sign of doomsday. Another agreed, and said 666 will actually represent the date and time the world will end: June 6 at 6 A.M.

Samir wondered how people had mixed myth with facts, and probably 666 had no meaning or interpretation!

There were no questions asked.

The next speaker was yet another mathematician, who spoke on the Fibonacci sequence and the 'Golden Ratio'.

He used his laptop and the presentation was projected onto the large screen.

"I am going to talk about God's number. But before I do that, let me give a very basic tutorial on the Fibonacci sequence.

"The Fibonacci sequence is named after an Italian mathematician Fibonacci. The Fibonacci number series is characterized by the fact that every number after the first two is the sum of the two preceding ones. The sequence goes like

1, 1, 2, 3, 5, 8, 13, 21, 34, 55, 89, 144…

"Fibonacci Day is celebrated on November 23, because it has the digits '1, 1, 2, 3' which is part of the sequence.

"When one makes squares with those widths, it becomes a nice spiral.

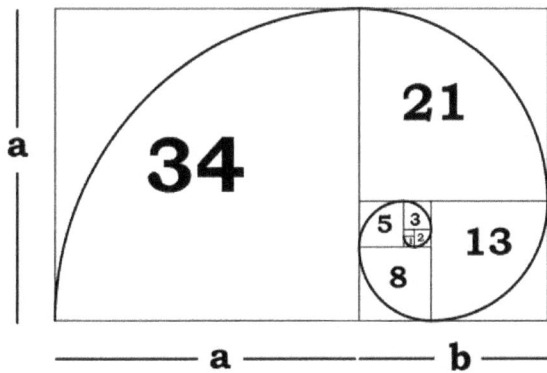

He paused for a moment to let the spiral sink in, and then continued.

"Most natural patterns, including life, follow the Golden Ratio."

He continued, "What is the Golden Ratio? When the ratio of any two successive Fibonacci numbers is taken, we get what is now called the Golden Ratio. It is the Greek 'φ', or phi, with a value of approximately 1.618034...

"Phi is also found by dividing a line into two parts so that the longer part divided by the smaller part is also equal to the whole length divided by the longer part. In other words:

$a/b = (a+b)/a = 1.6180339887498948420...$

"Phi is also the ratio of the circumference of a circle to its diameter.

"Phi is usually rounded off to 1.618.

"God has used Phi throughout the universe and in humans and plants!

He continued, "Phi has been used in the architecture of many ancient buildings, like the pyramids and the parthenon. In the pyramids, the ratio of the base to the height is roughly 1.5717, which is close to phi."

"Plato considered the Golden Ratio to be the most universally binding of mathematical relationships. Euclid linked the Golden Ratio to the construction of a pentagram.

He continued, "What is very well-known by the non-scientific community after the bestseller fiction, The Da Vinci Code, is that the divine proportion was picked up by Leonardo da Vinci. Da Vinci used the Golden Ratio in most of his paintings, including the Last Supper. The Golden Ratio also appears in da Vinci's Vitruvian Man.

"It also appears in the Mona Lisa. In addition, Leonardo da Vinci, other artists who have used the Golden Ratio include Michelangelo, Raphael, Rembrandt, Seurat, and Salvador Dal."

He paused for a moment to let the artistic information sink in.

"Now, I will tell you an even more interesting aspect of the Phi and the Golden Ratio in Islam. According to Islamic scholars, the Golden Ratio of the world is the city of Mecca."

The crowd was enthusiastic to hear more. Some even leaned forward on their seats.

"The ratio of distance between Mecca and North Pole to the distance between Mecca and South Pole is 1.618. Likewise, the ratio of the distance between South Pole and Mecca to the distance between both poles is again 1.618. The proportion of the western elongation of Mecca to the perimeter of the earth on this very latitude is 1.6. So, Mecca is the Golden Ratio point of the Earth according to Muslim scholars."

One could hear the exclamations of astonishment from the crowd.

He continued, "There is another aspect: In Chapter 3 Verse 96 is the location of the word Mecca in the Quran. The number of letters till the word Becca, which is the Arabic name for Mecca, are 29, and the number of letters after Becca are 18. The ratio is again 1.6. It places Mecca in the exact location in the verse as it does on earth."

"There is even more evidence of the mathematical miracles and the Golden Ratio in the Quran."

He went to the smart board to scribble on it, "If one were to add the chapter number to the total number of versus it contains, and separate these totals by even and odd numbers, one finds an equal number of evens and odds!

"Moreover, the total of the chapter numbers added together is equal to the total of the odd numbers added together, and the total number of verses added together is equal to the total number of evens added together.

"What is even more miraculous is if one adds all the repetitive numerical values, which equals 7,906, to the sum of the non-repetitive numerical values, which equals to 4885, and take their ratio, the final answer comes to 1.618, which is phi or the golden ratio!"

The crowd exclaimed! They were impressed with the information presented.

"All these evidences confirm the mathematical power of Allah, and the Quran sent by Allah 1,400 years ago, which is not found in any other holy book. It shows the uniqueness and the truthfulness of the Quran!"

Had God really created everything according to numbers and hidden these numbers in the Quran for men of understanding to decipher, Samir wondered.

Following the presentation, a few points were raised.

One pointed out that some scholars have a different viewpoint, arguing that Mecca is not at the location of the Golden Ratio. Many other cities can be made to appear at the location of the Golden Ratio.

Another said some Hebrew scholars disagree that Becca refers to Mecca. They claim no Hebrew prophet after Prophet Abraham, including Lot, Moses, Aaron, Jacob, Joseph, David, Solomon, John, and even Jesus have ever stepped into Mecca to perform pilgrimage, in spite of the fact that Becca is mentioned in Psalm 84. They claim Becca, which means to weep, is a place in Palestine.

A third one agreed saying Mecca is also referred to as Mecca in Chapter 48 Verse 24, along with Becca in Chapter 3 Verse 96, so clearly, they are two different cities.

He seemed to have a point. No one made any comment agreeing or disagreeing.

The last speaker for the math session spoke on numbers in national symbols of Islamic countries.

He said numbers have been used in national symbols as well. He first displayed the Pakistan Flag.

"The Pakistan Flag has a five-pointed star for the five pillars of Islam, and a crescent which symbolizes Islam. Its color is green which is the favorite color of the Prophet Muhammad and symbolizes Islam as well. The Prophet Muhammad mostly wore a green cloak and turban, and his writings are full of references to the color. In addition, Quran says that the dwellers of the paradise will be wearing green clothes."

Next, he displayed the Turkish Flag.

"The Turkish Flag also has a 5-pointed star, as well as a crescent for Islam. Red is the blood of the martyrs. Turkish national anthem has 571 syllables and 1,453 words. 571 is the year of the birth of the Prophet, and 1,453 is the year of the conquest of Istanbul."

His next projection was the Saudi Flag. "Likewise, the Saudi Flag is green as well, with an inscription of the 'shahada' or 'kalima', as commonly referred to, and is the basic acknowledgement of being a Muslim, on it. It also has a curved sword which was added in 1902."

Finally, he displayed the ISIS Flag. "On the other hand, the ISIS flag is black and uses the 'shahada' as well in white, but with 'Mohammed is the messenger of God' in a white circle with black writing. This is meant to resemble the Prophet's seal. It is also a symbol in Islamic eschatology, heralding the advent of the Mahdi, who will conquer the world. According to the Hadith, the emergence of the Mahdi would be signaled by black flags originating from Khorasan, and it will be the flag of the army that will fight Dajjal. ISIS has capitalized on the Hadith and the black flags to win the support of the Muslims worldwide. I am sure soon they will be declaring their leader as the Mahdi!"

The speaker had made a very important point, that of the emergence of the Mahdi from among the leadership of ISIS. If it did happen, would the Muslim world believe and follow them? Samir questioned himself. Would they resort to some other evidence to support their claim, one that the Muslims would believe?

There were no questions asked.

"Gentlemen and Ladies, we will reconvene after lunch to look at the aspects of Science in Islam."

Islam and Science

Samir welcomed the participants to the session after lunch which was to be on Islam and Science. He said the golden era of Islam was considered between the years 800 and 1,100, when Baghdad was the center of civilization, and Europe was in the dark ages. The new world America was not discovered yet by the Europeans.

There were significant developments that took place in the fields of Algebra, Astronomy, Algorithms, Medicine, and Navigation. He reminded the participants that both Algebra and Algorithms were Arabic words. Al-Khwarizmi in the 12th century is recognized as the father of Algebra.

Knowledge preservation and development was encouraged. The Islamic Civilization not only preserved Greek and Roman civilization, but studied and adopted it. Aristotle and Socrates were people that were looked up to by the Islamic scholars. The Muslim scholars passed on the knowledge to Europe during the Renaissance of 1300–1600 CE.

Samir gave a well-prepared talk, "The University of al-Qarawiyyin at Fez in Morocco, established in 859 CE, is the oldest and the first degree awarding educational institution in the world according to both UNESCO and Guinness World Records. It is still operating 1,200 years later.

"The first full-fledged hospital in the world was built around 800 CE in Baghdad.

"Ibn Sahl in 984 CE set out his understanding of how curved mirrors and lenses bend and focus light. Ibn Sahl is credited with first discovering the law of refraction. Ibn al-Haytham is known as the Father of Modern Optics. He wrote the first book on optics in 1027 CE, which lay the groundwork for the basic theories on optics and lasers.

"Then everything stopped, and Islamic countries started reverting to the dark ages. Why?

"The Muslim leaders became the biggest enemies of science and math. Imam Ghazali said playing with numbers is satanic. He associated math with the devil.

"Many scholars believed that the earth was fixed and does not rotate. A leading scholar from an Islamic university wrote, "If the earth is rotating, as they claim, the countries, the mountains, the trees, the rivers, and the oceans will have no bottom and the people will see the eastern countries move to the west, and the western countries move to the east. The earth is flat, and anyone claiming it is round is an atheist deserving punishment.

"When the printing press was developed 230 years ago, a well-respected Islamic leader gave a fatwa that the press is forbidden in Islam. As a result, we lost out on books, newspapers, literature, and exchange of knowledge.

"When the plane was invented, it was classified as haram due to its reaching heights. No one was allowed to reach out to the skies so as to reach God. They associated it with the Tower of Babel.

"When the radio was developed and the first transmission began, it was associated with the voice of Satan.

"Recently, a psychologist from an Islamic country claimed, 'Women who drive cars suffer from ovarian problems and rolled up pelvises giving rise to congenitally defective babies.'

"Yet, another Islamic scholar from a neighboring country said, 'Many women who do not dress modestly lead young men astray, corrupt their chastity, and spread adultery in the society, 'which increases earthquakes.'"

"And in our own country Pakistan, a leading Islamic figure said 'DNA test should not be used as evidence in rape cases'.

"Even today, many religious fanatics object to the use of camera, and of TV. They associate it as playing with the creation of God, as if man is trying to create another being. They forbid the taking of pictures.

"Blood transfusion is considered taboo with these fundos. So is polio vaccination. While we have still not made significant advances in genetic engineering, in human cloning, in 3D printing of human organs, there are already being opposed to by the religious fanatics.

"As a result, the growth of science in Islamic countries was stunted. As a result, out of a total of 325 Nobel Prizes given in Sciences so far, only two from Muslim countries have won these prizes: Dr. Ahmed Zewail in Chemistry of Egypt, and Dr. Abdus Salam in Physics of Pakistan. The irony is that Pakistan does not even count Dr. Abdus Salam as a Muslim. Both were awarded the prizes as a result of work they did outside their country of birth.

"Dr. Salam had emphasized that the Quran encourages us, sometimes even commands us, to reflect on the order of nature, and that is what science now is capable of doing, in a way never before possible.

"So, let the presentations begin!"

The keynote for the afternoon session was a science scholar from a university in Turkey. He noted that there have been many articles, and videos on YouTube, that as science progressed, there was no need to have a God who could have created the universe or this earth of life itself. The theories of evolution were getting stronger and introduced in every science subject and textbooks.

He said, however, a leading scholar from the West has argued that God's existence is necessary if scientific theories have to prevail.

"Even the great astronomer Carl Sagan wrote that there were two necessary criteria for a planet to support life: The right kind of star, and a planet the right distance from the star.

"According to Dr. Sagan, given the roughly one octillion, which is one followed by 24 zeros, planets in the universe, there should have been one septillion, one followed by 21 zeros, capable of supporting life. With such spectacular odds, scientists were of the optimistic opinion in 1960s that SETI, or the 'Search for Extra-Terrestrial Intelligence' should turn out something soon. With a vast radio telescope network, scientists listened for signals that represented coded intelligence, and listened, and as years passed, there was complete deafening silence."

He continued, "As our knowledge of the universe increased, it became clearer that there were more factors needed for life, let alone intelligent life, than Sagan supposed. Two grew to 20 which grew to over 50 parameters for life support, and consequently, the number of planets that could support life dropped to few thousands and kept on plummeting. Even SETI proponents acknowledged the problem. Peter Schenkel in 2006 wrote in the Inquirer that 'In light of new findings and insights, we should quietly admit that the early estimates may no longer be tenable'.

"The scholar wrote that today there are more than 200 known parameters necessary for a planet to support life. Every single one of them must be perfectly met or the whole thing falls apart. For example, without a massive gravity-rich planet like Jupiter nearby to attract the asteroids and protect earth, the earth would be like an inter-stellar dartboard. Simply put, the odds against life in the universe are astounding."

He let that sink in before continuing, "Could all parameters have been met by accident? At what point is it fair to admit that it is science itself that suggests that we cannot be the result of random forces."

"Doesn't assuming that an intelligence created the perfect condition in fact requires far less faith than life sustaining earth just happened to beat the inconceivable odds?" he asked.

The audience was mesmerized with his logical argument based on Sagan's theory. He continued, "The scholar has argued that astrophysicists now know that the values of the fundamental four forces gravity, electromagnetic, weak, and strong nuclear forces were determined less than one millionth of a second after the big bang. If the value of the ratio was altered by the tiniest of fraction, then no star or the universe could have been formed at all. That it just happened defies common sense. It would be like tossing a coin and it comes heads up 10 quintillion, one followed by 19 zeros, times in a row.

"Fred Hoyle, who coined the term 'Big Bang Theory', said his atheism was badly shaken by these developments.

"Paul Davies, world renowned theoretical physicist, said 'the appear of design is overwhelming'.

"Late Christopher Hitchens, a big aggressive proponent of atheism, conceded, 'without question, the fine-tuning argument was the most powerful argument of the other side'.

"Dr. John Lennox, Oxford University Professor of Mathematics, said, 'The more we get to know about our universe, the more the hypothesis that there is a creator gains incredibility as the best explanation of why we are here.'

"The scholar concluded with, and I fully agree, that the greatest miracle of all time is the universe. It is a miracle of all miracles, one that inescapably points to something or someone beyond itself."

Realizing that he had thrown a lot to the audience to ponder on, he concluded by saying, "This, ladies and gentlemen, is the proof that there is something much bigger than the universe itself, and it is God itself."

There was complete silence!

In the discussion section that followed, a participant fully agreed with the previous argument. "Even from a biologist's point of view, if the universe is 14 billion years old, the earth is 4.5 billion years old, and single celled life appeared 3.9 billion years ago, which is almost immediately on a relative scale. So, if life remained singe cell for the next three billion years, how come there was no evolution?"

He continued to comment, "Then in the Cambrian period, around 600 million years ago, there was an explosion of sophisticated life forms. This can only be attributed to God. And just within 100 million years, the oceans were full of fish, and the land had become populated. Nobody can explain how it happened, unless it can be attributed to God alone. Likewise, if dinosaurs were not wiped out 65 million years ago, and we don't know why and how, and by whatever, the earth would still be ruled by reptiles, and not man. So, intelligent life happened not because of evolution, but because of 'accidents'? Or clearly, life happened because of God!"

Everybody agreed that it could only be God that created life and the universe!

The next speaker, who was a physicist, spoke about the miracle that Prophet Muhammed spoke about: the sun rising from the West.

He said previously people would discard this as absurd but now scientists at NASA have found how it could happen. While observing Mars for a long time, they found that Mars, which rotates in the same direction of the Earth, appeared to rotate in the opposite direction, in which case the Sun would appear to rises from the west in the case of Mars.

"Every two years or so, there are a couple of months when Mar's position from night to night seems to change direction and move east to west. This strange behavior was very puzzling to early sky watchers. Did the planet really stop, back up, change its mind, and then continue to move forward? Did it have some weird, mystical meaning? Today, we know what's going on. It's an illusion, caused by the ways that Earth and Mars orbit the sun."

"This happens to all planets, and earth may be next."

One of the participants disagreed, saying it is only the relativity of motion between the Earth and Mars that makes it appear that the Mars is moving backwards. This phenomenon is named as Retrograde Motion. It does not mean that the Earth would rotate in the opposite direction.

The physicist could not defend his argument.

Another participant asked about the black hole, and how Islam explains what it is.

"First of all, let us agree to the belief that there are seven heavens. What we see around us, the complete universe, is part of the first heaven. We all know now, and agree, there are also multiverses.

"We think of the black hole as a dead, compressed star. On the other hand, the Star is like a ball, inflated by atomic explosions taking place inside. When stars die, that is when the explosions stop, then they are compressed to a small size, which is so dense, and has so much gravity. Due to this increased gravity, it keeps on collapsing, like a runaway train, till it becomes only a few miles in diameter, and is called a black hole. It has so much gravity that it sucks everything into it, gas, dust, even light! Or even space! As a result, it tears holes in the space fabric. These open holes could be openings to other universes! Prophet's travel to the other heavens could have been through them. They could also be time travel! As a result, no time elapsed when the Prophet traveled to heaven and returned back."

There were no comments on his presentation.

Another participant from a university in Karachi brought out the origin of the universe and the notion of the multiverse.

He said the Book of Genesis placed the creation of the world at 9 A.M. on October 27, 4004 BCE. Excavations take the existence of earth much before that. "Even the Indus Valley Civilization is 10,000 years old!

"On the other hand, the Hubble Telescope has found that stars are not uniformly distributed throughout space, but are gathered together in vast collections called galaxies. Hubble has also found that nearly all the galaxies are moving away from us. Moreover, the further galaxies are from us, the faster they are moving away. The universe was expanding, and the distance between distant galaxies was increasing with time. This expansion of the universe is a very important discovery."

He continued to present his argument, "Stephen Hawking has written that the beginning of the universe would be governed by the laws of science. It would be a bit like the formation of bubbles of steam in boiling water. Many small bubbles would appear, and then disappear again. These would correspond to mini universes that would expand but would collapse again while still of microscopic size. They are possible alternative universes but they are not of much interest since they do not last long enough to develop galaxies and stars, let alone intelligent life. A few of the little bubbles, however, grow to a certain size at which they are safe from recollapse. They will continue to expand at an ever-increasing rate, and will form the bubbles we see. They will correspond to universes that would start off expanding at an ever-increasing rate.

"This is called inflation by Hawking, like the way prices go up every year."

He looked around to see if everyone was following him, and continued, "Hawking wrote that the 'General Theory of Relativity' and the discovery of the expansion of the universe shatters the old theory of an ever existing and everlasting universe. Instead, general relativity predicts that the universe, and time itself, would begin in the big bang. It also predicted that time would come to an end in black holes.

"This compliments the Islamic theory on the beginning of the universe, and the end of it!"

Another attendee got up and added, "We cannot be sure of the future of the universe. Will it continue to expand forever? Is inflation a law of nature? Or will the universe eventually collapse again? Science is getting close to answering the age-old questions. Why are we here? Where did we come from? I am sure the final answer will concur with what the Quran says!"

The presenter nodded his head in the affirmative. There were no questions asked.

The third speaker, a physicist from Qatar, made some very interesting observations.

"Let me warn you upfront that some of my scientific views may strongly contradict with your beliefs. Like Dr. Samir emphasized in the beginning, the Quran encourages us to reflect on the order of nature."

Here are some of my views based on a book on Science and Islam written by a physics scholar. I agree with most of his views in the book, which is available at the front desk:

"On 'Quranic Healing', that is, the effect of the recitation of verses of the Quran on water, which then heals many ills in patients who drink it. Some explain the healing on the basis of 'the memory of water' effect, which is a long-discredited idea; while others explain it by some electromagnetic waves, carried by the 'vibrations' of the Quran being read, 'rearrange' the molecular structure of the water, giving it special 'energy', which is an overly abused word; while others invoke the concept of 'information content', which somehow gets passed on from the Quran to the water and then to the patient, especially if the Quran is read by quasi-saints; while others invoke telepathy; and some even base their claims on the 'theory' of homeopathy. Some claim that energy is transferred to the water by just placing one's finger in it and reciting verses aloud or in one's mind so the energy is stored in the water.

"One person even claims that he can transforms the energy into digital information, record it and even sends it by the Internet to anyone needing it anywhere in the world. This must certainly be 'a qualitative leap in the development of psychological immunity, and a quantum leap in the concept of miraculous Quranic technology, the first invention that combines the Holy Quran with modern technology', as the scholar has described it," he added with sarcasm.

"What no one mentions is the placebo effect or the mind's ability to trigger the release of medicinal chemicals, thereby leading to natural healing that looks quite miraculous sometimes.

"In regards to another miracle attributed to the Quran, that is the splitting of the moon.

"It is only mentioned briefly in a different context in the Quran in Chapter 54 Verses 1-2:

*'The Hour of Judgment is nigh, and the moon is cleft asunder
But if they see a Sign, they turn away, and say, "This is but transient magic."'*

"It is the Hadith that says that the splitting of the moon was one of a number of miracles performed by God during the time of Muhammad, and its purpose was to help convince people that he was a prophet.

"Some religious fanatics present evidence of a NASA picture showing a long indentation on the moon which was first discovered over 200 years ago with a small telescope. However, scientists believe they are remnants of ancient lava flows.

"In 2010, a NASA Lunar Science Institute staff scientist said, 'No current scientific evidence reports that the Moon was split into two or more parts and then reassembled at any point in the past.'

"It is, therefore, possible that the moon-splitting episode be the case of a huge meteoroid impact, the effect of which could have been described as a piece of the moon splitting from the main part. This will very clearly support what appeared to be a splitting of the moon and observed by the people during the time of the Prophet, and mentioned in the Quran. It may have happened during the time of the Prophet."

He continued, "There is yet another miracle attributed to the Quran where religious scientists have miscalculated.

"There is a calculation of the speed of light by a physicist from nothing but a few Quranic verses, which he presented as a paper. The calculation is based on one Quranic verse in Chapter 32 Verse 5:

'He rules all affairs from the heavens to the earth: in the end will all affairs go up to Him, on a day, the space whereof will be as a thousand years of your reckoning.'

"A full scrutiny of his paper shows it has many serious flaws. For example, the Quranic verse talks only about time, and no distance is mentioned. Obtaining a speed from this verse is therefore not possible. The flaws in his paper are detailed in the Islamic and Science book written by the physics scholar.

"Likewise, in another incorrect calculation based on the Quran for estimating the ages of the Earth and of the Universe, there was a similar flaw in the calculation. Here, the author refers to the Quranic verse in Chapter 70 Verse 4:

'The Angels and the spirit ascend unto Him in a day, the measure whereof is fifty thousand years.'

"He combines with other verses from Chapter 22 Verse 47:

'Yet, they ask thee to hasten on the punishment! But Allah will not fail in His promise. Verily, a day in the sight of thy Lord is like a thousand years of your reckoning.'

"And with Chapter 32 Verse 5:

'He rules all affairs from the heavens to the earth: in the end will all affairs go up to Him, on a Day, the space whereof will be as a thousand years of your reckoning.'

"He arrives at the age of the earth which conforms to what we estimate now as 4.5 billion years.

"His mumbo-jumbo calculations are also analyzed in the same book by the scholar."

He continued, "Regarding the supernatural creatures known as jinn, they could possibly be microbes, and the birds, which shot the Abyssinians invaders of Mecca the year Prophet Muhammad was born, could have been swarms of flies carrying diseases and infecting the army, and so on.

"Likewise, Jesus's healing of the blind may be imputed to the placebo effect induced by the mind, while Moses's parting of the red sea could somewhat easily be explained by sudden meteorological conditions which led to the wind blowing the red sea waters apart."

He continued, "I could go on and on, but I have run out of time. The book on Islam and Science is available at the registration desk for those who would like to see it."

The last speaker of the day spoke on the Prophet's journey to the heaven.

He said Muslims offer optional prayers all night during the evening of 'Miraj', called 'Shab-e-Mairaj', to celebrate the Prophet's journey to heaven. The 'Israa' and 'Miraj' are two parts of this journey. The israa is the journey that Prophet Muhammad took in one night from Mecca to the site of the Al-Aqsa Mosque in Jerusalem and back. The mairaj is the journey that the Prophet took from the Al-Aqsa Mosque in Jerusalem to the heavens.

Israa is mentioned in the Quran, in Chapter 17 Israa, called The Night Journey, Verse 1.

'Glory to Allah Who did take His servant for a Journey by night from the Sacred Mosque to the Farthest Mosque whose precincts We did bless, in order that We might show him some of Our Signs: for He is the One Who heareth and seeth all things.'

"Here, we are not discussing mairaj, which we do not doubt as Muslims, but the nature of the travel. What was the nature of this travel? Did it take place when the Prophet was asleep or when he was awake? Did he actually undertake a journey in the physical sense or did he have a spiritual vision while remaining in his own place? There are many schools of thoughts which say it was a spiritual journey to the seven heavens which God facilitated through the Angel Gabriel.

"Let us assume for a moment that he did go physically. The Hadith says he rode on Buraq, which was the heavenly horse with wings. Now forget the horse for a moment, which is only the mode of transport to make people of 1,400 years ago to understand time travel.

"Buraq is the plural of Barq, meaning light. Is travel at the speed of light possible? In theory, it is, according to Einstein's Theory of Relativity. When you do, time stops! We already have many Hollywood movies showing us that. If you recall the Star Trek movie, it used a Transporter. The Transporters converted a person or object into an energy, then 'beamed' it to a target, where it was reconverted into matter.

"Today, we are already conducting experiments to see if we can convert matter to energy, transport it at the speed of light, arrive at a destination, and convert it back to matter in one piece.

"And if one can travel at multiple speeds of light, which is Buraq, time can reverse! One could actually arrive at the destination in negative time!

"Today, it is possible to bring living objects as a hologram, or in light energy, at the speed of light right into your living room or on stage. This technology is already being used to deliver lectures to an audience, or simultaneously to many places, when a person can't be physically present there.

"Assume for a moment, if we are able to convert this light energy into matter, then transportation, and mairaj, becomes possible!"

He continued, "So, whether the Prophet had a spiritual experience, or a transported experience, it does not matter. What is mentioned in the Quran is very much possible according to science. One should not get into the nitty gritty of whether it was a winged horse, or it was a vision, or it was spiritual."

He continued, "I would also like to add that in another instance in the Quran, in Chapter 27, Verse 39, in the narrative about Solomon and the kingdom of Saba, one of the jinn, called Ifrit, who was an all-powerful jinn, volunteered to bring the throne of Saba in an instant. Here, we are mentioning of a distance from Yemen to Jerusalem. This could only be possible at super speed. Jinn are made of fire, which is energy. For energy to travel at the speed of light is very much possible. Plus, energy can pass through the walls and barriers, like radio waves do. Hence, we should not question what is in the Quran but only try to explain it through scientific theories!"

With that, he concluded his talk with an applause.

One participant got up and made a comment, "This is the problem with low educated Muslims, who are the majority, and who have been misguided by the mullas. It is possible that these were dreams and visions of the Prophet, but they have converted it into physical realities. The scientific community has not helped much either by explaining to the people that these miracles are very much possible and explainable by science. The result is that Muslims are going astray and becoming even more ignorant."

He continued lest he be accused of blasphemy, "No one is denying mairaj, but Islam is not a religion of fantasies and fairytales, it is a religion of realities and facts. Muslims need to be more educated in sciences to be able to understand and explain that."

The first day session ended. The moderator announced that dinner will be served in an hour on the front lawn.

Attack

The tables were laid out for over 200 people as a number of guests were expected to join for dinner. They were spread out across the front lawn. The main head table was reserved for Samir and the keynote speakers for both days, along with a few VCs, including both Latif and Hameed. A second round table next to it was reserved for other conference speakers.

The service was to be a buffet type of arrangement, with the salad and appetizers on one side, the main courses in the middle, and the desserts on the other side.

As the conference ended its sessions on the first day, the catering agency staff moved in to lay out the plates, silverware, and the glasses on the tables. Another group moved in to lay out the food on the side buffet tables.

Ali had come in earlier in the afternoon to the farmer's market with the other two Harmeen. They had bought the three vests with the verses of protection, the Ayat-ul-Kursi, printed on it from the kiosks at the local market without attracting any attention.

Their spiritual leader had met them at the market. He had brought three amulets with him and asked each one of them to wear one on their right arm.

"This will give you additional protection in addition to your vests."

He asked them to offer their prayers of forgiveness in case they die a martyr's death just in case anything went wrong. He had already placed about five kg of explosives in an empty aluminum cooking pot along with lots of nails and ball bearings to cause maximum damage when it exploded. It was then covered with bread and on top with a cloth to deceive anyone checking the pot.

They then placed the pot with explosives onto a Suzuki pick-up truck along with other food items that were to be loaded. This pot was marked with an 'X'.

"The remote is under the cloth. You will remove it as soon as you have placed the pot under the main table.

"I have told the owner you will be driving this vehicle to the venue, since Ali can drive. Other helpers will be following in a wagon."

Ali knew nothing would go wrong, and they would escape the venue before anyone would even realize it in the panic and chaos the explosion would cause. After all, they were the real Mujahidin.

As their spiritual leader waved them good bye, he knew his job had been done. He had already communicated the information to his masters.

As the three of them drove towards the venue of the conference, the logo on the vehicle was sufficient to let them pass through the main gate of the higher education secretariat.

"You are late already. The session ended about 15 minutes ago. Food should be served in 45 minutes," shouted the guard at the gate.

"No need to worry. The food is already cooked, warm and ready. The burners are already ready and laid out on the serving tables. It will only take us 30 minutes to lay out the food on the burners."

They went past the gate, and into the area where the guests would be arriving soon. They parked the truck close to the serving kitchen. The three jumped out.

An armed guard stopped them. He was patrolling the area, and appeared tired. It appeared he was waiting for the food to be served so he could dig in too with the left overs.

"We are here to serve the food. It is already late. Others are following."

He just waved them through.

They carried the pots containing the food to the serving tables. As soon as they had laid out a few, Ali came back to carry the pot marked 'X' and took it to the head table. He looked around to see if anybody was watching. All the other servers were busy laying out the food, and lighting the candles to the burners to heat the food. The armed guard was nowhere to be seen. He placed it under the head table, and carefully removed the remote from under the cloth, and put it in his pocket.

He walked back to the kitchen, patient that half the job was done. It was so easy. The istikhara was right. The venue and the timing was perfect. All he had to do was press the remote at the right moment and make their escape.

The food was now all laid out and the guests had started coming out from the hall, slowly trickling towards the tables. The heads table were still unoccupied. They would have to wait for the head-tables people to be seated.

He was getting impatient. The sooner done, the better. The world would soon know that Islam is not a science experiment. Islam has to be accepted at face value. There are no questions to be asked. Those who ask questions or challenge anything written in the Quran or the Hadith deserve death. They are all sinners and blasphemers, and the head of them all was the biggest one, an agent of the Jews and the Christians and satanic America. All the others who spoke at the conference deserved a dog's death.

The two others joined him near the kitchen, from where they could see the head tables. Most tables were by now fully occupied. Then a group of people emerged from the main hall and moved towards the tables. He could identify Samir in the middle of the crowd. He was the main target, the blasphemer, that had to be killed, and he would be blessed for it. He put his hand in his pocket to feel the remote. It felt warm. He felt confident that it will soon be over and they will make breaking news on all television channels.

All the guests were now seated. The two head tables were now fully occupied. No one suspected anything. Then someone spoke on a microphone welcoming everyone, and named the sponsors of the conference. The announcement lasted a few minutes. It ended by saying the food was ready and everyone could proceed to the serving tables.

Samir and the others got up to proceed to get the food. They were gone from the tables for about ten minutes. They returned back with their plates full of food.

Ali signaled to the other Harmeen to get ready to leave. They all walked towards the truck. Ali got into the driver's seat, and turned on the engine. Then he took the remote and, after taking a deep breath, said in a slightly loud tone 'Allah-o-Akbar'.

He pressed the button on the remote. Nothing happened. He pressed again expecting to hear a big bang. No sound, expect the sound of people eating the food. He tried third time. Nothing.

"What happened?" asked the other one in the front seat.

"Damn. Maybe it is the batteries in the remote." He opened and checked. They appeared quite new. He shook them around, put them back, and pressed again, expecting to hear a big bang. Nothing again.

"I will have to go and check the pot. Maybe there is a loose connection."

"How can you check? There are people eating at the table."

"We will get close as if we are checking on the quantity of the food. When they get up for dessert, I will pull the pot out and check the connection. You cover me so no one can see me do that. Then we try the remote again. I pray it explodes then. We will escape out of here as soon as we hear the explosion."

They walked out of the truck, towards the tables.

He directly approached the head table, with the two some distance behind. As they were all wearing server uniforms, no one suspected them getting close to the head table.

He asked about the quality of food. Everyone said it was fine. He walked to the next table, and the next one, till he saw a number of people getting up from the head table. He walked to the head table and waited till they all left to get the dessert. Then he signaled to his partners to cover him. They came and stood right behind him. He bent down as if picking something off the ground under the table. When he saw no one was close enough, he bent down to pull out the pot from under the table where he had placed it.

It was still intact. He removed the cloth cover and took out the bread quickly, threw it on the table, and fumbled around with the unit underneath. Everything looked okay. He pulled the bomb out of the box and started checking for any loose wiring.

"What is it you are looking for?" It was the armed guard who had earlier asked questions. He had appeared out of nowhere.

The other two tried to block him. Ali ignored the guard with the expectation that he will go away.

He did not. "Let me help you with the pot." He bent over and saw a device with wires in his hand.

There had been too many terrorist bombings in Pakistan for the guard not to realize that it could be a bomb. He could not take any chances and screamed at the top of his voice, while simultaneously pulling out his gun.

"Everyone, down! There is a bomb!"

But before the guard could pull out his gun, one of the Harmeen hit him hard on the head, and the guard went rolling down. People started to panic, running away towards the exit, while some hit the floor under the tables.

No one knew what happened next. There was a huge explosion!

Ali's hands severed off his body scattering his body parts all over the lawn. The two Harmeen covering him felt the impact of the explosion next. Their bodies went flying into the air, also parts breaking off their bodies. The guard's body also flew into mid-air and landed hard on the nearby head table. He appeared totally lifeless.

All others, including Samir and the keynote speakers, were at a safe distance near the food table, and had either hit the floor or run further away when the guard yelled. They all were at a safe distance, except for a few who were close by. Those close by were badly injured, some of them fatally, with the blast. The bomb had exploded outside the pot, and the nails and ball bearings inside the pot were left intact without causing serious damage over a much larger distance.

As the smoke and flying fragments of the dinnerware and the tables settled, Samir got up and looked around. It was the head table, exactly where he was sitting with the speakers that the bomb had exploded. He could not believe their lives had been saved by just a few minutes. Had the bomb exploded while they were all seated at the table, either a few minutes earlier, or a few minutes later, they would all have been blown into pieces by now. A lot more lives were saved somehow.

There was confusion all over. Some had started to panic, others were trying to help the injured. How could it have happened? Samir realized he should have taken security more seriously. He had been warned about it. Was he responsible for this attack?

He shrugged off the thought. To back off was to succumb to the terrorists. He could never have done that. Perhaps, he should have called for more security.

As he looked around, his mind rewound to what he had learnt in the last few days regarding protecting oneself from evil. How was it that no harm had come to him? It was obvious that he was the main target of the attack, since the explosion had taken place at the head table.

Was it the protection of the amulet or the aqeeq ring in his pocket, items in which he never believed in, or was it the prayers of protection, including the Ayat-ul-Kursi and the Qul that he regularly recited every morning, or the 99 names of God that he had recited that morning? Was it due to what Shaday prayed for him every day? Or was it his mother's prayers who had called that very morning to pray for his protection? Was it due to Bari Imam and the power of the shrines, in which he never believed, that he was safe? Or was it sheer luck? He would never know!

Samir thought these questions are best left unanswered as he could not say with certainty what saved his life, and of other speakers as well. But for the first time in his life, he felt as if a powerful force or aura was actually surrounding him and protecting him. He felt it was no one but God Himself who had protected him from evil forces, and nothing else! Everything converged to Him. He was the Supreme Being.

What Samir did not know but wanted to know was who were the terrorists who had attacked them and why? He would perhaps only know that after an inquiry was conducted by the intelligence agency and if the master-minds were brought to justice.

However, he was now becoming sure that the Islamists were misusing spiritual Islam for terrorism, He felt he wanted to go deeper into his investigations and learn more to stop these terrorists before they adopt other evil means like magic or perhaps use of other supernatural entities like the jinn for terrorism and before any major catastrophe took place. Timur had already warned him of that. Time was running out!

What Samir would never know is that why the attackers, despite the Istikhara, the amulets, the vests with the holy verses written on them, and the exact number of attackers used in the attack, failed. According to the attackers, they were attacking kafir who were blasphemous and believed in apostasy. So, why had they failed?

Samir was certain, however, that God would never allow prayers and ritual, and dreams based on istikhara, which are sacred prayers, and its interpretation, to be used for terrorism or to kill humans. Those who do so would definitely destroy themselves, not only in this world, but in the hereafter as well, where they will probably burn in hell forever.

Samir knew he would have to move fast to stop those wanting to use supernatural powers to cause more damage, and perhaps bring an end to this world. He was certain that the magic demonstrated by Timur in the training camp would be used in the next attack. But where could he begin or go next to learn more about magic, he was not sure!

Chapter 3
Black Magic

Say: I seek refuge with the Lord of the dawn
From the mischief of created things
From the mischief of darkness as it overspreads
From the mischief of those who practice secret arts
And from the mischief of the envious one as he practices envy
Al-Quran, Verses 113:1 to 113:5

Harut and Marut

"Haven't you heard the story about Harut and Marut in the Quran?" asked Hasan.

"I have, but never seriously read it," replied Samir.

"Well, Harut and Marut are the two angels mentioned in the second chapter of the Quran in Al-Baqarah Verse 102. They were present during the reign of the Prophet Solomon, and some believe they were present during the times of Prophet Idris as well, who is considered to be the second Prophet in Islam after Adam. The narrative is set around the ancient city of Babylon, where people used to worship the stars and planets, and where Satan taught people magic and sorcery if they kept them happy."

"How did the people keep Satan happy?" Samir was curious.

"They did all the wrong things for him, like remaining filthy, eating human flesh, which the magicians of today still do!

"Therefore, God sent Harut and Marut as a test for men. They were the most pious of angels. We know angels have no free will and cannot sin, however, the disobedience of men and jinn was so much that they were misled by them. Let me find the exact text for you from the Quran."

Hasan walked over to the bookshelf and pulled out a copy of the Quran with its English translation. He flopped over the pages to find the reference and read Chapter 2 Verse 102.

'They followed what the evil ones gave out falsely against the power of Solomon: the blasphemers were, not Solomon, but the evil ones, teaching men magic, and such things as came down at Babylon to the Angels Harut and Marut. But neither of these taught anyone such things without saying: "We are only for trial; so do not blaspheme." They learned from them the means to sow discord between man and wife. But they could not thus harm anyone except by Allah's permission. And they learned what harmed them, not what profited them. And they

knew that the buyers of magic would have no share in the happiness of the hereafter. And vile was the price for which they did sell their souls, if they but knew! If they had kept their faith and guarded themselves from evil, far better had been the reward from their Lord, if they but knew!'

He placed the Quran back on the shelf and continued, "Harut and Marut were sent as humans and both of them were not supposed to teach anyone anything. They were only to teach only after man had said that they are a trial, therefore, do not be a disbeliever. However, they faltered and taught what harmed the people. But they also knew whoever learnt and practiced magic, it was like they sold their own souls and would burn in hell forever. They taught men all the esoteric arts and branches of occult knowledge; astrology, alchemy, numerology, the healing arts, and magic."

"So, magic was really taught by the angels to man?"

"They didn't behave like angels at all. According to other narratives, God had commanded them to avoid wine, idolatry, fornication, and murder. But Harut and Marut eventually succumbed to human lusts and fell into all of these sins after seeing a young beautiful woman named Zohra. Consequently, God punished them for their transgressions. But before that, since they had become sinful anyway, they continued to teach magic to the people for a long time. Some also believe Zohra was refused entry into paradise and God made her the planet Venus."

"Zohra as Venus? This can't be true!" interrupted Samir.

Hasan shook his head, "When Solomon lost his kingdom, many a jinn and man renegaded against him, then stole the complete knowledge that God had provided to Solomon, and started practicing magic and sorcery. It was at this time that they wrote books on black magic. Black magic came to the earth through these jinn, who, after acquiring the new powers, would eavesdrop on the descending angels about matters decreed in the heavens. They were then shot at by the angels with the stars, much like shooting stars, to send them back. Once they knew they had nothing substantial to tell the people, the jinn and men would add lies of their own. The fortune tellers and astrologers would rely on the information the jinn would provide them. Half of it would be false.

"They would start predicting the future, on politics, on wars, on personal fortune. They would create methods how to have their wishes fulfilled. For example, they added how people could get some wishes fulfilled by standing and facing the sun and saying some words. They could also get other wishes fulfilled by standing with their back to the sun and repeating some other words. Men started believing them and regarded them as trustworthy. It is a sin to follow such practices. The word then spread among the people that the jinn had the knowledge about the future and the unseen, and they can change your fortune as well."

"Jinn are not trustworthy and always lie," commented Samir.

Hasan nodded his head, "The people of those times wrote all of this in a book and sealed it with a ring bearing the inscription found on Solomon's ring and placed it in a secret location.

"But when God restored to Solomon his kingdom, the jinn and men came back to follow him again. Here, Solomon decided not to trust anyone, located the book of magic from where the people had placed it, put it in a chest and hid it under his throne. All those who even tried to approach the chest were burned alive. Solomon took an even harder stance declaring that he would behead anyone who claimed that the devils knew the unseen."

"So, the magic was safe?"

"No! When Solomon died, a devil came in the form of a human being to the people and said: 'I will lead you to an everlasting treasure that will never run out.' He was referring to the writings of Solomon that were buried under the chest. Then Satan led the people to dig under Solomon's throne. To provide credibility to his word, he also offered to be killed if he was not correct in his claims."

"So, the people believed him?"

"Yes! And after the people dug out all the writings, the devil told them that it was these writings that had given Solomon power over mankind, the jinn, the animals, and the birds. The devil altered this book by adding magical and blasphemous writings. The devil wrote about different types of sorcery meant to fulfill different desires. The men and the jinn started to follow these scriptures and made it their religion."

"So, what we see today is the magic and witchcraft that was altered during Solomon's times. What happened to the book of magic?" Samir asked.

"That is a good question to ask, and there are many narrations. Some claim the scriptures are still with the devil which gives him the power, and he uses it through his followers in order to destroy mankind. Some claim the book was burnt by the Romans during their conquest of Jerusalem. Others claim it was buried back under the Temple of Solomon and remained protected by the Knight Templars, as some believed they were Satan worshippers. Many others think that eventually the Freemasons or the Illuminati got hold of it and have kept it in a secure place to use during the end of times."

"Were not the Knight Templars closely tied to the Crusades?"

"Yes! And the Freemasons have evolved from the Knight Templars. The Freemasons want to rebuild the Solomon's Temple in Jerusalem on the Temple Mount, once the Dome of the Rock, which is sacred for the Muslims, is gone. The Freemasons are planning to build the temple for the Masonic Christ, who will be Antichrist, on that site."

"So, the Knight Templars were satanic?"

"They worshipped Satan, and the symbol of Baphomet."

"Baphomet? Isn't that the symbol that looks like a goat?"

"Baphomet is the power of darkness and is a demonic head of a goat. The goat's head unites the characteristics of the dog, bull, and ass. The hands are human pointing at two lunar crescents. It has female breasts and the belly is scaled. The lower part of the body is veiled. On its forehead is the pentagram which was the seal of Solomon and of those who practice black magic."

"Aren't there many different images of the Baphomet?"

"Some Templars described it differently, like a frightful head, with long beard and sparkling eyes, others a man's skull, while others as having three faces. In any case, the Baphomet was worshipped under several different forms.

"The forces of evil, of magic, or sorcery, are just too strong and want to take over the world."

"You sound like you have read too many Harry Potter books," Samir commented with a frown on his face.

"You know, I love Harry Potter, and have read each one of these books. But that is all sorcery, and the world of wizards and witchcraft, and is fiction where Voldemort wants to take over the world. In this case, these are facts where the whore of Babylon wants to rule the world."

"What? Now, who is the whore of Babylon?"

"The whore of Babylon is actually from the Bible and not from the Quran. In Revelation 17:9 is a reference to a prostitute who sits on seven mountains and is covered in purple and scarlet color. She will have great powers to rule the world."

"Obviously, the whore must be a woman!"

"Most are also convinced that it does not refer to a woman but to a city on seven hills which will have the power to rule the world. The Iraqis were convinced it is Babylon itself, which led Saddam to delusions of grandeur to conquer the Middle East. Others argue it is Rome, or Vatican, where the power of Christianity is based. Some attribute it to Jerusalem, which is why Israel has forcibly occupied it to have the absolute power to rule the world, yet others attribute it to Manhattan, a financial power, which is also built on hills. Others believe it refers to Mecca."

"Mecca?"

"Yes, Mecca! It is also built on hills. Also, according to these believers, everything describing a woman fits the Kaaba; dress, pearls, jewels, and gold and silver threads across her attire. They say just the door of the Kaaba alone has 280 kilograms of pure gold, which is covered with a veil like the Muslim women."

"So, the Bible says Mecca will rule the world?"

"Not the Bible. Christians equate it with Rome since according to them, Rome is the city of seven hills. Muslims do not believe in this prophecy at all."

Samir wanted to know whether kabbalah is also magic.

"Is kabbalah considered magic too?"

"Kabbalah is a school of thought that originated in Judaism. It all depends upon who uses it and for what purpose. From its early Hebrew origins to later Christian, New Age, and Occult adaptations, kabbalah are teachings which explain the relationship between the infinite and finite, immortal and mortals, God and humans. It leads to spiritual realization."

"That is exactly what I said when I discussed kabbalah in my class during my Creative Leadership course."

"But that is not all! There are followers of the occult version which is called 'Practical Kabbalah."

"Have read about that too. What do you know about it?"

"Practical Kabbalah is a Jewish mystical practice that uses magic. At one time, it was called white magic by those who used it. It was only reserved for the rich and powerful, who could separate its spiritual source from the evil if a certain holy procedure was performed, while the majority of the Jews disapproved of it. Today, its use is more widespread among Jews, and it uses amulets like in Muslim and Hindu traditions."

"So, kabbalah is black magic?"

"Most kabbalists say practice of black magic is forbidden, but they practice it anyway, much like what the Muslims say about black magic but some practice it. People always try to reach out to a deity beyond God that they incorrectly think has powers. They try to reach them through prayers, dreams, amulets, astrology, spiritual ways, tarot cards, etc. The interest in supernatural knowledge has always excited men of all faith."

Samir wondered if Timur knew about the magic of kabbalah. After all, the TTP was funded by external forces and they would resort to the use of any negative force or magic to win their war.

Hasan interrupted his thought, "All is not negative in the use of magic. Right or wrong, magic was also practiced by the rabbis to cure people. The Talmud mentions the use of charms for healing."

"What about other references to magic in the Quran?" Samir asked.

"Yes, there is much more. When God banished Satan from the heaven, Satan wanted respite for a certain time when he said in Chapter 4 Verse 119 that he will mislead humans, and will create in them false desires. He further said he will order them to slit the ears of cattle, and to deface the fair nature created by Allah. All of this was to misguide man through the power of magic.

"Furthermore, there are four chapters in the Quran that relate to the story of Moses and Pharaoh. We all know the story because we have all watched the Hollywood classic 'The Ten Commandments' many times over. When Moses declared to Pharaoh that he was a Messenger from God, Pharaoh asked him to prove it. So, Moses threw his staff on the floor, and it became a snake."

He continued, "Pharaoh then assembled the best sorcerers in the country, and offered them rewards, including elevating them to a high position in the royal court, if they could defeat Moses's magic. They could not have expected anything better from the Pharaoh, who they worshipped as a god."

"Pharaoh always used to rely on his sorcerers."

"That was his strength. So, when the sorcerers gathered in the court, they were sure of their victory. Moses asked them to throw their staff first, which all became snakes due to their magic. Everyone in the court applauded expecting Moses to give up. These were the best of the sorcerers in the country.

"But then when Moses threw his staff, it became a much larger snake and swallowed all the other snakes."

Samir agreed, "Moses was more powerful because his power was from God. But where did the magic of the sorcerers come from? This story from the Quran confirms that there is magic on earth with the sorcerers and the magicians. Isn't this the same magic that is being practiced by the aamil?"

"Yes, Dad. Both the Bible and the Quran confirm that the fallen angels or Satan perform magic for their disciples."

"But surely, the power of God is much more!"

"Clearly, yes. Not only in this story, where Moses's snake was not only larger and stronger, but it also gobbled up the other snakes."

"Could that have been an illusion?"

"It is very much possible like other stories. But the miracles of Moses because of God go beyond the staff and the snake. The second sign that Moses displayed to Pharaoh was even more puzzling. Moses drew out his hand from the folds of his garments, and it was white and shining with divine light. This was to counter any suggestions of evil, which the snake in Egyptian mythology created.

"No Egyptian sorcerer could replicate this. Their magic was not as powerful. They then all fell down on the ground acknowledging God."

"What about the miracle of the parting of the Red Sea, when all of Pharaoh's army drowned while Moses and his people walked away safely to the other side?" Samir asked.

"Call it a miracle, or a natural phenomenon. It happened according to all beliefs, Jews, Christians, and Muslims, and they all accept it as a miracle performed by Moses. Surprisingly or as expected, even the scientific community does not deny it, and scientists today are still studying how that happened."

"There is always something on National Geographic on that!"

"Much has been explained. According to new findings, a moderate wind blowing constantly for about 10 hours at the northern end of the Red Sea, where the crossing occurred, could have caused the sea to recede about a mile and the water level to drop by about 10 feet, leaving dry land in the area. There has been a recent discovery of a ridge connecting the two sides of the sea in the same area, on which Moses and his people could have easily walked over. A sudden change in wind speed would have made the sea come crashing back into the area drowning the army. However, even if proven true, it still supports the story of Moses parting the Red Sea. God does miracles, but only through scientific means."

Samir was pleased Hasan thought so. "Didn't the unbelievers also say Prophet Muhammed was a magician?"

"Yes, they did so when he split the moon according to the Hadith. But there is always a scientific basis for all magic. We only need to understand it to replicate it."

"But wasn't Prophet Muhammad also affected with black magic. How can that be explained?"

"Yes! And that is the most unbelievable part, even for me. He was a Prophet of God, his last and favorite Prophet. The final message of God, the Quran, was bestowed through him. He was the living embodiment of a perfect human being. Praying, fasting, charity, love of God. All that most Muslims practice today, through the Hadith and following the sharia, are something that was just his daily life. He was the role model, the perfect human for all Muslims. Yet, he was stuck down with black magic which lasted for six months. If he could be affected, then who are we normal mortals?"

"I agree but what actually happened?"

Hasan had done his homework well whenever it came to spirituality and magic, "According to the narratives in the Hadith, some Jews visited Medina and met a famous magician, Labid bin Asam, and paid him three gold coins to cast a magic spell on Prophet Muhammad. They asked for a piece from his close body, like a hair. This was easy to obtain for them as a Jewish boy used to work as his attendant. Through him, they obtained a piece of the Prophet's comb with some hair stuck to it.

"Magic was worked on the hair and it was placed in the spathe of a date-tree hidden at the bottom of a well. The spell started working as the well started to dry, and the Prophet started to feel unwell. He felt he was melting away from within. He started getting illusions that he had done something, while he had not done it."

"Isn't that where the unbelievers started accusing him of narrating the Quran from his imagination? Or even forgetting the verses of the Quran? Some even say he was under a similar spell when he felt he was the chosen one," asked Samir.

"Only his personal life was affected, not his spiritual one, which is too high and powerful to have been affected by devils," Hasan corrected. "He used to do hijama, which is wet cupping, to get healed. He also prayed to God to be healed. He then had a vision in which God told him what to do: that he should recover the hair from the bottom of the well. The exact location was revealed to him."

Hasan continued, "He went with his companions, recovered the comb and hair, and also found a cord with eleven knots and a wax image with needles stuck in it."

"Why eleven knots?" Samir was curious.

"Eleven is considered a demonic number, so are its multiples. It expresses 1 besides 1, mean the Satan challenging God as His equal."

He continued, "The Angel Gabriel then came to him and told him to repeat the last two chapters of the Quran, which are the two Qul Al-Falaq and Al-Nas. As the Prophet repeated verse after verse, a knot was loosened and a needle taken out every time, till all the knots were loosened and all the needles removed, and he was entirely freed from the magic.

"That is why these last two chapters, Chapter 113 and Chapter 114, are considered the most powerful verses to break any Black Magic, one that is even as powerful as to consume the Prophet."

"How can real magic be explained by modern science?"

"We cannot yet, Dad. Science is too primitive while magic has been practiced for thousands of years. The scientists and the educated write it off. The pragmatists know magic exists!"

"And the terrorists are using it to their advantage while we are still disagreeing to its powers," Samir shook his head.

Samir was now sure there was black magic and it had its practitioners in every society. They were practicing devilish acts even though it was forbidden in all faiths. They were causing damage to individuals and to relationships. They were using it for all the wrong things.

He recalled Hameed had mentioned of terrorists becoming invisible and flying through the air. Timur had mentioned it, and he had seen a real demonstration of it at the training camp. These could be illusions but there were strong beliefs in these supernatural powers. The terrorists could attack the universities and the military bases using magic or after acquiring certain magical powers. If they have succeeded in the past, then nothing was going to stop them from acquiring more magical powers through the devil, and carry out more attacks in the future.

Samir shrugged his shoulder and went into denial mode. It could not be possible. He was certain these were illusions only. He, however, wanted to learn more about the practice of magic.

He decided to search on the net first if magicians did exist in the modern world.

Crowley

Samir spent the next few hours on the net searching about magic. He discarded most of what he read, and narrowed it down to a few events and individuals. The name Aleister Crowley appeared in most searches as a modern magician. Most sites called him the most wicked man in the world, some titled him 'The Beast'. He was a practitioner of kabbalah, and was born in 1875 and died in 1947. He was educated at Cambridge University, and became a member of a secret society called 'Hermetic Order of the Golden Dawn'. This is where he got trained in ceremonial magic, and then practiced Alchemy and Astrology. He found out there was a dark world beyond this superficial magic that the society practiced. Due to his desire to learn more and explore the dark world, he quit the Golden Dawn and started practicing real magic on his own.

He married Rose Edith Kelly in 1904 and they honeymooned in Cairo, Egypt. This is where Crowley claimed to have been contacted by supernatural forces, including a deity named Aiwass. According to Crowley, Aiwass was not a human and possessed far more knowledge than any human could possibly have. Aiwass could have been a jinn.

Aiwass dictated to him 'The Book of the Law' over the next three days. The Book of the Law is a sacred text that served as the basis for 'Thelema', which is a religion based on magic. Thelemic magick is a system of physical, mental, and spiritual exercises. Crowley spelled magick with a 'k' to distinguish it from stage magic

The book declared that its followers should adhere to the code of 'do what thou wilt' and align themselves with their will through the practice of magick. Crowley practiced magick for six months in Egypt to master the control of demons. At one point, it became very dangerous and Crowley had to stop his practices. However, many believe it was too late and he became possessed.

Aleister also conducted other rituals, including sex magic. He was twisted by dark supernatural forces, and his followers believe he knew more, which 'The Order' did not want others to know. He probably made Aiwass unhappy at some point and died a drug addict and in poverty.

Another site caught Samir's attention. It was mentioned that when Crowley was living in poverty in France, the grandmother of a former president of the US was in France and stayed with a common friend of Crowley. She became Crowley's magical assistant. When she returned back to the US, she gave birth to the president's mother. The site alleged that the president, who caused havoc in the Middle East and Afghanistan after 9/11, was Crowley's grandson!

Had the influence of magick penetrated the White House? Was the deity Aiwass a subordinate of Iblis? Was Iblis, through the deity, responsible for and controlling post 9/11 events? Was this all part of the master plan of Satan to lead events to the end of times and control the universe? It raised more questions than gave answers. It also led to more questions.

Was Iblis also controlling the events in Pakistan? Had the practices of magick also penetrated the power players in Pakistan?

Samir decided to do further investigation on magic and get more answers.

Pir

Samir flew into Karachi for a day to learn more about magic from Pir Wasim.

Wasim was a senior bureaucrat who had retired a couple of years ago, and was a highly educated person who was known to Samir from his earlier days at Karachi when they were neighbors. Wasim's father was a famous religious pir, who claimed he was a direct descendent of the Prophet Muhammed, and who had passed away many years back. He was buried in a mausoleum constructed by the son on family land outside the city.

Wasim had learnt many a prayers and sacred verses from his father to counter black magic practiced by many in the city. Many flocked to him for a spiritual cure. The verses he used against magic had been propagated though ages by word of mouth since the times of the Prophet to the times of his father, and from his father to him. Wasim claimed anyone who would recite the verses prescribed by him would protect them or their family against black magic. Such practices are known as white magic.

"Magic is real. Our former president used to practice magic!" Wasim told Samir.

"Even the president?"

"He wanted to feel protected in the presidency. You know he is still charged of many corruption cases against him, which he claims can never be proved in the court for lack of evidence. Many believe he had stashed billions in properties and in front-end companies under the names of his associates. Any single evidence unearthed could have sent him to jail for years.

"He believed the army did not like him, and neither did many others for personal reasons who wanted him bumped off. So, he resorted to magic while in the presidency to remain safe, and even does it now as well so he remains protected, and his properties and investments also remain safe and under his control."

"This is hocus-pocus! I do not think magic protects!"

"White magic does! Black magic harms!"

"How did he practice magic, black or white?"

"For starters, he did animal sacrifice. When at the presidency, he had a black goat slaughtered every day to ward off evil and to protect against black magic…"

Samir knew Marvi Brohi also regularly performed sadqa after returning to Pakistan and before she was killed in a suicide attack. He interrupted, "But this is sadqa, the ritual sacrifice of animals…"

"Sadqa is occasional. But when it is religiously done every single day, and black goats are killed, it is magical practice. He touched every single goat on the forehead before its blood was spilled on the driveway of the presidency. The outcome is that he had his party's government complete its full term, the first in our history. He weathered every storm, every political crisis, by sacrificing a goat every day of the year for all five years of his term. And he survived!"

"There have been newspaper reports on that."

"But it was not just confined to slaughtering black goats every day," Wasim continued, "a flock of black partridges were also kept in cages. However, the whole flock was electrocuted when a live wire fell on its cage," he smiled.

"Now what effects the partridge would have?" Samir asked.

"Black partridges are introduced there for their supposedly magical effects. The bird is associated with the goddess Athena in Greek mythology whom it served. Among the practitioners of magic, it is considered full of wisdom, and associated with lunar forces. It has access to the forces of the moon, both dark and bright."

"I have read that like the houbara bustard, a favorite of the Arabs, its meat also gives tremendous powers."

"Birds have a particular significance in alchemy. As one that is transformed from man to bird, certain birds hold tremendous powers, much like the legendry phoenix. These powers can be tapped by man for their benefit."

He winked, "That is not all. The president kept a couple of camels on the grounds of the presidency in order to drink its milk for protection from his enemies."

Samir snickered, "Looks like he had a zoo there. Who was the magician guiding him?"

"A certain pir who is famous for black magic. He claims he had met the former president in jail for the first time and had predicted then that he would soon become president. It was clearly not possible then. The former president took him seriously and they developed a 'magical relationship' between them.

"The pir claims that he enabled the president to recover the millions of dollars which were frozen in the president's Swiss bank account."

He looked at Samir to see how well he absorbed it, "The pir claimed this was a very difficult task to accomplish, that is to protect a president accused of high level corruption as well as to protect him from going to jail. He charged him a lot of money, and then meditated in Medina for a year. During the court's hearing, the pir was seen standing outside reciting certain verses. And it worked! The case was thrown out of court. The former president was made free and was also able to cash his check at the Swiss bank."

"I heard he had the president relocate a lot between cities during office?"

"That is correct! Whenever the pir would sense danger, or to ward off evil spirits dangling over his head, he would advise the president to go live in his house in Karachi by the ocean. Later, whenever he felt the danger has gone, he would advise him to return back to the hill in Islamabad."

Samir nodded, as he had heard all about it as well. The pir was seen walking freely all over the president's house like a free bird every day, and could walk into cabinet meetings without interruption, bearing a rosary in hand and muttering some verses. He was considered more powerful than even the prime minister or the governors. It was rumored that on his instance that the president changed the prime minister as well. Top bureaucrats were found sitting at the pir's feet all the time, even in their offices. Jokes about the pir were doing the rounds in all political gatherings, on the media, in army circles as well as in diplomatic receptions.

"At the end of the president's tenure, he said he had fulfilled his obligation of protecting him for five full years. He claimed he could have extended the stay of the president for another year, but the president refused as he did not want a premature dismissal and go to jail. So, he just walked away, joking that he has heard the former president now has a new live-in pir to ensure he gets back in office again for a full term."

"So, the pirs are influencing who becomes president?"

He smiled, "The use of magic to protect is not just confined to the former president but to the whole hierarchy in the government, present and past! Even the former prime minister was a believer when it came to superstitions and pirs. He was prematurely kicked out of office in the past, so he learnt his lessons fast, resorted to pirs and magic, and survived his next term."

"Was it the same pir as the president used?"

"He was a different one! The prime minister would be seen running to his dwelling at the top of a hill every time he faced a crisis to get his blessings. These visits to the pir were surely a blessing for the pir's fellow villagers, as the road leading to their village was built overnight and the village was electrified!" Wasim added with a smile.

Samir recalled Marvi had herself 'inherited' the same pir as was used by her opponent, to guide and assist her when she won the election and assumed office. There was no need for advisers or ministers to advice on the functions of the state, the pir knew it all! Her opponent's dismissal should have been a red flag, but she continued to visit the famed pir to seek his advice. The same pir claimed to cure terminally ill patients by spraying water on them with a garden hose. It was also reported that she had a helipad constructed to reach him quickly in times of turmoil or crisis. She was dismissed a year later!

When Marvi visited the White House the first time, she was accompanied by a stranger as a part of her very small entourage. Not only the Pakistani team, but even the American Secret Service was confused as to the identity of the visitor. Later, it was found that that he was a pir whose job was to ensure that she gets full support from the American administration. So, the pirs had been to the White House as well!

Wasim interrupted Samir's thoughts, "All politicians in Pakistan have a pir or two to guide them what to do, when to do, where to have the next 'jalsa', or gathering, and when to do 'dharna' or sit-in. I even know that one of the leaders of the opposition had black lentils rubbed all over himself to ward off a curse of black magic, which are preventing him from becoming the next prime minister."

Samir thought such stories are abundant. There are more fake pirs than real ones. As a result, among the poor and illiterate, the fake pirs exploit. Only recently, the local newspaper reported that a local pir raped the 15-year daughter of a couple after sending them to a butcher to buy a black goat's head that he said was needed to work his magic. He then threatened to curse the family with a dose of black magic if they told anyone what had happened. Everyone in the village believed the pir could cure people and solve everyone's problems.

In another newspaper story, a window dealer who 'moonlighted' as a pir cured a 60-year-old farmer who claimed to be possessed by a jinn. He told the farmer his brain and his whole body was in a state of dryness. He then suggested to stop smoking and stop drinking tea, and to give liquids, soup, and butter. In six months, the jinn was gone!

The use of magic is not just confined to pirs. At the 2011 World Cup cricket match with India, thousands did a collective prayer on the grounds of the stadium session to protect the local team from any black magic done by the Indian side. Regardless of the prayers, Pakistan lost! Maybe the black magic on the other side was more powerful!

Indians believe more on the power of the 'guru' or the holy man, who is their local pir. Recently, a guru, who was a self-styled messenger of god, was convicted by the court of raping two of his female devotees, and accused of multiple rapes and murders, and storing '400 pairs of testicles in his refrigerators cut from 400 devotees on the promise of getting them nirvana'. He claimed a large following of over 50 million people, including many politicians from the current government.

The belief is not just confined to politicians. Samir also knew that academics are divided whether magic as practiced by healers is real. Some academics believe there is room for jinn and spirits. Even a dean of arts and sciences at a leading university said it works at times. He said an acquaintance turned to a faith healer to treat severe abdominal pain. The healer found two jinn in her abdomen, exorcised them and cured her. Samir, however, believed many instances could be explained by the placebo effect, but in other cases cures takes place in which there are simply no explanations.

It was like Wasim read his mind, "There are things that are happening that cannot be explained by science or logic. Even cancer can be cured with white magic. These things are happening on a daily basis to millions all over the country."

"So, people really believe in magic?"

"Magic has been around since Harut and Marut were sent to this world. Prophet Solomon had magical knowledge. Magic is practiced in all cultures and regions of the world, whether it is voodoo in the Caribbean or through shamans in South America."

Wasim really believed in black magic, "There is a very strong presence of magic in our neighboring country, Oman, as well. Bahla is known as 'Madinat-Al-Sehr', or the 'City of Magic'. It is also known as the birthplace of jinn or black magic, a reputation that predates Islam. Legends about Bahla's magical past include tales of people being turned into cows or goats, haunted by spirits or vanishing when they stood in cursed places. Another one claims that spirits built the 7-mile long city wall in one night. Neighboring Nizwa enjoys a similar dubious reputation as the epicenter of black magic."

"How did these stories originate?"

"Before Islam arrived in Oman, black magic was practiced at Bahla which had its roots in Babylon. After Islam was introduced to the region, the chief practitioner was killed for practicing the dark arts, and a fort was built on his grave to prevent his followers from turning it into a shrine. It was after this that his spirit started appearing in the city and teaching everyone black magic. It continues to be practiced till today by many. Many of the locals travel to Nizwa and to neighboring regions to practice and teach black magic."

"So, black magic arrived in Pakistan from Oman?"

"Many Omanis are Baloch, as there always have been historical ties between Oman and Balochistan, which was a region independent of the sub-continent India. The port of Gwadar where the Chinese are building a big port actually belonged to Oman from 1783 till Pakistan purchased it in 1958 and amalgamated it into Balochistan. Black magic today is still strongly practiced in the coastal areas of Balochistan which lie closest to Oman."

"What about the famous Bengal black magic that is practiced all over India and Pakistan?"

"Bengal magic is very deadly, and originated thousands of years ago. They say it is more potent than any other type of magic practiced anywhere. If you go to any city in Pakistan, or even a very small village, you will see signs advertising Bengali magic which can do the impossible for you."

"So, black magic kills?"

"Most definitely yes, unless it is neutralized with the verses from the Quran!"

Samir asked the most pertinent question that he had come for, "What about use of black magic in terrorism?"

"Black magic is always used for negative reasons, whether you want to harm someone or kill someone. If it kills, it can certainly be used in terrorism. You can kill people through magic. You can convert a human into an animal or a bird. You can even make an object look alive, like was done by the sorcerers at the time of Prophet Moses. They converted their staffs into serpents. You can also make someone very ill or sick through magic. You can destroy business or make someone bankrupt through magic. You can destroy relationships through magic. This is even confirmed in the Quran.

"So, if magic can do these and many other things, a lot more can be done through its use, but only if someone has the right magical knowledge. Many claim they do, like many aamil, but very few know actual magic as was practiced in the past. The jinn are the entities who know real black magic from the times of Solomon, or what is recorded in the 'Book of Magic' and the aamil want to learn from them by selling their soul. Then the aamil pretend and act as if they know black magic. Most of them are actually creating illusions or fooling people."

"The terrorists are not Muslims! They are evil people who destroy lives by the hundreds," Samir commented.

Wasim nodded his head, "They are evil, but they believe they are fighting a jihad, so will probably resort to using it as a weapon. However, one should not practice it as the use of magic is prohibited in Islam."

Samir asked about what he had seen the terrorists do at the camp, "Can magic make one fly, or make one invisible?"

Pir looked Samir in the eye, waiting for a few seconds before replying, "There is so much to magic that is not all known. It has tremendous powers. To answer your question in short, yes magic can do that! Black magic can transport people to long distances at the speed of light."

He continued, "I have heard of magicians disappearing and reappearing at another place in an instant of a second! It was as if their whole body was converted into energy, transmitted to another place at the speed of light, passing through barriers, and converting back into bodily form! These real magicians must have access to the knowledge in the books of magic from the times of Prophet Solomon."

"What you are saying is really scary! If someone has access to the right black magic, then he can kill through it, he can fly, he can become invisible, and maybe do a lot more?"

"Yes! But I doubt if anyone has this knowledge in today's time, though there are many who claim they do, or want to acquire this knowledge."

Samir wished Wasim was right. He had heard enough and had got the answers he was seeking. Magic could do wonders. Magic could make people invisible. Magic could transport people to distant places at the speed of light. Magic could kill. Magic could do much more! But only if someone knew and practiced real magic!

He thanked Pir Wasim and walked back to his car. He recalled the Charsadda attack where terrorists, who had penetrated the campus were not seen or noticed by anyone despite the security cameras and the guards. That is what Hameed was warning about as well. Samir also remembered the training camp where Timur and his squad were walking over fire or flying through the air. He was not sure if they had succeeded to do that over longer distances or it was just an illusion created to make him believe it.

But one thing was very certain. Magic held tremendous power, and Samir was sure that there were magicians who could do a lot of damage. It was quite likely that the terrorists may have reached out to the real magicians to achieve their goals. After all, they were both evil, and birds of feather flock together.

But how could he reach out and find out which magicians were aiding them, what would be their next target, and how he could stop them? He wanted more answers, and knew where he could get at least some of these.

Astrologer

Samir's next stop was the famous astrologer Najumi Jamali. Even though Samir was not convinced that what astrologers usually forecasted was right, but there had been many a cases when what the astrologers predicted had actually happened. Maybe it was a coincidence or by chance. Anyway, he felt there was no harm in talking to Najumi. Perhaps he could give an insight into the terrorist's next activities.

Najumi was a third-generation astrologer and had a reputation that most of what he predicted always came true. People believed some supernatural forces in the universe were his guides and informers. He was usually invited to many talk shows on television, but mostly declined as he liked to keep a low profile. He was very much sought after by politicians, bureaucrats, army generals, and businessmen.

His father was also known to Samir's father, who had correctly predicted decades ago that Samir's father would quit his successful law practice and become a judge, when such a consideration was not even on the table. His father, within the family, had always quoted the elder Jamali many a times on his change of career. However, the astrologer had also predicted to Samir's father that he would become a judge of the superior court by such and such date, which did not happen. Samir had helped Najumi's son get his degree verification from the education ministry so the astrologer was indebted to him. He had asked Samir to come in the afternoon when it was his rest time when he would normally not see anyone.

"Glad to see you after such a long time. Do you want me to tell you if you will be the next prime minister of Pakistan?" Najumi asked with a smile.

"Najumi, I am not here to ask about my future but about the events that have been happening. Let me get straight to the point. Our country is going through many terrorist attacks, almost one every day. I fear something big may happen soon. You are known to predict unforeseen events in advance with a high degree of accuracy. I need your help. Where and when will the next attack take place?"

"I have been predicting these events all along, but no one cared to listen. All events on earth, and of individuals, are guided by the position of the stars. People don't take it seriously because they say in Islam one does not believe destiny is guided by the stars. But they don't realize that all destinies are made in the heavens."

Najumi picked a book from his shelf, opened a page and read, "In Chapter 26 Verse 61, Allah says,

'Blessed is He who made constellations in the skies, and placed therein a lamp and a moon giving light.'

"In Chapter 16, Verses 16-18, He says,

'It is We who have set out the zodiacal signs in the heavens, and made them fair seeming to all beholders. And moreover, We have guarded them from every evil spirit accursed. But any that gains a hearing by stealth, is pursued by a flaming fire, bright to see.'

"It is obvious from these verses that our destinies are decided and made in the heavens, and jinn eavesdrop and communicate these to their followers. Some men of magic ask the jinn for this information, while others try to interpret the heavens themselves."

"Do you get yours from the jinn?" Samir asked him a straightforward question.

Najumi did not answer. He turned to another page and read, "In Chapter 6 Verse 75, the Quran says,

'So also did We show Abraham the power and the laws of the heavens and the earth, that he might with understanding have certitude.'

"Prophet Abraham lived among the Chaldeans, who had great knowledge of the stars and heavenly bodies. But he got beyond that physical world and saw the spiritual world behind. But that doesn't mean the knowledge of the heavens does not exist!"

He continued, "The Babylonians learnt this knowledge from the jinn. They had astrological charts that enabled them to predict the future. The Greeks learnt it from the Babylonians, and through the studies of Plato, Aristotle, and many others, astrology came to be highly regarded as a science. Then it was learnt by the Romans. Today, we still use Roman names for the zodiacal signs. Finally, the Arabs learnt it from the Romans and spread it throughout the world."

"Don't Indian have a strong belief in astrology too?"

"It is almost like a religion to them. Jyotisha, meaning heavenly body, is the Vedic astrology. Vedanga Jyotisha is one of the earliest texts about astronomy within the Vedas, but was most likely influenced from the Greeks."

He paused for a moment and said, "We have more faith now in science now than what has been passed on to us through generations and over thousands of years. We have degenerated and transformed alchemy into chemistry and astrology into astronomy. We have moved from sciences of the soul to sciences of the material world. Some think of astrology as the occult and as mysticism, while in fact it is a primitive science that is complete and needs no further development if studied well."

He looked at Samir as if giving him an accusing look, and continued, "When the British decided to give independence to the sub-continent, called India then, and partition the region into a Hindu-India and Muslim-Pakistan, the Hindu astrologers reverted to the stars and did not favor the chosen date August 14, 1947. They saw political and economic turmoil, and instability, plague the nation that sought independence on his day. They chose freedom at midnight following this day, while the Muslims readily accepted being free on that day.

"What we see today in Pakistan is political instability, martial laws, the founder dying within a year of independence, prime ministers being assassinated or hanged, prime ministers being jailed or exiled, civil war and further breaking of the country into two: Pakistan and Bangladesh. We see continued unrest and terrorism. But we see none of that in India because they chose the right date! We should have consulted the stars then!"

Samir hesitantly nodded his head, "There may be certain elements of truth in this, whether we accept it or not. Our former prime minister Marvi herself was a staunch follower of astrology, of numerology and of many other predictive beliefs. At one point, she had even wanted to introduce this subject in the university curriculum."

"Indian universities teach astrology. We should too!"

Samir knew of this strong belief in astrology held by the Indians, "I recently saw the Bollywood movie 'PK' which showed how millions throng to these astrologers like they are gods! I also recall reading about how the Jantar Mantar monument in Jaipur, India, a collection of 19 architectural astronomical instruments built by the Rajput King Sawai Jai Singh in 1734 was used by subsequent rulers to learn about their destinies. I guess most Pakistanis have picked this up from the Hindus."

Could one really see the future through astrology, Samir wondered. If this was true, then Najumi would be able to give him the right answers.

He reverted back to the basic questions he had come to seek answers to, even though he wondered if he would really believe what Najumi would tell him, "Can you tell me if the terrorist's attacks will continue or stop in Pakistan? Will we be crippled as a nation? When and where will the next attack take place? What can we do to stop these attacks?"

Najumi became quiet for a moment. He then got up and walked to his cabinet of books and charts. He opened it to check a few charts, then finally pulled out one and lay it on the table.

"This covers the period since Pakistan was created. All major events that have occurred are clearly written here. I had warned the previous prime minister of what is coming, but he was less interested in administrating the country well and more in filling up his pockets."

He pointed to a corner of the map, which showed a planet, and had lines marked in red ink propagating in all directions, "I had warned of the break-up of Pakistan into Pakistan and Bangladesh if Bengalis were not given their rights. I warned of the killing of both leaders responsible for the break-up. I had warned of an earlier prime minister being sent in exile, and returning back to capture power. I had warned of the murder of Marvi Brohi, our beloved former prime minister," he almost choked.

Every astrologer claimed to have predicted the past accurately, Samir thought. It was the future he was more interested in.

"What can you tell us about the future?"

Najumi rolled up the chart, went to the cabinet, pulled out another chart, and laid it out on the table. It had many more markings in red ink: some lines, some circles, and many crosses.

"Are you ready to hear this?"

"Shoot!"

Najumi moved his finger on the chart, first along the lines, then the circle, and finally stopped at one of the crosses, "I see something terrible about to happen soon, a lot of agony and pain, many screaming with pain, many dying. There are evil forces!"

Samir was apprehensive but asked immediately, "Where and when? Can you please be clear? If it is so, how can we prevent it?"

"Destinies can be changed if the right measures are taken to counter them," Najumi replied with conviction.

Najumi then moved his fingers around till it stopped at a circle, "Islamabad will see great destruction soon. There are evil forces that are going to create havoc in the city. Nothing can stop them as they have the negative forces on their side."

Samir was at a loss of words. Islamabad and negative forces? He started to recall that Hasan had lectured him on that only yesterday.

He hesitated to ask him the next question, but did so as he was curious, "Can this destruction be prevented?"

"It can be prevented if the evil forces behind it can be countered. You need to find out first who is doing it and get to the bottom of where the evil is originating from!"

"Can you be more specific?"

"Wait…let me concentrate to what is causing it…I see more dead bodies…and these are not fresh bodies…they look like they are decaying…like after a burial. I see skeletons…it could be a graveyard. There is evil originating from it!"

He turned around to face Samir and added, "This is black magic! It means there is some evil planted in a graveyard to cause destruction in Islamabad."

Black magic? Samir had heard about black magic from many quarters, but he felt now was not the time to ask questions about it, but wanted to know how to stop further attacks.

"Can the evil be stopped?" Samir almost choked wanting to hear more from Najumi.

"You need to find the graveyard, and you need to take the evil out immediately to prevent the catastrophe!"

He concentrated for a few more moments and continued, "Black magic is being used for this attack. The magicians plant personal belongings or special symbols or writings within a corpse in a grave to inflict maximum damage. Objects are also planted within a grave or a corpse to give more power to the evil forces. You need to find the person, find the aamil doing it, and have him reverse it. Or you can stop it yourself by finding the grave, and taking out these objects yourself before it is too late."

"This is a long shot! We do not even know who the source is, who the aamil is, and where the graveyard or the grave is!"

Samir looked at his watch. He was running short of time. "I need to be at the airport within an hour to return back to Islamabad. I will certainly call you if I get any information that could be helpful to you or us in identifying the source." Maybe Hameed could be helpful in finding the aamil, Samir thought. He reminded himself to call up Hameed so they could meet up at the Islamabad airport.

"Tell me what more do you see into the future?" he hurriedly asked while getting up.

Najumi moved his fingers all around the crosses, "You don't want to know that. I see big destruction. A lot of it. And it is not just confined to one area or city. It is over a larger region, and across the rivers. There is blood in the rivers. There are many people dying. There is fire, and smoke and an earthquake. It is like a mini world war. It looks like an apocalypse!"

Samir was taken aback. He couldn't believe what he had heard. He had read about the end of times. He had also heard it from Timur at the madrassah, and from Latif at the university. Shah Naimatullah Wali had prophesized it too. Were they all predicting the same end? Or were they just using each other's information to predict the same future?

Samir wanted to know more. "When do you see that happening? Are the same evil forces behind it? Can we stop all that could happen?"

Najumi concentrated again with his fingers on the chart, "I see it not too far away. There are many evil forces. Many more. And much more evil than what we have encountered so far. They are resorting to a very powerful magic. Perhaps a superman or a being with supernatural powers. They are just too powerful and cannot be stopped…"

"Could it be a jinn?" Samir abruptly asked, "Can they use a jinn to cause destruction?"

Najumi stopped short of speaking and almost chocked. Samir could feel the stress in his voice, "I did not want to say that, but you took the words out of my mouth. If they use the jinn, you cannot win this war!"

It sounded like doomsday! The end of world. Jinn and men fighting! Who could stop it if the end of times was around the corner? Was Samir starting to believe in it all? Was he really beginning to believe in supernatural forces? Or was he just being afraid?

He knew he couldn't take any chances and live on his past beliefs that there was no magic, and that supernatural power like the jinn did not exist in Islam or in many other faiths, and that it could not be used for good or bad. What if all of this was true and for real? And what if it actually was being used for an evil purpose? And because of all this, the world could come to an end. Soon!

It had to be stopped! But how?

Institute

It was a cloudy and dark night with strong winds. Islamabad usually had rains once or twice a week. This season had been exceptionally dry with lesser rain as compared to the average for this time of the year. The water level at most lakes around Islamabad had depleted to their lowest levels causing significant water shortage in the city. The government was rationing the water supply, releasing it only for a few hours to each sub-locality in turns.

Tonight, the meteorology department had forecast a heavy thunderstorm with lightning which would begin late into the night then clear up by early morning. The dark clouds and thunderstorm were only showing for the region around Islamabad while the rest of the country appeared dry. This was very surprising and the meteorologists could not figure out where the clouds had appeared from. The weather commentators on each TV channel were doing their own analysis. Some even went to the extent of saying that local HAARP experiments to create artificial rain had finally succeeded for Pakistan. Whatever the reason, it was a welcome sign to most residents.

The National Institute for Agriculture was located on the banks of Lake Rawal, about 20 miles from Islamabad. It was a graduate institute under the federal government offering a number of academic programs in agriculture. It mostly had day students, about 750 of them, all pursuing their masters or doctorate. Most of them lived in the twin city of Islamabad-Rawalpindi. The campus was usually lively and active till about 9 P.M., when the last of the classes would end, mostly taught by visiting faculty in the evening. After 10 P.M., it would give a deserted look when everyone was gone. The gates would then shut down.

It was not heavily guarded as no secret or classified research was being conducted here, unlike the other military sponsored science and technology institutes in the area. After all, it only focused on agriculture research, which was within the domain of the civilian sector. During the day, there were only four security guards at the main gate for each of the two shifts, while during the night, when everybody had left, there were only two guards guarding the main gate.

The institute was otherwise secure in itself, mostly to keep the local population out. It was possible that there could be a break-in to steal the various drugs which were stored in a large fridge in the institute, some of which were expensive. After all, there were drug users and peddlers in all parts of the country. The periphery had a fence, about 10 feet high, with intermittent closed-circuit cameras and spot lights installed. At the top of the fence was running a 440-volt electric wire, supported by insulators, which was energized late at night till early morning. The cameras, lights and the electrification of the fence were controlled from within the guard room, which was inside the main gate. No untoward incident had recently happened at the institute, and there was even less reason to be concerned as there were no military personnel moving in and out to do any type of classified or secret research.

Among the number of agriculture labs, the institute had a radio-isotope laboratory used for research, in which various seedlings and saplings were irradiated to kill various parasites and pests before they were processed in the bio-technology labs next door to develop virus-resistant varieties. The laboratory normally carried a reasonable supply of radioactive fuel, locked away safely in a secure room, which were provided by the nearby institute of nuclear science working under the atomic energy commission.

The institute was usually frequented by foreign scientists to give guest lectures or sometimes to conduct joint research. No eyebrows were raised at such an activity. Likewise, a team of Chinese scientists was to arrive at the agriculture institute in the next couple of days to carry out some important experiments using a new irradiation technology developed by them. This was to be tested on a new variety of mangoes and few other fruits developed bio-genetically within the laboratories. With these new varieties, the shelf life of the fruits was expected to increase to months, making it viable to export to far away countries by sea. This would be a big boost to the fruit exports from Pakistan, turning it into a billion-dollar industry. It would give India a run for their money, who were Pakistan's largest competitor in terms of fruit exports.

The Chinese had requested around four kilograms of the radioactive material be made available at the time of their visit. It had warranted special permission from the chairman of the atomic energy commission. The agriculture minister had personally spoken to the prime minister for this permission, and had ensured this be made available at the institute prior to the arrival of the Chinese team.

There was some concern by the military over moving a few kilograms of nuclear material from the nearby nuclear institute to the agriculture institute. They were concerned about the transport, and its storage and its use for research, even though the radioactive fuel requested was not highly enriched and was not of weapons grade, which is normally over 90%. The fuel asked for was just about 20% enriched, which was still considered quite dense by civilian standards. However, after the assurances of the minister, and clearance from the intelligence agencies for the key scientists and staff working in the agriculture labs, they made arrangements for its safe transport, storage, and use at the institute. The Chinese were, after all, good friends and their scientists and engineers had cooperated on many projects before with their counterparts in Pakistan. However, the movement of the nuclear fuel was to be kept top secret as a precautionary measure.

Colonel Khalid was in charge for security and safety at the institute. He had a sound professional record and had taken an early retirement from the army. The atomic energy agency had sent him a detailed memo and manual to ensure additional steps are taken to safeguard and handle the nuclear fuel when it arrives. The memo had also added a clause that no visitors, other than the Chinese, should be allowed into the premises of the institute during the days of the experimentation, which was to last for a few days. Moreover, any left-over fuel would be picked up by the personnel of the nuclear institute and returned back to them after the foreign team had departed.

The fuel had arrived in a special van a few days earlier, escorted by two military jeeps, one in the front and one in the back. It was encapsulated in two special cylinders, made of lead, which were about one foot long and four inches in diameter. Including the weight of the fuel, which was about 2 kilograms each, the total weight of each cylinder was around 6 kilograms. It was stored in one of the buildings in a safe room and locked inside a small vault. The security had been asked to be extra vigilant during these days because of the fuel being stored here.

It was past 10 P.M., and like on a routine day, most of the research staff and graduate students had left. The main lights had been turned off, except for those used for security purpose. The cameras covered all open areas, including the entrances to most buildings. The electric fence around the perimeter was turned on after the security personnel had ensured everyone had left the premises.

The four guards from the second shift had left, and only one of the guards from the night shift had arrived. The other had called in sick. He had suddenly developed a high fever and was vomiting continuously as if he had contracted some type of stomach virus.

The first guard left a phone message with his supervisor that the second one will not be coming tonight. The supervisor informed Colonel Khalid that there is no back-up available and if it would be okay for tonight with only one guard. After all, the place was secure.

Khalid was not usually extra cautious with any lack of security. He would normally not be concerned, but because of the radioactive fuel stored at the institute, he was concerned. While this was kept a top secret, with very few people knowing of it, he reminded himself that he would himself visit the institute after dinner and drop his own personal guard to ensure there are two guards on duty. After all, he was responsible for the security of the institute.

Khalid's in-laws were visiting him from Karachi. He had invited his wife's sister and brother-in-law for dinner and the whole family had gathered for dinner. The dinner followed by tea and family chat would normally end late around midnight, but he felt it would be too late by then to go drop the guard at the institute. He asked to be excused due to an urgent matter as soon as the main servings and dessert were served.

The storm hit hard at around 11 P.M. just when Khalid was just leaving with his guard for the institute. It was unexceptionally heavy, with intense lightning and flash floods. He had never experienced such an intense storm before in recent years. It appeared as if the whole of Rawal Lake was turned upside down and emptying onto the roads. In low lying areas, the road was flooded with about a foot of water. However, his Toyota Land Cruiser was built to handle driving through high puddles and dirt roads. He reversed out of his driveway and hit the road cautiously driving through the flooded roads.

It was a 10-mile drive to the institute. It would normally take about 20 minutes, but tonight, it might take twice as long. It was a small single lane road which was a short-cut through the hills to reach the institute. The road was completely dark and deserted. There was not a single soul or vehicle on the road. The TV channels had a strong advisory to people not to venture out. Only someone crazy enough would take the risk of leaving their secure homes tonight. Khalid just wished he would arrive at the institute soon, drop the guard, and return back home safely.

There was lightning all over the sky. Some of the strokes extended all the way to the surrounding hills. He recalled reading about lightning in physics, how the ground or the nearby cloud gets oppositely charged, and when the potential difference becomes high enough, of the order of a few million volts, it breaks down the insulation of the wet air, leading to a strike. 90% of the lightning strikes are between clouds while only 10% are to the ground. Tonight, it appeared the law of physics were being defied. 90% of the strokes appeared to hit the ground.

A stroke of lightning hit the nearby trees, and a few others across the hill. It appeared as if all lightning was striking within the perimeter of a few miles. The wind was very strong, and the trees, mostly fir trees which were typical in the area, were bending heavily in the direction of the gushing wind, as if they were tearing apart at the roots.

Khalid turned a corner, and almost lost control of the vehicle. He slowed down, though he wished he would arrive soon, drop the guard, and return back to the comfort of his home. He was only halfway through. Somehow, he felt as if all forces of nature were out to stop him from arriving. He smiled at himself and thought he had been through worse when in the army practicing mock attacks in bad weather.

There was a big flash close by which almost blinded him. A sharp crackling sound followed, and in between the heavy patter of rain, and the sound of water flowing downhill on the inclined road, he could almost hear a falling tree. He braked almost immediately to slow down, and a huge tree crashed right in front of him. He screeched to a stop, and almost hit the trunk that had appeared out of nowhere right in front of him. He was glad the falling tree had missed him by inches.

He and the guard both got out of the vehicle to examine the situation. The tree was lying horizontally right in front, completely blocking the road. On one side was a steep hill, on which the tree top had come to a rest, and on the other side was a forest. It was continuing to rain heavily.

They assessed the situation and came to the quick conclusion that there was no way they could move forwards unless the tree was moved to one side.

Khalid and the guard looked at each other for a second, and it was as if they both agreed they should try to move the tree. They had already become completely soaked in the rain but the rain would not stop them. They both placed their palms on the tree trunk and tried to push it away. It would not budge as it was a huge tree. They gave up on it after a few minutes.

"Shall we try pushing it forward with the Land Cruiser?" asked the guard.

It sounded like a good idea. But with no other choice in hand, except to turn back, they had no other option.

Khalid shifted to four-wheel drive, slowly moved the vehicle forward and let the bumper touch the trunk. He then pressed on the accelerator, as the engine rolled, pressed it further. The vehicle moved forward by a few inches. He pressed on the accelerator further, and the trunk moved forward a few more inches. Then it jammed. The vehicle could not move forward any further. He tried again. No luck. He then reversed back by about a foot, swerved left, and tried at a slightly different angle. It moved a couple of inches again, but got stuck again. He gave up.

"If we go back to the highway, we should be able to take the longer road, and should be at the institute within an hour." He knew it would be very late by the time he would return home. He would call his wife and explain the situation.

He reversed and slowly turned around. The road had become very muddy due to mudslides. It was almost a foot of wet mud at some places. They could only move very slowly. He hoped he would arrive at the institute soon, drop the guard, and return to the comfort of his home soon.

Security

All the students and staff at the institute had left by 9.30 P.M. The lone guard at the facility was still awaiting another guard to join him as the first one had called in sick. He knew Colonel Khalid would be arriving soon to drop his personal guard, as no one else was available such at short notice, and that too on such a bad night.

It was raining heavily, and with strong lightning. The rain was welcome as it had not rained for so long. He had turned on all the security lights. The cameras were on all day anyway. There was no movement, and he was not expecting anything or anyone to come. No one would venture out to visit an institute this late in the night, especially when the weather was so bad.

The lightning seemed to have increased in intensity. He could see large flashes in the sky, streaking across for miles, followed by the sound of thunder. So many of them seemed to strike the ground. He stepped out of the guard room, and stood under the canopy, so as not to wet himself, as he watched the lightning dance in the sky. He had never seen anything so beautiful like that before.

There were a few strokes, one after the other, and one of them hit the lightning arrester on top of the tallest building in the premises. It was just four levels, but it stood out in this rural countryside as the tallest building. The arrester would attract any lightning stroke and ground the high voltage impact before it would cause any further damage. The campus had its own standby generator for back-up power.

The strikes seemed to be coming closer and closer. It appeared as if the institute would be surrounded by strikes. Another one hit the arrester, and yet another one. The arrester buckled away, and its towering rod dislocated from its base and fell crashing down on the roof of the building. Yet another strike struck the tall fence around the institute. There was a flash, and the electric wire carrying high energy cracked and broke. The lights went off simultaneously and grounds turned dark. It appeared the connection to both the lights and the security wire were from the same circuit breaker.

The guard went back in, and checked the controls. It showed zero volt on both the security wire and the outside lights. He checked the breaker. It had tripped. He flipped it back, and after a crackling sound, it flipped off again. It appeared there was a short circuit in the wiring outside which had to be fixed first. There was no electrician on duty this late in the night. No one would come in this bad weather either. It will have to wait till tomorrow. Anyway, the institute was closed and there was not a soul on campus so there was no urgency.

He checked on the monitor connected to the cameras, and there was just a plain fuzzy white screen. He fumbled with a few switches, and nothing happened. He wished the other guard, who knew more about electronics than he did, was present. But there was nothing to worry about. The back-up guard would be here soon with the colonel. There was no need to call for help.

He felt a cramp in his stomach. Was it that spicy food he had devoured at home before leaving for work, or was it just a grumbling sound due to fear? He composed himself. There was nothing to fear. It was just rain and lightning, and a power failure. It happens in Islamabad all the time. It had happened at the institute a number of times. This was just one of those routine electrical failures. By the morning, all will be well. He just wanted to make sure he documented that in the log book.

He felt like going to the washroom. It was just a block away on the other side of the workshop. It was raining, but he would take an umbrella. He reached for one that was hanging by the door, and unfolded it. He then stepped out into the rain.

It was 12 midnight.

Flying Men

The five were called in a week earlier to the recruiting center in Mingora. They were between the ages of 21 and 25, hailed from different parts of the country and had not met before. Each was trained in a skill which was required of the mission. They were chosen by the local TTP commanders in their region as those who were ready to give their lives for the mission if so required.

All had skill certification. Two of them had diplomas in computer programming, while the other three were trained as an electrician, an auto-mechanic, and a locksmith.

The man who briefed them at the center was a foreigner wearing a local dress and spoke in the local language with a strong accent. He seemed to know Islamabad and its surroundings very well. They knew he was a contractor perhaps from a foreign agency but they were not supposed to ask questions about his identity. He assigned a number to each team member. 1 and 2 for the programmer, 3 for the electrician, 4 for the auto-mechanic, and 5 for the locksmith. "Number one will be the leader of this group."

He then laid out a map of the region and pointed to the institute.

"This is where you will reach just before midnight in the car provided. There will only be two guards on duty in the guard room. No one else will be present in the institute, and there would be very little reason for anyone to be concerned of a break-in! There are closed circuit cameras all around the fence and inside the premises anyway, as well as security lights. The fence is also electrified."

He laid out another map which was a floor plan of the institute, "Number 4 and 5 will cause a distraction at the front gate to occupy the guards. The remaining three of you will reach this point towards the side, which is an isolated area. The light in this area would not be working, as it would have been taken care of by someone else sometime earlier. Number 3 will knock off the camera and cut the wires in this area where it is dark so you will not be seen. It will trigger an alarm inside the guard room, but there will be no one to monitor it as the guards will be busy with the other two at the front gate. 1, 2, and 3 will then cut the fence with the tools provided and enter the premises from the back."

"We have been told that we will become invisible and will be able to fly over the fence?"

The foreigner was skeptical, "You can certainly try that if it works!"

Although he had been informed by their local contact that they had made arrangements with a 'man of magic' to make the team become invisible and have them fly over the fence and enter the buildings through the windows, he did not believe in this hocus pocus. He had made his own fool proof plan for obtaining the fuel which he knew was stored inside the institute.

He focused on the map, "You will move in slowly from the back here and knock the guards out with special darts that we will provide you. You will open the gate and 2 and 4 will go around to bring the car inside. In the meantime, the remaining three of you will get the master keys from the guard room, which will be inside a locked cabinet marked 'keys'. The key to this cabinet will be with the guard, and if not, number 5 should be able to open it easily. The master key will open the door to building R." He pointed to a small building in the back.

"Number 5 is qualified in opening locks, he should be able to open it easily in case something goes wrong with the master key. It is an ordinary lock."

He moved his fingers on the map, "1, 2, and 5 will enter the building from the front, walk up to the second floor, and enter room R5. The master key will open it. If not, again number 5 is the back-up. Inside the room is a small vault that has been programmed to open. The security code of the vault is only available with the director and the chief scientist of the institute. However, we will provide you with a decoding device that would break any code. It is easy to learn and use, and has been made by the same company that made the vault. Number 1 and 2 will be able to learn it quickly."

He looked at numbers 1 and 2, suggesting they will be in charge of the decoding device and the opening of the vault. "Inside the vault will be two metal cylinders, approximately one foot long and four inches in diameter. Each weighs around 6 kg, and will have radioactive markings on it which look like a black fan with three wings on a yellow background, like this one." He showed them a sketch, "You will take them down to the car, where the others will be waiting, and drive out of the institute to reach this place."

He pointed to another location on the first map.

"We will give you exact directions and more details a day prior to the mission whom to contact. In the meantime, you will continue with your training for the mission at the camp with the tools you will be carrying, including the decoding device, the unlocking tools, and the use of the special darts.

"Are there any questions?"

"What about the security checkposts on the highway on our way to and back from the institute? What if we are stopped and searched?"

"You will have proper identity cards that will show you as students of the institute. There will already be relevant books in the car in case they check. You will answer that you are going to a farm house in the village to study, and on your way back, that you are returning back to Islamabad after studying at the friend's house. This is common practice anyway with the students who are out late at night. A contact name and phone number will be provided to you."

"What about the cylinders?"

"The car will have a large CNG cylinder in the trunk whose top can be unscrewed to open. You will place the two smaller cylinders inside the larger one and cap it. There will be dummy pipes coming out from the cylinder that will look like they are leading to the fuel injection system. In other words, it will look like a car that is being driven on compressed natural gas. It will not raise any eyebrows as there are many cars that plough the roads driven on CNG."

Due to petroleum shortage in Pakistan, many vehicles use compressed natural gas, or CNG, as fuel. These CNG cylinders are usually placed in the trunk and are connected to the engine, drawing no special attention.

He continued, "You will leave the darts behind at the institute after you have used them, as the mission would have been almost accomplished. In case there is an intensive road block and search, we would like the road security to stop and search you and let you pass."

The five men smiled. They knew this mission was more important than the normal suicide missions that friends they had known were involved with. This mission was something that would change the direction of the jihad. Their names would be written in golden words among the ghazi, those who survived the mission.

They had been waiting to do something big like this and become heroes. They could even become the next commanders of their regions.

Break-In

The five were provided with a 2008 model Toyota Corolla which was one of the most common car on the road so as not to draw any attention. It had a dummy CNG cylinder in the back which appeared connected to the engine through pipes but actually was not. They were shown earlier how to unscrew the top of the CNG cylinder and place the two cylinders containing the nuclear fuel inside. The trunk also carried other cutting and unlocking tools that were required for the mission, but would draw no attention if searched because the boys were all technicians. The decoding device was small and looked like a smart phone, which could be carried in the pocket. Inside the car were some books as well. It looked like a typical case of students returning back late after a joint study at a friend's place.

They left the safe house earlier around 10 P.M., and heard on the radio that heavy rains were expected later in the night, which was unexpected. As they passed a police checkpost on the way towards the institute, they were stopped, and after checking their identity cards and their car, they were let go without questions. There was nothing they carried that could draw suspicion. There were no other checkposts on the way to the institute.

They arrived within a couple of miles of the institute in less than an hour. Since it was early, they decided to stop at a petrol pump which had a small canteen for serving tea and biscuits. They took a short break and no one spoke. There was complete silence between them. Their thoughts were only focused onto the mission ahead.

By now, heavy clouds with strong winds had started building up in the sky, and the temperature had dropped considerably. A thunderstorm was expected. It started raining heavily around 11 P.M. They were not expecting such heavy rains.

"Should we move in now, or wait?"

"We move in another 30 minutes," Number 1 spoke with authority.

The five of them drove up to the institute around 11:30 P.M.

"Will we become invisible and be able to fly over the wall?" asked Number 3.

"We have been told that the aamil has succeeded in giving us that power for tonight. We shall be able to do it once we arrive at the wall!"

About a quarter mile away from the institute, the two, who were to approach the institute from the front, were dropped off on the road that led to the gate. The road curved past it to a nearby settlement a couple of miles away. These were agriculture lands, and local farmers lived with their families in small houses on the land itself. They would normally be seen walking past the gate and so would not draw any attention. Tonight, it was all completely dark on the road because of the power failure due to the storm.

The car, with the other three, drove past the gate and stopped past the corner where the fence had just turned inwards. It had become muddy and slushy because of the rain, but the ground was firm. They parked and turned off the headlights and decided to walk on foot for about a hundred yards to the spot where they were informed that the light would not be functioning. They were surprised to see that all the security lights were off, which was perhaps due to the electrical outage because of the storm. It was very dark both due to the lights not functioning and the storm. They felt at ease as they were now sure they could definitely not be seen by the cameras. They did not know that the cameras were not also working tonight due to the same power outage, which would have made them even more at ease.

Number 3 was confident he could fly over the fence. He ran to the fence, raised both his hands towards the sky and jumped up, as if to fly, like he had seen a superhero do in one of the science fiction movies on TV. He landed back on the ground on his two feet. Feeling embarrassed, he tried again, and again, he landed on his feet.

Number 2, on seeing him try to fly over the fence, commented that perhaps he was doing it all wrong.

"Watch me fly!" He raised both his arms, and tried jumping off his feet. He too after jumping about eight inches off the ground, landed on his feet.

"There is something wrong. The magic to fly is not working!"

"Perhaps you are not clean, that is why! You did go to the toilet at the petrol pump!" remarked Number 4 cynically. "You better go and wash up first!"

Number 1, who was more intelligent of the three, was abrupt and took charge of the situation, "Becoming invisible and flying means we will not be seen, so we can cross over the fence easily. Magic works in different ways, sometimes which we don't understand, and it has already worked because it is dark and we cannot be seen. We don't need to be invisible anymore. Let's see if we can cross the fence easily to the other side like we were flying."

He asked Number 3 to climb the fence and cut the cable connected to the camera with insulated pliers. Number 2 supported him on his shoulder to reach, and with one click, the cable was cut. They did not know there was already no power to the cameras.

Number 3 then moved to cut the electric wire. It was risky due to the rain, as everything was wet, from the pliers to the hands that were holding them, to the others providing support. He took out dry plastic gloves from his pocket and wore them quickly. As he touched the wire with the plier, there was no spark and he had a feeling there was no power in the wires. He tried again, and there was no spark and no power. He took out a small wire from his pocket, and created a short-cut between the fence and the wire. No spark again. There was definitely no power in the wire. He cut the wire anyway, and signaled to the others to let him down.

"It is our luck. There is no power, and there is no current in the wire. The lights are not working anyway and the camera has been disconnected. Allah be praised! It is all because of the magic. We can just cut through the fence and walk in."

They took out the cutting tools and started cutting through the metal. It took them ten minutes to cut through the fence an opening large enough to pass through. They crawled through to the other side.

"This is like flying through the air!" remarked Number 3 with a smile. "Black magic indeed has its ways!"

They started to make their way towards the guard room.

In the meantime, the two who had gotten dropped off on the road came up close to the main entrance, and one of them knocked at the gate. No answer. He tried again loudly.

The single guard was sitting comfortably out of rain in the guard room. He still had cramps in his stomach. He was expecting the colonel to show up any moment with the replacement guard so he could go lie down and take a rest. It had been raining heavily, and this had led to a power outage, so neither the cameras were working nor the lights. He did not know that there was no power in the wiring on the fence as well. He would inform the commander about these outages when he arrived. They could be fixed tomorrow only when the electrician arrived. It was a dead and wet night anyway so nothing could possibly go wrong.

He thought he heard something at the gate. The rain was too heavy and loud so he was not sure what is was. The cameras were not working so he could not even see what it was. He reluctantly decided to go out from the comfort of the room and check. He hated getting wet on this night especially when he was not feeling well.

He stepped out and walked to the gate, and opened the small window. He could see no one. It was dark. He called out, "Hello, is anyone there?"

Nothing. There was no one there.

His stomach cramped again. He wanted to rush to the washroom.

He turned to go back when he heard someone calling out loudly. He went back to the gate to look out. It couldn't be the colonel, he was sure. He would see and recognize his car. The colonel would anyway honk to have the gate opened. He looked again carefully through peephole, and saw two men.

Maybe they were the farmers from the adjoining land asking for some help. They might have been stuck in the rain. Maybe they wanted some milk for the children, as most shops were closed due to the storm and it was impossible to travel. Or perhaps they were seeking someone or something. He was not sure.

Normally, he would open the gate if there were two of them. Tonight, he was alone. He would not open the gate, especially when he had been advised to take some extra security this week.

"Who is it, and what do you want?" he called out loudly through the peephole.

"My brother here is very sick. We were on way to the farm when he threw up and vomited. We had food at the petrol pump down the road. It is likely it is a case of food poisoning. Can we stop in shelter till the rain stops?"

He could relate to the sickness as he himself was not feeling well. Surely, there was no harm in helping a fellow Muslim in this time of need. "Let me go and get the key, as the remote is not working."

As he turned around, he felt something hard hit him on the back of his head. He fell face down on the floor. He could only see some men behind him. Where did they come from, he was not sure. He blacked out.

Just a few minutes earlier, the other three had cut through the fence without interruption and without being seen. It was all dark inside, and they slowly walked through the premises to reach the gate. They saw the back of the guard talking to someone at the gate. The guard could not hear them due to the rain and thunder and lightning. Number 3 impulsively picked up a gardener's spade lying next to the guard room, and hit the guard hard on the head. There was no need to use the dart as it was easier and faster to hit him with the spade. The guard was knocked out. Number 3 hit him one more time on the head to ensure he did not come around quickly.

The other two pulled him onto the side, while the third rushed in to get the keys to open the gate. Luckily, the key cabinet was already open so they pulled out the gate key and the master key, and unlocked the gate. Number 2 and 4 then ran up to the parked car and drove it in.

Half the task was already done, Number 1 thought!

They drove the car to building R, which was in the back and less than 100 yards away. The master key unlocked the main door to the building. Number 1 and 2, who were both computer programmers, together with number 5, used a flash light and ran up to the second floor and knew where room R5 was from the map of the building they had earlier studied which was provided by the foreign contractor. The master key opened it easily.

They walked in the room, and the vault was exactly where it was supposed to be, in one corner of the room behind the desk. Number 1 took out the decoding device, and started working on the lock. It took him less than three minutes to open the vault. He had practiced it enough during the training period. It was a piece of cake.

They pulled open its door completely. Right in the middle was the treasure they had come looking for: the two metal cylinders which had the radioactive markings on it. There were a few other bottles filled with some liquid which they did not care about.

The two took one cylinder each, and rushed back down. The car was already waiting at the front door with the engine running. They opened the trunk, unscrewed the cap of the large cylinder in the back, inserted the two cylinders inside, and capped the large cylinder again. It just looked like a car with a normal CNG fuel tank.

They drove the car out of the gate and called their contact to inform him that the mission was successful, and that they were heading for the next destination to hand over the treasure. No one would discover about it till the next morning, when the replacement guards would arrive on duty.

They headed for their next destination. Number 1 was very happy that their mission would be accomplished as soon as they handed the cylinders to the agency man. The emir would be very happy with him once he finds out about it. He may even get promoted as chief in his home town.

It was around 1 A.M. when Khalid arrived at the institute. He had been driving slow as he wanted to take no more risks and wanted to ensure he dropped the guard at the institute and returned back home to the comfort of his own bed. He had already called up his wife and informed her he would be quite late, and not to wait for him.

It was still raining and dark when he pulled up in front of the main gate. It struck him very strange when he saw the front gate open. None of the security lights on the fence were on. He could sense something was terribly wrong, and immediately drove his car into the driveway and stopped it right next to the guard room. No one rushed out to greet him.

The whole premises of the institute was dark, and none of the security lights inside were on as well. They both jumped out of the vehicle, and rushed into the guard room. The emergency lights were on but the room was empty. There was no guard. The key cabinet was open, and he could immediately see the master key was missing. None of the closed-circuit camera monitors were showing any image except a fuzzy cloud.

He immediately knew something was wrong. Terribly wrong. He got onto his phone, and called up the military emergency number. It was immediately answered.

"This is Colonel Khalid, head of security at the National Institute for Agriculture. We have an emergency, there is a possible break-in at the institute. I have reason to believe, though not yet confirmed, that we may have some radioactive material stolen from here. I need assistance here immediately."

He hung up as he wanted to waste no more time. He rushed back to his vehicle and pulled out his automatic handgun from the glove compartment. It felt warm and loaded. He unlatched the safety on the gun.

He heard his guard scream out, "There is a man lying unconscious in the hallway…"

Khalid rushed to check. It was the security guard. He turned him over. There was blood behind his head. He was alive but knocked out. He hoped the emergency team would arrive soon to take care of him.

"You stay at the front gate while I go check the building inside," Khalid snapped at his guard, and moved into the dark premises of the institute. It was still raining and he got drenched but he did not care and rushed directly to building R, where the fuel was kept.

The front door was unlocked. He took his gun out and carefully entered. Not a sound. He turned the lights on which were supported by emergency backup power, and rushed in, and ran up the stairs. Room R5, where the fuel was, had its door fully ajar. He leapt inside, and saw the vault in the corner with its door open. He took out his flashlight and looked inside the safe. It was empty except for a few glass bottles!

There was no point in staying here further. He wondered what happened. Who and how many had gotten in? How long ago? Were they still around in the premises or in the proximity of the institute, or had made their getaway?

His phone rang. It was the military emergency number, "Help is on the way and should be there in another ten minutes at the max due to bad weather."

"I would like to request a roadblock of every road leading out of the institute. Every car is to be stopped and searched. Ask security to check for two cylinders, about one foot long, which are missing from the lab and have radioactive markings. They contain radioactive fuel!"

He wanted to give as much information upfront without being asked questions, and continued without interruption, "We do not know how many men, or in which car, till we check the closed-circuit camera footage. We do not know how long ago the incident happened, or in which direction they may have gone. They could still be in the adjoining farms, or nearby petrol pumps, or they could already have arrived at their destination. The men may be fully armed and dangerous, very dangerous…"

"Sir. Colonel Asad from anti-terrorist special forces is also on the line and wants to talk to you."

There was a small crackling sound, and it was a manly voice, "Colonel Khalid. I will immediately alert the nuclear emergency task force. It is a bad night, and very late, so it may take at least 30 minutes for those folks to get to you. Major Farooq is heading the task force. I have sent out a red alert emergency message to all our units in the area. They have all gone on alert. In the meantime, please stay away from the buildings. They may be booby-trapped for bombs."

There was nothing much Khalid could do at this time except wait for the emergency team to arrive. He called up the director of the institute, got him out of bed, and informed him of the theft. The director almost fell out of bed and said he would be there within an hour. Khalid rushed back to the guard room to check on the wounded guard to see if he could provide some assistance to him, and if he came around, to obtain any information that could be useful.

The nuclear emergency task force led by Major Farooq arrived within 30 minutes. They also had paramedics following them. They rushed to the guard while the armed personnel started doing a careful building-to-building search for any other casualties, for any radioactive contamination, or for any terrorists hiding. There was no contamination and there appeared to be absolutely no one else present. They found the metal fence cut through and the electric wire cut. The rain had washed away any markings on the outside or inside which could reveal any further information. There were no footprints or tracks of any vehicle.

Somewhere near the guard room on the floor were what looked like shooting darts, with a vial, which did not appear to have been used. The emergency team carefully placed it in a plastic bag for further testing.

"The guard is coming to his senses. He is ok and not in danger. A bandage to his head is all he may need for now till we move him to the hospital."

Colonel Khalid and Major Farooq wanted to get out as much as they could from the only person who was present.

"It was around midnight. I was waiting for Colonel Khalid to arrive with the other guard…it was raining heavily, and there was a power outage. The cameras stopped working and it became all dark on the grounds. I could see nothing…there was some noise at the gate, and I went to check assuming it is Colonel Khalid…I did not open the gate but looked through the peephole…there were two men, who wanted help as one of them appeared sick. It was at this moment that I felt something hitting me on the back of my head and I blacked out…I could not see their faces but they appeared young, in their twenties and the one who talked to me spoke in clear Punjabi. I had not even opened the gate. I am sorry, sir."

The major turned to Khalid, "It is obvious that others, who were part of the same group, entered by cutting the fence and the electric wire. There were no alarms due to power outage. A couple in the front distracted the guard long enough so the others could enter from the back and knock him out. I am surprised they spared his life."

"They took the master keys from the key cabinet in the guard room, and moved into building R, where they knew where exactly the radioactive fuel was," added Khalid, "But what amazes me still is how they were able to open the safe which held the fuel. The lock needs a security code to open."

"Hacking, cybercrime, and breaking codes are so easy today that even if a twelve-year-old has a smartphone with the right app, he could do it!"

He continued, "It could only have been an hour to 90 minutes. With this weather, they could not have gone far, not more than 30 miles at best. The roads leading out of here should have been all blocked by now."

Major Farooq got onto the phone and snapped an order, "We will be sending out an image of the two cylinders with radioactive markings that are stolen and contain nuclear fuel. We believe they could still be within a 30-mile radius of here. I want more teams out on the roads, bring everyone out. I also want the full nuclear emergency team to be on alert. It is quite possible that one or two of the terrorists may panic and blow themselves up with the cylinders if stopped and checked. There could be a lot of radioactivity spread if that happens and will be very dangerous, very dangerous indeed. We must avoid an armed confrontation and be very careful!"

He continued, "I am sure their ultimate goal is to, indeed, explode the cylinders as a dirty bomb in some crowded area, as the fuel is not enriched enough to make a nuclear device. It means they may wait it out till late morning when the weather clears. They will not risk waiting a few more days as time is not on their side and they would know road blocks are all set in. So, the target must definitely be some important building in Islamabad frequented by a lot of people. And they will do it soon!"

He called another number, "This is red alert emergency. Please inform the Military Headquarters to follow the standard operating procedures for radioactivity alert. It's urgent. I will be giving out more details soon."

He turned to Khalid, "The chiefs of the armed forces will be informed right away so will the heads of intelligence services, including the ISI and MI. The prime minister will also be alerted. The Foreign Ministry will alert friendly nations as well, though we don't know who we can trust and who we cannot."

He continued, "We have to keep the media out otherwise it will create a panic and mass exodus and panic from Rawalpindi and Islamabad. A large population of these twin cities live within 30 miles of here. Close to one million people are at risk!"

Khalid felt the ground had caved in under his feet. Whoever they were, if they succeeded, this would be the largest single disaster since Hiroshima and Nagasaki, where over 200,000 people had died. His own family, his wife and children, countless relatives and friends, who all lived in Islamabad, would suffer if a dirty bomb exploded. This would be like the Chernobyl accident with far more consequences.

He recollected that a dirty bomb is not considered a weapon of mass destruction but is a weapon of mass disruption. It would contaminate the area around the explosion with radioactivity, which could remain in the area for more than a year. It would create considerable psychological damage, mass panic and terror, and lead to a major economic and demographic fallout as one would see evacuation of businesses and residences in the area. In addition to causing instant deaths by the hundreds, thousands perhaps would die a slow and painful death, or suffer from post-blast complications, perhaps for the rest of their lives.

Safe House

It was past 2 A.M., and the rain had stopped. There were still dark clouds in the sky, and the lightning was beginning to die down. It was very quiet on the secluded street where the safe house was located. Harry was waiting anxiously for the team to arrive and deliver the cylinders. He had already been informed by Timur that the mission had been successfully completed, and was expecting the team to arrive with the cylinders any moment now. It was a fool-proof operation, and would be accomplished without anyone knowing that the fuel had been stolen till morning when the new guards would arrive on duty.

Harry was expecting to be handed over the two cylinders by the team. He knew his agency was expecting him to hand these cylinders to another team with new faces and in a different vehicle for transporting the cylinders to the tribal belt. Little did they know that he had his own personal agenda.

He had planned an operation with two suicide bombers, one a decoy, and the other with the dirty bomb. For the dirty bomb, he had asked Timur for a second vehicle with a dummy CNG cylinder to accommodate the two stolen cylinders. It would be driven by a well-trained suicide bomber. This bomber, who would have all the right identification and papers, would drive the car with the cylinders to the heart of Islamabad, where he would explode the vehicle with the nuclear fuel filled cylinders.

For the decoy bomber, Harry had asked Timur to arrange for a separate suicide bomber in a vehicle at Rawalpindi away from Islamabad. This suicide bomber would blow himself up about 30 minutes before the explosion of the dirty bomb in Islamabad. The military would assume the exploded vehicle carried the nuclear fuel, and the security forces would move to Rawalpindi leaving Islamabad vulnerable to move the nuclear fuel laden car in and explode the dirty bomb in the main target area at Islamabad. It would be a perfect decoy.

He knew that a conference was being held at the science institute across from the president's office in Islamabad. The papers that he had asked Timur to arrange for the suicide bomber carrying the cylinders included conference papers, name tag, and fake identity cards. These would give an identity and credibility to the bomber as he proceeded through security checks into Islamabad. Harry had also asked for a few kilograms of explosives to be packed into the CNG cylinder.

His personal agenda was to ensure that the bomber exploded the dirty bomb in the heart of Islamabad. This was well-planned by him, and the timing was perfect! The conference at the science institute gave the perfect excuse to drive to the venue in the explosive-laden car without attracting much attention. About 200 delegates were expected at the conference. There would be movement of a lot of people and paperwork into the venue. The bonus was that the president was to be the chief guest. One couldn't ask for a better target.

The real target was that there were a lot of VIP buildings within a one-mile radius of where the explosion was to take place, including the prime minister's and president's office, the supreme court, and the parliament. The federal secretariat was also less than two miles away. There would be a lot of casualties due to the nuclear fallout, and most of these buildings would become inhabitable for at least a year.

Harry, however, was not aware that there was a red alert already, and the army had set up road-blocks on all roads leading to Islamabad.

The five men arrived with the cylinders at the safe house.

Another car drove up at the same time. This was supposedly the car driven by the suicide bomber in which the cylinders were to be transferred. Timur was a fine commander and had it all arranged with precision accuracy. He had carried out many missions successfully in the past. TTP had been paid a lot of money for the fuel to be stolen. Harry had changed the plan. Timur did not care to ask why.

Harry walked out as soon as he heard the vehicles drive in. He walked up to the car with the five men. The man in the other car waited in his car.

"The skiing and camping equipment are all ready for you," Number 1 said. "Would you like to take them now?" He opened the trunk, shone a flashlight, and pointed to the gas cylinder.

Harry reached inside and unscrewed it. He asked Number 1 to direct the beam inside the cylinder. He wanted to verify the authenticity of the consignment. He carefully took out the two cylinders with the radioactive markings, checked the seal of the nuclear agency on it, read the serial numbers, grinned, and gave a satisfied look. He had seen the pictures of the cylinders before along with the markings sent to him by the agency, and knew exactly how the cylinders looked like. They carried the right serial numbers and were tightly screwed, held back by a latch.

"This is perfect. I will take charge of the cylinders now!"

He knew why the other car was there. He had asked for it from Timur for his own personal agenda, which even Timur did not know that it was his agenda and not that of the agency. After all, he was the only contact to Timur. He signaled to the other driver, who got out from his car and walked to him. He was young, well-dressed in western clothes, and clean shaved.

"Salam. I am known as Qari. I have been sent by Commander Timur whom you have been in contact with. He has asked me to carry out your mission, and I am ready for it," he spoke with a confident tone.

"I know Timur sends only his best men. Help me transfer these cylinders to your car."

They transferred the two cylinders to the Qari's car, which also had a dummy CNG tank which could unscrew to accommodate the two smaller cylinders. Timur had already arranged for it to be packed with explosives, which appeared to be about 5 kg to 7 kg of TNT. It could be triggered remotely from the cell phone carried by Qari.

The five men, satisfied that their part of the mission was over, got back into their car, exited the gate and headed north.

Harry had planned it well. If the Toyota, which had carried out the heist at the agriculture institute, was captured on any security camera in the area around the institute, a search of the car would yield nothing.

He knew he was pulling a fast one on his agency as they would also assume the cylinders containing the fuel are on their way to Afghanistan in another car with a new team. In just a few more hours, the world would be horrified to learn that a dirty bomb had exploded in Islamabad.

Harry had to brief Qari on the logistics of the mission before he left. He had it all worked out in advance with Timur. He asked Qari to wait in the car and keep an eye on any movement till he returned and gave the signal to move.

He walked back inside and called up his agency local number and informed them that the kits were already on their way to their destination. Would they be disappointed when the fuel would not arrive in Afghanistan?

The operator interrupted, "We have a message for you. You have an emergency back home. Your mother is very ill. She has asked you to return home by the first available flight. The office has arranged for your ticket for the 6:30 A.M. flight out of Islamabad to Dubai if you can make it."

Harry acknowledged the message and said he would leave around 4 A.M. for the airport and asked for an agency car and driver to take him to the airport.

He packed his belongings and looked at the watch. It was around 3:30 A.M. and had started drizzling. The car to take him to the airport would arrive soon. He walked down back to Qari to give the final precise briefing.

Harry was crisp and to the point, "You will leave for the science institute in Islamabad around 6 A.M. We don't want you to arrive too early. The gates of the institute will open at 6 A.M. so plan to arrive by 6:30 A.M.

"You are a student and a member of the local arrangement committee for the conference. You have the conference tags and your identity card. The trunk of your car has a lot of printed conference material in boxes, which you are bringing from your university in Taxila. You need to get to the registration desk before the participants arrive."

Qari was absorbing every word confidently and silently. Harry wondered how could someone who knew he was so close to death be so confident.

Harry continued to instruct him, "Your car has the main device hidden in the CNG cylinder, which is a small nuclear bomb. No one ever has carried out such a mission before. You have the remote with you which is the app on the cell phone, but be very careful with that. Any questions?"

Qari had no questions. "I have been waiting for this mission for a very long time. Allah has been kind that He provided me with this opportunity not only to achieve martyrdom but to go down in history as someone who has won the first battle leading to the end of times. Our mission will be achieved successfully inshallah."

Harry knew Qari was one of the best Timur had. This mission was very important and failure was not an option, so Qari was chosen. Harry continued to explain, "You will be checked and searched at the road block. There are enough boxes of papers in the trunk of your car to deliver on time to the conference that you will easily go through. If there are delays at the security checkpost, tell them that the president is to give the chief guest address, so you need to arrive early to set up the papers. You have the ID and the conference tag to show. There is nothing else in the car that will draw suspicion. The cylinders are specially built to prevent radioactivity being detected. They comply with international standards. No radioactivity can be detected unless both the CNG cylinder and the other cylinders are unscrewed."

Harry continued, "You will arrive at the institute around 6:30 A.M., when most of the conference staff would still not have arrived. You will enter through the back gate from where the supplies are normally delivered. Security at this time would be scarce, maybe just two or three persons. It will be early in the morning so you will get through without any problem. Park the car in the back-parking lot and wait. It will be a long wait, but no one will suspect you as you are one of the conference organizers.

"All cylinders have a latch that unlocks the screwing mechanism that keeps the cover tight. Just before you are ready to carry out your mission, you will unlatch them. The explosives are packed in the CNG cylinder.

"You will wait for the arrival of the president from the front gate, which will be around 9 A.M. This you will know from the police sirens. When everyone is focused on the arrival of the president at the front gate, you will start your car, and drive up through the narrow lane connecting the two parking lots. You will then drive as close as possible to the front side of the building, from where the president will be entering, and blow the explosives with the app on your cell phone."

Qari's mind was already rolling back to his last briefing from Timur. He had assured him that the mission will be successful, like all the others before this one, as magic had been invoked to provide him protection. Qari knew Timur had contacted one of the most famous aamil who practiced black magic adopted from the times of the Prophet, and one which always worked. He has assured Qari that he and his bombs would become invisible and would remain undetected to everyone, and they would pass by every road block and security check with ease.

Black magic had great powers. He had learnt that many of his comrades had resorted to such magic and had carried out successful missions in the past without being seen. He had heard from Timur on phone this morning that the five men who had stolen the two cylinders had remained undetected because the magic by the same aamil had made them invisible. This was just going to be a continuation of the same mission. Black magic will make him succeed.

He smiled as he thought the infidels always wondered how they could get in successfully and disappear after killing many of these unbelievers. After all, Allah, with all His powers, was on their side. One day, they will rule the world, and his name will go down in history in golden words as one who changed the fate of the Islamic world.

Qari also knew that the local American contractor had no idea that magic will be used today. He was not told because the Americans did not believe in it. They were living in a foolish world. This time they would know of the truth and believe in its powers after he had carried out the attack successfully. The world would then know of the powers of Islam.

Qari thought himself lucky that he had been chosen by Timur to carry out this operation. This was to be one of the most important mission anyone had ever carried out, more deadly than 9/11, where thousands will die, and millions will be evacuated from the area. His reward will be the highest level of paradise with 72 virgins. He just couldn't wait for it. He looked at his watch again, just a few more hours to go.

His mind was interrupted by a car that just drove in the parking. It was probably the car that would take the American to the airport. He would hear about the success of the operation after he arrived wherever he was going.

Harry walked out of the house with a small bag, and drove away without even looking back. He just wanted to be out of Islamabad and landed safely in Dubai before the world started reported about the dirty bomb. It would be breaking news all over the world. He would hear of it in Dubai. He knew he would have to answer to his superiors, but he was ready with his story, and was sure they would be pleased with the final outcome. After all, this was a better outcome than was planned by his agency. He would make up a story that they will believe.

He considered himself a genius.

Clues

Samir flight finally took off late from Karachi just around 1 A.M. due to bad weather at Islamabad. After a number of accidents at Islamabad, which couldn't handle landings in bad weather, all flights into Islamabad at the departure airport are usually delayed for take-off till the weatherman at the arrival airport gives the green light. He had informed Hameed that he would arrive late, and not to wait for him.

Samir had no idea that nuclear fuel had been stolen when he landed at Islamabad at around 3 A.M. He was surprised to see Hameed waiting for him at the airport. Hameed had a grave look on his face with desperation in his voice.

"They have broken into the National Institute for Agriculture and stolen two cylinders which contained around 4 kg of moderately enriched nuclear fuel…"

"What?" screamed Samir, "how could that be possible…"

"Even security is surprised how they got in undetected. It is only possible if they resorted to the use of black magic."

Samir shook his head, but he was at loss for words. His mind rewound to what the astrologer had warned him about.

"Najumi warned me of a similar catastrophe coming. He said many would die in Islamabad. He also warned that the evil forces are protected by some type of black magic. I never believe in these things, but Najumi predictions seem to be coming true!"

"What is most frightening is that if these cylinders are exploded in a populated area, it could take close to a thousand lives and the fallout would cover an area of a few square miles. Tens of thousands more would be affected, who could slowly die a painful death over the years. The whole area around the explosion for miles would not be habitable for many years," he almost choked.

Both were silent for a few minutes as Hameed drove out of the airport area.

"Who do you think is behind this? Timur and TTP? Cannot Timur be picked up by the intelligence agencies for questioning immediately," Samir asked.

"Nobody has claimed responsibility for the theft yet. It has only been a couple of hours I was just informed by our intelligence friends. The country still doesn't know about it. Anyway, most are sleeping which is good as it might otherwise create a nightmare to evacuate Islamabad in the middle of the night.

"We don't even know who did it, what the real target is, and when the attack would take place? We are keeping it very discreet otherwise it will cause a panic. The prime minister has been informed. The intelligence believes there are foreign hands in the operation. They are sure the fuel is still in Islamabad, and a red alert for the security agencies has been notified. The army has moved into action and is setting up road blocks all over Islamabad. The atomic energy agency folks have been called in as they are the only ones with the equipment to detect radioactivity. It is a nightmare!"

Samir's phone rang. It was the prime minister. He was not at all surprised to receive her call at 3 A.M. in the morning due to the severity of what had happened. She must have been informed, and sounded alarmed.

"Samir. I am shocked at the security at our institutes. Our security agencies have failed to stop the terrorists and the infiltrators in every case. But that I will discuss later with you. I have spoken to the army and the intelligence chief. They are both on their way to their headquarters to personally monitor the search operation. We cannot allow a nuclear disaster to happen, and that too in the heart of Islamabad. The army has taken charge of Islamabad but you know how risky that is. By the morning, all TV channels will be flashing news that the army has taken over the capital. It could also mean a reversal of democracy to military rule if we are not able to counter this as soon as possible."

She continued with panic in her voice, "The foreign office has already spoken to the Americans and the Chinese and have asked for their assistance. We know many of these terrorist groups operate from across the border and with foreign funding. We need to reach out to their commanders immediately through our friends to stop this insanity.

"You were trying to get to the bottom of this after the Charsadda attack! What happened?"

"Prime Minister. I am sure the solution lies within our borders this time, and that is what I am working on non-stop. I have just returned back from Karachi and have met several key people to get an insight on how they operate. These are not just plain militant attacks that can be stopped by security but there is much more to them than meets the eye. It is a world of magic and jinn which I can't even begin to explain to you over the phone."

"Stop talking nonsense!" she snapped, "get hold of our friends in US and ask them to help us! Most likely they may have an insight into this, but we need to move fast, very fast!"

"Trust me, Ms. Prime Minister, I am up to my neck into this, and on it without break. Foreign powers and friends won't be able to help in this case. We are helpless unless we play the same game and give the terrorists a taste of their own medicine. I will brief you on that when I see you, as right now, I am on way to the institute where the fuel was stolen to see if we find any clues that can lead us to the perpetuators."

"The atomic energy chief is on his way to my office. I have asked him to alert his staff. We need to stop this madness, even if we have to sit across the table to talk to these terrorists under the present circumstances. I cannot risk thousands of innocent lives, even if I need to step down…" her voice trailed off.

"Prime Minister. We cannot agree to the implementation of the sharia laws in the country. Beheadings, flogging, stoning to death? We cannot let our country be run by barbarians. Their agenda is to use nuclear armed Pakistan to destroy everything we believe in! We cannot allow that!"

She made no further comment as she hung up the phone.

Samir turned to Hameed, "We need to reach the institute and check with the chief of security if there are any hints they may have left behind which could lead us to them. We need to figure out where and when the attack could take place."

Hameed shifted gears and picked up speed. The rain had stopped but it was still dark. There were a number of army vehicles that they passed, including two road blocks. There were very few cars on the road, but each car was being stopped and checked. It slowed them down.

They arrived at the institute in under half an hour. Colonel Khalid came out to greet them. He had news.

"We received information that five men, all in their twenties, had stopped by a petrol pump a few miles off here at about 11 P.M. last night and had tea. The canteen owner reports they were all very quiet and hardly talked to each other. They were driving a white Toyota Corolla. They then drove off in the direction of the institute. The owner did not suspect anything funny as there are many farms in the area, and usually, there are cars going in that direction."

He continued, "We put out a red alert for the car, and only about 30 minutes back, they were apprehended about 60 miles north of here on the Peshawar motorway. First, they tried to run past the checkpost, but when security fired in the air, they quickly surrendered."

"This was a big risk they took!" Samir couldn't believe the foolishness of the checkpost personnel, "They could have panicked and exploded the radioactive fuel!"

"The men are careful not to create a panic! Anyway, they claimed they were all students and carried proper papers. When asked why they had not stopped, they claimed they were just nervous.

"However, the check-point security are well-trained and were suspicious, so a close search of the vehicle showed their CNG tank to be a dummy one. It had pipes going into the engine compartment but not really connected. The CNG cylinder had a latch, opening which unscrewed the top disclosing a large empty compartment. This was the giveaway and they were detained."

Hameed exclaimed, "This is excellent news. Who is interrogating them as we need to know if they were really behind the theft, and we need to do it fast?"

"They are being moved immediately to the anti-terrorist cell which is about 15 minutes from there. It is a small unit, and Captain Sabir is in charge."

Samir and Hameed asked to see the guard who was on duty last night. He had by now been relieved of his duties as he could provide no further useful information.

Samir turned to Hameed, "We need to get to the source of this! Najumi warned of the use of black magic by the terrorists, of bodies, of a graveyard, and an evil originating from it. He said to stop the attack, the graveyard and the grave needs to be found immediately and the evil taken out. Where can we start and how can we do it?"

Hameed looked at Samir, was silent for a moment, and said, "It appears you are beginning to believe in black magic after all."

"I never did, but it is certainly mentioned in the Quran. My younger son, Hasan, is convinced it exists from the Babylonian times. When we have no choices, and destruction and death is inevitable, then we need to adopt any way which can stop the killing, even if it is their way and we do not believe in it. If I had the time, I would go to Bahla in Oman and consult with the top magicians there.

"If you can't beat them, join them!" Samir added with desperation.

Samir told Hameed about what he had learnt in Karachi, "I was with Pir Wasim. He also said that since the terrorists believe they are fighting a jihad, they are probably resorting to using black magic as a weapon. Two evils make good friends."

Samir added, "The pir also believes that magic can make one fly, or make them invisible. What he said was really scary! If someone has access to the right magic, then he can do much more."

Hameed shook his head, "This is exactly what I had been telling you for a long time!"

They were quiet for a minute, when Samir suddenly exclaimed, "Oh my God! Timur's people were practicing flying through the air and walking on burning coal. We have seen a first-hand demonstration of it! They are using magic for their attacks. They may also have used it to steal the fuel. We need to find Timur, and talk to him fast!"

"We can't find him, but he can find us! I will message his contacts right away."

Hameed got on the phone and made a few calls in desperation. He left messages everywhere that it is urgent to talk to Timur, and if he could call him back. Hameed's usefulness came in moments like this. He knew whom to contact and when if the right contact had to be made.

They walked back towards the car to return back to Islamabad. Calling Najumi or Pir Wasim could help with some additional information, but it was early morning, and they would probably not wake up for another hour for morning prayers. Time was too critical and Samir wished time would stop!

They were halfway back towards Islamabad when Hameed's phone rang. It was a call from an anonymous number.

It was Timur! Hameed was not surprised.

'Timur. I am glad you called back urgently. Dr. Samir here would like to talk to you."

Hameed passed the phone to Samir.

"Timur. I will not beat around the bush. You know we have a very serious situation, and you know why we are contacting you. It is regarding the stealing of nuclear fuel from the institute. You and I know thousands of innocent people could die. If the army takes over the reins of the country, they will not accommodate any of your demands. Then it will be an all-out war between you and them. More people would die then than now, yours and ours! The army will not stop at anything till every single person working against our security is weeded out..."

Timur chuckled, "Dr. Samir. We have been very clear from the beginning. Pakistan was created so we could have an Islamic state. It did not happen because both the army and the politicians are corrupt and want to line their own pockets. Once we enforce an Islamic system, and implement the sharia law, there will be no more corruption. We will hang the corrupt and the stone the adulterers. We will chop off the hands of the thieves. We will become a model for the rest of the Islamic world. The rest of the Islamic countries will follow us, Caliphate will be introduced again, and we will defeat the Americans and Israelis in their own ground. There will be one flag of Islam all over the world. This has been prophesized in the Hadith and we will make it come true!"

"We can talk about your prophesies later. Can you for now stop your men from carrying out the attack wherever and whatever they are planning..."

"I told you when you visited us at the camp that nothing can stop us, and you did not believe us. I told you that we have now acquired powers to make us invisible, to fly through the air, you did not believe us. Our injured can heal themselves miraculously. Gunshots don't bother them. We can survive explosions without burning. We can fly though the air, as you yourself saw. We have the power, the magical powers now, and we are on our way to acquiring even more powers through jinn, and nothing can stop us. Be prepared for your own graveyard in the heart of Islamabad in just a few hours. The world will be on our feet within a few days."

With that he hung up the phone.

Samir felt he had got the lead he was looking for. Timur had spoken too much out of pride or his level of confidence. He had disclosed that the attack will take place in the heart of Islamabad in a few hours.

But where? Islamabad was a huge city. The airport? The Centaurus Mall? Jinnah Market? Blue Area?

Samir's mind immediately rewound back to that last meeting at the training camp. When Timur talked of magic, even at that time he had spoken too much. He had mentioned a Jadoo Baba from Hasan Abdal.

Samir abruptly asked Hameed to turn the car towards Hasan Abdal.

Captain Sabir was questioning the five men. Visually, they appeared to be clean and there was no evidence of them being involved in the heist of the nuclear fuel except that they were in the vicinity of the institute around the time when the fuel was stolen, and that the car had a dummy CNG cylinder large enough to accommodate the two cylinders. They were all young and claimed to be students with student cards, but what was strange was that their identities hailed from different parts of the country yet they were studying at the same institute from where the fuel was stolen. They claimed they were working on setting up a repair workshop together as a business. They were, however, not able to convince Captain Sabir as to what they were doing driving around that early in the morning, or having tea at a petrol pump. The car had no weapon of any sort, and they carried nothing with them that could make anyone suspicious of them.

However, when the dummy CNG tank was discovered by the security forces, they were immediately handcuffed, blindfolded, and moved into a high security cell. The captain was willing to take no chances. He kept questioning them about the dummy CNG tank as it was this part that did not fit into their stories.

Finally, they confessed, "We mean no harm. We are just young students trying to make some quick money. We have only been smuggling items from the tribal agencies to the cities and selling them for a profit."

This was a very common practice and in the knowledge of most police agencies, the customs, and the military as well. A lot of items brought in from across the border in Afghanistan and Iran at a much lesser price were smuggled across the porous border between them and Pakistan through the tribal areas, and sold in markets at a profit. Many would routinely drive across in their cars, fill a trunk load, bribe the inspector at the checkpost, and drive over. This practice had been going on for a very long time much before 9/11 and the Iran revolution. In recent years, the Afghan transit trade through Pakistan had provided a major opportunity of bringing smuggled goods in the country. The markets in the north were flooded with smuggled goods, many trickling their way into the south as well such as at Karachi Lea Market and Sohrab Goth.

Captain Sabir knew his job well and was tough, "The CNG cylinder is too small a container for you to make big money unless you smuggle some value-added goods, like drugs, foreign currency or gold. I don't think you were doing that. We will be transferring you and the vehicle to our headquarters in Rawalpindi to conduct some tests and ask more questions of you. We also need to ensure you are kept unharmed and safe from those who may wish to harm you, or kill you before you cooperate with us."

The captain knew that time was very critical. He had already sent out an alert asking for verification of their residential addresses and their student identity cards. However, it was only 5:30 A.M., and they may not hear anything till 9 or 10 A.M. Tests could be conducted on the dummy CNG tank urgently, and if they tested positive for any nuclear contamination, the men had to be broken down to confess and reveal more information. But time was crucial and was running out.

The five handcuffed men were immediately transferred to a small military truck and driven off in the direction of Rawalpindi. There was not much time to request a tow truck for the vehicle, so two drivers from the army were made to drive their car and follow the truck.

As Captain Sabir watched the car disappear into the horizon with the morning light appearing, he had a feeling that they were onto something big.

The early morning muezzin call for prayers could be heard from a distant mosque. Captain Sabir laid out his praying mat in the direction of Mecca and bowed his head to God asking for His blessings. He feared a major disaster was in the making!

Hasan Abdal

Samir and Hameed were on their way to Hasan Abdal to locate the aamil. It was just after 5:30 A.M. which was close to daybreak time, but it was still quite dark due to the clouds still hovering overhead. It had started to drizzle slightly again. Samir's thoughts flashed to what he had seen at the training camp and of men flying through the air, to what Pir Wasim had told him about magic, that most people, including those in power, and those who wanted to get into power, practice it. So what if the terrorists practiced it to achieve their own goals. It was like everyone was using magic to achieve what they wanted in life.

Najumi had told him about death and destruction in Islamabad due to some evil planted in a graveyard. Najumi had not known about the nuclear fuel being stolen, nor did Samir at that time. A dirty bomb would cause intense physical and psychological damage. It could trigger a major catastrophe. The possibilities were endless. It could trigger a nuclear war, it could trigger an apocalypse, the end of times,

Samir's mind raced back to the discussion his younger son, Hasan, had with him on black magic. Hasan was always very pragmatic and realistic. He believed in magic because there were stories about sorcerers in the Quran. The stories about Harut and Marut in Babylon were true, and everyone knew Solomon had tremendous powers given to him by God. What was not known was if there was indeed a book of knowledge, based on Solomon's magic, which had been passed down from generations to generations, and if this knowledge was now in the hands of terrorists.

Samir also remembered what Hasan had told him how the magic was performed on the Prophet, and which was reversed by finding and taking out the objects on which the magic has been performed. He tried calling him, but the message was the cell was off or out of the signal area. He would try later.

It was almost 6 A.M. as they entered Hasan Abdal. The early morning prayers in the mosque had just ended and a few devotees were trickling out of the mosque they had just passed.

Hameed pulled the car to one side, and asked to be excused for his morning worship, though he had missed the congregation by a few minutes. Samir said he would join him.

They both worshiped together in the mosque, facing Mecca, and prayed to God asking for His mercy against all evils the nation and the world was facing.

There were a few worshippers still present in the mosque reciting the Quran. Samir approached one of them who had grey hair and a long beard, "Salam. I am new here and we have come a long way from Islamabad. I have heard of a famous aamil who is a man of magic, who can make anything happen."

The old man looked at Samir in the eye and said, "Son, what you are saying is shirk, or a sin. Only Allah can make things happen. Believe in Him, and pray to Him, and all your desires will be fulfilled."

Samir should have been expecting this answer anyway from a man who looked pious and religious and was praying in the early morning hours in the mosque. Hameed came to his rescue. He spoke in Pashto to the man.

"Baba," which is a title of respect, meaning father, "we are both from the government. We have reason to believe, and fear, there are evil forces working against our people wanting to destroy it. I know you don't believe in it, neither does my friend here. But I have heard and seen enough with my ears and eyes that I believe in it. This is not the time to get into this discussion, but we need to get to this aamil to stop him from doing what he is doing. Can you help us?"

The man was taken back. "Yes, I have heard of a man of evil who lives in our city. I have also heard many flock to him to get evil things done through black magic. Whether he is able to do that or not, I do not know, but I can certainly have someone guide you to him if you follow me."

They walked out of the mosque, and nearby, under a tree, was a small tea stall which was just opening up. The vendor was lighting the fire to make early morning tea and hot bread for the early risers.

"Jatiya. Do you know the whereabouts of the aamil who I think is known by the name of Jadoo Baba? These gentlemen are looking for him and need to find him urgently."

Jatiya certainly had heard of and knew Jadoo Baba. Everyone in Hasan Abdal had heard of him. He directed them to the most crowded part of the city, "He works from a small house off a narrow lane which is full of shops near and in the main bazaar in the heart of the city. There is a mobile phone repair shop at the corner. Some of the shops in his street such as the milk and egg vendors will be open by now. Everybody in the city knows him. Ask any shop keeper and you will be directed to his house."

In this part of the world, all the addresses were identified by their proximity to something.

Samir and Hameed rushed back to their car and headed for the city center. There was hardly any traffic and they would be there in 15 minutes. It was already 6:15 A.M.

Qari had performed his morning prayers at the nearby mosque, which was a short walking distance from the safe house, and walked back to his car. He knew this could be his last worship in his temporary life. He was happy that he had finally arrived at what he always wanted to do for the last many years: martyrdom. This would not just be an ordinary act by blowing himself up and killing 50 others. He would be doing what no one ever had done on this earth before. He would be blowing a nuclear bomb and killing tens of thousands of people. Why do they call it a dirty bomb? It is dirty for all those infidels who are out to destroy Islam and conquer the land of the believers. But the Hadith was very clear on this. The Muslims would destroy the infidels, and the rivers of this land will become red with their blood. He would soon reach heaven and be blessed with the best fruits and food and women. He smiled.

He got into the car, and checked the trunk to see if the boxes of conference papers were all there, as if someone would have taken them, and quietly drove out into the road heading towards Islamabad. He pinned on his conference badge, and placed his fake university identity card and national identity card on the dashboard.

Half way towards Islamabad, he saw that the traffic was backed up in two lanes. There was a road block, and there was a military truck and a jeep parked on the side. A number of soldiers with their guns in their hands were searching every car. A few other men in white aprons who looked like they were from a laboratory were peeping inside each car. They held a device in in their hand which looked like a flashlight with an antenna. Some of them were wearing masks.

One could see the worried looks on the drivers and occupants of the car, who were asked to step out while the car was scanned and searched. Some were asking questions, but the military personnel were just waving them off as the cars were checked and cleared.

Qari became uneasy. He figured that the cat was out of the bag. It was obvious that the security had been alerted for a possible attack, except that the government had not yet announced it. He remembered that Timur had told him that magic done by their aamil will render him safe as well as make him invisible from the security forces. Despite that, when he saw the cars going through a check, with each occupant being asked to step outside the car, he started reading verses from the Quran for his safe conduct through the security barriers without the bomb being detected.

The traffic was moving very slowly, but being early in the morning, there was not much traffic. The trucks were not being allowed to go through, and only those who had valid reasons and identities were asked to park on the side for the time being. It was causing even more of a blockade to the traffic.

His car was next at the barrier. He kept reciting the verses from the Quran for protection. He was sure he would safely pass through this barrier as he was protected due to the magic of the aamil. The army personnel asked him for his identity and to open the trunk of the car. He then asked him to step out of the car and frisked him.

"What is in those boxes inside the trunk?"

He confidently replied, "I work at the science institute, and today, we have a conference beginning at 9 A.M. I am a member of the local organizing committee, and need to get all these papers and books at the registration desk before the guests and participants arrive by 8 A.M. The president is the chief guest who is expected to arrive around 9 A.M."

The army man reached inside to check the boxes, and dug his hands inside to find nothing but papers. He then asked the white aproned person to check inside the car and the trunk for any radioactivity. He inserted the detection antenna inside and moved it around. There was no signal, no radioactivity, no explosives detected.

Qari kept on reciting the verses. He was sure the magic would let him pass through undetected. He also knew the two inner cylinders were made air tight and secure by the atomic energy agency. Unless the latch was opened and the top unscrewed, there was no possibility of any radioactivity being detected. The larger cylinder was also airtight enough not to allow any residual air or fume leakage to come out. The TTP bomb people were very professional in making homemade devices and had prevented similar detection of explosives many times before. The detection equipment used by the security agencies were obsolete in any case, and mostly not working, like at the airports.

In the meantime, another person was checking the engine and underneath the car. If someone really checked the engine and the gas pipes closely, he would have found out they were not connected.

The army captain supervising the barrier walked up to the car, "What's in the boxes?"

The soldier replied attentively, "Sir. I already checked. Papers for a conference at the science institute in Islamabad. He works there."

The captain gave a friendly smile, "Once, I attended a guest lecture there when I was completing my training at the academy. They really bring in good speakers. Glad to meet someone from there. What is the conference about?"

"Technology!" That is all Qari knew. "The president is the chief guest. I am already getting late due to the road block…:"

"Let him go!" snapped the captain, and waved him forward.

Qari heaved another sigh of relief, got back in the car and drove towards the institute. The magic was already rendering him invisible to the security forces. Nothing could stop him now.

It took him another 20 minutes to reach the institute. There was hardly any traffic this early morning and due to the road block. He turned into the back avenue leading to the rear gate. He was glad he was using the rear entrance, because after the word had gotten out about the nuclear fuel missing, there would be an abundance of security on the main avenue where all the VIP buildings and offices were located.

There were two security guards at the rear entrance who were finishing their night shift. They already looked sleepless and tired. It was a rough night with heavy rains, and they were concerned about their family living in the low-lying areas where housing had been provided in some shanty quarters. They had called and found that the area had lost electric power all night due to rains. The children were restless and had not gone to school. The street leading to the neighborhood school was flooded.

Qari drove up and showed his conference batch, "I belong to the arrangements committee." He pointed to the box in the back, "All these papers have to be sorted and laid out at the registration table before the attendees arrive at 8 A.M. I am expecting others from my committee to arrive and help me sort the papers. I am early so I will just park and wait for them. They should be arriving soon."

The guards waved him in. They were in no mood to volunteer to help him after a bad night. They themselves wanted to be out of here as soon as the day guards arrived. It was already 6:30 A.M. They also knew there was going to be a major activity and protocol at the front gate, but only after 9 A.M. when the president was expected to arrive. Security would tighten as soon as the day guards arrived.

Qari drove in his car into the parking lot at the back side of the building. There were two other cars parked there, most probably of employees who might have left it there overnight. Because of the road barriers and checking today, he was not expecting anyone to arrive for another hour. He decided to lay back and relax.

It was just around this time that the five men in the intelligence headquarters were being grilled by a few other officers led by Major Osman. They were veterans in their jobs, and had been able to use various psychological techniques, without the use of torture, to read the minds of those detained to find out if they were guilty of something and would confess. They had achieved this skill over many sessions of training and being in the field for over 10 years. But this time, time was very critical and of essence. They knew time was critical, and if they were not able to have these men confess, then they would have no other lead.

After 30 minutes of intense interrogation, Major Osman knew that the one who was the electrician could be broken down. He appeared to have a soft corner against the killing of innocent people. The major took out his cell phone which had a recording from a few lines of the Quran from Chapter 5 Verse 32, and played it. The lines clearly conveyed what Allah had ordained: that if any one slew a person, it would be as if he slew the whole people, and if any one saved a life, it would be as if he saved the life of the whole people.

"Do you know there are thousands of innocent mothers and sisters and children out there who would be affected and killed by the nuclear holocaust? God will never forgive you for their deaths. Imagine if your own mother or daughter were out there and somebody else was doing it. What would you do? But if you save the life of even one person, you will have achieved your paradise. This is what Allah has promised in the Quran."

After this repeated persuasion, it did not take long for Number 3 to break down and start crying. "I never was meant to be a part of this mission. My uncle, who works in the madrassah, forced my father to send me to his madrassah, where I was given all these lessons…"

The major hugged him, "Its ok. We will talk about that later. Right now, we need to know where the cylinders are that you stole from the institute."

"We were asked to drop them to a certain place in Rawalpindi." He went on to describe the location of the place, and of the foreigner who was there, and one other person whom they had never seen or met before. The cylinders were transferred into the stranger's car in a similar type of large CNG cylinder. It was a white Suzuki Cultus. After that they had left and were asked to proceed towards Peshawar.

Major Osman immediately got onto his wireless and sent out another red alert describing the location of the house, the car, the person driving it, and the foreigner. He was not sure if there would be anyone at the location.

Within ten minutes, a contingent of two army trucks arrived at the house, and the soldiers jumped out and surrounded the place. As they slowly crawled in, they realized there was no one there except for the chef making breakfast for himself in the kitchen. He knew nobody and had met nobody except for a foreigner whom he had served coffee last night. He had no knowledge of any other person and appeared quite innocent. He was detained anyway.

A search of the place yielded no further information or clues. It was a guest house that was used by many for temporary accommodation. The foreigner had only arrived last night and had directly gone to his room. He had already left for the airport early morning. The information about him was immediately communicated to the airport but he had already boarded the flight to Dubai which had taken off.

The alert for the Suzuki car with a CNG cylinder was broadcast all over the city to all army, police, rangers, and intelligence units. It was intentionally not communicated to the civilian information ministry to avoid it being telecast on TV or radio yet. The army did not want them to broadcast it and create a stampede in the city. There was no point in doing it as they still did not know where and what the target was, and when the terrorists would strike.

Little did the security forces know that the suicide bomber had already arrived at the target location and was waiting for his high-profile target to arrive in a couple of hours. His car was safely parked, undetected, in the institute, thereby, avoiding detection.

As Samir and Hameed reached the city center, Samir's phone rang. It was Mike.

"Samir. I just heard from our friends that there is a severe threat of a dirty bomb exploding in Islamabad. Its exact location is not known yet, but we have asked our embassy's non-essential personnel to vacate as soon as possible."

Samir was not at all surprised how information on the heist had reached Washington so fast. Key governments were probably contacted last night, and the US must certainly be one of them. Also, since most of the terrorist organizations were financed from outside, the western intelligence agencies sometimes knew of impeding attacks much before the local agencies did.

"Don't worry. We are on it already, and have a run against time. We expect to defuse the crisis as I am on an important lead—call it spiritual if you could."

Samir had no time to explain any further, as they had already arrived in the vicinity of the aamil's neighborhood, and Hameed was inquiring as to the whereabouts of his house. He asked Mike if he could possibly get information through some of the agencies in the US who had possession of the fuel so they could negotiate a deal and it could be returned back to the government.

"You are not going to lay down your arms in front of the terrorists?" Mike was surprised.

"Not at all. We just want a little more time as I am sure I have reached the heart of the operation. Once we have clipped that, our countries will be a lot safer from the terrorists!"

Samir excused himself as he had arrived at his destination, and told Mike he will talk to him later.

It did not take long for them to find the aamil's house, as almost everyone in this neighborhood had heard of him or knew him. The neighbors were not surprised to find well-dressed gentlemen looking for him as it was a routine matter for the neighborhood. The aamil was well-known far and wide.

They walked up to his door and knocked. No answer. Another knock yet yielded no response. Finally, a few minutes later, a female voice asked who they were and what is it they wanted.

"We are here to see Jadoo Baba and have some urgent business with him."

"You need to come back in the afternoon. Baba stays awake all night, and sleeps after morning prayers till mid-day."

Samir looked at Hameed. He did not know what to do. It was not considered good anywhere to gate crash, and definitely not in this part of the world where a purdah-clad woman was answering the door.

Hameed decided to use some authority and spoke out loudly, "I am Major Hameed from the Army Headquarters. We would like to talk to Jadoo Baba urgently. Please let him know otherwise we will be forced to arrest him."

Some of the people who were probably neighbors on their way to work stopped to listen. It was typical in many Pakistani societies to listen in on everybody else especially when they felt the other was in trouble.

The woman chickened out when she heard the man was from the army. She asked them to wait outside for a minute so she can wake him up and get him. They said they will wait. Some of the neighbors came forward asking if anything was wrong. Hameed ignored them completely.

Finally, a tall and slim man who claimed to be Jadoo Baba appeared at the doorstep. He saw a small crowd of neighbors was already accumulating at his doorstep, so he invited the strangers inside to keep the discussion to himself. He wanted to retain his credibility among his neighbors.

"What can I do for you? Can you come back at 12 and I will see you first!"

Hameed spoke up sternly, "We know you well. We know you can do a lot through black magic. We are not interested in what you can do or not do. But we can have you arrested and sent behind bars for a hundred years if you don't cooperate with us!"

Jadoo Baba thought they were just some other customers who had connections in the right places and wanted to get things done for free, "Tell me what I can do for you. I can give pain to your enemies that they will never trouble you again..."

"We want information about something you had done for a man named Timur from the northern region. He may have asked you to give some evil power to his men and to steal something from an institute."

The aamil froze! He clearly remembered working for Timur many times before, and the men who usually represented him and who had given him a lot of money to steal something from a secure place. He tried to pretend ignorance.

"I know of no such man. Most of my customers are wanting a woman, a break-up in marriage, or to give an incurable disease to someone..."

"Perhaps you will cooperate after we take you to the detention center. We can have an army jeep here in 5 minutes if you don't cooperate!"

The word army jeep frightened him. He looked around and thought. There was no one listening. These men looked important, who claimed they were from the army. On the other hand, Timur was his regular client and a big source of money. He had given a large sum of money for this last job. If he disclosed his secret, he may never get his old customers again. It was also likely that Timur would have him killed if he ever found out he had disclosed his identity and the work he had wanted done. He knew Timur was a dangerous man.

However, he could mislead these men and they would never know the truth. That, he figured, would be the best strategy.

"Please have mercy on me. If they know or find out I talked to you, they will have me killed. There were a few men here last week, and they wanted to steal a treasure without naming it. I swear upon God I do not even know what treasure it was or where it was. Normally, people steal from shops or from homes. I had one person who wanted to steal from a bank. I thought this was a bank job and they wanted the security guard knocked out or unconscious. That is an easy job for me. They gave me money for it. I asked them for a personal item for the guard, which they brought for me. I usually read some magical verses and bury it with some dead body. It is now lying buried in some grave..."

Hameed interrupted, "We would like you to stop or reverse the magic. We know it can be done!"

"It may be too late…"

"We don't care. We would still like you to do it, and urgently. We know if what you have planted are taken out from the grave in time, the magic will reverse. We want you to take us to the graveyard now and do it in our presence!"

Jadoo realized he couldn't get out of that one. These men knew a lot. Right now, he may have no option except to take them to the graveyard otherwise he could end up in jail.

"It has rained very heavily last night. The Misri Shah graveyard is in a low-lying area. It is possible most of the graves are under water now, and it may be difficult to identify the grave even if we reach there…"

"Let us go now. We have very little time to waste."

He asked to be excused for a minute and went back in to get his umbrella in case it rained again. He also changed his shoes sandals to joggers as he said it was going to be very muddy at the graveyard.

As they walked back to the car, there was already commotion on the street, as many prying neighbors had already collected asking questions.

'Where are you heading to?"

"Are you going to kill someone?"

"Is he being arrested?"

He tried to console them that it was nothing, and they were just going to see someone who wanted a cure from a deadly disease.

Together, they left for the outskirts of the city, past the stadium, and then drove on a dirt track through agriculture lands and away from the motorway. The track was full of potholes flooded with water, and the driving was very treacherous, so Hameed had to be very careful to avoid getting stuck.

As they approached a narrow bend, they felt the car swerve and go down in a trench. Hameed tried moving it away but it would not turn in the opposite direction. He pressed the accelerator but even then, it would not move forward. Hameed tried to power it both forwards and backwards but it would not move. It appeared that the car had gotten stuck in one of the large potholes.

They knew they had to get down and try pushing it out. They all got down and tried, but it would not move. They were losing precious time. They looked around for some help, and finally, a Suzuki pick-up appeared carrying three men on its back. Hameed requested some help, and all three men jumped down to help push the car out. Hospitality and helping others was typical in the rural countryside. With the additional hands pushing, the car easily came out of the pothole, and Hameed thanked the men and started driving again towards the graveyard.

It took them another ten minutes and past a tea stall which had opened early in the morning to reach the graveyard. It was already around 8 A.M.

They entered the graveyard which was overflowing with graves with hardly any room to walk in between the graves. The rain and the mud made the walk even more difficult. Half the graves were immersed in rain water which looked like a large pool in the middle.

Jadoo Baba stopped. He had to stall for time and find an excuse, "Wait here. I need to find the caretaker, as I do not remember the grave myself now as they all look different in the water."

He walked up to a small shed on the side of the graveyard, and called out the caretaker's name. No one answered. He called again. No answer. Then he proceeded to knock on the small door in the front. It pushed itself inwards as if it was unbolted from inside. Jadoo Baba walked inside.

Samir and Hameed could hear someone talking inside, and it became louder as if there was an argument going on. They did not feel like going in to interrupt, but waited for Jadoo to come out. The argument was interrupted by a sound of a tussle followed by a gun shot. And another.

Samir froze in his shoes. Whoever was inside probably knew there were others outside, and they were unarmed. He looked over to Hameed wondering what they should do next. He saw Hameed was holding a handgun in his hand.

"One doesn't go to all these places in this part of the country without the means to defend yourself. Stay here! It is dangerous," He moved forward towards the shed and fired a couple of rounds in the air so as to frighten whosoever was inside.

He called out in Pashto, "Whoever is inside, walk out with your hands up."

Another shot was heard, and it came from inside the shed, and got Hameed on the shoulder. He twitched with pain, but he did not stop as he jolted towards the door. There appeared behind the door a hand holding a gun. Hameed shot three times in that direction, and a couple of shots were fired back. The hand disappeared. Hameed reached and pushed open the door, and saw a man down on his knees who was bleeding. Hameed pointed the gun at his forehead.

"Don't shoot him!" yelled Samir as he ran after Hameed. He had seen Hameed being shot, and had sprinted towards him in case he passed out, but saw him pointing his gun at the man's head.

Samir screamed, "We want him unharmed. He may have useful information!"

The man was frightened. "Please don't shoot. I am not a Taliban, but am only the caretaker of the graveyard. They forced me to work for them. They have taken my 15-year-old son away to some training camp and said they will kill him if I do not cooperate. It is Jadoo who has been working with them for a long time. He digs up the bodies and takes their body parts to do some magical rituals for them…"

"Tell us more, or we will let you die!" Hameed shouted.

The man took a deep breath as if to prevent himself from going into sub-consciousness, and then uttered, "Jadoo has been coming here on their behalf to practice other rituals as well, like making a chilla to make contact with the jinn…" his voice trailed off.

"What chilla? What jinn? Speak up!" screamed Hameed.

The man was in pain. "I don't know the details, but once Jadoo Baba had mentioned that he is helping a close relative by the name of Qabza Khan to make contact with the jinn, because jinn can cause far more destruction than what black magic does."

He struggled for words, "You know the chilla, if successfully completed, becomes the gateway to the jinn world and for them to contact men. I do not know of any more detail as I am just the caretaker of this graveyard. Please spare me and save my life!"

The man wanted help, but Samir knew it could be at least another 30 to 45 minutes before the ambulance could arrive.

"Why did you kill Jadoo Baba?" asked Hameed.

"Last night, one of them stopped by and asked me to kill Jadoo. He said Jadoo had done their work, but he knew too much and had to be eliminated…I was expecting Jadoo to come last night but he did not come probably due to bad weather. When I saw him this morning, I knew I had to kill him or else they would kill me and my son and my wife…"

He trailed off and lost consciousness. Hameed bent down to check his pulse. He was dead already. Inside the room, they saw the body of Jadoo Baba.

"They are both gone. What do we do?" asked Hameed.

"We know we are at the correct graveyard where magic was planted. We just need to find the grave and the corpse that was used to perform black magic! I don't know how, but we have to stop the destruction even if we have to dig up the whole graveyard. We don't know when and where they will use the dirty bomb, if they have not used it already. This is the only way we can reverse the magic and stop the destruction!"

Samir pointed to a couple of spades that were lying outside the shed. "You pick up one, I take the other, and we will be selective where we dig through only the fresh graves."

They were in luck as the majority of the graves appeared old and untouched. There were only a few fresh ones that looked like they were hardly a week old. These were on higher ground and a couple of hundred feet inside the graveyard and towards the back entrance. There could have been more fresh graves under the rain water. Samir hoped not, as it would be impossible to dig till the water dried off.

They both started digging away at the first of these graves. Samir had never expected himself to be doing such a job. Not only digging graves, but taking out corpses. He did not even know what he was looking for. But he was desperate to find the corpse which had the evil inserted inside, and fast!

He decided to call up Hasan one last time, who could be up by now. Hasan could sometimes surprise him with his knowledge of the mystical world. Perhaps he may have some insight on how the black magic can be detected and broken.

Hasan was up. "What's up, Dad. I noticed your missed call last night. I was just going to call you back."

"Hasan. Remember the black magic talk we had the other day. What are the typical items that the magicians plant when they do a magic spell?"

"Dad, what else but amulets, lemons stuck with needles, voodoo dolls, personal items, and specially items that are part of the body, including hair, nails, and even blood. Then items which have closely touched someone's body like a comb, underwear, vest, bras, and sanitary napkins. Just use your imagination!"

"Where would they plant it in a graveyard?"

"Where else but in a grave and inside a fresh corpse. Usually, their favorite places are the openings in humans, especially ones that are considered not clean, like where one does potty, the lower front opening for a woman, and sometimes even the mouth. It has to touch the inside of the corpse for maximum effectiveness. Some of the magicians cut open the body and plant it next to the liver or the heart where there is a lot of dried blood to make the magic more effective. This practice has carried over from Babylonian times."

"How does one break the spell or neutralize it?"

"The spell on the Prophet was broken by recovering the objects and reading the last two chapters of the Quran, the Qul Al-Falaq and Qul Al-Nas on it. If you see knots or needles, unknot them and take out one needle at a time by reading the Qul and blowing on them. If you see hair, burn it. But read the Qul under any circumstance, as it is only the power of the Qul that can not only break the magic but protect you from its evil as well as you try to undo it, otherwise it will enter your body as well!"

He was surprised as to how much his son knew. He may be a professor and a PhD, but there was so much to learn from his son about these mystical practices in various religions, and how magic was practiced from pre-Islamic to the present times, and how it had been adopted by the merchants of evil who incorrectly claim it has Islamic roots.

"Are you ok, Dad? You should have taken me with you so I could have guided you!"

"It is all right!" Samir did not want to have his son exposed to these dangers. As it was, his own life was threatened by fanatics.

Samir thought for a moment. How could they find the corpse with the planted items? There were at least ten or more graves that had to be dug up, and there was not enough time to dig them all.

Samir thought of the person who used maps and was a living spiritual GPS. He decided to give one last shot and call up Najumi. Perhaps, he could help.

Najumi was up practicing his rituals.

"Najumi: do you recall of the death and destruction you were talking about yesterday? You were absolutely right about the corpses and the graveyard. The evil forces are really at work here.

"I have even located the graveyard where the corpse is buried which has likely been used for the magic. The aamil told us an amulet or a personal item has been planted inside one of the corpses. Before he could guide us to the exact grave, he has been shot dead by the caretaker. We are now in a fix. We need to find that particular grave from among all these graves that has the corpse with the magical items inserted, and take them out to break the spell. Can you help us?"

Samir couldn't believe he was into all this, calling an astrologer to help him find a corpse. What would the faculty and his friends back in the US think of this? They would probably send him to a lunatic asylum.

Najumi was quiet for a moment, and then spoke, "It is a difficult task which I have never done before, so I will need to focus on it. Give me a moment and let me try if I can do that."

There was a rustling of some papers that could be heard on the phone. Najumi was probably referring to his notes. "Can you give me the names of the man who had wanted this done, and of the aamil who did this? I also need their location and your location as well."

"The man who wanted this done is Timur, and the aamil's name is Jadoo Baba. The aamil lives in Hasan Abdal in the center of the city, but right now he is lying dead in a shed at the Misri Shah graveyard in Hasan Abdal where I am standing. I do not know where Timur is or even lives."

"Hmmm. It may be a shot in the dark, but give me a few minutes while I read the charts and consult the stars. The stars know it all as they see it all from the sky. They are the witness to the burial itself."

It was the longest wait for Samir. He did not stop digging though. They had already dug out two corpses, and he had left it to Hameed to check the bodies, he could not bear the stench. There was nothing they could find yet.

It could have been forever when Najumi called back.

"I may have the answer for you! The grave you are looking for is located between two tall trees and has a brown stone marker. It lies next and to the right of a high mound of mud."

Samir looked around. He could see quite a few trees, but there were two tall ones that he could easily identify which were about 100 feet apart. Midway between the two was one grave with a brown stone. Next to it was a mud hill that had been partially washed away by the rain.

"That's it! I think we found it. Gotta dig now."

"Just one word of caution," interrupted Najumi, "I still find dark forces hovering in the sky above Islamabad. There is great evil in the air as if all the negative forces that have combined are ready to attack and destroy. They are concentrated in the area of the prime minister's office and the parliament. There is very little time. If not stopped, I see lots of bodies and blood and screaming…"

"I believe this evil magic is connected to all that killing. Inshallah we should be able to stop it if we are successful in reversing the magic." Samir hung up the phone and pointed to the grave, "That one. We need to dig fast."

They scraped away fast at the dirt, and in ten minutes had the corpse out. It appeared fresh as if it was just buried a few days ago. There was dried blood on the white sheet which covered it. It appeared as if it had been hurriedly rewrapped. Samir couldn't stop himself from tearing away at the sheet. It was horrifying to look at the corpse. Its belly was cut up, and inside was what appeared to be another piece of clothing which had been pushed in. He pulled it out. It had some hair and a lemon with needles stuck inside it.

"There is something sticking out of its mouth as well," screamed Hameed. He pried it open and found an amulet. They turned the body around and could not find anything else.

Hameed took the clothing and the objects from Samir, "Let me have these. I will open and unknot them, and burn the hair while reading the Qul, as I am still clean after my wash for the prayers."

They took all the objects to a high ground under the tree. Samir felt so exhausted that he almost passed out. Hameed looked at him and asked him to lie down while he started the procedure of breaking the spell of the evil magic. He started to read the Qul while unknotting the knots.

Samir lay on the ground and felt as if a demonic magical spirit was swooping down from the sky wanting to kill him. He screamed and covered his face with his hands and he could see no more.

He passed out. It was around 9 A.M.

Dirty Bomb

Qari looked at his watch. It was almost 9 A.M. There was already a lot of activity at the institute due to the conference. The car parking lot was full by now, as all those wanting to attend the conference had already shown up and were probably seated in the auditorium by now, waiting for the chief guest to arrive. No one had bothered him or asked him to move as he waited in his car. He attracted very little attention. Maybe he was invisible to others. The magic was fully working.

He slowly got out of the car, and walked back to the trunk to open it. He had this reassuring feeling that it will be only a few more minutes before he had accomplished his mission. Not only would he cause a lot of destruction but he would kill the president too. No one ever had accomplished that. He felt like he will soon be conquering the world, and Islam will reach to all corners of the globe because of what he will do today. He will go down in history as a martyr and a hero. He just couldn't wait to reach heaven, and certainly deserved the highest level of the seven heavens, the Jannat Firdous.

He reached out to the CNG cylinder to unlatch and unscrew it. As he tried, he felt it was stuck and he couldn't unlatch it. He tried again with some force, and it finally opened. He then unscrewed the top and felt comfortable when he saw the two inner cylinders and the explosives around it.

As he reached out to the inner cylinders to unlatch them as well, he saw a man come running from the parking lot in front of the building. He was from the reception committee to the president. He saw Qari with his badge of the conference and blurted out, "We just heard from the security personnel there has been a suicide bomb attack in Rawalpindi. It took place about 30 minutes back. The bomber was in a car, and blew himself and the car up to pieces."

"What were they targeting?"

"It is too early to say, but the radio is saying there appeared to be no particular target. Maybe he accidently blew himself up too early out of nervousness as it happens in most cases. There was no significant damage to the property around it, except a few passersby got killed."

He paused for a second to look at Qari trying to recognize him, then just continued, "They said the army has moved in, and are cordoning out the whole area, asking people to vacate houses and shops within a mile radius. It is not very clear why they are doing it, but there are rumors that there is some radio-activity involved."

"Where can such a rumor emerge from?"

He looked at Qari's badge again, trying to place him, "Didn't you see the check points coming into Islamabad? I am a physics graduate, and I knew they are carrying radioactivity detectors. They have been trying to detect radioactivity in cars, as if someone was carrying a load of radioactive material. It appears the suicide bomber was the one they were looking for. If it is so, it is scary as the explosion will spread a lot of radio-activity in the area. Let us hope this scare is over soon and we can start our conference."

He disappeared into the building wanting to be the first to break the news to the conference participants.

Qari could guess that this attack must have been done by a suicide bomber from his own organization and arranged by Timur in another part of the city to distract attention from this attack. Timur always had planned things perfectly. Because of this decoy bomber in Rawalpindi, everyone would assume that the danger to Islamabad had now been diffused, and all the extra security forces that had been assigned to this part of the city would start to move out to the site of the other explosion. What a perfect plan! He felt more relaxed now as he realized now he would easily be able to drive his car to the front of the building through the side lane when the president would enter, and then blow it up.

He heard some activity from the front side of the building and the sound of police sirens. He realized the president was on his way. He immediately rushed back again to unlatch the inner cylinders. Somehow this mechanism was also stuck. He tried again. It would not budge. He was sure he was doing it right. He had done it correctly with the outer one, which was assembled by his own people, but the inner ones were put together by the atomic energy agency people. Was there something else to it that the American had forgotten to mention? Maybe another twist, another turn, or another code? He had read that some of these devices have double unlocking mechanism.

The sirens died down. He could not afford to waste time figuring out how to unlatch and open the inner cylinders. He was running out of time. He closed the trunk, and walked around to the driver's seat. He started the engine, and drove the car into the narrow lane that connected to the front parking area. As he entered the lane, he realized he was stuck. He could not move forward as a number of cars had completely blocked the lane because of the VIP activity on the front of the building.

He decided to back off and try another approach to get to the front, but then another car stopped behind Qari's car, and he was really stuck. He could move neither forward nor backward. He had to make a quick decision. Either drop everything dead and forget the mission, or blow the explosives with the remote he was carrying right where he was.

He remembered Timur's word when he had parted. Go without fear. You will be invisible and fully protected. Timur had sought special powers for him from the aamil for the mission. He had told him the other boys had succeeded in stealing the cylinders despite the high security because of the magical powers given by the aamil. The aamil had performed the magic that they could become invisible and fly back over the boundary wall. He was sure he was invisible a few moments earlier as no one had seen him or asked questions in the parking lot. He was now confident he himself would also be able to fly over the cars and pass this blockade with ease, and nothing would be able to stop him.

He pressed on the accelerator expecting his car to fly magically over the cars. Instead he rammed hard into the car in front of him. He pressed the accelerator further and the car only pushed forward a little. The man in the front car got out of his car screaming at him. The one in the back also opened the door of his car to come out to see what was happening. Qari knew he had to make a quick decision.

He chanted, "Allah-o-Akbar," and pressed the app on his cell phone.

There was a big explosion and he passed out.

Dubai

Harry had safely landed in Dubai at around 8:30 A.M. local time which was around 9:30 A.M. Pakistan time. He had only carry-on luggage and was out of the airport within 15 minutes. His supervisor was in the car that came to pick him up. He was sure the cat was out of the bag. They would have known by now that there had been a dirty bomb in Islamabad. He was sure he would have a lot of explaining to do.

"The whole operation has been screwed up. Details are still hazy. Even though you did a good job in securing the consignment from the location, and passing it over to the boys to carry the consignment to the northern areas and into Kabul, it appears they passed it on to two of their boys to attack the president."

Harry took a sigh of relief.

"What happened?"

"It appears our associates tried to attack at two places simultaneously. Their goal perhaps was to create panic and cause maximum damage. One explosion was in Rawalpindi and the other was at an institute in Islamabad where the president was to be the chief guest at a conference. Details are still hazy and forthcoming but in either case, the cars carrying the bombers exploded. While the bombers died, along with some other fatalities and damage, there was no radioactivity in both cases."

Harry was surprised. He turned to look at his supervisor, "Then it is obvious that there were no nuclear cylinders in the cars, otherwise they would have exploded too!"

"Apparently that, or they did not explode. We should be getting more details as soon as we hear from our contacts down there. I am not sure who to trust now. It appears our key contacts at the TTP obviously had their own agenda and double-crossed us. They used our plan and our information to carry out their own attack. All got screwed up as a result." He shook his head, "We will need to review our partnership with them."

"They are the best ones we have."

"They have been screwing up lately. Our former associates are reaching out to us again as they are keen on reinforcing their hold in the region."

"By former associates you mean the Al-Qaeda?"

"Yes! But we can never trust them like we trust the TTP. We have information that they plan to steal a nuclear bomb from a base in Pakistan. However, this may be good for us as it fits in well with our plans."

"Did we not fall out with them after Osama? Are they back on track now?"

"They have been cornered as they now have a much stronger and larger competitor in the region. As a result, they are beginning to lose many of their fighters to ISIS. So, they want to do another 9/11 type of attack otherwise they will lose out their influence in Afghanistan and Pakistan. But we can't trust them yet."

"How is that?"

The agency really had some inside information, "We have learnt from our other sources that Al-Qaeda will tell us that the bomb which they plan to steal will be destined for India to force them into giving independence for Kashmir. One group within Al-Qaeda really wants to use it in Kashmir, yet the group led by their deputy emir wants to use it at the Bagram Air Base in Afghanistan against the Americans. They want to avenge the killing of Osama bin Laden."

"How can you be so sure?"

The supervisor was confident, "This is very credible information that we have received through the Mossad. None of the information they have provided us in the past has been incorrect. But the Al-Qaeda are the double-crossing bastards. This is where you come in."

"What is my assignment?

"The top Al-Qaeda honcho in Afghanistan is sure he will have the bomb in his hand in a few days. He has asked us for our help in arming it, as these guys do not know the technicalities of it. You are the only expert in the region who can do it."

"You want me to arm it so they can drop it at the American base?" Harry was surprised, but he knew there would be another plan up his agencies' sleeve.

"By cooperating with them before the bomb is actually stolen, we can find out from where and when the bomb will be stolen. Your mission is to ensure it does not cross into Afghanistan.

"We intend to double-cross the bastards by using the TTP against them. You will have the bomb intercepted somewhere in Pakistan using the TTP but after the Al-Qaeda have laid their hands on it. We will then expose the bomb within the borders of Pakistan by moving in the American forces from across the border to possess it!"

"Can we trust the TTP again?"

"We know TTP are mercenaries who will work for anyone who pays them more. You will have unlimited cash at your discretion to buy out the TTP so they double-cross the Al-Qaeda. I believe you have a good understanding with their top man, Timur."

"Timur is the best there is. Somehow, he screwed up the last operation."

"We will try them one last time." He looked at his watch as an indication that the briefing was over, "Pakistani intelligence will be on the lookout for you after what happened in Islamabad. They have a strong presence here in Dubai. You should get out of here immediately. You have a flight to Kabul in the next two hours. We will go around the block and drop you back at the airport. You will now travel on a different passport. There will be new instructions for you after you reach Afghanistan."

He handed over a new passport, with an envelope that carried a fake identity card for the Red Cross, some papers and cash.

"Please make sure you read these before you fly, and destroy them immediately afterwards."

The car swerved back towards the airport and dropped Harry at the business class curb.

Harry walked inside, went to the men's room, and in the toilet opened the envelope. There was a wad of hundred-dollar bills and a map of Moqor, a city between Kabul and Kandahar near the Pakistan border. An X was marked at a location on the map, and he knew he had to report there after arrival.

He shredded the map into small pieces and flushed it in the toilet.

He walked out of the toilet and moved towards the check-in area. He was happy his agency trusted him well and had another mission for him. But this time, he would make sure his personal agenda was carried through and that Muslims were wiped off from the face of this earth.

Iblis

The jinn had asked Qabza Khan to make the biggest sacrifice. If Prophet Abrahim was ready to sacrifice his son for the sake of God, then he should surely do something similar to gain the trust of Iblis.

Qabza was pleased he had already made contact with the leader and king of jinn. He had reached a level which very few aamil were able to. Most made fake claims that they had a jinn or a mukil in their possession. They were all liars. He knew he had undergone big pain and torture, both physical and psychological, to win the confidence of Iblis and make contact with him, and had succeeded. Now, the jinn wanted something big to gain his trust. He wanted a sacrifice. And Qabza was ready to give it!

He had a wife and two sons, aged 11 and 7. He had hoped one day his sons would learn magic from him and become better aamil. But now he knew he would have to sacrifice one of them, the one who was dearer to him. They were both equally close to him. Whenever he would return home late evening, they both would compete with each other for his time. They would also fight with each other out of jealousy for his attention. He could never think of the day when he would take a knife and slit one's throat.

He shrugged himself of the thought. He would be rewarded with another son. Maybe two. Iblis had tremendous power. He must do whatever he wants.

They had early dinner. He told his wife he needed to go out again after his readings so they can sleep. He went to the adjoining room and started reading his mantra to praise Iblis again.

"Oh, great one. I believe in you. You are the master. You asked me to make the biggest sacrifice for you. I can do anything for you if you raise me to the level of your servant and slave. I need your strength and your cooperation."

He kept on muttering the mantra for over an hour. By now, he knew his wife and the children must have gone to sleep. There was silence in the adjoining room.

He got up and checked. They had gone to sleep. He went into the kitchen and looked around for a knife. He found a cleaver which his wife used for cutting meat. He checked for its sharpness on his finger. It pinched him and a drop of blood came out. He immediately put his finger in his mouth and sucked on it. He was ready.

He walked into the bedroom quietly. His family was fast asleep. He had to decide which son was dearer to him. Ismail was the elder son to Abraham, so he must sacrifice the elder one.

He tiptoed close to where his elder son was sleeping on a small bed next to the window. He slowly lifted him up and carried him to the room where he had prayed to Iblis, then went back to close and bolt the door to the bedroom. Qabza looked at his son one last time. He felt no mercy. He was doing it to save the world from mankind. He was doing it to please Iblis.

He touched his neck, and found the jugular vein. He then put one hand on his son's mouth tightly, and immediately started slaughtering him with a back and forth movement. The blood started gushing out. The boy tried to scream and struggle, but couldn't. Qabza was much more larger and strong and had him pinned down. The blood flowed all over the bed and the floor. There was so much of it. The boy trembled and shivered, then slowly, his movement died down. No one next door heard the commotion. They were deep in their sleep.

Then he started severing off the boy's head from the body. It took him a few minutes to do that. He found a plastic bag, placed the head in, and covered the rest of the body with a blanket. He wiped his hands with a towel, then walked out of the house.

He took the path that went up the hill back to the same graveyard where he had made contact with the jinn. He reached the top to the same place where he had first made contact with Iblis. He lay the bag down on the ground, took the head out and looked up into the sky.

He held the head in both hands and cried out to the sky, "Oh, great one. Oh, Master. Oh, Iblis. I have carried out my part of the bargain. You had promised if I come back with the biggest sacrifice I can make, you will trust me and send me the strong one. I have sacrificed my dearest son for you. Here is his head that I offer to you. Now, you carry out your part of the bargain. You deliver the strong one to me."

He kept on repeating the same for over an hour, continuously looking up, hoping that Iblis would appear himself. Nothing happened. He did not give up. He kept on repeating the mantra again and again. Was Iblis not happy with his sacrifice? Or was he doing it incorrectly? Maybe need needed to place the head inside the chilla and then cry out to the jinn.

Suddenly, there appeared some dark clouds in the sky and the whole area turned dark. Lightning followed. He felt delighted that he was beginning to make contact with the jinn. He put the head down inside the chilla that he had marked and went down touching his forehead to the ground, repeating and calling out to Iblis.

There was suddenly a big lightning bolt, and he felt its heat. His skin burnt. He was sure Iblis was nearby, because the jinn are made of fire. He was appearing in the form of lightning like he had done before. Lightning gave more strength to the jinn.

There was a loud thunder, followed by a gust of strong wind. He felt the presence of something hot, as if someone had placed hot burning coals in front of him. He dared not look up. He continued to kneel with his head to the ground.

"Rise and accept my grace."

Was it someone whispering in his ears, or was he imagining these voices? He got up and looked up, and it appeared to him as if there was a burning fire in front of him. Was it Iblis himself in person, or was he imagining him?

He felt a blast of heat, and knew it had to be the jinn himself. He felt he heard the jinn speak.

"You have done your part of the deal and proved you are a slave to us. What would you like me to do for you?"

"I know you have tremendous powers. Before man was created, you were the prince of earth. You had your throne over the waters. You played beautiful music. Till men cheated you of your glory. I want to be your slave, and want to help you gain back your glory and your kingdom."

Qabza continued, "Men have been given a brain to think. You have been given the power. I would like to use my brain and be your slave, so with my planning and your power, we can together destroy mankind so the jinn can take over. You will rule the earth and the universe and I will serve you."

"What would you like me to do for you?"

"I have heard so much and read about your powers, your strength, and your speed. Only your faithful believe you have that power. Others do not! We will prove to them your powers. I would like to see a small show of your powers, oh great one."

The fire shot up a hundred feet in the air. Then it started swirling around like a tornado, and all the trees around started crackling and catching fire. The fire then leapt over to the adjoining hill, and the trees caught fire there too. It leapt back next to Qabza, and in an instant, all the fires were extinguished.

"What else do you need to see?"

"You are the king, and I believe in you. I don't need to see more of your powers. Let the world see your powers. But I need your help to help us win this war against mankind once and for always. I need your strong warrior to do this task. He is the powerful one but without knowledge, and he is known as Ifrit."

"Ifrit will do what I tell him to do. He lives in another galaxy, but I can have him here in a moment. What would you like him to do so I can rule the earth again?"

"Oh, my master. With your other slaves, we are working on a plan that will make you happy. It is almost finalized. Give me a little time, and tomorrow, I will be back with it. You are the king and don't need to be bothered with such small matters. Just send Ifrit here tomorrow when I worship you and call out your name. Ifrit and I will destroy mankind together, and then place you back on your throne."

There was another bolt of fire, and it burnt Qabza's skin, "By tomorrow, you must have a plan, as I cannot think like a man can. Do not waste any further time, because if Ifrit returns to your world, he will want to take revenge from mankind. He has been cheated out of his freedom by Solomon. But tomorrow, I will send Ifrit and tell him to follow your plan so he can take his revenge on mankind.

"If I become the king of the universe again, I will make you my most trusted servant."

With that, there was a gust of wind, the treetops rustled, then everything became quiet. Qabza looked up. There was nothing. The sky had started to clear up.

He was excited! He had finally achieved that which no one since Solomon was able to achieve. He had made contact with the king of jinn, the great Iblis himself. He had asked for Ifrit, the most powerful of the jinn, so together they could destroy mankind in one go. Iblis had agreed to send Ifrit to him to do what Qabza wanted. Ifrit would be a trusted jinn since he wanted to take his revenge on man anyway.

All other aamil who were reaching out to the jinn were foolish, asking for small things. They just wanted someone killed, someone destroyed, a bank stolen. He would ask for something very big, what even Solomon could not have asked for. He would be directly talking to Ifrit himself, something that no one had done in thousands of years.

But first, he had to find out what the men in black wanted him to do. They surely had a big plan to destroy mankind. He would use their plan and the power of Ifrit to install himself. He was certainly smart.

He got up and made a small hole in the ground with his bare hands. Next, he placed the head of his son in the hole and covered it. He had no regrets.

He ran down the hill, wanting to find the men in black. He would give them the good news, learn of their plan, and get more money from them. But he was pleased as beyond that, he would get power from the jinn directly. They will work together. While the jinn would rule the earth again, he will become their servant and confident aide and become the most powerful man on earth.

Safe

When Samir gained consciousness, he found himself lying under a tree at the Misri Shah graveyard. He knew he had passed out and was slowly recovering. He tried to recollect the events of the last few hours. He had no way of knowing whatever it was they were doing in the graveyard was just hocus pocus, or did it work.

Had he really started believing in black magic? Did he really believe that the aamil had so much power that they could do anything? Did he really believe that this aamil could make the terrorists invisible so they could fly in and out undetected and steal the nuclear fuel? Did they really use magic to get their suicide bombers into any location unseen? Is that what they did in Charsadda? In Islamabad? In Lahore? In Karachi? Had they done it again to get the nuclear fuel to wherever they were going to blow it up despite the army being on high alert?

He did not even know if the dirty bomb had exploded by now. Had thousands died? Was there a mass evacuation taking place? Had the army declared martial law and taken over the country? Was NATO or the United Nations already moving in troops to demilitarize and disarm Pakistan? Would there be severe sanctions?

He felt nauseated! He had no strength to even get up or make a phone call.

He looked up and saw Hameed walking around in circles and muttering something as if he had become mad. Maybe he had already received news of deaths and mass exodus. It appeared it was all over.

Hameed saw Samir wake up and heaved a sigh of relief. He walked up to him and blurted, "For a moment I thought the evil spirits had gotten to you. These things happen when we tread into the territory of the evil spirits and take their space. You had fainted after we tried reversing the black magic. I always wear my amulet for protection and worship to Allah five times a day. Something must have protected you too. Otherwise, it is impossible to come out of this alive."

"What happened? Is there any news from Islamabad?"

"Unfortunately, I lost my cell in the commotion when we were digging desperately. I checked your phone and its battery is dead. We can only try to go back and make a call to find out. Let us hope all is well."

Samir got up, and together, they walked over to the car. They drove back till they reached the tea stall they had passed earlier in the morning. As they got out of the car, the tea maker was shocked to see two men completely covered in mud. For a moment, he thought they had been kidnapped by some militant group and were on the run to safety.

Hameed spoke sternly in Pashto, and the man immediately handed him his phone. Hameed called the emergency number.

"This is VC Dr. Hameed from KP. The Education Advisor Dr. Samir Baloch is with me. We urgently need to speak to someone from the army disaster management center."

There was silence for about a minute, which seemed like the longest minute to them. It appeared time had stopped.

"This is Major Kaleem from the Intelligence. Where are you, Sir? We have been trying to locate you for the last 30 minutes."

Samir grabbed the phone from Hameed, "Is Islamabad safe?"

"Sir, very much so. There were two suicide car attacks. One was in Rawalpindi and there were a few casualties. We were almost sure there would be a radioactive leak in that area, but we were surprised there was none, and the area was cleared. The other one was more severe, at the science institute when the president was driving in to attend the conference. It appears that the nuclear fuel that was stolen was in that vehicle, but somehow the cylinders failed to explode. There appeared, however, minor cracks on the cylinder, which caused some radioactive leak. The agency and army moved in quickly to clear the area of all people. A major catastrophe was averted."

"Is everything else safe?"

"Yes sir. The army has asked the whole block to be cleared, and the atomic energy agency men have moved in with their equipment checking for radioactivity. There will be very little, I am told, as the cylinders carrying the nuclear fuel were intact except for a few cracks. They have been taken back by the agency already to be checked and disposed of safely."

Samir felt as if his life had returned back to him. He heaved a sigh of relief. They had successfully thwarted off a dirty bomb attack by the terrorists in Islamabad. They had defeated black magic with white magic.

But Samir was confused and shaken. His mind was a roller coaster. He was not even sure whether they had done it by reversing the magic, like what they were doing at the graveyard, digging out corpses, or was it a combination of luck and the efficiency of the Pakistan security forces that had saved thousands from dying.

Right now, it did not matter, as thousands of lives had been saved. Samir went down touching his forehead to the ground, thanking God. He knew man is too weak to fight evil unless he seeks help from God. What he had been witnessing in the last few days was a testimony to the fact that there is magic and evil, but prayers from the heart as ordained by God have the power to counter them.

Many questions were crossing his mind. Would the terrorists finally realize that they cannot fight good with evil and win, or would they revert to something more powerful and sinister in the future?

He recalled that both Timur and the caretaker at the graveyard were referring to the terrorists making contact with the jinn, because jinn can cause far more destruction than what magic does. Jinn were indeed an entity in the Quran with supernatural powers.

Samir had a feeling, his sixth sense was alerting him, that the worst was yet to come. There were certainly more powerful and evil forces, like the jinn, that the terrorists were capitalizing on. Jinn were after all the powerful evil forces that had taught magic to man.

But will the terrorists succeed in using the jinn? If they did, he was sure it will cause major destruction whatever their target would be.

They had to be stopped! And to do that, he had to learn a lot more about the jinn.

Chapter 4
Jinn

'Say: I seek refuge with the Lord and Cherisher of mankind
The King or Ruler of mankind
The Allah or Judge of mankind
From the mischief of the whisperer of evil, who withdraws after his whisper
The same who whispers into the hearts of mankind
Among jinn and among men'

Al-Quran, Verses 114:1 to 114:6

Shams

Shams Hashmi was a spiritual scholar known for his knowledge and religious insight into the supernatural. He had countless followers who were from the educated class and from middle earnings households. He was a well-known authority in Pakistan on the jinn and claimed his descent to the Prophet, who belonged to the Hashmi tribe.

Hasan, being a psychology graduate himself, had significant interest in parapsychology and metaphysics, having studied the subjects, and how possession and jinn could be explained by science. His friends from well-to-do households spoke high of Shams, a man who could provide a religious but pragmatic insight into supernatural entities like the jinn. Hasan had visited his spiritual center a number of times with his friends, had gotten into a discussion with Shams, and was much impressed with the man's knowledge, who could separate facts from myth. So, when Samir called up Hasan to inquire where he could get credible knowledge about jinn which is supported by Islamic beliefs, he immediately referred him to Shams.

"Dad. You must meet him first before you talk to anyone else. He is not a run-of-the-mill pir or religious scholar who does hocus pocus or give false information. He is well-balanced and separates facts from fiction. He is quite knowledgeable about jinn and will give you the factual information as it is in the Quran, the truth and nothing but the truth."

"How can you say that? We are not even sure if jinn do exist the way humans assume they do, or if they are just a figment of our imagination?"

"As Muslims, we must believe without an iota of doubt that jinn exist! There are, of course, many religious and spiritual angles to the jinn, and then there are scientific and psychological explanations as well. Shams will tell you who the jinn really are, and all your confusion will go away."

Samir had read and heard stories about the jinn, which were both good and horrifying, but were mostly evening tales. He had even watched a movie recently by the same name. Most stories were more or less housewives and children fables rather than anything else. So, with a pinch of salt, Samir took the next flight to Karachi to meet Shams.

He could not believe himself as he boarded the flight. He had read and believed in jinn the way everyone else believed in angels. None of that influenced his daily life, and as it was, if this world did exist, it did not affect their day to day living. But now, he was on his way to find out more about the jinn from an authority on jinn. Had he gone crazy or what?

His experience at the graveyard and with the aamil had convinced him that secret arts and hidden forces do exist within Islamic beliefs. All this was necessary for him to know and do if the next terrorist attack was to be carried out with the help of jinn, and this was the only way it could be thwarted. The next attack could possibly be worse than the previous one, which was avoided because he had worked with the antidotes and the verse which had made black magic ineffective.

Hasan had informed his dad it was usually very difficult to meet Shams, as the man was traveling most of the time. His large following spanned from Pakistan to Saudi Arabia to Morocco to Malaysia. However, Samir was lucky that Shams would be in Karachi for about a week before flying off to Saudi Arabia. Hasan had made a few phone calls to his friends who knew Shams like family and arranged an exclusive meeting for Samir with him at short notice.

Prior to boarding the plane, Samir searched on the net about the jinn and what they really are. He knew that jinn are mentioned in the Quran, but there is no mention of the jinn in the Bible or the Torah except as a demon. The power of the jinn, however, far exceeds that of a demon. He also knew and read about the Djinn and the Genie, which are popular western characters in children's books and movies, and the fictitious poltergeist on which a popular movie was made. He wanted to do some more exploration on the net on the origin and existence of the jinn outside the domain of what is mentioned in the Quran and the Hadith.

He found some interesting facts, but not a lot. Most Arabic dictionaries define jinn not only as spirits, but also as anything concealed through time, status, and even physical darkness. There was also a passing reference to ghouls as jinn, as they are believed to inhabit dark and isolated places and are feared. The word jinn most likely came from Aramaic, where Christians associated pagan gods with demons. However, the first mention of jinn dates back to pre-Zoroastrian mythology in Iran, where the Jaini was a wicked female spirit.

In Judeo-Christian mythology, the word or concept of jinn as such does not occur in the Old Testament, but the Arabic word jinn was often used in several old Persian and Arabic translations.

Earliest archeological evidence from northwestern Arabia indicate the worship of jinn much before Islam. Pre-Islamic Bedouin religions used to believe in spirits. An inscription from Beth Fasi'el near Palmyra pays tribute to the 'Jinnaye', the 'good and rewarding gods'.

There are also similar types of deities in the Canary Islands off the coast of Africa. In Guanche mythology from Tenerife in the Canary Islands, there exists a belief in beings like the maxios or dioses paredros, which are attendant gods, domestic and nature spirits, and tibicenas, considered evil genies, and the demon guayota, the aboriginal god of evil, that is identified as a genie. In certain aspects of Japanese religion and culture, the shinigami are gods or supernatural spirits that invite humans toward death. They have been described as monsters and helpers, creatures of darkness, and fallen angels.

In English, the word genie is borrowed from French, which is derived from the Latin word genius, which was a guardian spirit assigned to each person at their birth in the early 17th century. These beliefs eventually reverted to myths and folklore.

Other than a few folk stories showing the genie as a character, the most famous of these being that of Aladdin and the genie in the lamp, there was not much on the net except on Islamic sites which were flooded with the jinn. The west had not taken the jinn seriously to warrant any study or research, so any information about jinn could only be obtained from Islamic sites and scholars.

Samir landed well in time, and a car that came to pick him up and drove him straight to Sham's place.

Shams was a young man, in his mid-forties and lived near Guru Mandir in Karachi. Guru Mandir is a popular reference point among Karachites. It is a Hindu temple which was originally believed to be a Shiva temple, although there is no evidence of such history. Many people still don't know that there is actually a Hindu temple by this name when they refer to the mandir. The temple has a huge mosque on its right, and there are many who would want to change the name of the locality to the name of the mosque. The government in Sindh had so far resisted that.

Shams welcomed Samir into his modest home. There was no furniture or wall frames of any sort. The living room was carpeted, with fluffy pillows lying along the walls, and shoes were to be taken off outside the room.

He knew why Samir was here, so after exchanging pleasantries, he came to the main topic.

"There is so much myth and folklore surrounding jinn that it is difficult today to separate fact from fiction. A lot has been created by man, and by the jinn themselves, so we mortals have started to believe such stories are true."

"What do you mean by the jinn themselves? How do we even know that jinn really do exist?"

"If we are Muslims, and we believe in the Quran, then we must believe in the jinn. Chapter 72 in the Quran is even named after the jinn. Jinn are mentioned in the Quran in a number of places as an entity that Allah created along with humans and angels. Jinn were created before humans were created. While humans were created from clay, which is earthly matter, the angels and jinn were created from energy. While the angels were created from light, the jinn were created from a smokeless fire!"

"What do you mean by smokeless fire?" asked Samir.

"Smoke itself is matter, like carbon and soot. So, jinn are of the purest heat energy, maybe like a plasma. But in any case, while man is made of matter, jinn and angels are made of energy!"

He continued, "This gives jinn and angels an advantage over man! They can travel at the speed of light, perhaps even faster because they are made of energy. They can pass through matter, through walls, into the universe and deep into the earth and the stars, and are invisible to humans unless they decide to show themselves. The word jinn itself comes from an Arabic word 'janna' meaning to hide or conceal."

He took a breath and continued, "Jinn have tremendous strength, much above what humans or animals have! They live in a world parallel to ours, and in our world as well."

"Why did God create jinn?"

"The correct question is why did God create humans! Jinn were already created by God. They existed long before man was created, as mentioned in Chapter 15 Verse 27 of the Quran. They were created with free will; like humans, but unlike angels, who do not have free will and are free of sin. Jinn, however, have free will but were created to worship Allah, like the humans, which Allah mentions in Chapter 51 Verse 56:

'I have only created jinn and men, that they may serve Me.'"

Samir interrupted, "I have read that the demon and Satan are from the jinn?"

"The well-known jinn in the Quran is Iblis, popularly identified as 'Shaytan', Satan, or the master devil. He is considered the king and had belonged in the company of angels much before mankind was created, but was eventually thrown out of Allah's court for refusing to follow God's order! Now, most disbelieving jinn, and followers of Iblis, are called 'shayateen' which is the plural of shaytan. This is the equivalent of demons in Christianity."

"Is the jinn a fallen angel?"

"Fallen Angel is used by Christians for angels who have sinned, though the term is not mentioned in the Bible. Muslims believe this to be false, as angels are creations which cannot disobey the command of Allah. Iblis was a jinn and not an angel who had his free will, hence he disobeyed God."

"What happened?"

"The Quran is very clear on this episode. When God created Adam, he told the angels to bow down to him. Iblis, who was a jinn, refused to bow down to Adam. He told God that he was more superior to man as he was created from fire, while Adam was created from clay. This is well documented in Chapter 38 Verses 74 to 88 as follows:

'Not so Iblis: he was haughty, and became one of those who reject faith.

Allah said: "O Iblis! What prevents thee from prostrating thyself to one whom I have created with My hands? Art thou haughty? Or art thou one of the high and mighty ones?"

Iblis said: "I am better than he: thou createdst me from fire, and him thou createdst from clay."

Allah said: "Then get thee out from here: for thou art rejected, accursed. And My curse shall be on thee till the day of judgment."

Iblis said: "O my Lord! Give me then respite till the Day the dead are raised."

Allah said: "Respite then is granted thee—Till the day of the time appointed."

Iblis said: "Then, by Thy power, I will put them all in the wrong, Except Thy servants amongst them, sincere and purified by Thy grace."

Allah said: "Then it is just and fitting—and I say what is just and fitting—That I will certainly fill hell with thee and those that follow thee—every one. Say: No reward do I ask of you for this Quran, nor am I a pretender. This is no less than a message to all the worlds. And ye shall certainly know the truth of it all after a while."'"

"So Iblis, the jinn, refused to listen to God?"

"Not only that, but when God cursed him and banished him from heaven, he asked God to give him respite till the day of judgment, when the dead will be raised from their graves. He wanted to prove to God that His new creation was inferior and nothing but a mistake, and that he will lead them all astray, put them all in the wrong, and make them refuse to listen to God."

"And God agreed?"

"Yes. God accepted his challenge till the Day of Judgment when He would judge both mankind and jinn for their deeds. And that He would fill hell with those who follow Iblis, the jinn."

"Is Iblis the only jinn mentioned in the Quran?"

"Certainly, the only jinn who was honored to be in the company of angels in heaven. The other jinn that is mentioned is Ifrit who was a strong one and a commander in Prophet Solomon's army."

"Jinn were in Solomon's army?"

"I will come to that later. But let me tell you first about Iblis. There are countless myths and stories based on the Hadith about jinn inhabiting the earth before mankind was created. There is even mention of the war between the jinn and the angels, and how Iblis sided with angels to kill most of the bad jinn. Since these are Hadith stories and not in the Quran, I will not go into that. But certainly, most jinn follow Iblis."

"Was it Iblis who tempted Adam and Eve to become shameful and fall out of heaven?"

"Yes! The story is also mentioned in the Quran. Iblis suggested various things to them, like eat a forbidden fruit, which made them reveal their sex which was hidden from them. They then realized their mistake and immediately covered their body. But in actuality, Iblis tempted them, pretended to be their best friend and advisor, and told them that they will become immortals like the angels if they listened to him."

"I guess this deceiving by the jinn continues to the present day!"

"Iblis and his jinn are all around us every single moment to tempt us to do wrong things. Murder, rape, terrorism, wars, crime, corruption, you name it! That is why an increase in the occurrence of all these sins is considered the sign of the end of times, because Iblis asked for respite till this time. Now, it appears almost every single one of us has fallen into Iblis's trap. We are being led into terrorism and wars because it is Iblis and his jinn followers that are leading mankind to destruction. And if we continue to do so, very soon we will be fighting wars with each other and seeing the end of times and the day of judgment. God has promised that hell will be filled with the jinn and with those who follow the jinn."

"So, is it an all-out war where jinn want to prove themselves right by leading men astray to kill each other? Is that the only reference to the jinn in the Quran or is there more?"

"There are multiple references to the jinn in many chapters, that is why we must believe in the existence of jinn. But men, led astray by the jinn, have created many stories, many false and many based on local folklore. It makes them into an entity that controls our everyday life, including performing black magic and possession. It makes jinn a race of supermen that command tremendous power over humans. This is misleading, as it is humans that have the intelligence and knowledge, and not the jinn. They are just robots with strength, who can fly at super speed and are invisible."

"You said earlier that most disbelieving jinn are called shaytan. So, are there believing and good jinn also?"

"The Quran makes reference to some jinn who turned good after listening to the Quran. At the time of the Prophet Mohammed, it is mentioned in the Quran that a group of jinn were amazed by the recitation of the Quran, and believed in it after listening to it. They pledged to become right and not to associate partners with God. These jinn then returned to other jinn to warn them of their sins. I guess one could think of it as jinn who realized their mistakes and decided not to follow Iblis."

"So, we may have an army of good jinn that will not follow Iblis?"

"Jinn are not trustworthy! They are known to deceive. If their master can refuse to listen to God in His presence, certainly we should not trust any jinn even if they pretend to be our friend. They will most likely stab us in the back!"

"But did Solomon not have an army of jinn?"

"This is the part of the Quran that will interest you the most. An army of jinn! Yes! God gave Prophet Solomon a kingdom and power that He had not bestowed on anyone. He commanded an army of human, jinn, and animals and he could talk to each one of them! He had miraculous power over the winds, and could make them obey his orders. As a result, he had naval power over all the seas as well. But God gave him judgement and knowledge, so Solomon would never misuse his authority. There is even a reference in the Quran about how kind Solomon was and cared even for the small ants in his kingdom."

"Then how did Solomon trust the jinn? Could they not have overthrown his kingdom if there were so many in his army?

"Solomon had knowledge, intelligence and wit that God had bestowed upon him. He would keep track of every single individual in his nation and army, be they men, animals or jinn. That is why when once he was examining his army, and found only one bird, a hoopoe, missing, he immediately asked for it."

"Isn't that the famous story about Solomon and the Queen of Sheba, on which a Hollywood classic is based?"

"Sheba is referred to as Saba in the Quran. It is believed that the kingdom of Saba was in southern Arabia, most likely Yemen, and possibly ruled over Abyssinia as well, which is present day Ethiopia. The queen of Saba is identified as Bilqis in Arabic tradition and is left unnamed in the Quran, and even in the Bible. She is identified as Makeda in Ethiopian culture."

"So, what happened?"

"The hoopoe informed Solomon that it had travelled to a territory called Saba, which was unknown to Solomon, and where it had found a woman ruling over them. Her kingdom had all the riches and even her throne was magnificent However, they worshipped the sun and not the God of Solomon!"

Samir remembered the Hollywood classic. "They say her palace had 365 windows, and each day of the year, they would worship the rising sun through a window."

"These stories are folklore. In any case, Solomon asked the hoopoe to return back with his letter, and waited to see what they answered."

"What was the message?"

"As anticipated, the letter greeted her and requested her to submit to Allah."

He continued, "Like a leader of modern times, rather than a monarch, the queen consulted her minister, who advised her to go to war, as they had a huge army and the strength, but left the final decision to her. Intelligent as she was, she knew that war leads to destruction, so she decided to please Solomon by sending him exquisite gifts, and wait for his answer."

"So she thought she could win Solomon over, much like what Cleopatra did! Was Solomon impressed?"

"Solomon told the emissaries from Saba that what Allah had given him is far more and much superior to what the queen had sent, and he was now ready to wage war unless they come in submission."

"Solomon wanted to wage war?"

"Not at all. He was intelligent and knew that they would want to avoid war and would soon be coming to surrender and submit to Allah. But he wanted to show his strength to them as well in case they had other plans."

"What did he do?"

"He asked his commanders if anyone could bring her magnificent throne to him before they arrived! This was his way of showing the strength and magnificent powers that God had given him."

"How could they bring her throne before she arrived?"

"This is the most intriguing part which shows the power of the jinn. This is the other reference to the jinn in the Quran. One of his jinn commanders, called Ifrit, was the strongest amongst them. He volunteered to bring the throne before Solomon could rise from his council. Ifrit implied he had the speed and the strength to do it, and added that he may be trusted to do it."

Shams referred to the Quran, "The narration about Ifrit the strong jinn is mentioned in the Quran in Chapter 27 Verses 38 to 42:

'Solomon said to his own men: "Ye chiefs! Which of you can bring me her throne before they come to me in submission?"

Said an Ifrit of the Jinn: "I will bring it to thee before thou rise from thy council: indeed, I have full strength for the purpose, and may be trusted."

Said one who had knowledge of the Book: "I will bring it to thee within the twinkling of an eye!" Then when Solomon saw it placed firmly before him, he said: "This is by the grace of my Lord! To test me whether I am grateful or ungrateful! And if any is grateful, truly his gratitude is a gain for his own soul; but if any is ungrateful, truly my Lord is free of all needs, supreme in honor!"

He said: "Transform her throne out of all recognition by her: let us see whether she is guided to the truth or is one of those who receives no guidance."

So, when she arrived, she was asked, "Is this thy throne?" She said, "It was just like this; and knowledge was bestowed on us in advance of this, and we have submitted to Allah."'"

"So, Ifrit was one of the most powerful jinn in the army?" asked Samir.

"He had to be, since he was in the company of the commanders. However, being a jinn, Solomon knew he could not trust him."

"So, why was he a commander in his army?"

"Because he was one of the most powerful jinn, and someone had to command the other jinn in the army. However, Solomon was careful not to trust Ifrit if left alone on his own. Ifrit, if he had gone to Saba alone, could have conspired with the queen against Solomon."

"So, Solomon assigned the task to someone else?"

"To someone else who volunteered to bring it within the twinkling of the eye, one who was also knowledgeable. And indeed, within a moment, the throne of the queen appeared and was placed before Solomon!"

"This is amazing. It shows tremendous power and speed, and perhaps being invisible at the same time. Was the one who brought it a jinn also?

"It is not clear from the verses. While such a speed and power is only possible with the jinn, it is possible that it was a man who brought the throne, as only man are knowledgeable. But with time, men seem to have lost this skill!"

Shams continued with the story, "As you read the verses, you see that not only did Solomon had those in his army bring the throne in a jiffy of a second, but they also transformed it into something far more spectacular. So, when she arrived, she was not only shocked at seeing her throne appear before she arrived, but was also bedazzled by how it was transformed into something far more beautiful than she had ever imagined. Clearly, this task could only have been accomplished by the jinn at super speed, but under the watchful eyes of Solomon."

"That's amazing! The speed and power of the jinn!"

"The narration does not just end there. A palace was also placed right next to Solomon's palace, which had a glass floor over a lake of water, and when she entered, she lifted her skirt so her clothes could not become wet. She then realized how she had been tricked, first with the throne, then the palace. She then immediately submitted to God."

"So, what you are saying is that jinn are very much capable of moving buildings around if they want to do so, and transform them too?"

"Men have tried to contact jinn for hundreds, perhaps thousands of years, and control them too. If men can do this, they can rule the world!"

All of this was very useful information for Samir, but he wanted to learn more.

"Did not Solomon control the jinn?"

"There were jinn who worked for Solomon, and even then, they were not trustworthy. Any who deviated from the command were punished. Jinn are just like robots without a mind of their own. When Solomon died standing up while balanced on his staff, the jinn did not even realize he had died, and kept working away at the assigned tasks. They only realized that Solomon was dead when he fell down after a little ant gnawing away at the staff broke it."

"So, what you are saying is that jinn are powerful but have zero mind or intelligence of their own?"

"Yes. And definitely not trustworthy. They can perform miraculous tasks but if left on their own, they would come back and stab you!"

Shams got up to take a few strides in the room, looked at Samir, and said, "There is something else you may wish to know about the jinn. This is the part about fortune telling, and how they tempt man into following him."

"I heard black magic and fortune telling is from the jinn."

Shams nodded his head, "See what the Quranic verses say. In Chapter 15, Verses 16 to 18, God says,

'It is We who have set out the zodiacal signs in the heavens, and made them fair seeming to all beholders;
And moreover, We have guarded them from every evil spirit accursed
But any that gains a hearing by stealth, is pursued by a flaming fire, bright to see.'

"And in Chapter 37, Verses 6 to 10,
'We have indeed decked the lower heaven with beauty in the stars
For beauty and for guard against all obstinate rebellious evil spirits,
So, they should not strain their ears in the direction of the exalted assembly but be cast away from every side,
Repulsed, for they are under a perpetual penalty,
Except such as snatch away something by stealth, and they are pursued by a flaming fire, of piercing brightness.'

"And in Chapter 72, titled the Jinn, in Verses 8 and 9:
'And we pried into the secrets of heaven; but we found it filled with stern guards and flaming fires
We used, indeed, to sit there in hidden stations, to steal a hearing; but any who listen now will find a flaming fire watching him in ambush.'"

He paused for a moment to let that sink in and then explained, "All this implies is that jinn, who are the evil ones as referred to in the Quran, go up to heaven to eavesdrop what is being discussed amongst the angels. Earlier when Iblis was in the company of Allah, he could hear everything, but since the day he was thrown out, he or others in his army want to go up and listen about the future, but are stopped midway. Many believe the shooting stars are actually the flaming fire referred to in the Quran."

"So, what you are saying is that jinn do not have access to knowledge of the future, but they just make it up to create a following?"

"Jinn eavesdrop onto what the angels are speaking, and it is possible they pick a few things from them. They then return to earth and mislead their followers with half-baked lies. And in the process, those who learn from the jinn are evil men. They want to control the world themselves by reaching out to the jinn and making them do various tasks on their behalf."

"Do you think with what is happening around the world now, in terms of terrorism, or even 9/11, jinn were used, or can be used in the future by the terrorists to create havoc or lead the world to a war?"

"Yes! It is not only very much possible but is actually happening if you look around you. It is possible that they could have piloted the planes' directly or indirectly, that crashed into the Twin Towers. But it is a two-way street: Jinn want to control the earth and the heavens again, and the only way they can do so is by using men. Jinn have the strength, and men have the knowledge, and together, it is a very lethal combination. If evil men can manipulate the jinn to their advantage, not only they discern what is might happen in the future, but they can make them do impossible feats and rule the world. Likewise, the jinn can manipulate men with their evil whisperings and lead them to killing, terrorism, and war!"

Samir got to the main question he wanted to ask Shams.

"Can jinn be made to steal nuclear bombs?"

"My dear, sir! I have made it very clear by giving you references from the Quran, and not sourced from any folklore or grandmother's stories, that jinn have the power, the strength, can fly and become invisible, and move with tremendous speed! They have more powers and can do more than what your comic characters like superman can do, except that jinn are real, and superman is not! Jinn can not only steal nuclear bombs but can even trigger events around the world that can lead to a nuclear war!"

"So, what is preventing the jinn from doing so today?"

"Maybe the right contacts have not been made between evil men and jinn. I am sure there are many a man who would want to control the jinn to their advantage, likewise Iblis wants men to be led astray and work for him so he can rule the world again!"

Samir realized he had learnt a lot from Shams. If all this was possible and true, then what the graveyard caretaker at Hasan Abdal had mentioned about Jadoo Baba just before dying was that he was trying to make contact with the jinn. He had also mentioned someone by the name of Qabza Khan whom he was helping to control the jinn to do far more damage to mankind than what black magic could do.

Samir wondered if the terrorists had actually succeeded in making contact with the jinn through Jadoo Baba or Qabza Khan. And if they had, then one could only see destruction, death, and wars, much like what Najumi has prophesized.

He asked one last question of Shams, "Have you ever seen and talked to a jinn?"

Shams shook his head. "Our religion forbids us to make contact with the jinn. But I know of many people who do try to reach out. Many claim they have succeeded, but it may not necessarily be true. But it is likely that there are a few evil ones, real evil ones, who could have succeeded. But this does not mean that the jinn have not reached out to contact humans. The Quran implies that jinn do contact men to influence and control them!"

"Hmmm," said Samir, "what do we do if we are attacked by the jinn? You say they are very strong and invisible, and can fly at super speeds. So, how does one protect himself?"

"One should always seek protection of Allah by reciting,

'I seek refuge with Allah from Satan, the accursed'

which is how we usually start our praying. However, there is a very powerful verse in the Quran that protects one from the jinn. It is the last chapter of the Quran, Chapter 114 called The Mankind, or Al-Nas, with only six verses, which I am sure you know well by heart."

'Say: I seek refuge with the Lord and Cherisher of mankind
The King or Ruler of mankind
The Allah or Judge of mankind
From the mischief of the whisperer of evil, who withdraws after his whisper
The same who whispers into the hearts of mankind
Among jinn and among men.'

Samir nodded his head, "We were told when we were young to read these verses all the time to protect us from the jinn." He smiled and added, "I think I will soon require this protection when I confront the jinn."

Shams shook his head, "You should read it all the time, not just when you confront him. It will protect you from all evils and from any unexpected attacks as well."

"But that is not the only verse." He continued, "The Ayat-ul-Kursi, Chapter 2 Verse 255, is equally powerful to quash the power of the jinn. So are the last three verses of Chapter 2 Al-Baqarah. No jinn can face the power of all three combined."

"I will certainly remember to use them if attacked by the jinn!

"Well, to sum what I told you, jinn exists! They are powerful entities and can fly. They are invisible since we can't see them, unless they decide to be seen or heard. They are made of fire. They have asked for respite from God till the day of judgment to mislead men. They do evil whisperings and can lead men astray and have them kill other men or go to war with each other. There are a lot of folklore and narrations from the Hadith out there, and a lot more has been added to the conversation based on make believe and maybe some real stories based on experience."

Samir shook his head, "We do not know how much truth there is in these conversations. But what I would definitely want to know and understand is the psychology and the personality of the jinn, and how they operate, and how they come in contact with humans. To fight an enemy, one needs to understand them first. Whom should I see to get that information?"

"The best person who can give you that information is Pir Wasim. He interacts with a lot of people who have black magic and jinn problems, but he is a good religious guide who knows a lot about magic and jinn!"

Samir knew Pir Wasim well. They just had a long discussion a few days back on black magic, which the terrorists were using to fight their wars, and which had turned out to be very useful in fighting this evil. But now, Samir had realized that terrorists could possibly be using the jinn to fight their wars.

It was time to pay another visit to Pir Wasim and learn more about the jinn.

Moqor

Harry had safely landed in Kabul, and found the agency car waiting for him. There was a Red Cross decal on the vehicle which would allow them to go through most security barriers. The fake identity papers he was carrying facilitated him in passing through the multiple check points. He was travelling as someone working for the Red Cross to provide assistance to the worn-torn victims in the area. The agency driver had also handed him a Glock and Thorium X satellite tablet upgraded to send encrypted messages to the agency.

Moqor was about 150 miles south of Kabul and on the way to Kandahar. It would take about four hours to get there, assuming they were not stopped for checking multiple times. It was also close to the Pakistan border, and the area was infested with Taliban. There had been multiple attacks by the Taliban on Afghan security convoys in this area. Last year ISIS, which had been spreading its influence in Afghanistan, wanted to take over Moqor, but the Taliban had given them a run for their money, and many ISIS fighters were killed in the battle. Since then, ISIS had not returned back to Moqor in force but had moved north to the Tora Bora mountains which had now become their new haven.

Harry recalled only recently the Americans had dropped the Mother-of-all-Bomb in Tora Bora. The Americans had claimed it was used against ISIS but Harry knew that it was only to weed out the Taliban so the area could be cleared of them. There were unconfirmed reports that the only casualties were of 14 Indians from Kerala who were just workers employed in the area. The Pakistan agencies, however, believed the bomb was thrown to facilitate ISIS into moving in, as they were being routed out of Raqqa in Syria. Al-Qaeda, on the other hand, had a strong influence in Moqor, and it was reported that its deputy emir was based in Moqor. Al-Qaeda had an understanding with the Taliban to be given sanctuary in Moqor, from where it had positioned itself for attacks on the American and NATO forces.

Moqor was, therefore, a hotbed of activities and a center of negotiations between the various militant groups, including the Taliban, Al-Qaeda, ISIS and the TTP. The Taliban were strong here, with their headquarters around the corner in Kandahar. Al-Qaeda was now headquartered here, with the deputy emir frequenting Moqor regularly. ISIS, though, had lost a major battle in Moqor, and were moving fighters to Tora Bora into the north of Afghanistan after they were uprooted from Dabiq and were facing strong resistance in Mosul. The khalifa of ISIS, claiming to be the leader of all Islamist forces, was reaching out to Al-Qaeda and the Taliban at Moqor through his representative in the Tora Bora region for a truce. The TTP in Pakistan had their sanctuaries in Moqor whenever they were on the run from the Pakistan armed forces. They were basically mercenaries who would fight anyone or for any group for money. They had also been known to work for a number of foreign forces in advancing their agenda in this region. In other words, all these terrorist organizations had a strong presence in Moqor. When not fighting each other, all of them could be seen socializing in local tea shops, and yet nobody trusted each other. There were hardly any families or peaceful civilians left in Moqor. They had all emigrated away to nearby Kandahar. Moqor was a 'trigger happy town' much like the Wild West but full of terrorists.

The Al-Qaeda people recently had become very upset at the TTP despite paying them a lot of money to do their tasks. Their deputy emir Wazir had sometimes cursed Timur in his meetings, calling him a pig and a dog, for messing up with the dirty bomb assignment. This word had gotten around to Timur. The dirty bomb attack, if it had succeeded, would have created a sensation around the world.

Timur was offended by Wazir's remarks. He did not like it, as he believed it was only due to him that all targets in Pakistan were successfully hit, while Wazir got all the credit. If at all, Timur deserved to be recognized and appreciated by the emir, and made the deputy emir for the region instead of Wazir.

Likewise, Al-Qaeda was still angry at the Taliban leader Mulla Omar for messing up after 9/11 as a result of which they were heavily bombed in the Tora Bora caves. As a result, the stronghold they had built up in Afghanistan prior to 9/11 had to be dismantled and they were on the run, making Moqor their new headquarters. Their leader Osama bin Laden was in hiding in Tora Bora for so many years that many commanders and fighter had lost contact with him. Some had speculated that he was dead. There had been complete silence for about two years prior to the American raid at Abbottabad in Pakistan in which they claimed he was killed. Many suspected he had actually died a natural death in the Tora Bora mountains due to kidney failure.

Harry arrived at the place marked on his map and found it was a safe house which the agency had acquired a few months back. This was their key point of contact with the TTP. The agency had to be extra careful in this hornet's nest of activities. It was worse than the old western towns, and one always had to watch their backs from each other.

The man at the counter, who appeared to be a Pashtun, greeted him and told him his friends had been waiting for him since the morning in the house across the street. He then led him to his room. It was a crabby room with a small bed and table, no phone, a small stand-alone wardrobe, a sink, and an attached toilet with a shower head in one corner. Harry knew this was the best comfort he could get in this shanty town, but at least it was safe. The Pashtun had a code of honor in which a guest would be protected with one's life. Here, it appeared he was the guest of every terror group operating out of Moqor.

Harry freshened up, tucked his Glock under his belt, walked out of the safe house, and was greeted by another armed man waiting outside, who led him to the house across. There were four men with guns at the entrance who let him go through. His identity mark being an American was enough as identification. He doubted if there was any other American here. He entered the house into the main receiving area, and saw three men sitting around a table. He identified Timur as one as he had worked regularly with him, and a man he could trust.

Timur got up to shake his hand, and made no comment. The other two men also got up, and Harry could feel that one of them had authority. He was tall, and was wearing a black local suit. Timur introduced him as the deputy emir whose real name was Wazir. Harry sensed some sarcasm in Timur's tone. He figured there must be some differences or animosity between the two commanders over some operational issues.

Harry had heard of the deputy emir, who belonged to Al-Qaeda. He was in charge of operations in Afghanistan and Pakistan, while Timur, who was from TTP, handled mostly Pakistan's northern region.

Wazir spoke up, "We have a new and much larger mission to carry out after the last operation was unfortunately messed up in Pakistan."

He glanced at Timur for a second, as if blaming him for the failure, and continued, "This time, we will explode a big bomb in Kashmir. A nuclear bomb!"

That double-crossing bastard and liar, thought Harry, *he is giving me a cock and bull story.*

Wazir paused for a moment to let it sink in, and noting no reaction from Harry continued, "There is already a lot of unrest in Kashmir among the local population against the Indian atrocities and rule. There will be an explosion near the Indian army base, with a lot of casualties, probably in the thousands. The Indians will call it a major act of terrorism, point the finger at Pakistan and arm its own nuclear weapons for an attack on Pakistan. The world will move in quickly, and there will be a call for immediate sanctions on Pakistan. As a result, Pakistan will be forced to dismantle its nuclear program to prevent an all-out nuclear war."

Harry had heard that before many times. This was certainly always a wishful thinking of all terrorist organizations, from ISIS to Al-Qaeda to TTP, to steal a bomb, but it was impossible for them to lay their hands on the nuke. They had been trying it for years, but the nuclear arsenal was very well guarded by the Pakistan forces. They had put in all fail-safe mechanisms in place. The deputy emir must be living in a fantasy world. But he let him continue to learn more about their operation.

Wazir looked at Harry, and asked, "Isn't that the agenda of your government as well—to put sanctions on Pakistan and have them roll back their program because your friend Israel is threatened by it as well? Well, now we can work together on one platform with one agenda."

Harry smiled to himself as he wondered since when was it an Al-Qaeda agenda to work with the Americans to denuclearize Pakistan. After all, he knew that the real target of the Al-Qaeda attack—the Bagram Air Base, which his agency had warned him about.

"If you are carrying out this operation and have planned it well, why do you need us?" he asked.

"We don't have the technology to ensure the bomb is armed and triggered. I have been told by our sponsors that there is a program which has to be punched into the triggering device, and depending on what is needed, it will set the bomb to explode at a particular time. We know that you are one of the few experts on an assignment in Pakistan who can do it. That is why you have been sent by your agency to Pakistan—to create conditions for sanctions and roll-back for Pakistan. We are both on the same side, and your and our sponsors are the same. But we need your help to program the weapon. We plan to bring the bomb to Moqor, and all arrangements have been made to steal them off the Pakistani base."

Harry knew the bombs were well protected by the Pakistani forces, and it was impossible for Al-Qaeda to steal it off their base. However, he let Wazir continue.

"You must be thinking this is nothing new, and you have heard it many times before from us. Let me tell you this time it is different and we have made special arrangements which will not fail. I am not at liberty to disclose these with you but you will see it for yourself when the bomb arrives in Moqor within a few days."

"How will you get it across the border?" asked Harry.

"We have also made special arrangements that it will pass the borders without detection."

He smiled and added, "Just assume it will be flown here by a superman."

Harry couldn't believe this bull shit, but he played along.

"So, what do you want me to do?"

"We need your help to arm it here, since we cannot do that. After it is armed, our fighters will take it to Kashmir."

Harry thought Wazir was crazy. There was absolutely no way they could steal the bomb, and that too so soon. Secondly, even if they did manage to get their hands on it, they would never be able to bring it across the border into Afghanistan with the Pakistan army being on full alert after the heist. They must clearly have something else up their sleeve. Maybe they had bought off a key person in the Pakistan command structure. That that was impossible too, as Pakistan followed the US style Personnel Reliability Program for safety of its nuclear arsenal.

But then he also knew Wazir was lying, as the Al-Qaeda had no plan to take the bomb to India to explode. It was meant for the Bagram Air Base north of Kabul as he had been informed by his agency. The Al-Qaeda was playing a double game and planning to use an American against an American base.

He had to play along, and agree to the task, whether the bomb was successfully stolen or not. He knew it was impossible. But assuming one chance in a million that they did manage to get their hands on it, his assignment was to have it hijacked along the way to be exposed within Pakistan and then possessed by NATO forces.

But his mind was confused! What mechanism was Wazir talking about to transport the bomb here, as there were countless military checkposts along the way and on the Pakistan Afghanistan border? Surely, the Pakistan army would be on full alert.

He shook his head. It was not possible.

"How do you plan to steal it from one of the most well guarded bases in Pakistan?"

"Mr. Harry. Did we not carry out successfully the last operation in which we acquired dirty fuel from right under the eyes of Pakistan security? Not only that, we were also successful in attacking the convoy of the Pakistani president right in the red zone of Islamabad, and would have destroyed them all if it had not been for the follies of some of our friends." He looked at Timur again and continued, "The current operation is already well-planned, but I can't tell you the details. I personally intend to supervise it from here. There will be no mistakes this time. Be assured the bomb will arrive here in a day or two, and the world will soon realize our strength and we will bring it to its knees!"

Harry realized if the current operation was already planned and in place, which Wazir was confirming, then he had to inform his agency immediately as they would just have a day to plan to hijack the bomb from Al-Qaeda if at all they were successful in stealing it. There was no time left. He also knew that Timur would come in very handy in providing the timing and location of the operation, and could create a road block to give them extra time, till the NATO forces could move in to possess it. They had less than 24 hours to complete their arrangements. Every single minute was important.

Timur was the key. He had to talk to Timur alone, who he was sure would go along with him since he would want the deputy emir to fail too.

"We are ready to cooperate with you if it means denuclearizing Pakistan. It will not be difficult to arm the bomb. I will be in Moqor till you need me."

Harry got up to shake his hand. Wazir held out his hand, and remarked, "This is great. It is great to work together for a change."

He then got up, and the other person who seemed to be his guard, followed him out of the house.

Harry waited for a few moments till he could hear them down the steps and walk away with the four others that were waiting outside. He turned to Timur and asked him if there is a tea shop nearby as he badly wanted to have a cup of tea after the long dusty travel. Timur nodded in the affirmative and told him to follow him. Timur could read Harry's body language that he wanted to talk to him also.

They walked for a block till he found one that was out in the open, with a few tables and benches sprawled out. They took the furthest one away, away from the group of Afghans that were having their afternoon tea. He ordered two Afghani teas, something which tasted like green tea, but was far healthier.

Harry knew Timur well enough to come straight to the point. They had worked together on many missions before and could trust him. He knew Timur had a price for everything.

Harry looked over the shoulder to ensure everyone else was out of hearing range and let it in without wasting any time. He spoke softly just in case somebody wanted to eavesdrop.

"Timur. The agency has always worked with your group for many years now. We have an understanding and have reached a point that we trust you more than anyone else in this region. We wish you become the deputy emir one day for all the sacrifices you and your men have made."

The last sentence got Timur's attention. The way he looked at Harry clearly displayed he liked what Harry was saying.

Harry continued, "We don't want your fellow Muslims, who have been part of your jihad, dying in Kashmir because the Indian forces will retaliate with a vengeance. I personally don't think your friend, the deputy emir, can pull off this operation, but if they do, it will make you look bad and inefficient."

Timur nodded but did not say anything wanting to hear first what the American was proposing.

"We can have the bomb intercepted in Pakistan. This will make a failure of Wazir's operation."

The last sentence got Timur's attention. He leaned forward to hear more.

Harry lowered his voice to a whisper, "To do that we need your help. Actually, we just want it held up just for a few hours before it crosses over to Afghanistan so our forces can move in from across the border. We can pay any price upfront whatever you seek."

Timur was not at all surprised at this plan. He knew the Americans and Al-Qaeda has a love-hate relationship. In many a strategic matters, they were partners, as the Al-Qaeda supreme leader Osama bin Laden himself had been on the American payroll for a long time till their relationship fell apart after 9/11. Now, they had developed a deep resentment for each other. The TTP, on the other hand, always enjoyed good relationship with various American agencies, and they had worked with contractors like Harry many times before.

Timur felt this was a God-sent opportunity for him. God had always been kind to him. This was surely because he was a sincere soldier of Islam, and he believed God would never let him down. Here, he had the American asking him to fail the operation being planned by the deputy emir, and on top of that the American was willing to pay a lot of money upfront. If this big operation failed, the deputy emir would definitely be disgraced and beheaded by the khalifa. This would be his opportunity to become the deputy emir, a position he had always aspired. He would be in charge of the whole region and would also get to travel beyond the borders of Pakistan and Afghanistan into Iraq and Syria and other countries as well as an emissary of the khalifa.

Timur looked at Harry and wondered if he really knew that the real target of Al-Qaeda was the American base in Afghanistan and not Kashmir. He also knew this operation was being planned to be carried out by jinn, whom he had heard had been successfully contacted by the aamil. But he also knew the Americans would never believe that. There was no point in trying to explain that to them as they had never even known or had heard of the jinn and their powers. The Bible made no mention of them. They only believed in demons, and jinn and demon are not the same, as the jinn has more power than a demon and has an identity like that of a human. This operation was planned and was being executed by the deputy emir using jinn for the first time, which was a new war strategy never carried out before. Nobody would believe it, and he had no intention to give a lesson on jinn to Harry. There was no need or time to do so.

He also knew that if this mission was being done by jinn, it could never fail. No one could stop the power of the jinn. The bomb would not even be transported by road. It would be flying through the air, carried by a jinn, and dropped onto the target. There would be nothing to intercept.

But then he knew that jinn do not have a mind or intelligence of their own. They certainly have superhuman strength, and can fly and take the bomb with them, but could they arm it to explode? Certainly not! That is why the deputy emir wanted the jinn to bring the bomb to Moqor first where Harry would arm it, and then their fighters or the jinn would carry it to Bagram.

Harry had asked him to intercept it for a few hours within Pakistan. How could that be possible if the bomb was being carried by a jinn? It could definitely not be stopped on the highway in Pakistan as the bomb would not even be transported by road! He can't block a jinn from carrying the bomb in midair!

He started thinking of other possibilities. He certainly wanted the deputy emir to fail. Maybe he could provide this information in advance to the Pakistan intelligence agencies, so they could relocate the bomb from where it currently is stored. Perhaps the Pakistan Army could intercept it in Moqor, as Pakistan is right across the border, and fail the operation. Perhaps NATO forces could take possession of the bomb in Moqor as soon as it arrived here. He had no quick answers, but right now, he realized he must say yes to Harry and play along.

"It is very much doable, depending upon the level of secrecy between you and me and the amount!"

"You know the TTP has worked together with us many times before and we can trust each other. Would one million dollars do it? Half million dollars in cash, delivered by tonight to wherever you want to do it, and another half million the day the operation succeeds!"

"Two million. Half in advance."

"One and a half million, divided equally. Let it be a done deal. This is within the limits of my authority and I can arrange to have the money sent tonight."

"Done." Timur got up to shake Harry's hand. "I will get you the details of where the money is to be sent in Kabul. But you know, if this word ever leaks out, you and I will both be beheaded! I must take your leave now before others get suspicious."

Harry wanted him to get more details of the operation from some of the deputy emir's associates, who were being very secretive about it. He knew his men could get them to talk after smoking some hash together.

They walked away in different directions. Harry walked back alone to his room. He had to use his satellite tablet to immediately communicate the outcome of his meetings with both of them. He had to inform the agency of the Al-Qaeda plan to steal the nukes within the next few days. They had to plan for the interception of the bomb and be on standby. He knew the agency would think he had gone crazy, but he could take no chance. He had to tell them also to arrange the money and transfer it tonight.

As he walked up to his room, the sound of the evening muezzin came up loud on the speakers, calling the faithful to pray.

The bastards wanted to kill Americans at Bagram, he thought. Ideally, he should let the bomb go to Kashmir and explode there. It will also kill a few thousand Muslims when it exploded, which would be ideal. But he knew that was not their plan. They had already screwed up last time with the dirty bomb. This time, he wanted to ensure that if the bomb was really stolen by them as they were claiming, it had to be intercepted on the highway near the Pakistan base by the NATO forces, much like another Osama bin Laden type of operation. That would be sufficient to denuclearize Pakistan. Perhaps he would find another day to kill the Muslim population.

Pir Wasim

Samir stopped by Pir Wasim's next to find out more about jinn, and drove over to see him at his parent's mausoleum outside Karachi on the highway to Hyderabad. Wasim was wearing a white suit and had just finished his sermon. He took Samir to his private quarters, and ordered two cups of tea with some biscuits.

"I knew you would be back to ask me about the real source of black magic. While magic is practiced by men, it is really the jinn that have taught them the art of black magic. Black magic originates from the jinn!"

"Hold on! Could you please start from ground zero and tell me how they are connected? Please detail me what the jinn really are?"

"Each and every society believes in the supernatural. And they believe in evil forces: ghosts, demons, Satan, Iblis, Jinn, Lucifer, Azazel, you name it. Even Hollywood has its trolls and many beast-like creatures. We Muslims believe in jinn, and Iblis, or Satan, is their leader and king, while the other jinn and demons are their followers. The primary meaning of jinn is 'to hide' as they are considered invisible. Some in their western folklore call it djinn or genies, like in a lamp. But in reality, they are nowhere near how they are visualized by the west—just as a cartoon character!"

He knew a lot about jinn, "Jinn had always existed since prehistoric times. They were created by God from the flame of a huge fire much before man was created. Angels were created from the light of that fire. According to some beliefs, the very first jinn that was created was called Marij, and his wife was called Marija. They raised their family to over 70,000 jinn. Azazel, whom we call Iblis, was born much later.

"Jinn were given a new lease of life and importance among the Muslims after the Quran was revealed, as they were mentioned in the Quran in a number of places. It described them as being made of a smokeless fire, like humans were made of clay and the angels made of light. Jinn have been described to have strength, they can fly, are evil, and are not trustworthy. Since they are made of energy, they can travel at the speed of light and have hundreds and thousands of years of lifetime. They have no intelligence of their own and are not knowledgeable or emotional. Humans have more intelligence and wisdom. However, subsequent Hadith and folklore describe the jinn in much more detail. Most of it is possibly made up by man over the years."

"What is the general belief about jinn?"

"Jinn are a complete entity having communities like humans. Jinn can be Muslim or non-Muslim, with the majority of them being non-Muslim due to their nature of being created from fire. Like humans, jinn will be judged for their deeds on the final day of judgment. In any case, whether good or bad, they cannot be trusted."

He continued to educate Samir, "Generally, there are three types of jinn: one that flies in the air, one that appears like snakes and dogs, and the third that wanders about isolated and dark places, particularly the impure places or graveyards. Jinn are shapeless as they are made of energy but can take the shape of humans or animals. They live in remote areas, mountains, seas, trees, and the air, and in their own communities. They eat, drink, marry, have children, and die. They are very different from humans and can rapidly multiply. It is reported that the female jinn can give birth after every three months, and up to 40 jinn at a time. The baby jinn can walk within one hour of the birth. Jinn can live up to hundreds and thousands of years."

Samir could not believe all this! Wasim must be crazy to believe all this!

"Jinn can hide behind barriers, from humans and even from angels by becoming invisible. They are invisible from you, but you are clearly visible to them. But like I said, they can take shape of humans or animals as well. However, if they do, they are susceptible to the same living conditions, meaning they can be killed when in human or animal form, not otherwise. A popular female jinn is the 'churail' which many assume to be the witch. Jinn can also have animals as pets, however, we do not know who these animals are or in what form they live.

"There is a jinn attached to every human, so they know you closely and very well. Therefore, they can impersonate you or any of your close relatives or friends; wife, husband, father, mother, brother, sister, friend, etc., and can play games to misguide and deceive you. They can easily make friends with you, without your knowing who they are, and do you favors with the intent of winning you over. Once they make friends with you or get close to you, they will possess you and make you their slave, and if you resist, they can even kill you. Animals, somehow, have an instinct and can identify them. When a dog barks or a donkey brays unnecessarily, it means they have encountered a jinn."

Samir shook his head, "All of that sounds unbelievable and a figment of someone's imagination. So, are you telling me that we cannot distinguish between a real person and a jinn, and that they can impersonate your relative, your friend, your boss, or even a commander in a military base?"

"That and much more! Except that they have no intelligence or mind of their own so they can be detected. Humans trump them because brains are superior to brawns. Allah had blessed Adam over Iblis with intelligence and knowledge. It is also a widely held Muslim belief that there is a jinn assigned to each person, except to the Prophet. But then there is a guardian angel assigned to every person for good at the same time to counter the evil forces."

"You make it sound as if we are surrounded by jinn all the time, whether impersonating as loved ones, or as animals…"

"They personally have no physical shape, as they are made of energy. However, like I said, they live and appear like humans and animals. Even during the times of our Prophet, Iblis came in the form of one of the companions of the Prophet to deceive people. When encountered with a jinn, one should never fear them, for if they sense fear in you, they will either attack you or capture you."

This is so weird, Samir thought. Wasim, however, continued to impart his knowledge.

"They usually eat with their left hand. Bones are their favorite food, and if you see a black dog or snake eating a bone in a dark desolate place, you can be assured it is a jinn. You must immediately recite the Ayat-ul-Kursi, Chapter 2:255, or the last Chapter 114 of the Quran, called Mankind, to ward off evil. These, and the last three verses of the second Chapter Al-Baqarah, are the most powerful antidote to protect from the jinn. These three work together very efficiently to counter the effect of jinn."

"Yes. Shams told me that too."

"You mentioned he is invisible and made of energy without shape. How and in what shape do they enter our world?"

"They can enter any time by giving themselves a shape, any shape, and becoming visible. However, we can invite them to enter our world through 'chillas', which is a circular type of stargate or portal that evil men and soothsayers use to contact them. Chillas are usually made and practiced in isolated graveyards which the jinn usually frequent or live in them. The aamil walks around the chilla, on one foot in a clockwise direction, for 40 nights to make contact with the jinn."

"Why clockwise?"

"Because at Mecca, the pilgrimage around the Kaaba is done anticlockwise. The aamil moves clockwise in reverse direction to counter that. They are also required to sacrifice someone they love and read the relevant Quranic verses backwards to make the jinn happy so they can come in contact with them."

"Would moving in the opposite direction in the chilla reverse the spell?" Samir was curious.

"Yes! Contact will be broken and the jinn can be sent back into his world if one moves around the chilla in an anticlockwise manner and simultaneously reads the verses from the Quran which protects one from the jinn. But before that, the jinn will try to distract you, and if you get distracted, possibly kill you if he loses his cool."

"If one makes contact with the jinn through these chillas, they can be made to do any task?"

"That is the general belief. But first of all, hardly a few out of thousands successfully complete the chilla and make contact. They are distracted by the jinn in every possible way. They may appear in the form of a pretty young sexy female and offer you sex, or show themselves up as a loved one seeking your help as if they are bleeding to death. Those who are lured or leave it midway either become mad, die an unnatural death, or are killed by the jinn in most cases. Hence, it is not advisable to do the chilla if one cannot complete it. Many evil men lie that have succeeded in competing the chilla and are now in control of a jinn. That cannot be true as even the Prophet was not in control of the jinn."

"I believe he had an encounter with one?"

"He reported that once an Ifrit jinn tried to distract him while he was praying. He immediately overpowered him and tied him to the pillar of the mosque. But then he remembered Solomon's prayer to God that only he should have the power to control jinn, so he let the jinn go. It is even reported that the Prophet once wrote a letter to the jinn asking them not to bother mankind. Some even today keep a copy of this letter in their amulet to protect themselves from the jinn.

"Chapter 72 is named after the jinn. In it is mentioned that an assembly of jinn came and listened to the Quran, and converted from non-believers to believers. There have been other stories also of the nine jinn, who were Jews, who first accepted Islam, and became companions to the Prophet, while others joined later. They say up to 70,000 jinn came at one time to see the Prophet. There is also a world conference of jinn reported. Even in the war of Badr at the time of the Prophet, Iblis is said to have come to the aid of the enemies, and claimed no one can defeat them as he will be their protector. But when the Prophet picked up a handful of dust and threw it into their faces, they turned and fled."

"If Iblis was a jinn, why was he in the company of angels when Adam was created?"

"When Iblis was born, he was the king of jinn and his throne was over the water. To make Allah happy, he used to fly to all corners of the universe and worship Him. For every thousands of years of worship, he was rewarded by being raised a level, till he was raised to the level of the seventh heaven.

"Most of the jinn from his tribe, who still lived on earth at that time, and being made of fire, were short-tempered and of the angry type. They were always in quarrel and fighting with each other and eventually started killing each other. Then just like for the present civilizations, God sent to them over 800 jinn prophets to reform them, but instead, they started killing each prophet as they were sent, and became totally rebellious. This continued for over 100,000 years. God finally ordered the angels to kill the jinn, and Iblis, faithful as he was to God, sided with the angels to kill the jinn. This was called the jinn war. Most rebellious died but a few were left who hid in caves and forests. Iblis was rewarded and was elevated to join the company of angels in God's court."

He continued, "This was when God decided to create Adam from the same earth that Iblis ruled at one time. Iblis was unhappy and would not bow to a creature made from the same earth which he ruled, as he considered himself superior to man. He was the first racist ever. He was made of fire and man of earth. He also wanted to become the ruler of the earth again, so he rebelled and challenged God that mankind would follow the same path of other jinn and would not be obedient to him. But what he did not realize was that God had given intelligence to man and the power to acquire knowledge, which he did not have. The rest is history."

"So, he was thrown out of heaven? Can Iblis go back to the same levels of universe that he once could fly to?"

"No. He is now trapped on earth and within the first universe. He cannot travel to the highest level of the universe now. Freedom to travel up to the highest level of universe, the seventh level, is now only allowed to the angels, where the fortunes of individuals are discussed and the future is decided, including on the day of judgment. Iblis would very much like to know of the future, so he and his companions hide behind the stars and eavesdrop on the angels, typically at sunset and sunrise when there is a changing shift of the angels. When they are discovered, stars are thrown at them to scare them away, which we see as shooting stars in the universe. They then come down from the first level of universe to their followers on earth, and claim they have heard all. They say they know of the future, and can change their fortune. With this, they create a following on earth. 99% of what they say are lies. The false whispering, as is mentioned in Al-Nas, which is the last Chapter of the Quran, Chapter 114, which I am sure we all know by heart. After all, their agenda is to make people believe in them and eventually gain control of the earth once more, and make mankind their slaves."

"You mentioned his companions. Where did they come from?"

"Iblis had nine sons, and the other jinn who had hidden in the caves and dark places during the jinn war have joined him on earth. Each of his sons have been assigned jinn followers and a task. For example, one jinn is responsible to create wars and riots, another to mislead you not to pray, another to commit sin, and so on."

"And there are people who are led astray by them and follow them?"

"Yes. The soothsayers, the aamil, the fortune tellers, the astrologers, are their ready-made clients. They try to influence other people too, either by possessing them, or by showing themselves as good jinn, befriending them in the form of humans, offering to help them, and in the process misleading them. They ask the people to please them, and in exchange, they would do anything for them, including giving them everlasting life."

"Having everlasting life has always been man's weakness over the ages. What about the people who practice black magic? Is that from the jinn too?"

"Black magic was taught by the jinn to the people at the time of Solomon, when they were serving in his army. Even today, People who are involved in magic make contact with the world of jinn, even though it is forbidden for men to contact jinn and vice versa. One cannot control the jinn, but sometimes an understanding, a collaboration, a partnership, is developed between evil men and jinn when they reach out to each other. The jinn ask them to do certain acts of sin to appease them and to check their level of determination. For example, they may want you to commit the murder of a loved one, or to bring the liver of a 10-year-old. They may ask you to clean your toilet with the sacred pages of the Quran. Anything that would seem impossible to do. Only if one passes those tests would a jinn make contact with you and be willing to do what you require. It is a 'you scratch my back, I scratch your back' arrangement. But even then they cannot be trusted because they are made of fire and are therefore hot tempered. They will take the first opportunity to betray you and stab you in the back."

"What about Solomon and his control over the jinn?"

"That was the power given by God Himself after Solomon prayed to God for a kingdom never before given to anyone nor in the future. Jinn were his subjects, and he used their labor to build palaces and temples, and to fight wars. The jinn were scared of him. Many thought Solomon was a magician because he could control the jinn. A magic ring called the 'Seal of Solomon' was given to Solomon which gave him power over the jinn. Solomon's knowledge was written in a book, but was stolen by jinn and men who started practicing black magic. It was eventually recovered by Solomon who placed it under his throne. When Solomon died, the people dug out the book and started practicing what was written in the book. They learnt how to do black magic and control the jinn. This has become the basis of all sorcery today."

Samir nodded his head, "I have heard that one before. Some claim the book was first possessed by the Knight Templars and is now with the secret societies such as the Freemasons and the Illuminati, who are using the knowledge of the book to make contact with and worship the devil. They would like the devil to rule the world again. Others say it is still being searched in places like under the Temple of Solomon and the Dome of the Rock in Jerusalem where the Ark of the Covenant is also hidden. Some say it is in Ethiopia, where the son of Solomon Menelik I from the Queen of Sheba ruled. Some even claim the book was eventually found in Babylon, and is in the possession of ISIS now."

Wasim seemed to know a lot about black magic, "The evil empires of the world have always wanted to get their hands-on Solomon's book of magic and the Ark of the Covenant. The Nazis very much wanted to locate them, and had even dug up half of Egypt trying to find them."

Samir couldn't believe all that he was hearing. If all this knowledge given to Solomon to control the jinn was written in a book, and if this book was now in the hands of an evil empire or a terror group, they could easily control or destroy this world and all mankind with the help of jinn.

Was this the end-of-times narrated in Islamic eschatology and what is sermoned in lectures by terrorists like Timur? If they could control only one jinn, especially the Ifrit who was a powerful jinn, that would be sufficient to rule the world!

Samir wanted to know more about the Ifrit. "Who or what are the Ifrit?"

"The Ifrit is a commander jinn mentioned in the Quran, who was very powerful, who volunteered to Solomon to bring the throne of Saba, or Sheba, in an instant, adding that he could be trusted. Of course, even Solomon did not trust him, because he knew once he lets the Ifrit go to a far way land of a different empire, he would conspire with them a better deal and rebel against Solomon with an army of jinn. Solomon was wise not to fall into his trap."

He continued, "Ifrit are a clan of powerful jinn known for their strength and speed and being wicked as well. They are not what one could call average but are a super jinn. There are also myths associated with the Ifrit, who is believed to be an enormous winged creature of fire, much like flying dinosaurs, that lives in caves and dark places.

"The jinn can have sex and marry humans as well," he added with a smile and continued.

"No army or modern weapons can have power over them, but they can be captured and controlled by magic. No one has been known to succeed in controlling an Ifrit yet, though quite a few have tried over the years and lost their lives. It is believed that unless one has the knowledge of Solomon's book of magic, a jinn cannot be captured."

"What about jinn possessing humans?"

"Jinn have the power to possess humans, especially if the human has weak will power. Exorcism is practiced in all faiths. Whether the body is possessed by the devil, Satan or the demon, it is one and the same thing. We believe it is the jinn that captures the body. Most of the victims are females captured by the unbelieving male jinn. It could be to make them work as slaves, or for sex or marriage. They are usually exorcized by reading the verses from the Quran, in particular the last Chapter 114, the Ayat-ul-Kursi, and the last three verses of the second Chapter Al-Baqarah. Spraying the holy water from Zamzam works too as the jinn is made of fire, and water is an antidote and extinguishes fire. Amulets with strange symbols or writings are not allowed in Islam, as they mostly come from the magic that was practiced in Babylon. The aamil insert evil words within the verses of the Quran to make their magic work. No other remedy works better, even though there are a lot of soothsayers and religious men out there who would tell you different techniques to exorcise. One needs to be wary of them, as they are most likely working for the jinn themselves. These individuals could even be the jinn himself posing as a spiritual guide. The remedy works in some cases and becomes worse in others."

"I believe these are mostly cases of schizophrenia, cases of split personality or epilepsy instead of possession."

"Not always. When the possessed starts speaking a language he or she does not know, or starts speaking of places never visited, or talks of people never met, but who really exist, one begins to wonder if these are really mental disorders or jinn possessions."

"So, how does one know if it is a mental disorder or a possession?"

"If you see a sudden change in personality, a split personality, changes in facial structure and voice, speaking of a foreign language, hallucinations, or increased physical strength, then it is most likely a possession by a jinn."

"Are jinn the only supernatural creatures in Islam?"

"There are other types of jinn, like the 'marid'. Then there are angels, of course, created from light, who only follow Allah's orders and worship Him. 'Jibril', known as Gabriel in Christianity, is an angel too. There is 'Buraq', which is a noble white steed with the head of human and the wings of an eagle, which can move at the speed of lightning and with a single step can reach the horizon. He served as a mode of transportation for the various prophets of Islam, and in particular transported our Prophet to the seventh heaven and back during his famous night journey of 'mairaj'. Then there is the 'Beast', who will appear before the end of times. When the Sun will rise in the west, the beast will emerge from the ground, which will carry the staff of Moses in one hand, and in the other it will wear the ring of Solomon which controlled the jinn. There are also the 'houris', female beings who will accompany the faithful in heaven. They are often associated with the 72 virgins…"

Samir thought Wasim was getting too far-fetched. He interrupted, "Getting back to jinn, I have read a lot of tales in papers where people also believe they are contacted by the jinn and who want them to do an evil act in exchange for something they need. Only yesterday there was this news item that a possessed man got three years jail for killing his father. The man claimed he had received a message from a jinn to kill his father. Clearly, he had a mental problem.

"There are many Hollywood type stories one hears every day." Samir asserted, "A friend of mine had strange voices come from the basement of his house for over a month. Finally, he decided to call in a spiritual guide, who was a known expert in exorcising jinn from a house. He immediately went down and caught a jinn by the neck and took him out of the house. No one could see the jinn, but the body language of the guide showed he was struggling with someone invisible wanting to get away, and holding him tight. One would not believe this, but then no more voices could be heard from the basement anymore."

Wasim nodded his head in agreement, "All these are facts. You scientists think we are crazy when we communicate such stories, that jinn have taken over a person, or even a locality. A whole region in Karachi was subject to jinn sightings, because it was built on barren land which was their settlement. Families of jinn were living there. Finally, we were called in to request them to leave the area and move outside the city. I am glad they agreed without resorting to violence. The area has been quiet since then.

"In another incident, in a case of possession of a whole household by a very powerful jinn, I had to seek the assistance of a whole team of spiritual guides known to me, and we had to recite the holy verses for weeks to counter the possession. In the process, we were also attacked by them, and two of our guides suffered serious injuries. But in the end, we were able to make them leave the house and leave the individuals alone."

Samir wondered whether Wasim had gone bonkers, or was telling the truth. Samir thought he should share his own experience with Wasim as well about how these aamil lie.

"Well. It's not always a case of jinn versus men. Sometimes, men think they can seek and get assistance from the jinn as well. It has become a booming business especially in areas where people are mostly illiterate and poor.

"I had once, out of curiosity, visited an aamil in a poverty-stricken area who claimed he controlled jinn and could answer any question. The house was crowded with people, who were paying money to ask questions or discuss their problems with the jinn. The jinn in this case was a ninja-clad woman sitting in one corner whom the guide claimed had a jinn trapped in her body. When one posed a question to her directly, she would answer with a hissing sound and the guide would interpret the answer. When I asked my 'test question', she hissed but the aamil could not answer it correctly which confirmed my notion that they were lying.

"Clearly, these are cases of fraud where the public is cheated of their hard-earned money, but there is a huge clientele out there who believe in jinn, and why not, since they are mentioned in both the Quran and the Hadith. You can't argue with them, otherwise, in this age and country, you never know what you could be accused of."

"One could be accused of blasphemy!"

Samir shook his head, "Only recently we had a case of falsely accusing a young university student of blasphemy. He was lynched and killed because someone else wanted him dead for a different reason, and what better way to get him killed then through a false allegation of blasphemy. They just hacked his Facebook page and posted something controversial on his wall. That was enough to get him killed by a mob of over 50 people while a few hundred watched."

"One has to be very careful in these times. These crazy fanatics are self-proclaimed judge, jury, and executioners."

Samir reverted back to the reason he was here. "Is the book of Solomon the only source of magic and jinn? Could the magicians be using other books too?"

"There have been many books, and many have claimed to have the magic knowledge, and the knowledge to control jinn. While most of them could be false claims, there is one book that possibly has this knowledge. It was written by Al-Ghazali and is called the 'Book of Knowledge'."

Samir had heard of Al-Ghazali but not of the book.

"What book?"

Wasim walked over to his book shelves, which displayed hundreds of books on spiritual thoughts, Sufism, jinn and black magic, but he unlocked a small cabinet in its middle, and took out a book which he had kept safe with a few other books which all appeared very fragile as if they were hundreds of years old.

"The Book of Knowledge, written by Imam Ghazali! He was a Persian philosopher and mystic who lived in the 11th century, and is considered to be a 'mujaddid' or a renewer of the faith, who, according to tradition, appears once in a few hundred years to restore the faith of the community. He has sometimes been referred to as the most influential Muslim after the Prophet. He brought the orthodox version of Islam and Sufism closer, and wrote more than 70 books on sciences, Islamic philosophy and Sufism.

"The Book of Knowledge is the foundation of the 40 books of the revival of the religious sciences. It is said that only the ones with a brave heart and superior intelligence can understand and master it, and gain from it for the benefit of the mankind, others would just misuse it. When one masters this book, they can actually call down the spirits. So, one has to be strong enough to do that. One can also undo black magic with the knowledge in the book, including that which a black magician cannot undo."

He continued, "With this book, you can understand the jinn and can even talk to them. There is nothing magical in it. It is only about understanding life, which consists of four elements: earth, water, air, and fire. These elements keep a balance in the universe and the body. Any variation in this balance will end in natural disaster, and illness in the body. Black magic is practiced using the same forces of nature and so is communication with the jinn."

"So, Imam Ghazali understood magic?"

"He knew playing with numbers is satanic, and associated math with the devil. His writings were later re-written in a 14th century manuscript called the 'Kitab al-Bulhan' or the 'Book of Wonders', which covered many aspects of astronomy, astrology, and magic."

"I am sure this book will come in handy if we need to communicate with the jinn."

With this, Samir realized he had learnt a lot and added, asking for permission to leave, "I will be in touch with you if the need arises. Could you please be available at short notice on your phone in case I need your guidance on any matter related to the jinn?"

"You know I am always available to help you at any time. But after giving you this information, I feel I could be attacked by a jinn anytime if they feel I am a barrier to their plans. But I am not afraid as I have never feared jinn. It is God that one must seek the protection of. I read the last chapter of the Quran, the Ayat-ul-Kursi and the last three verses of the Chapter 2 Al-Baqarah every time to protect myself, and so should you, as you are moving into the dangerous territory of the jinn. They will just kill you. You must not forget that!"

Samir had heard that before. He was shaken with all the knowledge he had gained about the jinn but was not afraid. Fear is only of God, he reminded himself.

He felt he had learnt enough about the jinn from both Shams and Wasim. While Shams's views were based on the Quran, which every Muslim should believe in without an iota of doubt, Wasim's interpretation of the jinn was based on the Hadith and on countless stories and myths making the rounds among everyday Pakistanis, who religiously believed in them.

He was almost beginning to believe that a jinn could be exploited by evil men and terrorists to serve a purpose, even to aid in terrorism, if it led to the destruction of mankind. Clearly, a nexus was fast building up between them. It had to be stopped otherwise evil men and jinn would rule the earth again.

Najumi

Samir stopped by Najumi's place again on the way to the airport, who had been very helpful in identifying the time and location when black magic was used by terrorists in an earlier attack. Samir wanted to know if Najumi could provide some insight into the jinn as well as many believed the astrologers are in contact with the jinn, from whom they get their predictions from.

"I am so glad you stopped by. I have been getting very strong vibrations for the last few days that there is yet a much more severe debacle around the corner, but I can't seem to focus on it as if there are more powerful forces blocking my vision."

"Please read your charts again for me," requested Samir, "What you read last time was very accurate."

Najumi was determined to help. It was as if he had vibes of the nature of events to come.

"I will certainly try to do so," he said as he walked up to his charts. "But I am getting very blurry visions, and each time I try to do a reading, I don't seem to see far into the future. It is as if a dark force is blocking my vision."

He pulled out a large chart, which had a constellation printed on it and looked similar to the one he had used the last time, laid it out on the table, and moved his fingers around. His fingers would not glide beyond a point. He tried again, but no luck.

"There is a force blocking my reading…"

"Najumi: Have you ever sought the help of jinn in your fortune telling?"

Najumi was taken aback, "Never! I know I can reach out to the jinn if I want to, and learn a lot more, but I will not trust what they will tell me. It is also a sin to do so."

"So, where have you learnt your art from?"

"From the wisdom of the ancient astrologers. From my father and his collection of books and charts…"

He suddenly got up, "Wait. There are a few charts that my father left me that are based on the knowledge of the stars left by from the days of the pharaohs and his astrologers. The jinn had taught them the art of making these charts. We know the pharaohs were ahead of their time in construction and had built the pyramids. People only wonder how it was possible when there were no cranes."

"I believe the jinn built it for them!"

He let that sink into Samir before he continued, "I have never used these charts before; because my father said never use it unless you feel your knowledge is being blocked by unseen forces, and then only revert to the knowledge of these charts. He also said that there is a risk of misinterpreting these charts, as there are forces who may try to block your vision and mislead you. I believe he was referring to the jinn.

"These are replicas of the similar ones used by those astrologers and have been carried down by the word of mouth much like the tarot cards. I am sure this will help us now because it takes a thief to catch a thief."

Samir could feel Najumi's uneasiness as he got up and walked over to his safe, unlocked it, and inserted his hand to the very back to pull out what appeared to be an old worn out diary and a few large charts. He carefully pulled them out, unrolled a chart, and laid it out on the table. Samir could see that it had some very strange symbols which he had never seen before.

"I need to remember what these symbols mean, since I have never used this chart before." He walked over to his bookshelf, and pulled out a large thick book which looked like an encyclopedia.

"These are the collection of most symbols found from pre-medieval to the present times. There are thousands of such symbols in existence today, on old buildings, temples, castles, caves, and inscribed on stones. We still cannot understand what many of them mean. It is the science of symbiology, and even the scholars in the west are trying to decipher them. A few hundred have been decoded and interpreted over the years, but not all. My father also did a lot of research in trying to interpret many of the symbols of which we do not know the meaning. He spent years travelling to Egypt and Iraq tracking their origins, and was able to decipher quite a few which he wrote down in his personal diary. They have never been published. Many other symbols are used in Tarot cards, the interpretation of which has been carried down by travelers and gypsies since those times. This book could come in handy to understand what some of these symbols mean."

He then started to circle his fingers on the chart, which had stars and what appeared to be planets, with some symbols placed in between. He stopped at one point over a star, then moved it again over another and stopped over a symbol. He continued a few more times, noting down the star and the symbol. Then he opened the book of symbols to match the right symbol.

"Some of the symbols have the interpretation in the book, but others do not. Let me check if my father was able to decode them."

He opened the diary carefully, turned a few pages, and started matching the symbols to the ones drawn by hand in the diary with some narration written in front of it in what appeared to be Arabic.

He smiled, but then immediately frowned. One could see the worry on his face.

"What is it? Do we have an answer?"

"The chart and the symbols are based on what was taught by the jinn to the astrologers of those times, so we are reading the mind of the jinn themselves!"

Samir was impatient, "What do the charts say?"

"Apocalypse!" He said in a hoarse voice, "I see death and destruction on a very large scale not seen before for a very long time. I see a big cloud of smoke. I see fire all over. I had predicted the same last time you were here. I could see the destruction then. I see it again but on a larger scale. It is all over this region. There is an earthquake…"

His voice trailed off.

"Where and when…" Samir almost choked.

Najumi moved his fingers over the stars again, and pointed his finger at a planet. He then rolled out the second chart, which had a hand drawn map of what appeared to be a map of Asia and Africa, somewhat fairly accurately depicting it, with more symbols on it. He moved his fingers with his eyes closed and stopped at a point. He opened his eyes to stare in disbelief.

"What is it?" Samir raised his voice.

"I see destruction." He placed his finger on an exact spot in the map, "It is probably not in Pakistan. It could be right across the border maybe in Afghanistan or Iran. It is across the mountains of Balochistan on the other side. You know these are not modern maps that one could find out the exact location through latitude and longitude. And the destruction is very close, and very soon!"

"Oh my God," exclaimed Samir, "what can we do to stop it this time? Can we change the destiny this time too like we did the last time? What is the antidote to stop it?"

"These negative forces are far more powerful. Far more than the black magic we encountered last time. We can perhaps stop it only if we know the origin of these negative forces, like before, and then try to reverse it!"

"Can you not focus and find out the origin?"

He closed his eyes for about a minute as if to concentrate hard on his vision and blurted out, "The jinn! They are using jinn for this destruction. Oh, Allah, forgive us! Once someone uses jinn for a destructive purpose, the jinn are not going to go back easily to their world. It's like the saying, 'The genie is out of the bottle.'"

"Can we locate the source from where they are contacting the jinn? Pir Wasim mentioned that they make these contact through chillas…"

"Yes…that's it. Find the chilla and the aamil they are using to contact the jinn. I will need to concentrate on it. But the remedy is to reverse it. You need to talk to Pir Wasim who is knowledgeable enough to reverse it or even to protect you."

"Yes! Both Shams and Pir Wasim have given me the right antidotes to seek their protection from the jinn."

Suddenly, Samir realized there was much more to it. His mind reverted back to the lecture by Timur at the Madrasah. Even though Timur had said and thought they could use the jinn for their acts of terror, it was perhaps the jinn who were conspiring to put an end to humanity. It would be just the way Iblis wanted it: to conquer and rule the world.

If it was true, then it appeared the prophesies were becoming true, and the end of times were fast approaching, whether it was through black magic or jinn. And on top of that, the terrorists were facilitating their takeover of the world.

Islamic eschatology was real and doomsday was fast approaching, if the jinn were to take over the world!

"How much time do we have?"

"Not a lot. The evil forces are already out there contacting the jinn, and once they are able to please them, it may just be a few days away."

Samir knew he had to rush back to Islamabad to see if he could find out more about the mastermind who was planning to use the jinn for his evil designs, and find the evil aamil who was doing the chillas to control them. They had to reverse the chilla and break the nexus between the jinn and the terrorists. The jinn had to be sent back to his universe before they controlled the earth and let loose their reign on it.

He bade a quick farewell to Najumi and rushed to the airport.

On his way to the airport, Samir's mind thought more of the jinn. What or who were they really? Were jinn spiritual only? Or could there be a scientific explanation to their existence? And if so, was there a scientific solution to it?

Samir recalled Nafis Alibhoy, who was a well-known theoretical physicist working at a university in Islamabad, and one who had always rejected the existence of supernatural as spirits in many conferences and discussions. Samir had known Nafis for years when he was completing his PhD at Princeton.

He called up Nafis as he boarded the flight and asked if he could stop by late at night as he needed his input on an issue of grave concern. Nafis knew Samir would never call him to see him that late in the night unless it was really critical. He said it was fine as he was always a late worker, usually going to bed at 2 A.M., so Samir could stop by his home any time before that.

That settled, Samir next called up Hameed and asked him to be on standby, and told him he would call him again as soon as he landed in Islamabad.

Science

While Samir waited for the flight to take off, his mind kept on drifting to the thought whether the jinn was a spiritual, scientific or a psychological phenomenon. Could they be explained and controlled by parapsychology or metaphysics?

Samir thought that before he met Nafis, he wanted to hear what Hasan thought of it. He knew Hasan had done a capstone project in the psychology of the supernatural. Hasan might be able to throw some additional insight into jinn.

He called up Hasan, and asked him to meet him at the airport in Islamabad saying it was important. Hasan knew his father's urgency sometimes so did not question him as to why.

Hasan already knew the jinn were on his father's mind because he has especially flown to Karachi to meet Shams. He was already waiting in the arrival lounge in Islamabad when the plane landed. They drove back together and Samir told him briefly about his meeting with Shams, and then asked him what he thought of the jinn from a psychological or scientific viewpoint.

"Dad. There are multiple theories of what the jinn really are, and what they are made up of. The Quran says they are made up of smokeless fire. That has to be our basis of explanation."

"Can science explain what the jinn are?"

"We, in the east, are too primitive in our understanding of sciences. Science is only a few hundred years old while jinn have existed for millions of years. The west is also not interested in this phenomenon as they do not believe in jinn. So, we have to rely on theories of some lame duck eastern scientists who try to explain the jinn from their perspective. I can lay out some of these theories which I have read about but do not necessarily believe in them."

He blurted out what he had written in his final year project about the jinn, "There are many possible explanations. According to one theory, jinn are made from some light or heat source, charged particles like the photons or electrons in a high energy state. When they jump from one level to the other, they emit heat and light in the process, much like nuclear fission. Electromagnetic waves are also emitted during this process. When the waves are in a visible spectrum, having wavelengths in the range of 400–700 nanometers, or a frequency of roughly 430–750 terahertz, we can see them. You know nano is to the power of minus nine, and tera is to the power of plus twelve. This bandwidth is between the infrared and the ultraviolet waves, which are visible. When the jinn jump to a lower frequency, they move into the infrared region, which is the region of heat and the smokeless fire. So, the jinns are nothing but electromagnetic energy that exists between visible light and infrared, when they become invisible. As electromagnetic energy, they can pass through walls and travel at the speed of light as well. It also explains when in movies like Ghostbuster, they use electromagnetic field detectors to detect the ghost."

Such a theory was appealing to Samir. "Can it explain their physical strength?"

"Every matter, force or energy we know of has three dimensions: mass, length, and time. Einstein's theory of relativity is based on this notion, which is that matter can be converted to energy and vice versa. Jinn can convert to one or another form at will. They can then travel at the speed of light when in high energy states. This is like the transporter in the Star Trek movies. I believe that humans, jinns and angels have more than three dimensions if we include consciousness and the spirit as well. They can move between these dimensions as well, and when they move into a different dimension, we can't see them. It is an art that we as humans are still trying to learn. Psychologists and neurologists are still trying to understand these dimensions. When jinn move between dimensions, they can create the right force if they so desire, they can create speed or consciousness.

"The jinn masters believe our stargate to connect to the other dimension and communicate with them is the chilla. But we can't explain the chilla through science unless we visualize it like another black hole."

"Hmm," Samir thought for a moment, "there is so much to learn to understand the jinn. Could jinn possibly be like plasma, which is a high temperature medium?"

"There is yet another theory by another physicist who says all living beings need energy to live. Our energy comes from the food we eat and from the oxygen we breathe. Likewise, if there are other creatures in the universe, they would need energy too to live. In very hot places, like the sun, where the surface temperature is over 6,000 degrees Celsius, and over several million degrees at the core, all matter would be ionized, which is breaking into positive and negative ions. This state of matter is called plasma. There are scientists who say there could be life on the sun or stars in the form of plasma, which can be very hot and like a smokeless fire. That is basically what the jinn are. The ions in the plasma, which are nothing but charged particles, create an electromagnetic force. This plasma then could be the jinn living on the stars, or even in the core of the earth. But this theory stops here and does not explain more about the jinn."

"You mentioned the black hole. How do you explain that?"

"Astronomers and space scientists are only beginning to understand what black holes are and their origin. Are these a cemetery of stars, a star cruncher, or where new stars and universes are born on the other side? Did our own universe originate out of a black hole? Likewise, those who try to explain jinn but have less of an understanding of the universe associate black holes to jinn as well. They are, after all, very dense matter or energy, emit radioactivity and are very hot in temperatures, all characteristics of a jinn. So, is the black hole a portal to the jinn? We do not know that, not yet at least!"

"What about the UFO and the ETs? Is it possible that the UFOs or the aliens which people report to have seen could be jinn? Is Area 51 a refuge or settlement for jinn?"

"I am sure you must have read the best sellers written by Erich von Daniken when you were in college. He made claims about extraterrestrial influences on early human culture, but these are rejected by a majority of scientists and academics. However, instead of hypothesizing that these visitors were or are aliens, it is likely that these visitors could possibly be jinn. Erich probably had never heard of jinn otherwise he would have hypothesized about them too in his books."

"Then maybe the jinn are probably extraterrestrials visiting earth," Samir thought of that as a possibility and added, "Even what some call the shadow people, could possibly be the jinn!"

Hasan thought for a moment, and then asked, "Have you heard of the 'Ascended Masters'?"

Samir knew, as a student of psychology and being an inquisitive student of spiritual sciences, Hasan easily could connect science to psychology to spiritualism to history.

"Just a little. How could they be jinn?"

"Ascended masters were normal human beings who have ascended in subsequent incarnated lives to a higher state through spiritual transformations. According to these teachings, a shaman or spiritual master has taken the fifth initiation and dwells in the fifth dimension, while an ascended master has taken the sixth initiation dwells in the sixth dimension. There are up to nine initiations, where a 'Lord of the World' is a human being, or a being of some other lifeform who has taken the ninth initiation, which is the highest. Examples of ascended masters include Jesus, Confucius, Buddha, and many others. It is likely that jinn could be the eighth dimension of ascended masters.

"That is a theory only."

"Then there are also the Archons, which in gnostic theory are a species of inorganic beings that emerged in the solar system prior to the formation of the earth. Like the jinn, they existed before the humans. In 1947, there was an archeological finding of a cache of rare gnostic texts at Nag Hammadi in Egypt. Gnostics Christians were targeted as heretics because they did not believe in many of the traditional beliefs including Christ's resurrection but believed in supernatural. They experienced altered states and developed siddhis, occult skills such as clairaudience and remote viewing. Gnosis became a kind of yogic noetic science melded with parapsychology, and explains how these inorganic beings called the archons, who possibly were the jinn, were present in our universe."

He continued with his knowledge on the subject, "These beings were created in our solar system before the Earth was formed, and inhabited the complete solar system. Archons can affect our minds as well through an intellectual virus or false ideology pertaining to religion. They are also violent and predatory, which fits in well with the characteristics of the jinn."

"This is interesting," commented Samir. "So, even though the Christians do not believe in jinn, but the gnostic Christians of earlier times believed in jinn in the form of archons?"

Hasan nodded, "Many Christians don't know about the existence of the jinn. The Old Testament, Ezekiel 1: 1–28, confirms that, which says, 'And out of the midst of fire came the likeness of four living creatures. And this was their appearance: they had the likeness of a man…their appearance was like coals of fire…and there was brightness to the fire, and out of the fire went forth lightning. And the living creatures ran and returned as the appearance of a flash of lightning…' This confirms jinn were mentioned even in the Old Testament."

"Amazing! So, jinn are a reality in all Abrahamic religions?"

"Not only in Abrahamic, but jinn can have a presence in other faiths as well. There are similar gods in Africa, and in certain South American and Far Eastern cultures as well. Hindus scriptures have many classes of demons and gods differing in power and influence. They also have a God of Fire, who they call 'Agni Devta', agni meaning fire in Sanskrit. They believe in reincarnation, and a moving up to a higher level or lower level. Souls can enter any living creature. Those who are good are rewarded to a higher state till they reach the level of the creator and are merged into it. This is also the equivalent of heaven. On the other hand, those who are bad or evil are punished to a lower level, including becoming animals like dogs and snakes, and possibly a jinn…"

"It makes sense but still does not explain the superpowers of the jinn, including becoming invisible or flying through the air."

"We are only beginning to understand the jinn now. There are other possible scientific representations too. Jinn could be multidimensional creatures that breathe in air, exhale deadly gases like sarin and cough out antimatter. Some fictional writers have shown that such supernatural or aliens could disrupt brainwaves, interfere with ability to think, and create dreams or hallucinations. They could stop our heart from beating, or produce sound vibration that would shatter our bones. They could kill chloroplast so plants could no longer convert sunlight and humanity would be wiped out due to lack of plantation. These creatures would be no less than jinn that we believe in."

"Disrupt brainwaves, interfere with ability to think, and create dreams or hallucinations. Certainly, that shows their ability to create terrorists out of normal human beings."

"If the brain waves can be altered, from alpha to beta to theta, then one could be made to do superhuman feats as well. Theta occurs in deep sleep, dreaming and meditation. In theta, our senses are withdrawn from the external world and focused on signals originating from within, which are beyond our normal conscious awareness. The yamabushi mountain monks are known to lower their brain waves to theta so they can take a dip in a thundering, ice-cold waterfall and then take a wet stroll up the mountain."

Samir recalled the terrorists training themselves in their camp, "Likewise, those who walk on burning coal, like the terrorists I saw at a training camp, possibly do the same by meditating through prayers, or even calling out to the jinn, who temper their brainwaves so that the fire does not feel hot to their soles."

"Very much possible," added Hasan.

Samir felt he had learnt enough about jinn. He was now quite convinced that jinn, who were supernatural creatures, could be used in the next terrorist attack. He had also learnt from Najumi that the attack is possibly imminent, perhaps in the next few days, and the destruction would be widespread across the border in Afghanistan or Iran.

Should their embassies be alerted? He had no evidence to that effect, only what Najumi had prophesized. They would probably laugh at him, and the prime minister would think he was crazy.

Najumi had also talked of death and destruction on a very large scale, and a big cloud of smoke and fire all over. He had talked of an earthquake taking place. This could only mean a nuclear explosion, nothing less! All signs were indicative of a nuclear device exploding.

Afghanistan and Iran were not nuclear enabled. Only Pakistan was. The terrorists were fairly successful few days back to get their hands on nuclear fuel through a combination of black magic and skills, and of course the failure of security on their part. So, it was likely that their next goal could be to acquire a nuclear bomb. The west was already very much concerned that Pakistan's nuclear assets could fall in the hands of terrorists. They had always pressurized Pakistan to roll back its nuclear program or face sanctions. Pakistan's military and political governments had, till now, successfully resisted the pressure, and despite the carrot-and-stick approach by the west, Pakistan was not going to part with its nuclear assets.

The terrorists getting their hands on an armed nuclear device was next to impossible. First of all, the locations were kept secret, and they were moved around frequently. Secondly, security was provided by Special Forces who were trained to thwart off any attack on these devices. There were counter layers of security. It was a fool proof mechanism where no man or beast could penetrate a base where the devices were stored.

No beast? What about the jinn? Samir wondered.

If a jinn was used to steal the bomb, and deliver it to its destination, like the throne of Saba was carried by the Ifrit, would the military even be able to detect it or even stop it? Clearly, not! They will never be able to stop a jinn.

It was very important to stop the jinn from stealing the device. But how? It was perhaps only possible if one could locate the source and the contact.

Where were the jinn being contacted from? Who was doing it? He recalled what Wasim had told him. He had mentioned the chilla, much like a stargate, which would most likely be at an isolated graveyard. Samir's mind also went back to the caretaker at the graveyard at Hasan Abdal, who had said Jadoo Baba, the aamil, was helping a close relative, Qabza Khan, to make contact with the jinn. He had also confirmed that the jinn would cause much more destruction than what black magic could do.

Hameed was very connected in the northern areas. Perhaps he could get some information on Qabza Khan and his whereabouts. He called up Hameed.

Hameed answered the phone immediately after one ring. Samir went straight to the point.

"Jadoo Baba has a close relative by the name of Qabza Khan who is also an aamil. The caretaker at Misri Shah graveyard had mentioned this when we were there. It is important and urgent that we locate the whereabouts of Qabza Khan immediately. Can you send someone as soon as possible to get this information from Jadoo's wife or any other close relatives who may be in Hasan Abdal. Try to keep it discreet so no eyebrows are raised."

Hameed was on the mark, "Right away! I have a trustworthy university staffer whose family lives in Hasan Abdal. I will contact him and Inshallah get this information within an hour. I will call you immediately afterwards."

Samir knew he would, at best, have a few moments with Nafis before he would be on the road to locate the chilla and possibly destroy it before the jinn destroyed them first.

He told Hasan to drive fast to Nafis's residence.

Fiction

Nafis was up and waiting for him. Samir came straight to the point.

"Samir. Have you lost your mind? There are no jinn or whatsoever. All these black magic and jinn are just a figment of imagination and have been created by the merchants of Islam to make a quick buck and to have their hold on the illiterate population of this country. I am also very surprised that a large number of academics have started believing this imaginary world of jinn, and you on top of that?"

"Jinn do have existence in the Quran," Samir commented. "They don't interfere in our lives, nor we in theirs. They are just a parallel world of supernatural."

"That may be quite likely, as one should not question the Quran. But this country is going bonkers. When a leading university in Islamabad starts organizing a workshop on 'Black Magic and Jinn', and there is standing room only, then one knows something is wrong with the mind of these people."

"That's interesting. I would readily fund such a study. What was discussed at the workshop?"

Nafis looked unbelievingly at Samir and added, "A spiritual cardiologist was the main speaker who spoke for three hours. Logic was used to prove the existence of jinn. He spoke about three types of jinn: those that fly; those that change shape and appearance depending upon circumstance; and those that find abode in garbage or dark places. No one challenged him."

"Well. Many in the west believe in ET and the shadow people. Hollywood makes a lot of trash movies on vampires, werewolves, and zombies, don't they? Most of America believes in them, don't they? Some even make billions at the box office."

"So does Lord of the Rings and Star Wars! Crazy ideas were discussed at this conference, like creating a jinn-based telecommunications network or developing radar-evading jinn-powered cruise missiles. Someone suggested the host university to pursue research into replacing fossil and nuclear fuels with jinn power, which incidentally was proposed in the 70s by a leading nuclear scientist from Pakistan in an interview to a leading western journal. He said that he could draw electricity from a captured jinn."

"Now, that could easily solve our energy problems," Samir commented cynically.

Nafis looked at Samir again not believing his responses, "At another leading university in Lahore, a professor argued that it was jinn power that made a nuclear bomb explode, or a nuclear reactor produce electric power? Jinn, surely! Another senior faculty from the same university claimed that reciting or listening to certain holy verses can control genes and metabolites. He even suggested placing audio-visual equipment in hospitals to treat terminally ill patients."

"You may be surprised, but I actually have been to one of these treatment centers, and it works! It is also happening at a major government hospital in Lahore, where the Chapter 55 Ar-Rahman is played on CDs in the wards. The hospital claims it works effectively."

Nafis shook his head, "Placebo effect, probably. Honestly, these leading scientists and academics at our universities believe that mental disorders like epilepsy and schizophrenia, can be cured through a pir with a six-inch beard because the jinn are responsible for it. They also believe that jinn are responsible for weather changes, including hurricanes and tsunamis. What is mind boggling is that heads of some far-right political parties believe earthquakes occur because we as a nation are on the wrong path by following western traditions and practices. They have all turned mad!"

With a strong note of disapproval, he added, "It is in our culture and genes. Historically, we have always believed in supernatural powers. There are many stories that people believe in. For example, in the early 19th century, when Bhopal was attacked by Rajputs and Marathas and the ruler was not well-equipped with arms, his deputy went to a spiritual pir in a trance who pointed to a cave where a lot of weapons were discovered. The pir said that a jinn had told him about the weapons. The attack was thwarted off, and the ruler then started believing in pirs and jinn. His followers do to the present day. They must all be crazy!"

Samir reminded Nafis, "We also had heard many such stories during the 1965 war with India, where jinn could be seen in the sky shooting down Indian planes. As children, we used to believe them too."

Nafis agreed, "As a child, it is understandable to believe in the boogeyman. But when grown-up adults do that, and that too a large segment of the population, including scientists and academicians, then I think this country has gone bonkers!"

He shook his head and continued, "There are some who actually believe another war between Pakistan and India took place in 1975, which was kept a secret by both countries. In this war, they believe neither side used conventional weapons. India used nuclear-powered chariots that were discovered in caves and built thousands of years ago using the knowledge of the Vedas, whereas the Pakistani side used saucer-shaped flying objects fueled by the power of the jinn. Some even reported seeing dog fights over Lahore and Delhi between the chariots and the flying saucers. It is believed that Pakistan has a secret program to manufacture jinn-powered flying saucers which will be used in a future war with India. Some even believe some of that technology was leaked out, and the planes that crashed into the twin towers in New York were jinn powered."

Samir shook his head, "Surely, the world does not believe that, and neither do we!"

"We may not, but there is a whole world out there who believes we can capitalize on the energy and power of the jinn. These weirdos not only include the mullah but scientists as well."

Samir agreed, "Let them believe so, and take admission in a lunatic asylum. Science does not support any of these hypotheses. This is nothing but science fiction.

"However, your criticism of those who believe in jinn, sane as it may sound, is not helping me. We were just attacked in Islamabad the other day by terrorists who used black magic. You will say black magic does not exist. I have personally gone through it. Our Prophet experienced it, and thousands of others experience it on a daily basis. Likewise, there is a definite existence of jinn in the Quran, Iblis being the king and Ifrit being the powerful one. The Quran narrates how Ifrit transported the throne of Saba within seconds thousands of miles away, supposedly from Yemen to Jerusalem."

"There could be other explanations," commented Nafis.

"I agree, but today, we are faced with a very serious threat. Your denying what exists or does not exist means nothing to me, and is not helping me. I believe that a jinn will be used by the terrorists to steal and use a nuclear device within the next few days, and explode it. There are real evil forces out there who want to use the jinn to fight wars, and not the fictitious 1975 war you talked about. If a nuclear war between India and Pakistan does break out, millions will die. And it will happen out just because we did not believe in the jinn!"

Nafis had to know that the other world does exist, "When I started out on this journey, I did not believe in any of this hocus pocus, like you do. But as I explored and discovered more about these supernatural powers, I got sucked into it more and more to the point of believing in them, and into the possibility that they can and will cause severe destruction. Do you even have an idea of the destruction this nuclear war, if triggered, would cause?"

"I do, and only recently I read about it, and it is horrifying!" replied Nafis.

Nafis walked up to his laptop, typed a few words on google search, and read into the screen, "According to a study by researchers from the US, over 20 million people would die. Another two billion around the world would face severe starvation due to the climatic effects of this nuclear war."

Samir shook his head, "I would rather make a fool of myself and believe in the jinn and try to stop them and prevent this apocalypse instead of waiting for a few million people to die. It is a damned if I do, damned if I don't situation."

Nafis just shook his head. He was too much of a theoretical physicist to believe in all this and could be of no further help as he lived in his world of theoretical science which mostly conflicted with religious and spiritual beliefs.

Samir realized he would not get much out of Nafis, so he bade him goodbye and walked back to his car, hoping that Hameed would get some information on the aamil and the location of his chilla. Once he had the information, they would need to rush to reach and stop him. He realized they would need a faster mode of transportation to reach wherever they were to find the chilla, perhaps on some obscure mountain top.

He called up the prime minister's office and requested the staff to urgently requisition a chopper on standby at Islamabad airport. The staff knew of the level of trust the prime minister placed on Samir, and in these times of terror, confirmed that the chopper would be available in thirty minutes.

Samir headed back in the direction of the airport, and on the way, called up Hameed asking him to meet him there. Samir hoped that by the time he arrived at the airport, Hameed would have the required information about Qabza Khan and his whereabouts.

Operation Sting

Timur's moles were active with the Al-Qaeda boys in trying to get details of the next attack. Some of the Al-Qaeda boys in Moqor were very excited as they had an idea of the next big attack, which would be on the Americans, and would place them on their knees begging for mercy. The local grapevine had it that 'an atom bomb' had successfully been stolen which would destroy the 'farangis' and finally evict them from the Muslim lands. This would be the mother of all wars and their greatest victory, much more than what 9/11 attack was. They also heard that immediately following the attack, the caliphate would be declared under one flag of the khalifa. They would be in accordance with the Hadith which had mentioned that the armies of 80 countries will be led by their black flag.

They had always known that the jinn had tremendous power, and could destroy anyone if one so desired. However, it was very difficult to contact the jinn and control them; only the aamil could do that. They had also heard that the deputy emir had been trying to contact the jinn through different aamil since the last few months, but all aamil had failed in reaching out to jinn, and in the process, the jinn had killed them all. Contacting and controlling the jinn was not an easy task. Others who claimed they had succeeded were found to be fake and were beheaded by Al-Qaeda. Hence, no aamil had agreed for this task.

Now, there was excitement in the camp as they had learnt that a famous aamil by the name of Qabza Khan in the tribal areas of North Waziristan, who was well-known by the title of jinn master, had succeeded in contacting the jinn. Before he had taken on the task, many had warned him not to, as even his cousin, who was very senior to him could only complete it for five days, and was thrown off the cliff by a jinn. However, this aamil had agreed to do so because not only did he think he was the best but the price paid to him by the deputy emir was abnormally high. They said he had successfully completed the chilla a few days back, and a jinn was now under his control.

There was complete rejoicing in the Al-Qaeda camp. They were all talking about how the jinn will now fight the war with the Americans, and soon the mother of all bombs, the 'atom bomb' will be used in their next attack. They had heard that a bomb will soon be stolen from a Pakistan army base by the jinn and brought to Moqor. They were desperately waiting for that moment.

Timur had also learnt that the bomb would be stolen within the next few days. But he did not know from where. Even Harry or his agency did not know of the actual location and timing, or how the bomb would be stolen. He had agreed to find out from the deputy emir and inform Harry about the location and timing of the heist for the large amount of money he had charged. He had also committed for a price that his people will block the bomb on the highway, after it is stolen, for at least a few hours till the NATO forces arrived to take possession.

However, the truth was different from what he would tell Harry. He knew that even if he found out from which base and when the bomb would be stolen, the road block by his people would fail as the bomb would be 'flown' by the jinn above everyone's heads and brought to Moqor. They will find nothing to intercept or block, and the NATO forces waiting for their raid would be very disappointed as no bomb would show up on the road.

He just couldn't tell Harry about the jinn as he would not believe him.

He suddenly saw his trusted aide come running and was very excited as he blurted. "The bomb will be stolen from Chakwal tonight."

Chakwal! Timur smiled. No one could have guessed the nuclear devices were stored at Chakwal, which was very close to Islamabad. Chakwal was just about 40 miles from the famous Khewra Salt Ranges, which were among the largest deposits of rock salt in the world. These underground deposits extended all the way to Chakwal. The army knew that the rock salt would prevent any detection of these devices from the air even by the most sophisticated satellites or drones. Chakwal was also close to Khushab, where the nuclear fuel was enriched, and to Sargodha, which had the largest air force base in Punjab. Most F-16s and Mirages were stationed there. In case of war, the jets could easily be nuclear armed within a few hours.

He was surprised as to how Al-Qaeda had gotten this information that nukes were stored at Chakwal. Normally, parts and fuel are stored in different locations. They must have their sources through the ISIS or perhaps even India or Israel. But he did not care. He had gotten what he wanted. Now, he had to inform Harry immediately.

He rushed off towards the place that Harry was staying. It was late at night and it was all dark and quiet in the streets, and no one saw him. There was an armed attendant outside the place, who knew Timur well so he did not stop him. He saw the light in Harry's room was on, and walked up to the door and knocked.

Harry was expecting him. Timur walked in and immediately closed the door behind him.

"It will be Chakwal tonight." He then added a make-believe scenario to give credence to his story as he couldn't mention the jinn, "It will be hidden in the tank of an oil tanker and travel by road to Bannu and cross the border at Khost into Afghanistan. I will arrange for my men to intercept them just after the tanker crosses Bannu."

Harry had known this operation was imminent and could happen any one of these days, but was not expecting that Al-Qaeda would move in that fast. There was so little time left for NATO to move and intercept if, at all, the bomb was stolen. He still doubted whether Al-Qaeda could steal the bomb from under the security of the Pakistan forces, but could take no chance.

"That is a very important piece of information you have provided. You have always been a trusted friend."

Timur, however, wanted to make sure he had received the money before Harry found out the truth. He handed Harry a small piece of paper with something scribbled on it by hand.

"Please send the money to this address by early morning. Someone will receive it. I need to move our people to Bannu by early morning as well. There is very little time, as we need to choose our people well who are ready for martyrdom. We also need to cross many roadblocks to reach there with our weapons. It will not be easy but will be done.

"We should be able to hold the Al-Qaeda fighters transporting the bomb easily for a couple of hours in a gun battle. Please make sure your men get there during this time as we will only be able to hold them for a couple of hours! It won't take long for the Pakistan army to move in and whisk the bomb away."

That is all Harry wanted, "That is ample time for our forces to arrive from across the border by choppers."

Timur turned around and walked out of the room before someone could notice he was there. He also knew he had to arrange a mock road block in Bannu, knowing very well that there would not be any oil tanker carrying any device or passing through there. But he had to show their presence to the agency for the price they had charged. They would not be responsible if the bomb did not show up and transported by air by the jinn. When the bomb would explode in Bagram, it would be the beginning of the end-of-times and the rule of Islam as promised in the Hadith.

Harry waited till Timur had left the room then pulled out his satellite tablet and transmitted the information to the agency. The messages sent were safe as they were encrypted by the tablet, and on top of that the agency had its own coded language to enable operators to send secret messages where encryption was not available. Harry knew there was very little time to arrange for the NATO forces to be ready to move into Pakistan.

As soon as the satellites and the drones had tracked the oil tanker moving out of Chakwal, he was sure the TTP would block the tanker for a couple of hours, during which time, NATO forces would move in on choppers. They would, of course, inform the Pakistan forces in advance that they are coming in to aid in the recovery of the stolen nuclear weapons. Pakistan forces would have discovered the heist by then and would have no choice but to seek the help of NATO for this operation as they would need to show to the world that they were on the side of right.

Once the weapons were recovered, the US base in Bagram would be safe. It would make breaking news all over the world that a nuclear weapon, that Al-Qaeda stole to use in Afghanistan, was recovered by NATO forces. He knew NATO forces would not go back till Pakistan had rolled back and dismantled its nuclear program. He called it 'Operation Sting'.

It was going to be a perfect operation and a win-win situation. Within 24 hours, the world would be a much safer place from the terrorists of Pakistan.

Chakwal

The base commander at Chakwal knew he had one of the most difficult talks in the country. A colonel by rank, Zamin was one of the top officers who was soon up for promotion to the rank of a brigadier. He was currently leading a team of the best SSG commandos in the country at the base. He knew the largest arsenal of assembled nuclear weapons in Pakistan was left to his protective custody at the Chakwal base, and he was proud of it. Patriotism ran high in his veins.

He knew that normally the nuclear warheads were kept in disassembled form with key parts kept at different physical locations. This builds up a time delay, making unauthorized use or an accident less likely. In a crisis, the National Command Authority at the General Headquarters would give the order to assemble a weapon. Chakwal was the exception, which was a highly-guarded secret. Assembled nukes were kept here in case the assembled bombs were needed at very short notice, such as the Nasr, which was developed as a quick response to the 'Cold Start Doctrine' of India. A limited supply of these nuclear mounted mobile missile systems, but of much less than 1 kiloton yield, were stored here. This was sufficient to cause theater damage. Only a handful of top military commanders were privy to this secret.

He was proud and confident of fulfilling his responsibilities. He knew the right checks and balances were in place, because since 2005, Pakistan had followed much more than the US style 'Personnel Reliability Program' for safety of its nuclear arsenal.

He also knew he also had to protect this arsenal not only from India but from the terrorist groups wanting to lay their hands on it as well as from any western plan to capture and destroy these assets.

He had been briefed that the Pentagon had developed a set of highly detailed plans to destroy these nuclear weapons. It would be a joint US Central Command and US Pacific Command operation, as the scale of operation would be too large to be handled by the US Special Operations alone. The Joint Special Operations Command, or JSOC in short, accompanied by civilian experts, would lead the operation. The US Delta Force and SEAL team had done many practice runs in mock Pashtun villages on the East Coast, and in Nevada using extremely sensitive radiological detection devices which could detect even the minutest amounts of nuclear material and thus locate the precise spot where the weapons were. They were also prepared for any inevitable coup, where US forces would rush across the borders as well as parachute out of planes to secure nuclear weapon sites. The teams were trained to destroy a nuclear weapon without setting it off. Once the weapons were disabled and nuclear material secured, the US forces would evacuate quickly. These would be followed up by precision missile strikes on the nuclear bunkers, including the use of the mother-of-all-bombs, which was recently tested near the Pakistan border.

Chakwal, located about 60 miles south east of Islamabad, was a martial town in the Potohar region of Punjab. During the British occupation of the sub-continent, and during the uprising against the British in 1857, the residents of Chakwal had shown their sincerity and faithfulness to the British forces by siding with them. Since then, Chakwal had always been a recruiting ground for the army, first by the British, and later by Pakistan. Every single household in Chakwal had sent soldiers to generals to the forces for the last 150 years, and each house displayed medals, framed pictures in black and white from the British times to colored pictures of the current times. The cemetery was full of serving soldiers who had lost their lives defending the homeland. Many Chakwal soldiers had never returned, perhaps lying buried in tombs of the unknown soldiers in places as far away as Burma and Morocco, and even in unmarked graveyards of Saudi Arabia fighting for the British. It appeared that the whole region was a garrison town where each person was a soldier or a former soldier. There could be no other place more secure for nuclear weapons than Chakwal. The people of Chakwal took pride in their heritage and would do anything to protect the arsenal. There could be no infiltration of spies in Chakwal, like what had happened at Abbottabad where Osama was killed. There could be no one on the CIA payroll here. Any stranger snooping around would be caught within a day. Chakwal was no Abbottabad where Osama was located by CIA contractors and killed.

Chakwal district is also home to the Katasraj Temples, which are dedicated to Lord Shiva and have existed since the days of Mahabharata. According to Hindu mythology, the Pandava brothers, who are the five acknowledged sons of Pandu by his two wives, are also believed to have spent a substantial part of their exile at the site, and the Hindu deity Krishna is said to have laid the foundation of this temple, and established his handmade shiv ling, considered a symbol of the energy and potential of Shiva himself, in it. The former Prime Minister of India Manmohan Singh also hailed from Chakwal.

The Khewra Salt Ranges, yielding prehistoric finds, are believed to have a huge collection of archaeological treasure still hidden in them. The fossils discovered are estimated to be dated between 6,000 and 7,000 BCE. A number of bones of giant animals resembling the extinct mammoths and dinosaurs have also been found. The site warrants a large archeological team to excavate and discover its hidden wealth. However, due to the strategic nature of Chakwal, no foreign teams are allowed anywhere near the military areas.

The district had huge tracts of lands cordoned off for the base with barbed wires that ran over 12 feet high with checkposts every few hundred yards. A multilayered system was at place to protect the arsenal. There were no posted signs. With a heavily guarded gate, there were cameras mounted at the gate and on the checkposts. They were connected to a control center inside the premises and to another control center at the National Command Authority under the Strategic Plans Division. The division administered all nuclear and ballistic missile related activities in the country, and was established in 1998 shortly after Pakistan tested six nuclear devices. There was an occasional drone belonging to the Pakistan army that would hover above the cordoned off area. A second electrified fence ran a few hundred feet inside the first fence. Beyond the second fence were a number of hills, and the barracks of the elite SSG. On each hill were army posts, each having a radar that was continuously scanning the skies. The airspace was off limits to all civilian flights, and the commercial planes would take a diversion around Chakwal before landing in Islamabad. Behind the barracks was a well secured road entering what appeared to be an opening in one of the hills. Nothing else was visible or known to the outside world. Right inside the opening, and not visible from outside, was a metallic gate that looked like an entrance to a large vault, secured in place by a coded electrical lock, which could only be unlocked remotely from the headquarters in Rawalpindi. There was also a physical padlock holding the gate as a fail-safe mechanism, one which could only be unlocked by the local base commander.

Beyond this gate, hidden from prying eyes, was a tunnel dug deep into the mountain which went underground through seams of hard rock salt, ending into a larger vault that stored the nuclear weapons. There were cameras and laser beams throughout the tunnel leading to the main vault, which could only be opened from the main control room at the headquarters. It was not possible for anyone to cross the tunnel without alarms sounding at the control room above and at the headquarters. In case of any alarm sounding, Special Forces could be there within ten minutes from headquarters and from another military base about five miles away.

Colonel Zamin's biggest responsibility was to guard the nuclear arsenal. He knew each one of his guards were die-hard commandos and patriotic Pakistanis. The guards were allowed to keep long beards, pray five times a day and vote for religious parties. But they were not religious extremists, as each one had been checked and double checked for their past, and their beliefs, by the security division at the military headquarters. The system could distinguish between an Islamist extremist and one who is simply religious. Even after recruitment, all were eavesdropped on, their telephone calls monitored and recorded, and were subject to periodic psychological tests before being placed at strategic locations. The country had learnt from its past experience when a number of scientists were found to have met or sold secrets to some extremist groups. Now, it was more important to weed out those who had sympathies with Islamists or had extremist Islamic views. The Personnel Reliability Program allowed weeding out those who could compromise on national security for greed, lust, depression or similar other characteristics. Above all, all the men had sworn on the Quran to give their lives fighting if the arsenal was threatened or attacked in any way.

Zamin also knew that the US had a contingency plan in which the American Special Forces operating in Afghanistan could take over the arsenal in case there was an Islamist type of coup in the country. To protect them, the military had ensured that their nuclear assets were dispersed at various locations across the country, but that also made them more vulnerable. Chakwal was the only one where fully assembled nukes were placed since it was in a highly secure and a strategic location. The Salt Ranges would also ensure that even if the Mother of All Bombs would be dropped at this site, the arsenal would still be safe.

There were other fail-safe mechanisms. The army had 11 corps, headed by lieutenant generals. The 11th one, called the Army Strategic Force Command, was considered the elite corps and was responsible for bearing and protecting the national strategic and nuclear assets. It was within striking distance of Chakwal in case of an emergency.

Despite safeguards, it was also a matter of fact that no country has been immune from mishaps. The UK nuclear weapons convoys have had 180 mishaps in 16 years. The US department of defense lists 32 accidents involving nuclear weapons. Five times the US almost nuked itself. The Russians, on the other hand, had countless mishaps, including even losing a nuclear submarine with nuclear weapons on board.

Pakistan's credibility of protecting its weapons program was tarnished when a leading nuclear scientist, called the father of the nuclear bomb, was placed under house arrest for allegedly selling nuclear secrets to North Korea, Iran, and Libya. In the past, two retired nuclear scientists were detained for allegedly meeting the Al-Qaeda leadership in Afghanistan, including Osama Bin Laden, just after the 9/11 attacks on at least two occasions. One of them, a former director at the Pakistan Atomic Energy Commission, had even suggested that the energy of the jinn could be used to produce electric power. He firmly believed in the jinn, and in an interview to a leading American journal in 1998, he had said, "I think that if we develop our souls, we can develop communication with them." The former scientist was also accused of sketching a rough diagram of the nuclear bomb for Osama during his meeting with him.

Zamin knew and understood the severity of the destruction that would be caused if a nuclear war ever broke out between Pakistan and India. He knew Pakistan had over 150 nuclear warheads, with the world's fastest growing arsenal. It has three nuclear enrichment plants which were churning away fuel without stopping, and had its own supply of uranium in Dera Ghazi Khan. India, on the other hand, was estimated to have around 120 nuclear warheads.

The majority of Pakistani nuclear warheads were mounted on land-based ballistic missiles. The Shaheen III ballistic missile and the Ababeel with multiple warheads and a range of 1,500 miles could strike deep into the heart of India. They were considered medium-range ballistic missiles, or MRBM, and could carry nuclear weapons. Pakistan was further developing the range of its ballistic missiles, as it is only beyond a range of 3,400 miles that a missile is considered an intercontinental ballistic missile or ICBM.

Zamin had been to the war games at the defense university in Islamabad and had read Indian intelligence reports on Pakistan's nuclear capability. The Indians believed a major attack by Pakistan's MRBMs would likely target India's four major metropolitan cities—New Delhi, Mumbai, Bengaluru, and Chennai as well as the major commands of the Indian army. They also believed that nearly half of Pakistan's ballistic missile warheads can be mounted onto the Ghauri missile, which has a range of around 800 miles and could hit Delhi, Jaipur, Ahmedabad, Mumbai, Pune, Nagpur, Bhopal, and Lucknow. Eight warheads which could be mounted onto the Shaheen, which could target all Indian cities, including Kolkata on the east coast. Another 16 warheads could be fired with the shorter range Ghaznavi missile, which could target Ludhiana and Ahmedabad near the Pakistan border.

In case of an Indian conventional attack into the heartland of Pakistan, called the Cold Start Doctrine, Pakistan could defend itself with the Nasr missiles, with a range of 40 miles, and which are nuclear armed but with limited destructive capability. These tactical nuclear missiles could stop the Indian advance right in their shoes.

An estimated 40 nuclear warheads, accounting for nearly 25% of Pakistan's total, could be delivered using the F-16 and the Mirage jet fighters.

On the other hand, the report mentioned India has 56 Prithvi and Agni series of surface to surface ballistic missiles, which is roughly half its nuclear arsenal, with a maximum strike capability of 1,500 miles. There are also an estimated 12 submarine-launched ballistic missiles. Indian jets can also be mounted with half of its nuclear weapons. They can be delivered using Jaguar and Mirage fighter.

India could easily hit the twin cities of Islamabad-Rawalpindi, Lahore, and Karachi and possibly many of the corps headquarters. However, all cities in Pakistan, including Multan, Peshawar, Quetta, and Gwadar are within striking range of India.

In case of a nuclear war, the fallout would not just be restricted to the Indian and Pakistani territories, but could affect neighboring countries as well depending on the wind direction.

Zamin had to be on alert round the clock as not only tensions with India had increased due to the fragile situation in Kashmir, but the number of terrorist activities had gone up to an all-time high. He used to get daily memos from the intelligence agencies reporting on chatter relating to the nuclear assets. What had concerned him more recently was that the chatter had gone up significantly in the last one week. There had already been a dirty bomb attack in Islamabad, which had failed, and the government had kept a tight lid on the leakage of this news for fear of panic caused among the masses. However, the most recent chatter in the last two days related to the Chakwal facility. A few of them even made reference to jinn. He knew many Muslims believed in jinn, and were frightened by them. Jinn are also known to possess people. Other than that, why would a reference to the jinn would be used in a chatter relating to Chakwal?

He had heard that there were certain hills in Chakwal that were haunted. Old residents had sold their property and agriculture lands, as there had been strange sightings and sounds in the area. Other than that, there was no further connection between jinn and Chakwal. Maybe the chatter was related to some increased abnormal activity there.

But he could not write it off his mind. There was something in the chatter about jinn that was bothering him.

Miranshah

Samir's phone rang as he returned to Islamabad airport. It was Hameed.

"My man has located Qabza Khan through Jadoo's wife. Qabza is a well-known aamil and lives in Miranshah in North Waziristan, about 200 miles from here."

"That is excellent progress. I am already at the airport and we have a chopper ready. We need to leave immediately for Miranshah. How long will you take to get here?"

"I am at the traffic light and will be at the airport in just ten minutes."

"And please bring your toy with you. It proved very handy last time at Hasan Abdal…"

"I never move without my gun, but am not sure if any gun will prove handy against the jinn. But we will certainly be armed with the right weapons." Hameed smiled and hung up.

Samir reminded himself that he had to keep reciting the Chapter 114 Al-Nas in case he is attacked by the jinn.

They took off for Miranshah. It would take them an hour and a half to get there. The military secretary to the prime minister had arranged for a Jeep with an escort vehicle to greet them on arrival. Travel in the tribal belt was not considered safe especially at night. A Captain Tariq would receive them and guide them to wherever they would want to go. Samir called up the captain to give him a heads up on their arrival.

"We are locating an aamil by the name of Qabza Khan. Please locate him and keep an eye on him. But be cautioned as he may be very dangerous."

Captain Tariq was at the heliport when they landed to greet them.

"Dr. Baloch. We found where Qabza Khan lives, off in a remote corner of the village. He is known as the jinn master. The local villagers say he is hardly at home and has been spending a lot of time at an old graveyard up in the hill for the last many weeks. They think he is doing a chilla. No one has seen his family too, but one person said his wife and one son were seen leaving the home in a hurry yesterday. The wife appeared as if she had gone mad as she was beating her chest. They have not been seen since then. She might have gone to her own parents. There is even a very strong stench coming from the house since yesterday. No one dares go to his house, as they all believe it is haunted by evil spirits and jinn. Everybody is afraid of him."

"Let us go and check the house first."

They drove off in the direction of the village and arrived at the house in under ten minutes. It was quiet and dark. Not a sound could be heard except the rustling of dead leaves under the shoes as the team walked up to the house.

The front door was open. They walked in and a strong pungent smell hit them hard. It smelt like a dead animal which had been decaying for days.

The lounge was all dark. Captain Tariq turned on his flashlight and searched for a light switch. He found it right next to the door and flipped it on. There was no power.

He shone the flashlight into the lounge, circling it around the far corner, and immediately stopped at what appeared as someone sleeping under a blanket on a cot in the corner. He cautioned others to stay back, took out his gun, and moved closer slowly,

The blanket was soaked in dry blood, and there was a pool of dried blood under the cot as well. Tariq cautioned Samir and Hameed to stay back and slowly lifted the blanket off the body. It was what appeared to be a small body, but without a head. The head had been severed off the body.

Tariq stepped back cautiously and snapped an order.

"Check the other room and see if there is anyone. Call up the local police station and inform them that there is a dead body with a severed head in the house."

There was nothing much in the other room. Most of the belongings in the house were old booklets with strange symbols on them, candles, matches, old scarves, amulets, and similar other objects expected at an aamil's house. There was one locked closet in the room.

"Check what is inside the closet."

It took only a minute to break the lock and look inside. Same old magical stuff, but in one corner was a box that was filled with money.

"There appear to be at last 50,000 rupees here. Money for the dirty tasks he does." They put the money back where it belonged.

Samir realized there was not much here. Qabza had to be found, and the only place he could be would be at the top of the mountain doing the chilla.

"We need to go up the mountain to the old graveyard. It is an hour's walk to reach up there through a long twisting trail."

They immediately left the house without wasting any more time and walked up to the jeep to take them to the trail. Strong winds had started building up by then.

"We had better hurry. There is a storm build-up and we may not be able to go up the trail if it gets rough."

As they got off the jeep at the foot of the trail, a light drizzle had started.

Samir, Hameed, Captain Tariq, and three other men got off the vehicle and started the long walk to go up the mountain to the graveyards. The others were asked to wait with the vehicles.

Ifrit

Earlier in the day, Qabza had excitedly communicated to the men in black that he had not only completed the chilla successfully, but had also talked to Iblis the King of Jinn. Iblis was ready to have his jinn do any task for him because he had delivered on his promise to the jinn and made him happy by doing whatever he desired of him.

He could now only visualize himself as the most powerful aamil in the whole region who could talk to Iblis. He had asked for Ifrit, who is a powerful jinn, to do a certain task for him which the men in black wanted him to do. However, he still did not know what the task was.

The men in black, all five of them, came back late that night looking for him. They were all carrying guns under their shawls, and their faces were covered.

"Qabza: We want our assignment done tonight which can't wait any longer. You have to go back to the mountain, and we need to come with you as well."

"My dear, sirs! It is very dangerous for you to be present. The jinn may not bear your presence and may kill you all."

"How else can we be sure that you have contacted the jinn and are controlling them? We need to see this with our own eyes and only then will you give them the command which we will tell you. But if we see that you have lied to us, then you know the consequences."

Qabza went down on his knees and touched his forehead to the ground, "Forgive me, my masters, if I am lying. I am only saying this to protect you. But if you wish to accompany me, you can do so but I am warning you it is very dangerous."

"We have seen more dangers than you can imagine. Let us go. We must not waste any time. You lead and we will follow you."

With that, they started their long walk up the hill. It took them an hour through the trail to reach the top where the graveyard was located.

Qabza had his bag of supplies, which included candles and matches, in a brown jute bag next to the chilla at the graveyard. The chilla and the star were still clearly etched in the hard soil at the top of the mountain.

"Let me know what you want Ifrit to do as I will be reaching out to him now."

They looked at each other, and one of them, who appeared to be their leader, nodded his head.

The other man blurted out what they wanted done, "We want the jinn to steal an atom bomb from the base in Chakwal where they are stored, and deliver it to our deputy emir at Moqor in Afghanistan. The jinn must then pick it up again after a short time and drop the bomb at Bagram."

"That should not be a difficult task for him to do. Now, if you will all sit down under the tall tree, I can start my chilla to reach out to him. But try not to see him directly with your naked eye, as you may become blind from the lightning, which is what the jinn may show up as."

It was a still night with a clear sky. Qabza was wearing his red attire. He then started his ritual of first lighting up the six tall candles, and placing them around the points of the Star of David with strange symbols inside.

He took off his shoes, moved into the chilla, and started his barefoot dance on one foot in rhythmic motion in a clock-wise motion around the graves which were inside the chilla.

Qabza started to speak up as well, talking to the sky, and calling out to the devil, "Oh, great one. Oh, Master. Oh, Iblis. I have sacrificed all for you which you know and only wish to serve you. I want to make you king of the earth, I now have a task that will make you king. The task is, however, too small for you. You can have any one of your soldiers do it for you. Ifrit is the powerful one. Send Ifrit to me and I will tell him what to do for he is the strong one."

Qabza kept moving around and reciting his magic mantra as well, continuing for almost an hour without break, while looking up occasionally into the sky. Nothing happened.

He wondered what happened. Iblis should be contacting him, and if not Iblis, maybe he had already sent Ifrit here who perhaps was having difficulty communicating with humans after thousands of years since the times of Solomon. He wondered, *What if contact was not made tonight?* He was afraid there could be no second chance as he would most probably be killed by the men in black if the jinn did not show up. But he was not lying. He had talked to Iblis, and had done whatever he wanted him to do. He had to succeed. He must keep doing the chilla. The jinn will surely come.

The men were getting impatient. They had already waited for an hour watching the magician dance on one foot, and there was no movement in the sky. All they could hear was the mumbling of the mantra and the call to the jinn on Qabza's lips.

How long should they wait? This was important and they could not afford to fail. They had already informed the deputy emir of the success of the operation, who must have informed the khalifa by now. If there was any failure tonight, not only would they kill Qabza but their own lives would be in jeopardy. Maybe the deputy emir would be called back as well and a new one appointed. This was too serious. They knew jinn could only be contacted in the dark of the night and not during the day. They may have to wait till dawn.

Qabza continued his mantra and dance without stopping. As time went by, his movement and sound became more and more aggressive, as if he was starting to get desperate. Another hour went by and yet the night stood still. It would be dawn in a few hours.

He was now beginning to fear that the jinn may not come tonight. Maybe he had done something wrong. He reverted back in his thoughts trying to figure out if he had left anything out. There was nothing he could think of.

Suddenly, he felt a breeze, and the leaves on the trees started to make a rustling sound. His eyes flared. Was it just the wind, or was it the jinn coming? He found new vigor and energy in his dance and mantra. He continued to move around the chilla and increased the pitch of his voice.

"Oh, great one. Oh, Master. Oh, Iblis. I want to make you king of the earth, I have a task that will make you king. You will rule the earth again. Send Ifrit to me and I will tell him what to do."

The tree tops started to sway in the breeze which had now turned into a light wind. Clouds started to appear in the sky from nowhere and it started to get darker. One could now hear the sound of thunder at a distance.

The five men now got up from where they were sitting. They moved out from under the tree and looked up expecting a large fiery jinn to descend from the skies.

There was a sudden bolt of lightning, followed by a loud thunder. The intensity of the wind suddenly increased, and blew out the candles. It felt like a tornado was approaching. There were a few more bolts in the sky, followed by a bright bolt of lightning.

The men in black were excited yet had a degree of fear in them. They had never seen a jinn before in their life. The jinn in the form of lightning was certainly here, but what did a jinn look like in real life? Would he be like an ugly monster, or would he look like a dog or a snake? They were curious, and moved out to under the open skies, looking up with searching eyes, scanning the sky for any sign of the jinn.

There were several more bolts of lightning, then there was a severe bolt of lightning that seemed to be directed at the men. It was a very bright flash, and before the men could cover their eyes, the flash hit them right in the faces. One could only hear the screams originating from their mouths, and within seconds, their clothes had caught fire and the men's bodies had burned severely. The men danced with pain and agony, screaming at the top of their voices, and within a minute, they fell down on the ground in a heap of blackened bodies.

Qabza felt the intense heat and saw them burn, but he did not show his concern, or slow down his mantra and dancing. He had after all warned them. They never seemed to understand the power of the jinn. The jinn was unhappy at these men watching him and had attacked them as he felt threatened.

Qabza could feel heat all around him, and his skin started to burn, yet, he was unmoved. He knew the jinn was close by, so gathered up his energy to continue with the chilla. Soon, he felt he heard a growling voice from the sky, "I am Ifrit. My lord Iblis has sent me to you. What can I do for you?"

He could not believe his ears. It was Ifrit! No one ever since the times of Solomon, for thousands of years, had been able to see him or feel him or even make contact with him. He was the first man to do so. Ifrit was the most powerful of all jinn. If Ifrit alone could listen to him and come under his control, he could rule the world with Iblis. But to do so, he had to get the jinn to do something. These jinn were all dumb, and he could easily manipulate them and call the shots himself. He smiled to himself.

"Oh, great Ifrit. The most powerful one. The commander from Solomon's army. Sometime back, you had volunteered to bring a throne from the land of Saba to your master Solomon. Your master did not trust you then and asked someone else to do it."

It appeared as if it was the thunder that was speaking, "It was not right for our master not to trust me and to give this task to someone else." It was Ifrit, "He always had the feeling I wanted to escape him with the other jinn. We were certainly scheming to take over the world and rule again. He was wise and somehow sensed it so he did not let me go and instead sent someone else. Men have always betrayed us!

"Solomon made us work as slaves and build his temple. But when he died, I finally escaped with many other jinn to a far-out galaxy. Since then I have waited for thousands of years to hear from our King Iblis as to how we can come back and conquer Earth which we rightfully own. Iblis said you have a plan so I have come back. We have the strength and speed to do whatever you tell us to do."

"Oh, great one, the all-powerful, my plan will destroy mankind and make you rulers of this world again!"

"Let me know what to do, and it will be done since my king told me to do it. But if your plan doesn't work, he told me to cut you up in a thousand pieces and feed each of your body parts to the young hungry jinn."

"It will work if you do what I tell you. It is very easy."

"Your wish is my command!"

"We want you to steal an atom bomb from under the hill at Chakwal where they are stored, and deliver it to our deputy emir at Moqor in Afghanistan."

There was silence. Was Ifrit listening?

Qabza was determined to explain, "After a short while, which is the time it will take us men to take a walk from here to that far away hill," he pointed to a nearby hill, "you will go back and pick up it again and drop it off at Bagram a short distance away."

The sound of thunder came back, "This is an easy task. I can do it faster than you can even wink. However, Iblis ordered me to first tell him what the task is before I do it. He would like to make sure it is not a trick you humans are playing on us to capture us and make us your slaves again like Solomon did."

"Do it by all means, for I know Iblis will be very happy when he hears of our plan. Once you drop the bomb at Bagram, there will be a huge explosion, one that will shake and destroy mountains. Thousands of men will die, and it will lead to many more explosions like this when men will drop bombs on each other and mankind will be completely destroyed. You will be free to walk and rule the earth again.

"I am only doing it for you jinn!"

"Consider it done then before the sun rises. But I need to ask my master first and see if he approves it. If not, you die!"

With another sound of thunder and a bright blinding flash, Ifrit disappeared in an instant. Again, there was a huge thunderclap much like a jet breaking the sonic barrier at low altitude, and the wind started howling at high speed like a tornado. The trees started to bend over as they would almost break.

But this time, the wind did not die down nor the thunder and lightning stopped. It started to rain heavily out of nowhere, starting a whole series of flash floods in the mountains.

Qabza knew he must quickly start his descent back before he gets trapped here in the mountains. He started to make his journey downhill to reach the safety of his home.

He wondered who would now give him his remaining money after the men in black had been burnt to death by Ifrit. But he cared less, because he knew the khalifa himself would reach out to him and reward him. After all, he is now their only link to the jinn. After all the kafir have been destroyed by the bombs, he could double-cross the khalifa and become the khalifa himself with the help of the jinn and rule the world with them. It was destined in the Hadith that those who will talk with the jinn will rule the world.

What a master stroke, he thought and patted himself on the back. Tomorrow, when mankind is out to destroy itself, would be a new beginning for him.

Heist

Zamin got up from the middle of his sleep at the barracks for his early morning prayers. It was almost 5 A.M. and would be dawn in another hour. A devout Muslim, he had never missed any of his prayers. Neither had most of the other SSG commandos at the base. There was a small mosque right next door to the sleeping quarters, and after washing up, he would be able to catch the congregation in 15 minutes.

It had started to rain in the middle of the night and it was still pouring. There was the regular sound of thunder, with continuous lightning all over the sky. He grabbed his umbrella to step out of his quarters, and stepped out to go to the mosque. It was an intense downpour which he had never experienced before. He looked up, and the lightning flashes were very bright connecting one end of the sky to the other. Some of them reached out to touch the ground. He figured lightning was striking the earth somewhere close by. He had seen some images of long and bright lightning flashes on the internet and in the National Geographic magazine, but they were nothing like what he was seeing now.

He felt a little uneasy in this weather. Were all the security systems working fine? He went back inside for a moment to call up the control room to check if everything was fine.

"All is okay and all security systems are working fine. We have not lost any electricity anywhere, the security fencing is still fully electrified, the security lights are all working, the cameras are all functioning, and everything is under control."

"What about the laser beams at the entrance and the tunnel, and the cameras inside the vaults?"

"All systems checking fine. Nothing to worry about."

With that, Zamin let in a sigh of relief. He had enough experience in the past that he knew nights like these set the perfect stage for any misfortunes. It had happened only a few nights back, when the nuclear fuel was stolen from an institute. But then the security at that institute was nothing compared to what he had here. At the institute, the civilians and visitors were allowed access during the day, while here, not even a bird would be able to fly past the outer barriers. He knew in today's technology, there were drones that looked like birds, or even insects, and had cameras installed in them to record everything, so he made sure that in these vaults, not even a large insect could pass the tunnel without making sure what it was.

Zamin stepped out again of his quarters and walked to the mosque. At that very moment, there was a big bang and a huge bolt of lightning hit the entrance to the vault. The sound was deafening! He had never seen lightning like this before.

All lights went out!

"May Day! May Day! May Day!" screamed the operator at the control desk, but no one could hear him on the speakers, as all power had completely disappeared from the console and the microphone, and even the room had turned completely dark. The operator immediately reached for his emergency flashlight and tried turning it on. It would not turn on!

He grabbed the emergency intercom which operated on rechargeable batteries. It would also not turn on. He rushed out of the room into yet more darkness of the outer hall.

Zamin immediately felt something was wrong. It was dark all over. They had never lost power ever for even a second. Every system in the base was supported by a back-up uninterrupted power supply. He ran towards the control room, and saw the operator and a few other guards coming out of the main control door. He wondered if the headquarters and the nearby base was alerted. He took his mobile phone out of his pocket, but it would not turn on either. That was not possible. He had just charged it all night. His second in command immediately offered him his phone, but it did not take more than a few seconds to figure out that even the other phone was not working.

By now, every man at the Chakwal base was on high alert. Zamin screamed at the top of his voice for some men to secure the entrance to the base, and others to move to the vault. The men rushed towards both ends, while Zamin rushed towards the vault. There was no indication of any break-in. The gate was securely closed and the padlock was still in place. Maybe just the electrical system had failed. Zamin heaved a sigh of relief.

He wondered if the powerful lightning flash had generated a strong electromagnetic wave to blow out all the electrical systems, including the phones. He had read about that in an electronics course he had taken at the university. He looked up at the sky, and saw that the lightning flashes were starting to move away from the base. He wanted to reach out to headquarters and inform them of the power failure but he had no way of doing it. Only when the lights were up, they would be able to check and ensure if the arsenal was secure and in place. Till then he could do little.

He realized that headquarters would have known by now as they would have lost all contacts with the base as well. He was sure, within a few minutes, there would be special forces arriving from the headquarters as well as the nearby base to check on them and aid them if needed. Only then he would be able to move in and check if the nukes were safe.

He had to wait for them, and for directives from the main headquarters. Only then he would risk walking past the gate and into the tunnel.

A moment later, he could hear the sound of helicopters in the sky. It was risky flight in this weather and normally such flights would not take place. All choppers would need prior clearance to land here. However, this was an emergency and the special forces from headquarters were trained to take all risks. Two helicopters with Pakistan army markings landed. Zamin walked up to the heliport to greet them. There were a total of about 10 men, all fully armed to the teeth. The man in charge was a Brigadier Aftab who at one time was Zamin's superior officer and knew him well. They had both attended the same army course at the defense university on securing nuclear assets.

He greeted Zamin, and asked if all was in order, "We have been trying to reach your base, but there is complete radio silence. We expect additional forces to arrive by road in another ten minutes from the nearby base."

"None of the systems are working. The cameras in the tunnel are not working and there is no light inside the vaults as well. I believe we have lost power due to an electromagnetic surge caused by severe lightning, but I presume everything inside is safe and in place as the outer gate is still secure and padlocked."

"We need to physically verify that before the power is fully restored. I had received these instructions while leaving the base that we need to go in together. But before we open the gate, I want your men to cover all entrances to the base."

"My men are already in place and on full alert."

It took them a few minutes to open the padlocks. The electrical power failure had somehow disrupted the remote locking mechanism, and the gates automatically swayed open a few inches due to their weight.

"A normal power failure will never unlock the gates by themselves. It is, therefore, probable that the internal electrical system is burnt out due to the lightning flash. We would need to have the electrical system repaired immediately," commented Zamin. He snapped an order to his men to have a team from the army engineers sent in immediately.

The gates, which were made of heavy metal and very sturdy, pulled outwards on rollers. Each side of the gate was about 10 feet wide, and 15 feet high. When fully opened, they were wide enough that a special truck could be reversed inside the tunnel to load the bombs. The men pulled the gates open. Inside, it was completely dark. No emergency spotlights were on, no cameras were flashing, and no laser beams could be seen, it was quiet and pitch dark.

Four specially trained commandos took up positions with their sub-machineguns pointed inside, while one of Brigadier Aftab's men directed his flashlight into the tunnel. Three other armed men joined in with their flashlights to illuminate the tunnel wall. They scanned the ceiling as well as the side walls, and the floor till as far as their beams could go. It was all clear without any sign of any intrusion or tunnels being damaged or dug on any side. All was intact and appeared safe to move in.

Aftab ordered his men to proceed inside slowly and carefully. They could hear the sound of a convoy of vehicles arriving at a distance, most likely from the nearby base. Those men knew they were required to secure the periphery of the base and cover all exit points as soon as they arrived, unless alternate instructions were given by the base commander.

Steadily and slowly, they entered the tunnel, which was about 15 feet wide and 15 feet high. A fully metaled road led inside which connected the outside road to the main inner vault inside. After the inner vault was also unlocked and opened by remote control from the headquarters, the bombs could easily be rolled on a mechanized trolley and mounted onto the trucks taking about 15 minutes per bomb. The base commandos had practiced these mock runs many times before.

They reached the end of the tunnel, and arrived at the main inner vault gate. One of the guards shone his flashlight onto the gate, and around its periphery.

"It is all secure, sir!"

Zamin and Aftab reached for the handle on the gate, which would unlatch the gate only if it was activated from the control room at the headquarters to open it. It turned clockwise without much effort.

"It's open! The locking mechanism has failed here too!"

"It is expected, as it is the same electrical system running all over the tunnel."

It did not take them long to open the inner vault gate, and Zamin couldn't help himself reaching for a flashlight from one of the men, and stepping in first. He could almost hear his heart beating loudly.

The place had a strong pungent smell like rotten eggs. He had never smelt that before. One could hear the sound of prayers being murmured from Zamin's lips, "In the name of God, the Most Gracious, the Most Merciful," the Bismillah which most Muslims utter when starting any task in the name of Allah and hoping for the best.

It was all pitch dark. He shone the light inside, as he and Aftab walked into a huge salt cavern. Other guards followed and shone their flashlights inside as well as it was pitch dark and much more light was needed. What they could see in the front of them was an array of wooden crates placed next to each other, each one numbered with a large letter, and with a flag of Pakistan painted on it. These were the nuclear bombs that every Pakistani protected with his life and was willing to die for.

Zamin and Aftab moved together, making sure all crates were secure and in place. They started from one corner and read the numbers out loudly in unison, "1, 2, 3, 4, 5…7…"

"Number 6 is missing!" shouted Zamin.

Aftab shone his flashlight around to make sure it had not moved or was placed in another location. They checked out the other numbers too. Every other bomb was intact and in place. They verified and reverified. There were only 9 of the 10 crates present. Number 6 was missing!'

The other men in the meantime checked every inch of the cavern for any opening or tunnel. There was no other crate to be found and there were no openings or tunnels dug into the wall!

"It is not possible! There are no tunnels or openings in here or in the tunnel outside. The padlock outside was secure and locked. The cameras were all working just prior to the lightning strike. There has been no intrusion. Neither the base nor the headquarters has reported any movement in the tunnel or the cavern…" Zamin's voice trailed off and almost choked.

"We need to immediately inform headquarters," snapped Aftab, "get on our radio quick. We need to talk to director general security as soon as possible."

"I want four men to stand guard here, and four at the outer gate, till our electrical systems are working again. I want the electrical team sent in urgently and power restored, as the arsenal needs to be made fully secure. I want all recordings to be seen again for any abnormal movement around the base camp."

They rushed out back to the open, shining the flashlight along the walls of the tunnel and the floor as if they might have missed an opening or a crate on their way in. There was absolutely no hint that even a fly or an ant could have penetrated the tunnels. The only peculiar thing they could not understand was the strong pungent smell inside the cavern which was unbearable.

One bomb was clearly missing, and they did not even have the faintest idea who, how, where or when it could have gone!

Bannu

It was June 6. June 6 combined with another 6 becomes 666, and is considered by many as the sign of the devil, of the Satan, and of Iblis.

666 was considered by many to be a sign that Iblis will take over the world.

Today, it made the perfect combination if the missing bomb number 6 was added to the date. 666.

Today, nuke number 6 went missing from the Chakwal base!

Today could become the day when the world could end!

Today, TTP Bannu had been directed by their local commander to keep an eye on the local highway. There was a possibility of a truck carrying nukes and moving in the general direction of the Afghanistan border. They were to set up a roadblock and stop its movement for a couple of hours. They would be informed in advance of the identity of the truck. However, there had been no movement of any military convoy on that road all night.

Today, across the border, NATO forces were put on full alert at Bagram Air Base when they were alerted by intelligence experts both at the Pentagon and NSA that they had received credible information late last night that Al-Qaeda operatives or their surrogates would be stealing a nuclear bomb from Chakwal, and transporting it through Bannu and across the border to Khost into Afghanistan.

Special SEAL commandos from the US forces were on standby and full alert. There were about ten helicopters ready to take them into Pakistan as the need arose. A few F-18 fighters stood by also on alert if any air coverage was required. Drones had been in action all morning taking off one after the other, intruding into Pakistan, keeping the road near Bannu into Afghanistan under full observation. There was regular traffic and nothing unusual. There was nothing that warranted special attention.

Local informers of the American forces were also told to be on high alert. They were moving in and around Bannu and into the road leading all the way into Afghanistan. As the sun rose, routine day traffic had started, and there was nothing that warranted reporting any peculiar movement to their sponsors.

As early morning broke, suddenly, there was a lot of radio chatter coming from and near the Chakwal base. Normally, such chatter took place when there was bomb movement by the Pakistan forces. This time, it was not clear what the chatter was about, as no bombs or military trucks had been observed to move into or out of base. Something must have certainly happened. But nothing that looked like the nukes being transported out of the base.

The local American Embassy in Islamabad, Bagram Air Base and CENTCOM headquarter were already on alert since last night. But it was unclear what this chatter was about. Informers around Chakwal eavesdropping on civilian communication started reporting a lot of movement in and around the Chakwal base in the early morning at daybreak. Special forces had moved into Chakwal from a nearby base. There was a series of helicopter movement between the Army headquarters in Rawalpindi and Chakwal. There was information that the army chief was perhaps also on his way to Chakwal.

Piecing together all the information, the US intelligence agencies were certain there was an emergency, perhaps to the extent that there was a break-in, and that a bomb or nuclear fuel had been stolen, and taken elsewhere instead of Bannu.

They were puzzled as to how the bomb or fuel could have disappeared, and were trying to quickly put together pieces of information where the bomb could have been transported if it had indeed been stolen. This was a very serious nuclear threat but the Pakistani government needed to confirm that first. All possibilities were being worked out but there were no reports of any movement on any road leading to Chakwal other than the Pakistan military vehicles all moving in the direction of the Chakwal base.

The Pentagon was in touch with the Pakistan army headquarters. Intelligence was shared. The brigadier at the Pakistan desk finally conceded that they were still trying to verify if any of the bombs were missing. He insisted that if such was indeed the case, then most probably it was a book-keeping and inventory control error, and they were hopeful they would be able to locate it elsewhere. The brigadier tried to assure his counterpart in the Pentagon that most likely the bomb was still at Kalabagh where it was probably not moved out with the last movement to bring it to Chakwal. If any bomb was indeed missing, which he doubted, they would immediately inform the Pentagon and other allies right away.

The Pentagon urgently communicated this information to the White House and the state department, and to CENTCOM and the ISAF forces in Afghanistan.

It was clear that if a bomb was indeed missing, and if it was not found soon enough, Pakistan could face the worst sanctions it could imagine. It would have no choice except to roll back its nuclear program.

Pakistan military was put on full alert.

The Bomb

They had announced that right after the early morning prayers, which is just before dawn breaks, the deputy emir would address the congregation and make an important announcement. As a result, the mosque at Moqor was very crowded despite the bad weather. It appeared that everyone living in the city had shown up for prayers. It would be an honor for everyone to listen to such a distinguished leader.

Moqor had become the United Nations of the terrorists. There were regional commanders from ISIS, Al-Qaeda, TTP, and many other militant organizations operating in and out of Afghanistan, Iran, Pakistan, Kashmir, and many from Central Asian republics as well. Everyone showed up at the congregation to hear the deputy emir.

The word had already gotten around that the mother of all bombs, an 'atom bomb' would soon be arriving at Moqor. They all knew the mastermind behind this was the deputy emir. There would be a celebration and everyone would offer prayers of thankfulness. The bomb would then be sent off to another location to explode. This would be the mother of all attacks, never having happened before. 9/11 would be a firecracker compared to what was to come. Thousands of kafir will die. The world will be on its knees. Islam would prevail and the golden era will start when Muslims will rule the world.

Harry could not sleep as he wondered whether Al-Qaeda, first of all, would succeed in stealing the bomb, and if they indeed did, whether the TTP would be able to block it. Would the NATO forces be able to move in quickly and possess the bomb? Would sanctions be immediately announced for Pakistan or would it lead to an all-out war between Pakistan forces and the militants, or perhaps even with India who would take advantage of the situation to attack Pakistan? There were many questions on his mind, but he had no answers. In any case, it would lead to Muslims dying on all sides. But if nothing happened, would he or Timur be exposed, and if so, would he be able to make a quick get away from Moqor or be beheaded?

Harry wanted to remain in his room next to his phone and tablet in case there was any news from Bagram.

It was still dark in early morning when the deputy emir spoke at the mosque, "My dear Muslim brothers. Today is a very important day in our Islamic history when good will finally prevail over the bad. We have suffered over hundreds of years, first by the Jews, then the Christians, the British, the Americans, the

Spanish, and the Portuguese, the Russians, and the Chinese. The khalifa has communicated through me that the bad days of the Muslims are finally over."

He paused to take a breath, "Today, we will see a new beginning. Today will mark a day that we will punish the kafir and farangi with something they created themselves to rule the world. Today, their own technology will destroy them. Today, they will remember forever as the day they were brought down on their knees. Today, they will bow to us!"

The crowd was enthusiastic to hear more from the deputy emir.

"The west has introduced to the world all forms of evils, which are sin and haram. They drink liquor, they eat pork, they gamble in the biggest casinos of the world, they listen to music, they send their women to work and talk to other men, their women show off their bodies on beaches and clubs, they have open sex with others, they think of Jesus as God…"

There was a murmur of disapproval from all those listening.

He continued, "They curse our Holy Prophet by making cartoons of him, they make friends with the Zionists and the Hindus to kills our Palestinian and Kashmiri brothers. Now, they are killing millions of Afghanis, Iraqi, Syrians, Yemeni, and Libyan brothers. This cannot go forever. Now, it is time for us to take revenge and kill them by the millions.

"We will destroy their land and their property. We will possess all their women as slaves."

The crowd yelled with sounds of 'Allah-o-Akbar'. His bodyguards fired a barrage of shots in the air. Others followed. The noise was deafening.

He was supercharged as he spoke, "The Prophet spoke of this time when he said Muslim forces from the east will defeat the unbelievers. Today, there will be a big graveyard of the unbelievers. But today is only the beginning. We will drive out all the infidels from Afghanistan, and Pakistan will fall to our mujahidin. We will then proceed west to drive them out from Iraq, Syria, and Turkey, and then take over Israel."

There were more chants of 'Allah-o-Akbar' and more firing in the air.

Having delivered his sermon, he walked down from the podium, shaking the hands of everyone sitting in the front row. He was delighted that he will go down in history as the savior of Islam in this region. They were all congratulating him, and it appeared that all terrorist organizations had forgotten their past grievances against each other and had become one under him. He was now their undisputed leader. The khalifa would be pleased with him for uniting all the factions.

The rain, by now, had increased in intensity and everyone standing outside the mosque was drenched. Nobody seemed to mind it as rain was rare in the hot month of June, and this would considerably cool the weather. It would also be good for the gardens of pomegranate in nearby Kandahar, and for the poppy fields, which was a cash crop minting hundreds of millions of dollars for their arms purchases and to fund terrorism in the region. There were a few bolts of lightning in succession.

The deputy emir walked out of the mosque and looked up towards the sky, expecting to see a flying jinn carry down a bomb in his hands and lay it at his feet. The sky was all dark and gray with occasional bolts of lightning. There was nothing that even closely resembled a flying object, except for the lightning in the sky.

He was still confident that a miracle will happen and a jinn would appear with the bomb. He had risked his whole reputation on the power of the jinn. After all, the Quran had confirmed that so he couldn't be wrong. He had not given up, not yet!

As he waited patiently, there was another big bolt of lightning, and the sound of thunder was deafening. The lightning had struck a huge tree which stood about 500 yards away from the mosque, and the tree caught fire and cracked to fall down at the same time.

He immediately recalled what he had learnt about the jinn, that they are made of fire. Maybe this is how the jinn will appear in the sky, in the form of lightning!

An 18-year-old Afghan boy excitedly rushed towards the burning tree to watch the fire closely. Two other boys followed him. As they reached the burning tree, one of the boys yelled at the top of his voice, "Khalifa. There is a big box under the tree!" They all called their leader as khalifa.

The deputy emir stopped in his tracks. He could not believe his ears. Had the miracle he was waiting for finally happened? His face lit up as he turned around and ran in the direction of the burning tree. Timur followed him and so did his guards. As he saw the box, it took the deputy emir only a few moments to realize that they had succeeded in having the bomb stolen and delivered by the jinn.

"Allah-o-Akbar," shouted the deputy emir at the top of his voice. Everyone joined him. This was certainly a miracle of God. Some started firing their weapons in the air. There was complete jubilation and it appeared everyone was celebrating a big victory already.

"Everybody stand back and do not touch the box. It is dangerous!" shouted Timur. Though he appeared excited, but inside he was cursing the success of the deputy emir. His dreams of becoming the deputy emir had been shattered!

The rain increased in intensity and became severe. There were powerful bolts of lightning striking the ground every few minutes which appeared to go around in circles. It was like the sky was tearing apart.

The deputy emir and Timur walked to the box, drenched in the rain, and examined it closely. It was about 15 feet long, 6 feet wide and 4 feet high. It had a serial number written on it, with a flag of Pakistan painted on the wooden box. There was a big '6' painted on top of the box. The box had a lid cover with hinges on one side which could be lifted up to open the box. It was just soaked in rain but the box was fully intact.

The deputy emir raised his hands towards the sky as if praying and loudly recited, 'Bismillah-ar-Rahman-ar-Rahim' and unbolted and lifted the hinged cover to check the contents inside.

Inside the box was a grey metallic rectangular box of a smaller size than the box outside. On top of it was another small hinged lid, about six inches by one foot. The deputy emir's face lit up. He knew he had succeeded. He was looking at a real bomb and touching it, something that no other person from his organization had ever done since they had declared jihad decades ago. The sole credit went to him!

He slowly lifted the smaller lid, and under it was what looked like a digital clock with numbers and a key pad. There were two small push buttons on the side, one red and the other green.

The deputy emir went down on his knees and bowed to the sky. He then started to talk to the lightning because he was sure it was the jinn.

"Thank you, my master. Today, we have made friends after thousands of years. We are sorry for whatever you had to endure because of us. Now, together we will destroy the bad from this world, and those who were responsible to eject you from heaven and from this world. Together, we will rule the world."

The crowd looked up into the sky expecting to see a winged jinn, but there were only bolts of lightning.

He continued to address the lightning as he knew he was talking to the jinn, "I know you are impatient to complete the task so mankind is destroyed. So are we. We just need a little time to make it work, then you can take it and drop it at the farangi base at Bagram a little further away towards that side." He pointed north as if the jinn was listening and watching him.

He got up and turned around to face the crowd.

"Khalifa. How do we carry it and fire it at the enemy?" asked one enthusiastic militant.

"Do not worry. God willing, everything will happen just the way it was brought here. The jinn will do it for us."

He turned around to one of his guards, and snapped an order, "Get the Amreeki from his room."

He then turned around to the others, and spoke in a commanding voice, "In a few moments, our enemies will be destroyed. All their planes and jets and drones and tanks will be destroyed. The infidels will fall flat on their face and will burn in hell. We will take over Afghanistan and the rest of the world and show them we are destined to rule them."

The crowd was jubilant and continued to shout, "Allah-o-Akbar," at the top of their voice.

The crowd was, however, still puzzled and continued asking, "Khalifa, where will this bomb be thrown, and how will we carry it?"

"Leave that to me. Whoever has brought it here will carry it to where we want it to go."

Harry was still in his room and was cut off from all these happenings. He was restless that night. First of all, he was not even sure if the Al-Qaeda would be able to steal the nuke. He very much doubted that. But since the information had been provided not just by his own agency but also 'straight from the horse's mouth', his agency could not take the risk of writing it off.

He had sent word to his agency of the impeding operation at Chakwal, and for the NATO forces to intercept it at the right moment just before it crossed over to Afghanistan and possess it. He was sure if the nukes were rolled out of Chakwal, TTP would be able to hold them off for a few hours at Bannu. After all, he had paid them handsomely, and Timur was a reliable and good commander. He just couldn't wait to receive word on his satellite tablet if the nukes were indeed stolen and if so, had they been intercepted successfully. Either way, it would be good for him.

A heavy thunderstorm had built up that night with severe lightning which did not seem to stop. In the distance, he felt he could hear a crowd chanting and raising some slogans, but they normally did that whenever they heard of some good news, even if it was killing one 'kafir'.

He realized that was just past the early morning prayer time, and the local crowd must have assembled at the mosque's steps to exchange news from around the world and have an early tea at the local stall. The Afghanis usually started their day with the morning prayers and local gossip over breakfast and tea. But today, it must be exceptionally good news since they were jeering so much. He wondered if they had indeed succeeded in stealing the nukes! He shook his head again. Not possible.

He heard the front door to the house open and the sound of running footsteps and excited voices. There was a knock on his door. He got up and pulled out his Glock just in case, and asked who it was.

"Khalifa wants to see you right away."

He wondered why at this early hour of the morning. Maybe he wanted to give him some other news, and also tell him that the operation to steal the nukes has been delayed instead of admitting failure.

He wore his denim jacket, tucked his Glock under his belt so that it was not visible under his T-shirt, and opened the door.

Two of the deputy emir's guards with half a dozen other men stood outside his door. They were all very excited and all were speaking at the same time. There was some excitement about the bomb and some 'jinn'.

He stepped out and followed them into the rain which had been pouring without break for the last few hours.

There was another bolt of lightning. The whole sky lit up, and he could see a big jubilant crowd of the locals at a distance. He really wanted to know what the commotion was all about, and was now beginning to feel uneasy wondering if they had indeed succeeded in stealing a bomb.

Timur was the first to reach out for him. He seemed to have a disappointed look on his face and it appeared he was shaking his head. He did not utter any word.

The deputy emir called out loud to Harry. He was jubilant. "Come here, my American friend, and see for yourself what we have got here."

Harry walked up to him who looked so happy as if he had hit the jackpot and won ten million dollars. He was standing next to a large wooden box with serial numbers and a Pakistani flag on it. There was a large '6' written on it.

The deputy emir lifted the cover off the box, and inside it was what certainly appeared to be a nuke. Harry had seen pictures of these grey metallic rectangular boxes and crates in his briefings at the agency so he could not be mistaken. It was indeed a nuke unless it was a dummy.

He was confused and was not even sure which base it came from as it would not have been possible to bring it from Chakwal with the TTP and NATO on the lookout for it. There was no way they could have gotten their hands on the nuke at Chakwal, or even from any other base for that matter. But it was here right in front of him.

The truth hit him hard in the belly. Al-Qaeda had, indeed, pulled it off by stealing a nuke from a highly secure Pakistan base and even bringing it across the Pakistan border into Afghanistan. A border that was highly secured and guarded. How could they have done it?

He was sure there must have been red alerts sounded all over the country. This was a big box that could not be hidden in the CNG tank of a car or a horseback. It could only have been brought in a truck or an oil tanker as was planned.

His thoughts were interrupted by the deputy emir. "We want you to arm it to explode in one hour!"

Anti Chilla

It was a long and treacherous walk up the mountain to the graveyard at Miranshah. It was raining heavily by now, and completely dark, and the six of them, led by Captain Tariq followed by Samir then Hameed and then by three other army men started their journey uphill. They had to be careful not to step too much on the side of the valley, as it was almost like a 500 foot drop to the side, and the ground was soft and slippery. Had it not been for their flashlights, they would not have been able to make the climb in the dark and rainy night.

The graveyard was lying abandoned for many years and so not many villagers had walked up the trail or had cared to clean it of the overgrown shrubbery and weeds. Till only a few months back, it had been frequented by strange men and aamil who only cared to go up there to try out or learn new magic. However, since Qabza had started doing his rituals since last month, no one had dared to go up. Qabza was a dangerous man, and his reputation went far and wide. No one wanted to cross his path.

They walked for almost an hour but had still not reached the top due to the bad weather. They were using two flashlights at a time, one at the front by Captain Tariq and another at the back by an army man to guide those walking in front, and by now, they were on their second set of batteries. The LED types lasted much longer than the old-fashioned ones which used a tungsten filament. They figured it would take them perhaps another 15 minutes to reach the graveyard at the top.

Dawn was now almost beginning to break, and they could see the grey sky and the dark clouds as the tall trees started to thin out. The wind was still howling. Suddenly, Captain Tariq, who was in the lead, turned off his flashlight, and turned around and asked everyone to be quiet and lie low. They could hear the sound of someone singing. Then footsteps could be heard which seemed to be getting closer. They all held their breath, as a man appeared from around the corner, unaware that there could be others coming in the opposite direction.

He was singing and limping along slightly as he came closer. He was wearing a red dress. He suddenly stopped and was frightened as he saw a uniformed man right in front of him. There were more men behind him, and some of them wore the army uniform. For a second, he decided to turn around and run, but then on second thought, he realized they could just be troops on patrol. After all, Miranshah was a hotbed of terrorists, and there were regular army patrols in the village and combing the surrounding areas.

He gathered some strength and said, "Salam alaikum."

"Walikum Salam," replied Captain Tariq, "Who are you and what are you doing up here this late in this rainy night?"

These men obviously knew nothing about the jinn and the chillas, thought Qabza. "I am a local villager from Miranshah and I usually come up here to pray at my grandfather's grave."

Captain Tariq knew the man was lying. No one in their right mind would go to the top of the mountain in this ghastly weather. And that too wearing a red dress which was a typical color wore by the aamil. He was most likely the man they were looking for.

"What is your name?"

The man hesitated for a few seconds. Should he tell them his real name? Then he realized these men had never met him so they have probably never heard of him.

"My name is Qabza Khan and I have lived in the village down the hill since my birth. I have not seen or made contacts with any terrorists or with any Afghanis from across the border…"

"Let us go back up to the top. We have a few more questions to ask you!"

Qabza realized he had no choice. It was a single-track trail, and he couldn't run down past these men. It was like a dead end one way up. He turned around and said, "As you desire, sahib."

They turned around and walked for another ten minutes before they reached the top. It was still dark and raining lightly and it appeared that the sky may begin to clear up.

They came to an old graveyard at the top. It had many unmarked graves, but what caught Tariq's immediate attention was a circle and a star etched on the ground, and a jute bag that was lying next to a grave. Tariq picked it up and checked inside. It had some candles and matches.

'Is this yours?" Captain Tariq asked with authority.

"Yes, sir. These are just some candles I use when it gets dark…"

Hameed stepped forward and interrupted Tariq. Time was crucial.

"Qabza Khan. We know who you are. Jadoo Baba is in our custody and he has confessed everything. We know you are an aamil master from Miranshah. Everyone has heard of you…"

Qabza put both his palms together as if begging for mercy, "I can do magic for you if you like. I can bring your wife or your lover at your feet. I can bring about a divorce between any married couple. I can bring a business loss to anyone. I can do anything for you without any money. Just let me go…"

Hameed interrupted him harshly, "We know that. But you also probably know why we are here. We know of your chillas and why you have been doing them. We also know and are checking about the headless body in your house, and will soon know everything."

Hameed paused to let that sink in for a moment. Qabza was shaken with this information. How could anyone have known that?

Hameed continued with an authoritative tone, "We also know people from across the border have been in contact with you, and have paid you a lot of money to do something for them. All of this will be of no use to you once you are sentenced by the military court for terrorism. As you know, it is a quick trial, and the sentence is death. You will hang in two weeks unless you cooperate with us."

Qabza was shaken. He knew immediately that the game was up. He knew he was not a terrorist but was only doing a task for money. Perhaps he could convince them to let him go free.

He fell down on the floor and caught the feet of Captain Tariq, "Forgive me. I am a poor villager who just did a small task for someone who offered me money. What can I do for you? Please let me go."

Samir interrupted, "Tell us everything you know and have been asked to do."

Qabza sat down on the floor, put both hands on his head, and started to cry loudly, "It was them who contacted me and told me to contact the jinn. I told them it was a very difficult task. Many pretend they have done it and create lies and make money. They offered me a lot of money but told me they will chop off my head if I lied. I discussed with other aamil who also told me it is impossible, but they also said if anyone could do it, I could. So, I took the risk. I knew if I succeeded, I could become the most powerful person on earth. Who wouldn't want to be that?"

He paused to take a breath. "I learnt about the chilla and the special symbols marked inside the star, and the impossible tasks we have to go through to please the jinn from my father and uncle. It is a secret art and a very difficult task, one that is impossible to do. Many die in the process to control the jinn. However, finally after 40 days of hard labor and chilla, and despite the distractions caused by the jinn, I was able to complete it successfully and please the great jinn."

"What did these men want you to do?"

"They wanted the jinn to steal a bomb for them from some army base in Chakwal and deliver it to some place in Afghanistan."

"How could you be sure it was the jinn you contacted? These could be hallucinations or a figment of your imagination."

"I have personally talked to two of them, Iblis the king of jinn and Ifrit the powerful one. You people don't believe in jinn, but Ifrit told me he will steal the bomb and deliver it before the day breaks, because jinn are active only in the night. I am sure it must already have been stolen and must have arrived in Afghanistan by now because the jinn can never fail."

Samir looked at the captain and said, "I never believed in this stuff till I talked to others who are knowledgeable about jinn. What he is saying is not only very much possible but may actually have happened by now. Can we can verify from Chakwal, or from the army headquarters if nukes are missing?"

"Sir. The signals are too weak here on top of the mountain. Our jeep is at the base. It will be another hour before we can reach down and make contact."

Hameed shook his head, "It will be too late by then if the nukes have already been taken by the jinn to the terrorists in Afghanistan. It is already approaching dawn. Now it is only a matter of time that the terrorists will be able to arm it and drop it on their target, maybe again through the jinn, wherever the target may be…"

"Yes. I had asked the jinn to drop it someplace in Afghanistan…"

Hameed caught the aamil by the collar, "Can you call the jinn back? We need to stop the jinn from delivering the bomb, if there is a way…"

Samir suddenly recalled what Pir Wasim had told him, "Wait. There is a way. I think we can break the spell if we try!"

Hameed shook his head in disbelief, "Why did I not think of that earlier. Yes, it can be done!"

The captain got impatient, "What can we do here? We are cut off from the rest of the world…"

Samir was quick to recall what Shams and Wasim had told him, "The three antidote verses from the Quran! If each one of us recites one of each, and we rotate around the chilla in an anti-clockwise direction without stopping, I am sure we will be able to send the jinn back to wherever he came from! At least we can take a chance as we are totally helpless otherwise."

Qabza immediately interrupted, "You are taking a big risk. This could annoy the jinn. Once he loses his temper, he can never be trusted. He may either kill all three of you or do something opposite or more disastrous of what he has been asked to do."

All three of them completely ignored Qabza. They all knew it was a do or die moment. They were ready to give their lives to save humanity.

Hameed was a hafiz, or one who knew the Quran by heart. "I will recite the last three verses of the second Chapter, which are the longest of these three, as I am presuming you do not know these by heart. You can take the other two which I believe everyone knows."

The captain agreed and volunteered to read the Ayat-ul-Kursi, which almost every Muslim knows by heart. Samir agreed to read the last chapter of the Quran, the Al-Nas, which is about the jinn.

They took off their shoes and told the other soldiers to keep an eye on Qabza. Hameed next erased the star with the strange symbols inside while simultaneously reciting the Quls. Then with a prayer to God, the Bismillah, in their heart and on their lips, the three of them stepped onto the chilla. They knew it could be dangerous and they could be attacked by the jinn.

They started to move in an anti-clockwise direction chanting the three verses loudly and looking up to the sky, praying to God to destroy the jinn or send him back to his universe.

They were into the chilla for hardly ten minutes when suddenly the weather started getting severe. Severe lightning and thunder reappeared, but the three continued their encircling the chilla and reading the verses again and again. Samir knew the jinn were made of fire, so he knew that the jinn was appearing in the form of lightning. He had also been warned that the jinn would distract them in many ways.

Samir heard a voice. It was Hasan standing outside the chilla and calling out to him. He appeared badly injured and was holding out his arms. For a moment, Samir felt like it was real, then he immediately recalled he had been warned of the distraction. He realized it was nothing but a hallucination, so he immediately closed his eyes and continued with the recitation in a louder tone. The voice continued to call him, but Samir completely ignored it. When Samir opened his eyes again, he was gone.

A flash of lightning struck the ground right next to the chilla, and the three of them could feel the intense heat. There were two other strokes directed at the chilla, but that did not distract them.

Qabza became terrified and started screaming at the top of his voice asking everyone to run, "We need to get out of here quickly otherwise we all will be killed by the jinn…"

He was interrupted by what looked like a giant black creature, much like a flying dinosaur with a wing span of almost 10 feet, having sharp claws, large red eyes and emitting fire from the mouth sweeping down from the sky in their direction. The creature landed right next to the chilla but dared not enter it. It moved in the direction of Qabza while ignoring the other men.

"Help me! It is Ifrit himself. He is going to kill us all..."

He was interrupted by one of the men firing at the creature, but that did not stop it from moving in the direction of Qabza. It seemed to want only Qabza, and snatched him with its claws and immediately took off again into the sky. One could only hear Qabza screaming as the creature disappeared from view among the treetops.

None of the men had even experienced such a terrifying moment. They had heard tales about the jinn but never seen him ever. This creature could only have been a jinn!

The men continued with their chanting and the chilla. They were cut off from the rest of the world, not knowing if the world was any more safe or on the verge of destruction!

The first break of daylight started to appear in the sky.

Explosion

Harry knelt down next to the nuke. He still could not believe that he was looking at the weapon that the Americans and his agency had been trying to get their hand on since 1998 when Pakistan carried out its five nuclear tests. He wished he could somehow communicate to his agency that he was touching it right now with his bare hands.

The deputy emir had asked him to program it so that it would explode in an hour. Harry wondered how it got here so fast, and how it had crossed Bannu and the border uninterrupted. Had the TTP and the NATO forces failed? Had the Pakistan army also failed to stop it from crossing over into Afghanistan?

He dared not ask these questions, which was less important now. The answers could wait. He was looking at the bomb and had been asked to program it. Should he or should he not? The deputy emir had said it was destined for Kashmir. His agency had informed him it was meant for Bagram. If he pretended to arm it, would they know? He was sure they would detain him in Moqor till the bomb exploded. If it did not explode, he would be killed. If it exploded, many more innocent lives would be lost.

"Hurry up! What are you waiting for? We hardly have enough time," yelled the Deputy Emir.

There was another severe flash of lightening, followed by two more very close ones that Harry could feel the heat of the flash. He wanted to gain some time till he could think of a way out. Maybe the NATO forces would arrive here. He pretended to fiddle with the keyboard.

His thoughts were interrupted by the deputy emir, "We don't have a lot of time. I can see my carrier is getting impatient." He cocked his automatic and placed it at Harry's temple, "Let there be no tricks. We want to have it done now and fast."

Harry could arm it to explode and kill everyone here right now, or he could arm it not to explode. But he would definitely not arm it to explode in an hour. That would mean countless American lives would be lost at the Bagram Air Base.

His thoughts were interrupted by another lightning flash. And yet another. He started to feel the pounding of the flashes in his head. His mind started to go dizzy. He felt as if the flashes were burning in his body. He started to perspire and tremble. His body was on fire.

"Can I have something to drink?" he asked one of the guards.

"Get him some water!" shouted the guard to another.

Harry reverted back to the keyboard. His fingers started trembling. He tried to stop them but couldn't. He was losing control. He felt like something was trying to control him. He felt as if something had entered his body and was controlling his mind and movement.

The glass of water arrived. He gobbled it up in a second but the flashes that were burning in his mind had become more severe. He was burning from the inside and his fingers started to touch the keyboard. He seemed to have no control over his fingers or his mind.

What was happening, he wondered. Had they drugged him with the food in his room, or was it in the water? He felt like a zombie that had lost control of his mind and movement. Was he getting possessed by an invisible force which was controlling his thinking power?

The fingers started to punch in a code on the keyboard. He had lost control over them. He did not even remember or feel what he was punching. He started to black out and lose his senses.

He looked at his watch. It was 6 A.M. As he punched in a few more digits, there was a beeping sound, and the number 666 appeared on the control. They started to roll back in reverse order very fast, moving about ten numbers in one second. He did not even know how these numbers appeared. He couldn't even stop them.

Harry started to tremble, and as the number reached 066, there was one more bright flash in the sky, which retracted in the opposite direction as if it was directed towards the sky instead of the earth.

With the number 000, another huge flash appeared, but this flash was not in the sky, it originated from the box in front of Harry.

It was all darkness after that.

The bomb had exploded.

Moqor was wiped off the face of earth.

It was 666! June 6 at 6 A.M.

The Beginning

It was past dawn when the chilla at the graveyard was interrupted by a young lieutenant who had run uphill to break the news.

"We just received a news flash on our radio that a nuke was stolen in the early hours of this morning from the Chakwal base. There has also been a terrible explosion across the border in Afghanistan near Kandahar about an hour back..."

The three of them stopped mid-track.

"Oh my God!" exclaimed Hameed. "So, it happened and we were not able to stop it."

"Our meteorological office first announced it was a small earthquake of the order of 4.1 on the Richter scale, but other reports have come in fast on the BBC and the CNN that a nuclear weapon has been detonated above ground. Moqor has been identified as the epicenter where the detonation has taken place…"

"Moqor," Hameed interrupted, "it is considered the capital of the terrorists!"

Samir's mind was quick to grasp the events as they unfolded, "The bomb was stolen by the jinn and taken to Moqor. It is apparent from the scale of the tremor that they got their hands on a small bomb instead of a large one, thank God for that. If a large bomb would have reached its final destination, tens of thousands of civilians would have died. The target could have been Kabul or Karachi or Kashmir. It was not important who or where. The idea was to yield maximum deaths and destruction and create a global panic to show the capability of the terrorists with their newly acquired power."

Hameed shook his head in disbelief, "It looks like we did reverse the spell and saved millions of innocent lives with the verses from the Quran, and in the process, killed all the terrorists. Allah is great and all powerful!"

Samir remembered what Shams had told him, "The jinn cannot be trusted. Ifrit could not be trusted by Solomon. The terrorists did a big mistake by trusting the jinn, and in the meantime, we were able to reverse the spell. Ifrit killed them all, and they all got wiped off from the face of the earth."

They were still in confusion when the sky cleared and the sun appeared. They wanted to reach the bottom and immediately started their slow and long journey down the mountain.

Samir assumed most of the terrorists had died in the explosion at Moqor. He could never be sure, but what was certain was that the terrorists had indeed succeeded in stealing a nuke and exploding it. It was perhaps only due to their praying the anti-jinn verses that their plan to kill thousands had backfired and a major catastrophe was prevented.

But then Samir wondered if this would lead to sanctions on Pakistan till it rolls back its nuclear program? Would it end terrorism across Pakistan, or would it increase it further? Would the terrorists resort to other means?

But the most pressing question on his mind was about the jinn! Had the jinn returned back to their own universe, or had the chilla opened up a portal to more jinns invading earth to destroy mankind? There already was a large presence of jinn on earth. Would the jinn team up to attack mankind?

Was this the beginning, or was this the end?

Only time would tell!

Chapter 5
Apocalypse

'Then, when one blast is sounded on the trumpet
And the earth is moved, and its mountains, and they are crushed to powder at one stroke
On that day shall the great event come to pass'

Al-Quran, Verses 69:13 to 69:15

Khalifa

The world was still reeling back from the nuclear explosion at Moqor. Relief teams had arrived from the west, as well as from India, US, and Europe. Pakistan had offered to send to its team from the national disaster management authority, but the offer was declined by Afghanistan.

The explosion had caused a huge crater, and radioactive dust had spread to over 50 miles, the westerly winds taking them further into Balochistan and towards Southern Sindh. There was complete panic in Karachi, a city of over 20 million residents. The weather men at television stations were tracing the nuclear dust, hoping it would bypass Karachi safely into the Arabian Sea. Monsoon rains were not due till end July at least, which could have cleared the dust. .

There was compete chaos, with all possible rumors spreading. The western media had already reported, as a part of its investigative journalism, that the bomb was destined for another target, possibly the Bagram Air Base north of Kabul, which would have caused major casualties and a severe setback to the American forces fighting the Taliban in Afghanistan. Over a thousand Americans and ISAF troops were stationed there. The western media had somehow speculated that the bomb had exploded prematurely at Moqor causing deaths of over a thousand hardcore fighters from the Taliban, TTP, Al-Qaeda, and ISIS, including many of their commanders, in the bomb blast.

NATO forces were put on full alert, even though they were already put on standby to intercept and possess the bomb near Bannu in Pakistan. It was not at all clear how the bomb had managed to travel across northern Pakistan, and then cross the border into Afghanistan.

The Pakistan cabinet was in an emergency meeting for the last two hours yet there were no explanations coming from the government. The military had been put on the back foot by the civilian government, and the army and intelligence chiefs were called to the cabinet meeting to explain how the weapon had been stolen and had made its way across the border into Afghanistan.

The Afghanistan government was up in arms and was clearly pointing fingers at Pakistan. They had called an emergency session of their national security council. At the council meeting, it did not take long for them to ask the United Nations Security Council to convene immediately. They wanted a resolution to be approved imposing complete sanctions on Pakistan unless it opens up all its nuclear facilities to the United Nations for inspection, leading to a roll back and then complete denuclearization of the Pakistan nuclear program.

The militants and terrorists spread out across Pakistan and Afghanistan were in complete disarray. There seemed to be no central command to take charge or talk about avenging the blast at Moqor. It appeared that many of their regional top leadership along with the commanders had died in the blast.

The khalifa, who was heading ISIS at Tora Bora in Afghanistan, identifying his organization with the name of Islamic State Khorasan Province or ISKP, the chapter of Islamic State in Afghanistan, Pakistan and Central Asia, was quick to capitalize on the blast and declare himself the supreme leader in the region. His video immediately came up on the web, showing him addressing his followers with the black flag of ISIS in the background. He revealed that the bomb was actually destined for Bagram to kill thousands of kafirs, and teach them a lesson they would never forget. However, the Americans had somehow reprogrammed it to explode at Moqor killing many of their fighters for which there will be a severe retaliation.

"ISIS will avenge the deaths of thousands of our brothers who have achieved martyrdom at the hands of the kafirs. All of what is happening around the world today is what the Prophet had disclosed 1,400 years ago. The signs are very clear now, and even the blind can see them. We are waiting for the day when Allah will send the Mahdi as our leader, who will then announce himself to us at the right time. Let me assure you that day is not far.

"The wars which are already happening all around us, in Afghanistan, Yemen, Syria, and Iraq were already prophesized. Now, we are witnessing the final signs as well, including the 'malhama' or the apocalypse, which started in Afghanistan at Moqor and will now engulf the whole world in its fold.

"Afghanistan will be a graveyard for the kafir!" he declared

"Once Mahdi appears, all Muslim forces from around the world will join him. Under his black flag, the kafirs will fall everywhere, and Mahdi will lead our forces to complete victory.

"The signs of the end of times are already here.

"It is mentioned in the Quran that swarms of these people will come out from behind the wall, which will be among the final signs for the world to end. Gog and Magog people from China are taking over Pakistan. But before the end of world, we will attack the Gog and Magog people in their backyard and send them back behind their great wall where they have lived in isolation for thousands of years!"

He next fired about a dozen rounds from his gun at an image of the American president.

"Dajjal is already in our midst. He will be annihilated by Mahdi under command of our black flag. Allah has his ways to lead us to victory. America is acting like god, and has killed tens of thousands of our brothers and sisters, but is under threat of its own annihilation by North Korea. Inshallah, kafir America will be destroyed soon."

He then raised his gun above his head like a victory sign to make an important revelation.

"We are not alone in our jihad. It is in the Quran that Allah created us to rule over all his other creations, including the jinn. The shaytan Iblis did not agree to our creation, and defied Allah. He wanted to be the superior creature. Allah knew what he knew not, and threw him out of His court. Now, as a result of the enmity between the jinn and men, both of us have suffered for thousands of years. Let me tell you that those days are now over!

"It is in the Hadith that Mahdi and his loyal followers will communicate with the jinn and will be assisted by them to have Muslims rule the world."

He let that sink in for a moment before he continued, "I want to make an important revelation today that we are already communicating with the jinn, and have made truce with them. We are no more at war with them, but together we are at war with the kafir who have set us apart.

"The bomb at Moqor was stolen and carried by the greatest jinn warrior, Ifrit, the powerful one, who has returned back to our world and is now on our side. No one can defeat us now, not America, not Israel, not China, not India. We will win, and all these countries will be destroyed!

"Under the Mahdi there will be one flag of Islam around the world!"

Cabinet

Samir watched the video in total disbelief. The region was already at the threshold of anarchy, and all law and order had broken down in Pakistan. The country was under threat of sanctions if it did not agree to the UN restrictions that could be imposed on it. Now, ISIS had also announced it was going to step up its activities by attacking the Chinese in Pakistan. And on top of that they were claiming they had the jinn on their side.

Hordes of people started to flood the supermarkets, small stores, and street vendors to stock up on food supplies, and other emergency items like the batteries, candles, first aid boxes, and medicine if sanctions were imposed or war was declared. There was complete chaos on the streets.

The social media including WhatsApp, Twitter, and Facebook was making it worse. The explosion at Moqor, and the khalifa address in which he claimed teaming up with the jinn, became the focus of speculation. It led to many more fake postings which started circulating, and which made bizarre claims. The one that caught the attention of the world community was that more than a dozen bombs had been stolen by the terrorists from the military base at Chakwal, which the Pakistan government was keeping as a closely guarded secret. These bombs were now on the verge of being distributed to various terrorist groups around the world, and were destined for many kafir countries around the world, including America, Israel, and India.

In Kashmir, the various militant groups, including Lashkar-e-Taiba, the 'Army of the Pure', Jaish-e-Mohammed, the 'Army of Muhammad' and Hizb-ul-Mujahidin, the 'Party of Holy Warriors' were already claiming on social media that they will soon have their hands on the bomb. They were announcing that a major attack will soon be launched against the Indian military bases in Kashmir, who will see the worst attack in recent history, in which hundreds of thousands will die, unless India withdraws its forces from Kashmir and gives it independence.

In Iran, the Jundallah 'Soldiers of God', a Sunni militant organization, were declaring that very soon they will target a major Shia shrine with a nuclear bomb which will teach them a lesson they will never forget for killing countless Sunnis.

In Syria, the Sunni powers, backed by Saudi Arabia and Turkey, who were screaming for President Assad's blood for killing Sunnis in Aleppo, were vowing to annihilate his presidential palace with a nuclear explosion.

The military chiefs were summoned to the cabinet meeting in Islamabad, who swore at the meeting that only one bomb went missing from Chakwal, and all these claims being made by the various terrorist and social media were incorrect. They had absolutely no idea how the terrorists were able to penetrate Chakwal, or even leave, as there was no evidence of any gunfight, or any movement recorded on the cameras. They had heard of the khalifa's proclamation about the jinn stealing the bomb, but could not believe it or that jinn could be made to do such a task. It looked like some 'invisible' hands and penetrated the base, and one bomb had somehow vanished in thin air and reappeared in Afghanistan to explode.

Samir had requested that he be allowed to speak to the cabinet with the military chiefs present, as he may be able to throw some light on the bomb that was stolen and propose a possible course of action.

"Madam Prime Minister, ministers and military chiefs. What I will present to you today is something that will make you think I have lost my mind and should be admitted to a lunatic asylum. We know for a fact that we lost one bomb without a trace. It showed up in Afghanistan crossing countless police and military checkposts, including crossing the border within a very short time. The explosion at Moqor was a nuclear explosion of approximately the same yield as the bomb that was stolen.

"Khalifa, the ISIS leader in Afghanistan, has already claimed it was stolen by a jinn who carried it to Moqor, which most of you doubt. If you recall, nuclear fuel was also stolen from the agriculture institute few days back, and there was an attempt to explode a dirty bomb in the heart of Islamabad and target the president as well. Even in those cases, we did not know how they were able to penetrate the institute and bring the fuel undetected to the heart of Islamabad. They would have succeeded if the cylinder carrying the fuel had completely exploded. If it had, hundreds would have died, and half of Islamabad would have been evacuated, including the building where we are currently holding this meeting."

Samir paused to let his message sink in, "We expect by tomorrow, the Security Council would most likely pass a unanimous resolution putting sanctions on us, unless we open up all our bases to the United Nations, and start dismantling our nuclear assets. India and Israel are probably the countries that are most excited at this development.

"The world has a reason to be gravely concerned, because they don't believe us anymore. On the contrary, they believe a dozen bombs are already on their way to various capitals of the world. The way the bomb arrived at Moqor, undetected, is probably how they think the other bombs will arrive on their shores in due course of time. They are not going to take our word that only one bomb is missing…"

The prime minister interrupted, "We know all of that. What else would you like to tell us?"

Samir went straight to the point, "The master terrorist of all, Khalifa, in his video address this morning talked about the jinn. We as Muslims believe in this supernatural entity because it is in the Quran. Denying the existence of the jinn means denying we are Muslims.

"The TTP commander in Pakistan had personally mentioned to me they are resorting to black magic and will soon control the jinn which will turn the war in their favor!"

Samir looked around to check if he had gotten everyone's attention. Some were shaking their head in disbelief. Most of the ministers, however, were leaning forward and sitting at the edge of their seats.

"I have every reason to believe that the terrorist groups, led by ISIS and Al-Qaeda, have succeeded in controlling the jinn. The bomb that went missing from Chakwal was stolen and transported undetected by a jinn to explode at Moqor! What the khalifa is claiming is 100% correct!"

There was complete silence.

Samir continued, "The West needs to understand that it is a completely different ball game now. The issue is not about denuclearizing Pakistan anymore. Like they say, 'The genie is out of the bottle.' The jinn, whom we know as Ifrit, is out to destroy and rule the world in league with the terrorists. Other jinn may join them. If the jinn can steal a weapon from under the watchful eyes of the Pakistan elite forces, they can not only steal all of Pakistan's nuclear arsenal but can do it from any country of the world. They can explode the most powerful bomb at any place of their choosing at any time!

The silence was deafening!

Samir continued, "I expect the world geopolitical situation to change rapidly, because the jinn Ifrit is now freely roaming on earth. He is after all a trained commander from the days of Prophet Solomon, and can mobilize other jinn on earth to serve under him. As a jinn, he can also influence events around the world. Verse 114 says it all. Jinns have powers to influence evil through their whisperings. I expect many hotspots will flare up in no time around the world under his evil influence, and we could be on the verge of World War III!"

Nobody spoke for some time. Finally, the minister for faiths and beliefs spoke up, "Allow me to add, Madam Prime Minister, what the Advisor for Education has just conveyed is not only possible but most likely true. The Quran talks of the creation of the jinn from a smokeless fire before man was created. The jinn are invisible, have enormous strength and can travel at the speed of light. They live for thousands of years. There are many stories in the Quran and Hadith attributed to jinn, and Ifrit is just one of them. If we are believing Muslims, then we must not doubt any of these stories. The jinn were practitioners of black magic which they taught to the aamil, and this magic is being practiced even today."

He stopped to recite a verse which was inaudible and then continued, "If Ifrit, who is a powerful jinn, could volunteer to bring the throne of the Queen of Saba from Yemen to Jerusalem in an instant of a second, then he certainly can bring any bomb from anywhere to anywhere!

"Chapter 114 of the Quran, which is Al-Nas, says the jinn can induce evil thought in men. The jinn can take men to wars, terrorism, murder, rape and have them do all evils of this world. What the advisor is saying is possible and correct.

The jinn will influence events around the world, and wars will flare up in no time. Unless we stop the jinn, we could be days away from total annihilation!"

The prime minister mustered up the strength to speak, "First of all, I don't think all of what you are saying is possible and believable in today's time. But then I know how much enlightened you, as a minister of faiths, are in all religious matters, and would never give wrong advice or make a statement unless it is 100% backed by the Quran. I also personally know Samir as a scientist who has worked in the top laboratories of the world for so many years. I know he has credibility, and can never muster up such stories unless he has investigated them himself."

She looked around, and then directed the question to the foreign minister, "How can one even begin to convince the world leaders that what we are saying is true, and we need to act together to end this evil alliance between terrorists and jinn? The world needs to understand that it is not about our nukes getting stolen, and it is not about denuclearizing Pakistan, as these bombs can be stolen from anywhere by the jinn, but it is now about mankind fighting the jinn."

"All religions believe in the end of times," the foreign minister finally spoke, "Yet, everyone believes these stories are fictional. Are you proposing we present this case to the UN Security Council?"

"Tell them that sanctions and denuclearizing of Pakistan will not make an iota of difference to the events that are about to take place in the foreseeable future!" The prime minister added, "The world needs to understand our position and unite forces against the jinn otherwise the apocalypse is upon us."

With that, she asked her principal secretary to connect her urgently to the US president announcing the meeting will reconvene in 30 minutes.

Kabul

The Afghan National Security Council had called another emergency session at a few hours' notice and outright blamed the nuclear explosion at Moqor on Pakistan. The hard liners were out for Pakistan's blood, and wanted immediate military action to be taken against Pakistan. Others wanted to wait first for the United Nations Security Council to pass a resolution asking Pakistan to denuclearize its nuclear program.

The hawks were very outspoken and blamed Pakistan's military for all its troubles since December 1979 when the Soviets invaded Afghanistan. They pointed out that they had an excellent opportunity in December 1971 when the Pakistan forces were fully occupied with India during the Bangladesh war, and over 90,000 were made POWs as a result of their losing the war. The Soviets had at that time asked their King Zahir Shah to attack Pakistan which he refused, and an opportunity was lost in which they could have captured the complete Pashtun belt in Pakistan and had a united Pashtunistan. Within two years, the king's cousin Sardar Daoud toppled the monarchy. This act heralded the era of instability in Afghanistan which continues to the present day, and Pakistan is responsible for this.

The interior minister reminded that the day Pakistan was created as an Islamic nation state in 1947, many Afghanis were looking up to the new nation, and thousands of fathers named their newborn sons after Mohammad Ali the founder of Pakistan. Most Afghans' yearning for Islamic caliphate saw their dream come true in the manifestation of Pakistan. The Hadith had mentioned the emergence of a new nation east of Khorasan which will lead the Islamic nation after the 14th century. Most assumed it was Pakistan, but now it is clear that it is the Pashtun's from Afghanistan, and not from Pakistan, that will lead the new nation. He said intelligence had provided his ministry with the information that most Pashtun in Pakistan are frustrated with the Punjabi attitude of ruling the country, and are interested in carving their own homeland. He said the time is now right, and he proposed attacking Pakistan. He was sure that the Pashtun from across the border would welcome the Afghan troops and join them as well, just like the Bengalis did in 1947.

The intelligence chief briefed the meeting that they have reached out to the Taliban, who are mostly Pashtun Afghans. They have managed to bribe the Taliban that an Islamic caliphate could formed if they could align themselves with the Afghan forces to help them capture large areas of Pashtun land across the border. Since the Taliban enjoy a good understanding with the Pashtun in the Pakistan army as well as the Pashtun population at large in Pakistan, there is a strong possibility that all Pashtun forces will combine under their flag and Afghanistan could become the largest Pashtun nation on earth, and possibly the headquarter of the Islamic caliphate with Kabul as its capital.

The defense minister pointed out that with the Indian forces keeping the Pakistan army fully occupied on its eastern borders with India, and one should not lose this golden opportunity which has come after a long time after 1971, when King Zahir Shah did not take the Soviet advice and they lost on the opportunity.

The president, after hearing to all sides of the argument, agreed that attacking Pakistan is a good strategy to pursue, but said the time is not ripe right now till the nuclear weapons are first removed from Pakistan. He also wanted to get a feedback from the American intelligence on this plan. He directed the Afghanistan military chiefs to be on full alert in case their forces are needed to go across into Pakistan and support the US Special Forces as they move in to denuclearize the country.

In a formal resolution, the Afghan National Security Council reiterated their demand for the United Nations Security Council to convene immediately to put complete sanctions on Pakistan and to denuclearize its nuclear program, failing which the Afghan government would be free to pursue its own course for its defense, including moving its troops inside Pakistan to clear out 'threats to its national security under UN flag'. All options were on the table and nothing could be ruled out."

Following the meeting, the Afghan military was ordered to mobilize and move reinforcements towards the Pakistani border. The UN Security Council and the neighboring countries were informed of this move by the Afghans.

The Indian prime minister was the first one to call the Afghanistan president and congratulate him on this bold decision. He assured him of all possible logistics and intelligence support, adding that, "If push comes to shove, India would put all its military personnel on the border with Pakistan, and support the Afghan forces if necessary." He said he had already directed its air force and navy to be on full alert in case Pakistan resists the UN forces who may seek to denuclearize it.

Kashmir

Immediately following the Pakistan cabinet session, there was breaking news on Indian TV channels that there was a sudden uprising in Kashmir by the local Muslim population against the Indian government. Despite over half a million Indian troops present in Kashmir, the protests had turned violent, looting shops, banks, and ransacking the government offices. Cars and buses were set on fire, and the green and white Pakistan flags were raised on top of key government offices. Some demonstrators carried weapons, who fired upon the security forces trying to control the mob.

The Indians were not anticipating an uprising in Kashmir to be that quick and violent, and immediately pointed the finger at Pakistan. The prime minister called the Kashmir chief minister, who showed his helplessness in crushing the uprising through the use of local police.

"We urgently need federal assistance, otherwise I fear we will lose control of Kashmir to the Muslim fanatics!"

The Indian prime minister was quick to respond. He ordered the military, which was already stationed in Kashmir, to 'take action as appropriate' to safeguard lives and property of the Indian citizen. The troops were quick to retaliate, firing back at the crowd, and leaving a multitude of bodies lying around on roadsides and inside buildings. Curfew was declared in most parts of Kashmir with an order of 'shoot to kill' anyone who violates the curfew.

The militants were quick to respond, and the Lashkar-e-Taiba, Jaish-e-Mohammed and Hizb-ul-Mujahidin supporters started using various mosque speakers asking people to pick up arms and declare jihad against the Indian occupiers of Kashmir. As the Indian army moved into the cities of Srinagar and Jammu in large numbers, many of the militants who had taken refuge in mosques, started firing back at the troops. Kashmir started turning red with the blood of 'martyrs' on both sides!

The Indian government immediately accused Pakistan for flaring up the insurgency, blaming it of sending in armed military personnel in civilian's clothes to aid the local militants. Pakistan, on the other hand, accused India of firing upon innocent and unarmed citizens.

By mid-afternoon, TV news from Pakistan reported that as many as 120 civilians, including women and children, had died as a result of Indian fire, and more bodies were being counted. Indian TV, on the other hand, reported that over 200 Hindus in Kashmir were mobbed to death by the separatists, many of them lynched or burnt alive.

The US secretary of state, British and the Russian foreign minister were on phone calls to the prime ministers of both countries asking for restraint. While the Indian prime minister openly accused Pakistan of terrorism, including being responsible for thousands of deaths in the nuclear explosion in Afghanistan, the Pakistani prime minister was quick to point out that India was responsible for the death of thousands of Kashmiris, including many forced disappearances, mass torture, and sexual violence. She also reminded them that under the United Nations Security Council Resolution 47, a plebiscite was to decide the fate of Kashmir, which has never taken place up to now, thereby leading to abuse of human rights in Kashmir. Had the plebiscite taken place, hundreds of thousands of lives would have been saved since independence, and the hundreds of billions of dollars both countries had spent on defense would have been spent on the people in improving civic services and infrastructure.

Neither India nor Pakistan was willing to concede their position, and each blamed the other for the four wars that have taken place between them. These countries, both nuclear armed, were now on the verge of yet another war.

An emergency session of the Indian cabinet was called, and within 30 minutes of deliberations, India was quick to accuse Pakistan of not only inciting violence in Kashmir, including being responsible for over 200 deaths since insurgency began this morning, but also of sending its troops across the border dressed as civilians who were involved in looting and burning of buildings, firing upon innocent civilians, and raping young girls and married women. Pakistan's action was considered a direct attack on the sovereignty of India, which therefore reserved the right to protect itself.

Pakistan, on the other hand, denied these accusations, and instead accused India of brutalities and mass killing of Muslims in Kashmir, Gujrat, and Mumbai, as well as accusing it of inciting trouble and violence in Balochistan and Karachi. It blamed India for the thousands of deaths in Karachi and Balochistan through its various surrogate terrorist organizations. The official communique further added that an Indian spy recently arrested confessed to the support of terrorists in Pakistan on national television.

It further accused India of killing over 70,000 civilians, with over 8,000 forced disappearances, and sexually abusing and raping over thousands of young girls and women in Kashmir since its occupation. Additionally, India was responsible for many human rights abuses, including killings of lower caste Hindus, and the lynching of many Muslims across India who were killed for storing or eating beef. It further added that just in the most recent uprising, there have been reported deaths of over 120 deaths in Indian-held Kashmir since this morning, and more bodies were still being recovered and counted.

By 4 P.M., the Indian prime minister was on national TV declaring that India believes Pakistan is behind all the unrest and killings in Kashmir, and has violated the sovereignty of India. He further went a step forward making Pakistan responsible for the nuclear explosion in Afghanistan, in which many thousands had died, and declared Pakistan to be a terrorist state. He declared that India needs to teach Pakistan a lesson which it had still not learnt since the brave Bengalis rose against it and declared their independence in 1971. He also mentioned the Kargil war of July 1999 where Pakistan had been taught a lesson, and November 2008 Mumbai attacks in which Lashkar-e-Taiba was facilitated by the Pakistani ISI to carry out that act of terrorism, in which over 150 innocent civilians had lost their lives. He said it is time the brave Baloch in Balochistan, Muhajir in Karachi, Sindhi in Sindh, and the Pashtun in KP province pick up arms against the Punjabi establishment and declare independence from the terrorist state of Pakistan and join the peaceful comity of world nations. India would welcome them all and provide all possible assistance where and when needed.

By 5 P.M., the uprising in Kashmir had become very violent and bloody. Thousands of armed Kashmiris had defied the curfew and occupied all government buildings, and had started looting banks, burning cars, and attacking Indian forces.

There was frequent use of rocket launchers as well. The Indian forces had to back off and were forced to retreat to outside the city.

The military commanders were already in an emergency session at the prime minister's office in New Delhi. Kashmir would be lost unless they moved fast and attacked Pakistan across its borders to inflict major loss and capture some territory. They compared the present conditions to exactly what had happened prior to the 1965 war with Pakistan, when Pakistan had instigated an uprising in Kashmir. India had retaliated and attacked Pakistan in return across its whole borders, intruding deep into its territory.

The director general military operation, however, was quick to point out that this time it would be different as Pakistan is fully prepared against any Indian attack. He also added that Pakistan had in its arsenal low yield nuclear missiles Nasr, which they would use in the face of an advancing Indian Army. There could be significant loss of lives on the Indian side.

The army chief disagreed by saying that India is also nuclear armed this time, and Pakistan knows that any use of Nasr on their part would provoke India to arm their nuclear missiles. He said the possibility of Pakistan using Nasr existed only in war games.

The other generals agreed. Orders were then issued for an intrusion of Indian forces into Pakistan at the Lahore and Bahawalpur borders, where four Indian divisions were already on full alert. The armored corps would move to the front and lead the attacks.

The Indian 'Cold Start Doctrine' to inflict maximum damage in the shortest possible time was given the go-ahead to allow India's conventional forces to perform holding and shallow attacks into Pakistan. Since Pakistan and India were both nuclear states, the cold start doctrine was a strategy to prevent a nuclear retaliation from Pakistan.

The Indian generals had, however, underestimated Pakistan's preparedness and response. Satellite images provided by China to Pakistan showed large scale mobilization and movement of troops to Lahore and Bahawalpur borders.

Pakistan's Nasr low yield nuclear tipped missiles, which were stored at Chakwal in battle-ready condition, were immediately armed, and ordered to be transported to the battlefields without delay.

Samir's cell phone rang as he stepped into the prime minister's outer lounge. It was Mike.

"You are making a grave mistake. Mobilizing the Nasr is no solution to the crisis. It has to be resolved diplomatically!" He seemed to have gotten the information right away.

Samir agreed, "Moqor is no fault of ours. I cannot even begin to explain how it happened, as you would not understand. India needs to understand that all issues can be settled amicably and diplomatically. They have no reason to deploy their troops across our border. We have learnt from 1965 and 1971 that we can't wait for them to attack first this time. You know we have hawks too in our armed forces who want our flag to be unfurled on the Red Fort in Delhi."

Mike pointed out Pakistan's advantage, "You have your troops who are fully prepared this time. It cannot be a surprise attack from India anymore. They know if they attack, there are going to be heavy casualties on both sides. It will be an expensive war which none of you will be able to sustain."

Samir was apprehensive, "We do not want war, let alone a nuclear one. But India has a much larger conventional army than we do. Over 1.4 million versus 600,000 for Pakistan. They also have much better armament, as India spends over $50 billion on defense every year, against $9 billion for Pakistan.

"We cannot even begin to compare our conventional forces with theirs. Just their strike force consists of thirteen corps, three armored divisions, four infantry divisions, 18 infantry divisions and ten mountain divisions. They have two surface-to-surface missile units, and over 4,000 battle tanks, 2,000 armored personnel carriers, 4,300 artillery pieces and 200 light helicopters, while we hardly have half as much. You know we cannot hold them for long in a conventional war even though we believe our forces are better trained. Nasr was, therefore, developed by us to counter the balance of power in conventional forces. It is only theater defense, without causing any damage to the civilian population, and the Pentagon knows that!"

Mike disagreed, "One thing leads to another. Even the firing of a single Nasr will lead to serious ramifications!"

"I am at the prime minister's office, and will be bringing these up with her."

"Please tell her that this very moment, our Secretary of State Robert Forster is flying over from Istanbul to Islamabad and Delhi to talk to both prime ministers to diffuse the crisis!"

"That might be too late. You need to pressurize the world powers to call off the Security Council session!"

"I cannot promise, but will try."

With that, he hung up the phone.

The prime minister was in a meeting with the chiefs of the armed forces and the defense minister. The military secretary knew that she would always see Samir even without an appointment. He communicated to her Samir wanting to see her, and she asked him to join them inside the meeting room.

"I am glad the chiefs are all here," Samir took the opportunity to express his viewpoint, "I believe we are on the verge of a major war with India. We have been made to believe through generations that we have a better fighting force than they are, yet we lost half our country in 1971."

The generals felt uncomfortable at this comment, and shifted their positions wanting to say something.

Samir continued, "India has the advantage of numbers and better weaponry. The war will cost each one of us tens of thousands of lives, and billions of dollars in damages. We believe the nuclear tipped Nasr missile will hold out the Indian advance for some time, but there are major risks associated with its use, including escalation of the conflict to a full-fledged nuclear war. Our country may possibly disintegrate even if we win, but I believe there will be no winners."

The army chief spoke up, "India needs to move its forces away from our borders first."

"I fully agree. That is why we need to resolve this diplomatically. The US secretary of state is on his way here, and will arrive within a few hours. The Security Council is to meet tomorrow, wanting to put sanctions on us, and denuclearize us…"

"Why only us?" the intelligence chief interrupted, "we are not all of South Asia, why not India or for that matter Israel?"

The prime minister lifted her hand gesturing everyone to be quiet, "I just talked to the Chinese prime minister. Their foreign minister is also on his way here and will arrive at night right after the US secretary of state visit. We can certainly have a dialogue tonight between the Indian, Pakistani, American, and Chinese foreign ministers. The Russians and the British have already been informed of the latest developments by our foreign office. I believe we can diffuse the crisis through diplomacy if the Indians are cooperative. We have only two demands: UN session to be called off and India to pull back its troops."

Samir nodded his head, "That will be ideal, Madam Prime Minister, but the danger is not only confined to this region. The accident at Moqor will pull in many Islamic terrorist groups into the fold…from Kashmir to Iran to Syria.

"The jinn are now the players in this war led by the powerful jinn Ifrit, who has arrived on earth. This crisis between Pakistan and India is only the tip of the iceberg. I believe the jinn have already embarked on his agenda of initiating new wars around the world. As I expressed earlier this morning in the Cabinet meeting, I believe we will soon see many other crisis's around the world which may lead to a nuclear world war and complete annihilation of our race."

Samir took a deep breath and continued, "The ISIS head is already claiming in his video address that they have control of the jinn. He is also saying it has been prophesized that the jinn will aid the Mahdi in destroying the non-believers, and Islam will rule the world. This is a very frightening scenario, as here we are not talking about radical Islam but apocalyptic Islam!"

The prime minister shook her head, "How do you convince the western leaders that apocalyptic Islam is the threat? That jinn are the threat? Even I as a Muslim doubt that most of the times, and to make them believe that there are jinn who are now controlled by the terrorists and are out there to steal every single nuclear bomb in the world and fire them at us?"

Samir was adamant, "No! We cannot convince them! That is why we need to act urgently to end this evil alliance between terrorists and jinn, otherwise the whole world will be annihilated! Pakistan and India are just the tip of the iceberg!"

"How do you end this alliance?" asked the prime minister.

Samir took a deep breath, wondering whether they will log into what he was going to say next, "There are antidotes in the Quran, call it what you may, that will neutralize the jinn. You may think I am crazy, but it is true! We have tried it before, once to end the influence of black magic, and the second time to neutralize the jinn that took the bomb to Moqor."

There was complete silence in the room. Everyone present was trying to digest this information. Finally, the army chief spoke up.

"But the bomb did explode in Moqor! How can you claim the antidote worked?"

"I cannot prove it, but the khalifa in his address claimed it was destined for Bagram Air Base. It is also likely that the bomb was destined for another destination, maybe Kabul or Karachi or Delhi, we don't know that. Many civilians by the thousands would have died in that case. It would have created a global panic, and would have shown the newly acquired capability of the terrorists. Something caused the bomb not to explode at Bagram but at Moqor.

"I personally believe we reversed the jinn spell with the antidote verses from the Quran and the chilla, and saved perhaps thousands of innocent lives. In the process, the terrorists instead got killed. Perhaps we can do it again!"

The prime minister shook her head, "I don't know what you are up to, but please do anything you can do that can stop the jinn or the terrorists from acquiring any more bombs or exploding them. I do not even want to know what you are doing. I have enough worries and a diplomatic challenge on my head trying to prevent a conventional war, let alone a nuclear one, and to convince the US secretary of state, the Chinese foreign minister, and the UN Security Council that we will support any global action to rid our countries of terrorists."

Samir was relieved that the prime minister at least trusted him. He thanked the prime minister and asked permission to leave, and as she nodded her head, walked out of the office.

As he walked to his car, he was worried that if the khalifa was really in control of the jinn who had returned from the outer universe, then no one could defeat them, other than the power of God. All diplomacy, even at the highest level, will fail if the jinn wanted the war.

He recalled what Shams and Wasim had told him, "The three anti-dote verses from the Quran! If they are recited, and one rotates around the chilla in a clockwise direction without stopping, it would be possible to send the jinn back to their universe!" He remembered he had recited these with Hameed and the captain at the chilla in Miranshah.

However, if the powerful jinn Ifrit stole more nuclear weapons and lined up other jinn to attack mankind, it would lead to a war of the army of jinn versus man! The jinn would certainly win. If so, they would definitely need more than the chilla to defeat them!

What other forces could they use in addition to the chilla to defeat the jinn?

Shams had emphasized on the power of the Quranic verses, Allama Malik and Latif were convinced in the power of prayers, while his son Hasan believed in the power of spiritualism.

All of them were needed now to fight the jinn!

They had already resorted to the chilla to influence the jinn! Would it work again when the threat was far more severe? Would they need a larger chilla, or perhaps multiple chillas? Or would they need something more, something different, something new?

Could the jinn be stopped or sent back by an 'army of men' doing both the prayers and the chillas if there was a human-jinn war, Samir wondered.

His mind travelled to another dimension. Was there a possibility that some other entity other than men, like the angels, or any other spiritual forces, fight the war with the jinn and win? Was that a possible solution?

Samir shook his head. Angels were not created to fight but to love and pray to God and follow his instructions.

The jinn must be defeated at any cost, otherwise it will be all over for mankind.

CPEC

Much prior to all these happenings, more than 7,000 Chinese engineers and workers had arrived in Pakistan in addition to the 5,000 already present as a part of the $62 billion investment in China Pakistan Economic Corridor, or CPEC. The corridor was under development from the Chinese border to Gwadar with a major thrust on developing highways, power plants and the seaport at Gwadar.

The detailed plan called for a deep and broad-based penetration of most sectors of Pakistan's economy as well as its society by Chinese enterprises and culture, including leasing out thousands of acres of agricultural land to Chinese entrepreneurs. Work had already commenced on the laying of a national fibreoptic backbone for internet traffic as well as broadcast TV, which will cooperate with Chinese media in the 'dissemination of Chinese culture'. All major cities from Peshawar to Karachi would have 2-hour video recordings on roads and marketplaces for monitoring and surveillance. Major Chinese multinationals would have exclusive rights in manufacturing and mining. A number of industrial parks, or special economic zones with first rights to the Chinese, were to be built which 'must meet specified conditions, including availability of water, perfect infrastructure, sufficient supply of energy and the capacity of self-service power'.

It appeared the whole country was being handed over to China!

There were more spoilers of CPEC than those favoring it. CPEC had made the Americans, Russians, Indians, and Gulf countries very unhappy. With direct access of Chinese goods to the warm waters of the Arabian Sea through a modern port which rivalled Dubai, most neighboring countries would feel an economic pinch. The Americans were concerned that CPEC allowed an alternate route to the Strait of Malacca which was patrolled and controlled by US Navy. The Russians were concerned that the Chinese had accomplished peacefully what the Soviets could not through the invasion of Afghanistan in 1979, and their designs on Balochistan. India's dream of becoming an economic superpower would be jeopardized if CPEC became a reality. India had already objected to the portion of CPEC passing through Gilgit-Baltistan in Pakistan, which India considered a disputed territory. The Indian prime minister had already boycotted the OBOR meeting of heads of states held recently in China.

The Pakistan Military, on the other hand, had vowed that they would provide full assistance and security to the Chinese during the development of the corridor.

This is when the abductions and killing of Chinese engineers and other personnel in Pakistan started as the project progressed. A couple was kidnapped and killed in Balochistan, which ISIS claimed responsibility on its news agency, Amaq. Pakistan was quick to play down the killing as well as the terrorist group's role.

This killing was followed up with two more Chinese mining engineers who were abducted near Miranshah and whose bodies were found near the Tora Bora region of the Pakistan-Afghanistan border. The area across the border had mostly been in control of the Islamic State Khorasan Province or ISKP, the chapter of Islamic State in Afghanistan, Pakistan, and Central Asia, since the last few years, and again ISIS claimed responsibility for these killings.

The Chinese government showed its concern for lack of security provided by Pakistan for its personnel working in northern areas. Pakistan was quick to point out that although it was the responsibility of the Pakistan government to provide adequate security to the Chinese, but most of the northern areas near the Afghanistan border were off limits to Chinese unless escorted by the military. The Chinese engineers had gone beyond the region assigned to them for their surveys.

Within days, there was another major abduction of five Chinese engineers at Taxila when they were visiting the Buddhist monastery. Taxila is generally considered a safe area as it is close to Islamabad. Within a few hours, their mutilated bodies were recovered from the River Indus near Attock.

The Chinese government asked all their personnel to stay at their headquarters till further notice.

Latif called up Samir, "Do you recall the prophesies of Shah Naimatullah Wali which I had earlier mentioned to you? There will be bloodshed. River Attock will become red with the blood of the kafir."

"But had he not prophesized that an army of Muslim warriors, including the Chinese, will come in the aid of Pakistan? So, why are the Chinese being killed?"

Latif was quick to explain, "Our interest in CPEC was that the Chinese population in its northwest region called the Xinjiang Uyghur Autonomous Region would benefit. The Uyghur are mostly ethnically Turkic Muslims, and China, over its 69-year rule of Xinjiang, has persecuted Uyghurs and restricted Muslim worship, attire, and names.

"Xinjiang is the largest Chinese administrative division spanning over 640,000 square miles and borders Mongolia, Russia, Kazakhstan, Kyrgyzstan, Tajikistan, Afghanistan, Pakistan, and India. In recent decades, abundant oil and mineral reserves have also been found in Xinjiang, and it is currently China's largest natural gas-producing region."

Latif continued, "The Uyghur are suppressed people. Over 300,000 have escaped persecution in China and are now settled in Turkey. Both Pakistan and the Uyghur Chinese found CPEC as a way of improving the economic conditions of Xinjiang. The ISIS eyes Xinjiang as a significant prize, and therefore Chinese from other parts of China are not acceptable to ISIS. These killings are to serve as a warning to the Chinese."

"But that is clearly not the only reason Chinese are being killed," asked Samir. He knew and was briefed well by the intelligence agencies on the geopolitical importance of CPEC, which would shake some of the economic foundations of US, India, Russia, Afghanistan, Iran, and the Gulf countries.

"Of course, ISIS is a mercenary force as well and has multitude of other interests," added Latif, "CPEC is clearly in China's and Pakistan's interests, and all others want to sabotage it."

He took a deep breath before he continued, "If the Pakistan forces are not able to protect the lives of the Chinese, I expect the Chinese will move some of their forces to do the job! Call it an invasion of Pakistan by the Gog and Magog people! It is in the Quran anyway."

"Are you suggesting that the Chinese are the Gog Magog people mentioned in the Quran?" Samir remembered the Gog Magog have been associated with so many different groups in the past: the Israelis, Pashtuns, and the Chinese.

"Yes! In Chapter 18. The Cave in Verses 94 and in Chapter 21. The Prophets in Verse 96, there are clear references to Gog and Magog.

"In Verse 18:94 God says,

'They said: 'O Zul-Qarnain! The Gog and Magog people do great mischief on earth: shall we then render thee tribute in order that thou mightest erect a barrier between us and them?'

"In Verse 21:96 God says,

'Until the Gog and Magog people are let through their barrier, and they swiftly swarm from every hill.'"

He added, "Gog and Magog were suppressed by Zul-Qarnain, who was a king and a conqueror. Many associate him with Alexander of Macedonia while others call him a prophet. It has two meanings in Arabic: the one who has two horns, and the one who affects two ages. When Zul-Qarnain travelled during his conquests to the ends of the world, he met people who sought his help in building a wall that would separate them from the Gog and Magog, who will 'do great mischief on earth'. He agreed to build it for them, but warned them that when the time comes, Allah will remove the wall and Gog and Magog will swarm the earth. We know for sure that the Great Wall of China that has kept the Chinese at bay for thousands of years."

He took a deep breath and added, "The invasion by Gog and Magog is a major sign of the end of times. It is among the ten major signs that will herald in the end of the world."

"So, we are at the end of times according to Islamic eschatology?" asked Samir.

"Very much so. Gog and Magog have already started swarming the earth in large numbers, exactly the way the Quran has described it. In the past, we thought Dajjal was the prime minister of Israel, but now we think it is the president of America. We now also have a racist beast in India who is bent on killing Muslims and minorities. Due to the war, there are so many fires out of Yemen, and the recent explosion at Moqor has caused an earthquake in the east followed by a cloud of smoke. Soon, we will experience earthquakes in Arabia and the west as well. If the jinn continue to dominate, then it is only a matter of time that someone will claim he is Mahdi, and the Muslim world will follow him blindly."

Events followed exactly as predicted in the Hadith. Following the killings of the Chinese engineers by ISIS, a battalion of the Chinese Army moved across the Kashgar border into the south into Pakistan. The Chinese government made it clear to Pakistan that if its security forces could not provide protection to the Chinese staff, then they would take up security of the Chinese in their own hands.

India was the first to react. They strongly objected to the presence of the Chinese troops in Pakistan. They accused the ISI of being responsible for the murders of the Chinese, which gave an excuse to the Chinese forces to move in. They accused Pakistan of a premediated move so that the Chinese could be drawn into the conflict in case of increased hostilities between India and Pakistan. The Chinese were their insurance in case of a war with India.

Following the developments after the Moqor explosion, the Indian foreign office warned China not to interfere in the dispute between India and Pakistan, or to provide any assistance to Pakistan in case of war. It would be in China's best interest and safety to withdraw all Chinese personnel from Pakistan.

Samir knew both the Chinese foreign minister and the American secretary of state were on their way here, and would land in a couple of hours. These issues would be settled once they arrived. But would they be able to hold off on further escalation of tension till they arrived? Or would the jinn create further mischief by 'whispering evil' in the ears of the military commanders.

If a full-fledged nuclear war broke out between India and Pakistan, would this be the apocalypse for the millions of people in South Asia?

Mahdi

Khalifa was up in arms at Tora Bora. He knew the time had come and he would soon have to move his forces into Pakistan and bring the Pashtun land under his control before the Afghans moved in. He was aware that the Afghans had similar designs, and had also deployed their forces along the border. He wanted to beat them at their own game.

Khalifa knew the Afghan army was no match for the Pakistan army. However, since most of the Pakistan army was now on its eastern border with India, he figured Afghans had a window of opportunity to attack Pakistan and intrude inside their territory with least resistance. But he had an advantage over the Afghans: he had the jinn on their side which the Afghans did not.

He knew deep in his heart he was not in direct contact with the jinn, but somehow had a feeling that the jinn were reading his mind. It appeared everything was happening according to a certain scripted plan. He was sure Ifrit was making things happen: from the insurgency in Kashmir to the killing of Chinese engineers to the facing off of over a million Indian and Pakistani forces at their borders. He was sure the jinn had exploded the bomb at Moqor instead of at Bagram but he did not know why. He had lost many a good people, including Wazir, but other organizations had lost many more fighters and commanders. He was lucky because most of his people were at Tora Bora instead of Moqor.

But now, the time had come for them to move across the border into Pakistan. He had already claimed that he was in contact with the jinn. His following, and perhaps others too from their associates, including the Al-Qaeda and TTP, believed he was in full control of Ifrit. Nobody other than him knew he was not in direct contact with him. Maybe he could take advantage of this. If only he could communicate with the jinn directly without going through any intermediary, he could implement his own agenda of ruling the Islamic world. He could declare himself the Mahdi.

And why not, he thought! If he could communicate with the jinn, directly or indirectly, and make him fight his wars, he indeed deserved to be Mahdi. That is what the Hadith had said anyway: that Mahdi will communicate with the jinn. Maybe he was indeed the Mahdi!

Yes! He was the Mahdi!

It was time to proclaim this to the world!

He sent out a message that he would be addressing his followers again to make an important announcement to the Muslims of the world.

His message was loud and clear.

"I have just received a message from the jinn that the time has come for us to unite under the black flag. Ifrit, the powerful warrior jinn, has asked me to consolidate our forces, and has asked for all brother groups to merge into ISIS which he wants to command.

"The jinn has also addressed me as the Mahdi! The Hadith is very clear on the Mahdi: the jinn will communicate with the Mahdi and his loyal followers, and they will help Muslims prevail throughout the world.

"I accept with humility the title that the jinn has addressed me with, as it is Allah's will, and take pride in announcing that the Mahdi is among you now."

With that he fired a few shots in the air.

"I would also like to declare that our flag will now be the flag of our new kingdom, the Islamic Emirates of Khorasan, which will include all Pashtun territory in Afghanistan, Pakistan, and Iran. Your Mahdi will rule the emirates, and the forces of the emirates will be under the warrior command of Ifrit, who will set out to dominate Muslim land first from Indus to the Levant, and from Arabia all the way to the Maghreb. Our emirates will be far larger than the caliphates under the Umayyad or the Abbasid.

"We will revive the glory of Islam around the world one more time under the black flag. The jinn has declared me to be the Mahdi which completes the last of the ten minor signs. We will now accomplish what God has destined us to do: declare jihad across the Muslim world.

"We will conquer Jerusalem and Istanbul, and I will impose real Islam under my caliphate. The Hadith prophesizes that Prophet Jesus will then descend from the heaven and lead us to conquer the rest of the world from India to America. Together, we will kill the Dajjal and the Beast. Allah will lead us to victory, and the whole world will be under our feet. There will be only one flag of Islam around the world!"

Khalifa then looked up to the sky as if he was addressing the jinn, "Oh, Ifrit! Oh, great one! I accept the title of Mahdi which you have conveyed to me. You know more than what we on earth know, since you can venture out to the stars and listen where our fortunes are made, and where the future is decided. You know what we know not!

"It is in the saying of our Prophet that you will communicate with the Mahdi, and you have indeed chosen to do so with me. I accept this title given by Allah to lead the Muslim world into victory, and you will help us as our commander so Muslims can prevail throughout the world.

"In accordance with the Hadith, I have declared today the Islamic Emirates of Khorasan, to include all Pashtun territory in Afghanistan, Pakistan, and Iran. Once we unite all Pashtun under the flag of the emirates, we will set out to conquer the rest of the Muslim world from the Indus to the Maghreb."

He turned to address the Chinese next, "Oh, the Gog and Magog people. You have been cursed from the time of Prophet Zul-Qarnain, who had built the Great Wall around you to keep your mischief in, but it appears you have not learnt your lessons and have again broken through it. These are the signs of the end of times as narrated in the Quran. However, if you believe you will conquer our lands, then you are greatly mistaken. We will teach you a lesson you will never forget.

"We will instead liberate the Muslim Uyghur from their occupiers, and together we will create the largest empire since the Mongols!"

Khalifa fired a barrage of shots in the air, while his followers raised slogans of 'Allah-o-Akbar' and filled the air with additional gunfire.

The noise was deafening.

He raised his hand asking the crowd to be silent, then declared, "Today, we will move east in Pakistan. No one will be able to stop us as we will be led by Ifrit. I call upon all Pashtun and other Muslims to join us. Together, we will defeat the Gog Magog, the Jews, the Christians, and the Hindus. Islam will now rule the world under your Mahdi."

There was more ceremonial firing in the air.

False Leader

Samir remembered Pir Wasim was well-rehearsed in the Hadith, He called him up to get his views on the self-proclaimed Mahdi.

"Did you hear the Khalifa of ISIS has claimed to be Mahdi, the promised leader of the Muslims who will rule the world?"

"He is a lunatic! Many like him have claimed to be Mahdi in history, more than two dozen so far! The Quran mentions nothing about a Mahdi leading the Muslim world before the end of times. It is only mentioned in the Hadith that a Mahdi will appear to lead the Muslims to victory, which would be followed by Prophet Jesus who will descend to earth at Damascus."

"I have heard that many times before. Did we also not have someone claiming himself to be the Mahdi not too long ago in Saudi Arabia?"

"Certain fanatics took over the Grand Mosque in Mecca led by a man claiming to be Mahdi. They were all killed but only after a few hundred lives were lost."

Samir had read about the Mahdi, but wanted to know if Wasim had some additional information that could prove the man was a fraud, "How can we prove this man is a fake?"

"First of all, if we were to believe in the particular Hadith, then we all know that Mahdi's real name will be Muhammad who will be born in a Quraish tribe. His father's name will be Abdullah. He will be born in Medina and will come to Mecca to perform Haj at the time of a major war. At Mecca, he will be chosen as a leader by the people themselves to lead them to victory," reaffirmed Wasim.

"Are not we already in the middle of so many wars in the Middle East, and we don't even know what this man's real name is or where he was born? How can we prove he is not Mahdi? Hasn't he also been chosen by his people to lead them?"

Wasim disagreed, "The declaration of Mahdi will be in Mecca, and by the people themselves, and not by a self-claimed leader."

Samir wanted to be sure of the information that he had read about the Mahdi, "They say Mahdi will be joined by Muslim forces from the East, from Khorasan, bearing black flags, who will announce that they are joining him for jihad. They will conquer Jerusalem, and Islam will rule the world. Isn't that what Khalifa is projecting himself to be, a self-proclaimed leader of the Muslim world under the black flag?"

"They are only capitalizing on what is in the Hadith!"

"What about the Gog and Magog, who are mentioned in the Quran as the mischievous people? He claims they are the Chinese and wants to teach them a lesson!"

"You can fool some of the people all the time but you cannot fool all the people all the time! We are not even sure who Gog and Magog are in these times.

Some believe they will be from the east, from the Levant or even from Khorasan, and will come to destroy Israel. Others identify them to be Chinese since China has emerged as an economic superpower! Yet, many hard-core fundamentalists identify them to be the Jews. It is wrong to label anyone as Gog and Magog.

"What about the Dajjal?"

"Likewise, there have been many Dajjals in history. During the Yom Kippur war, many thought it was the Israeli Defense Minister Moshe Dayan, since the Hadith mentions him as one-eyed."

Samir was glad that Wasim had confirmed what he already knew. But the real issue here was about the jinn, whom Khalifa was claiming to control. While Wasim was the Hadith expert, it was Shams who was the Quranic expert in the matters of the jinn. If Samir could only get hold of Shams.

It did not take long for Samir to get hold of Shams on phone.

"I was just thinking of calling you after I heard that someone is claiming to be Mahdi after a jinn has addressed him as such!

"Let me be explicit here and tell you that no jinn has the authority or power to declare anyone to be a Mahdi or whosoever! We are not even sure there will be a Mahdi!"

Samir heaved a sigh of relief, "What about him declaring that he is communicating with the jinn?"

"Jinn have been in communication with men over the ages since the times of Babylon. They have taught them black magic. They have uttered evil in their ears. They have led all evil on this earth. There is no denying that it is not happening now!"

"What about Ifrit? Will he lead the command of the terrorists, like this so-called Mahdi is claiming, and will set out to conquer the Muslim world?"

"Ifrit is a very ambitious and strong jinn. He was the commander of jinn in Solomon's army. Like all jinn are, Ifrit is evil and can do anything to harm mankind, whom they hold responsible for being thrown out of Allah's court."

"That is scary! So, what you are saying is that even if the man is not Mahdi, and is faking it, Ifrit could be communicating with him and influencing events to lead to wars and destroy mankind?"

"Yes! Very much possible and much more. Jinn do the evil whispering in our ears!"

Samir heaved a deep breath and let out whatever had accumulated in his mind in one go, "Could Ifrit be leading Khalifa and all other militants, including TTP, Al-Qaeda, and ISIS, to attack Pakistan? Could Ifrit be responsible in instigating the Afghans to attack Pakistan? Could Ifrit be responsible for the killings of Chinese in Pakistan, and thereafter making the Chinese forces move in? Could Ifrit be responsible for the insurgency in Kashmir? Could Ifrit be responsible for the military standoff between India and Pakistan? Could Ifrit lead Pakistan and India into a nuclear war?"

"Yes!"

Samir's knees buckled. He could not stand and collapsed onto a chair. Shams felt the silence and could sense the stress coming from the other end of the line.

"There is a silver lining though! Like all jinn, Ifrit is no one's friend and cannot be trusted. All jinn are made of fire and are short-tempered. One cannot force them to do anything if it is against their will, or if they don't like something they hear!"

"What do you mean?"

"Khalifa claims it was Ifrit who declared him to be the Mahdi! Khalifa is lying, as a jinn can certainly whisper evil and can destroy, but they cannot scheme or plan. They have no brain or intelligence. They can't think for themselves. They are strong and are just a workhorse. In this case, Khalifa has misquoted Ifrit for his ulterior motives. A jinn will never forgive him for that!"

"You mean Ifrit may not carry out his orders because he lied?"

"Most likely will not! Jinn have been known to kill their benefactors. I would suspect this to be the case now! Khalifa has invited the wrath of Ifrit who is already loose on earth!"

"What about the other thousands of jinn who already inhabitate our earth?"

"They have always been around before man was created. They do cause mischief and do evil, but are in no way as evil and powerful as Ifrit. No doubt all other jinn will assemble under Ifrit, as they have found a leader after millions of years, but it is mainly Ifrit we need to worry about! With no leadership, the other jinn are all lost and astray."

"What about Iblis? Would he not want to take charge?"

"Iblis is the king. He would certainly watch but not get involved directly. He would be certain the jinn will win, and at the end, he will reward those who fought well and punish those who were scared!"

Samir heaved a sigh of relief, "So, what can we do to contain Ifrit?"

"Same advice that I gave you last time. Recite the sacred verses that can control and contain the jinn, but with much more intensity as we are dealing with much more evil. We need collective prayers this time!"

Samir recalled reciting these verses on the mountaintop with Hameed and the captain, while doing the chilla in reverse. He still did not know, and was not sure, if it was indeed their prayers that had thwarted the big nuclear attack on Bagram or a city in Kashmir, Pakistan or India, or instead it was Ifrit who had done exactly what Shams was conveying: double-crossing one's own benefactors and exploding the bomb on them. No one knew, and certainly no one could trust the jinn.

He had one last request of Shams, "Can you arrange for collective praying of the verses so that Ifrit is controlled?"

"If it is a nuclear war we are trying to prevent, or an apocalypse, then we need a lot of good men to do so. We have very little time, but I will try to arrange it at the earliest at my madrassah and at other places I know.

"You may also want to talk to Pir Wasim as well who has a large network of followers who are into reading the anti-jinn verses and do many other antidotes as per Hadith."

Samir was determined, "Certainly will do so right away!"

Samir got on the phone with Wasim again. This time Wasim had conjured up his own solution on tackling the jinn.

"If Ifrit is back on earth, we need to take advantage of this opportunity and contact him and try to control him instead of the khalifa doing so. If we can make the jinn listen and work for us, think of the endless possibilities!"

"You mean opening a dialogue with him?" asked Samir.

"Yes! Don't we as men have the intelligence and the art of diplomacy? If we can control him, we can start by telling the jinn to kill Khalifa first. Likewise, we can fool him to get rid of all the other terrorist leaders around the world!"

Wasim was being very blunt and far-fetched, "We can then ask him to put an end to all wars taking place on earth by putting pressure on their leaders to do so, failing which we will have the jinn remove them. We can ask the jinn to remove every nuclear weapon and missile from the inventory of both the developed nations and the rogue countries and have them dropped to a distant planet or star."

"Jinn are evil! Why would they side with good to destroy evil?" asked Samir.

"Elementary, my dear Watson. It will not be difficult to convince the jinn as they don't have a brain or intelligence, while we do!"

Wasim's eyes shone, "Jinn made the Pyramids and the Temple of Solomon. Who knows what other structures they have made on earth working for men, such as the Gardens of Babylon and the Inca temples? Perhaps even the Taj Mahal. We can have jinn make new cities in no time so all the refugees of the world can find a place to live in which they can call home. We can ask the jinn to solve the energy crisis by creating electric power. With the excessive and cheap energy, we can desalinate sea water and warm up greenhouses in cold countries. There will be no more food shortages. On the contrary, we can grow an abundance of food, making prices fall further and within the reach of the poor."

Samir thought Wasim was crazy but he let him go on.

"It will be the reverse of the jinn war that took place millions of years ago, when the angels fought the jinn. This time, the humans will befriend the jinn and make them work for us. Allah will really be happy with us that we have well utilized the intelligence and the wisdom He gave us. This time we will be utilizing their energies for a better cause…"

Samir cut him short, "These are all fancy ideas, and I do hope you make them work! Right now, we have a crisis, which you may have heard of. We have the Afghan army assembled on our western border, ready to attack from our rear once the Indians attack us. Our armies, both India and Pakistan, are fully deployed and are facing each other. ISIS leader Khalifa in Afghanistan is claiming he is the Mahdi, and that the jinn are working for him. He is all set to move his forces into Pakistan and create a new caliphate. All these are probably Ifrit's doing. We need to stop Ifrit in his tracks!

"Shams suggested that we recite the sacred verses that can control and contain the jinn, but collectively and with much more intensity and vigor."

Wasim agreed, "I agree that we need collective power. This is the best way one can control the jinn, whether one wants to defeat him or stop him in his tracks, or to make him work for you!"

"Can you arrange as many men as possible to start the collective prayers at the mosques and madrassahs wherever possible? We need to reverse the spell so that Khalifa is stopped in his tracks."

"I will do that right away. But from what I have been hearing and following, Khalifa is claiming to be Mahdi because he is saying the jinn told him so. That is a big lie. He should not underestimate the vengeance of the jinn if he is turned off. The whole plan could backfire on him, and Ifrit may just go back and kill Khalifa. We just need to tell Ifrit he is being used by Khalifa!"

Samir agreed, "Shams was saying something similar. You do what you think will work that can stop him. For me, Khalifa is only the tip of the iceberg. The jinn could start a nuclear war between India and Pakistan. We need to stop that!"

"Let me try my own approach to contact and convince Ifrit that Khalifa has misused him, and not to listen to him. In the meantime, I will reach out to my people as well to start collecting at madrassahs and mosques to read the prayers."

Samir called up Latif next and ask him to spread the word around in Islamabad that collective prayers are needed to control Ifrit. Latif said he will talk to the caretaker of Bari Imam to have as many worshippers start reading the verses right away. He said he would also be calling up the caretakers of the other shrines whom he knows personally, including Data Ganj in Lahore, Shams Tabrizi in Multan and Lal Shahbaz Qalandar in Sehwan, to start the recitations as well.

Samir heaved a sigh of relief. He wondered if he really believed in the good men versus evil jinn war. Only a few days back just before the Charsadda attack, he never believed in all these shenanigans, dreams, black magic and jinn, and today, he had become a believer that there were certainly evil powers, but the power of prayers can defeat them all.

Prayers

The whole country was by now aware of the developments that had taken place since the Moqor explosion. All radio and TV stations and social media were broadcasting minute to minute developments and commentaries. The declaration of the Mahdi, the advancing of ISIS forces towards Pakistan to create a new caliphate, the deployment of Afghan forces on the Pakistan border, the confrontation between the Indian and Pakistan armies, which could lead to a nuclear standoff, and above all, if true, the arrival of Ifrit on earth and his mobilization of the army of jinn to attack mankind and destroy them, were enough to create a panic across the country.

It had become a national emergency where everyone had forgotten their differences. Collective prayers had started at many madrassahs, mosques, and shrines all over the country. People were reading the verses that would bring peace to the region and neutralize the influence of jinn.

Unaware of all these developments taking place across Pakistan's mosques, shrines, and madrassahs, Khalifa's men, about 500 of them, and armed to the teeth with sophisticated weaponry, including shoulder-launched missiles, were preparing to move out from the Tora Bora caves and head east towards Pakistan. Some of them were mounting the black flags onto their convoy of vehicles consisting of pick-up trucks as they would move their caravan across the border into Pakistan.

Khalifa was least worried about the small number of his forces, as he was sure many more would join his jihad along the way towards Pakistan. He was certain that with Ifrit on his side, thousands in the Pakistan army would revolt against their government and join him. Soon, the whole of northern region would welcome them as heroes and liberators. Within no time, the black flag would be unfurled in all government buildings in Peshawar and across all major cities of Pakistan in the north.

Soon, he would have his emirates and become its undisputed leader.

Wasim arrived at his parent's mausoleum outside Karachi carrying a small bag. As soon as he arrived, he let the word out to neighboring settlements that they will soon be starting collective prayers for Pakistan's welfare, including preventing the

India-Pakistan war, and people should join him in large numbers. Since he was well-known and respected as a pir, many started flocking to join him to pray.

He led the night prayers, and then prayed to God with his palms open asking for His blessings for all mankind.

He knew he had another mission to carry out tonight. It was a dark night, and he walked over to the back of the mausoleum with his bag, and placed it on a raised stone under a lighted lamp post. He opened the bag to take out a book which looked very old and fragile as if it would fall apart. The title in Persian was half faded, but he could read it. 'The Book of Knowledge', written by Imam Ghazali. The book was originally written a thousand years ago by the Imam who is considered one of the leading Muslim scholars. He flipped the pages softly so as not to damage them, and turned the pages to where the text described ways to communicate with the jinn and its appropriate verses.

There were about three pages of verses that had to be read out loud seven times after the night prayers. There were instructions following these verses on how to address the jinn, but it also said that if done incorrectly or left incomplete, the reader could annoy the jinn and be possessed by him or even killed. The reading had to be done inside a chilla for protection from the jinn while one faced Mecca.

He had never done it before, but one had to take the chance. The terrorists were using the jinn for their evil designs, and they had to be stopped even at the cost of his life. He etched a circle about 10 feet in diameter on the ground, and stood inside it facing west, which was the direction of Mecca. There was just enough light from the lamp post to read from the book.

He read the pages out, and as he read them each time, he could feel some invisible power, something evil getting closer to him, as if preventing him from reading further. After each reading, he started sweating and his legs started shaking more and more, but he did not stop. He knew he could not stop in the middle of calling out to the jinn, because if he did, the jinn would be annoyed and could harm him.

By the time he had read the relevant pages seven times, he felt as if an invisible evil and ghastly looking jinn was standing right outside the circle looking at him and wanting to attack and kill him. The chilla protected him, and he knew if he stepped out, he would be killed.

He mustered up just enough energy to address the jinn, "Oh, Ifrit! Man has betrayed you many times over in the past. You were promised to be crowned the leader and commander of Khalifa's advancing army, but Khalifa has cheated on you and has declared himself as the leader. He had also lied to others that you have declared him to be Mahdi. Khalifa is a liar, cheater, and opportunist! He has deprived you of your position.

"When we were first created thousands of years ago, your King Iblis had told the Creator that your race was superior to ours, and warned the Creator not to trust us, but instead he was thrown out of the heaven. Since then, he had ordered you not to trust men."

Wasim was short of breath, and thought he could not go on, and would collapse. He heard a growl coming from all around him, and realized he must continue, or be killed.

"You yourself have been double-crossed thousands of years ago by Solomon, another man, when you were expecting you would be allowed out of captivity and go to the land of Saba to bring the throne. You were not trusted and instead someone else was sent. Your people were then forced to make Solomon's temple till such time he died, and then all of you made your escape.

"It is now after thousands of years you have been called back by men to do what? Give you the crown? No! It is a lie. They just want you to serve them! They lie using your name! They want you to be their slave! Do you accept this role?"

Wasim paused talking to the jinn as if expecting an answer. There was none. Instead, the growling stopped. There was silence. He looked up to see if the jinn was still there. There was no one. Wasim was not sure whether he should continue addressing the jinn or stop, whether he had gotten his message across or not. He waited for a while, but there continued to be complete silence, except for the distant hum of the worshippers reciting the verses on the other side of the mausoleum.

He was not sure if he would be attacked by the jinn since he had stopped. He immediately read the verses from the Quran for protection from the jinn, and while reciting these verses, slowly stepped out of the chilla.

Nothing happened. No one attacked him. He was safe!

The jinn had already gone. He wasn't even sure whether his plan to convince the jinn to dump Khalifa had worked or not. Only time would tell.

He put the book back in his bag and walked around the mausoleum back to joining his followers reciting the verses.

Samir made one more call, this time to Najumi, who answered right after one ring as if he had been expecting the call.

"I am glad you called yourself, as I was just going to call you with something good for you for a change."

"Najumi! How can it be good? We are in the pits. You know the country is going through the worst crisis in its 70-year-old history. We are being attacked by terrorists who claim they are controlling the jinn. Their leader claims to be the Mahdi who is declaring the end of times is near. The Chinese are being killed in Pakistan by terrorists. The world wants to put sanctions on us while denuclearizing us at the same time. We have the Afghan forces on our border, and on top of that we are on the verge of a nuclear war with India. How can things be good?"

"What I have seen is not bad!"

"I hope what you are saying is true! You were right before about Islamabad, and we were able to thwart off the destruction by locating the evil with your help. You were also right about the terrorists using the jinn and about the destruction at Moqor. Who could have thought of that?

"You know we have another mega crisis at hand. Shams and Wasim have advised us to do collective praying and recite anti-jinn verses, which we are already doing at the mosques, madrassahs, and shrines. Now, what else do you see regarding the crisis and what can we do to come out of it?"

"Somehow, I always see death and destruction. I see it again this time near the Afghanistan Pakistan border in the north!"

"But how can that be good? Isn't it the same destruction you saw last time? Are we talking about yet another explosion in Afghanistan? Do you mean Khalifa will be able to get hold of another nuclear bomb through the jinn like they did before, and use it on us? Or would it explode again in their hideout?"

Najumi let Samir finish his assumptions before continuing, "I see a big aura of negative energy emancipating from some mountainous terrain between Pakistan and Afghanistan. I also see a bird flying and dropping a big pellet on it, much like what is mentioned in the Quran when the birds dropped pellets on an army from Yemen wanting to invade Mecca and destroy it. The pellets killed them all. I see similarity when the invaders will be killed in a similar fashion. I see a huge explosion, lots of dust and smoke and then the negative aura disappearing! When the dust finally clears, I see death all over!"

"How can the negative aura disappear followed by death? Doesn't negativity disappearing lead to something positive?"

"Whatever bad is emancipating from those mountains will be destroyed by something, maybe a huge pellet, dropping out of the sky! I consulted a number of charts and they all point to the same incident."

Samir shook his head, "These can only be the terrorists who are hiding in the mountains in Tora Bora between Afghanistan and Pakistan. In the past, they could not be weeded out by the Soviets and neither by the Americans despite heavy bombing by their planes. Osama was able to successfully hide for years in these treacherous mountains. Any number of bombs falling from the sky makes no difference to them, unless we throw a nuclear bomb, which is perhaps your huge pellet, but that is out of question!"

"The prophecy cannot be wrong!"

Samir hoped he was right. Only a miracle could stop ISIS forces and the jinn to not cross into Pakistan.

Tora Bora

US Captain John and his co-pilot Second Lieutenant Tom were on a routine flight in their Hercules C-130 from the Bagram Air Base. The C-130 is the work horse of the air force. It was originally designed as a troop and cargo transport aircraft, but can also be used as a gunship, for airborne assault, search and rescue, and for aerial firefighting among others. One of its big advantage is that it can land and take off from non-conventional runaways.

John would normally fly reconnaissance flights over south eastern Afghanistan. It was considered the hotbed of terrorist activities, but he would fly high enough to be out of the range of their rockets. There would normally be regular drone flights in this area. Intelligence information conveyed the area was buzzing with a large number of militants and vehicles. He had been informed that ISIS had moved in large numbers to this area, but that was none of his concern or assignment, as they had never been fired upon during any of their flights in this area. His job was to make sure the payload he was carrying was always in functioning order.

The payload was one of the largest bombs ever made for the US military. Commonly known as the 'Mother of All Bombs', abbreviated MOAB, it was the most powerful non-nuclear weapon available with the military. The bomb, which is around 30 feet long and 40 inches in diameter, weighs around 21,000 pounds. It is loaded onto the plane on cradles and is dropped onto the target by parachutes, thereafter a GPS satellite-guidance takes over to guide the bomb to its target. The MOAB is made to explode in air just above the intended target and destroy an extended area in rough and impossible to reach terrains like a deep canyon or within a cave. Its blast is roughly equal to 11 tons of TNT affecting a radius of around 500 to 1,000 feet radius depending on the terrain it is dropped onto. Earlier this year, they had already tested the MOAB against terrorists in the same mountain ranges.

John was all fine before he took off from his flight but as he circled the base to head south, he started to feel a little dizzy. It couldn't have been the mocktails he had at the bar the night before, as he only had a couple of drinks. Last night, everyone at the bar was celebrating how they have lived to yet another day, after they heard that the nuclear bomb that was meant for Bagram actually exploded at Moqor. No one really knew why or how it happened, but it had put them all on high alert.

They knew the Afghan forces had been mobilized and had assembled at the Pakistan border. The ISIS terrorists were threatening to move into Pakistan as well, and their leader was talking about being some Mahdi and having some jinn under his control. He reminded himself to read up on these items when he returned to base.

The weather was clear and visibility was around 50 miles. He had been asked to stay away from the Moqor area as there could still be some radioactivity in the area.

As he started turning around, he felt something lugging at his controls wanting him to go into a particular direction. He checked his controls, and found all systems functioning well. The plane was on a steady straight course back to Bagram, yet he felt it was turning and swaying to the right. It was years of his training and flying the C-130 that his sixth sense told him something was not right.

"Is something wrong?" Tom asked him as he realized John was struggling with the controls.

"Nothing really!" he replied, "We are straight on course to Bagram and should arrive in 20 minutes."

The plane continued to sway and turn right, and visually, it was clear it was making a sharp turn heading towards the Pakistan border in the east. Tom noticed that, and gripped the control tight turning it slightly to the left. The plane continued turning right.

"Sir! There is something wrong with the instruments. It is telling us we are on course to Bagram, yet we have turned right and are flying over some mountainous territory. Should we ask base to verify our position and trajectory?"

"Yes, please do. Something is not right. We seem to be losing height too, yet it is not showing on the altimeter. There is certainly something wrong with the systems."

Tom got on the wireless and was immediately in touch with the air controller there.

"Could you confirm our trajectory?"

"You are heading towards the Tora Bora mountain region. You should immediately return back as you may steer into Pakistani territory."

John took over the mic, "All our navigation systems are telling us we are headed towards the base. Yet, we are turning right and you are also confirming the same. We are also losing height fast! I cannot even steer it left!"

"I will send out a distress call to our fighters in the area. We will also immediately inform the Pakistan air headquarters that due to a navigation error, one of our planes has steered off course and will turn around and return back. Please stay on line."

The plane was now flying dangerously low, around 5,000 feet above the mountain tops. Tora Bora region was among the most 'impregnable cave fortress' which was developed as a CIA-financed complex built for the Mujahedin. The complex had ammunition storage rooms, ventilation system, and roads wide enough to drive a truck. There were intelligence reports that the labyrinths of caves currently housed 500–600 ISIS fighters.

John again reverted back to the base, "We are losing height fast, and could just be a few thousand feet above the mountain tops, yet the instruments are saying we are at cruising altitude…"

As the plane swooped low over the mountain tops, John felt the ramp was opening by itself. The control showed the ramp to be secure and closed. It was obvious that none of the electronics were working. A stream of fresh air hit the cockpit as the plane swayed in the high wind pressure. John double-checked the controls but all showed normal conditions.

"Oh my God! What is going on? There is definitely something wrong happening here. The instruments are showing the ramp is closed, yet it seems to have opened up by itself…"

"May Day! May Day!" screamed Tom at the controls.

Suddenly, the plane felt light as it immediately started gaining altitude. The MOAB had unlatched by itself from the plane, rolled on the cradles towards the open ramp, and was now freely falling towards the Tora Bora caves!

John panicked! "That cannot be possible!" he uttered impulsively into the microphone.

He knew an explosion was perhaps imminent, and immediately pulled back the throttle for maximum altitude, also turning north-west towards Bagram, and suddenly, the instruments started working. As the plane tilted sideways turning left, they could see a huge ball of fire rising from among the mountains. The sound of the blast came about 10 seconds later, convulsing the plane from left to right. They could see a huge cloud of dust had started building up at the site of the explosion.

"Oh my God! What happened? We did not drop the bomb. How could it fall by itself?" John impulsively questioned himself and was clearly nervous. He prayed there was no civilian population down there. He could see himself facing an enquiry, and perhaps a sentence and a dishonorable discharge from service if they were held responsible for any civilian deaths.

John immediately got onto the microphone and passed out the message, "The payload has somehow dropped by itself onto a location few miles south of where we currently are. We had no control over the flight and the way the bomb dropped by itself, as if it was remotely controlled by some external force, or by magic! A huge ball of fire is visible which has now given way to a large cloud of dust. We do not know where the bomb has fallen. Our systems are somehow functioning again automatically, and we are immediately returning to base."

John knew he would have a lot of explaining to do, but he just hoped most of the activity would have been recorded by the black box on board which would clear them of the charge as there would certainly be an enquiry why and how the bomb was dropped.

The plane flew back into Bagram.

The Pakistan Army post at Parachinar border was fully prepared and expecting ISIS fighters to attack them. Instead, they were the first to hear a loud explosion. The exact location of the explosion could not be determined. They immediately communicated the information to army headquarters. It was another ten minutes when headquarters informed them that an explosion had taken place at the Tora Bora caves, and that they were still trying to get additional information from both their American and Chinese counterparts.

It took an hour for the CENTCOM to communicate to both Pakistan and Afghanistan that an American C-130, which had taken off from Bagram, had dropped a MOAB on the ISIS terrorists who were responsible for the Moqor incident and were moving towards Pakistan in large numbers to attack them. The CENTCOM claimed miles of caves had collapsed due to the bombing, causing death of hundreds of ISIS fighters, including many of their top commanders. They were presently trying to confirm if the ISIS leader Khalifa, the man claiming to be 'The Mahdi' and prophesized to be the leader of the Islamic world, was also among those who had died. They added in their communication that none of the Muslim world leaders had accepted him as Mahdi. They said it would be another hour or two before they may be able to get a close-up view and footage through their drones to be able to confirm the severity of the destruction caused by the American bombing.

The Americans had cleverly and politically taken a position to make themselves look good in the international community. Instead of admitting their error, they took the credit for bombing ISIS in Tora Bora, and getting rid of the fake Mahdi for the Muslim world. This would also remove the doubts of the Pakistan intelligence community that ISIS was brought into Tora Bora by the Americans, or that Mahdi was their creation. Pentagon immediately gave a news briefing of the bombing to major TV channels showing charts where they had dropped the MOAB.

Many leaders from the Muslim world immediately welcomed the bombing in which the self-claimed Mahdi had died.

Samir heard the flashing news as he was heading towards the prime minister's office. He could not believe what he had heard. Najumi was correct in his predictions again! The death of evil! He reminded himself to call him up later and thank him as he had other urgent matters to take care of first.

He remembered what Wasim had told him: that Khalifa should not underestimate the vengeance of the jinn if he is turned off. He had said that the whole plan of Khalifa could backfire if Ifrit found out that he was being used by Khalifa, in which case Ifrit would just go back and kill Khalifa. Wasim had said he would try communicating with Ifrit and let him know how his name was being misused. Perhaps Wasim was successful in communicating with the jinn and convincing him to dump Khalifa! Maybe that is why the jinn killed Khalifa through the American bombing. He had no way of knowing and would check on that later as well.

Right now, he was more worried about the Indian and Pakistani forces facing each other. If Ifrit could influence events in that battlefield, which he was certainly trying to do, it would lead to a nuclear war! No diplomacy would work in this case.

He looked at his watch. The US secretary of state would soon be meeting the prime minister in about 30 minutes. He would need to brief her immediately on the recent bombing at Tora Bora and why it happened and how. She would need these discussion points with the secretary to have an upper-hand in her diplomatic talks, which clearly the army chief may not be able to brief her on.

He called her secretary with an urgent message that he needed to speak to her before the secretary of state saw her.

She could carry out her diplomatic initiatives, but he had to find a spiritual solution to the Ifrit crisis!

Secretary of State

Samir got about ten minutes of talk on the phone with the prime minister before the US secretary of state's meeting. He quickly gave her the run down on the Tora Bora incident, and the strong possibility of the jinn being vengeful and responsible for the incident. The good news was that the fake 'Mahdi' was also killed in the explosion, otherwise he would have created major problems among the millions of illiterate Muslim population who were waiting for the Mahdi to appear and bring them salvation.

She was doubtful, "Samir, even I am not convinced when you keep blaming everything on this supernatural thing called the jinn which no one has seen, and which the rest of the world does not even believe in. Even many Muslims believe in the jinn with a pinch of salt. And now this Mahdi thing is another dimension which I am glad is over before it reached our land. The secretary would think I am crazy when I try explaining the jinn. Anyway, I may give it a wild shot if he is listening since our only other option is sanctions or war!

"I will give you an update after I meet him."

With that she hung the phone.

The US Secretary of State Robert Forster arrived on time for the meeting, and got straight to the point. "Madam Prime Minister. The Security Council is meeting tomorrow morning. I am sure you know all the permanent members will be voting in favor of the Afghanistan resolution putting sanctions on Pakistan unless it denuclearizes itself under the observation of international inspectors."

The prime minister was neither surprised nor shaken, "Mr. Secretary. We have already explained our position to you and others on the accident at Moqor. How it happened is something you would not understand. However, at least the positive outcome was that it eliminated many of the terrorists operating out of Afghanistan that were hurting both our countries."

He shook his head, "I sympathize with you but who would believe that some flying genie stole the bomb and exploded it in Afghanistan!"

She decided to take her chance at the gamble, looked at the secretary straight in the eye to catch his reaction at the bombshell she dropped next, "The US has just exploded a huge bomb at Tora Bora and are claiming they have done us and the Muslim world a big favor by taking out the ISIS terrorists, including their self-claimed fake 'Mahdi', that were on their way to attack Pakistan. I am sure the US government is itself trying to figure out how it happened as we know Pentagon did not order that attack or the bomb to be dropped on them!"

The secretary was taken off-guard. His jaw dropped and he did not know how to respond right away.

She continued without giving him a chance to recover from the shock, "We have every reason to believe that both the incidents of Moqor and Tora Bora were identical. What caused the accident at Moqor was exactly the same reason which caused the accident at Tora Bora. If Pakistan was responsible for the nuclear explosion at Moqor, then US is responsible for the MOAB dropping at Tora Bora.

"We both know that in both cases, it was out of our hands as it was the jinn who did that!"

She paused for a moment to let that sink, and then continued, "The jinn are a reality in all Abrahamic religions. The Old Testament mentions of creatures whose appearance is like that of fire. Our sacred book, the Quran, also mentions the jinn."

The secretary tried to digest this information, debating in his mind whether to accept or deny the similarity between the explosions. He finally struggled with words to speak, "I am not at liberty to disclose what I am about to disclose, but looking at the severity of the crisis, where we have the possibility of a nuclear war erupting within a few hours, let me tell you that there is certainly some classified work going on funded by DARPA exploring the possibility of supernatural entities like the jinn.

"Regarding the Tora Bora incident, the information we currently have is still very hazy and confusing. We are investigating the cause of the bombing, and technical data available so far, including from the black box. What we have figured out so far, which is still not conclusive, is that there was, indeed, something strange that happened which caused the bomb to drop and explode. I cannot officially confirm, but what you are saying could possibly be right!"

He thought for a moment what his next words should be and then let it out slowly, "It is possible, or even quite likely, that something remote, or even something magic, as the pilots themselves called it, caused the C-130 to fly over the Tora Bora region and drop the bomb. The pilots, who are both very experienced and seasoned with thousands of hours of flying and combat hours, are still in a state of shock. There will be a detailed investigation and enquiry, which will take some time, but we have heard the recordings of the conversations of the two pilots, and checked the data on the black box. It only leads to confirm what you are saying. But that cannot be our official position."

"So, privately, you do admit the possibility of some supernatural forces at play here?"

"Certainly, suspecting that it is a remote possibility till we have more information to confirm that. However, how can we even present this hypothetical or fictional case of jinn, or whatever you call it, to members of the Security Council, or even to the leaders of other countries to vindicate your position?"

The prime minister was stern in what she wanted, "We would want you to veto the Security Council resolution!"

"We can certainly consider moving in that direction after the unexplained Tora Bora incident, but it is a long shot that others will believe your case. I will talk to the president that we can delay voting on the resolution, pending further enquiry into the Moqor incident, much to the annoyance of India and Afghanistan, but you also need to talk to the Chinese foreign minister as well, who I understand is on his way here, and take him on board. In the meantime, I need you to commit to us that you would hold back on the Nasr. Deploying the Nasr is no solution to the India Pakistan crisis. It has to be resolved diplomatically!"

She thought for a moment and reluctantly agreed, but was concerned about India, "India also needs to understand that all issues can be settled amicably and diplomatically. They have no reason to deploy their troops across our border. We have neither threatened them nor there has been an aggression or violation of ceasefire across our line of control.

"We all know India has a much larger army. We do not wish to be taken at a disadvantage if attacked when we have weapons that we can defend with. If India attacks first and intrudes into our territory, I will not be able to prevent our generals for using Nasr for our defense!"

"I will talk to the Indian prime minister to hold on to their forces as soon as I arrive there in around two hours."

Secretary Forster looked at his watch, "I had better be going. The Indian government is steaming mad right now. We need to extinguish their tempers right away!"

With that, he left for the airport to go to Delhi.

War

The US secretary of state had hardly taken off from Islamabad airport when the first shots were fired from the Indian side at Wagah border in Lahore. The Pakistan forces were quick to retaliate, and an exchange of artillery firing erupted.

The firing quickly expanded to the Bahawalpur sector, and dozens of tanks from both sides soon started rolling in preparedness for a full-blown war on the ten thousand square miles of Cholistan desert. This could be the largest tank war ever since World War II.

The prime minister called up Samir to update him on her discussions with the secretary.

"There is some hope the talks may succeed," she was optimistic.

Samir shook his head, "It is already failing. Our tanks are already facing each other in battle ready formation, and I am convinced the jinn will ensure the shots fired are escalated even before the US secretary lands in India!

"The jinn are out to take revenge, and wants mankind to destroy itself so they can rule earth again. Ifrit may have mobilized all the other jinn on earth as well to join his army!"

Samir continued, "The jinn, Ifrit, is responsible for the stand-off between India and Pakistan, and will not back off. He has the power of what we call 'evil whisperings', and can induce evil thoughts and actions in our commanders leading them to war. He is already working on his agenda, and it is possible he would succeed in starting the war between India and Pakistan even before there is any headway in talks. He can, and most probably will, induce the Pakistan army chief to fire the nuclear tipped missile Nasr at them. He can have both India and Pakistan destroy each other ten times over with nuclear weapons!"

"Why did the jinn drop the bomb at Tora Bora? He should have preferred the war!" the prime minister was confused.

"The khalifa from ISIS Afghanistan, who was the one who had the jinn contacted, declared he was the Mahdi, because he falsely claimed the 'jinn' told him so. This lie was enough to turn off the jinn and kill him for misusing his name. The jinn can't think much beyond that."

Samir continued, "According to Islamic eschatology, Mahdi will lead the Islamic forces from Khorasan, which is in Afghanistan, and conquer the Muslim world…Afghanistan, Pakistan, Iran, moving east to Iraq, Syria, Jordan, Israel, and Turkey. He will conquer both Jerusalem and Istanbul, then move towards Saudi Arabia and conquer Mecca and Medina. It is prophesized that Mahdi will then rule the world for seven years till Jesus takes over from him.

"Khalifa thought he could become the Mahdi by using the power of jinn! His first step was to have India and Pakistan destroy each other first using the power of the jinn so he could easily conquer and rule the sub-continent. Then he would have proceeded west.

"His plan back-fired!"

The prime minster was confused, "Samir, from what you are telling me, and you seem to be sure of that, is that all diplomatic efforts will fail unless we tackle the jinn first."

"Well, you are already deep down into it. Like you said, you do what you need to do to stop the jinn spiritually, and we will try to use our diplomatic channels in parallel. Maybe something will work out in unison."

"We will try to make the jinn go back to his universe! But there is a risk. Either he goes back if we succeed, or he destroys the whole world, not just India and Pakistan if we fail, and he is aggravated. The risk is apocalypse and an end of times!

"But we cannot give up at this stage. I firmly believe in my heart that good will win over evil!"

Samir wished the prime minister the best in her initiatives and hung up the phone.

Next, he called up Hameed. Hameed was always useful to give a better insight as Samir was very confused as to what his next move ought to be.

Hamed knew of the developments. "I have heard from my friends at the intelligence community and understand the jinn Ifrit, whom we tried to control, is now on the loose after Moqor, and now he is responsible for the bombing at Tora Bora."

The news does travel fast, thought Samir. "That is correct. The problem is even more severe now India and Pakistan are at the brink of a war! Most likely it is Ifrit and his evil whisperings."

Hameed agreed, "There can be no other explanation how events could have erupted so fast. It is just beyond human imagination and control. But the war will not just end here. I am sure the jinn will soon lead our two countries to fire nuclear weapons at each other's cities. This will be exactly what he wants: the beginning of the apocalypse and the end of times. Humanity will soon destroy itself and the jinn will take over the earth!"

"At least the fake Mahdi is dead…" added Samir.

"There will be many more Mahdi to take advantage of these events," interrupted Hameed, "all circumstances are pointing to what the Hadith says. There will be many more wars, perhaps all incited by the jinn, and they will lead to the end of times!"

"Are you prophesizing the end is near?" asked Samir.

"Allah Says in the Holy Quran Chapter 84 Al-Inshiqaq, The Rending Asunder, in Verses 1-5:

'When the sky is rent asunder
And hearkens to the command of its Lord, and it must needs do so
And when the earth is flattened out
And casts forth what is within it and becomes clean empty
And hearkens to the command of its Lord, and it must needs do so, then will come home the full reality of the Day of Resurrection'

"But this is a reference to doomsday, which is inevitable, and not a reference to the present times! How can we stop the jinn or send him back?"

"There are already many powerful and evil leaders today who are helping the jinn carry out his agenda to destroy humanity. We have a beast prime minister in the east and the Dajjal president in the west. They are his agents. They are leading us quickly to the end of times and doomsday!

"However, Islam does provide many solutions to all the evils of this world. Among them is repentance from our sins, asking for His forgiveness and praying to Him with sincerity. We have lost our ways and deviated from the good!"

Samir sighed, "All religions preach the same good. Both Indians and Pakistanis are probably praying to their gods right now. But this is the same old talk we keep hearing over and over again. Please give me a practical solution!"

"Shams and Wasim are currently your best bets. They are the jinn experts. You talk to them first. I am available with whatever you want me to do, but now the matter has gone much beyond my contacts in the north."

Samir told him he has already talked to Shams and Wasim, and they have arranged prayers across the country to control the jinn. Hameed said he knew that, as he had also asked students across all KP universities to join the collective prayers as well on their campus mosques.

"We should do another big chilla, perhaps a much larger one, or even multiple chillas. We should not leave any stone unturned at this stage. One of them is bound to overcome the jinn!"

Hamid continued, "I will give immediate instructions to start large chillas at each of our campuses. I will ask them to repeat what we did on the mountaintop. It is also dangerous, as the jinn, or their army of jinn, may feel threatened and attack them simultaneously, like they wanted to distract us as well…"

"Please don't jeopardize the security of our students…"

Hamid interrupted, "It is our collective responsibility to save mankind. We started this by keeping our eyes closed when we were being imposed with fundamentalist thought, and threatened by extremists and militants, and the result is we are seeing so much terrorism today, not only in Pakistan but in the whole region and around the world. We created the mess and we must clean it now!"

Samir couldn't believe this was coming from a man who was considered a die-hard religious fundamentalist. With intellectuals like Hameed joining their ranks, and fighting this war against all evil forces, be they terrorists or the jinn, there was hope for mankind after all.

Samir thanked him and asked him to start the chillas as soon as possible. Perhaps the prayers at the chillas will be able to send the jinn back to his universe.

He next called up the director military operations and found out that the situation at the battlefront in the meantime was getting worse. The Pakistan military commanders were quick to sense the war mood of the Indian army as tanks on both sides were mobilized in Cholistan. Orders were given to arm the Nasr and be battle ready to fire in case the Indian tanks move across the desert. Time was running out.

The Indians were already prepared for the arming of Nasr by Pakistan. They would not be taken for sitting ducks while Pakistan fired the nuclear tipped weapons at them. They ordered for the arming of their nuclear missiles.

Samir's phone logged in many missed calls while he was talking on the phone. There were a number of calls from Mike, his son, Hasan and Allama Malik. He called back Mike first as it might have something to do with the secretary of state's visit.

Mike told Samir he had discussed with the secretary of state the volatile situation before he had arrived in Islamabad. Mike was very concerned at the escalating crisis between India and Pakistan.

"Our intelligence has just told us that India is already arming their nuclear weapons as they know Pakistan is doing the same! Can you imagine what will happen if they face off their Prithvi and Agni missiles against your Shaheen and Ghauri? I also wish to share with you, which I am sure your intelligence knows by now, that they are mounting nuclear missiles on their submarines, putting all of 20 million people of Karachi and the port of Gwadar at risk."

"It is my plea to you to deescalate the crisis!"

"Mike. The prime minister has already assured the US secretary of state that if India holds back on attacking Pakistan, we will not be launching our Nasr. He is on board the plane to talk to the Indians now."

Mike was a good and sincere friend, but there was little he could do to resolve the issues at hand. Mike said he would call back as soon as he heard something new from the secretary of state or from Washington.

Samir called up Hasan next. Hasan would be a consolation in this crisis and he knew Hasan sometimes would throw some creative solution right off the right half of his brain.

"Dad. Its jinn versus men! Men have intelligence but their strength is no match with the jinn, even if you bring in all your whole army."

"So, are you proposing we lay down arms and give up?"

"No, Dad. It's the fight of evil versus good. Good always wins in the end. You have not even pitched our good against their evil!"

"There are men praying and reciting the verses at the mosques, shrine, and madrassahs."

"Praying is one thing. But where is the battle? Where are your warriors? Whom have you pitched against the jinn? You don't even have an army!"

"I don't get it! Men can't fight jinn, just like you said. Jinn are too powerful."

"The good can fight evil. Our best goods are the saints and the Sufis. The saints can fight evil but they need to be approached! God has ordained the saints to protect mankind from all evil. We are only surviving because of their good deeds and the protection their souls are according to us even after they are gone and are not in this world anymore.

"Remember how you told me Bari Imam warned you of the danger from the bomb that was to explode at your feet? That was because you approached him. Bari Imam is closer to God than you and I are. He communicated with God your problems, and God told him to protect you. I suggest you contact and request the saints to take their orders directly from God and fight the jinn!"

"What?" Samir couldn't figure out what Hasan was hinting at.

"Go to the shrines. Ask Allah's help, and get the attention of the saints. Ask them to fight the jinn and throw them back to where they came from! The saints can do that as they are as powerful as the jinn!"

"You are crazier than I am! I must have got my genes from you. How do you suggest I do that?"

"Let me give you a suggestion. There is not enough time to visit a lot of shrines, but go to the one where your roots come from." He was referring to Lal Shahbaz Qalandar, whom he claimed his great-great-grandfather was named after. "Lal Shahbaz Qalandar has among the highest order among many saints of this region. He is the savior saint of both Muslims and Hindus. He has spiritual strength, and can fight for both Pakistan and India. But you need to go to his shrine in person to seek his attention. Ask him to protect both his Muslim and Hindu followers. He will certainly do that if you ask of him from the bottom of your heart.

"Only when you are there in his presence will you get his attention and make him happy to win him over. But you need to go to Sehwan right away, join his devotees and do the dhamaal to get his attention. I am sure he will listen to you if you ask him for his help. He will honor that.

"I know he will listen to your wishes and desire but only if you go to his shrine and indulge in his ecstasy. Once he knows you have come all the way to pay respect to him and seek his help, I am sure he will fight the jinn for you and send him back to his universe!"

Samir was flabbergasted! Leave it to Hasan to give all sort of crazy and creative ideas.

Before he could comment, Samir's phone rang again while he was on the line with Hasan. It was Allama.

"I will call you back," he told Hasan and hung up.

Allama was quick with his advice, "I have been trying to reach you. The whole country is up in arms, I mean they are all praying to counter the jinn. It is a war of good versus evil. Men versus jinn. But we need much more than that! We need more power to fight the jinn."

"What do you mean by more power?"

"Men can't fight the jinn. We are too weak and materialistic! We are overrun by greed and are sinful ourselves. We need spiritual power. We need Sufi power!"

It appeared as if he was listening in to his conversation with Hasan, "We need our saints to fight the jinn. It is only through the saints that we connect not only to our inner self but to the Almighty as well. Only God can help us under the present circumstances. But reaching out to Him through the saints is faster and perhaps more effective. I believe this is the only solution!"

"I am surprised you brought it up as Hasan, my son, was just advising me the same. You two must be on the same wavelength or talking to each other. What do you suggest we do?"

It appeared as if there was a spiritual force leading the way.

"I am already at the shrine of Lal Shahbaz Qalandar. Come here and indulge in God! Seek His guidance."

"You must have read Hasan's mind. Isn't there already a lot of praying taking place at the shrines which is enough?"

"I am talking of indulging oneself personally to connect to the saint and through him to God! Connect yourself to Him through spiritual ecstasy induced by His remembrance while hearing the recitation of the Quranic verses. You will feel the difference then. God listens to those who go into a trance when they indulge in Him."

He was talking of going into a dhamaal at the shrine of Lal Shahbaz Qalandar, exactly what Hasan was proposing. Samir knew collective prayers had already started at many of the mosques, shrines, and madrassahs across the country. People in large numbers were reading the verses that would bring peace to the region and neutralize the influence of jinn. Would going to a Sufi shrine, doing the dhamaal in ecstasy, and praying to God at the same time make a difference and add value to one's praying and connect to God faster? Would the saint carry forth the wish to God? Would the saint fight the jinn and send him back to his universe?

One would never know, but there was no harm in trying what Allama and Hasan were proposing. Was there any other course left?

He decided to follow up on Allama's and Hasan's advice because there was no other option left. Beggars couldn't be choosers especially at this critical time.

Samir called up the prime minister's secretary and requested her official plane urgently so he could go to the Shrine of Lal Shahbaz Qalandar and join the devotees in praying before the night was over. The secretary could sense the urgency in Samir's voice and replied she would inform the prime minister and it would be done right away.

On his way to the airport, he called up Hasan and said he would pick him up from home in 20 minutes.

Hasan was pleased, "I am glad you are finally beginning to see the spiritual side of things. You will be surprised at its powers. All cannot be explained by science!"

Samir wondered what he was getting into. He was a nerd and scientist at heart but now following Sufism and the saints. Was he becoming crazy one more time like he once went to the graveyard to dig out a corpse to end black magic, or had done the chilla before to counter the jinn? Those remedies or antidotes had most probably worked, but he would never know that.

Did he have any other choice? Probably not at this time, as he knew by tomorrow, it would be too late!

He will take this chance one last time before tomorrow. If there would be a tomorrow!

Qalandar

Lal Shahbaz Qalandar was born in the year 1177 in Marwand, Iran, and died in 1275 at Sehwan at the age of 98. He lived around the same time as Jalaluddin Rumi, Shams Tabrizi, Bahauddin Zakria, Baba Fariduddin Ganjshakar, and Syed Jalaluddin Bukhari, all renowned Sufis.

His 'urs' or 3-day 'celebration' of his death anniversary, is held on the 18th of Shaaban, the eighth month of the Muslim lunar calendar. During the 3-day celebration, the city is packed with over a million devotees from all faiths who travel from all corners of Pakistan, India, Bangladesh, Afghanistan, Iran, and Nepal, making their way to the shrine to commune with the saint, offer tributes, ask for their wishes, pray to their God, sing and do the traditional ecstatic dance 'dhamaal' all day and night to the tune of the traditional Sindhi folk song 'Dama Dam Mast Qalandar'. The urs is popularly attended by celebrities and movie stars, politicians, students, fakirs, and people from all walks of like, most of them wearing the red or 'lal' attire that the saint wore all his life.

The shrine was built in 1356 and decorated with Sindhi 'kashi-tiles', mirror-work and a gold-plated door donated by the late Shah of Iran and installed by the former prime minister of Pakistan. The inner sanctum is about 100 square yards with the silver-canopied grave of Qalandar in the middle. The outer courtyard is much larger and is usually packed with devotees, singers, and dancers doing the dhamaal.

The shrine was, last year, attacked by suicide bombers of ISIS in which at least 90 people were killed and over 300 injured. The very next morning, the shrine's bell was rung by the caretaker at its routine time of 3:30 A.M who defiantly vowed that they would not be intimidated by terrorists, followed by the resumption of the dhamaal the very next evening following the attack.

The plane landed near the shrine of Lal Shahbaz Qalandar. Allama met Samir and Hasan at the airport wearing a red attire which was the color of the devotees of Lal Shahbaz Qalandar, 'lal' meaning red. He had brought for them also a red attire and a traditional yellow neck garland to wear and change into at the airport lounge.

Devotees were praying for peace between India and Pakistan, and between Afghanistan and Pakistan. At the nearby mosque, they could hear the muezzin continuously calling out on mosque speakers, asking men to come join in the collective praying. It was causing more men to rush to the mosque and join others in the middle of the night. The threat of nuclear war was looming in the air.

The Verse Al-Nas, the verse of the Jinn, could be heard over the speakers:

'Say: I seek refuge with the Lord and Cherisher of mankind
The King or Ruler of mankind
The Allah or Judge of mankind
From the mischief of the whisperer of evil, who withdraws after his whisper
The same who whispers into the hearts of mankind
Among jinn and among men.'

Worshippers were also reading the Ayat-ul-Kursi as well as the last three verses of Al-Baqarah, which were the other two antidotes to the jinn. The message to the jinn was very clear: stop the evil whisperings in men's ears. Stop inducing people to fight wars.

No jinn could face the power of all three combined!

But who could fight him and send him back to his universe? Could Lal Shahbaz Qalandar do that?

Samir, Allama, and Hasan drove to the shrine which was about 10 miles away from the airstrip. As they got closer to the shrine, one could see a flood of people surrounding it. They managed to park about half a mile from the front gate, and walk to the shrine.

Allama had already informed the caretaker or sajjada nasheen of the shrine, Rasool Bux, of Samir's arrival. He came out to greet them.

"Ya Qalandar! Ya Ali! It is an honor to us that you are here today among millions of devotees. Qalandar had told me you would come. Let me take you inside to greet him and pray first."

Rasool Bux was around 75 years old, a thin and fragile man, with grey hair and beard. He was born in the quarters connected to the shrine as his father was also the caretaker, from whom he had taken over when he died when Rasool Bux was 55 years old. He had played as a child every day right in the shrine courtyard, and had also travelled to all other shrines in the region. He was extremely respected by all other caretakers of shrines and by politicians and generals alike, but he had never sought any favor from them.

They wriggled through the crowd to pass the main courtyard where hundreds were dancing and doing the dhamaal.

"Do you know the famous Sufi folk singer Tahira Parveen is here also to sing to the Qalandar? She will be beginning in a few minutes."

"Dad! Tahira is the most famous Sufi singer in all of South Asia. When she sings the Sufi songs, one feels the soul has left the body to connect with the Qalandar."

They walked together into the main building where the grave of Lal Shahbaz Qalandar was located. Allama handed both Samir and Hasan a red 'chaadar' or large scarf made of satin with golden threads having Quranic inscriptions to lay on the grave of Qalandar, greet him and pray to bless him first, and then ask whatever they desired.

They lay the red chaadar on the grave. The caretaker put his hand on Samir's shoulder, "Qalandar is pleased you have come here. He is ready to listen to your plea."

Samir remembered the last time he was at the shrine of Bari Imam, he had wondered whether people prayed to God or to the saint. If they desired their wishes from the saint, then did the saint really have the power to fulfill their desires? Now, it was getting clear to him that the saint was much closer to God than most men were, and therefore, he could easily convey their desires to God to be fulfilled. So, it really did not matter whom the devotees were addressing, the final power laid with God. It was God who would tell the saint what to do to fulfill the wishes of the devotee.

They all raised their hands towards the sky to pray.

Samir knew what he wanted this time. He addressed Lal Shahbaz Qalandar loudly so others could also listen and follow the same prayer, "O Qalandar. O one who loves God like we do, but is closer to Him then we are. We ask of you to help us.

"Ifrit the jinn has returned to earth and is mobilizing all the other jinn on earth who were hiding in caves and graveyards. He wants to avenge himself and his king Iblis, the Satan, by destroying mankind so jinn can rule the earth again. He is whispering evil in men's ears and leading countries to fight with each other. He is whispering evil in men's ears so we attack each other with nuclear bombs. If a nuclear war erupts between our two neighboring countries, millions of your devotees, Muslims and Hindus, and many others will die. God's humanity will die. The war will soon spread to the rest of the world. Humanity will destroy itself.

"We men are not as powerful as the jinn. You are! God has given you strength. We seek your help to fight the jinn. We know you will only do what God wants you to do as He has given you the strength. He is your God and ours as well. Please go to the seventh heaven and speak to God, as we cannot reach that level. God will listen to you. Please tell Him we need you to fight the jinn. Please overcome Ifrit and send him back to his universe. We know you can do it.

"Please also tell God that we men are all sinners. We are thankless creatures who fight each other instead of spreading love. God's message to us, whether in the Quran, or Bible, or the Torah, or the Bhagavad Gita, is for humanity to love each other. We were taught that lesson, but in the materialistic world, we forgot why You created us…to make this world a better place for others to live. Save mankind one last time please. We beg of You. Amen."

They all then rubbed their open palms to their face, and the caretaker offered Samir and others a drink in a clay pot from a large barrel which was chained to the pillar.

"Drink the sacred water. This will give you the energy for dhamaal."

Samir could feel something entering his body. The caretaker looked at him with deep penetrating eyes and nodded his head in the affirmative.

"Would you like to join the dhamaal now?"

"Yes! We would like to!" replied Allama.

They walked out to the courtyard to join the thousands of devotees doing the dhamaal. The voice of popular folk singer Tahira Parveen could be clearly heard on the speakers surrounding the courtyard singing the famous Sufi qawwali 'Dama Dam Mast Qalandar'. The opening lines went like these:

"*O Lal Meri Pat Rakhio Bhala Jhulelalan, Sindhri Da Sehwan Da, Sakhi Shahbaz Qalandar, Dama Dam Mast Qalandar, Ali Dam Dam De Andar.*"

One could see the devotees were already in a trance dancing the dhamaal to the tune of the popular song. It was like they were all intoxicated with hash or bhang, which is the local marijuana.

"Dad. This is the wajd or the haal, when people are connected to God. One loses their senses completely and it feels as if you are connected to the infinite. Do you know the translation? It goes something like this:

'*O the red robed! May I always have your benign protection, O Jhulelal, O the lord, the friend and the sire of Sindh and Sehwan. The red robed God-intoxicated Qalandar, Ali breathes in you.*'"

Hasan jumped into the crowd to join the dancers, with Allama following. The caretaker looked at Samir and said, "Connect to him and he will fulfil your desires."

Samir let himself go and joined the frenzy of dancers. They were all going around in circles, shaking and convulsing. He felt himself a misfit, wearing a red attire and dancing with a crowd of unknowns, Muslims, Hindus, and Christians, all swaying to the sound of drums and the voice of Tahira, like they were high on hash.

But as he circled around the courtyard, within a few minutes, he started feeling like he was losing control of his body. He felt like his spirit was starting to leave his body and move up into the universe. Everyone around him was beginning to become hazy and invisible, and he his mind was beginning to lose all conscious thoughts of who he was, except the sound of 'dama dam mast qalandar'. Soon the world around him started to disappear, and he felt he was gliding among the clouds with a blank mind, except for the thought of the Supreme, whose presence he could feel.

He felt he was floating higher and higher among the clouds, and felt as if a red robed man, whose face was as white as snow and had glowing eyes with long grey hair that reached out to his shoulders, appear from within the clouds and approach him. The man extended his hand and offered him something to drink in a silver crucible. Samir took a sip and felt that a new energy, a new vigor had entered his body, as if he just drank from the elixir of life. The red robed man smiled and then disappeared back into the clouds from where he came from.

Samir felt like following the man, but then he saw himself spiraling back to earth, and soon the sound of music and the dhamaal reappeared. He was back with the dancers and going round in circles in a frenzy. The music had reached its climax with loud drums and Tahira was herself swirling on the stage with her arms extended towards the sky.

As the music reached its finale and ended with the loud beat of the drums, all devotees fell down on their knees with their arms extending up and exclaiming, "Ya Qalandar Ya Ali Madad," addressing both Qalandar and the Caliph Ali, the cousin and son-in-law of the Prophet, from whom many believe the power comes to mortals from God.

The caretaker was the first to reach out to Samir, "Did you feel or see something?"

"I saw a red robed man offer me a drink in a silver crucible from which I took a sip!"

"Ya Qalandar. Allah be praised. Qalandar offers a drink only to a few lucky ones. It means your desire will be fulfilled. You will get what you want! Why don't you honor us by ringing the shrine bell, which is traditionally always rung at this very hour?"

They walked back to the main entrance, and Samir picked up the large metal ladle and struck at the bell which was hanging above the main door. The noise was piercing, but somehow, it gave a consolatory feeling that for whatever desire they had come for to the shrine of Lal Shahbaz Qalandar was fulfilled.

As they slowly walked back to the car, Samir wondered if he was really floating in space during the dhamaal, or was he hallucinating? Was there something in the drink that the caretaker had offered him inside the shrine? He just shrugged his shoulders to think about it later as he still did not know the outcome of making his presence at Qalandar. But he felt inner peace like he had not felt since there was threat of war.

As they sat in the car to return to the airstrip, the caretaker tapped on the window asking him to roll down the glass. He put his hand on Samir's shoulder and spoke softly so others would not hear, "I just heard from the Qalandar. He said your prayers have been answered and your desire will be fulfilled!"

Many questions immediately started going through Samir's mind. Had Qalandar really accepted their plea? Would he really fight the jinn? If so, would he be able to defeat him and send him back to his universe? Would the evil whisperings from the jinn stop and will the world become more peaceful? Would it stop India and Afghanistan from attacking Pakistan? Would it prevent the nuclear war from erupting? Could the apocalypse and the end of times be delayed?

He hoped to know the answers once he was back in Islamabad.

Islamabad

Samir had arrived back in the early hours of the morning and rushed to the prime minister's office. The meeting with the Chinese foreign minister had already taken place, and the prime minister was in a session with the defense minister, the foreign minister, the national security advisor and the chiefs of the armed forces. He was asked to join the meeting.

"We have agreed to the Chinese minister's request to hold back on the firing of the Nasr. We have assured him that for the time being we will stop further processing of enriched fuel, but only if we receive assurances from the US secretary of state that the Indians will do the same and hold talks on Kashmir.

"The US secretary of state called just now and informed us that he met the Indian prime minister and his counterpart, and was able to convince them to hold back on attacking Pakistan across all fronts. He said he has also asked them to roll back on their arming of nuclear weapons.

"He has proposed quad-lateral talks between India, Pakistan, the US, and China, and the Indian prime minister had agreed to present this peace initiative to his cabinet and the parliament. I told him that we want Kashmir to be included in the agenda, which the Indians are still not willing to concede. However, the Indians have agreed to bilateral talks with Pakistan at the foreign minister level as soon as possible, with the two prime ministers meeting immediately afterwards.

"The US secretary of state is now flying into Kabul and will ask them to withdraw their resolution from the United Nations. With tens of billions of aid pouring into that country from the US, and with the presence of over 10,000 American troops in Afghanistan, he is positive that the Afghanis will concede."

Samir could feel that his mind was going round and round. From an onset of a nuclear war to a complete diffusion of the crisis leading to peace talks in such a short time was something that only the prayers of good men and sufis, and a sincere effort by those who lead their nations could accomplish.

He felt dizzy and asked to be excused from the meeting, and walked out of the building where one could only see and feel the beauty of the Margalla Hills over the horizon.

As Samir sat outside on the front lawn on a bench with the stars slowly beginning to fade out, with the sun to rise soon from the east, he could hear the sound of a distant muezzin calling the faithful to early morning prayers.

He was thankful to God that the prayers of millions across both sides of the border were answered and there would be peace soon in the region. He was now sure the recitation of the jinn verses from the Quran had contained the jinn. He was also sure that the pious, the Sufi, and saints like Qalandar and many more had defeated the jinn and kept them away from mankind and the earth. He also knew and was convinced that many other good men, like Hameed, Shams, Latif, Najumi, and countless unnamed more had all played their role in keeping mankind safe from the evils that confront us on a daily basis and lead men to fight and kill each other. He was a scientist and an academic who thought he knew all, but it took someone like his son, Hasan, to teach him the power of spirituality!

The good had won over the evil!

He was sure Ifrit had been banished back to his universe. But for how long? He was not sure.

Would the good that men do be able to keep Ifrit there for long, or would he be able to return again to lead the jinn to avenge mankind, only time would tell!

Ingram Content Group UK Ltd.
Milton Keynes UK
UKHW021824280323
419318UK00005B/52